Rose Wyn, Editor

What was the shocking connection between the Secret Agent and the white-robed crime king, the Resurrectionist? And why was this weird villain murdering men, only to raise them from the dead? True, he was out to enrich himself, since he plundered on a grand scale. But he was really out for power and control. Such dominion would he gain only after he had acquired that most closely guarded of secrets—the real identity of Secret Agent X. And the Man of a Thousand Faces realized that even he might finally have run out of time—and surprises.

Introduction

By Tom Johnson

WHEN George Thomas Fleming Roberts took over the helm of the Secret Agent X series, he brought with him a flair for mystery and unique storytelling. He did not rely so much on mood, like Paul Chadwick, or gun blazing action like Emile Tepperman. A turn of phrase and a twist in the mystery were more his style. He also humanized the Agent and his brave team of crimefighters, making us care about them. All of it he did with ease.

Unlike his predecessors Chadwick and Tepperman, Fleming-Roberts gave the women in his stories more attention, too. They were not merely gun molls or women without substance; they were femme fatales, and often overshadowed the main villains.

Still he created his share of memorable ones, weird foes like the Ghoul, Shaitan, Emperor Zero, the Brain, the Scorpion, and Thoth. For almost four years these criminal masterminds and numerous others plagued the Secret Agent, from *The Corpse Cavalcade* (June 1935) to *Yoke of the Crimson Coterie* (March 1939). Almost every time they used bizarre super weapons against him and their assorted victims, and *every* time, the Agent defeated them and exposed their real identities.

In the early part of his run on *Secret Agent X*, Fleming-Roberts penned longer novels, works of roughly 40,000–45,000 words. Rather quickly into his tenure, though, he reduced the length of his stories. And there may be a perfectly logical reason for their decreased word count.

It is highly suspected that the final stories were edited down from longer manuscripts, and what we ended up with were mere novelettes instead of full novels. Some of that editing likely eliminated numerous quick changes in disguise, and other scenes deemed unnecessary in the editing office. It's a shame we don't have the original manuscripts to examine. I would love to see those stories published as Roberts had intended.

Although the Secret Agent X series continued into the 1950s in Greece, the one story I read left a lot to be desired. However, in 1996 through '98, Stephen Payne brought the Agent back in three brand new novel length adventures. These were *The Freezing Fiends*, published in *Classic Pulp Fiction Stories* in six parts: #12, 13, 14, 15, 16 & 17 (May through October, 1996). *Master of Madness* was published in three parts in *Double Danger Tales*: #1, 2 & 3 (February through April, 1997), and the third novel *Halo of Horror* was published in three parts in *Double Danger Tales*: #21, 22 & 23 (October through December, 1998). These were the first new novels in the US since 1939.

Those three stories also proved that Steve was the logical choice as the new scribe for the Secret Agent X series. He studied not only the Fleming-Roberts stories; he also studied those by other authors in the series, and brought his own flair to Secret Agent X, while staying true to the character, and especially to those stories by Fleming-Roberts. In constructing "The Resurrectionist," Steve looked at other stories by Fleming-Roberts, culling ideas that he might have used in his Secret Agent X stories, but never got the chance. One such gimmick was the "life from death" aspect that you will find in this story. Yes, it was a Fleming-Roberts idea.

Steve also reaches back for an old villain in this adventure, and uses another Fleming-Roberts trick in disguising him. In fact, a lot of the aspects of this story are culled from previous adventures of X, as well as other Fleming-Roberts' outings in other genres. Many readers will likely miss these "Easter eggs," but you don't have to be a Secret Agent X/Fleming-Roberts expert to enjoy this tale.

Coming in at something over 170,000 words, this is truly an epic Secret Agent X tale. It is one that readers will not want to miss.

Happy Reading!

Tom Johnson
December 2013

The Resurrection Ring

By Stephen Payne

Author of "Master of Madness," "Halo of Horror," etc.

Another Amazing Exploit of Secret Agent X

What was the shocking connection between the Secret Agent and the white-robed crime king, the Resurrectionist? And why was this weird villain murdering men, only to raise them from the dead? True, he was out to enrich himself, since he plundered on a grand scale. But he was really out for power and control. Such dominion would he gain only after he had acquired that most closely guarded of secrets—the real identity of Secret Agent X. And the Man of a Thousand Faces realized that even he might finally have run out of time—and surprises.

PROLOGUE
POSTHUMOUS MEMOIR

I died seventy-six hours ago—or so I've been told. Nonexistence—how to describe it? There are no words. I leave that question and the entire Great Guess to the philosophers, the theologians, and the ministers. This is all I know: I was; I was not; I was again.

It was perhaps four hours ago when I came back. Apparently everything worked according to the proverbial Hoyle. Well, almost everything. Seems that my friend only now discovered the hitch in our plan—and he's not really telling me what it is. Says that it's simply too early to be sure of what happened. But his manner reveals that it's puzzling and disturbing. If I didn't know better, I'd think that he looked at me with pity in his eyes when he first brought me back.

He gave me a mourner's sad smile, as though I were really, truly the "dearly departed," not someone who's—

The man—he'd stretched his form across a bed and written these thoughts by flickering candlelight—paused for a moment, startled. At first he thought he heard sudden moaning, or perhaps a wailing. Then he cocked his head to one side. His ears detected a siren, of all things, its song loud as a banshee's wail.

It was a radio, blaring a newsflash about a felon who had eluded the police dragnet, only to be recaptured by a dogged and courageous Federal rookie. Apparently whenever a sensational crime occurred, the radio station would air a Bakelite recording of a wailing siren, to grab listeners' attention. It was a silly gimmick, but in the case of the writing man, it had worked.

The segment kept the writing man engrossed in the narrative, more for the criminal's identity and his threat to the public, than for his, the writer's, concern for himself or a need for sensational reportage.

According to the announcer, Fred William Joliet, the perpetrator, had once served the country as a crack agent for the F.B.I. Unfortunately the fellow had also moonlighted as a master forger and a counterfeiter, not to mention a devotee to the protection racket.

The radio voice continued, *"Unvarnished greed had driven Joliet to commit his crimes, of course. And elimination of his competition was the means he used to achieve his ends. However he realized that mere forgery and counterfeiting wouldn't bring him the money he so desired. Nor would protection schemes work in their support. So he resorted to a new invention that would enrich his coffers in a most deadly way.*

"In April of last year he came into possession of a supply of a new colloidal pyrotechnic substance which promised fantastic results. Like the famed thermite, this material would burn metal. But thanks to an improvement in the Goldschmidt process, this new wonder worker would light much more easily than does thermite. Also this new material would blaze with far more intensity, that is, reach higher temperatures than 3000° F, or more than thermite could achieve. Too, the substance, being a semi-solid, could be poured from a container, at which time the pyrotechnic would stick to the surface to be melted.

"The unfortunates at the First Mercantile Bank of Chicago learned these facts, all too well, in August of the same year. With a large group of masked confederates, Joilet melted his way into First Mercantile Bank, snagged over $2,000,000 in cash, and made a daring getaway. After the trial and conviction of Joilet, someone smuggled more of the stuff into his jail cell and staged a break-out. It was only a matter of months until he was up to his same old tricks.

The writer shook his head. He remembered, with great vividness, a similarly devilish device other criminals had commandeered not so very long ago. But thankfully they had been captured, later. As the radio scribe reported, this criminal's luck had run out, too, earlier today, to be more precise. By a piece of great good fortune, a young Treasury officer had recognized Joliet, who had posed as a tourist with a group visiting the Bureau of Engraving. Clearly, Joilet had been casing the place. But the Treasury fellow, a uniformed man, had collared the former Federal man. In that very moment he had been quietly walking away from the rest of the visitors.

The scribbling man had heard enough. Someone at least had stopped Joliet, he thought. *But what if he escaped once more? And what about the next criminal?*

Then the writer's pen *scritched* across the page again, recording, in code, more private musings. For some reason known only to himself, he tore this last piece of paper from the bottom of the page, folded it, then rammed the scrap into his pocket. Then he resumed on the next page:

Why in heaven's name am I so uneasy? Is it Joliet? Maybe so. But it's really our program. We've planned for every contingency. This is going to work. It—is—going—to—work. It has to. Everyone and everything are depending on us.....

The wordsmith skidded his pen to a halt this time, the implement's nib carving a long, deep groove into the paper's surface. Something might have emitted a whispering sound outside his door, which stood perhaps ten paces away. His eyes whipped around the room with its scientific apparatus: beakers, Bunsen burners, jars of chemicals, microscopes, electrical devices, racks of tools. Even a superficial examination revealed the writing man's environs to be part laboratory.

The writer smiled to himself. He scribbled more on the paper, despite the furrow he had plowed into it. *Maybe it's nothing. Maybe I'm just worrying for no good reason. After all, I'm beginning a new life, one with new and exciting challenges and opportunities to be welcomed. I.....*

The door to the room creaked open, a veritable coffin's lid unloading its deathly occupant. A Nosferatu-like figure in silhouette stood framed by the narrow doorway. Worse yet a set of clawing digits fumbled for a light switch, whereupon feeble white light eased its painstaking way into the room.

The individual slowly closed the door. In the room's pale glow he stood revealed as a tall, singular-looking man, one not soon forgotten by an observer. This fellow had one of those long faces—deeply lined cheeks, pendulous lips, sharp nose—that looked perpetually blue. Also, he combed his thinning salt and pepper hair all the way over to his right ear, in order that he might hide an ever-increasing bald spot. All in all, he resembled an animated corpse, with the only difference being that he didn't yet own a space in a six-foot-by-three foot room with the requisite narrow bed and dirt for a floor.

"I changed the lighting in this place before I brought you back," he whispered as though plotting court intrigue in the palace of Henry VIII. "I installed a rheostat, too, in order to diminish the brilliance of the bulbs in here. Figured your eyes would thank me, since you've been underground in a casket for the past three days. Can't be too careful, you know," he advised. "And besides, we have to keep you healthy for what's coming next. But you knew that already, Captain," he concluded, his whisper carrying a bit of New England—and his medical alma mater, Harvard—in its huskiness.

Clouds of seriousness covered the erstwhile writer in silence. So the newcomer tried to put him at ease with a compliment: "I must confess that since meeting you last year, I've wondered what you *don't* know. There's my field of medicine, for instance; and you seem to have studied as much as I have—my M.D. and advanced training in microbiology notwithstanding. Pharmacology? You know it as well as Schmeideberg himself. Botany? You might have written a text as authoritative as Bailey's *Cyclopedia of American Horticulture*. And lest I forget, there are your courage, and your uncanny talent for man—"

Embarrassed, the Captain forcefully cleared his throat to halt the other man's paean. The medico stopped his laudatory recitation, though each and every word of it was true. Namely, the young patient was a veritable polymath, housing an expert's knowledge of a number of fields in his capacious brain.

Over the next few seconds silence continued its reign. The nervous doctor occupied the time by tapping a well-worn pencil against the underside of a metal clipboard. He caught himself when he noticed that his listener, although smiling kindly, watched him with unusual keenness.

This wasn't an easy task for the patient at

first, what with his gray eyes' extreme sensitivity to light. Still he gradually reacquainted his optics with the chamber's illuminating rays, and, as slowly, re-established their friendship with the light. That same radiance did something else, something far more revelatory.

It haloed his lustrous brown hair and his handsome, youngish face. And yet those same features showed another quality when he inclined his head. They displayed a curiously mature aspect, as though he had seen much of life, tragedy and triumph alike. Those experiences had molded him, not marring those features but lending them a dignity and a seriousness that were unmistakable. The kindness in that face was just as undeniable. And then there were those eerie gray eyes, diamond-like orbs that could bore deep into every person or situation that they encountered.

Even the doctor himself felt their compelling power. He questioned, almost mechanically, as though entranced by them: "Are you okeh, Captain?"

The erstwhile patient nodded slowly to the physician. His affirmative was grave: "Yes, Doctor Osben. I'm fine. But no more titles or names, now, please. That's in the past, as far as we're both concerned."

He paused for a moment, weighing his words to the aging medico. He resumed, "I appreciate what you've done. You've been more than kind, helping me to execute each stage of our plan. And it hasn't been an easy one, at that."

Doctor Osben agreed. He curled his lips into a tight smile which vanished as soon as it appeared. His right hand fumbled absently at his side, then began tapping again on the back of the clipboard.

The wordsmith groped for his next words. He cut his eyes away from the doctor, trained those orbs on the tile floor. When they returned to the doctor's face, those eyes had acquired a supernatural intensity.

"So we start the next phase now, I assume?" he quizzed.

"Ye—yes, of course, Captain," he inadvertently addressed the man by his former rank. The older man looked away, as if saddened to his core. Something was amiss. He faced his patient again. "You're dead, to all intents and purposes. You can start fresh now, do what you've been planning to do for several months. And there's no one more qualified than you to undertake the task ahead. Maybe this world of ours will have a real chance at peace, now...."

His voice trailed off, and his head turned away for a second time. Silence had briefly regained the throne.

To himself the wordsmith thought, *Osben is tap-dancing around everything. Something is wrong—horribly wrong. And I'd wager it has* everything *to do with the procedure I've undergone, a few days ago.*

"What is it, Doctor? You've got to tell me what's bothering you!" He shot upwards from the bed where he had been sitting. His right hand shook a bit as he urged, "Tell me, Osben. What is it?"

"There are complications, as I feared when I first awakened you," Doctor Osben looked down, his watery blue eyes haunted. "The drug and the process both were untried. I—I'm—I don't know what to say, except something is wrong. I—I'm so sorry...." The flow of his words trickled to a halt.

In the midst of this unsettling report, a tall fellow and a curvaceous young woman of medium height strode purposefully along the softly-lit hallway, halting in front of the room occupied by the resurrected man. Their attire, a lab coat for the man and a nurse's whites for the woman, branded them, like Osben, as members of the medical profession.

The lab-coated man knuckled the door three times. No one answered his request for entry, so he made a second attempt.

Doctor Osben ignored this attempt, as well. Finally, he delivered a sharp response: "Come in!"

Those newcomers marched decisively into the room. The area's soft light disclosed the man as someone with a shock of dark brown hair and a tall robust frame. To his detriment, however, he possessed heavy black brows which looked remarkably like a pair of squirming caterpillars. A set of drooping, or heavy, features adorned his face. And the bump at his nose bridge hinted at a severe break, despite the plastic surgeon's otherwise expert job of repair.

His mouth though was another story. His thick lips were fixed perpetually in a killer's sneer. That maw would have easily lent itself to vocal delivery of the "dese, dem, and dose" school which Hollywood so often projected onto the silver screen. Indeed on the strength of his physicality alone, he might have portrayed a terrific villain in a Hollywood crime picture. Still his cultured accent would have betrayed him as a learned man. Proof of those credentials lay in his doctor of medicine in plastic surgery, earned at the University of Heidelberg. And he, like Osben, had taken advanced study in Soviet Russia, the newcomer having conducted his research in chemistry and a special new area of human physiology.

The woman accompanying him presented, if anything, a stark contrast to the man, a regular beauty to his beast. Thick, wavy hair of deepest brown accentuated a perfect ivory complexion and a perfect, heart-shaped face. In addition, those features complemented her nearly black eyes, her sculpted cheekbones, the faint cleft in her chin, and her slightly upturned nose. She was positively breathtaking.

Through a set of perfectly molded lips, the woman—her name was Teresa Fox—informed in a rich alto, "Doctor Osben, now that he's back among the living, shouldn't we examine those readings you ordered? And complete that next round of tests?"

"She's right," her companion reported, the impatience of the fellow's tone sharper than a lancet. "How much longer are you going to be here, when we have other work to do?"

Head bowed, Doctor Osben remained silent, preoccupied with the report he couldn't bring himself to share with his charge. After a time he raised his head and fixed the visitor with a tired gaze.

"We'll be with you in a moment, Emel. It's just that I'm trying to frame my words. Trying to show this man some human decency, some compassion. Can't you understand that?"

The beautiful young woman rolled her black eyes in utter contempt.

"Sure, I understand, Doctor. We're supposed to be his nurse maids, too," she screwed her beautiful features into a contemptuous sneer. Her next words were even harder, more ruthless: "This just proves I should have stayed with my first career, not switched into—"

Iron undergirding his words, Osben lectured, "All right, Nurse Fox. No one is forcing you to remain here at gunpoint."

Beautiful features now terrible with fury, she pivoted around, stormed away from them and towards the door. Emel tried to stop her; but oddly shuttering her right eye a single time, she left their presence, ostensibly for her own chambers down the hall. In actuality she hovered like an angry spirit outside the door to the room. Finally she departed for Emel's spacious office at the opposite end of the corridor.

That chamber of Dr. Emel would have struck most observers as a typical place for a sawbones. It contained its share of examining equipment; the requisite lab coat, stained; bottles of chemicals; and so forth. It also housed a desk, on which he wrote his observations, kept baskets of incoming and outgoing papers, and parked his telephone.

But in other respects, Emel's part of the building looked like an artist's studio. An easel with attached canvas, for instance, occupied one section of its real estate. A couple of pots of brushes stood adjacent. Several paint-filled jars served as their next-door neighbors.

A series of small busts, each one only inches tall, also lived in this neighborhood. There were Mayor La Guardia of New York and Charles Lindbergh, among the famous; and Clyde Barrow, Al Capone, even Dillinger among the infamous. There were figures of obscurity, too, mostly men who would have been known only by parents or friends; cops or creditors.

Emel maintained the area, so he said, to escape the pressures of the profession, to obtain a bit of relaxation by engaging in creative pursuits.

Teresa shot a quick look around these environs. Then she fixed her gaze upon a bookshelf at her eye level, that is, somewhat over five and one half feet above the floor. On it parked an oblong brown case of two feet in length, one foot in width, one and one half feet in height. Down it came into her waiting hands. Once Teresa had popped open its lid, she quickly shoved the busts into special slots of tan velvet, all arrayed on shelves inside the case. All the while a smile like poisoned honey adorned her lovely face.

Emel's desk then took the case off her hands. Next she gathered some of Emel's papers—files and such—from his cabinet, along with several of his medical and other books from a different shelf. These she crammed inside a pair of oversized black leather briefcases, formerly beside the desk. Suddenly, Teresa Fox knew she must have forgetten something, perhaps even more than *one* something. She pointed her gaze back towards the file cabinet. One particular manila folder squatted atop the appliance. The young beauty realized it was the *something* in question, or at least one of them. She snatched it down and shoved this folder into one of the over-large briefcases. However, she could never remember what the other *something* might have been. It probably wasn't important, anyway, she reasoned.

Throughout this affair, it was obvious that something was up. Teresa's level of alacrity and her resolute expression proved this point. Still, exactly what was happening, only she knew.

Whatever it was, it inspired Teresa, the container of busts in one hand and her small white purse in another, to depart immediately, taking a side door out of Emel's chamber. In turn, this portal fed onto a different hallway and out into a parking area where a couple of automobiles, a black Ford sedan and a dirty, gray Chrysler coupe, rested. She took a key from her purse, unlocked the Ford's trunk, and slipped the larger case into the compartment.

Easing the trunk shut once more, she marched back towards the office, again by the same route. She used it as a mere passage, however, since a few steps carried her, speedily, back out onto that original hallway.

Meanwhile, back in the former patient's room, Charles Darwin Osben commented to Emel, his tone one of resignation, "Well, I suppose that's the end of Teresa. I rather expected it, since she's been threatening to leave us, since the project started."

Gray eyes glittering like frost, Emel posed his question with fury: " 'You rather expected it'? This is *your* fault, Charles, upsetting her as you've done!"

"My fault, Emel? She's been volatile ever since we hired her—or rather, since *you* hired her."

A curious look in his eyes, Emel insisted, "She's my *niece*, Charles. My sister pressured me to employ her after she had finished nurses' training."

"But with her background, Emel? She's consorted with mobsters for years. Frankly, I *knew* this would come to a poor end, bringing her on board a project like this one. I simply can't believe I let you talk me into this."

Weary beyond belief, he shook his head and rubbed his temples.

Their former patient, the Captain, stopped their bickering, with a voice that cracked like a whip: "Look—let's get down to cases, here. What about my return? And what about the plan, for that matter?"

"What *about* your plan?" Emel probed, his caterpillar brows bunching curiously. "Your plan is dubious, at best, especially your 'taking the war to the enemy' approach to the world's ills. It all reads like a cheap melodrama. And your so-called 'Project An—'"

"—That will be *quite* enough, Emel," Charles Osben made an abrupt, horizontal slashing motion with one hand and fixed a stern gaze upon his colleague.

"No, it's *not* quite enough, Charles," Emel countered with a severity of his own. "We're standing here, wasting time, money, and effort. I simply want to finish going over these results with the two of you, so that this thing can come to an end. You'll find, Charles, that this grand 'project' hasn't turned out quite as you've planned."

"I *know* that already, Emel. Moreover, I've already told him that something was wrong."

It was the turn of the former scribe now. Despite his nerves, he forced his lips into a smile. "Give it to me, Doctor Osben. Am I going to turn into a giant fly, or maybe a spider?"

Osben said nothing. His stony silence caused the younger man to exclaim, "Doctor Osben—Charles, please! Don't mince words with me!"

The other doctor, Emel, stood there, looking strangely unfazed. Then with a shrug of his shoulders, he said, his voice transforming to a cynical baritone: "All right. Here's the 'real dope,' as all the kids say. You're going to die again—and soon. So you may as well get your affairs in order. 'Eat, drink, and be merry,' as they say."

"Now, wait a minute, Emel. That *may* be the case," Doctor Osben qualified, offended by the man's bluntness. "But we don't yet *know* that for sure. And you're showing the height of irresponsibility and inhumanity, by telling him in such an insensitive manner."

Storm clouds gathering in his dark blue eyes, Doctor Emel insisted to the young man: "You *are* going to die again. Pure and simple. And this time we can't bring you back. No cheating death this time—no life from death for you. No beating the Grim Reaper. This time, you'll stay dead."

The young patient, a philosophical look in his gray optics, noted, "Everybody dies. I concede that. But what do you mean by saying, 'No cheating death for you this time,' and 'This time you'll stay dead'"?

Doctor Emel spoke through a set of clenched teeth. "It's that drug and the process we used to inject you. At first I thought this would work. But after a while, I had bad feelings about the results!" he complained bitterly. "Now we have nothing to show for our labor, other than a failed experiment."

"He's *certainly* not to blame for the problem, Emel. This is *our* fault," Osben defended the young patient. The medical man pivoted his head at the man he'd called Captain: "We simply weren't ready to try any of this on you. And for that I can only apologize to you and to the many people who were depending so much on all of us."

Eyes glittering with fury, Doctor Emel muttered a string of words, only one of which, "file," was intelligible.

Of a sudden, Osben, closer to Emel, trained his watery blue eyes on his colleague. "What did you just say?"

"Nothing at all!" the man barked. "I'm just frustrated, is all—with this experiment, with you, everything. Sick to death of it all, to be honest. I just don't see the point of any of this business—especially the secrecy." He bestowed a particularly venomous look on the young man. Then Emel turned back to Osben. "You and I could have gone far with this thing, not depended on Washington's backing—much less your plodding fashion and your bogus sense of ethics. We could have—"

"—continued on *your* path and not discovered the flaw in our approach. Or we could have continued to do things *my* way, the methodical way, and balanced *that* concern with the fact that a human life was involved. *That*, Emel, is proper and ethical science. I've told you that, countless times. And it seems for one reason or another, you have yet to grasp that concept."

Emel mumbled something about the word "file" again, spitting out these next words by way of conclusion: "Oh, yes, I grasp it, all right. I also grasp the idea that you, Charles, are a plodder, and that you will never get anywhere. And neither," he glared at the younger fellow, "will you."

"Are you finished, Emel?" Osben offered a glare of his own. "Because we have work to complete, not least of which is checking back over our figures. Work with me—work with both of us—" he indicated the patient, "and it will take your mind of Teresa. Plus, you may help us to find the problem with the formula or the process, and thus help our young friend. Will you do this—listen to reason, and to conscience?"

The other doctor *pshawed*, "Maybe *you* will do it, Charles. But I'm done with you *and* him. Especially him and his grandiose ideas about public service."

He stormed from the room. Not far down the hall he encountered his young niece Teresa, who clutched the cases housing the medical tomes. While he grabbed the heavier of the two receptacles, she opened her lovely mouth to say something to him. Immediately he *shushed* her with the index finger of his left hand. This done, he formed his right index finger and thumb into a circle, signifying everything was a-okeh. She nodded and moved around the corner and towards another door.

Not many more minutes ticked from the clock. In that period of time Emel had entered his office, grabbed additional materials from it, and stashed the lot of them into two more cases.

"Get my car from the back," he told her. "Bring it to the front entrance of the facility."

"You should have told me that, when I first left," she glared at him, her slender hands going to her hips. Acid dripped from her next words: "Especially since you're supposed to be such a great planner."

"I *am*, my dear. I've been biding my time for this moment. I've even duplicated many of Osben's and that other man's files for quite some time and secreted them in that safe place. We *will* have our day. Now, hold that famous temper of yours. And get the car."

Teresa pinned him to the wall with her eyes once more, although she begrudgingly complied. But she was cursing a blue streak when she left.

As she did this, Emel made a final circuit of the office, ensuring that nothing of value remained behind. He heard an outer door crash open. Emel ventured onto that main hallway, where he found Teresa already waiting.

About that time Charles Darwin Osben entered the corridor. He made a final attempt to dissuade Emel from leaving. But the man remained adamant.

Osben watched them, sadly, as he turned and trudged back towards the patient's room. He was sorry to lose Emel, and on reflection, almost as sorry to have lost his niece. Maybe they could have worked with her. Maybe— things would have turned out differently. Maybe....

In the doorway the former dead man had come to see what the hold-up might be. Dr. Osben turned the conversation back to the project. As he did, he and his patient caught the final portion of a conversation originating from the door.

The first voice was male, clearly that of Emel: "...correct art supplies?"

"You mean the *special* ones?" came the female's—obviously Teresa's—query.

"Yes—those. I don't give a damn about the rest of them. He can burn them for all I care. Hell, he can join them, on the way to the fires and—"

They went through the door and out of earshot.

Moving towards Emel's black Ford, an animated Teresa scolded him: "Don't get your tail feathers in an uproar! I've got *everything* you need. Even the formula for that stuff the patient developed, Uncle Emel."

"Fine. That will be put to good use, as well. Along with the—"

The cranking of the sedan's engine drowned out the rest of his response. And the two people zoomed away.

Back inside the patient's room, silence had ruled the day, ever since the two relatives had departed. The two remaining men sat in folding chairs, opposite each other.

Finally, the erstwhile Captain remarked with a shrug of his broad shoulders, "So, that's that, I guess."

The medico shook his head. "It seems so, doesn't it? A pity—he had such potential, such brilliance. Washington had great plans for him. But I suppose you knew that already."

The young man nodded agreement. "Yes. He was to be given a director's position in the Criminal Investigation Division. He would have spearheaded one of the new scientific branches, in fact."

"It was your recommendation, wasn't it, which obtained him the post?" Osben asked.

Affirmation came from the lips of the former Captain. "They had already started the paperwork that would have made him the head of forensic medicine. He would have been an asset to the Department of Justice."

"But that is over and done. Now, I ask you for the final time," he urged, his tone insistent and his gray eyes compelling, "what can I expect from our project?"

Osben had been watching the younger fellow during part of the business with Emel. But Dr. Osben hadn't wanted the former Captain to see him, the physician, doing so. There was good reason for his secret observation, and that was the trembling in the man's hand. This symptom and its cause inspired the doctor to evade the question, thus: "I don't know what to tell you, son. I've a myriad of tests to run on you yet, and not much time to complete them, I'd suspect."

The patient wasn't satisfied with such indirectness. He pressed the man once more. "Be more specific, please. I have the right to know *as far as possible* what is going on—and you have a moral and an ethical responsibility to share that information with me."

Osben became thoughtful, his voice grave. "Touché, Captain. All right. Here's what I can tell you now. I've already noticed the shaking in your hand."

"Nerves?" the former patient asked him. "That must be it, correct?"

"Perhaps. But more likely, you've already developed an involuntary tremor which will only progress over time. It will probably attack your facial muscles and head, too, perhaps cause bulging of the eyes. This will all become worse, I'm afraid. Then you'll begin to have a craving for the medication I used to return you to life. You'll have to take more and more of the drug, simply to function. Eventually, your body will reach a point of satiation, such that the drug won't work.

"I estimate that you have three, at the outside, four months to live—even with the drug used to revive you. In the meantime, if you overtax your body, at any point, you will die even more quickly. Here is what will happen. Your immune system will begin attacking itself. Your system will eventually shut down, with the liver and pancreas failing first, and the kidneys following close behind them. You'll find breathing difficult, impossible, eventually. And your heart will go, before everything is said and done.

"Your death won't be a pretty one..." he trailed off. He shook his head, his face growing longer. "And your body will...."

He trudged over to a bookcase next to the wall. From it he pulled a thick text of several hundred pages. Once he'd cracked open the volume, he ran his right index finger down the table of contents, until he'd located the list of illustrations. When he'd found the proper one, he flipped to it.

Into the patient's hand the doctor transferred the heavy tome. The image depicted was too grim, too horrible for the average mind to conceive.

Surprisingly, the young patient didn't suffer a tingle of horror at such a picture—or at the ones equally as awful on the subsequent pages. His thoughts went to higher things as he shook his head, rubbed his temples with long, slender fingers. *All of our preparations, all of them.* Clouds of sadness gathered in his eyes. His thoughts resumed: *And all of those people, who depended on the success of this endeavor....*

He looked, pleadingly, at Charles Osben, "Surely the process can be arrested, or maybe even—even reversed. Maybe *that* would work. Maybe we could go forward after you corrected the problem...."

"Well, as I tried to tell you earlier, there's always that chance. That might even be the case here, despite what seems inevitable at first glance. Maybe, as is often the case, nature has built in a corrective mechanism; and we simply haven't found it yet."

His voice took on graveyard grimness. Osben averted his head, dropping his decibel level yet again, "Or maybe we're too damned smart for our own good...." The medico stopped for a moment, head turned away from his listener's gaze. The doctor's tone, barely above his customary whisper, assumed a strange humbleness, even a philosophical bent.

"It's funny. We medical folks are only human, after all—even though many of us—my colleagues not to mention many laymen—think that science will save us. And damned if I didn't think the same thing when I was a young sawbones...."

The younger man drew a halt to such musings. These reflections would accomplish little at this late stage, now that the deed was done. The resurrected man had other ideas in mind.

"We'll get on with everything, then," he asserted, gray fires kindling anew in his weird eyes, lines of resolve carved into his features.

Was he certain that he wanted to proceed? asked Osben, pie-eyed with surprise. Yes, Osben's erstwhile patient affirmed. The former dead man was alive to this plan, no matter the consequences that might lie ahead. People's lives were, after all, depending on their actions that night. Indeed, a nation's fate might eventually rest upon their decisions; so they must do all the good they could, while they could.

Osben agreed, drawn to the man's magnetic personality. This young fellow's iron will, his courage, and his goodness all rivaled that of his former police patient, a young gunshot victim, back home in Massachusetts, several months ago. He could see a day when this present young man might attain a higher status than that fellow. He might, in fact, become a hero of epic proportions like a Washington or a Lincoln.

In the coming days, Osben wouldn't be the only one to make such a comparison.

The resurrected man rising from the chair, he started to depart Doctor Osben's laboratory. Before doing so, he recalled something left behind there. He whipped his body into an abrupt pivot and snatched his leather-bound notebook from the bed. Gray diamond eyes drilling the page, he encoded several lines of text. Then he concluded with a curious sentence at the bottom of the page. It was a statement dramatic for its very brevity.

The coded words read simply, *The good work begins.*

Back into his pants pocket went the small notebook. He reflected a final moment over coming events. Then favoring the aging doctor with a single, resolute nod, the now and forever nameless younger fellow marched from the room, Osben close behind.

An unknown man facing uncertain future—yet confident and courageous the while—thus was the way of this nameless individual. Only the future could know he would become a legend in the annals of heroism, the sword in the hand of Lady Justice... Secret Agent X!

CHAPTER I
CRIME'S CONVENTION

THE Secret Agent's reputation had grown since that day in 1932, when Dr. Osben had raised the master man-hunter from the grave. But superman of detection that the Agent was, even he could not have foreseen the way this latest case would unfold, or the lives it would eventually affect. And certainly the Secret Agent couldn't have known about the original ball set in motion by this latest case.

Out of the country at the time, X didn't know about the tragic death of Charles Darwin Osben by suicide, one and one half years later. Nor did the detective know about the mysterious gunman who had shot Emel and his niece dead, back in 1935. Police had never solved the case.

The next year, 1936, was on its way to becoming history. On a November night the pale moonlight threw its sickly glow over gray, cloudy skies. Forecasters had predicted an excellent chance of rain for this cool, fall darkness. But while the skies were gloomy, the hearts of people were cheerful. And their faces reflected a mounting excitement and expectancy.

On that night Franklin Roosevelt was sweeping to a second Presidential term. Not surprisingly that news had penetrated even the gray stone walls of a prison, the notorious State Penitentiary of New York, in Attica, no less. Like the populace outside, guards and staff concentrated their attention on radios, eager to hear the latest news coming from Washington. The President's victory set them to asking the question on all minds: Just what new policies might Roosevelt implement, to bring continued relief from the business depression that had shattered so many lives in the past seven years?

For the hundreds of men incarcerated in the prison, however, this wasn't a day of triumph, much less tragedy. It was just another day behind those craggy walls. There was a good reason the place housed the most dangerous felons. These were, after all, the most violent men—murderers, bank robbers, gangsters, hoodlums all. They all deserved the State's punishment. They had earned a just recompense for their offenses against the honest people beyond the stony ramparts.

One of these men was a tall, young-looking blond fellow with classic features, a modern Adonis. Cigarette companies would have loved to use him for their ads, so handsome he looked. Too, the moving picture companies would have killed to star him in their celluloid productions. He might even have been a well-known personage in the world away from Attica. But here he was a non-entity. Official records listed him as Prisoner in the State Penitentiary of New York (PSPNY), Number 2575. He had become an inmate, a nameless man known by his number, like all of his fellows in Attica. Indeed, living in freedom as we do, most of us completely disregard the loss of a name as a punishment.

Yet conviction for a crime inevitably exacts that steep price, loss of freedom and thus identity, on the hoodlum.

None of this dawned on 2575, though. Certainly none of the heartache or tragedy he caused had stamped any sense of remorse upon his soul. For 2575 the only tragedy of his life was his own incarceration.

Why should he be imprisoned—merely because others had blocked his way on the path to wealth and power? He suffered no remorse over his illegal scientific experiments, horrible surgical procedures on his fellows, in the outside world. Nor did qualms of conscience plague him over those victims' loss of their very humanity, their degeneration into *things*.

All of 2575's crimes mattered to the members of the jury, however. For those malevolent acts 2575 had committed, the jury had handed down a guilty verdict after only thirty minutes of deliberation. In the sentencing phase of the trial, the judge had punished the man with the maximum sentence: life without parole. He had dodged a date with the hotseat *only* because he had confessed to his crimes.

Now he was barely over a year into his prison sentence at the State Penitentiary. And in the midst of Roosevelt's re-election and the inmates' indifference, he was smiling, no, out and out smirking.

He smirked all that day, strangely enough, the smug smile decorating his classic features in a most unsettling fashion.

On this Election Night of November, he seemed to come to life in this place of emotional death.

How surprising it was that he came to life in the very place of his own murder.

An obese criminal, a French-Canadian thug named *Petit Homme* or "Little Man," rode shotgun over the affair. A multiple murderer and bank robber, he had watched 2575 all day, eyeballing the blond man too closely for the French-Canadian's observation to be one of common interest. For his own part 2575 sensed that Little Man was scrutinizing him and had been doing so for quite some time.

Inexplicably, Little Man's staring didn't rattle 2575 in the least. The good-looking prisoner simply tended to his own garden, so to speak.

He continued to behave in this way until the afternoon when he, 2575, presented himself, unexpectedly, at the concrete confines of the prison basketball court. There a large group of men, ten in all, shot baskets with more than a trace of athletic prowess, and an equal amount of unfriendly rivalry. In the gray concrete bleachers off to one side, a much larger congregation of men watched the game, cheering with a fanatic's enthusiasm for their chosen warriors of the concrete battlefield.

Over to those bleachers 2575 marched, his long legs and tall, slender body moving with an easy, confident grace, his thick blond locks tousled by a slight wind. Several of his fellow inmates offered gruff *hellos*.

"Hello, all," he saluted in the tones of a cultured man. He intended to say something else, but he needed to stop, in order to clear his throat. After no little difficulty in this regard, he stated, "I thought I might take in a game with everyone on this fall night."

Not standing on ceremony, they promptly informed him to plant his tail on one of the hard-surfaced benches so they could get back to watching the game.

Two slots down from Little Man, the blond fellow took a seat. There he might gain a better view of the combat between the opposing squadrons of basketballers. In moving to his seat in the bleachers, he dragged one of his rather large feet across the outstretched leg of Little Man, falling into a none-too-graceful sprawl.

For his all his massive bulk, Little Man abruptly flew to his feet, the force of his sudden motion rolling 2575 back to the hard concrete. Stunned a second time, 2575 shook his head and curled his lips into a pained grimace.

Meanwhile, Little Man bared his teeth at him like a wild animal ready to attack.

"*Sacre bleu!*" he screamed, his Gallic origins never clearer. "What is ze beeg *idée*, *mon beau garçon*? It ees that you cannot watch where you're going, *non*? I show you how *le vrai gentilhomme* acts à *le terrain de basket!*"

Beau Garçon or Pretty Boy, the Anglicized name the prison's worthies had dubbed him, backed away, not wanting to cause a ruckus among this tough crowd. His blue eyes were wide as pizza pans.

"Look, it was an accident, Little Man," he insisted with courtesy that seemed an utter incongruity in this place of iron bars and prison walls. He presented a manner of genuine regret over his clumsiness. "I'm—I'm sorry that I caused you embarrassment or injury. Please accept my apologies—" he put up plaintive hands to show his good faith.

" '*Vous voudrez bien m'excuser*,' " Little Man mimicked the apology in French, adding a pinch of sarcasm to the mix. "I'll show you *excuses, idiot!*" he cocked back a ham of a hand, balled it into a fist, and airmailed the thing straight for 2575's handsome face.

Pretty Boy, 2575, tried to sidestep the blow, but came out on the short end. The thrust knocked out one of the man's canines, blood and the tooth performing a skydive to the gray concrete. Not much of a pugilist, Pretty Boy did his best to retreat from the man before he could deliver another of those sledgehammer blows.

And then it began. Other men jumped to Pretty Boy's defense, attacking the obese French Canadian. Little Man had his own partisans, as well; and these hoods joined the battle to defend their confederate. Arms flew, legs kicked, and teeth bit. One thug would deliver a blow only to have the thrust countered by another, sometimes even one on his own side of the combat. As by sleight-of-hand, a few of the convicts produced weapons like brass knuckles and saps. Some of the last implements the offenders had fashioned from socks filled with ball bearings from the machine shop, tying the opened ends of the socks in knots. In the correct hands these makeshift weapons could and did deliver devastating punishment against enemies, breaking a number of bones and cracking almost as many skulls. In addition, many of the criminals produced homemade weapons, especially shivs or homemade knives, stabbing or cutting their opponents. The result would send many of the hoods gashed and bleeding to the prison hospital.

Police guards raced into the fray to stop the violence; yet they could do little. Most of them, if armed at all, packed no more than pistols. Hence, as far as stopping the fight went, they stood as little a chance as a snowman in hell. Even worse, some of the officers actually lost their service revolvers to the hoodlums, who swept over the bluecoats like a human tidal wave.

Disorder ruled the day, and as though matters couldn't deteriorate more, one man's hand traveled to his waistband. From it he unhitched a gun, actually a pistol of some sort. The weapon might have been a target model, though that wasn't certain. After all, the man, a tall bulky hood with Coke bottle glasses and effeminate lips, had deliberately covered most of the grip and a portion of the chamber with his huge hand. And to his advantage, the mounting chaos of the prison yard also prevented a clear view of the weapon's manufacturer.

That was the way Prisoner 3671—they called him Specs—liked it, anyhow. He was in the joint for fraud, according to prison scuttlebutt, a couple of high-dollar crimes within the funeral industry. Still fraud and forgery were merely the terms describing his particular offense. They failed miserably in characterizing his personality.

He was a bully, weak in himself, but prone to choose targets that wouldn't stand up to him. With those tougher than he, Prisoner 3671 contrived ways to become indispensable to them. Using his money—scads of it in smuggled from the outside world—he would buy them contraband and thus put them in his debt, usually with appeals to their need for friendship. That wasn't his only tack. Playing on his targets' emotions, especially their vanity, was his next frequent approach. He often flattered his brother inmates with appeals to their supposed intelligence or extravagant claims about their criminal prowess. Cynic and mercenary that he was, he found both methods highly effective.

One of his flunkies, a man with rock-hard muscles and a head just as hard, had earned much of Specs' largess on both fronts. So this fellow accompanied 3671 as they pushed and shoved their way through this criminal mob. Closer and closer he and his lapdog—Specs called him "Herman"—inched towards Specs' quarry. Along the way, Specs held his own with the men smaller than himself, of course, shoving them out of the way. But this didn't work every time. So when he or his henchman encountered someone bigger or tougher than Specs himself, then Prisoner 3671 resorted to his simple solution. He simply sicced Herman on the offender. Herman made an excellent junkyard dog.

By now he and his pet thug had reached a point close enough to carry out their plan. And this was critical, as they must be near to the victim. Very near.

With only eight feet separating him from his target, Specs aimed his pistol at his victim's neck and squeezed the trigger. As though silenced, the gun uttered only a slight *cough* from its barrel.

His target jackknifed instantly to the concrete.

From several feet away the shooter spotted a thin, horribly disfigured man, apparently a confederate. This worthy gave a wink to the pistol wielder, following which the thin felon repeated the motion for benefit of another man who showed the same interest in the recent shooting. Miraculously the crowd backed away to allow passage for this criminal, a dignified, gray-locked oldster who might have passed for a rich banker on the outside. At that point the gunman executed a pickpocket's trick and passed the handgun to the old-timer. This man did something with the weapon, though in this melee, no one could have discerned its nature.

Within another minute the graying convict

shifted the gun to the waiting paw of the thin criminal. Then the scrawny fellow performed something totally unexpected.

He turned the target pistol upon the original gunman, whereupon it *coughed* a second round at the original wielder, that is, Specs! He, too, swayed once or twice and then wilted to the concrete.

Someone apparently wasn't satisfied with his death, as that same person, grinning like a death's head, kicked him, hard in the side of the head, just as his body went down. Then the mysterious convict, clearly an old adversary, ran off into the throng of convicts.

In the meantime, his right hand curiously free of powder burns, Mr. Scrawny executed a pickpocket's move of his own to another man, a rat-faced hood with a rodent's skulking manner, to boot. Once the gun had gone into the hands of Rat-Face, the weapon became a metallic infection of sorts, passing from one hand to the next in that rioting crowd.

Those eyes of Mr. Scrawny caught the orbs of Rat-Face, with both of them bobbing their heads in acknowledgment. This pistol wouldn't turn up later, for the simple reason that the final holder would disassemble it. Then he would scatter the parts by the simple expedient of sending it out, piecemeal, as prison rubbish aboard the garbage trucks that rolled through, twice per week.

Penitentiary guards meanwhile had radioed their brother officers' plight from the guard tower to the main building. The clarion call went out. To the prison armory a large force of police sprinted, unlimbering rifles and filling their chambers with tear gas cartridges. Likewise they donned gas masks. Out onto that basketball court they galloped, their rifles belching tear gas cartridges into that prison mob.

At first the jailbirds did not realize the nature of this new foe attacking them. As a consequence, some of the miscreants tried to continue their battle with the commandeered pistols and the homemade weaponry. Now the clouds of gray-white smoke mushroomed in their midst. Spasms of coughing and floods of tears overwhelmed the gray-garbed men before they knew what was going on.

But eventually the police completed their criminal rodeo, corralling the offenders and herding them back to their cells.

The final toll was thirty-five wounded, some critically. One of them was Mr. Scrawny. In his attempt to cut himself loose from the skein of bodies, he made the mistake of tangling his own thin frame with that of a man he had wronged years before. Foolishly the jailbird had thought the man, a fellow with a hyena's laugh and pock-marked skin, had let bygones be bygones. Without warning the fellow had buried and then twisted his shiv, handle deep, in Mr. Scrawny's lower right back. Horrible as the wound proved to be, Mr. Scrawny was expected to live. He would be joined by the rest of the thirty-five, precisely eighteen of them, who had incurred wounds of much less severity.

These men were the lucky ones, as some fifteen men met their demise. One of them was the Gallic miscreant Little Man, who tangled with a foeman clutching a homemade sap. This head cracker, a sock crammed to the brim with coins, dealt him a terrible blow to the side of the skull. As soon as the man went down, Little Man's assailant leaped on him, pressing his advantage with repeated blows to the cranium of Little Man. Prison guards would eventually recover him from the yard, but their efforts to save him produced no result. He died from massive head trauma.

And Pretty Boy, he of the clumsy feet, paid the ultimate price too that day, having been the victim of the gunman Specs. To retrieve Pretty Boy's corpse, police had yanked coughing, tear gassed battlers from their private war, following which the officers carried his body and the rest of the corpses to the penitentiary's morgue. While the prison guards were transporting his body, one of the officers noticed something strange.

A hint of a smile yet accentuated Pretty Boy's handsome visage, as though the convict knew a secret to which no one else was privy. Most likely, that secret likely had nothing to do with the next life. It prompted much speculation on the part of those who witnessed his pleased expression, but they quickly dropped their musings on account of the job at hand.

In no time they had trundled his body and all of the others to the morgue. There the prison sawbones could determine specific causes of death and tag the remains of the miscreants.

Then a team of felons initiated the process of preparing the dead for burial: building coffins and digging graves there at the prison. Burying the bodies within the walls of Attica perfectly satisfied a number of people, as a matter of fact. Back home, many of the families wanted nothing to do with people who had disgraced their names. And many other felons lacked any relatives.

Yet some with kin made the trek to Attica and retrieved the bodies of their dearly departed. One of those casualties was Prisoner 3671. He was the bulky Specs, perpetrator of the second murder and himself a victim of a gunshot.

On the third evening subsequent to the riots, a long, black hearse, a battered older model, rumbled up to Attica's main gate. There a tall, gray sentry box with a single guard, rock-jawed and blue gray-eyed, stood watch. Once he arose from his seat, he could spy the driver, though the man in the back was huddled in shadows. Thus the guard could make out only a dark fedora clamped down on the passenger's head, in addition to a trench coat which enshrouded his shoulders.

The door of the sentry post popped outward, the guard ventured outside and with his left hand stopped the hearse. His right hand he allowed to hug the butt of his state-issued .45 caliber Colt.

Out of the car hopped, like a jack-in-the box, the car's huge black-garbed driver. He sported tousled brown hair and coarse, bulldog features incongruous with his immaculate attire. He shoved the proper documents into the hands of the stern-mouthed duty guard. This officer, still hyper-vigilant from the late riots, gazed with a skeptical eye on the hearse and the two visitors. He therefore phoned the office of Warden Vance Hallan for further instructions. After a brief interval, Hallan took the line and ordered the men to be admitted. With cautious eyes, the guard waved them through the gate, itching to comment but afraid to buck his warden's directive.

The hearse and its occupants rolled inside, halting, after the brief drive, in front of Warden Hallan's office. The hearse disgorged only one of that pair of travelers, the huge chauffeur. His trench-coated passenger remained in shadow in the back seat, his identity still a mystery.

He waited in the hearse for only a short space. In roughly fifteen minutes the tousled-haired driver reappeared, this time with two guards who pushed a gurney and some sheet-covered cargo in front of them. The three fellows maneuvered the rolling bed to the rear of the hearse. They hefted the cargo—it must have been a body—into the hearse's confines and shut the door behind that silent—and grim—new passenger. Then the driver in black retook his former position. He cranked the machine and turned the wheel away from the warden's office, intending to transport all of this crew from Attica. Before they could move the vehicle, however, the hefty Warden Hallan, older, patrician, and kindly, strode from his office.

In a moment he had reached the hearse's, and leaned his beefy frame against it. He pointed his head at the rear seat of the vehicle and there let his eyes rest on the man in shadows.

"It's been a long time hasn't it?" he questioned the passenger.

The occupant slowly rolled down his window, perhaps six or eight inches.

"Yes," was the fellow's monosyllabic—and barely civil—reply, one delivered as from a deep well. "A long time."

"You're re-established, then—on the outside, I mean?"

The man in the auto stated through clenched teeth, "I'm making a comeback, if that's what you're asking. As if you'd care...."

"I *do* care. And I'm sorry about your son, too. I'd hoped he would have learned his lesson and rejoined society as a more respectable citizen. But—"

The father cut him off with no hesitation: "I'm not here for a sermon, Warden Hallan. I'm here to recover my son's body so that I can take him home for a proper burial."

"Yes, I understand that," Hallan nodded. "I wish I could offer you comfort."

"I spit on your comfort, Warden," the father gritted. "Have you made your point now?"

Warden Hallan shook his head with frustration. This was becoming uncomfortable for both of them.

"You haven't changed, have you, after all this time?"

The traveler refused to answer. Hallan grasped the pointlessness of going forward with this man. He stated, resignedly, "Very well. I can say only 'Good luck' to you."

At a whisper from the man in the back seat, the hearse finished its original turn, reached the outer gate, and regained the highway.

The next evening, two more people came to collect the body of a loved one, some distant cousin, apparently.

It happened this way.

Outside the prison's gate, a different hearse arrived, this one a rarity, a white model. It put forth a much better face than the previous one had done. In the first place its paint was bright and crisp in the pale yellow lights of the prison. And in the second, its sides were smooth as glass, with chrome trim edging all of the doors. Some body—literally—would be traveling in style, this night.

In a moment, its driver, immaculate in a white suit, made a request for entry to the officer from the night before. The blue-clad gentleman followed the same procedure he'd traced with the other hearse. And in a moment, Warden Hallan allowed entry to the machine and its human cargo, a driver and two passengers.

From the rear seat the man whispered some order to the driver, who nodded his understanding. This directive he mouthed, immediately before they pulled up in front of the warden's office.

Warden Vance Hallan met three of them this time, that young driver with his barely-wet-behind-the-ears baby face, freckles and all; and his two passengers, an older couple.

The man, a tall, slender gent, looked distinguished in his tailored English suit of charcoal gray. It complemented, magnificently, his healthy head of iron gray hair combed neatly to the side and his neat Van Dyke, also gray. In addition wrinkles deep as crevices cut deeply across his brow. His patrician nose carried its own share of indentations and wrinkles, especially around the bridge. As for his shoulders, they stooped only slightly, as though he were an aging Atlas who might still have carried the world for a brief time. His entire person bespoke sophistication, even down to his precise, though friendly and vibrant, manner of speaking. Those qualities drew Warden Hallan to him like a magnet, despite the tragic circumstances bringing him to Attica.

The traveler's wife presented a distinct contrast to her husband. For one she didn't speak in as pleasing a manner, her voice being adenoidal, not to mention nasal in its quality. Frankly, it produced an effect about as lovely as a honking goose, flying overhead. Still, she did wear expensive garb, in this case, a pricey mourning dress of black. Someone had carefully tailored her garment, too, since dressmakers normally found it a challenge to fit a woman of her tall, hefty frame. It was a distinct comedown, this present appearance of hers, as her sky blue eyes, high cheekbones, and perfect lips might once have created a veritable whirlwind of attention among the males of the community. But the winds of time had buffeted her face most harshly, toughening her cheeks like old boot leather. She didn't help matters by coiffing her grayed, formerly ash blonde hair into a most severe bun. The effect made it seem that the woman's forehead were tighter than the bark on a tree.

She didn't exactly brim with vim, vigor, and vitality, either, she told the warden. And there was a good reason for her pain. Her feet hurt her like the devil, the resultant agony etching horrible lines of discomfort across her face. It was no wonder that she wore orthopedic shoes, not heels, for those fallen arches of hers. That way, at least her feet would be in comfort. Maybe then the rest of her body—and for that matter, her spirit—wouldn't suffering so at the thought of retrieving the remains of this dearly departed cousin.

She quietly removed a handkerchief from her black handbag, held the linen article to her eyes. Shortly, tears, a flood of them in fact, poured from her bright blue orbs. The woman, a Mrs. Ramond, apologized, saying that she was too overcome with emotion to speak. Mr. Ramond, her husband, would have to do the talking from now on.

Kindly Warden Hallan understood perfectly, he told her, as he put a friendly hand on her trembling shoulders. Thankfully, Mr. Ramond was better at keeping his composure during this difficult time. He allowed a polite smile to adorn his bearded lips, as he requested Hallan to relate what had happened here in Attica.

In that soft-spoken way of his, the warden

began to deliver a narrative of the prison riot. This story went forward in a relatively mundane way, albeit not for long. Shaking his head, Hallan expressed utter amazement over the fact that the bullet, the one killing their cousin, had never turned up. It was, in Warden Hallan's words, "the damnedest thing he'd ever seen."

Mrs. Ramond let out a moan of agony, whereupon her husband requested the driver to take her back to their car and then return to help him recover the body.

"N—no, no," she honked to Mr. Ramond. "I must see him! I must...."

Clasping both of her hands in his, Warden Hallan consoled her, "There, there, Mrs. Ramond. I can see this is too much for you. Perhaps your husband and I should go with the driver, and leave you here."

"I insist on seeing my cousin! It's the last act of kindness I can bestow on him."

"Very well. We'll go immediately."

During the trip to the prison's morgue, Mrs. Ramond suffered the worst ordeal because of those aching feet. That meant constant starting and stopping for the entire distance. Finally the tiny band resumed its march, at which time Mr. Ramond related some of the young murder victim's story. In brief, when his parents had died in a tragic automobile crash, no one else in the family had the means to take him in. Hence it fell to Mrs. Ramond and her husband to do the right thing, and make the boy a part of their own family. Even then, that hadn't been enough to steer him away from a life of crime.

"I understand your wife's sadness and grief perfectly, Mr. Ramond," Warden Hallan nodded. "It *is* terrible, her cousin's tragic end. However, you did your best by him. I wish only that more family members thought and acted as you two have done."

The little party finally reached the morgue, the remains of Prisoner 2575 laid out on wheeled table. Immediately they noticed that fatal bullet wound to his neck, something more along the line of a tiny hole surrounded by a marked bruise of Concord grape vividness. Further bruises splotched the cheeks, encircled the eyes. And the assemblage couldn't fail to spot a number of additional contusions covering his torso. One oddity persisted, however on his handsome features: that slight smile still decorated them.

Mr. Ramond shook his head over this man's fate, wished that the fellow hadn't come to such a horrible end. It was bad enough, Ramond murmured, being sent to prison. But to die in a place like this merely because he tripped over someone's feet?

Suddenly, poor Mrs. Ramond couldn't take any more of these sordid events. She promptly fainted, crumpling to the floor with little more than a whimper.

On seeing her, Mr. Ramond himself became flustered, briefly unable to function. He barely choked out an order to the hearse's driver to carry her back to the comfort of their vehicle. There she could wait until they had loaded both the body of the prisoner and Mr. Ramond himself aboard.

Finally a distraught Mr. Ramond composed himself too, such that Warden Hallan could lead him to a nearby chair.

"I probably should have warned you and Mrs. Ramond about the sights you would see, here in this morgue," Warden Hallan put a friendly hand on his visitor's shoulder.

"It's not a pretty place to visit, a state prison. Especially for older civilians like yourselves to see. Imagine, if you will, what it does to us, the staff: the state of being on constant alert. The ever-present aura of violence hovering around us. Then put yourself in the shoes of the inmates, who face minor assaults every day, and major ones almost as often. It all comes down to power, raw power, the thirst which never is unquenched. They constantly jockey for it, and when someone wrongs them—or seems to do so—they never forget that offense, whether it's a grudge against their fellows, or against one of us, the staff."

Mr. Ramond murmured, "So I've heard. I—I just didn't know prison was so *awful.* My wife's cousin spoke only of the outside, of his desire to leave this place. He positively obsessed over it."

"Prison takes away a person's choice, Mr. Ramond, his free will. That is the most devastating aspect of incarceration. It hit your relative harder than most."

He stopped briefly, as though reflecting on Prisoner 2575. Then he resumed: "I won't preach to you about your loved one except to say that we had high hopes for him—even with the sentence he'd received from the judge.

"Your wife's cousin wasn't like many of the men here, you know. He had too much promise to—" He was about to say " 'waste himself in the penitentiary,' " but he backed off, realizing that such editorializing wasn't appropriate, least of all at a time like this. Instead he shook his head with more than a little sadness in his kindly blue eyes.

The warden stuck out a hand for Mr. Ramond, who returned the gesture and offered a head shake of his own. He pulled a neat white handkerchief, monogrammed, from his left pants pocket, daubed at his left eye. It was then that a single tear escaped the prison of his left eyelid and fled down his cheek. He dejectedly replaced the handkerchief in its pocket.

Warden Hallan noticed the man's act, and once more offered a comforting hand. At the same time he detected an odd something in the air, a pleasant, almost sweet fragrance.

Mr. Ramond thanked Warden Hallan for his kindness towards the deceased man, and he signaled the driver of the hearse. With some help from a morgue attendant, the driver hefted the corpse aboard a gurney for transport back to the hearse and for eventual burial.

The morgue attendant did his work quickly, whereupon Warden Hallan accompanied Mr. Ramond back to the waiting hearse.

Both men exchanged a final few words, as the gloomy visit drew to a conclusion. Their hands clasped in a gesture of respect, Mr. Ramond and Warden Hallan said their goodbyes. Mr. Ramond boarded the gasoline chariot, and the driver pulled away from the warden's office towards the main highway.

From the back seat of the hearse, Mr. Ramond swiveled his bearded head at Mrs. Ramond.

"Still sad, my dear?" he questioned.

"More than you can ever imagine," she formed her lips into a slight pout. Out of her black handbag came her own handkerchief again. She passed the linen piece under her eyes, while tears pooled, then overflowed their lidded barriers as they had done in the warden's office. This done, she cut her eyes knowingly around to Mr. Ramond. And she presented him with a crafty smile.

This observation she then offered, "Time isn't the only thing that heals all wounds, Mr. Ramond."

"How true, how true," he agreed, somewhat cryptically.

Ramond followed by retrieving his own fancy handkerchief, which slid easily from his pocket. Training now-dried coffee eyes on the expensive piece of linen, he rubbed calloused fingers over a strange piece of a soft, white material adhering to the fibers. He wiped the handkerchief under his eyes for the second time, too; and again tears collected around those optics. In addition, a mildly sweet fragrance permeated the air of the hearse's back seat. That scent was identical with the one Hallan had detected in the prison.

One fact was more singular than all the rest, however. Not unlike Prisoner 2575, Mr. Ramond also wore a strange smile, despite his tears. He folded and crammed the linen handkerchief back into his left pant pocket. And if it were possible, his smile grew even bigger.

Swiveling her head towards Mr. Ramond, Mrs. Ramond opined, "I'd say taking lives is a good way to make a living—wouldn't you?"

"None better—except maybe for giving life back...."

CHAPTER II
THE UNDERHANDED UNDERTAKER

THE Ramonds and a handful of others quietly buried Prisoner 2575, Pretty Boy, in a family plot in his hometown outside of New York. Some little-known funeral home conducted the services. As far as the authorities were concerned, that was that. The world was better off without someone of the prisoner's ilk. Newspapers and radio stations treated the story in the same way, referring to him with contempt for a time, but finally dropping all references to the inmate after his violent demise and burial. As far as they were concerned, Prisoner 2575 was yesterday's news. Specs, that is, Prisoner 3671, shared the same fate with him. His father buried him in a family plot beside his deceased mother. Oddly the sire's bitterness, like water droplets on a hot stove, had evaporated. Perhaps he had finally made peace with his son's death.

Of course, no one would have tied the killings of either man to the string of murders that would follow three years later, beginning in mid-June 1939 and ending that July. Nor would any of the public have foreseen the symphony of chaos and death on a grand scale that would be performed in New York.

At one particular place, only the second of these events, death, ever bothered a certain group of people. And death interested them, only insofar as it made them money.

But that was to be expected, since Caledonian Memorial Gardens was a funeral home of the "you-plug-'em-we-plant-'em" variety. That, is, if someone had the money, they would bury that person. Moreover, they would ask no questions regarding the career of the decedent or the cause of death. For Caledonian, the whole rigamarole of final arrangements was all simply a business transaction.

For too many years to count, Caledonian Memorial Gardens had followed this policy, or at least Victor McGrieve, its owner, had. That didn't mean that his son Jay-Jay agreed with such sentiments. McGrieve the Younger had too often told his father, in no uncertain terms, of his true thoughts about some of their clientele. And the last couple of months had seen Jay-Jay grow much more vocal—exponentially so—in his denunciations of his father's business practices.

He'd preached to his father—for sermonizing it was—that he, Victor McGrieve, had no more given up the old life, his criminal ways, than a fox could give up its taste for chickens. Jay-Jay McGrieve was singing the umpteenth verse of this song, right now, as he and Caledonian's young associate Dean P. Morston quickly gathered the tools and chemicals for embalming a body, a Mr. Leakey. In life the gray-haired oldster had been a prominent neighborhood grocer who loved his food in more ways than one, if his ample waistline were any proof.

At work the day before, he had fallen victim, suddenly, to a massive heart attack—no surprise, this—and his doting wife and children had wanted a rush job on the embalming and burial. There was as little surprise here, either. The speedier that the McGrieves did their job, the more quickly Mrs. Leakey and her children could go ahead and read the man's will, aiming to come into the man's considerable inheritance.

Pushing Mr. Leakey's cap back from his head, Jay-Jay removed Leakey's dingy blue shirt, with Dean Morston pulling off the trousers of the corpse. They also removed his expensive pocket watch, a gold Elgin model with a diamond inset at each numeral. This watch they catalogued in a ledger, along with his other personal effects: a handful of pocket change, a penknife, and a wallet with considerable cash. This procedure now complete, they set about removing his undershirt, socks, shoes, and undershorts. In a trice they had denuded his body of everything, prior to the embalming.

They knew that they would have to work like demons right now, and with good reason. In a short time they would have to shift gears quickly to the preparation of another client's body. Only moments ago, Jay-Jay and Dean had learned this information. Drivers for the funeral home would soon bring the remains of Roddy Shingle, a murdered racketeer, to Caledonian Memorial Gardens.

Therefore, Jay-Jay McGrieve and Dean Morston pulled long, white cotton aprons from a nearby storage locker, a capacious affair of green-painted steel.

Tying one of the cotton garments around Dean P. Morston's waist, the tall, muscular, and blond Jay-Jay McGrieve offered seemingly interminable commentary about his father's questionable business practices through the years. Angry over them, he briefly rolled his sapphire blue eyes and pursed his delicate, almost feminine lips. The action caused him to acquire the ridiculous semblance of fish just hooked. It was a distinct contrast to his usual good looks, which he shared, in striking degree, with the actor Robert Donat.

"Hell, Dean," he cursed in a strained, hyper-tense tenor, "I meant to grab a pair of surgical masks for this job. If Dad comes in here and finds us unprepared on the least detail for Mr. Leakey, he'll give us what for."

He stopped all of his preparations and began to hold forth about his disgust with his father.

Dean P. Morston offered a pleasant word of agreement and said everything would be just fine, that Jay-Jay shouldn't worry. They would get everything done on time. In that vein, his, Morston's, firm lips gradually took on an encouraging smile. This show of support lent more attraction to his handsome face: wholrsome features, a firm jaw, and bright hazel green eyes. Such complete obliviousness to his own good looks, however, gave Dean P. Morston much of his allure with the ladies. An almost comical inability to tame his light brown hair also lent him a certain boyishness. Women loved the fact that those strands kept falling into his eyes. They craved, much more, the chance to help them fall into his eyes. Most women would have been pleased because several of those locks did so now, in fact. So he used his fingers as a comb to force those hairs back into place.

"Going to have to build a pen around this stuff, to corral the runaway strands," he muttered, with an embarrassed laugh. "I know how your dad is, too, about our appearance. Got to look professional at all times—and treat all of our clients like they were members of our family. Not that I disagree with him, mind you. We have an impression to make on people."

"Well, I think that he's the *wrong* one to be doling out that kind of advice," Jay-Jay McGrieve opined, scouring a drawer for those masks. "His criminal connections did nothing but drive my mother to an early grave, is what they did. Hell, he steered my brother towards.... Well, anyhow, Dad is as responsible for her death, as a murderer with a pistol would be."

Morston was becoming visibly uncomfortable with this discussion of the McGrieve clan and their past troubles. He removed a package of cigarettes from his shirt pocket and shook out one of the paper tubes.

"Family issues aside, I think I'll take a smoke before he comes in, Jay-Jay," Morston stated in a warm, friendly baritone. "Maybe you should do the same. It'll calm your nerves, you know."

Jay-Jay McGrieve came back, "Maybe so, Dean."

He fired one of Dean's coffin nails. Jay-Jay continued with these words, "I'll tell you something, though: If the old man catches us smoking and not working, he'll raise more hell than the devil tormenting a sinner. Lots of combustible chemicals in here, don't forget. Besides that, he wants to get these jobs right the first time. Old connections to Leakey. This clown, Shingle, too."

He went back to his search for the masks, still unable to find them.

In the meantime, Morston nodded. "I guess so. But this Shingle fellow—is he really as bad as you've said?"

Jay-Jay retorted, "I'll say! Roddy Shingle was one of the worst racketeers in New York. Ran one of the biggest gambling joints in the city. The Jazzy Kat, they called it. A big swing and jazz club in the front, all for respectability's sake. But he ran a regular high-rollers' casino in the back."

His voice acquired a conspiratorial air: "They say he was raking in over half a million a year, and growing. And he operated an enormous racket, which dealt in extortion and blackmail, as well as a bit of forgery, his original 'career.' Word is that he had sunken his hooks into more than one politician at City Hall, getting dirt on them, wringing money from them, and so forth. His kind of criminal operation would have necessitated that kind of thing, I suspect."

"For crying out loud, Jay-Jay!" Morston exclaimed, hazel green eyes wide with shock. "He was a serious crime czar!"

McGrieve agreed, angrily, "That he was."

"And your dad knew this guy, I mean, knew him personally?"

"Let's just say that they're 'old friends from the neighborhood.' It makes me mad as nobody's business, to think that Dad has chums like these."

He went silent for several seconds. Then he launched a new diatribe. And his denunciation was as shocking as waking up beside a corpse—something the younger McGrieve probably wouldn't have put past his sire, either.

"More than once, he's been in trouble for not embalming bodies properly. Had to pay his share of fines for it, too, as a consequence. Did I ever tell you about that little detail?" Jay-Jay was saying, as he ferreted out one of the surgical masks from a drawer and tied the piece of cotton material around his handsome face.

Young Dean Morston shook his head. "No, I hadn't heard that part of his past."

Trying to keep Jay-Jay focused on the task ahead, Morston pointed at the drawer, "Say, would you grab one of those masks for me, too?"

"Sure," Jay-Jay McGrieve nodded. He tossed a second cotton covering to his friend and continued his train of thought.

"It's an issue of public health, you know, proper preparation and burial of the dead. But Dad's done worse: Burying corpses in caskets made of substandard materials is just one example of his shenanigans. The coffins leak because the gaskets won't properly seal. The remains then leach into the soil, as you're aware. Most likely, the decomposed bodies—the flesh is gelatinous now—will ooze into the water table, too, especially after a good storm."

"Let's hope he's finally learned his lesson, Jay-Jay!" a wide-eyed Dean Morston stated with fervor.

"Are you kidding me? It only gets worse. He's been known to bury empty caskets and then dump the actual remains in mass graves out in the sticks. And this didn't even count the fraud he'd conducted with certain life insurance policies. Some he had failed to honor, saying they'd expired. He pocketed the proceeds—the premiums, in other words. Others he has had rewritten, to aggrandize himself. You know—to name himself the beneficiary, so that he could collect on them."

The list, Jay-Jay shook his head, went on and on. His father had beaten some of those charges and scored out-of-court settlements on some of the others. Of course, he had served time and paid fines for some of his little stunts. And saying that these events had been sometime back, or that he'd had his last sentence reduced, or that he'd gotten time off for good behavior, didn't mitigate the man's guilt, in the eyes of his son Jay-Jay.

"My God!" the shocked Morston exclaimed, his eyes bulging. "No wonder you and your father don't get along! I wouldn't have gone to work here, if I'd known your father was engaged in this. My friends back home will keel over dead if they discover a *third* of what he's done, or what he might be doing again. And God only knows what my *mother* will do if she hears such things!"

Jay-Jay McGrieve pivoted his head in Morston's direction, almost pitying the man. "Well, you always have looked for the best in people, Dean. And that's a good quality, as far as it goes. You were also fresh out of Dad's old alma mater, the Indiana College of Mortuary Science, and that made everything even better, as far as he was concerned," he reminded his friend with a slight shake of the head and a sad little smile. "Add to that your need for a job, and the rough business situation; and I think you were eager to grasp the opened hand, this place with Dad.

"So you got this position, and Dad got something else: the prestige of hiring another person from his College and a man with the imprimatur of the College's own President, besides. But that was just part of the fringe benefits 'Mr. Victor McGrieve' earned. Dad also erected another pillar to help him rebuild that monstrosity called his 'reputation in the community,'" McGrieve the Younger ranted, huge drops of cynicism falling from his words. "With you and his lapdog, that so-called 'assistant' of his, he could still run this company, from behind the scenes. I can't believe 'Old Creepy' let Dad talk him into selling insurance again, much less spending the kind of money he doles out for 'company improvements.'"

"I thought," Dean stated, "that selling insurance was Viola's job."

"On the surface it is. But she's little more than a figurehead for Old Creepy and, for that matter, Dad, as far as I'm concerned. Trust me: Dad's up to his old tricks again."

Suddenly he realized he'd been killing time with his history and commentary, and not locating a final instrument they'd need for Mr. Leakey's corpse, and Shingle's remains, later. So Jay-Jay started pulling cardboard boxes from a second shelf over to his left. He checked several of them in the process. But none of them was the correct item.

Dean Morston realized his colleague and friend was upset over the prospect of embalming such a criminal such as Roddy Shingle. So Morston made the search for the implement which McGrieve couldn't find. Unfortunately he fared no better, the object refusing to submit to his discovery either.

By now Jay-Jay McGrieve was boiling like a tea kettle atop a hot stove, since they had been unable to ferret out the missing thingamajig. He even let out some choice expletives before Dean Morston could calm him down. Emotions now reined in, Jay-Jay stalked over to an interoffice communications device—it was one of several in the funeral home—and he twisted a button clockwise.

"Viola, I need you down in Embalming Room One for a bit," he requested.

The woman in question, Viola, ignored the incipient simmer in his voice and returned in a pleasant contralto, "Sure thing, Jay-Jay. If I'm not there in a minute, then I'm not worth a nickel."

"Good enough," Jay-Jay told her, switching off the communications device.

In less than a minute Viola appeared at the door to the embalming room.

She came and stood behind Victor McGrieve's frustrated son, unbeknownst to him. When he failed to turn around, she tapped him lightly on his right shoulder. Startled, Jay-Jay pivoted to face her. For a few seconds he stood there practically gaping at her, speechless and indeed fascinated now, in a foolish kind of manner. It was as he had behaved when she first went to work for his father's funeral home, back in '37. And there was good reason for his reaction to her.

Despite her average height, she was a dynamo of energy, this Viola Vye. Electricity—no, ball lightning—seemed to pulse from her very form. She was always in motion and always so *alive*, doing things around Caledonian. Never had Jay-Jay seen a woman so downright exciting, whatever the activity. If that weren't enough, her compelling beauty was enough to wake a dead man.

Lustrous waves of honey-gold hair crowned her head, and light brown, almost amber eyes peered back at him, twinkling with excitement. Nature had blessed her with a peaches and cream complexion. Her face was positively breathtaking, being shaped like an oval. It fell short in the chin itself, which was slightly out-thrust. Still, the slight flaw bestowed that much more character to her beauty, made her that much more real, more earthy—and thus more attainable. Then there were her cheeks, which dimpled whenever her soft, tempting lips formed a smile. This was one of those times, as she reached forward her arms to kiss him.

Young Jay-Jay stopped her with an out-thrust arm, peering down at his wristwatch.

"Well, am I worth that nickel, or not?" she repeated, puzzled by his action.

"Waiting for that minute to tick past," he peered upwards and winked at her.

"Time up yet?" her adoring voice whispered at him.

McGrieve reached into his pocket for that buffalo piece.

"Stop it, you!" Viola pecked him instantly on the tip of his nose. "Now, what is it?"

Impatience colored Jay-Jay's features. He sighed to her, "Those trocs. We thought you might know where they were, since you received the last shipment from the manufacturer."

"Angry at your father, again, Jay-Jay?" the young woman asked him, more rhetorically than anything else. In reality, she was trying to bring some calm to an already tense situation.

Smiling sweetly, she went on: "Just leave it to Viola." She looked first at him, next at Dean Morston.

These words were her next ones: "You men can't do anything without me. You can't conduct your correspondence without my help. You can't sell a burial policy or a life insurance policy without me, either. And it goes without saying that you can't schedule the funerals without me. For goodness' sake, sometimes you fellows even need me to help with the embalming."

Eager to please, Dean Morston spoke up, albeit timidly, "I'm just glad you're—you're working here, Miss Vye. I'm kind of embarr—"

"I *know*," she wagged her right index finger at him. In the next instant, she gave a sassy shake of her honey-gold hair, the tresses flaring outward most enticingly. Never angry for long, she reassured the two men, especially Jay-Jay: "That's okeh, even if you are like *two little boys*. Or maybe chickens with their heads cut off, just running around here, not knowing what to do next.

"Now, let's see," she placed her slender left index finger against her chin. Light brown eyes twinkling with mischief, she recalled, "I know that I put those trocs somewhere in this place. Just a minute—I think I know where they are."

Viola strode over to another shelf the men had overlooked. After shifting a couple of larger boxes to one side, she produced the container in question, a third rectangular box some ten inches in length. From it she pulled a hollow tube perhaps six inches long, its tip fitted with a point like an arrow. Known as a trocar, it would later be attached to an aspirator, a tube-like instrument through which a vacuum would be created to draw tissues and fluids from a dead body.

"The object in question, gentlemen!" Viola

announced with a flourish. "Now, let's get to work. Trust me—it will take your mind off your frustration."

So there in the larger embalming room, Viola Vye, Dean P. Morston, and a disgusted and barely compliant Jay-Jay McGrieve began placing the remaining implements on the nearby table. They positioned four different kinds of scissors with two pairs for each of them, in orderly rows on the platform's metal surface. These instruments resembled troops arrayed for battle, so orderly had they been arranged. The first were small artery and vein scissors. These bladed tools would enable them to cut through the arteries and veins of the deceased. To slice through clothing or bandages, on the other hand, they would use specialized angular bandage scissors. Tissues and ligatures would require another kind of blade, a pair of all-purpose or utility scissors, which in turn might be dull or sharp, depending on the job to be done. And a final device, two trusty pairs of embalming scissors, would allow them to cut into arteries. In that way the young trio might inject embalming fluid into the remains.

As they gathered the tools, they concentrated on a dry-run of the process itself. Jay-Jay quickly became so agitated over the subject of the embalming, Roddy Shingle, that the younger McGrieve had to stop. Viola Vye then gently reminded him of the procedure they would need to follow in the minutes to come. And Dean Morston went so far as to tell him that he could sit on the bench for this particular game.

"After all," he acknowledged with a bashful smile, "Miss Vye, here, is a crackerjack embalmer herself."

At first Jay-Jay refused the offer from the young woman. However, Viola persuaded him to compromise. That is, they would all three embalm Shingle's remains. It would speed their work; plus she, Viola, could give Jay-Jay some good company.

When she phrased it this way, young McGrieve happily agreed.

To commence their embalming work on a body, they began to prepare the body of Mr. Leakey. First they stripped his corpse. Next they extracted the decedent's eyes. Then they slipped embalmers', or mortuary, putty into the cavity to give the illusion that the dearly departed, old man Leakey, slept peacefully. They knew that if they failed to add the pasty material, Leakey's lids would collapse upon the hollows thus exposed in the eye sockets.

Next the three young people set about gluing Leakey's lids shut. Not doing so would practically ensure that lids' natural retraction and thereby reveal the concealed putty. Nor could they leave the mouth untreated in the embalming procedure. It would necessitate stapling along the gum line, in addition to the mouth's re-formation with mortuary putty and cotton balls. This way, the lips wouldn't pop open and thus shock the life out of the already-aggrieved mourners.

Now the undertakers could start the actual embalming stage, a two-step process comprised of arterial embalming and cavity embalming.

Viola's presence there would render this stage much easier.

The young people cut a slit, or injection site, in the person's neck, in order that they might remove the carotid artery. They then resorted to a set of chemicals stored on a series of sturdy, easy-to-reach metal shelves. On these they found glass bottles of formaldehyde, which, when combined with a small quantity of ethanol and methanol, would replace the blood extracted from the arteries.

By way of the injection site, they employed an embalming machine, to which a hose had been attached. Through this tube, they extracted all of the blood and fluids remaining in the corpse. When they missed some of it, as they did because of their speed, they cut another tiny slit or two to complete the process. This finally enabled them to start the second and final stage, cavity embalming.

Here they hurled the trocar into the battle. The embalmers inserted the tube into the abdomen of the corpse; then they moved it in every direction within the opening. Such motion punctured and eviscerated the organs of the dead grocer. His heart, lung, stomach, and other organs they then sucked through the trocar. Once they had emptied the cavity, they stuffed it with filler, which provided a natural appearance. A quantity of cotton or putty filled the other orifices; and the embalmers had, by now, finished their job. Hopefully, its quality would earn high marks from the family and friends of the deceased.

Jay-Jay McGrieve had regained some of his composure by this time. The work had proved to be the best tonic for his anxiety and his anger towards his father. Of course, the company of that little sparkler, Viola Vye, also lit the way for his return to a place of calm.

So the three young people were now ready to move forward with the embalming procedure on the dead racketeer. And by now a pair of Caledonian's drivers had trundled the remains of Roddy Shingle into the room.

They moved the table of tools and chemicals next to the gurney holding Shingle. Immediately, they noticed that someone had shot the man in the neck. Curiously, however, the back of Shingle's neck contained no exit wound. And to make matters more strange, the bullet had bored only the shallowest of holes in his flesh.

If Roddy Shingle's wound struck the young workers as unusual, then his status as a gang leader, no matter how high, seemed positively ridiculous, if appearance counted for anything. In life he had been a short, rusty-haired fellow, his locks cut in a military crew style. And his hair was stiff for all that, wiry, indeed, as boar's bristles. Dean Morston pulled back Shingle's eyelids—it was standard procedure as much as curiosity—and discovered a set of light brown eyes that were almost amber in color. Eerie they were, for those optics were slightly lighter, even, than the eyes of Viola Vye.

At the time of his murder, Roddy Shingle was still wearing one of the loud suits for which he was infamous. This one, a double-breasted number, was lime green, with an atrocious bottle green shirt and a hideous yellow necktie. Hicks often donned such garments when they visited the big city, not knowing that two-bit punks wore them too. Maybe, Jay-Jay mused to himself, *that* was the reason Roddy Shingle was sporting such garb....

Dean Morston tonged a pair of the angular scissors in his right hand with the intention of attacking Roddy Shingle's ghastly coat. At the same time, with those other angular scissors, Jay-Jay McGrieve slid one of the blades into the waistband of the corpse's trousers.

As it turned out, he gave them only minimal trouble as they removed him, manually, from his ghastly togs.

Suddenly, Jay-Jay stopped for a moment,

the job not quite done. He decided that a bit of music would make the job more pleasant. He whispered a word to Viola, to bring the radio closer to them. Consequently she strode over to a wall, where a different table rested. On the object's surface a large radio parked. This machine she unplugged from the socket near the floor. Next she moved the radio away from the wall and atop a different table, one nearer the working men. The radio's console closer to them, it would better project the sounds into their midst. Its position must have satisfied them when she turned it on, since they both began to smile broadly. In addition, they started to keep time to some swing number blaring through its speaker. Now they could really finish removing Shingle's clothing and recording his effects in their ledger.

Dean Morston and Jay-Jay McGrieve had no more than stripped Roddy Shingle of his outer wear, when a newcomer barged into the embalming room.

He was a tall man, and he owned a distinctive basso voice. That was readily apparent from the so-called tune, a rendition of a popular love song, which boomed from his throat. It thundered more loudly, if possible, than the radio. It was immaterial that the device was broadcasting a number with lots of booming drums to undergird that swing melody.

Engrossed in that ditty and the world of his own thoughts, this new arrival aimed himself towards the embalming room's shelves. He seemed completely unaware that Dean Morston and Jay-Jay McGrieve had already amassed the necessary equipment for the current job.

In utter surprise the two young men and the young woman watched, open-mouthed and silent, as this unhealthy-looking specimen, rapidly scanned the shelves for something else he couldn't seem to find.

He looked to be a sickly fellow, this man, someone who'd grown up in a sunless place. Perhaps it had been a basement, based on his pallid skin. Furthermore, he was as ugly as homemade sin. *Hideous* was in fact the better term to describe his ghastly appearance. The man looked like a fictional undertaker come to life, one who might have haunted the pages of some Victorian novel or short story. His head was a veritable cranium with a bit of skin stretched over it. His grin was one of the rictus variety, about as inviting as the toothsome smile of a skull. A tonsure of wispy hair, formerly brown but now some murky chocolate hue, ringed the area above his ears. And lastly, he possessed a body as thin as any scarecrow's frame, lacking only the ragged clothes, floppy felt hat, and acres of cornfields to complete the picture.

None of this was even relevant, however, to his level of vitality, much less to his desire to make money.

"There's been a change of plans, men—oh, and you, too, Miss Vye," he announced matter-of-factly. "I'll be handling Roddy Shingle, personally. You two can tend to the body of Mr. Murtagh in one of our other embalming rooms. Miss Vye will be staying behind, here, with me and my assistant."

Viola Vye opened her mouth to respond in protest, but she couldn't find the proper words. So she simply nodded at him and smiled—like a beautiful rose dying before his eyes.

For his part Dean P. Morston didn't quite know what to say

Certainly Jay-Jay McGrieve wasn't at a loss for words.

Fists balling, he gritted, "Going to be another one of your patented quickies, Dad—this 'service' for Roddy Shingle? That why you're getting us out of here, right now? Huh?"

Glowering, he marched over towards his father. In the next second he shoved his jaw right into his father's face. In turn the older McGrieve puffed up his skeletal chest, such that he now resembled a scarecrow with a helium balloon shoved inside its ribcage.

Off to the side, young Morston nervously ran his fingers through his light brown hair. This family squabble was going in a most unsettling direction. Indeed to Morston's view it was traveling the high road to hell. And he found himself wondering why, exactly, he'd taken this position with Caledonian Memorial Gardens. Maybe he *didn't* need the job as badly as he'd once thought....

Meanwhile, Victor McGrieve spread his lips in a skeletal smile. "There'll be no arguments about this, Jay-Jay. You'll do as I say, and tend to Mr. Murtagh. Do I make myself clear?"

The son muttered something, the meaning of which no one could discern. He concluded with this: "So, it's you, Viola, and 'Old Creepy' for this one, then, eh?"

" 'Old Creepy,' as you called him, is my friend. My *close* friend and most trusted advisor, I might add. And I insist that you call him by his proper name and that you show him proper respect."

"I frankly don't care what *you* insist I call him. And I care even less about showing him 'proper respect,' " he pshawed. "That man is still 'Old Creepy' to me—and that's all he'll ever be."

Viola Vye went to Jay-Jay's side, attempted to soothe him with an arm around his waist. He continued to glare, his eyes like white-hot spotlights blazing on a formerly darkened highway.

"Maybe your father is right, Jay-Jay," Dean Morston finally spoke up, his tone tremulous and his hazel green eyes shuttering and unshuttering in fits and spurts. "Maybe we should go on to the next room and embalm Mr. Murtagh. That way, there won't be any trouble between you and your father. It will keep the family peace. And that's important to me because I just can't stand conflict. It's more than my constitution can take."

McGrieve the elder smiled again in his rictus fashion. "This is the correct attitude to take, Dean." He fixed his son with a stern look for a few seconds, but Jay-Jay made no audible comment. Head pointed downward and teeth clamped in an angry grimace, he simply muttered a series of condemnatory phrases more appropriate to the alehouse, rather than the church-house.

The father of Jay-Jay McGrieve went on, "You ignore the fact, Jay-Jay, that my friend is my most trusted advisor. He's helped get us through some tough times. And he's brought some valuable new ideas to our business."

Jay-Jay stated, huge drops of sarcasm falling from his tones, "I'll say he has. Helping an old crook like you to cheat more people. That's helping someone through tough times, all right. And as for those new ideas—"

"—Now, wait just a minute!" a snarling Victor McGrieve cut him off with an abrupt horizontal slash of the hand underneath his, Victor's, throat. "I didn't yet have my license restored. So he helped me to run the business before I could regain my license."

"Yes, he served as your proxy—but so did Viola Vye, who is the embodiment of honesty."

"She's all right, at least, for the job she does," the older gentleman opined, amidst a hurt look from Viola Vye.

McGrieve's son wasn't finished. "Oh, she's just 'all right'? As if 'Old Creepy' is better than sliced bread?"

Victor McGrieve rolled his eyes, molded his lips into a thin, grim line. "I'm tired of hearing this, Jay-Jay. He is valuable to me, beyond measure."

"He'll cause the law to crack down on you again, and you know it."

"This discussion is going nowhere, Jay-Jay. Now, I ask you again to get out, so that I can embalm Roddy Shingle's remains. We have to do this quickly."

"Uh-huh. It's one of Old Creepy's so-called 'new' ideas you've adopted. I know a little about it."

"Oh, you do, do you?" anger whetted Victor McGrieve's voice to dagger sharpness. "And what do *you* know about it?"

"I know that this process works only on a person newly dead. I overheard Old Creepy say that much to you, only last week. I figure that it explains, rather neatly, your need to execute the procedure with speed. And I've realized something else, too. I've discovered that you use it only on people with criminal records, or those alleged to have committed crimes. It's strange to me that *every one* of them shares some type of connection with you. Funny, isn't it?"

"They have as much right to a decent burial as the next person does."

"I'm not saying that they don't. What I *am* saying is that you're doing it for—for—"

"For what, Jay-Jay? Why do you have such qualms about what I'm doing?"

"To fatten your own wallet," he said. "And to do it by *any* means necessary. It's immoral and it's probably illegal."

"You have no proof to bolster your accusations, Jay-Jay. And besides—would you begrudge me, your father, his livelihood?"

"I'm not trying to do that, either. I simply think you're acting secretive, lately. Too secretive for my tastes. And I think you *just might* be up to your old tricks again."

Victor McGrieve shook his head. "Just because of this process. You have a suspicious nature, just like your mother."

"Well, I have good reason for it!" Jay-Jay insisted. "You *have* served some time. And as a consequence, you *did* lose that mortician's license of yours. Not to mention your license to sell life insurance."

"All in the past. I've regained both of them, on a provisional basis. Besides, it was a nobody of a private detective who brought those charges against me. A gumshoe whose word was, at best, dubious."

"A gumshoe who gathered some incontrovertible evidence, Dad," a furious Jay-Jay McGrieve insisted. "He showed, pretty convincingly, that you'd forged signatures and completed phony life insurance claims."

"Well, I'm clean now—that private gumshoe notwithstanding."

"That's *not* the point, Dad. You were guilty because you violated the law—not because that detective exposed you."

"Well, be that as it may, that's why Miss Vye, here, is running the insurance part of our operation as a quasi-independent entity. She keeps us out of trouble."

"Keeps *you* out of trouble, you mean. You'll need that kind of help if you go down the road where I think you're going."

"Oh, and I suppose you're precognitive, now?" his father boomed.

"Let's say this: A jury of your peers convicted you and your son once before," Jay-Jay recounted, not even honoring the other McGrieve with the title "brother." "You got a light sentence because of your age. But trust me when I tell you," he promised, "the law will nail *you* to the cross, the second time around, because *he* won't be there to take the fall for you."

The older man *pshawed*. "I doubt what you say."

"Rest assured, a jury will not," Jay-Jay stated again. "When I get to the bottom of your present scheme, you and Old Creepy will be done in this business."

Victor McGrieve thundered, "I should disown you, Dean! No—now that I think about it, that should have been *you* that died in Attica, not your brother Malcolm! He was far from perfect, God knows; but at least he had a modicum of respect for his father!"

"I'll *say* he had respect for you. He was a crook *and* dope addict! Maybe you've forgotten those minor details, hmm, Dad? Maybe you're under the misapprehension he was on a little vacation, albeit at state's expense? Taking in the sights, maybe?" In a mocking tone he asked, leaning towards his father, "You think he was sending out postcards like this: 'Attica's winters are to die for?' Or how does this one hit you: 'Wish you were here'?"

He concluded, "Want to know what I think?"

"Oh, I'm just dying to know," his father rumbled, his volcanic anger threatening to erupt.

"Fine. I'll tell you the reason that crumb was in the pokey: He was there because he was the patsy for *you*. He was a soldier loyal to the bitter end. That's what I'm thinking—he was paying for your crimes."

The older McGrieve's blood pressure must have shot from the scale, since the man was shaking like a patient with palsy. He exclaimed, finger wagging and eyes blazing, "Sniping at me at every turn! Harping on my past! Choosing my friends for me! *My God!* I know what should be done. *I should fire, and* then *disown you!* Then you'll learn some humility and respect!"

He ceased his rant, body still quivering with the strain. Finally he croaked, "At least Dean, here, doesn't contradict me. He's as loyal to me as my friend—"

From the doorway to the embalming room, a pleasant voice reassured, "I appreciate that strong vote of confidence, Victor. But it's a waste of valuable time when we need to be following Mr. Shingle's final request. Isn't that right, Dean?" he asked, walking towards the young associate mortician with outstretched hand.

Not knowing how to handle this touchy situation, Dean Morston simply shook the proffered member with the warmth of a cold fish. Then he murmured, "Yes—yes, sir, that's right."

The tall, slender fellow, a man with a headful of gray locks and matching chin shrubbery, pointed, in fact, sauntered over to one of the many sets of metal drawers lining the walls. From one, he drew a pair of black rubber gloves. In the next moment he scared up another of the cotton aprons to cover his body. Once he had tied the white covering about his waist, he covered his left hand with the first of the rubber gloves. Simultaneously, he adopted a mysterious smile, "You have the right spirit for this kind of work, Dean. But now, you and Jay-Jay need to step back, so a couple of masters like Victor and I can get to work.

"Oh, and I don't mean to slight you, Miss Vye. Your presence is always welcome."

He offered her a hand which she took only lightly.

In the next second he moved nearer the body of Roddy Shingle. Downward the fellow reached out his ungloved right hand to feel the flesh of the deceased.

"Tragically cut down by a murderer's bullet," the man observed, seeming to mourn. He went on with a couple of questions: "Isn't it marvelous, though, how well preserved Mr. Shingle is? Don't you agree, Victor?"

"Yes, that's true. He should be a most fit candidate for the—the secret process we have here at Caledonian Gardens," he stated, his manner so unctuous that floor around him might have seemed greasy.

Nodding, the gloved man mentioned that the method was far more lifelike than any other procedure for preserving the dead.

"Yes," the fellow agreed, his manner cryptic. "He looks like the very life from death, in fact. Incidentally, Miss Ramos will be here tomorrow for the graveside service. I understand she is his um—ah—what is the criminal parlance for a gangster's love interest?"

Victor McGrieve replied, "A moll, isn't it?"

"You *would* know something like that, Dad," Jay-Jay sneered at his father.

"Be that as it may," came a soft laugh from Old Creepy, "his 'moll,' a Miss Ramos, will be most pleased tomorrow, when she sees the body."

In the next moment Old Creepy removed a white handkerchief from a pocket, daubed his eyes with the article. Immediately after he had blotted those orbs, they teared somewhat. But that was no surprise, for he'd done the same thing and achieved the same result, some years before.

He was the mysterious Mr. Ramond, the older man who'd helped to bury his wife's cousin after the prison riot at Attica Penitentiary!

CHAPTER III
THE CARROT-TOPPED MAN

AFTER Mr. Ramond and Victor McGrieve subjected Shingle's corpse to the special process, that hoodlum underwent his funeral, the very next day.

On the grounds of Caledonian Memorial Gardens, they'd even raised a new pair of Scottish flags—the famous white St. Andrew's cross on a blue field—to signify the criminal's death. Some people might have considered this an oddity, this connection with Scotland, of all places. However, Shingle cited Scottish forebears in his lineage, just like Victor McGrieve. And while the old flag dangled from a pole at the center of the grounds, the new colors, according to Victor McGrieve's orders, bounded the entrance to Caledonian, as countless mourners entered the place.

As predicted by McGrieve's assistant, the moll, the beautiful Miss D. Ramos, attended the funeral. The present solemn occasion propelled the flamboyant Latin woman completely out of her usual element, the world of the sleazy nightclub. In that setting she would have poured herself into a form-fitting, bright red or maroon evening dress to highlight her gorgeous olive skin, her curvaceous figure, her feline grace. Here, however, the darkly beautiful woman had exercised a bit of restraint. She had donned the traditional mourning black: a conservative dress, a modest hat, and a fine-meshed veil, to hide her features and her grief.

Back of Miss Ramos, several mob "notables" had joined her to pay their respects, those hoods a distinct contrast to the dignified atmosphere of a funeral.

Heads swiveled as one particular pair, a romantic couple, strode into the chapel at Caledonian. They found seating some five pews in advance of the door.

The woman, moving with obvious hauteur, had clad her slinky form in a most inappropriate dress of blood red, the garment low cut and slit up the side, nearly to her thighs. She had topped her dress with a glittering, silvery necklace and a pair of earrings of equal flash and color. Sad to say, none of her adornments were real, but rather paste she had bragged would make her "presentable" for the "high-steppers" she perceived would be in attendance.

In that same vein the woman had arranged her red-gold tresses in a long, coiled affair, and piled them into a sophisticated roll atop her head. Her hair style would have suggested sophistication to some onlookers. But her dark roots, some deep shade of brown, would have betrayed her pressing need to visit the beauty shop, post-haste.

If her hair were an adornment of dubious distinction, her features paced them in the same artificial manner. True enough, they were pretty in a child-like sort of way. Her face was slightly round, for instance; and her cheekbones were delicate. Her lips were voluptuous, inviting. Moreover, her complexion seemed creamy and unblemished, rather like that of a doll. Up close, though, an observer could discern that she heavily powdered her face, to hide a few tell-tale blemishes. And she borrowed her eyebrows from the same chemical preparation, slightly diluted, that colored her hair. Those same brows arched sharply above pale blue optics she used for seeing—and being seen. Such was the accepted "look," she supposed, for mob royalty.

Perhaps her elevated view of herself explained her next action.

She rose from her seat in the pew, whereupon she told her male companion that she wanted to wait in the car. Just now, she couldn't bear to be seen in this kind of "jernt."

Next she cupped her slender hand around her fellow's ear and stated in coarse tones: "Can't let 'em see a *lady* cryin', right, Butchie? Ya unnerstand, doncha, ya bein' a gentleman, an' all?"

A dubious example of a "gentleman," Butchie wrapped a beefy paw over her hand, calling her his "sugah" and telling her that crying definitely wouldn't do. Not with a "look" like hers. And taking into account who he was, the statement represented a rare expression of truth—or perhaps animalistic desire. The second option was probably the more accurate of the two, since he was the infamous gambling czar and drug lord, Butch Spangler.

Butch could have taken a bite out of his woman, Monica Willens, who sashayed like a burlesque queen out of the chapel and towards Spangler's fancy machine on the street.

Spangler regarded her as the perfect for

himself. She'd caught his eye some two months ago when she'd come in his casino, seeking work. Then he'd hired her as a croupier girl in his "jernt." And already he'd elevated her to his moll. Most of Spangler's associates regarded his move with suspicion. She could do nothing for him, so they said, except bring him rivals and, maybe, a bullet for his trouble. But Spangler disagreed. Indeed, he had patted himself on the back for exercising such restraint and for waiting an entire two months to make his play. In his mind he was getting a little wiser, maybe even sentimental, in these middle years. And that was an accomplishment for a fellow as hard-bitten and ruthless as he was—and, tellingly, as he looked.

This fellow, a gambling rival to Shingle, was a textbook example of the New York mobster, what with his slightly better than six feet of height and bulky frame. He pomaded his dark chocolate locks and parted them sharply to the left. Except for Monica, he watched everyone and everything with a set of sea green eyes, deep set and suspicious, which bookended his boxer's flattened nose. Jowly cheeks and hard, sneering lips lent him yet more of an appearance of boldness, one accentuated by his loud, though tailored suits. For this event he'd donned a particularly tasteless outfit, a $750 number, all in deep purple, like an old bruise. The front of a lavender shirt and slightly darker tie peeped from behind the wall that was his purple-lapelled chest. Most hideous, his shoes partook of the same bruised color as the suit. He was mob deluxe, if you liked your men on the thuggish side. On some level, Miss Monica Willens apparently did. To her, Butch surpassed a shaved ice in July.

So there were Butch and the other mobbies, not to mention some prominent members of the City's business community, gathered to send Roddy Shingle into the Great Guess.

A carrot-topped man of turned-up nose, freckles, and pleasant features had also seated himself in their midst. He looked to be a former tight end for some college football club, if those broad shoulders and narrow hips meant anything. And he put forth a friendly, easy-going manner, shaking hands with many funeral-goers. From some source he must have gained particularly detailed knowledge about the life of the decedent. But strangely enough, he wouldn't cough up anything about himself, other than the sobriquet "Red Semple."

Onlookers regarded him as a member of the City's tireless press corps. Two bits of evidence indicated this much. One was a small piece of white cardboard in his battered brown fedora. And the other was a compact camera whose leather strap had been hung around the collar of his tan, rumpled suitcoat.

Through a pair of steel gray optics he observed the chapel and the assemblage itself, his eyes growing ever more intent as the minutes ticked by.

Eventually, Red and the other people in attendance grew quiet as a tall, distinguished man of patrician features and black suit, a Presbyterian minister as it happened, arose and moved towards the pulpit at the chapel's head. Someone had tapped him to deliver the eulogy for Roddy Shingle. Though saying Shingle's life had been one well lived would be worse than ludicrous.

Still the parson had to say *something* good about Roddy—it *was* a funeral—so, in a great *non sequitur* of sorts, the minister remarked that Roddy had always loved his mother. The odor of this pronouncement set the eyes of a few women there to tearing. Yet it also inspired more than a few snickers from the hard-bitten males in the chapel. The divine, meanwhile, ignored their scorn and admonished them all with these words: "Love your mothers, truly." This tack lasted only as long as it took for water to boil, and he sat down.

In the next moment three of the mobbies offered their own praise. They delivered equally absurd comments, hailing his "persuasive powers" at the business table. Their encomia were worse than disgusting.

Eventually the service ended. And now came the moment when mourners filed by the casket.

Many of them uttered the requisite lines one so often hears at a funeral: "Doesn't he look natural?" Some of them moaned, "Oh, he looks just like himself."

By this time Red, the fellow of the carroty mop, had reached the casket, to pay his respects. Or, at least, it appeared thus.

Red allowed his gray eyes to play over every piece of exposed flesh on the corpse. Shingle's hands seemed completely ordinary, save for the calluses frequent gun-holders suffered between index finger and thumb, or on the index, or trigger, finger of his right hand.

What *did* interest Red was this: a tiny indentation in the neck, most likely a bit of mortician's putty which hadn't quite covered an entry wound of some sort. This detail might play a critical role later on, so Red filed it in his memory.

Upon seeing that indentation, Red did something which funeral goers often perform. He delicately reached forward his right hand and touched the corresponding wrist of the dead man, Shingle. An onlooker might have regarded the press man as a friend or acquaintance who offered this final good-bye.

Sure enough, the man behind him, the Presbyterian minister, observed that Red must have held Roddy Shingle in high regard. He, the other man, could understand the difficulty in telling a friend farewell—even if that friend had traveled down the wrong path.

Gray eyes lancet sharp, Red offered a polite nod but said nothing. He alone knew that he was really examining the man for signs of life. Yet, it was clear the man was quite dead. His lack of inspiration and expiration, the rising and falling of his chest called respiration, showed that. Moreover, his absence of pulse and thus no contractions of the heart further corroborated the man's death.

He eased away from the casket and out into the foyer of the Caledonian Memorial Gardens, an impassive look on his pleasant face. But behind those emotionless features, a storm began to swirl within his intense, almost hypnotic gray eyes. In light of their owner, it was no wonder that this tempest was forming inside him.

He was the fabled Man of a Thousand Faces, Secret Agent X.

Relentless man-hunter that he was, he'd returned only two days before from wrapping up a case in central Europe, specifically in the country of Teutschland.* And now, though

*** AUTHOR'S NOTE: In YOKE OF THE CRIMSON COTERIE, X had battled a young woman, Madam Death, or Naida, who could kill her victims with a mere touch. However she was a dupe of the Master, the infamous dictator of the central European nation, Teutschland. On a top-secret mission the Secret Agent flew to the Master's very lair, *Schwarzberg*, or Black Mountain, to end the Master's plans. To delve more deeply into the particulars of this case, HELL'S HAVEN, is presently not advisable,**

still tired and more than a bit shaken from his experiences there, he'd taken this new assignment from his superior K9, in Washington.*

K9 had dispatched the Secret Agent here with good reason: to learn the who, why, and how of a mob leader's death, just at the moment when the man was facing Federal prosecution. The local authorities had tried, multiple times, to nail the man for his illegal activities. But he'd repeatedly beaten back their attempts by virtue of his high-priced mouthpieces, not to mention his share of blackmailing state officials and tampering with juries. So Washington had decided to get Roddy Shingle by the same maneuver the Federal authorities had used against mobster Al Capone. That is, Uncle Sammy had intended to prosecute Shingle for income tax evasion. But he'd been murdered, thereby spelling The End to that plan.

In the same vein, two other men had perished at the hands of gunmen's bullets, some two weeks ago. Wayne Helmer, the first of them, had been a wealthy, respected business titan, the owner and operator of W.H. Textiles. Helmer had founded one of the largest independent textile outfits in New York. Across the Northeast it enjoyed a reputation for being a revolutionary manufacturer of woven fabrics, smaller, perhaps than a Burlington, but a hard-charging and visionary concern nonetheless.

since I have not yet been given permission to report it to the readers of Secret Agent X. The Agent assures me that after he has cleared its more confidential details with his superior K9, I will have Agent X's authorization to report this thrilling exploit to the American public.

*** AUTHOR'S NOTE: K9 is Ronald Holme, the name by which he prefers to be known. He was once an intelligence officer himself, but these days he is a high official in Washington. Holme is the Secret Agent's official sponsor, though I believe that he carries some additional influence, perhaps with the President himself. K9 most recently appeared in the novel CORPSE CONTRABAND.**

For Wayne Helmer, commercial success required a relentless search for the coming thing. One example was a special textile with insulating properties he'd invented for Alpine skiers or for parties engaged in mountain rescues. The new fabric was head and shoulders above most material of its type because it conserved the wearer's body heat. Plus it weighed very little, in comparison to an equal amount of textile. Because of its wondrous new qualities, the textile lessened the amount of heavy clothing a wearer needed to don. Helmer also claimed the development of a new kind of fiber which gave protection against gas attacks, specifically those which assaulted a victim through the skin. He had introduced a new fiber which itself acted as a giant filter to stop such gases and thus protect its wearer. These were but two of his innovations, laudable ones because of the honest hard work they entailed.

But he'd attained the rest of his accomplishments by engaging in criminal acts. One of them involved the practice of good, old-fashioned industrial espionage, especially theft of others' inventions. He'd done this enough times that it had become old-hat for him, or rather for his agents. He also crushed his competitors through undercutting their sales prices of bulk textiles. In both kinds of cases he was neither forthcoming about his thefts, nor about the earnings which they annually garnered for him. It was no wonder that he'd gained the attention of the Federal government.

And then there was another man who had considered himself as "respectable" as Wayne Helmer and who had found himself facing a

Federal investigation too. Not perhaps coincidentally, he, too, was just as dead. The gentleman in question was Henry Terran, the owner of Terran's Own Candle and Soap Works. This outfit manufactured all sorts of exotic candles, some of them impregnated with a base of ambergris to fix the scent, as in perfumes. Terran also had perfected the products Procter & Gamble had introduced, some six years ago, the first synthetic soaps brought to the American public. Yes, Terran, like Helmer, was a visionary of sorts. But the shady reputation of Henry Terran preceded him, much as it did with his textile counterpart.

Indeed, Terran, through his company, had promised that his soaps would cure certain skin ailments and leave the epidermis "baby smooth." In actuality those bars *burned* the skin because of their high alkalinity. He had dodged jail time in this case by settling out of court and by paying for the victims' medical bills. And in another episode he had allegedly swindled investors with his promise to bring a new soap factory to a depressed district of New York. At the last minute he had claimed his negotiator had skipped out with his backers' money, which, incidentally, pulled a permanent vanishing act. He whined to this group of victims that he was "sorry, truly sorry," that he had engaged such a person for his services. So he mollified the backers by throwing a little county business their way. He prefaced his offers with warnings about the many people who knew dirt on the fine, upstanding folk who'd funded his own investment-construction scam. It went without saying that not a one of them refused his kind offer of assistance.

Agent X was recalling all of these details as he moved several feet from the casket. He was also bringing to mind more information, this intelligence regarding Victor McGrieve. This material his lieutenant Harvey Bates had discovered immediately in advance of X's entry on the case.*

Harvey had dug up much of the dirt about McGrieve's past legal troubles—his criminal connections, his trial and conviction, and certainly his time in jail. The square-jawed giant had also ferreted out news clippings and police reports, not to mention some wire recordings and newsreel footage. All of the evidence begged the question: Had Victor McGrieve gone clean? Or was he still leading a life of crime?

As an observer of Shingle's funeral, X hoped McGrieve himself would answer this riddle. Plus the Agent was developing additional questions for anyone else who might figure in this thing.

Right now, however, there was a whole heap of nothing going on. From many feet away Butch Spangler, for instance, eyed him with that trademark suspicious look, adding a pinch of contempt to the mix, while he engaged other shady characters who lingered in Caledonian's foyer.

Stu Lothian, a businessman of questionable reputation, behaved more aggressively. Indeed over the next few seconds he expressed vehement disdain for a curious person like the Secret Agent. To the Secret Agent, such an attitude was no surprise coming from Lothian. A trucking magnate and the owner of Lothian Trucking Limited, he was notorious for his boorishness. Moreover, he was

*** AUTHOR'S NOTE: Readers may remember Harvey Bates, head of the Bates Detective Agency, as one of the most trusted lieutenants in the network of Agent X's operatives. Bates last assisted his chief in the recent HALO OF HORROR.**

accustomed to being obeyed in his little fiefdom, a portion of the Meatpacking District, on the New York side of the river, southeast of Hoboken.

When he noticed the Agent's stern gray eyes fixed on his own sky blue orbs, however, he felt a strength of will which was palpable and a touch frightening. Quickly he muttered a hasty good-bye to his fellows and aimed himself towards the exit, where another group of men were gabbing.

Now Butch Spangler decided to come a bit closer to the detective. That way, the bulky hood could determine the reason for the Agent's interest in their group.

At first the casino lord stood there in silence. But he kept his sea-green eyes on the Secret Agent after he, Spangler, noticed the name "Red Semple" emblazoned on the detective's press card. So when X asked him to tell about the gambling czar's relationship with Shingle, Spangler shoved the Agent backward. Then in a voice redolent of cheap whiskey and cheaper cigarettes, he growled, "Peddle yer papers somewheres else, punk! See, I gotta take my 'sugah' for a spin in my new Auburn Speedster," he shot his green eyes towards his wristwatch. "Got somewheres to be, unnerstan'?"

Smiling, the Secret Agent remained insistent. "Our *Herald* readers want a comment on your presence here. It would beat my simply reporting your attendance, thus inviting speculation about it. Rest assured, our readers are informed citizens. And they *will* ask questions. Especially when it comes to a pair of fellows like yourself and the deceased. Were you rivals, or maybe pals?"

The mob chieftain sneered. "He was none o' that ta me, champ. He was just another successful businessman like me—and that's all he was. So my comin' here's a sign o' that—a show o' respect for a competitor. See, he knew his business, plain and simple. He knew how ta give da customers what dey wanted."

"He did, eh?" the disguised Man of a Thousand Faces inquired, his steel-gray eyes crackling with electricity. Cocking his carroty head backwards a little, he quizzed, "And what was it, exactly, that his customers wanted?"

Agent X watched as Butch Spangler turned away from him. An untutored person, especially one ignorant of Spangler's temper, might have concluded this was the way the gangster would end his business with the Agent. Some strange sixth sense warned X otherwise, however.

Suddenly, the gambling lord swiveled around and grabbed the man-hunter's coat lapels. Next Spangler yanked the detective in close to himself. Calmly, Agent X formed his pleasant features into a grin, of all things, while the hood informed him: "What da hell da ya think Roddy Shingle's customers was wantin', champ? The suckers who waltz inta his joints think they're comin' ta win at the tables, or on the damn' wheels. And he let some o' them do that. Hell's bells, I do that, myself—let some of 'em win, in other words. It's good for business, since it keeps the rubes comin' back for more. But ya wanna know why the folks *really* come to a gambling joint, Shingle's or mine? 'Cause it's a thrill for the men, and an escape for the frails. That's what all of 'em was wantin'. See, winnin' some o' Roddy's money's—or mine—is just icin' on the cake for 'em. And me? I'm happy ta supply th' icin'—as long as they keep buyin' the rest o' the ingredients from me."

He laughed with a cruelty that would have shocked Simon Legree himself.

X's eyes grew frosty. "I'll bet you *do* like supplying them with ingredients. And I bet I know who supplied the 'icin' and the cake to you," Agent X commented, his disguised lips still smiling.

"Yeah? Yer a wiseguy, are ya, Red?" Butch Spangler sneered.

"Let's just say I'm an observer of nature—especially the lower life forms."

Spangler gritted in his bourbon voice: "I'll make ya think 'lower life forms,' ya big galoot—"

He airmailed his enormous paw right towards the Secret Agent's face.

Human lightning, the Man of a Thousand Faces, still smiling placidly, flashed to his left. Butch thrust out another, similar blow. And once again, the smiling Agent X favored him with a different move. He simply pivoted, as though he were some matador in the ring with *el toro*. With the third aim of Butch's fist, the Agent snatched the member from the air and held it in an adamantine grip. Worse yet, he tightened his hold on the man's hand, such that pain burned its scarlet brand across Spangler's ugly features.

He exclaimed, "My Ga—gawd! Nobody's ever dodged one of my punches before! What are you? Some kinda damn' superman, like that laughin' mook what dresses in black and prowls around at night?"

Eerie gray optics glittering coldly, the Agent uttered a whispery laugh. "Oh, I wouldn't say that, Butch," the Agent replied. "I'm just a simple newsman, trying to get a story. Now, what about it? Your attendance at this funeral has to do with something more than respect, doesn't it?"

The man wouldn't say anything. His hand hurt too much to respond with anything, save a grunt of pain.

"Well?" the Agent insisted, his grip constricting yet again.

"Shouldn't answer this," Butch gritted to him, his hand more than he'd thought humanly possible. Finally he offered, "I'll tell you this much, if you'll leggo my hand."

X did as Spangler had requested. Then the detective's ears heard this scheme: "Shingle and me, we was thinkin' about consolidatin' our operations, awhile back. Didn't—didn't go through with it, though," he gritted, hand still smarting. He rubbed that hand and stammered, "He got a better—better offer than I—could ever give 'im. But somebody offed him, I guess, before—before he could go through with it."

He grew pensive. Then, massaging that sore hand, he resumed with this: " 'Course, I gotta admit somethin'. Teamin' up with Shingle was a good idea, as long as it lasted."

"Let's go back to something you said, a moment ago. Who made the offer to him?"

"You must think I'm a damn' mind reader, like that Captain Whatsisname, huh?"

Gaining this man's cooperation would be akin to asking a wild bear for a tame kiss, the master detective decided. So he stated, "Fine. Let me take a different tack then. Neither you nor Shingle would join forces, unless both of you had something to gain. Am I right?" X prodded.

Spangler grinned like a donkey eating briars. "Hell, yeah! I mean, Shingle cleared a little more than a hunnert grand a year. And I have a good take from my three casinos, too. They pull in just a little less than Roddy's did."

"Uh-huh," X nodded. His eyes acquired a

shrewdness, indicating he was much more in the know that the usual newsman. "Those gambling halls are the *legal* arm of your business. Word on the street says you're pulling in much more from those door prizes for your preferred customers. I've heard that you provide them little samples, 'enticements.' The kinds you shoot in the arm. If they like your product, they slip you cash. Sound familiar?

"Or what about one of your other, more despicable habits, selling dope to kids? Remember?"

Spangler knew that the Man of a Thousand Faces had hit too close. The gambling and dope king realized that someone had put this snoop wise to a certain kind of dope that he had begun to distribute. Drugs had been his money maker, but this new stuff would become the real cash cow—as long as two-bit reporters like this Red Semple stayed away. So, he, Butch, would close the spigot of information to the newshound.

Sneering, Butch tucked his tail as he moved away from the Man of a Thousand Faces. But the racketeer warned the Secret Agent, "Better not get much closer, newshawk. You may not like the headline I write for you: '*Herald* Reporter Red Semple Found Dead in Truck."

Taunting Spangler with a cold, soft laugh, Agent X informed, "Oh, I'm not too worried about your scare heads, Butch. If I were you, I'd be more worried about the smart guy who zeroed in on Roddy Shingle. Something tells me the odds are stacked much more in favor of Roddy's murderer than they are in yours. But, then, you know *all about* the odds, don't you?"

Spangler was set to make good his departure, that is, join his lover Monica Willens in that Auburn Speedster, his supercar parked on the street.

As Spangler transferred his frame to the doorway, Stu Lothian and some other men shouted for Spangler to join them. As the Secret Agent watched, his former opponent briefly—and unintentionally—acquired a less harried, if not pleased look at this latest development. At the same time he aimed his big form in the direction of Spangler, Lothian, and those other men.

X knew something was going on, here, what with the gangster's secretive manner, as well as Lothian's request for the gambling lord to join them. But by habit, the detective wasn't yet ready to form a real theory about these events. His philosophy was to wait until more facts rolled in. In the meantime, he would engage in some people-watching. To that end, he sidled over to a nearby water cooler and reached for a nearby papercup. As he turned the cooler's spigot, he heard a woman's scream, keening from within the chapel.

The sound emanated from the lips of Miss D. Ramos. She wailed that life had lost all meaning for her. Furthermore, she couldn't, *simply couldn't,* bear the thought of going through life without her beloved Roddy.

X whipped back through the chapel's door, halted slightly to the left of the grieving woman. She had yanked back her veil, to reveal perfect features and waves of jet black hair that fell just above her olive shoulders. Her dark brown eyes were fixed on the form of her dead lover.

"*Rodrigo es vivo!*" she exclaimed in a low, throaty voice. At the same time she thrust out a perfectly manicured hand to caress his dead flesh. "Roderick is alive!"

That was impossible, X thought to himself.

He'd already studied the dead man to see if he were still breathing. And he'd felt the crime king's pulse, besides. Still, Miss Ramos' fervent outcry made the Secret Agent doubt the evidence of his own keen senses. The next development left him puzzled once more.

Rodrick "Roddy" Shingle was sadly dead, a deep voice informed her. The Secret Agent and Miss D. Ramos wheeled around. The Latin American woman's eyes alit on the funeral home's owner, who had popped up, off to the right. Immediately, he gently patted the trembling shoulders of the Latin beauty.

McGrieve rumbled a litany of platitudes: "It was his time, Miss Ramos. Death comes to all of us. 'Ask not for whom the bell tolls,' you know. Why, I've had to face the Reaper many times, myself. I had to bury my own wife, far too early. And I've buried a son, too. So I know how you must feel."

These were clichés even to the foreign-born woman. In her Spanish accent she squealed at him, "How darrre chew tell me chew know how I fil! *Rodrigo es mi vida!* Rodrick ees my life! Can chew not understan' that?"

She doubled a trembling fist, as if to smite him, Roddy having schooled her well.

For once the Man of a Thousand Faces was growing rather antsy, hoping he wouldn't need to intervene and save not the woman, but the man, in order to keep the peace. Agent X knew would she would tear McGrieve up one side and down the other.

Off to one side appeared Viola Vye, the distaff member of Caledonian's staff. The dynamic young woman immediately came to Victor McGrieve's rescue.

"There, now, Miss Ramos," she comforted, patting the woman's gloved right hand. "Come with me, to the hospitality room; and I'll get you something. Perhaps a snack and a soda for you to drink? Would you like that?"

For the moment Miss Ramos ignored Viola's ministrations. The Spanish moll opened the purse she carried in her left hand, and she searched its contents. However, she came up short, being unable to locate the object of her quest. Looking heavenward, she wailed, "Oh, Rodrigo! *Mi pobrecito*! My poor little one!"

The beautiful Spanish nightclub singer wailed again. She must have thought that if her touch wouldn't waken Rodrigo, then her cries would do as effectively. "Oh, Mees Vye, I'm afraid I have no—how chew call him? *El pañuelo.*"

"Oh, dear, I'm afraid I can't understand Spanish," Viola complained, a scowl marring her pretty features. Miss Ramos, frustrated, pantomimed what she meant, blotting her brown eyes with her black-clad right hand. Instantly Viola knew what the woman had meant by the Spanish phrase.

"You mean you need a *handkerchief*! That's it!"

"*Si, el pañuelo.* I mean, the 'andkercheef!"

Viola resorted to her own purse at this juncture. From it she extracted the object in question. With the linen appurtenance she daubed the river of tears which were by now were flowing from Miss Ramos' heavily mascaraed brown optics.

"The hospitality room?" Viola asked again. "That is, will you come there with me?"

"I—on second thought, would chew get me the soda and snack and then escorrrt me to my automobile? I don't theenk I can stand the graveside serrrvice."

Viola Vye understood perfectly. In a

moment the two of them were departing the chapel, with a quick stop at the hospitality room on the way out. In the midst of their leave-taking, Viola offered Miss Ramos a knowing nod and a comforting smile that only another woman would understand. In so doing, Viola had preserved the reputation for loving care that marked the staff of Caledonian Memorial Gardens.

Thankfully the women's departure left the Secret Agent free, the better to discuss certain events like Shingle's death with Victor McGrieve.

The master man-hunter had noticed him off to the side, trying to regain his calm.

Playing the role of the smooth, though determined reporter to the hilt, the Secret Agent had intended to march over to the owner and question him.

Before the Agent could accomplish this end, Butch Spangler, showed he couldn't resist coming back inside the building. He made a point to stroll past the detective. Next the casino king gave Agent X the obligatory sneer and clapped him on the back, a tad too smartly for the act to be a friendly one. "We'll dance again, Red," he undertoned to the man of mystery. "And you won't step on my feet next time. That's a promise."

X chuckled a bit, just enough to let Spangler know that the detective was far from worried over the prospect. Shrewd as he was in his understanding of "lower life forms," the man of mystery knew exactly the means of needling the egotistical Spangler for maximum effect.

In the meanwhile, Spangler had moved close to a knot of men some ten feet away from Agent X, and less than that distance from the undertaker. Of a sudden the funeral home's head honcho stopped Spangler, assumed a friendly air, and rumbled, "Well, well—Butch Spangler. I'm surprised to see you here, but you're certainly welcome, of course."

Pivoting his head towards McGrieve, Spangler took McGrieve's proffered hand, muttered the most perfunctory of greetings. For three or four minutes, he whispered words to Spangler. And the Agent could tell that Butch, though generally crude and arrogant, somehow acquired a warmer, friendlier air in keeping with the undertaker's own. Eventually McGrieve stated his good-byes, and with a closing handclasp, he sent the gangster marching, finally, towards the front entrance.

To the mind of Secret Agent X, Butch had confirmed a connection between himself and Shingle. And now the evidence indicated another one between Spangler and McGrieve. A veritable wave of curiosity thus washed over the Man of a Thousand Faces.

In what context did the casino owner and the undertaker know each other? Also how had they met in the first place? Furthermore, how, exactly, did Shingle and McGrieve share an acquaintance? Had the funeral owner merely conducted the man's final arrangements, as he would do for another client? Or was there something else to their story?

The detective must find the truth.

Finally catching Caledonian's proprietor away from his other guests, the forceful Agent took the bull by the horns and thrust out his hand. "Red Semple of the *Herald*. I'm told you're Mr. Victor McGrieve, the owner of Caledonian?"

Returning the Secret Agent's handshake, McGrieve bassoed, "Victor McGrieve. Pleased to meet you." He allowed his eyes to travel up to the battered brown fedora and the press card, slipped inside the hatband.

"So you're with the *Herald*, eh?"

"That's right. Best paper in town."

"That a fact? The *Herald* has been known to give some people a hard time, hasn't it?"

Agent X knew this to be the case. In fact he'd intentionally chosen this role as one of that paper's reporters. But he shared none of this intelligence with McGrieve. Instead the Man of a Thousand Faces answered him cryptically: "Maybe we do. But it depends on what kind of people you mean."

His eyes stern, the funeral owner related, "Your paper gave me hell when I was undergoing prosecution, Semple. Gave it to my son Malcolm, as well. So you can imagine that you're not terribly welcome around my establishment."

"Perhaps so. But I'm here for something else. I'd like to speak with you, regarding your connection to Roddy Shingle. For example, when did you meet him?

"He's—he's an old friend. We met in the old neighborhood when we were younger. Of course, I'm older than he, by some ten or fifteen years."

"So how well acquainted, then, were you?"

"We didn't 'pal around,' as the younger set says. But we were friendly. Actually I knew his father and mother much better."

"Really? Apparently he knew you well enough to serve as a character witness at your trial, some years ago. And, if I recall correctly, he also knew your son Malcolm. Weren't he and Roddy—"

"That's all past history," Victor McGrieve stated, his tone becoming grave. This man was touching a spot more sore than a canker.

Secret Agent X, meanwhile, went on: "All right. So it's all in the past. Then, what about your connection with Butch Spangler? He from the old neighborhood too—or didn't he hire the lawyer who defended you?"

"That's part of the public record, so, certainly, I'll admit to that."

"His return on the dollar wasn't that successful, was it, though? In other words, the State of New York still stripped you, for a time, of both your mortician's license and your license to sell insurance."

"So what? I've come back."

"You have indeed, it seems," Agent X affirmed, looking around the Caledonian's sumptuous environs. Suddenly he noticed that McGrieve was pinning him with his needle-sharp gaze. Obviously he meant to intimidate the supposed newshound into halting the march of his questions. The cool-witted detective fixed the man with a steely look of his own and made another observation: "Funny how your comeback involves throwing open the doors to mobbies like the dead man. Could it be you're planning on burying his admirers like Spangler and Lothian?"

Making his scrawny frame even more erect, McGrieve thundered, "That, sir, is a baseless accusation! You are," he volunteered, "more suspicious than my own son Jay-Jay!"

"I think not," X countered. "One of my contacts tells me that several of Shingle's kind also have some sort of relationship with you. And that every one of them was hoping, or *is* hoping, to avoid Federal prosecution."

"It's immaterial to me, what your contacts think. As far as I'm concerned, they—and you—can—"

The lights in the place abruptly gave a flicker, as of dying flames from a fire. They popped on again after three repetitions of this routine.

Accompanied by Dean Morston, Victor McGrieve's son Jay-Jay strode up to his father in that moment.

"Electrical system is acting strange. I can't understand what—"

A loud *pop* assailed their ears. It came through the funeral home's audio system, by which they piped music into the chapels. In this case no comforting melodies rippled through the air. And not unexpectedly, the lights all failed. And all present heard this declaration: "*I am the Resurrectionist! I am here among you, now, to show my power extends everywhere! And I am here to remind you of the one I have claimed for my own—Roddy Shingle, the next one to experience the life from death! He will join my unbeatable army, and none of you will stop him—or me! Which one of you will follow him as a recruit for this league of living dead men? Watch and see!*"

A second loud *pop* emanated from the home's loudspeakers. The lights flickered and returned to life. But the entire episode left McGrieve wild-eyed and shaking, as though he had palsy. His son and Dean Morston had to remove him quickly to his office. Once inside it, they removed an Army cot from his closet, unfolded the appliance, and placed him atop it.

Outside, the people in the funeral home didn't know quite what to do. The next event, which happened five minutes or so later, simply worsened what they'd just heard.

Everyone there found out exactly *who* had bought it, thanks to the mysterious Resurrectionist.

It happened thus.

Another funeral-goer, a scrawny, balding member of Lothian's entourage, raced in from the street. His face was flushed, and his skin seemed to be blistered for some strange reason. After the people in the funeral home had calmed him somewhat, he revealed what had occurred outside. His boss had gone to the street to chew the fat with people he knew. Then he'd intended to pick up his car and leave.

"We weren't lookin' for this ta happen!" Lothian's hood exclaimed, his voice as appealing as fingernails on slate. "Honest ta God, we weren't! Some weird-lookin' characters like snowmen in a white truck drove up out front; then two o' them fellows hopped out of the cab. Before we knew it, this red-headed guy Petey Tetwilder—I *know* that's who he was—well, he drew some funny-lookin' pistol from a shoulder holster. And he shot Stu dead! Tetwilder's eyes were jumpin' like there was no tomorrow, too! Looked like a damn' hophead! Then him and them other guys set fire to several cars and some people. They used some odd gimmick from the back of the truck to do the dirty work. Damn' bunch got away before anyone could do a damn' thing!"

The news almost knocked the Agent off his feet. Such a wave of mass murder was, by itself, enough to drown his mind. But one other detail shocked him like a trip to the electric chair. And it was this fact: Petey Tetwilder was dead! And from his associate Bates, the Man of a Thousand Faces knew that Victor McGrieve had buried him, some three weeks earlier!

CHAPTER IV
ONE BAD THING AFTER TEN

IN a trice the intrepid investigator hit the street, standing amidst the witnesses to the murder.

Several blackened bodies lay where they had fallen, victims of some unknown device. In addition more unfortunates, also horribly burned, were gasping out their last breaths. Like the ones killed instantly, these people had passed beyond hope, too, waiting only for the final quantities of air to seep from their seared lungs. And X, unable to help them, mentally cursed himself that he hadn't been more foresighted in his planning.

Off to one side he spotted a small crowd which had encircled a survivor. Commanding in his presence, Agent X cut through this knot of humanity to provide him succor.

X found a man who sat cross-legged on the pavement while he rocked back and forth. At the same time he was bawling and grimacing with everything he had. Bespectacled, he was a young man, possessed of sharply receding, dark blond hair and a thick, light brown mustache. His lip shrubbery had acted as a net, trapping gobs of blood there. Still more of the scarlet fluid smeared his mouth and cheeks. Near him a bystander, a teen-aged boy with stringy, hay-colored hair and acne, told X what he, the youth, thought had happened.

This blond guy had strolled by during the murder and burning. The blond man had raised Cain, trying to stop the killers. For his trouble, he'd suffered a pistol blow across the face. And the assault had left more than one of the poor fellow's choppers on the street. In addition, the severity of the blow had knocked him off his feet, so that he'd joined his teeth on the pavement. After those hoodlums had left, a small crowd had formed a circle around the injured man, but not a one of them knew any first aid. So the wretched man was screaming in pain when the Secret Agent found him.

Agent X ordered them all back, whereupon he knelt by the victim of the pistol whipping. Next he placed a firm, though friendly, hand upon the shoulder of the fellow. "I'm Red Semple, a reporter with the *Herald*. What's your name?"

The injured gentleman stammered, "It's—it's B—Buck. Buck Martel."

"Well, Buck, I'm going to get you a doctor," he promised, his tone encouraging. He locked eyes with the teen-aged boy and sent him back inside the funeral home. From a telephone inside he could summon ambulances out here as quickly as possible. Just how many did they need? the teen asked. X told him to dispatch at least six of them to the site.

Then he turned his attention back to the injured man. "I've got something here, which will give you some relief."

He reached a hand inside his rumpled suit. From a hidden pouch there he removed his pocket medical kit. After snapping open the lid, he removed a small bottle of white pills. They were powerful pain-killers which would alleviate some of the victim's suffering. One of them he slipped into the hand of this young target of crime. At the detective's urging, the survivor swallowed the pill.

Now X asked, "What kind of truck were these criminals driving?"

"Well, it was white and big, maybe more like those rigs that deliver groceries around town," the man spoke in a low, pained voice.

After a bit, the Secret Agent posed another question: "How did your assailant look?"

"He—he was a—big guy," his respondent declared, "a shade taller than you are, and probably heavier. And he was dressed all in a white suit of some kind. Well, actually, it was almost silvery white. It glittered, in a way, like nothing I've ever seen before. And it was bulkier than a regular suit of clothes. It sort of reminded me of a snowman walking around. No, that's not right. More like some *thing* from another world. But he was perfectly human."

The Agent's gray eyes became gimlets boring into the other's very soul. "You're certain of that fact, eh?"

"Absolutely. I mean, he wore a protective hood over his head," the man stated, growing more animated. "But he removed the hood affair for a bit because—and I'm just guessing—that something had gotten into his eyes. Guess that was why he was wiping them with a handkerchief. Anyway, I got a fairly good look at a headful of shaggy, black hair. It was touching his eyebrows and his collar, too. I figured he hadn't gotten a haircut anytime recently. Oh, and he had wild, dark eyes. They were the wildest ones I've ever seen, darting back and forth like minnows in a barrel. He reminded me of a dope fiend, I hope to tell you!"

"What about that gun he used to hit you? Was it the same one that he used to kill the other fellow?"

"Well, the scrawny man did the actual killing. That big man was the one who smacked the daylights out of me. Wish I could get him back for it, too," he gave vent to an angry fantasy. This character owned his share of grit, the Agent decided; but the young victim of assault needed to harness it to a more productive purpose.

"I'm sure you're angry over what happened, Buck—"

"—Hell, yeah, I am!" he interrupted. "I'm not working right now; and I was on my way to a job interview. I'm practically broke and I need that job—"

"—But you can help me, the police, and yourself by giving me more information. That's the only way we'll catch his kind. So please continue your story. You left off with the pistol."

"That's right, Mr. Semple. Well, that thing looked like a kid's toy. At least, I thought it was at first. Barrel wasn't too long. Had kind of a squared clip, too, at kind of an angle to the rest of the gun. Oh, and what looked to be a smaller grip, too. It didn't seem to be as big as a .45 or a .38. Funny thing, though, about that gun."

"How so?"

"I thought I saw something glinting from it. Maybe it was the sun, causing it to shine."

"If that were the case, then what might have been the composition of the gun?"

"I'd say it was metal. Maybe the entire barrel was. But then, I'm no gun expert."

The detective nodded. "You've done fine with your observations, Buck. But say, I should get over here and take a look at that murder victim. You'll be okeh until the doctors arrive, won't you?"

"Sure, Mr. Semple. I'll be fine," he nodded his head and offered a bloodied, but brave smile to this Good Samaritan.

"You hang in there," he urged, rising to his feet.

X sidled over to the body in question. The fellow was Stu Lothian, all right, deader than a fossil. But strangely smiling? It was completely bizarre, this killing.

Ever the detective, he bent over the body of the dead man, to find the entry wound. Oddly enough, no blood covered any point on his garments. Agent X *did* find a strange little scarlet dot—it was like a pinprick—on the neck of the trucking king. It bled only minimally, of itself nothing that would cause murder. Yet Lothian *was* dead. His present state of nonbeing set Agent X to wondering if a poisoned dart could have sent the man into the next life.

Outward the Secret Agent thrust his right hand, towards the neck wound. His searching fingers found a mysterious *something*, plunged deeply of the skin, to the left of Lothian's Adam's apple. It could be a needle. But here at the very murder scene, he lacked the proper tools to perform an autopsy of the body.

Quickly the Agent sent his eagle eyes on a flight around the body itself. Near the head and torso the detective discovered nothing of interest. The same was true of the area around Stu Lothian's waist. X finally focused his attention on the pavement around the man's feet. He moved to that place with such singlemindedness that he almost slipped down in the process.

X turned his head downward. There on the macadam beside Lothian's left shoulder, something captured his attention.

It was a smudge of some sort. Something urged him to lift his right shoe. On the sole he spotted a tan, pointed object, slightly mashed. Bits of grit and grime from the street peppered its surface.

Agent X looked closely at the thing for a few seconds. Then he knelt beside that blotch at his feet. At its center he spotted several crumbs of the same tannish material. He scooped some of the stuff into the palm of his left hand. Next he rubbed the unknown material between the thumb and forefinger of his right hand. He did the same with the gob of foreign matter from his shoe. On comparing the two, he immediately noted both specimens' oily consistency. In a way they reminded the Secret Agent of petroleum jelly, though this stuff wasn't quite that oleaginous.

He needed to study these clues in much greater detail and with much more quiet and reflection. So the Man of a Thousand Faces extracted a tiny paper envelope from the left pocket of his coat. Carried always for such circumstances as these, the hungry pouch opened wide its mouth for the Agent. And it greedily devoured every morsel of the tan stuff, crumbs and lump, which X fed it.

That task done, the Man of a Thousand Faces next contented himself with a search for clues among the corpse's effects. His initial recovery proved ordinary: some $2.73 in change from Lothian's pocket, being first. Also he retrieved a knife, actually a switchblade, as the next. Surprisingly, this article shocked him not at all. Stu Lothian, after all, traveled with some pretty rugged customers, coming from a trucking background like his. Men in his industry often needed protection against enemies. And of course, some truckers employed such weapons—and worse ones—to snatch forcibly what wasn't theirs in the first place. This switchblade might well be a signpost indicating that same path in Lothian's life. The Agent would need to check on this angle with some of his operatives to find out if it were true.

Secret Agent X ventured next to the man's back left pocket, where Lothian carried an overstuffed pouch of fine black cowhide.

The cash slot coughed up quite the wad of

dough, $1000 of it in total. To X's mind, this was definitely not walking around money. Its presence revealed a man extremely proud of his ability to carry such large sums—or maybe ignorant of its advisability.

More of the wallet's compartments disclosed some receipts, which he pocketed for future reference. He fished through the requisite business cards, too; but these, for the most part, held little interest for him. However, one of them engraved an odd mark, as of puzzlement, on his disguised features.

The Man of a Thousand Faces lifted the oblong in question. His eyes immediately noticed the gilt edging that bordered all four of its sides. This adornment led him to believe this surface might have been the front of the card, its obverse. However, no text of any kind announced a message on this pasteboard's face. The reverse, the opposite side of the card, though, told a different story.

Indeed it announced a strange message: LILAC—04.

Without another word he slipped the thing into his own wallet. After more thought, he decided, of a sudden, to cram Lothian's wallet, as well, into the inside pocket of his rumpled brown suit.

Rising once more, the man-hunter peered around the assemblage. His hope was to question one final eyewitness before seeking out that white truck. He hoped, further, that the murder vehicle itself wouldn't wreak more havoc in advance of his efforts to stop it.

X sent his gray eyes on a quick tour of the crowd. His optics stopped upon a tall, gaunt, aging man with faded blue eyes. This man's skin, too, bore that scalded appearance, likely placing him close enough to the burning device to cause such blistering.

At the fellow's side the Agent introduced himself as a reporter with the *Herald*. Had the fellow been burned by the same people who murdered the trucking king, Stu Lothian?

"Damn' right Ah was!" he twanged in the tones of old Kentucky. "Wish Ah had my ol' shotgun right about now, and Ah'd—say, you said Lothian?"

"That's right. He was the murder victim. Did you see what he was doing, when they killed him?"

"Waal, Lothian had stopped on the sidewalk back h'yar," he thrust his left thumb over his shoulder. "He was a-sayin' something, Ah guess, to a big, burly guy who was a-headin' for a car with a woman already inside it."

That would be Monica Willens, the Agent thought to himself. "Please go on."

The gaunt, blistered man did. That car, he related, pulled away in a rush, and zoomed off in the opposite direction.

A bit too convenient, Secret Agent X stated to the oldster. The man himself thought so, too. Well, anyway, as he related, a white truck drove up from a side street, a few minutes later. That was when the shaggy-haired man and a scrawny fellow jumped from the cab; and the scrawny one killed Stu Lothian.

Suddenly the first three of the ambulances delivered its whining complaint from down the block. They arrived there in mere heartbeats, so the Secret Agent herded the gaunt fellow to an ambulance for treatment of his own burns. X slipped some money into the man's hand to help him pay for his medical expenses, once he'd arrived at the hospital. The Agent also helped the attendants load the victim of the pistol whipping aboard the same vehicle. While the crew was doing its job, the detective quietly removed a pencil from his pocket and scribbled something on the back of a business card. This he then slipped into the blond fellow's pocket, a couple of C-notes cloaking the oblong bit of pasteboard.

The driver and his two attendants moved back to the cab, readying themselves to transport their patient to the hospital.

Just before they departed, the young assault victim, curious, removed the card from his pocket, whereupon he saw the image on the front. It was a black X, which slowly disappeared before his eyes.

Pie-eyed with shock he husked, "You're—you're that guy—"

Curling his lips into a smile, Agent X nodded. "Take care of yourself now," he clasped the fellow's hand briefly.

The driver of the ambulance, a hefty, older man with graying hair and dark brown eyes, came back around to the Agent. Thankfully, the ambulance jockey had witnessed nothing of the exchange from previous moments. But he had heard something terrifying.

In frantic tones he informed, "Come up here to the cab, Sir! Radio just said something about a big white truck, what torched part of a street, three blocks away!"

Storms whirling in his steel-gray eyes, Agent X said nothing. Instead he sprinted across the street to his black coupe. Thrusting himself under the wheel, he stabbed his right index finger into a special button to the right of the steering column. Instantly the action cranked the automobile, and he executed a tight U-turn in the middle of the street. In the process he barely avoided hitting a bread truck and a pair of pedestrians who were crossing the broad concourse.

Quickly he switched on his radio, turning it to the police band. A police dispatcher reported news more horrible than the ambulance jockey had related. Two men had thrown open the back of the truck, in order to reveal a cannon-like device. With it they had unleashed a hell-fire of destruction on a number of innocent bystanders gathered at a bank. And it wasn't simply *any* lending institution, either. It was a branch office of the First National Bank!*

The police radio's bulletin only worsened in the course of telling. While the cannon's operators fired that stream of hell-fire at the First National, more of their number, all dressed in that color of silvery white, bulky suits and hoods, were storming into the burning building itself. They did not fear the fires, either, but actually welcomed them!

X continued to follow the unfolding horror reported by the police dispatcher. From outside the bank, bystanders could see that the marauders were robbing tellers at will. As quickly as they could snatch bags of money, they would run out of the flaming structure, only to return for more.

The Man of a Thousand Faces shook his head at the human tragedy. Traffic, meanwhile, slowed to a screeching halt, a good half-block before Agent X could reach the Bank's location. He would either have to wait for it to clear, or he'd have to snatch opportunity by the forelock.

He shot his head to either side of the street, specifically to the now-emptied sidewalks themselves. Jerking his steering wheel hard

*** AUTHOR'S NOTE: Agent X uses its parent institution, of course, to deposit funds under the cognomen of Elisha Pond. Ten wealthy, public-spirited men have contributed to a fund in that name, and with this money the Secret Agent wages his ceaseless war on crime and criminals.**

to the right, the resourceful man-hunter shot his coupe over the curb and down the wide pedestrian path. Now the detective and his super machine zoomed into battle with their hellish opponents.

And then it happened.

He reached a point within twenty feet of the large white truck. There he spotted that cannon-like affair which jutted from the back of the machine.

Puzzled, he watched a fountain of silvery mist spew from one barrel of the gadget. In the next instant a clear mist married it. The child they birthed must have been a hell-spawn, as a bluish-white fire shot forth, engulfed the front end of the Secret Agent's black coupe!

CHAPTER V
TRAIL OF DANGER

X, fighting to stay alive, clambered into the rear seat. Once there, he tonged the release lever, thereby unlatching the left rear passenger door. Through it he bolted towards the doorway of the nearest building, a dealer in men's wear. In the meantime, the operators of the cannon, more of the men in the bulky silver-white suits, battled their own weapon. Bulky as the thing was, they could not simply turn it on a dime. As X and several customers watched from the clothier's place, the men finally swiveled the cannon into a new position. At once, they set more of the bluish-white flames loose upon numerous cars in their line of fire. Some people had still sat in those vehicles. And an iron hand of terror clutched every one of them in its awful grasp.

That same terror cost all of them their lives. The tongues of the bluish flames licked hungrily at the victims. Wailing like the souls of the damned, the men, women, and even a handful of children transformed into blackened husks, mockeries of humanity. It was devilish, this business. And it was made more so because the perpetrators of this crime were laughing all the while.

Eventually they had reduced much of the immediate area to a crisped or a blackened hell, thanks to the blue-white flames. Cool-headedness enabled Secret Agent X to take charge of the situation in the clothier's shop. Inspired by his example, its clients and owners successfully escaped through the building's rear. Then all of them raced into an alley and spotted other innocent people who'd fled to safety. Agent X continued to lead the way as they marched to the service door of a restaurant on the rear street. This area had, for the present, escaped the wrath of the white suits.

What none of them presently realized, however, was that the police simply had no defense against such a terrible device. So on the other street the men in white continued to unleash mayhem and murder. Finally they ended their merciless assault and drove on, unmolested.

Police prowl cars eventually threaded their way down the street of burned vehicles and dead civilians.

Agent X watched all of this closely, the detective having sneaked back to the site of the original battle. From his location behind a still-burning pick-up truck, he spotted a familiar personage unlimbering from a police auto. The individual was Timothy Scallot, of the New York Police Department.*

*** AUTHOR'S NOTE: Timothy Scallot, designated "T.S." in Agent X's records, acts as a spy in police headquarters, answering directly to Harvey Bates. Scallot believes he works for the Federal government by gathering information about crime and**

Up went the Agent's hand, to remove the press card from his hatband. He resorted to some quick changes—prodding here and pinching there—which rendered his features more commonplace than previously. Next he pulled a sandy toupee from his pocket makeup kit. After he combed his hair back, he slipped the hairy mass over his scalp.

Stepping from behind the burning pick-up, he strolled confidently over to Scallot.

"Good to see you again, Detective," he addressed Scallot with a smile.

Scallot formed his harsh mouth into a grin. "Special Agent Weston! It's been some time!" *

"It has, that. You know that I'm not a detective anymore, don't you?" he asked. In the next breath he removed his wallet, which held a bright, new badge. It designated him an Assistant Inspector.

The detective exclaimed, "I'm glad to hear about this! But I must admit that I didn't know about it. I've been working elsewhere," which was technically true, "so I'm somewhat out of touch with things. How did this come about?"

"One of these days Inspector Burks will retire. So they're trying to train me for that day. Meanwhile, I guess you're here to find out about these killings and fires?"

"More properly, they found me already. Some of them burned my car, a few blocks from here," he narrated, while he fanned his face with his fedora.

criminals. He does not realize that he is in the employ of Secret Agent X, himself a Federal man of sorts. Scallot last appeared in MASTER OF MADNESS.

*** AUTHOR'S NOTE: The real Special Agent Weston is a sometime ally of the Secret Agent, having first encountered the Man of a Thousand Faces in THE MURDER BRAIN and again in SLAVES OF THE SCORPION. Since Scallot regards his role as an adjunct to Federal law enforcement, it makes sense that X would adopt such a guise to meet him.**

"Ruthless bunch, aren't they?"

"That they are. What do you know about these fires, Scallot?"

"I should back up a bit and tell you about their assaults on several jewelry stores in downtown, last week."

"So, this has been going on for that long, then?" the Secret Agent's tone was grave.

"That's right. These white suits made off with some pricey merchandise at each one of the stores: thousands of dollars in diamonds, a treasure trove of rubies and emeralds. Losses will be through the roof, from what the owners have told me.

"Obviously that wasn't enough for this greedy crowd," the mysterious man-hunter commented to his colleague from the police.

"I'll say!" Scallot nodded his agreement. "That's what makes their next targets, those branches of the First National Bank, seem so logical, doesn't it?"

X stopped him briefly. "How many have they struck before now?"

"Three previously, bringing the total to four. Here's where everything gets odd, though, Weston."

"How so?" the Man of a Thousand Faces raised one eyebrow in quizzical fashion, his steely eyes flashing with interest.

"They went inside two of the previous branches, so witnesses said, seeking someone by name."

X hated to ask this next question, but circumstances forced him to do so. "Who were they hunting?"

"Said they were out shaking the bushes for that millionaire philanthropist, Elisha Pond. It's a miracle he wasn't at any of the branches when the white suits hit the banks with their 'Wrath of God.'"

" 'Wrath of God'?" X repeated.

"That's what they're calling their flame device. When they struck those previous banks, they said it was time for Pond to pay for his sins, to face the Wrath."

"It's a personal vendetta they have against him, then?" Agent X quizzed, tone solemn.

"Seems to be the case. Inspector Burks tapped me to figure out why. So I've been combing through a list of anyone who might have it in for him."

"Business rivals?"

"Yes. He may have encountered his share of them, you know, men who consider themselves more entitled to success—or even recognition—than he is. You might be surprised to know about the rivalry among some people in the philanthropic community."

X merely grunted at this suggestion. Inwardly, he knew that Scallot's analysis was off-base, and with good reason. Indeed the Secret Agent had assumed the Pond identity after the World War, when the real man had gone missing in action.* So to think that he had rivals from the years prior to the World War was unlikely, to say the least.

Here was another possible—and more likely—explanation for the Resurrectionist's war on Pond, according to the man of mystery. And, unsettling as his supposition might be, he had to share it: "Maybe this new crime czar is another kind of enemy, a man who might want Elisha Pond dead. After all, I would know from my Washington contacts," he concluded, eyes twinkling a bit, "that Pond isn't facing any kind of Federal prosecution—in distinct contrast to some of the men who have already died."

* **AUTHOR'S NOTE: This was first reported, of course, in HALO OF HORROR.**

"Say, that makes sense!" Scallot snapped his fingers. "That fits much more closely with the killing of Stu Lothian."

X bobbed his head. "Yes. And after his murder, it seems obvious to me that his death, the killings of those other men, and the hunt for Pond are all connected, too. And here's another little tidbit: Someone apparently rubbed out that drug king, Petey Tetwilder, some three weeks back. But he turned up, alive, from what a witness told me, a few moments ago."

"Tetwilder?" the eyes of Scallot widened with shock. "That can't be, Weston! I went to the funeral myself!"

"Nevertheless, Scallot, he was very much alive—and looking at a Federal prosecution like his predecessors. But what was this you were saying about those previous dead men?"

"Yes. So, this so-called 'Resurrectionist,' as he calls himself, shot Lothian and the rest. Or rather, his 'Resurrection Ring,' some of his operatives, did the dirty work. In the case of Elisha Pond, though, this Resurrectionist was seemingly out to burn Pond to death.

"It begs the question, again, 'Why?' doesn't it, Weston?"

The Man of a Thousand Faces bobbed his head. He asked the newly-minted Assistant Inspector to give him a ride downtown, to the offices of the *Herald*. The disguised Agent had another contact there, he informed, whose information might also prove invaluable. Scallot happily obliged his fellow law enforcement operative.

Scallot guided his police auto through the maze of burned machines until he'd reached the offices of the *Herald*. On arrival there he mouthed a quick thank you and a request for further information, should Scallot learn anything new. Then the detective hopped out of the police chariot and marched towards the front entrance. More seconds passed as his elevator rumbled to the top floor of this towering office building.

Once outside he strode purposefully towards a particular office. His knuckles rapped a quick tattoo on the door, and a pleasant female voice invited him inside.

She was Betty Dale.* And to the unsettled eyes of Secret Agent, the beautiful young blonde was a beacon of hope and stability in this ever-growing storm.

"Can I help you, Sir?" she politely inquired, under the impression he was an advertiser or a reader of her paper.

He crossed both index fingers in an X, a symbol she would instantly recognize.

Her sapphire eyes instantly became pools of moistness. "Oh, it's you!"

She ran to his arms, hugging him close to her. They kissed tenderly, then passionately, as two starving people finally sitting down to a sumptuous banquet. Finally they stopped for a time. Peering up into his face, she whispered, the tears flowing freely, "I—I hadn't seen you in weeks. I thought, for a while, that—that something had happened to you.

"My mind ranged over the worst outcomes. Maybe someone had captured you. Subjected you to awful torture. Or perhaps killed you—slowly. I couldn't sleep for days on end. You can't imagine what I—what I went through—the torment I suffered."

Agent X, ashamed, realized he had no excuse for not having reached her sooner. He could offer Betty only a heartfelt apology for his actions.

Betty, still teary eyed, remained silent for a number of seconds. Eventually she extended her forgiveness. After that she told him, "Several days ago I read a wire report about those events in Teutschland. I knew at that point that you must have been involved. You were with that adventurer, that Hazzard fellow, weren't you?"

"That's right."

"He looked so *arrogant* in that picture. As if he were God's gift to the world, or, worse, one of those goose-steppers. He was certainly wearing the boots for it."

"Well, dear, if it's any consolation, I had to wear the disguise of a Teutsch military man for a brief time while I was over there," he came back.

Shocked, Betty stammered, "I—I see."

"And besides, Hazzard was—is—a valuable ally. I wouldn't have won through without him. He even saved Bates' life over there."

She softened somewhat over this news about the faithful giant. "Bates is okeh now?"

"He's fine."

"And you?" her voice broke, ever so slightly.

"I'm fine, too, darling," he favored her with a shy smile, pulled her close again. He didn't want to tell her of the horrors he'd seen over there. Much less did he want to worry her about the Master's plans against the rest of the world, especially this country and her allies. As a consequence, he paused many seconds before he spoke this: "Still, it was a horrible business over there, what the Master was planning for the rest of the world."

"The report said that his castle was de-

*** AUTHOR'S NOTE: All followers of the Agent's exploits are familiar with Betty Dale, reporter on the *Herald*, and X's companion through many perilous adventures. Of all living people, Betty Dale alone has seen the real face of Secret Agent X. Betty, more than anyone else, knows the courage, kindliness, and resourcefulness of the Man of a Thousand Faces.**

stroyed, along with some weird equipment he'd stockpiled. And that he up and resigned. No explanations or anything."

"That was on purpose. It's classified, dear, what he intended to do. I *can* tell you this: The War Department put a gag order on the particulars of the affair because all of Europe is an armed camp right now."

She could feel the tremor from X's hands which were visibly shaking on her shoulders.

"Oh, dearest! What can I do for you? Is there anything I—?"

"Something's coming, Betty," he asserted, staring off at some horrible prospect only he could see. "Something terrible that will change our world, I'm afraid, permanently, since I—I didn't quite finish what I'd been assigned to do...."

He rubbed the fingers of his left hand slowly across his brow, shook his head.

Neither of them said anything more for quite some time. Holding each other, for those moments, was all that mattered to the couple.

When Agent X broke the silence, it was by deed, as much as it was by word.

His right hand traveled into the pocket of his shirt, whereupon his fingers returned with the odd business card.

"Recognize it?" he questioned, his manner still grave.

Betty peered closely at the pasteboard slip. "Strange, that someone would gild one side of this card and leave it otherwise blank. I've never seen anything like—"

She absently flipped it to the other side. "What's this reference to 'LILAC-04'? What could it mean?"

"I haven't the faintest idea—not at present, anyway. It might be a phone number, for instance, ineptly disguised. Or it could be something else entirely. All I know for certain is that Stu Lothian was carrying it on his person when someone murdered him."

"The police radio in my editor's office picked up that call! Someone had just done the deed."

"That's right. So I want you to do some checking for me. Write down the number on the back of the card."

After she'd done so, the Agent continued, "I'll keep this thing for myself, so that I can do a chemical analysis of it. In the meanwhile, approach some of your police and criminal contacts. Find out what you can about this card. It's likely that the other men were carrying them, as well.

"Who?"

"Why, Wayne Helmer, Henry Terran, Roddy Shingle, and Petey Tetwilder, of course. They all met their ends, because of gunshot wounds to the neck."

"Petey Tetwilder, eh?" Betty touched her perfect chin, pointed her head upward. "I remember when they buried him, a few weeks ago. You remember that he's that drug kingpin, maybe one of the biggest in town, after that Shingle fellow."

X certainly did. Tetwilder's sudden appearance on the scene had shocked the Agent like sticking a fork into an electrical socket.

When Betty overcame her own incredulity, the young police reporter went on: "They're saying that this business involves 'sugar.' Something dealing with cocaine, I suppose?"

"It could be," Agent X lightly bit his lower lip, his tone pensive. "If that *is* the case, then I'm dealing with a high-dollar operation. So here's something else you can do for me, since you mentioned this 'sugar.' You know about Shingle's lady friend, Miss D. Ramos?"

"Certainly, darling. She's the 'girl singer' over at the Jazzy Kat. Really popular, as I understand. You're thinking I should—"

"That's right," he agreed, slipping an arm around her slender shoulders. "Get out there, and find out what you can about Miss D. Ramos. In other words, when did she first meet Roddy Shingle? Under what circumstance? And what might she stand to gain, since his death?"

Betty would be glad to help him, she said. Then, taking both of his hands into her own slender hands, she offered an additional morsel of information to him: "You know that one of Shingle's old rivals frequents that place, quite a bit, don't you?"

Since Tetwilder was dead, that left only one other person. "You mean Butch Spangler?" he inquired, steely eyes glinting with interest. When she corroborated his conclusion, he said, "Ask about Butch Spangler's connection with all of this, too. It might help to know that he and Roddy were planning to consolidate their enterprises. But Shingle's death scotched that scheme."

"Okeh. So I'll get cracking on this thing, starting to-night. How will I reach you, when I've dug up the appropriate dirt?"

"Contact the Bates Detective Agency. Harvey or one of his associates will relay the message to me."

This plan was agreeable to her. Agent X, therefore, planted a quick peck on her cheek; and he, after phoning a cab, left her office. Once downstairs he would direct the hack to transport him to a garage containing several of his other vehicles.

That afternoon, Betty did as promised, albeit not quite in the way that the Secret Agent would have suspected—much less approved. She checked a phone directory to locate the woman's address. When she'd located it, she traveled out there in her trim, powder blue Cord Sportsman. Ringing the bell at the Ramos woman's apartment produced no results, however.

Ever resourceful, Betty accosted a neighbor, an elderly woman of brittle features. When Betty told her she was doing a newspaper story, the oldster informed Betty that she, the neighbor, thought it completely inappropriate for a young woman to work on one of those "awful newspapers" when she should be teaching children or finding a husband.

Though she profoundly disagreed with the woman, Betty offered her no commentary. The prudish, old soul cranked out a few more unsolicited pieces of advice to the young blonde before Betty could steer her back to the present matter. Finally the woman informed Betty that Miss D. Ramos was probably at that "awful nightspot," as she termed it, the Jazzy Kat. Betty thanked the woman and, gratefully, took her leave. Having reached her Cord, she faced a clear choice. Betty could either wait until the next morning, thus wasting valuable time; or she could act on her own initiative.

She chose the latter. That night she motored out to the nightspot in her sporty little chariot. At the Jazzy Kat's front door, a duded-up mob gorilla, tuxedoed, stopped her there. When he stepped into the harsh yellow glare of a street light, she noticed that the hood was as appealing as a case of athlete's foot fungus, certainly as dirty, if those heavily pomaded locks; harsh, leering mouth; pockmarked skin; and that threadbare tux were proof of anything.

For her part it was all Betty could do to charm him with her gorgeous smile. But she disappointed the thug with a polite "No, thank you," when it came to moving her vehicle. Now out of his sight, she tooled her car to the rear. She thought to herself that she had spent too many hard-earned dollars to allow a dirty dog like this one to bring his fleas into her car....

She parked her machine, and aimed herself towards the club. At the doorway, a waiter met her, whereupon he escorted her down the darkened hallway and into the large dance area. Here she caught the eyes of the club's male clientele. And there was good reason for their fascination with her.

The young police reporter had clothed herself in a turquoise dress of conservative cut which still could not hide her loveliness of form. Too, the dress' very color accentuated the perfection of her ivory complexion. A small leather handbag, also turquoise, further underscored her simple elegance. That bag worked wonderfully with the small ring of pearls which encircled her lovely neck. And the modest yet tasteful watch on her wrist completed this portrait of a modern, sophisticated young woman, enjoying a night on the town.

Betty presented a refined contrast to the glitzy, gaudy collection of criminal types who surrounded her in this nightclub. From her table many feet back and left of the bandstand, she could observe her fellow patrons practically unnoticed. Immediately she spotted a number of mob thugs, including some crime bosses, who tried to outdo one another with their loud suits of linen, $500 a pop and up. Still others of their fraternity had donned tuxedos and even white dinner jackets, each of which cost an arm and a leg for someone—other than the wearers. Their women too had clad their forms in expensive, though gaudy wear. In most cases, sleazier versions of dresses worn by Hollywood movie queens covered their shapely shoulders. And pricey gold jewelry—most of it probably hot, or stolen merchandise—adorned their necks and ears.

Above the patrons' tables, tiny chandeliers emitted soft lights which haloed the club-goers with their gentle radiance, ironic, to say the least with thugs and their molls on the scene.

Away from the patrons shiny brass trim edged the long bar itself, with a bartender who looked death on anyone who smudged his bar's cedar surface or spilled liquor thereon.

And at the front of the place, a large swing band performed some popular dance number from the radio. Several couples were gyrating to the musical selection, to be sure. But most of them waited for the band's girl singer, Miss D. Ramos, to take the microphone.

As it happened, they would be waiting a little longer, as Betty found out from a tuxedo-wearing waiter. He informed her Miss Ramos was taking a break. She would not sing her next set for another fifteen minutes.

Betty didn't mind. She could pump the woman for information, after which X's companion could report to the Secret Agent. And Betty wanted to do so without delay. He had seemed unsettled, much more so, in fact, than what he had revealed to her. Something else must be wrong with him. And he couldn't hide it from Betty....

Around the semi-darkness of the room she swiveled her sapphire blue eyes. After a time they alit on a table well where D. Ramos, the Latin nightclub singer, sat.

The fiery Latin beauty had allowed her thick, jet hair to fall in a cascade onto her olive shoulders. Gold hoop earrings dangled from her lobes. An orange dress of sheerest witchery hugged the form of Roddy Shingle's former love. The low cut of the garment displayed everything but the price of tea in China—and she might have shown that too, if they cared to inquire.

Betty casually walked over and invited herself to sit down. Before the woman could question her or offer an objection, Agent X's smiling companion took command of the situation.

"I'm Betty Dale, Miss Ramos. I'm a reporter for the *Herald.* One of the waiters told me that you were taking a break between sets. Might we talk?"

The woman, surprised at Betty's self-assured demeanor, couldn't speak for a moment. Her lack of words allowed Betty to press her advantage even further.

Her hands touching those of Miss Ramos, Betty addressed her tenderly, "I know that you've suffered quite the loss, with the death of Roddy Shingle. And I'm here to get to know the real you, Miss Ramos—not some creation of the sensational rags. I believe that this way, my readers can understand the real people, back of the news headlines."

Such words caused the Latin singer to squeeze Betty's hands, as though she, Miss Ramos, had found a friend. Unbidden, however, her body slumped, like a marionette whose strings had been severed. When she peered upward at Betty again, the sad-eyed Miss Ramos slowly shook her head. Then she stated, wistfully, "*Rodrigo*—he—he was the kindest *hombre* I have everrr known...."

Her voice caught before she could say anything more. The woman turned her head downward to her orange purse, which perched beside her on the table. The black clasp of the leather accessory unfastened, she retrieved her handkerchief.

"Rodrigo bought thees *pañuelo* forrr me," she curled her beautifully molded lips into a sorrowful smile. "That ees why thees, eh, thees 'andkercheef is so—so, how you say *preciado*?" she groped for the correct English word.

After she daubed her dark eyes, pools of tears collected while Betty guessed, "Are you trying to say 'precious,' perhaps? Is that what you mean?"

"*Si,* prrrecious! It was a gift from *mi vida, mi Rodrigo*!" she exclaimed, her eyes plaintive.

"I understand gifts of the heart," Betty replied fervently, while she wrapped her slender arms around the woman's shoulders and sweetly hugged her close. In that instant she caught wind of a most pleasant scent—likely Miss Ramos' perfume, and asked the Latin woman, "So tell me: How long had you and Roddy known each other?"

"We met, eh, fourrr months ago. *Un amigo* told him to come to the club to hearrr *mi música*. Our eyes met, and, *caramba! Amor, mi amiga!*" she exclaimed to Betty. "*Nada pero amor*!"

"That, too, I can understand," noted a sweetly smiling Betty. She need not have been a Spanish speaker to fathom the woman's deep devotion to Roddy Shingle. The Latin beauty's sentiments reminded Betty of her own deep love for the Secret Agent. She related, "You met, then, here. What did the two of you enjoy doing together, when you weren't singing here at the Jazzy Kat?"

As the two women became better acquainted, a group of three men, hats obscuring their features, sat in a booth which cloaked them, intentionally and almost completely, in shadow. Their gloomy vantage point guarded a position some ten feet or more from Betty and Miss Ramos. The darkness surrounding the men wasn't a simple case of blowing out a candle and hence eliminating a source of light for the patrons. Rather, a small dome light on the wall would normally have afforded further illumination to the booth, via a bright bulb of titanium whiteness. But one of the men had pulled the cord to switch off the light, sometime before.

Hands tapping the table, they feigned a love of the tunes the band continued to play. Nevertheless, they weren't at all interested in the peppy music syncopating its way from the bandstand. And already knowing one another—too well, in contrast to Betty Dale and Miss Ramos—these fellows weren't interested in an evening of convivial conversation. Instead they cared only about the two women themselves, especially Betty Dale.

The first of them was a big fellow, a trifle over six feet in height, and bulky like an oil field worker or perhaps an Oklahoma cowpoke. His features might have been fine, or they might have been coarse. With the lack of light, it was simply impossible to discern them with any certainty. He sat beside another rather large, though more slender character to the first one's right. This second individual was patting the table with a fury that matched that of the band's drummer, so deeply engrossed in the music did he seem. His actions were actually a mere front for the words issuing from Betty Dale's mouth.

"...discussed anything about flowers?" X's companion had asked. "That is, has Roddy ever expressed an interest in them to you?"

"*Flors*?" the Spanish beauty's eyebrows grew more arched. "As a matter of fact, he rrrarely gave them to me—until rrright before he was murdered."

"Really? What kind did he purchase for you?"

"They were lilacs...."

Instantly the supposed music lover came erect in his seat, as did the man two slots away from him, to the left of the seeming oil field rowdy.

This one was a being whose features were also obscured. However, in his case, he happened to lean forward across the table to make his point. In so doing, his face eased briefly into the pale circle of light projected from the bulb set at an oblique angle from them.

It might have been real, that visage of his. Certainly, it was well-molded, handsome, even, in a preternatural fashion. But it was entirely immobile, and thus unnatural, by its very perfection.

"You heard what the Dale woman just asked?" he stated in an menacing tone. "Her presence here is not a coincidence. It means *he* is getting close to us. Far too close. I cannot permit this."

His intense eyes almost matched the rapidity of the second man's tapping hands. "You know what to do, of course?"

"Follow her?" the oil field lookalike suggested.

"Yes, follow her, along with the Ramos woman. But pay particular attention to Betty Dale. If she gets too close, then you know what to do...."

The shadowy men would be following these orders, though later than they thought.

Miss Ramos later took her leave of Betty Dale, that she, the Latin singer, might perform her last set for the evening. With her whole heart she sang of love and loss, of joy and pain, in a way only the bereaved could accomplish. There was something savage, even primal, about the way she interpreted her music. It was raw, powerful, authentic. And her listeners knew they had experienced something akin to true artistry that night.

At least, most of them did.

For the three who intended evil against Betty Dale, it wouldn't have mattered if they'd heard a divine trying to preach them away from hell-fire. They would still have marched willingly towards those flames. They would eagerly have pursued their own path, simply because of the promises their leader, the masked Resurrectionist, had made to them....

CHAPTER VI
DANGEROUS INTELLIGENCE

WHEN Agent X departed Betty Dale's office earlier that day, he could not have foreseen he had sent the reporter into the maw of danger and sudden death. Had he done so, he would have come unglued. To his way of thinking, it wasn't so much that he distrusted Betty's ability. It was the fact, rather, that he was supposed to protect her, like the knights of old protected their kings, queens—and certainly the fair maidens. Unrealistic as this might sound, that was simply his code.

The Secret Agent had retrieved another of his autos from a city garage which stored some of them in the names of his many aliases. He used his present machine, a cream-colored coupe, to transport himself to one of his hideouts in the city.* En-route to the site, he stabbed his right index finger into a small stud, countersunk into the dashboard. His action closed a circuit, which in turn opened a small, concealed door to the left of the glove compartment. From this hidden area, a tiny UHF sending unit slid out, along a ball-bearing track.

The Agent's fingers placed the microphone next to his disguised lips.

"X to Bates. X to Bates. Do you read?"

At that time the square-jawed Harvey Bates had been sitting at a desk at his agency. Squared pipe between his lips, he had wrapped his huge, square fingers around a battered pouch of pipe tobacco. He'd intended to enjoy a pipeful of his favorite brand before returning to his duty. On hearing X's radio hail, he dropped the leathern container onto his desk and snatched up the microphone parked on his desk.

"Here, Sir. Got some new information about this Resurrectionist and his latest criminal Ring."

"I'm ready."

Bates clipped, *"That Wrath of God the Resurrectionist and his men are using, Sir. Burned three more branches of the First National Bank."*

"How many casualties did he cause, this time?"

"Killed three tellers at the first bank, as well as five at the second, and two more at the last one. Burned, but didn't kill, fifteen more employees. My contacts say he murdered another twen-

*** AUTHOR'S NOTE: The Agent maintains many hideouts all over New York, as well as in every state capital and large city in this country. In each of them he has stashed an extensive wardrobe, in addition to makeup apparatus and crime-fighting gear. Moreover, this present hideaway plays host to a sophisticated a crime laboratory, rendering the place a more complete outpost guarding the borderlands of justice. Only the Agent's Montgomery Mansion headquarters outstrips it for breadth and depth of equipment.**

ty-five patrons of the firm and injured double that many, if you add all of the banks together."

The Man of a Thousand Faces shook his head, his eyes growing flinty and his features hardening to stone. This thing was growing worse by the day. And at this moment, he couldn't predict the head miscreant's next move, much less bring him to the bar of justice.

"What do you know about a possible connection with this case and the dope trade, Bates?"

"Sir?"

"Have you or any of your associates heard the term 'sugar' bandied about, in relation to the Resurrectionist?"

"Know that 'sugar' is a word for cocaine. Also I'm hearing the criminals brag about the stuff—the euphoria it produces—and the possible connection to this new mastermind the Resurrectionist. Just heard something else: One of my operatives just informed me about that killing of Stu Lothian by Petey Tetwilder. Don't put much stock in that *kind of thing, though, Boss."*

"Perhaps not. But someone answering Tetwilder's description purportedly *did* commit that murder. Butch Spangler is becoming involved in this affair, too."

"Real up-and-comer, isn't he?" Bates asked, his voice uncharacteristically sarcastic. When he spoke again, he was offering new information to his chief: *"Heard about the lilacs, too, then, Sir?"*

Here it was, again, that mysterious reference to the flower. "How did you learn about them?"

"Picked up more chatter off the police radios. Scallot's told me the same thing, too. Oh, and Miss Arden—one of my best associates—eavesdropped on something else. One of our field men planted a listening device in that thug joint, the Pink Rat.

"That low-life's taproom, correct?"

"That's the one. Well, Miss Arden heard a group of criminals, there, jabbering through the microphone. Most of the conversation was useless. But started crowing and laughing about lilacs. Said they needed to buy some for themselves, but that the things were awfully expensive."

"Interesting. Tell me this: Could Miss Arden determine whether they were communicating with a UHF device like the two we're using right now?"

"Suspect so, Sir, since she told me the reception was so crisp and clear."

X put a hand to his chin; his voice acquired a contemplative tone: "That fits with UHF, all right. Those units transmit their signals much more faithfully than the older models do. Of course, these UHF machines aren't cheap, either. And if this Resurrectionist has one or more, that's more proof we're dealing with a well-financed operation.

"Let's consider something else for a moment, Bates. What makes the lilac so significant to these fellows?"

"Can't say. Can't imagine hoodlums who grow flowers—or love them. Still," he continued, with more confidence in his voice, *"Miss Arden might find the answer to that. Give me a moment or two?"* he finished.

"Certainly. I'm stopping at a hideout right now."

"Good enough, Sir. Bates out."

The detective parked his machine on the street in front of his sanctuary, an apartment building in the Tenderloin, one of the seamier parts of the city. There he could and often did pass as a criminal type, right under their noses. Though this means was a dangerous one, it was a bold and effective, much like the Secret Agent himself.

He popped out of his machine and within seconds stood at the building's front door. Through this portal, he next scampered up the stairs to the third floor, the site of his hideout.

When he was certain no one was nearby, he marched several paces down the hall from the door to his hideout. There his steel-gray eyes settled on a small panel of lead-colored metal which protruded somewhat from the wall's otherwise cinder-blocked surface. Its rectangular shape would have struck the untutored observer as a covering for some sort of electrical apparatus, perhaps a hallway fuse box. Certainly it was large enough to serve that purpose. And a lever on the doorway's left side would have lent further credibility to such a conclusion.

It was completely erroneous.

Rather than grasp and pull the lever, X reached probing fingers to one particular spot on the box's underside. He caressed a switch with hair trigger sensitivity. Abruptly the apartment's door eased open, and he stepped inside.

He had outfitted the apartment's four rooms—sitting area, kitchen, living quarters, and a sizeable storage room—to meet his own exacting specifications. Right now he marched to the storage area, which doubled as his crime laboratory and radio room. He chose the nearest of the three radios in the room and there seated his broad-shouldered frame in a bottle-green swivel chair. Then he resumed the conversation he'd begun, some moments before.

"X here, Bates. What did Miss Arden find?"

"I'll let her tell you, Sir," Bates came back. *"She's more knowledgeable about such things than I am."*

Miss Arden, a young woman with a pleasant voice, was one of the new breed of Agent X's associates, a young woman who had studied accounting at a business college. She exuded intelligence, resourcefulness, and industriousness, as the next moment revealed.

"I'm holding a volume about flowers here, Mr. X; and it discusses the ways they've been employed in symbolism. People have used them, since ancient times, to symbolize love, according to the writer of this particular book. Thus gentlemen would bestow them on their ladies. And some Christian churches have associated lilacs with resurrection, since—"

"—the flowers bloom near the Christian holiday of Easter…." the Secret Agent murmured with an abbreviated bob of his head. "That makes sense, as far as it goes. But I wonder if something else—"

A call sounded from the radio designated Tenderloin 2. X signed off with Miss Arden and wheeled the chair over in front of the second UHF machine. On its frequency an associate with the Hobart Detective Agency was hailing him with the urgency of a radio weatherman warning of an impending cyclone.*

The voice rasped, *"Calling A.J. Martin! Calling A.J. Martin! Urgent! Can you read? This*

*** AUTHOR'S NOTE: Secret Agent X recruited Jim Hobart, a red-haired, raw-boned detective, some years ago, in the chronicle OCTOPUS OF CRIME. Previously, Hobart had served a suburb of Boston as a police officer, until a vicious racketeer framed him for graft, thereby discrediting him. After a rigorous investigation and the discovery of some new evidence, the Secret Agent cleared the young Hobart of all charges. In addition the generous public defender established him in an organization of his own, the Hobart Detective Agency, known far and wide as one of the best in the United States. Jim last appeared in MASTER OF MADNESS.**

is Sloan. Can you read?"

"Martin here," the Agent answered in the newspaperman's tones. "Go ahead, Sloan." He thought fondly of this fellow, a plodding though faithful detective who'd worked in the Boston office for some years. Indeed he had served there prior to the efforts of Hobart himself. Later, Sloan had gone to work for Hobart's agency as its Boston head and thus remained in the Secret Agent's service.*

"Have some news for you, Mr. Martin," Sloan announced. *"It's about this case you're following with the Resurrectionist. Jim even brought me in from Boston because the information was so sensitive. He thought I was the only one he could trust with it."*

That was strange, that Jim didn't contact the Bates Agency. After all, the two *did* know each other. And though they'd rarely worked together, X wondered why Jim hadn't decided to share some of the material in question with another ally.

Before he could follow this thought, Sloan dropped his bombshell: *"Jim has planted a contact in the Resurrectionist's own organization."*

Rarely this excited, the Agent drew his chair closer to the desk, his gray eyes glittering like pale diamonds in the overhead lamp of his desk.

Sloan stated, *"The contact says that the Resurrectionist is out to get Pond. And that he wants someone else's blood too. It's that mystery man, Secret Agent X. This Resurrectionist holds X responsible for his imprisonment years ago. He says that it's time for him to pay the ultimate price."*

Thoughts raced through the man-hunter's head. Did the Resurrectionist think the two beings, Pond and X, were connected somehow, as allies? Or did he know the truth, that they were actually one and the same?

*** AUTHOR'S NOTE: For newer readers of X's adventures, Sloan came onboard the Agent's organization sometime prior to OCTOPUS OF CRIME.**

And why was Jim acting through an intermediary? Something fishy was going on, all right. So the Agent hypothesized: "Jim is worried about someone's safety; otherwise he wouldn't have turned over his agency's operation to someone else—even another operative. Am I assuming correctly?"

"That's what he told me by phone, Sir. He won't say who this guy—this contact—might be. He'd tell me only that you would know who the fellow was. Let me see," he said, while he stood up from the table where his own UHF device was parked. *"I think I have the clue in my wallet."*

While he rummaged for the object in question, the Agent continued to pore over this mystery.

In the next breath, the man Sloan supplied another piece to the puzzle: *"Here it is, Mr. Martin. Jim says, 'One of the twins is out of the big house, and on the case.' That mean anything to you?"*

X pondered the words in silence for a moment.

The light of revelation slowly rose in his eyes when he realized what Jim Hobart had relayed to Sloan.

He took an abrupt break from Sloan, in order that he, the Secret Agent, might untangle this complicated—and deadly—skein.

The Secret Agent strode over to a nearby bookcase. It housed a few of his reference books, some in criminology, and others which provided capsulated versions of his more significant cases. X selected one of these second kinds of books from the shelf, thumbed its pages.

His fingers ran down the list of investigations, this particular book arranging them chronologically. And there it was, an episode which had occurred in mid-1934. That year he had squared off against a set of twins, Walt and Arch Fingeroth, who had been part of a vast, deadly criminal ring.

Police had dubbed them the Twins of Trouble. They had been hired gorillas for the slickest counterfeiting ring that the Secret Agent had ever encountered. Indeed this funny money operation had come within a heartbeat of destabilizing the American money supply.

He had finally defeated the duo by trickery of his own, deceiving Walt into thinking that Arch had turned on him. X's subterfuge had achieved success, with himself and Jim Hobart narrowly escaping death. Walt Fingeroth, the more violent and vicious of the twins, hadn't enjoyed the same good fortune. Walt suffered a terrible end: death in an electric furnace used for melting metals into alloys. And Arch, the surviving brother, had traveled up the river to a Federal pen. Arch had cheated the chair because although he was a thug, he wasn't a murderer like his twin. Arch, instead, earned convictions for counterfeiting, as well as aggravated assault and some other charges.

Finished with his research, X ventured back to the UHF device now. "Sloan, scan your reference books. Find all you can about a possible release from Sing-Sing for Arch Fingeroth, the surviving brother of the Twins of Trouble."

"Sure thing, Mr. Martin."

Sloan rummaged through some of the reference books at the Hobart Agency, as well as some bound copies of newspaper clippings. In a moment he had found the information that X sought.

"I'm holding a digest of his parole officer's last report, from two months back. Says here that Fingeroth got an early release."

"I see," was the Agent's response. He stroked his chin as his gray eyes danced with interest. "What does your source report, in terms of his whereabouts?"

"Hmm. That's odd. There's no sign of him, Mr. Martin. He might have dropped off the face of the earth, as far as the parole officer is concerned."

Perhaps that *was* the case, from the public official's perspective. But the public defender suspected Hobart had arranged the man's release, in order that he, Jim, could have the man infiltrate the Resurrectionist Ring. For a character like Arch Fingeroth, eager to be free again, the prospect of freedom, of life on the "outside," must have been far more of an enticement than the drudgery of existence behind bars.

Human life was *about* freedom, X mused to himself—never mind whether the said life was a lengthy one or not. And knowing the Resurrectionist's predilection for murder and mayhem, the Agent calculated Fingeroth's lifespan to be roughly that of a fish in a barrel....

CHAPTER VII
LETTERS FROM THE DEAD

ACROSS town that same night, a dramatic war on crime wasn't the sole conflict to wrack the city. Some of the clashes then, though not as fantastic, were no less discomposing to the parties involved.

Such was the case with the McGrieves, father and son, who still feuded in the wake of Shingle's funeral.

Indeed, Victor McGrieve and his son

hardly spoke during the service for the mobster. Dean Morston and Mr. Ramond had assayed the role of peacemakers in this family war, yet they knew the two men disdained such efforts. Finally on the day after the funeral, the McGrieve men called an uneasy truce, after the men had exchanged a new spell of accusations and curses. Still all parties at the Caledonian Memorial Gardens realized it was only a matter of a few days before such bickering started again.

This was especially true, now that Stu Lothian, another connection of Victor McGrieve, had been murdered right outside the funeral home. Jay-Jay knew that this man, too, had made his final arrangements through Caledonian. This meant the fellow had purchased a burial policy with the firm; plus he'd scheduled his funeral under their auspices. Likely *his* embalming, too, would include that so-called "secret process" which Mr. Ramond had developed. Jay-Jay's father had seemed eager enough to use the thing, at least as far as the son could discern.

However, to his mind, his father and Mr. Ramond treated it almost as a military secret for the War Department. And their very secrecy over it raised a bump of curiosity on the head of Jay-Jay.

But that didn't mean that the son of Victor McGrieve couldn't learn the truth. He *did* think he had a right to know about it, since he was the owner's son. Or maybe he desired revenge against his father for old grudges he thought he'd suffered in their relationship. He wondered which of the two told the real story.

Whatever the case, he decided he would scour the firm's records and get to the bottom of everything. And if his dad caught him, then he, Jay-Jay, would let the Devil—or his dad—take the hind parts.

Nine o'clock at night had rolled around. The staff, exhausted after the latest funeral and its attendant preparations, had decided to call it a day. Indeed Viola Vye had already left the building some time back. Before walking out, she had begged him to leave, as well, on account of the late hour. He gave her some lame excuse, and she left him, albeit reluctantly. Now Mr. Ramond stepped into Jay-Jay's office and offered a slimy good-bye of his own. Jay-Jay McGrieve barely acknowledged it, deciding he'd rather slash his wrists than shake hands with that man once more. Dean P. Morston stopped by, as those other colleagues had done. There Dean found Victor McGrieve's son huddled over the desk, laboring over a stack of papers. They were burial policies, including one made out in the name of Shingle.

Ever dutiful, Morston asked whether Jay-Jay needed any assistance. McGrieve the Younger thanked him, but said he could handle everything solo. When Morston reminded him this was technically Viola's job, Jay-Jay replied that he realized that, but that the work must be finished. At least, Morston acknowledged, the job was getting done. He was too bushed to do it, after their hard day at work. Sleep, he concluded, would be most welcome this night.

"Your eyes do look bloodshot, about now," Jay-Jay commented, his features lit with concern for his friend.

Dean P. Morston agreed. "I'll say they are. These allergies and the late hours here will do me in, before my time."

He heard from Jay-Jay, "Well, go home and grab some shut-eye. It'll do you a world of good."

"That it will. Good night," Morston smilingly offered to his friend.

He departed.

Several more minutes passed. When Jay-Jay cast his eyes upon his desk clock, the timepiece read nine forty-five. Apart from the corpses still there, Jay-Jay was the only living being in that house of the dead. He continued his work on Shingle's burial policy, and then shifted gears to the policy of another client. He mused briefly that he'd rather do it correctly—and honestly—than see his father or Old Creepy falsify the records.

From outside the building a heavy vehicle rumbled by and rolled around a corner. It was eerie, that deathly silence which intervened. It lasted for many minutes until a handful of bread trucks commenced their nightly rounds to the area's groceries. More minutes ticked by. Now a lone truck, likely another delivery vehicle of some sort, eased past, eventually grinding to a halt immediately outside, its doors slamming loudly. When the hood of the thing went up, Jay-Jay inferred that the machine must be suffering from engine problems. He listened to an angry someone damn the battery, the truck's manufacturer, and finally the world. Four or five more minutes elapsed. Eventually the person, cursing again, slammed the truck's hood and restarted the machine. Jay-Jay, meanwhile, lost himself, once more, in that stack of papers.

He reasoned it would be only a matter of time before the moll, Miss D. Ramos, came in, to collect on Roddy Shingle's life insurance policy, the other product Shingle had bought, along with the one for his burial. Caledonian couldn't avoid paying out a claim on either of them, he realized. And much as it rankled him, they *certainly* couldn't shirk paying a claim on his death. The man hadn't committed suicide, after all. He was dead, murdered at criminal hands. *So be it*, he thought to himself. *I'll let Dad fret over this foolishness.*

Finally he decided he could give his father's office the once-over. Perhaps there he could dig up some clues about that "secret process" and something else he had suspected, but had never voiced to a living soul. Namely, he regarded his father as merely one piece of a crime puzzle. If Victor's offspring were correct, that box of pre-formed and interlocked cardboards contained additional ones awaiting their appropriate place in the picture.

To that end Jay-Jay switched out the light. A mantle of blackness now cloaked the Caledonian Memorial Gardens.

In the half-light from the street outside, Jay-Jay felt his way down the long hall, passing the offices of Old Creepy, Mr. Ramond; Viola Vye; and his friend Dean Morston.

He stopped at the entrance of his father's space. Normally the old man would have locked the door behind him, but tonight he had forgotten that precaution, as Jay-Jay quickly discovered on twisting the knob.

Jay-Jay stepped through his sire's door. In the compartment beyond, an arrow of pale yellow light shot through the window from the street, coming to rest on the floor some feet away to his right. Still it provided more than enough illumination to accomplish his goal: a search of his father's desk and his files.

Under a sharp-eyed gaze, McGrieve the Younger pinned his father's desk. This would be the first point of interest for Jay-Jay.

Atop the desk he noted a gray wire basket of papers. A quick search of these documents showed absolutely nothing. However this wasn't surprising to Jay-Jay. He didn't think his father would be so careless as to leave incriminating materials out in the open. Therefore, Jay-Jay let his hands tour other parts of this wooden territory.

The rest of the desktop disclosed nothing of import. McGrieve the son was growing frustrated now. He wanted to discover the truth, or so he told other people—and himself. And yet, and yet, perhaps he *was* merely out for revenge against his father. Maybe he *did* want to see him swing, was his bitterest thought.

He believed this second option was the case as he parked his frame in the chair nestled behind the desk. From this vantage point, he started hunting game in the desk's drawers. In no more than a few seconds, he ran across a pair of framed pictures of the family. The first of them depicted his father; his mother Millie; his brother Mal, and himself, as a teenaged Jay-Jay. The four of them were posed in front of the old house in Sutton Place, before they'd picked up stakes for the Upper West Side. The second of the photos showed them in front of a large flower garden at the rear of the house. That plot of land served as home to a number of different flowers, but roses—probably red and white varieties—and lilacs—likely both the bluish-purple and the white kinds—grew most prominently in that plot.

These two photos set him to thinking about the old man, his relationship with both sons, all of the old slights and indignities he, Jay-Jay, *thought* he had suffered. To Jay-Jay's thinking, Victor McGrieve had openly favored his much older son Malcolm while the mother had parceled out her attention equally to both of her children. Still, for Jay-Jay, what he regarded as favoritism by his father was bound to spark rivalry and jealousy on his, the younger son's, part; and it had. No matter the good things he did, Jay-Jay believed he couldn't gain his father's respect, much less his affection. As far as Jay-Jay McGrieve was concerned, the typical comment from their father was "Mal is the tops." And from Mal to their father, it was ever a case of "Dad, I just want to *please* you," with Mal having crossed his fingers when he said it, or having looked cynically askance at Jay-Jay, as if the younger offspring were in on his little scheme.

Mal the sycophant, Jay-Jay gritted to himself. *The old man couldn't—or wouldn't—see through his son's pose*. Or maybe he had. Now that McGrieve the Younger thought about it, the father had groomed Mal for the funeral business *because* he, the father, was himself a fundamentally dishonest man. And he'd merely recognized the same character flaw in his son Malcolm. That *had* to be the case, as far as Jay-Jay could see.

Now he recalled episodes from his days in junior high school, concurrent with his brother's days in college. His memory conjured up old ghosts: the constant complaints his mother had made about Malcolm's cheating, as well as his lying and his petty confidence games. In addition there were the constant attempts to defend him that his father undertook.

While he stewed there in the darkness, Jay-Jay noticed something singular about the framed family portrait: It protruded much too far from its cardboard backing. Clearly a certain *something* hid behind that processed and squared fragment from the forest.

He could break the glass and thus make it

obvious he'd been snooping around. Victor's son determined instead to check the back of the portrait. There he spied a series of four clasps which held the contents immobile. Carefully he pried them upwards, then eased the cardboard sheet from the frame itself.

The edges of the picture were there, for the entire world to see. They lay *underneath* a sheaf of folded yellow legal sheets which someone had crammed into the picture frame. This progeny of Victor McGrieve liberated all of these captives from their glass-and-wood prison, laid the picture aside, and unfolded the papers. They were something he hadn't seen in years. And they were all damning.

Concrete evidence of Malcolm's shady thoughts and plans, these papers had fallen accidentally into his mother's hands. She had stumbled upon them while throwing out some of his old things, after his completion of college at Rensselaer. Millie McGrieve had thought the papers were some old notes of his. But they described schemes for fraud, ways that he and his father could make money, dishonestly, on the backs of the aggrieved. She knew he'd been engaging in youthful devilment for years. But that seed had finally come to flower with this kind of criminal plotting.

Jay-Jay, young and naïve, hadn't realized the sheets' significance. He knew only that something had upset his mother, and that he needed to comfort her. After the fact, he somehow learned that she'd confronted Malcolm, who, supported by his father, laughed off her objections to his plans. The youngest McGrieve knew that this episode and subsequent ones probably helped send Millie McGrieve to her grave.

And his brother marched forward with his criminality alongside their father, himself no model of civic virtue. They had a great record, all right; and Victor was still going at it, still consorting with the likes of Roddy Shingle, Stu Lothian, and God knew who else.

In utter disgust, the youngest McGrieve slammed the yellow pages onto the desktop, his teeth grinding the while. Only Mal's much-deserved death in that prison riot had spelled *finis* to such a sorry career.

Or had it? Was he mysteriously alive? Was there really something to those mysterious phone calls he'd received over the past few months? And what was he to think about that strange, sepulchral voice which had alternately threatened and begged him? Was it truly his brother's deep tones?

Such was Jay-Jay's thought when an unknown batch of papers, a pair of envelopes and more yellow legal sheets, broke free from their adhesive tether on the back of the last page.

That first envelope carried a stamp with an image of the Baseball Centennial, in Cooperstown, New York. In addition it bore a postmark of New York, dated May 15, 1939. Another stamp showed the same image, also with a postmark from New York and a date of ten days later.

This information wasn't so shocking, being conventional fare from the Post Office. But the intelligence from the letters therein couldn't have been more explosive: Malcolm McGrieve *was* alive. He'd even scribbled a cartoonish lilac and some object like a fish with its head pointed leftward, the two of them at the top of the page. To Jay-Jay and to his father, both symbols were signs that the letter had originated from Malcolm's own hand.

But he had renounced his old name, it seemed; and he had returned as someone new.

He now called himself the Resurrectionist. And like their McGrieve ancestor he cited from the American Revolution, he had undertaken a holy war of vengeance against his enemies of days a-gone.

The State of New York would suffer his wrath, most certainly. So too would the police who had arrested him. They would enjoy their share of torment. He wouldn't omit his family, either—especially his father, for whom he'd served as the fall guy and gone to prison. But last of all, he would go after the man who had taken so many years of his life. He, more than anyone, would know the meaning of hell.

Many feet down the hall, the closing of a door *clicked* a soft word of warning to Jay-Jay. Two people had entered the building with him! And here he was, scouring this office after hours. Unnerved, he slipped all of the incriminating materials under his coat. In a moment of inspiration he snatched from the desk a heavy lead-glass paperweight. Then with all his considerable might he hurled the object through a sizeable window glaring onto the street beyond. Came a loud crash! Shards of glass exploded into the hot, humid air outside. And Jay-Jay McGrieve likewise exploded from his original position to a sheltering closet only five feet from the window. Unbeknownst to him, a fugitive piece of paper escaped from his grasp, coming slowly to rest on the floor of the office.

Meanwhile, the unexpected noise drew the duo down the hall, like iron filings jerked forward by an electromagnet. Body rigid as a pole, eyes glittering like those of a terrified animal, Jay-Jay barely breathed within his place of concealment. Would his ruse fool them, or would they discover his presence?

He found out soon enough. Now in the office, the holder of an electric torch cast the beam slowly around the enclosed space, much as a cameraman would pan his lens around a movie soundstage.

The fellow, clearly the other's underling, observed, his voice slightly muffled, "Guess that the faked engine trouble worked only for the people on the street."

His listener overlooked the remark, speculating, in a cold, deep voice: "Who could have been searching through this office? Have any of your men reported leaks in the chain of command?"

"N—no, they haven't."

Shoe heels clicked across the floor.

That voice like a radio host abruptly dropped several more degrees in temperature: "There are several different people who might have breached this room. You realize that?"

"Yes, Sir, I do," his henchman affirmed, his tone becoming a trifle nervous. That strange quality of the other fellow's voice, or maybe the potential threat he posed, caused goose pimples to rise on the man's arms.

Jay-Jay McGrieve's ears detected more footfalls in the office.

"Come over here, Sir," whispered the underling of the other man, who stood near the window. "Glass is shattered outward, so he must have jumped through the thing." At the same time, the electric torch's goblin of light hopped from one place to the next.

One of his ears Jay-Jay rammed closer to the closet door, so as better to hear the goings-on outside.

From a point elsewhere in the room, a fabric of some sort scraped across a piece of furniture. And footsteps of the other intruder became louder, indicative of his closer proximity to the closet. Additionally, they signified that the listener had joined his fellow in front of the shattered pane of glass. Neither man said anything for several seconds. Finally the listener of previous moments answered, "Perhaps he's gone. That paperweight on the ground indicates as much. But stay alert. We can't afford discovery—least of all now."

"Hey, Sir," the voice of the underling drew his chief's attention. "Looks like the guy left this behind."

These words husked in the ears of Jay-Jay: "Words from the past!"

The speaker of them turned over the yellow legal sheet Jay-Jay had dropped on the floor, the papers crackling a bit as lifted them. Then he shined the light across their surface. "So this burglar thinks he has discovered the truth about my plans. Fool! He has learned nothing of import. Nothing that will stop my *real* schemes for this city and for the hated one!"

Inside the closet Jay-Jay couldn't fail to hear the man's muttered curses. *The hated one!* Who, exactly, was the hated one? was Jay-Jay's question.

With frightening abruptness, the desk chair emitted a squeal of protest. Because the appliance continued its complaints, Jay-Jay inferred that the person sat in the thing. Sure enough the hard opening and closing of drawers confirmed his thoughts.

"Find anything else, Sir?" was the question from the underling.

"Nothing. Our position is much stronger than I initially thought. Especially since he didn't find *this*."

Whatever *this* was, the speaker didn't reveal. It was only something which caused a peal of eerie mirth to escape his lips.

The laughing man's henchman asked, "Think he connects it with the lilacs?"

"Why should he, Tiny?" the laugher came back. "He knows only what he knows. Nothing more. The glare from his resentment of Victor McGrieve will blind him to the truth until it is too late. And by then, neither he nor anyone else will be able to stop me."

The underling snickered. "Not you-know-who."

"Certainly not *him*."

"Bet he won't see what's coming. Especially the life from death or the Wrath of God."

"Speak not of my power, fool!" the other one commanded. "When the time is right, then all will see these miracles. And not a moment sooner...."

Another rustling of fabric met the ears of Jay-Jay McGrieve. And he was growing cramped and sweaty from standing in the hot confines of the closet. How much longer would they remain here? And would he survive, long enough to get help?

McGrieve pondered these questions for only seconds before the leader of the two men spoke.

"Let us leave now, as we have removed the evidence connecting us with the vengeance to follow."

The leader's henchman uttered a grunt of assent, and the two of them crossed the room. Next the door softly closed. And within the closet, Jay-Jay McGrieve breathed a bit easier.

He eased open the door of his refuge. Less than an eighth of an inch did he move it forward, to peer into the space beyond.

This was his first mistake, the idea that enough time had transpired for him to flee the office.

He committed the second error in creeping not to the broken window, but to the very door through which the intruders had passed.

Immediately on the heels of his outward movement, the door to the office blasted open again.

It was the two men who'd entered in the darkness! They'd been waiting for some action like this, and unsophisticated in the arts of deception, Jay-Jay McGrieve hadn't disappointed them.

Something clutched in his hand, one of the invaders proved to be the henchman, an enormous figure dressed in some light-colored business suit, possibly white in color. Though lacking sheer bulk, a tall, strangely hooded figure accompanied him, and this personage might also have worn white.

"Kill him!" the hooded man shrilled. "Kill him immediately!"

Upward and outward the underling thrust his pistol. The gun cracked out a round amidst a plume of orange and red flame.

On the hooded man's order, McGrieve had already sidestepped to the left. Now he backpedaled towards the window. So hurriedly were his legs pumping that he didn't bother to pivot when he reached the broken pane. As he finally flipped his back in the direction of his attackers, the hooded man's underling squeezed the trigger of his weapon for a second and then a third time. With that third shot, Jay-Jay went stiff; and his form toppled through the window.

The hooded man and his satellite sprinted to the opened portal. Reaching into a pocket of his coat, the henchman retrieved his electric torch. He pointed the beam of the object onto the ground beyond. The grass of the lawn revealed a patch of blood, a sure sign that the bullet had drilled the man, or that the broken glass had sliced his flesh in his escape.

That light from the torch revealed one other striking detail.

No one was there outside the building! The man had somehow escaped, despite his wound.

Shaking because he feared reprisal over his failure, the henchman in the light-colored suit inched away from the window. Now the silhouette of his cursing chief stood revealed, however briefly, in the remnants of the broken window. He strode closer to the broken window and gazed outside.

"Damn you, Jay-Jay McGrieve!" the man in the hood whispered, his fists clenching and unclenching till they were white-knuckled like the titanium hood covering his head. "I promise—I *promise* that you will face the wrath of the Resurrectionist!"

CHAPTER VIII
THE DEVIL WEARS WHITE

THREE more nights passed, that warm June. And at some secret location in New York, a strange figure hunched in shadow over a large metal desk. An aura of impending doom, of deathly silence, permeated the air around him and his writing surface.

Resting atop that space, a lamp of low wattage projected a tiny cone of white light. And on a nearby rectangular box, an array of blinking bulbs pulsed red and blue flickers of their own, deepening the mystery surrounding this unearthly being.

Nothing of his true identity could an observer have discerned, despite that onlooker's best efforts. In the first place that weird individual reclined in shadow, away from the lights themselves. Thus he might have seemed an indeterminate mass dropped into the room, entirely by blind chance. Moreover, he still wore that hooded arrangement, which entirely covered his head. But his most curious feature became apparent in the next moment, when he moved his chair into the edge of the light. For though his vocal cords issued a voice, the lips of that being, momentarily revealed, never moved!

"My Resurgos are ready to raise my newest children from death, are they not?" the curious fellow coldly intoned into an electronic device, a black radio microphone cast from one of the newest plastics, polystyrene.*

Through the ether a metallic voice responded: *"Yes, Resurrectionist. They can't wait to get going on this thing."*

"Then they need wait no longer. It will go forward tonight, according to plan, since our real enemy is getting too close to us. Our golden opportunity, our time of no real opposition, is done. Still, so be it. The hated one has already experienced a taste of my power. Tonight and in the days to come he will find out what I can *really* do. My next three murder victims will underscore that fact."

"The demonstrations may require other killings, too, down the road."

From the shadows, this Resurrectionist came back, unconcerned, "Oh, yes, it will require you and your men to kill."

*** AUTHOR'S NOTE: Only two years ago, the Dow Chemical Company first released polystyrene to the market. A thermoplastic, polystyrene may be heated like a candle, at which point the substance will melt. When cooled, the material will regain its hardness. Polystyrene promises many uses, in addition to cases for microphones and housings for radios. Someday chemists will begin to use it for cases of clocks, insulation for electrical wiring, and even housewares. One day it will be as ubiquitous in our lives as metallic and glass containers were in the lives of our grandparents.**

The voice of the other man probed: *"Like you did with Jay-Jay, then?"*

"No—it's what I *should* have done to him," returned the fellow in the hood. "Now, he's already out of the hospital, despite that injury he received."

The Resurrectionist spat out several words of profanity. Then bars of iron resolve closed over his emotions as he resumed, tonelessly, "I aimed for his head. But I was firing in semidarkness. So the bullet hit him in the shoulder instead. The doctors extracted that bullet, according to one of my spies at the hospital."

"And his present condition?" clipped the Resurrectionist's etheric correspondent.

"The doctors injected him with some new drug—I think my spy called it a sulfanomide—and they say he'll stage a full recovery.** They also managed to close up his wounds from the broken glass. A pity, this."

This was the response the Resurrectionist heard over his shortwave: *"At least he's out of the way. He's just a minor inconvenience, anyway, when it's all said and done."*

"That's true. Jay-Jay is nothing to worry about—like any other minor obstacle which

**** AUTHOR'S NOTE: The sulfanomides are a promising, new class of drugs produced from a combination of sulfur, oxygen, hydrogen, and nitrogen. With a sulfanomide, physicians can greatly inhibit the growth of bacteria which might attack a person, as a result of a wound or a burn. Science has known about sulfanomides since 1908, when a German chemist named Paul Gelmo first stumbled upon them while seeking better dyes for woolen products. Some scientists realized the possible medical benefits of sulfanomides even then. However, it was not until 1931 that another German bacteriologist Dr. Gerhard Domagk synthesized a derivative of a sulfanomide, Prontosil, and used it to kill a form of streptococcal bacteria, *Streptococcus pyogenes*, which he had injected into mice. Only a short time later, in 1935, did I.G. Farben, apply Dr. Domagk's discovery to human use, bringing it to the market and using it to treat infectious bacteria in human beings. Secret Agent X informs me that doctors will find ever more uses for sulfanomide in the coming years.**

might temporarily sidetrack us. So from now on, I will delegate such minor matters to you, trusting to your hand."

"Yes, I appreciate that—and some of the men have an appetite for murder, anyhow. And the entire affair, every aspect of it, goes forward. Providing none of the men make any trouble, of course. If they don't, then everything will move like clockwork."

"You've encountered difficulties at some point in the plan?"

The other fellow paused for several seconds before answering the query. Then offhandedly, he remarked, *"Oh, one of the men has been asking all sorts of questions from those truck drivers you've enlisted."*

"Yes, the people of Stu Lothian, another subject to be released from death's prison. Go on, please."

"I have reason to believe this man is not quite what he seems to be. But maybe I'm worried about nothing."

"Perhaps so. But tell me: Who is this man with the inquiring spirit? And what do you know about him?"

"Well, his name's Arch Fingeroth."

"The name is familiar to me for some reason," he stated, as though the fellow at the other end of the shortwave had stirred the waters of his memory. He allowed several more seconds to tick past before he asked, "Is he an import from Boston, by chance?"

"How did you know that, Sir?"

The Resurrectionist bobbed his head slowly and answered most cryptically: "Already this brings us close to *him*."

"Excuse me, Sir?"

"Never mind. Tell me what else you know about this man Fingeroth."

"Well, I've heard that he used to be a gorilla for a gang of counterfeiters, back in Beantown."

"He *was* a practitioner of that art, some years back."

"I thought it was Lowry's mob, but it might have been Goren's bunch. I've heard him mention one gang leader's name to one man, and the other leader's name to a second or third."

"That sounds suspicious, since Lowry's mob is no more—indeed for quite some time now. Have you a photo of Mr. Fingeroth?"

*"I do, Sir. Three of them, in fact. I can send them immediately by facsimile, if you would like."**

"Do that, then."

Off to one side the ugly gray and black machine began to clatter, the first one of the original pictures from the other side being reproduced, dot by dot, on the Resurrectionist's machine. Finally after two more repetitions of this routine, the electronic device ceased its racket. At this point the Resurrectionist pulled the finished products from the facsimile's revolving cylinder. He scrutinized them with great interest for several

*** AUTHOR'S NOTE: During the late nineteenth and early twentieth centuries, American and European inventors developed the facsimile, mostly as a means of transmitting photos, via wire or radio waves. Facsimiles work in this manner: At the transmitting site a person wraps the photo or picture around the surface of a revolving cylinder. Within the machine itself a minute light ray passes over the image. In turn a photoelectric cell catches the light's reflection, transforming this into electrical current. Lighter portions of the picture reflect more light and a corresponding increase in current. On the other hand, the darker ones reflect less light and a concomitant drop in current. Thus electricity itself replicates the picture, its light and dark patches. When the receiving set then intercepts the signal, it travels along several stages, beginning with a printer blade; moving to specially treated, dampened paper; and reaching, finally, a wire encircling the cylinder. Chemicals in the paper then produce a reaction. This reaction races along the blade, then to the paper, and last to the wire. If the current is a strong one, it results in a dark spot. In contrast, a weak one concludes in a lighter spot. In this manner, the paper's image replicates the gradations of light and dark in the original picture.**

seconds. Something in them made him nod gravely, as if he recognized one person or the other from those pictures. So he went to a folder perched on a nearby bookshelf. For several seconds his fingers quested through that manila container. His results were rewarded when he finally located a quartet of specific photographic prints. These he removed from their former residence.

Comparing the four of them side by side, he next laid them on a table alongside the other pictures from the facsimile. All of the photos depicted the same man—or someone purportedly that individual—posed in various styles and shot in entirely different settings. Some of the prints also depicted him with another man of nondescript features, perhaps light hair. A harsh fanatic's glare lit the blue eyes of the Resurrectionist. Some detail of the photos had obviously captured his attention.

Into the microphone he asked, "You're certain of Fingeroth's story that he's done some strong-arm work in the past?"

"He was *insistent about it. Did some time for it, too. But he's out of the joint now, looking for work,"* the Resurrectionist's mysterious partner-in-crime slipped, unintentionally, into jailhouse parlance.

"Interesting, that piece of information. My own intelligence here shows something quite the contrary to your own report."

That voice at the other end was dying to ask what exactly had grabbed the Resurrectionist's interest. But he'd learned not to force his master to volunteer information. Instead the voice informed him, *"You might want to know something else: Somebody arranged an early release for Fingeroth, not long ago. I'm thinking it was his mouthpiece, maybe with some moneybags, behind the scenes somewhere, tossing the dollars."*

"And he came here to New York, looking for new work. How extremely convenient for him was it that *we* were available, eh?"

"Yes, Sir. He hooked up with Jonesy right after his arrival, and—"

"Ah. The illustrious Mr. Jones. Have him keep a close eye on this Arch Fingeroth."

"Klinker's had something to do with this character, too. They've gotten pretty chummy, getting lunch together and what-not."

"Then they can both watch Fingeroth for any suspicious activity. Preferably without his knowledge, of course. And I want to know more about his background, too. Perhaps we can find more use for him, in the future. If not, we can find, eh, *other* uses for him. He might become an excellent adjunct to our friend from the cab company."

"That coward you've mentioned to me? How can you use him?"

"He can lead us to the hated one. With the proper persuasion, of course."

"Want me to have a talk with him?"

" 'Persuade' him of the necessity of cooperation. Appeal to his greed, if you think that will work. If it doesn't, then appeal to his sense of self preservation. That will certainly produce results. Then be ready to bring him here when I've given you the word. Now, have you any other news to report?" the Resurrectionist concluded.

"Well, some of the men are having trouble with the 'sugar.' Hell, for that matter, so am I."

"Indeed," stated the voice, curious and stern at the same time. "What kind of trouble?"

"Oh, it's—it's nothing to be concerned about. Maybe the 'sugar' wears off sooner than we thought."

"You and they should, perhaps, take *more* of it, then; shouldn't you?"

"I—I guess so," he stammered, though inside he was skeptical. However, in another second he doffed that emotional garment and resumed with this: *"Everything will work out just fine. The men just need to do what* I've *told them, to the letter, not forgetting their doses of 'sugar' or wasting any time on their jobs. Of course, if they don't, then* I *may have to get rough with some of them. That'll spook them out of their skins, is the way I look at it.*

Throughout that pronouncement he had emphasized some variant of the personal pronoun "I" in his statements, and his listener caught those slip-ups. He also construed them as a challenge to his own power, saying, "I see, Resurgos One. I am concerned that you did not bring this problem to my attention any earlier. I suppose you are under a misapprehension regarding your proper place in my plan?

"Be careful, lest you run afoul of me. Remember, I am the Resurrectionist! I am the life from death and the death from life. Moreover, it is I, not you, who controls the very Wrath of God!"

"Ye—yes! I wasn't trying to challenge your leadership. And I wasn't trying to hold anything back from you...."

Now the hooded chap fell silent for a bit. When he spoke again, an air of eerie calm settled over his words: "Very well. Let me correct you about something else. Your 'men,' as you so vulgarly referred to them, are *my* Resurgos, *mine alone.*

"Now, pay close attention. The plan goes forward tonight. I have built an engine powered by men's greed and desperation, then supercharged by my desire for revenge. We have a most unbeatable combination here, Resurgos One. I bid you success."

The hooded man uttered a cruel laugh through his immobile lips, at which point he broke his connection. Arising from his chair, the Resurrectionist replaced his microphone and its long, snaky cord upon the desk, beside the radio. Muttering indistinct words, he flicked the lamp's toggle switch to the "off" position and departed this place.

In the outer hallway, the Resurrectionist gloated to himself. *I will finally get what I have wanted for such a long time. But my detestable enemy will get what he has so long—and so richly—deserved. And it will all come about unexpectedly, from a foe he thought dead. Truly, there is a part to be played for all of us in this grand tale of revenge—as long as* I *am the director....*

More hours dragged by on that hot, steamy night, a time that might have prefigured hell.

In a lonely, ancient graveyard out in Long Island, a hedge of low-grown shrubbery, poorly kept, described a rectangle around that necropolis. Many feet behind that wall of greenery, a rusted, wrought-iron fence hugged a family plot nearly as old as the cemetery itself. Most of the headstones had toppled to the ground, casualties, like their graves' occupants, to the all-conquering march of time. But some of markers stood there defiantly, as if to show that nothing, not even time itself, could vanquish them.

Among the graves of this family plot, a mound of dark, newly turned earth swelled the ground. And there, hovering over that piece of hallowed soil, a small body of men had assembled. Most of them wore dirty work clothes: denims and light cotton work shirts, heavy brogans on the feet. A few of them, however, had donned silver-white suits for this occasion, albeit these were dress suits, not those bulky things a witness had mistaken for the animated snowmen. They might have gathered there to pay their respects to the dearly departed. But as would rapidly become apparent, neither piety nor devotion had anything to do with their presence here.

One man, the Resurrectionist of that mysterious radio exchange, stood at the head of the group. He continued to avoid the lights, in this case, the rays of the electric torches. Hence only his general shape—hooded head, above average height, and silver-white robes—stood out. Still his confident tone must have impressed them; certainly his bold declaration worked that effect.

"You know what I intend to do here, on this hallowed ground! You are to be my first observers, no, my first *witnesses* to the life from death! You will proclaim this event to all who follow!"

At his signal, four of the men yanked forth a squat new person, one surrounded earlier and thus blocked from the others' view. Moreover, the features of this newcomer they had completely hidden underneath an eyeless hood. They meant for his identity to remain secret. At the same time they intended for him not to see any of their faces, until a more propitious time. If nothing else, the Resurrectionist showed flair both for the secret and for the dramatic.

He addressed them in that moment, blue eyes blinking rapidly: "I know that some of you might question what I intend to do now and in the days to come. Know, then, I have already raised one man from the dead! And he stands here, now, for all of you to see!"

Turning, the Resurrectionist faced the hooded fellow immediately to his rear.

"Come forward, my newest disciple!" the white-hooded criminal demanded. "Come and show how I repay faithfulness to me and my cause! Show these men the life from death!"

Suddenly, the man in white jerked the hood from the man's head. In the next instant the formerly unknown individual shot a pair of wild gray eyes at first one man and then the other. A strange *something* inside him had made him think he could go bear hunting with a stick. It must be the effects of the "sugar" that rendered Wayne Helmer, respected owner and operator of W.H. Textiles, such an emblem of bravery.

"Do you come here in good faith, ready to experience the life from death?" the Resurrectionist asked the thickset personage.

Eagerly, the squat man intoned, surprisingly, in a basso of immense proportions, "I do, Resurrectionist. I am," he somewhat pompously drew up his frame, "fully committed to you, a loyal disciple of the life from death!"

Amidst these dark proceedings, a pair of bitter blue optics whipped from Wayne Helmer to the Resurrectionist with an intensity barely concealed. The features of that man projected an equal intensity, despite the heavy blue-black beard and mustache which enshrubbed his cheeks and chin.

To the mind of this observer, anyone could make up like Helmer—Black Beard knew this firsthand. But this new devotee to the Resurrectionist bore all of the earmarks of the real industrialist. He was certainly short, squirrel-cheeked, and squinty-eyed as was Helmer himself. He was, in addition, pompous enough and, because of ill-fitting dentures, comical enough in his delivery to be Wayne Helmer. His very authenticity provided the perfect warm-up act for the Resurrectionist's next trick, the source of which Black Beard had noticed over his left shoulder.

There he'd spotted a pair of fresh mounds, one of them only six or eight feet away. The other one squatted to the left of this group. They went, for some reason, to the one on the left. Deep into the black soil, someone had stabbed a small silvery metallic marker. Of itself this token meant little, since newly dug graves typically carried such indicators. Funeral homes used them to help families and friends locate their departed loved ones in a necropolis. The funeral homes employed these markers, too, to show the masons where to position finished headstones or other monuments over the deceased.

One feature tipped Black Beard to the fact that this marker was not an ordinary one.

It contained a stylized flower of some sort, into which the name of the decedent had been engraved. And below the name someone had also etched a word, *LILAC*, and a number, 02, into the metal surface. In that moment Black Beard knew that they had met here by design, in order that the Resurrectionist might also raise this corpse from the dead.

Sure enough, in the next moment the man in the white robes pointed to a quartet of shovels, lying nearby. Four worthies, two in white suits and the other two in work clothes, grabbed the implements and commenced an assault on the earthen fortress at their feet. In a short time they had converted that dirt, into a pile off to one side. In turn their labors had also exposed a long coffin. In color it was a rich reddish brown affair, a promise of more lavishness to come.

A lover of beauty—likely few of this crowd—would not have suffered disappointment in the next moments.

The coffin's manufacturer had applied a gilt edging to its wooden surfaces, all crafted from the finest mahogany. As further adornment twenty-four karat gold plating covered all of the handles. Finally the maker had capped the box with ornate side panels depicting the occupant's family crest.

Truly this owner wasn't a mere zero, but a man of consequence.

Two of the working men ran to one of the cars and removed a portable block and tackle. With it they hefted the casket from its grave, planting the bone box on the ground. At a new command from the white-robed leader of the group, one of the men in white produced a bladed device to cut the coffin's gasket and thus break its seal. Now the white suit did his job, whereupon the body inside the casket was exposed to the hot, humid night air.

Men of the Resurrection Ring stepped aside for their chief. At the head of the group once again, he thundered, a mysterious rod clutched in his hand: "The dearly departed, Mr. Henry Terran, of Terran Candle and Soap Works."

One of the white suits threw back the coffin's lid.

He was a middle-aged man, this Henry Terran. However, he'd reached the age of fifty in a well-preserved condition that even the undertaker couldn't have improved. He owned sharp cheekbones, an aquiline nose, and a firm jaw. Tanned cheeks, a sign of good health, marked him as a man who loved the outdoors. And a thick mane of dark chocolate hair topped his head, the locks combed backward to accentuate his sharp widow's peak. He was handsome in a Mephistophelian kind of way—if you liked a guy with a sinister touch. Death had not prevented his lips from curling slightly in a smile that promised holy hell to anybody who might stand in his way.

From behind his strange mask, the Resurrectionist sent forth a soft chuckle. He understood the power that Terran's death and resurrection would bestow upon him, the crime czar, among the criminal class. So, head upturned to the heavens, he built their anticipation and suspense. Eventually he ordered an underfed hoodlum of horse face and teeth to match to produce a mirror from a pocket of his white suit. Then he ordered the oblong of silvered glass to be placed over Terran's mouth. All could see that no breath leaked from the man's mouth or nose.

"Check his pulse, too, then, Resurgos 12," the Resurrectionist ordered his flunky. "It must be obvious to all comers, especially our newest recruits, that this man is dead."

The scrawny fellow reached towards the man's left wrist. He did the same thing at the decedent's neck.

These actions completed, the villain's assistant looked up once more at his boss. "He's still takin' a dirt nap."

Among the observers, a stocky man, young despite his chubby features and balding head, watched the proceedings. He was practically chomping at the bit for the next scene of this drama to unfold.

The Resurrectionist did not disappoint him.

That mirror holder's last statement his cue, he latched his fingers around the lance with an adamantine grip. Next he moved directly to the dead man's left. In high seriousness, with the shadows partially obscuring his features, he trained his gaze downward. He might have seemed to pity the departed one, so long did he look upon the man. Slowly, he raised eyes upward towards the beclouded night sky. At the same time he uttered strange words, apparently something from a foreign tongue. Right hand held above the midpoint of the lance, and left hand below, he slammed the blunt end of the weapon directly into the chest of the dead man!

Followers of the Resurrectionist stood there, not knowing what would happen next.

All of a sudden, a loud intake of air, a gasp, permeated the air of that forlorn graveyard.

Abruptly the observers gathered in a knot. But they wouldn't approach the coffin's side, a tether of fear—and awe—preventing them from moving any closer.

At the Resurrectionist's goading, the men came closer. And then they could see the miracle within its confines. There, pinkish eyelids fluttered, then popped open. And chocolate brown eyes once again peered onto the world.

Over one month after his murder, Henry Terran, owner of Terran Candle and Soap Works, had arisen from the dead! Gradually he lifted his torso upwards, such that he could peer out at the many gaping onlookers there in the cemetery.

The Resurrectionist bobbed his head, pleased with his miracle. For a moment the white light of the electric torches illumined the eyes of the white-robed villain. And those titanium rays showed bright blue eyes which blinked with growing rapidity and glittered with wildness.

Those eyes and Terran's resurrection almost caused the black-bearded man to swallow his own tongue, so great was his shock.

While the black-headed man recovered his composure, the Resurrectionist delivered new orders. Thus six of his henchmen, three white suits and three working men, hoisted the casket of Henry Terran into a large white delivery truck parked at the gates to the cemetery. They had to do a bit of work to push the bone box past a sizeable object cloaked with a great quantity of silver-white canvas. But pushing and turning the casket, they accomplished this acrobatic act. Next they assisted both the soap king Terran and the textile man Helmer into the diesel chariot's trailer. A finger twisted the key in the vehicle's ignition, firing the engine; and the truck transported that portion of the crew from the scene.

In the meantime, Black Beard, in reality, Arch Fingeroth; a fellow of average height named Stringer; and another man calling himself Jonesy took the front seats of a white Chrysler Imperial. Tall and muscular, Jonesy was possessed of a dead, chalk-white face, white hair, and eerie pinkish eyes. He was an albino. Stringer, on the other hand, was ruddy-hued, like someone who does back-breaking field work, then burns to a crisp in the process. While Stringer was taciturn, Jonesy was a regular squawker, talking ninety to nothing—and twitching like mad as all of them prepared to leave this place.

"Told you this would be the job for ya, didn't I, Blackie?" he said to Fingeroth. "Make a man outta ya! And make ya some real jack, in the process."

"Hope so," Black Beard replied, earnestly. "Need some work. Papa needs new shoes, you know."

The twitching albino uttered a foolish laugh at Fingeroth's attempt at wit. "That's rich, Blackie! That's rich!"

While all of this transpired, they watched as the Resurrectionist and three other worthies climbed aboard a Chevy sedan, also white. These chariots also zoomed away, clouds of dark dust billowing from behind them.

After another fifteen minutes had passed, they found their way to the second and final cemetery of the night. Here the Resurrectionist would perform his last miracle and raise one more man from the grave.

All of the fellows in the individual machines switched off their headlights. Yet they drove unerringly through the cemetery's gate and down a deeply rutted path. It made a logging trail seem like a city street. Several more seconds elapsed before they located the proper grave, the heaped, darkened earth being the clue, of course, to the tomb's freshness.

The Resurrectionist and his body of travelers, shovels in tow, boiled from the Chevy sedan, as did the motorists from the white delivery truck and the Chrysler Imperial.

Once again they wasted no time in their movement through the cemetery. Indeed once again, they marched directly towards one of the markers stamped with a flower and the word-number designation, in this case *LILAC-05*. Clearly they'd located another member of the Resurrection Ring.

They halted here in front of this mound of black earth, their shovels at the ready.

"He is *here*, my Resurgos! Here, awaiting the life from death. Here, ready to become part of my invincible army; and ready to vanquish, forever, Secret Agent X!"

At his signal the men commenced their

digging. In short order the team of six had excavated another of the expensive coffins and lifted it from its earthen well.

In the present instance the occupant had chosen a box of finest oak, polished to the highest luster, then stained with a deep brown color. A St. George's cross, the saltire or X, and crossed swords inside the X, decorated the top of the casket. Like his predecessor Terran, this occupant had also picked gold-plated handles for either end of the casket, as well as for the sides at right angles to them. And last the owner had requested brass fittings for each side of the bone box. It was quite the affair.

They popped its lid, exposing the deceased man.

With great pomp, the Resurrectionist came and hovered before the opened container. He spoke the words in that mysterious foreign tongue, hoisted that lance-like gadget high into the air.

Down it flew, like a shaft of lightning, crashing into the chest of the corpse.

Came a gasp. Then came a cough, followed by a sneeze.

And Stu Lothian, trucking racketeer lived again!

Wide-eyed, he peered around the assemblage. Lothian suspected the nearby white-robed figure was the Resurrectionist, though that being's voice was all Lothian had ever heard.

His features weirdly immobile, the Resurrectionist laughed weirdly. Next the being in white questioned, "Now do you doubt my power, Stu Lothian? Do you believe that I have given you the life from death?"

A Cheshire cat's grin crawled over Stu Lothian's lips in that moment. It was somehow fitting when Lothian beamed in that way. It always presaged something he believed would later work to his own advantage—at the expense, of course, of someone else.

He said, "Gotta give it to you, Resurrectionist. If I'd have known bein' dead was this much fun, I'd have done it before now."

The Resurrectionist offered more of his soft mirth. At that point he directed the transfer of Lothian's casket to the white delivery truck. There it rested alongside the former final resting place of Henry Terran.

Before they all had boarded their respective vehicles, a twitching Jonesy came near Fingeroth and elbowed the ribs of the larger man. "Yeah, ya can't beat this job! Didn't I tell ya that, while you was pokin' around Lothian's joint? Didn't I?"

"Yeah, you did," Blackie stated, growing impatient. "But we'd better get going now—or we won't *have* a job."

Jonesy boarded the car.

When the machine's dome light popped on, Stu Lothian happened to get a closer look at Black Beard, that is, Fingeroth. They had stopped right outside its door when this exchange occurred:

"Seen you somewheres before, ain't I?" Lothian turned, of a sudden, in Fingeroth's direction.

Black Beard affirmed, "Yeah, guess so. I was around your trucking operation recently."

"Yeah, you were. But I've seen you, before then. Ain't you one of the Fingeroths, who worked with that counterfeiting ring, a long time back?"

"That's right."

"And earlier, did you do jobs for Goren's mob?"

"With Lowry, you mean?"

Lothian remarked, "Oh, yeah. That's right. How was the big house?"

"You don't know?" Black Beard asked. When Lothian pled ignorance, Black Beard stated, his words now icy: "Then you don't want to know."

The trucking racketeer twisted his mouth into a sneer, though he said nothing. However, he decided he'd be watching Fingeroth, from then on.

Meanwhile, Fingeroth stepped into the Chrysler. And that was that—for now.

In seconds they were tooling their chariots from the cemetery. Within the Chevy sedan the man in white took the microphone of the UHF radio. With it he issued fresh orders. As he spoke, the man with the blue-black hair sent his right hand on an innocent mission to his pants pocket. That same hand jingled a few coins before it returned to the outside world with a book of matches and a cellophane package of cigarettes in tow. As he fired one of the paper tubes, he mused grimly to himself. This was *quite* the job, all right, like that man Jonesy had promised him. And it might, just *might*, be quite the trip to hell, besides....

CHAPTER IX
THE FRIEND OF LABOR

ANOTHER three days passed. In the interim New York slipped into a period of relative silence on the crime front. In the meanwhile, the mercury continued to register high temperatures, among the hottest on record, in fact, for this third week of June. To make matters worse, the weather folks promised July temperatures which would be more blistering than those of the previous month.

Some waggish newspaper writers joked that the present heat wave should have made the diabolical Resurrectionist feel right at home. It was their way, of course, to mask the nervousness—no, the fear—that the being in white had engendered in the city.

Agent X spent his time in neither fear nor speculation about the villain's activities. Instead he pursued his investigation of this case with the same vigor, no matter the fact that it was late at night.

In a radio transmission Agent X, in the voice of Martin, had gained new information from the snitch Arch Fingeroth, by way of the Hobart Detective Agency. The Resurrectionist had dropped references to his men that he had located a certain criminal *someone*. And according to the villain's hints, the Man of a Thousand Faces wouldn't be thrilled about the ally he, the white-robed miscreant, had found.

"Couldn't Fingeroth be more specific about the person's identity?" a puzzled Agent X inquired of Hobart's operative Sloan.

Frustrated over his own lack of knowledge, his respondent stated, *"I don't think so. Fingeroth said that neither he nor any of the Resurrectionist's 'Resurgos,' in other words, his men, know the guy's identity. The head honcho is keeping everything close to the vest."*

Agent X pondered this development in silence. Clearly his enemy had a reason for holding back such information about his new ally. But the precise reason why he did so, the Agent could not yet determine. Thus the Agent followed a new direction in his line of questioning: "What has Hobart's informant said about the Resurrectionist's purpose in acquiring this new ally?"

"Well, Jim's boy Fingeroth thinks the Resur-

rectionist is scrounging around for the Agent's greatest secrets. And believe me, it's not the fact that Mr. X prefers pancakes to waffles. Fingeroth sent me a coded message—all of the messages come that way—which said that only the Resurrectionist's new friend would know the answers that the crimelord seeks. Also Fingeroth said another person might stand to gain just as much from the Resurrectionist's information."

"As though the Resurrectionist might act as an intelligence broker and sell the secret, eh?"

"That's exactly what Fingeroth thought, sir."

"Does the message say anything else—any speculation about what those secrets might actually be?" the man of mystery nervously inquired.

"Let me see," he paused for a moment. Clearly he was searching the message for more news of value. Finally he related, *"Here it is. Fingeroth thought the secrets might be the location of X's headquarters and maybe his real name...."*

Icy claws of fear raked down the back of the public defender. This Resurrectionist was getting too close to him. Much too close....

"He's waited to find this man who can reveal hidden truths," X stated. "He's also waited to perpetrate any new murders of criminals and shady types. Does the snitch know who the next victim might be?"

"Jim's man is pretty certain on that one, sir. He says it's going to be that labor boss, Pat Calvert," Sloan shared. *"He's facing prosecution too, for violating some Federal labor laws, as well as not paying Federal income tax for several years. The last coded message said that the Resurrectionist would knock off Calvert, come tomorrow."*

X's voice came back, tight as piano wire: "Fine, then. I think someone needs to arrange for an interruption of those plans. That's all. Martin out."

He made another call to the Bates Detective Agency, giving highly specific instructions to Harvey Bates, in addition to a sometime associate, Hiram Beckwith, whom the shaggy-haired giant could contact.*

This call completed, the Man of a Thousand Faces put through a telephonic communication, to Betty Dale, at the *Herald*. When he'd reached her, he questioned the woman about her recent conversation with Miss D. Ramos.

Betty related the details of their confab, along with this tidbit about Shingle: "He wasn't one for buying flowers. But all of a sudden he bought her lilacs. Lots of them, according to Miss Ramos. When she asked him what they meant, he was celebratory. He said they were his ticket to life. They were, I quote, 'the life from death.'"

"That slogan of the Resurrectionist!" X exclaimed.

Betty affirmed, "Right, dear. He told her that every part of this affair was all about life. He went on to say that he had her to thank for making him see the value of life."

"I see. Did she follow up on this sudden philosophical bent of Shingle's? He wasn't,"

*** AUTHOR'S NOTE: Beckwith, a fat cab driver, is a prime example of a book whose contents differ from the cover. A tough-talking character, he has earned a Columbia degree, in classical literature. He is also a most formidable fighter and a deadly marksman, especially with a rifle. In that vein, the Agent informs me that he has chided Beckwith, in the past, about his tendency to solve problems with firearms, not with his wits, as do the most expert investigators. Beckwith most recently assisted the disguised X in the novel MASTER OF MADNESS, against the ruthless Fool. Because the cabbie provided such invaluable service, X financed the man's establishment of his own company, Fat Cat's Cabs, actually a front for the Agent's relentless war on crime.**

the detective chuckled, "especially known for his metaphysical insights."

Betty too laughed, the tinkling sound mindful of a small bell's toll. "She *did* say to me that she'd warned Roddy to be careful, because of the company he kept and the dangers he constantly faced."

"*Not* Roddy Shingle," Agent X chuckled again. "He was such an upstanding member of our community."

Laughing again, Betty came back, "Well, whatever the case, Miss Ramos seemed to be holding something back, as if she knew more than what she was sharing with me."

"That makes me think something is up, too, Betty. Call on her again, if possible, at her home. Get to the bottom of her warnings to Roddy, as quickly as you can," he concluded, a ghost of worry haunting his tone.

She noticed that trace of tenseness in his words, a replay of his earlier manner towards her, days ago. "Dear, are you—"

Not wanting to trouble her, he answered a bit too quickly, "It's okeh. I—I'll be fine. Will you do this—I mean, see Miss Ramos?"

Troubled by his evasiveness, she reiterated that she would. And X, upon thanking her, broke the connection.

He pulled a file from one of the bookshelves, perused the contents of its pages. When he was satisfied, he moved to the area for his hideout's disguise apparatus: the table and mirror, his large makeup kit, and the wardrobe holding his clothing.

Into the makeup box his hand roved. It returned bearing the proper pigments, a toupee, a set of mouth appliances, and of course, a couple of tubes of his volatile plastic.

He spent most of the next half hour in duplicating the features of his subject, a man well-known in New York's labor community. The fellow was perceived as both a figure of loyalty and a man not immune from controversy—or fearful of danger.

Nodding slowly at his choice of disguise, the Secret Agent grabbed one of the tubes of volatile material and squeezed a gob of the stuff on either cheek. He spread the stuff over his features, such that it was thick in some places, thin in others. Next he fixed those mouth appliances in place. When he had completed his work, he cast a critical eye in the triple-folding mirror. One thing remained to be done. He must disguise his unique eyes for his masquerade to work.

Thus from the makeup kit, he produced a small, oval-shaped container. Once opened its twin wells disclosed a pair of colored lenses, special invisible glasses, or "contact lenses," to hide his own steel-gray optics. He applied the devices. When he'd blinked his eyes a couple of times, the optical devices came to rest over his irises. He cast his orbs towards the mirror. Those gray peepers, normally alive, now appeared blacker—and deader—than a shark's eyes. As he arose from the table, he knew they would work perfectly....

The night passed into the morning of the next day, what was to be the end of this present life for Pat Calvert. And he, like his predecessors, wouldn't be a conventional murder victim, either.

With his pearly whites and his preternatural handsomeness—high cheekbones, dark green eyes, saucy black brows, thick ebon hair, and arch smile—Calvert looked more like a devil-may-care matinee idol. His obsession with so-called "physical culture" lent an additional dimension to his allure, giving him a face and a build like Errol Flynn. Indeed more than one admiring member of the female species had shared such intelligence with Calvert. And more than a few of them had treated him accordingly—despite the fact that he was hard of hearing in one ear and practically deaf in the other.

This little flaw didn't stop him from enjoying the adulation of the opposite sex. It gave him a sense of power over them, that he could use them, as he willed. And he lusted after this sense of control more than an addict craved his dope. Indeed this feeling of power competed constantly with his love for money. He would have been hard-pressed to determine which of them he most desired.

Those two loves of his—power and money—translated into an inordinate desire for the finer things in life: expensive autos, tailored suits, pricey homes. Even this fancy office in an elegant old brownstone fell into the same category: high price and lots of class. The office was his, pink slip and all; but so was the brownstone itself. It was his personal preserve, and had been for quite a number of years. He figured he'd worked hard enough for the place, so society owed it to him to enjoy the fruits of his labor. And in this regard he differed not at all from others of his criminal ilk.

Stated bluntly Pat Calvert was a racketeer. He was one of the worst kinds in the business because he preyed off the proceeds of hard-working folks, still struggling to rise up from the late business depression and the recession of two years past.

Ostensibly he served as a union leader, head of the teamsters' outfit for New York and suburban New Jersey. At his command men would work their jobs and obtain a fair wage for their labor. At his command, too, the men would strike because of unfair or unsafe working conditions. To them and to the newshounds, he was the "friend of labor," known throughout the Empire State for his crusades for the working folk.

On their face his struggles with managers looked fair-minded enough. Tirelessly, Pat Calvert would negotiate better contracts for his "boys," as he called them; but Pat Calvert played a deeper game. He always rigged the contracts. He always made certain to set the union's dues or its insurance too high, for instance. Just enough, mind you, to enable him to skim his own cream from the top of the churn. Multiplied by the thousands who worked as teamsters, Calvert was earning money hand over fist.

And Pat Calvert's hand could double into a fist of iron that matched his forceful voice.

If a local union leader demurred at Calvert's negotiations, then the handsome union leader had ways of "persuading" said labor boss. Some of Calvert's goons might start with intimidation of the wayward soul. They would promise to stop their threats, if the man paid up a bit of kale for his trouble. He might still refuse. This approach might then progress to mild physical violence, perhaps a bit of shoving or pushing. Next it might progress to a knife attack or the business end of a baseball bat. Usually most of them caved in at this point. If they did not, then more of Calvert's men would arrange an accident for the poor scoundrel. He might find the brakes of his automobile cut, for instance, or might take the proverbial "ride."

With such a person out of the way, most of his fellows gave Pat Calvert their wholehearted support. For their part they provided him with advertisements better than the largest billboards or the most frequent radio announcements in the city.

Yes, the crooked life had smiled on Pat Calvert. And on this late June morning, as he strolled into his office, he spread his handsome features into a pronounced smile of his own. He bragged, *molto voce*, that business was booming. Unfortunately because of his hearing loss, he couldn't hear the slamming door in the office beyond his own. Nor could he detect the series of loud crashes which thundered from the same side room.

Pat Calvert went on, instead, with his boasts over his latest "commercial endeavor," as he'd taken euphemistically to calling it. He had lately begun to muscle in on the crime bosses themselves, in the fashion of a classic protection racket.

He knew that this was the kind that the criminals themselves feared. After all, they couldn't very well go to the police with their troubles, and thus risk exposure of their own criminal activities. Hence, for all their tough talk, they were completely at the mercy of such racketeers.

Glancing up towards the opposite wall, he noted the date on a large calendar, his eyes lingering there a bit too long. And in the next moment he peered just as closely at his watch. Then he resumed talking, as it became apparent, to someone other than himself.

"You listening to me, Luke?" he raised his head from the desk and his voice to an unseen listener.

From the next room "Luke" shouted back, "Yeah, I'm listenin'. Just had something to take care of, back here. Damn, who did this knucklehead think he was, comin' in here without permission from the big man hisself?"

There came a choked sound, as of a man being throttled.

"What do you think you're doin' in here?" the voice choked out.

Surprisingly the voice seemed to be talking to itself, when it rasped, "It's nothin' to ya!"

Then a sound like a fist smashing against bone penetrated to the outer office.

The first voice screamed, "I said, 'What do you think you're doin'?' Who do you think you are, showin' up in here, in broad open daylight, lookin'—"

The duplicate suddenly interrupted in the same sandpapery tone: "Damn it to hell! Stop your squawkin'! I got somethin' that'll settle you!" hollered the voice again.

"Yeah?" the man rasped his question.

An odd something provided sibilant accompaniment to his response, though Calvert couldn't hear it, of course. The light closing of a door, soft as a lover's kiss, escaped his notice for the same reason. Calvert could hear only the louder noises, like the smacking of fists; and these gave him much pleasure.

Pearly whites gleaming, Calvert chuckled at the conflict in that side room. This kind of thing happened frequently, when "unannounced" visitors showed up. Luke, Calvert's *aide-de-camp*, had standing orders to give them the bum's rush, especially if they showed signs of belligerence. For this reason the labor racketeer simply sat tight. Luke could certainly "handle things."

Pat Calvert continued to grin for another couple of seconds. Then he grew suddenly serious. He thought to himself, *It pays to have a fellow like Luke around—if he doesn't get too big for his britches, that is. And Luke* does *have that tendency. That, and the idea that he's always going to win a fight or an argument, no matter what. But there were two things that neither Luke nor I could ever beat. And neither could anyone else. At least until now. With this new guy in the game, maybe we can beat one of them.* One saucy eyebrow climbed up in the manner that had tantalized so many of the fairer sex. His smile crawled slowly back over that handsome face. But it grew in size until it was more of a death's head grin, a sign of impending menace.

Pat Calvert turned his head towards the side office, which stood more than thirty feet from his desk. "I could die a happy man now, Luke. A truckload of people would be glad to see me go, too. 'Course, people like you would be glad to keep me around a bit longer, eh? What with the good money I'm paying you, and so forth."

It was a speak-of-the-devil moment as Luke Cordray ambled through the door of the side office, only to stop in front of Pat Calvert's own desk.

But the man wasn't Cordray at all. In reality he was the Secret Agent. He had assumed the present disguise, in order to observe and perhaps to stymie the next thrust of the Resurrectionist.

Masterful as this impersonation was, however, it was also highly dangerous. Calvert's naturally suspicious nature rendered it thus. Indeed Pat Calvert gazed sharply at his seeming assistant, at his shark's dead black eyes and his straw-colored hair. The labor boss watched just as closely as the supposed Cordray angrily shoved the tail of his pastel blue shirt into the waistband of his medium blue pants, fashioned from his trademark seersucker. He followed this action by straightening the collar of his coat. Finally he repositioned his pale blue tie and silver clasp which had evidently come undone, the result of that mysterious episode in the side office.

"Damned creep!" Cordray exclaimed to Pat Calvert. "Who'd he think he was, comin' in here, actin' like he could push me around?"

Cordray sent a strong right hand up to the left sleeve of his coat, jerked the fabric back down to his wrist.

In the process, Pat Calvert caught a glimpse of a silvery band which encircled the third finger of Luke Cordray's left hand.

Calvert questioned in a loud voice, "Who do you mean?"

"That clown what showed up a few minutes ago. Thinkin' he had some kinda dirt on me," was Cordray's response. "I'll make him *think* he could blackmail me, that guy!"

Luke's manner betrayed the fact that the experience had unnerved him. He was repeatedly clenching and unclenching his jaws, so much so that the muscles in his neck stood out like cords. Calvert stated thought Luke Cordray had broken this habit, sometime ago. It was too dangerous, Calvert had often told him, because it tended to forecast Cordray's intent, no matter what his features might suggest.

The labor racketeer went on with this question, "What did you do with him?"

"I sent him on his damn' way, was what I did!" Cordray replied, his voice passionate. "You said you weren't to be disturbed today. So I was seein' to it that you weren't disturbed. Got to protect you."

He bestowed a hasty laugh on Pat Calvert.

Something funny was going on with Luke, Pat Calvert decided. The man had never struck his gang chieftain as a fellow with much of a sense of humor. Moreover, he had never been known to wear rings. Yet he had donned one on his left hand.

It had been like this since he, Calvert, had decided, at Luke's urging, to buy that

Calvert gave Cordray a batch of papers, next year's budget, to examine while he, Calvert stood by to observe what happened next.

Certainly Calvert thought Luke looked every bit himself: a big man, maybe a former college linebacker, who'd muscled his way into the world of labor racketeering. Despite a bit of a paunch, the big fellow still retained a degree of his physicality. He still wouldn't hesitate to give Calvert's enemies the business, whether he had to use knives, brass knuckles, or the occasional firearm to make Pat Calvert's point.

But he wasn't all muscle, as the trucking racketeer knew. Luke could be smart when he needed to advise his chief on various affairs, like this budget.

This man Calvert thought was Luke continued to look at the papers, wordlessly, until finally he replied, "Looks okeh to me."

"That's funny," Calvert stated, puzzled. He ordered the Agent to sit down while he, Calvert, passed the budget over to him. "Just yesterday you suggested I up the percentage that all of the men pay in union dues. You even said it would bring me more of the green stuff. Remember that?"

Uneasy, X lied, "Oh, yeah. Sure, I do. I'm all for makin' more money."

"Well, you were even *more* for it, last week. It was the miscellaneous expenses that you thought were too high. Suppose you've come around to my way of thinking, right?"

Privately the Agent knew this business about an increase in the man's miscellaneous expenses might be a lead. But he sidestepped this accusation against Luke Cordray's life with this: "I—I'm not thinkin' straight today. It's that moron who came in the office a few minutes ago."

The labor racketeer took the sheets back from his subordinate. Pat Calvert could tell something was going on with his assistant. Could the husky fellow have discovered what he, the labor racketeer, had colluded to do, with the Resurrectionist?

A sudden ringing of the telephone halted Calvert's current train of thought. He favored his wrist watch with a quick look. Then he ordered Luke out of the office for a bit.

"And shut the door to your office while you're at it!" he commanded in his usual loud voice, while his right hand lifted the phone.

In the meanwhile, big Luke Cordray, the Secret Agent, obeyed the directive without question, when normally he would have desired to stick around, possibly to listen or to give commentary to his chief. As Cordray left the office, Calvert trained his green optics briefly on the man's departing form. Luke's failure to protest struck Pat Calvert as another suspicious angle requiring investigation. But that would come soon enough.

Pat Calvert was not the only one with suspicions. Agent X, too, knew that more than a patina of skullduggery colored the racketeer's latest dealings.

Out of sight in Cordray's office, he shot over to the side of the closed door. From his left coat pocket he flicked a small toggle switch on one of his UHF transceivers, activating the thing.

The disguised eyes of the Agent acquired dagger keenness. His dexterous finger tapped out a quick message on the speaker's surface. When he received the expected reply from an operative, he allowed himself a brief smile. That task done, he switched to another frequency and transmitted a different message to a second operative. It too produced a quick reply and a second smile. Everything about the case was shaping up so far.

Back into his pocket he transferred the gadget. However, he didn't switch it off.

Next he thrust his right hand inside the right pocket of his coat to retrieve a seemingly harmless object. It was a box-like affair in the shape of a camera. In actuality the contrivance, a mere shell, concealed a sophisticated listening device. Agent X often used the thing when he wished to be a concealed third party to a quarry's conversations or actions.

Quickly he unspooled a thin length of black insulated wire and a red suction cup from the hollow camera. After attaching the rubber cup to the door, he adjusted a tiny stud, actually a rheostat, to supply more volume to his listening gadget.

The device produced no sound for a moment, the result of a dead battery. He suddenly recalled he had used the thing many times over in Europe. As a consequence, he must have completely depleted the battery's charge.

That wasn't like him, to allow a piece of equipment to operate at less than normal capacity. However, the aftermath of the European trip still affected him, as did the troubling nature of the current investigation. He mustn't let it cripple his effectiveness, though—especially since he wanted to stop the Resurrectionist's threat.

Invigorated by his desire for justice, he thrust his left hand back into a coat pocket for a fresh energy cell. This he then used to replace the exhausted one, which went back to his pocket.

He committed a new error when he cranked up the rheostat much too high. A loud noise, as of a megaphone's blare, sent far too much sound traveling down the wire and through the earpiece. The detective adjusted the rheostat in a counterclockwise direction, the sound dropping to a more reasonable level.

Absolutely still, X focused his attention on any noises emanating from the other side of the closed portal.

There was still nothing, despite his change of battery. Evidently the other party was doing the talking right now.

Suddenly Agent X's ears detected words.

"I can't hear you, dammit!" Calvert exclaimed. *"Let me adjust the volume on this phone!"*

The voice on the opposite end must have said something else. Swearing like a dock hand, Calvert told him he couldn't hear this either. But angrily fumbling with the telephone's volume control, he managed to rejoin his telephonic visitor.

"What do you mean, the price has gone up? I thought we had agreed upon—"

His respondent must have offered an objection because Calvert shot back with more protests. *"Well, I'll tell you what you are!"* he shouted a series of obscenities through the phone's mouthpiece, *"you're a damn no-good—!"*

The mysterious voice—it was Mr. Ramond—stated something else which apparently placated Calvert. The labor racketeer responded, *"Well, that's more like it."*

More words came, as Calvert grew silent.

Then the Agent's ears heard this: *"Yeah,*

he's in the next room. I sent him out when you called."

Calvert's caller must have posed a question about Luke Cordray, given the reply of Calvert himself: *"Hell, yeah! I think he's acting suspicious this morning, too. He in cahoots with you?"*

Pat Calvert received oily reassurance from Mr. Ramond that Cordray was merely like any good friend—concerned about his comrade's welfare. As a result, Calvert's smile returned. Did Luke have to see what they intended to happen? Calvert asked.

Apparently Mr. Ramond said that he did, since Calvert resumed his silence. At some point Calvert spoke again: *"What do I need to do to get ready?"* More silence occurred. Then X's machine transmitted these words through the door: *"You're coming in ten minutes? That's—"* he glanced at his watch. Shrugging his massive shoulders, he grudgingly stated, *"Well, all right. Come ahead."*

He replaced the phone on its cradle.

Still turned towards the closed door, X scrambled to gather his gear. When he'd finished, he reached a hand inside the opposite coat pocket.

At the same time he heard a couple of sounds, both of them disconcerting.

The first was one he knew would come: Pat Calvert ordered him to come into the outer office. They needed to continue the budgetary discussion of moments ago.

X informed the man he, the Agent, would be there shortly.

The second of the two sounds was one familiar to his ears.

It was the *click* of a trigger.

He pivoted, to see the real Luke Cordray, conscious and fully recovered from the assault of the Secret Agent's anesthetic gas gun!

CHAPTER X
THE VOLATILE SITUATION

LUKE Cordray must have avoided the full charge of the Agent's weapon! And worse, the man had escaped his bonds! This last outcome wasn't the result of carelessness on the Agent's part, either. No dumb lug, the fellow had actually cut through his bonds, something which rarely happened when the Agent tied a man. Still, he had taken another precaution, which he had executed as a fallback maneuver. And, given the present danger, its effectiveness would quickly become apparent.

"Thought you was slick, didn't you, fella, comin' in here, lookin' like me," the real Cordray sneered at the Secret Agent. "Thought you were even smarter, shootin' me with that funny little pistol of yours and then tyin' me up?"

The resourceful public defender seemed strangely unconcerned about his situation. As if to underscore his calm, a hint of mirth passed his lips. Then it vanished as quickly as it had appeared.

"You should have checked more closely when you threw me in the closet over there," the real Cordray indicated the opened door with his right thumb. "I didn't breathe enough of that gas, or whatever it was, to do me any harm. And I always—*always*—carry a couple o' holdouts up my sleeves."

He pointed to his right arm and slid back the sleeve of his light green seersucker suit, as well as the shirtsleeve underneath. Luke had directed a tailor to make both sleeves slightly oversized, and with good reason.

There on his forearm he had strapped a "holdout," a metal and leather track contrivance, spring-loaded, which could deliver a playing card, a knife, or, in this present case, a gun into the hands of the user. Luke did the same with the other sleeve of his coat, to reveal a knife which he'd squirreled away in another of the contraptions. Old-time gamblers on the Mississippi River had carried such gadgets as one of their most vital pieces of equipment—along with loaded decks and special eyeglasses for reading marked cards.

"Apparently you're an old hand at this kind of thing," the Secret Agent offered, nonchalantly. "Guess I'll have to take that into account, next go-around, eh?"

"Yeah, bet you will, at that, fella," Luke Cordray agreed with the cornered detective. "Next time, don't make it so easy for fella ta snap his knife inta his wrist and untie himself—kinda like I did. Real surprisin' ta me that somebody with a reputation like yours could let that happen. It's even more surprising that you'd get trapped so easily, isn't it, *Mr. X*? 'Cause I'm bettin' that's who you are—Secret Agent X, the famous Man of a Thousand Faces."

The bold man-hunter countered, "You sure about that, Cordray? I say that *you* were out for a while, after our struggle and that *you're* the one who's confused. Fact is, *I'm* the real Luke Cordray."

"Yeah, that's rich. I guess you think I'm some kinda dope, too, Mr. X." Well, we'll see about that." He paused for a moment; then he shouted, "Hey, Pat! Got a guy in here you gotta see. Claims he's me, in the flesh. But he's really Secret Agent X, that fella who's always stealin' somebody else's face. And this time he's pinchin' mine, good looks and all!"

This last remark traveled deeply into the territory of self-satisfaction. It was typical of the real Cordray: great resourcefulness, not to mention extreme self-confidence. Here again it emphasized the danger X had assumed in borrowing Cordray's identity, particularly on such short notice. For perfect as X's impersonation might have seemed, it fell short on some of the fine details of the man's life. But after all, he had taken on the role merely to gain entrée to Calvert and his circle. X's pose might still work, for the simple fact that he always planned for such eventualities.

The present moment, in fact, counted as one of them.

Cordray, the real McCoy, thought he had his man, X, dead to rights. When Pat Calvert entered, he immediately realized something strange was going on. What neither of them could have foreseen was the possibility that the Agent might bring reinforcements. And that he had summoned them, already, by tapping out a coded message on the UHF transceiver.

From across the street two of them awaited the detective's signal.

The first of them was Harvey Bates, the black-haired, square-jawed giant. He parked his large frame on the front passenger seat of a battered New York hack. The vehicle's hood concealed a super-charged engine, a twelve cylinder, of immense power.

Behind the wheel of the same cab sat an immense piece of flesh, one Hiram Beckwith. A balding, cheerful sort with a love for the latest swing tunes, potbellied Beckwith sat there with a bag of candied orange slices clutched in one hand and two of the sugary morsels in the other. He crammed the sugar-dusted, conjoined items, Siamese twins they were, into his mouth and smacked them with relish.

With his sausage-like—and sticky—right index finger, he increased the volume of his radio. "Mind if I toin up dis juke box a little? Fella can't heah a damned thing, wot wit' dis traffic on da street," he commented to Bates.

At first Harvey Bates, a more taciturn sort, said nothing, giving only a curt nod as his reply. However this time was different, and words were necessary. Of a sudden his sharp ears had detected a rhythmic *clicking* from his coat pocket.

"Chief's UHF unit," he clipped to Beckwith. "Might want to back off on that Dorsey tune, Beckwith," Bates suggested. "Might have missed some of the Chief's message."

Instantly Beckwith twisted the radio's volume to the "off" position. Sharply he turned his head to his passenger and questioned, "Wot's he say, Bates?"

Bates translated the entirety of the message on the second go-around: " 'Wait ten minutes. Then come looking, if you don't hear from me. And use anesthetizing gas—no guns.' "

Beckwith gave a nod. But he seemed genuinely crestfallen when he said, "Damn, but I hate it when Diamond Jim," that was Beckwith's nickname for the Agent, "don't let us go in, guns blazin', like da G-men...."

Harvey Bates gave a sidelong glance towards his corpulent ally, and though Bates' dark eyes were twinkling ever so slightly, he said nothing.

He and Beckwith unfastened their doors. But they remained briefly in the cab because they'd seen a mysterious white delivery truck.

"Funny, that transport over there. Ever seen a delivery vehicle like that one?" Bates quizzed, suddenly interested.

Beckwith leaned his bulk across Harvey Bates' own giant frame, squinted at the white machine.

The obese cabbie commented, "It's not like any delivery truck *I've* ever seen, that's for shuah. See the damn' front end?" He pointed his thick left index finger at the fore of diesel chariot. "It looks more like a batterin' ram, if ya ast me. Means it's constructed, most likely with steel. And take a look at the sides of that bus, while yer at it."

Bates did as Beckwith suggested.

Bates clipped, "Bulletproofed!"

"Damn' right! Seein' that thing, I'd swear it was 1929, all over again, and I was behind the wheel of that thing...."

About that time a quintet of men disembarked from the truck—two from the cab and four from the right side panel, which slid back as if on bearings.

Dark eyes sharp as daggers, Bates rapped, "Up to no good, this bunch. Chief's in that place too."

Beckwith slowly nodded. He and Bates eased from the hack and watched the next proceedings with incredulity.

Like their vehicle the driver and his five passengers wore suits of silver-white material which fairly gleamed. And they dressed in the self-same fabric, including hoods, which they'd employed in those earlier assaults, not the stuff they'd worn in that graveyard.

Despite the bulk of their outfits, they moved with a precision that would do credit to a military unit.

Bates and Beckwith observed their driver, a short, heavily-built fellow, hustle four of the men from the vehicle until their leader could urge them to their devilish task. Had X's men been able to see underneath the man's hood, they would have discovered a man of chubby cheeks and ruddy complexion, a personage flabby of body, besides. More than anything else, he resembled a French chef who'd sampled one too many of his creations.

Now their leader, a big-boned, massive fellow came to the head of the group.

Beneath his hood, this man sported a swarthy skin tone, as well as a full head of shaggy black hair, rather like Harvey Bates' own locks. Where the features of Bates were more nondescript, though, this man was handsome, indeed exceptionally so. Some people might have called his features heroic, since they were chiseled and his lips, perfect.

The third fellow, fair and blond, carried his head like a king, waiting for his subjects' obeisance. He needn't have worried about looking heroic, though, or brave, much less handsome. This character owned a pimply complexion, a receding chin, and a bent beak, or nose, the result of a bad break and worse setting by a doctor.

Man number four would have been quite the physical specimen, divested of his strange silver-white garb. With his heavily pomaded brown hair, bronzed visage, and muscular frame, he might have been a stand-in for Charles Atlas. Certainly he looked as if he had spent hour upon hour underneath one of those sun-lamps so popular with the younger set. Also he had probably spent as much time, building that magnificent body of his. This Atlas lookalike had had ample time to do so, what with the hard time he'd done, breaking up rocks in the State pen.

Stripped of his own gear, gentleman number five could have doubled for one of those aging wizards from the Brothers Grimm. He owned, for instance, a shock of salt and pepper hair which formed a sharp widow's peak on his Mephistophelian brow. Moreover, his brows were arched in most arrogant fashion, one in particular, as if he might be trying to impress someone with his intellect or his other abilities. That facial skin of his was too tight, as well. It made a person think that someone had grabbed his face from behind and pulled it taut as a drum. Such tension stretched his already ample mouth much wider than ever, such that he could have admitted a freight train through that cavity.

When he was not so strangely dressed, the final man owned a skinny form. In truth he seemed an animate scarecrow, with flame-colored hair as though he'd stepped from a blast furnace. His complexion was nearly as ruddy as that hair of his, suggestive of some English, Irish, or English forebears. His eyes were enormous, wide-set. Parked in between those peepers was a nose which, at best, might be described as bulbous, at worse, as a small potato. Those lips of his were no better, being full, perch-like. He always gave the appearance of being ready to smooch any female he encountered. But he was perpetually telling everyone he met that he was a fighter, not a lover. If his non-stop talk were an indicator of his physical prowess, then he must have been a regular jim-dandy.

Such were the criminals Harvey Bates and Hiram Beckwith observed, however incompletely.

A shame it was, too, that the Agent's associates couldn't see the men's most important characteristic: their eyes.

There was a savagery, no, a madness in all of their peepers. Those optics looked wilder than wild, like the orbs of dope fiends. The eyes of the fat man, for example, were greenish yellow and resembled the eyes of a wildcat on the prowl, that is, merciless, kill-crazy. The big man, in contrast, showed forth a set of coffee brown eyes which burned with devilish intent. That third character, he of the blondish locks, watched the street with too-interested slate gray visual sensors, his head pivoting constantly. Man number four's violet irises glittered unnaturally, showing his anticipation of something less wholesome than a downtown shopping jaunt. And the last individual, Flame Hair, observed the world through a zealot's pair of restless blues. With them he gave a viewer the idea he might, with no provocation, hop onto a soapbox and harangue a crowd, more for the sake of hearing his own voice, than for pushing a just or worthy cause. Worse yet, he evinced an uncontrollable tic of some sort, one that could diminish his ability to function.

Their leader, the big fellow, ordered the men through the front door of the brownstone.

Pat Calvert did not yet realize what was unfolding outside. Neither did his *aide-de-camp* Luke Cordray or the Secret Agent yet suspect any of the unfolding events on the street.

Calvert had marched across the room and through the door into the side office. It was this compartment where Luke Cordray normally held forth. The shock of all shocks greeted Calvert in that room: two Luke Cordrays! On his right wrist, he wore a narrow band of some sort. And in the corresponding hand he clutched a small .25 caliber automatic. The other fellow shot a black-eyed shark's gaze at the pistol's wielder.

"Well, what have we here?" Calvert allowed a sly grin to creep across his handsome features. "The Prince and the Pauper, eh? One of you is Secret Agent X, and the other is the real Luke Cordray?" he quizzed. His tone grew brittle. "I don't have time to figure out who's who."

Ever daring, the bold public defender took the bull by the horns. "No need for you to do anything, Pat," he stated, his voice an exact duplicate of Cordray's tones. "I'm Luke Cordray. And I can prove it."

The real Luke Cordray exclaimed, "That's a laugh! I'd like to see him prove he's me."

"It's easier than buyin' a Chicago politician, Pat," a grinning X remarked with supreme confidence. "Just take a close look at his forehead, and you'll see exactly what I mean. And while you're at it, scope out his jawline, too."

"What about my face and my jawline, fella?" Luke Cordray sneered at the Secret Agent. Contempt dripped from his next words: "You're just stallin' for time, is what you're doin'. And I for one—"

"Can it, Luke," Pat Calvert ordered, in a tone of suggestive of a parent scolding an incorrigible child.

X maintained his relaxed pose there beside that door. In this way he showed clearly that the situation hadn't rattled him. And his plan would have time to bear fruit....

In the meantime, Pat Calvert sidled over to the real Cordray.

"This better not be a game, Luke," he peered over his shoulder and warned the false Cordray, Agent X. Slowly Calvert's frustration was peeping from behind his wall of calm, as he declared, "You're already on thin ice with me, when it comes to that budget. Damned thin ice, in fact."

The real Cordray stood there like a hundred-year oak, immoveable. But his face betrayed his confidence the situation would turn in his favor.

Now Pat Calvert took a step directly in front of the beefy Cordray. The labor racketeer trained his gaze directly on Luke's forehead and jaws. The pitch of his voice climbed the scale in direct proportion to his mounting vexation: "Can't quite see what you want me to find here, Cordray. I'm beginning to think it's a trick—"

"It *is!*" the ex-football player insisted, his cockiness disappearing and his teeth now showing like the fangs of a rabid canine. "Can't you see it, Pat? It's a damn' trick!"

A sharpness suddenly entered Calvert's dark green eyes. His mouth abruptly opened like a trapdoor.

With equal speed his muscular right index finger rocketed to the real Cordray's forehead, scratched it. When that digit fled the scene of its crime, the nail carried something strange under its edge. Calvert performed the same act with the right and then the left jawline of his assistant.

To the utter disbelief of Calvert, the tip of his fingernail accumulated a small quantity of the mysterious stuff.

It was a flesh-colored substance, lightweight, and extremely flexible.

That stuff was the Secret Agent's volatile plastic! And it masked a dark stain, removable only with a solvent. The olive tint gave Cordray the illusion of a man who'd gained a rich tropical tan, one of X's own physical characteristics in point of fact.

Little did Luke Cordray, or for that matter Pat Calvert, suspect that the Agent had rubbed a small quantity of skin dye on the fairer man's face and neck. This trait would suggest a man of the outdoors, perhaps an adventurer of some kind. In addition, he'd spread some of his volatile plastic over the man's features. Agent X had smeared just enough of the substance there, in fact, to lead an observer to an erroneous conclusion: He, Agent X, had crafted an incomplete disguise for his olive features. Perhaps he had intended to finish his masquerade as Luke Cordray upon arrival at Calvert's office. But he had first tangled with the genuine article there. And thus he had failed to achieve his goal of supplanting the ex-football player.

Pat Calvert drew this very conclusion, regarding his assistant.

The labor boss rolled some of the volatile plastic into a miniature ball, allowed the stuff to fall into the palm of his right hand.

"So you're not Agent X, eh, Luke?" Calvert accused the man. "Seems like that's not the right answer now, is it? Especially with this," he brought the rolled volatile plastic before Luke Cordray's frightened black eyes, "*this damned stuff that is Secret Agent X's stock in trade!*"

As if by magic he drew a .45 caliber Colt, a black slab of a pistol, aimed it directly at the now-cringing Luke Cordray!

The satellite begged, "Now, wait a minute, Pat! You can't do this! Sure, I've been—I've been...."

Calvert megaphoned, "You've been *what*? You've been spying on me, Agent X, is what you've been doing!"

"Damn' right it's what he's been doing!" Agent X chimed in, a sneer of contempt drawing up his disguised lip.

"I've a good mind to kill you on the spot, Mr. X," Pat Calvert magically changed his countenance from one of handsomeness to the cruel face of a Borgia. Ramming the gun into Luke's right nostril, he cynically informed the other two men, "I'd be doing everybody a favor, you know. Hell, John Law would probably give me a medal for it. I'll bet his nibs, Inspector John Burks would even pin it on me. Maybe even Commissioner Charlie Foster himself would do the honors! Yeah—giving Secret Agent X the bump is the way to go, I think."

This plan of the Agent was going much too well, now. And X, for all his hatred of crime, couldn't simply allow the man to commit cold-blooded murder. It did not matter that Luke Cordray was as crummy a piece of humanity as Pat Calvert himself. Only a judge and a jury could try the two men and determine their guilt or not.

As Calvert continued to menace Luke Cordray, the detective abruptly stepped in closer. From his new position he could, if necessary, bat the .45 from Pat Calvert's eager hand.

"Look, Pat!" Agent X urged in Luke Cordray's voice. "You can't haul off and drill this X character! Why don't you let me pump him for information? They say he's got some connections with Washington, that he's some kinda G-man. Maybe I can pry his plans from him, you know. Maybe he'll listen to a little persuasion...."

The labor racketeer sang a counterpoint to X's song. For his part, he remained intent on doing in Secret Agent X, actually the man he misapprehended to be X, despite the best efforts of the Man of a Thousand Faces.

A devious smile on his handsome face, he sucked his teeth a couple of times, as though deep in thought.

While this business was going on, the real Luke Cordray trained his glaring black eyes on Pat Calvert and the Agent.

He wasn't waiting any longer, not with his very life in jeopardy. Without warning he ducked his head and launched his body directly at Secret Agent X.

The detective had already seen the glower which had invaded Cordray's black shark's eyes. As the man leaped at the Agent, the brilliant detective hopped into the man's path and threw up his left arm. That act warded off the man's attack. The same motion also stymied Cordray from going after his erstwhile chief.

"Get out of here now, Pat!" the Agent commanded, his head pointed over his shoulder at the gang leader.

"But I can't leave, Luke! I've got to—"

Eyes huge, Pat Calvert paused for a brief second and not just at the Agent's behest. He was still thinking of the time, as indicated by his glance at his watch. Then he fled the room and ran to the front. And all of a sudden, from outside, hell broke loose!

CHAPTER XI
COME, SWEET DEATH

GUNS cracked. Voices shouted curses. Furniture splintered and overturned. Awaiting a conference with their leader in a side room, a quartet of Calvert's labor thugs thundered onto the scene. There they made a stand against the invasion of the white-suited men.

One of Calvert's toughs, a fat older man with a cue-ball for a head and an "O" for a mouth, pumped a couple of rounds into the chest of the wizard-like thug, who instantly collapsed in an unnatural sprawl on the floor.

The bronzed Charles Atlas, too, caught his share of hell, when a bullet grazed his left shoulder. Another of Calvert's men, a greasy-haired young Turk with blood in his eye, shot the hood in the gut. The man would cash in his chips, quickly, without medical attention. In revenge his four thuggish comrades cut loose with their own weapons, two of which were C96 Mauser pistols of the Bolo variety.*

The result was predictable.

One after the other of Calvert's toughs collapsed, screaming, fountains of crimson gushing from their lips.

In short order the white suits had ended any opposition from Calvert's men. They seemed poised to advance, unmolested, to the inner chambers, location of Agent X and the rest.

Two individuals, however, tried to resist the building's inevitable fall to the invading force: Harvey Bates and Hiram Beckwith.

The gun battle was subsiding. Thus the Agent's assistants had stolen into that room of dying men. Bates and Beckwith had moved in via the same street entrance through which the gunmen had invaded. Now Bates and Beckwith huddled behind an overturned metal desk. From either side of it, they had fired several shots of their own, resorting to regular firearms because of their opponents' semiautomatic weapons. In so doing, they had managed to delay the white-suited quintet, but only briefly. Suddenly, from that long hallway leading to Pat Calvert's office, the white suits lobbed round after round at the heavy rectangular desk. When able, Bates peeped over the desk and squeezed off his own rounds. But he shot mainly to disable his opponents rather than to kill them.

That was not the case with the fair-haired blond criminal, the fellow of the kingly manner, Prince Albert. Quickly he revealed his bloodlust. He failed to realize that either newcomer had anything to do with Calvert's hoods. Of course, had he known their association with the Secret Agent, he most likely would have doubled the fury of his assault.

As it was, his fresh attack was vicious enough. With his Bolo Mauser, Prince Albert fired potshots around the room, simply to intimidate Beckwith and Bates. And on the heels of the gunshots, he emitted a twisted choking sound, a travesty of laughter, from the depths of his throat. He was likely a dope fiend, a man who would enjoy bringing harm or doom to another person.

Everyone heard a peremptory shout from Prince Albert's leader, the olive-complexioned giant. Prince Albert ran back down the hall. His chief whispered to the blond man not to waste more time, but to kill Bates and Beckwith immediately.

Prince Albert promptly found cover behind a quartet of luxuriant plants in tall, heavy stone pots. This bulwark enabled him to face Agent X's men. After offering some weird rant, he uttered a statement he, the Prince, thought particularly crafty. He shouted an order for Bates and Beckwith to drop their weapons. If they complied, then he and his fellows would allow the two safe passage from the building. Both of X's men knew the man's offer to be a false one, of course. Beckwith undertoned that this blond was the type who would as soon murder his

*** AUTHOR'S NOTE: A compact version of the famed "broomhandle" Mauser, the Bolo variety, equipped with its short barrel and small grip, offers easy concealment. Moreover, like its larger sibling, the Bolo, also a semiautomatic, fires rounds with deadly stopping power. Indeed, only a weapon firing a .357 Magnum cartridge can match it for lethality.**

own parents as look at them.

Bates nobbed his head slightly but offered no comment to Hiram Beckwith. The giant Bates *did* pull a tiny notebook from a pocket, whereupon he scribbled a brief message to Beckwith. They must reinforce Agent X quickly and thus halt this bunch's murderous rampage.

Meanwhile, the blond killer offered them quarter for a second time. They could still leave the building, no questions asked. This affair didn't pertain to any of them, the man informed. It involved Pat Calvert and him alone.

Harvey Bates, usually a taciturn sort, shouted back to their enemy, "Not interested in the offer! Smart thing for you and your pals to do is to drop your own weapons!"

His pistol a metal snake, the man slithered the object between two of the stone pots. From that vantage point, he pumped half a dozen fresh rounds in the direction of Bates and his comrade. Fortunately none of them even hit either of X's men. Harvey Bates then offered Prince Albert several leaden reasons of his own why the battle wasn't yet done. Prince Albert spewed a fountain of curses from beneath his protective hood. And in his fury he grew much more careless. Because of his heavier firepower, he thought he should peer over the top of the pots. True, this move gave him a more panoramic view of the battlefield. But that tactic exposed his upper body.

Prince Albert ducked before they could fire at him. He resorted to his makeshift gunports, the slots between the plants, again, and lobbed more rounds at Beckwith and Bates. Then, foolishly, he arose to peer at the desk.

This gave Harvey Bates an idea. Like the Secret Agent, the giant carried a handful of marbles and something else: several magnesium flares. The devices, small canisters, could light an entire area with a brilliant, white light. The user, however, could as easily blind himself for a space, if he had not tightly shut his eyes in advance of discharging the flare.

On the sheet of notebook paper, Bates scribbled his plan to Hiram Beckwith. The fat cab driver didn't know what to expect, having never witnessed a flare in action. Nevertheless, he did as Bates had directed. Suddenly the shaggy-haired giant hurled a couple of clear glass marbles across the room and to his right, that is, to the left of Prince Albert. They *clackety-clack-clacked* to the floor, just outside Prince Albert's line of sight.

Abruptly, the wild-eyed blond reared up from behind his protective barrier. He pumped more shots at his foes.

Bates arced the small canister up and over the heavy metal desk. The cylindrical object *plopped* against the floor. Instantly a blinding light exploded in the room.

The man's shooting continued by reflex, until he had exhausted the Mauser's clip. Agent X's men heard the melody of a trigger's repeated *click* against the Mauser's firing pin. More curses provided harmony to this tune. Nonetheless, it was music, sweet music to the beleaguered friends of Secret Agent X.

To celebrate their minor victory, Bates strode across the room and retrieved the blinded man. Beckwith produced a length of strong, thin cord. The fat cabbie sliced a short length of it from the main piece, reserving it for some future purpose. Next Bates roughly threw the criminal onto his stomach. The giant followed that move by yanking the man's hands backward and tying them firmly.

He completed the entire procedure by lashing Prince Albert's ankles to his wrists. Beckwith removed the hood from the man's face, balled a dirty handkerchief from his pocket, and rammed the thing into the tough's mouth. With the cord he'd reserved, he looped the section around Prince Albert's mouth and knotted the thing in the back.

"Don't recognize this guy at all," Hiram Beckwith commented.

Bates wasn't as ready to offer an observation. He simply grunted while he and Beckwith awaited word from their chief.

Down the hall, the labor racketeer had raced into a compartment at right angles to the scene of the assault, a capacious storage area leading from his office. But once in the new room, he scrambled to a position of relative safety. To the right of the door, he saw a pair of filing cabinets standing at slight angles. A tight squeeze of his muscular frame enabled him to slip behind the two of them. There he heard the invasion as it unfolded: His foes fought a heated gun battle for a time, his own men coming up short. This had better be what he expected. Otherwise he would be in for a surprise.

In the meantime, Prince Albert's confederates pushed down the hall and into the space outside Calvert's own chambers.

There was Chef Jules, the driver of the white truck; and Flame Hair, the thug with the fanatic's wild eyes and the odd tics. Tiny, the giant with the shaggy black hair, still generaled the survivors.

Each of the men still carried his firearm, a conventional pistol like a .45 Colt, or, in the case of Flame Hair, the remaining Bolo Mauser.

Tiny and Flame Hair, however, packed more unique weapons, in addition to those others..

The two things, steel crafted, were handguns of a sort, perhaps something along the line of a .45 automatic, but with a rounder barrel. In addition the manufacturer had affixed another metallic piece, a long tube, along the barrel—or what might have been the barrel.

The quartet stepped into the filing area. Once inside, Tiny cupped a hand around his mouth. Hurling preliminaries to the wind, he informed the labor racketeer in a deep-pitched tone, "It's your time now, Calvert."

Calvert still huddled behind the shelter of the metal cabinet. Finally, he squeezed out a stammered, "N—now? How can I be sure that yo—you're...."

The giant criminal tittered for a couple of seconds. Then he replied, "Everybody's going to face the Reaper sometime, Calvert. It's either now or later. You knew this ahead of the game...."

Struggling from behind the file cabinets, the labor racketeer faced the men in white. He protested, "I've—I've got to be sure about this....You're one of his—"

The racketeer reached inside a black leather wallet as the men held him at gunpoint. From a cellophane sleeve inside the leathern pouch, he extracted a small gold embossed card, its obverse etched with a word in a foreign tongue and a sentence in English. Its other side, the reverse, contained a picture—it might have been a flower—and a number.

Shaking, he inched the piece of pasteboard over to Tiny.

A large right hand, that of Tiny, wiped smudges from the clear covering of the bulky hood. The giant acknowledged the image with a curt "yes." He immediately shoved the card back into Calvert's hand. The labor crook promptly crammed the thing back into his wallet.

"This is it, all right, Calvert," Tiny remarked, cold as a witch's kiss. "Good thing you didn't expose it to air for too long, or it wouldn't have been visible. And that would have been too damn' bad for you...."

Then a strange smile suddenly invaded the territory that was Pat Calvert's handsome visage. Paradoxically, he seemed to have regained his composure.

"Do what you have to do, then," Calvert commanded the man. "And while you're at it, you can go in there and finish off Agent X; then help my man Cordray. He's wearin'—"

"—I don't care what he's wearing, Calvert. We don't have time to do you any favors," Tiny interrupted with a wave of his hand. He glanced quickly at a watch strapped to his wrist and suddenly replaced his silvery-white hood. "We're on a timetable, and finishing the Man of a Thousand Faces isn't part of your package. Besides, when the Resurrectionist is ready, he'll deal with Mr. X, personally."

The giant criminal raised the strange pistol he held. He aimed, point-blank, at the intended victim's throat. Strangely the gun emitted nothing so much as a weird cough of sorts. In response, Pat Calvert opened his trap and emitted an odd exclamation, though not exactly a scream.

In that side room off Calvert's chambers, in Luke Cordray's office, Secret Agent X had been battling for his life with the real Cordray.

Calvert's satellite and the detective had been thrashing about on the floor, with neither presently able to gain the advantage. For the Man of a Thousand Faces something worse was going on. More than a trace of Cordray's former prowess lent him the ability to deliver a few powerful blows to the Secret Agent. And the man wasn't a mere brawler, either. He knew how to deliver a punch that would cause maximum damage.

Right now he did that.

Luke Cordray had heard, long ago, that the Secret Agent had suffered a terrible injury below his heart, during the World War. Indeed that same wound had brought him to the very outer court of the Reaper's throne room. It was only his indomitable will that had allowed him to survive and, eventually, to become the brilliant crime crusher, Secret Agent X. Even then the remnants of the wound, an X-shaped cicatrix and the source of his name, caused him occasional and sometimes crushing pain, a constant reminder of his brush with death.*

Cordray mailed his enormous fist directly into the geography below the detective's heart.

Abruptly the cruel blow sank the Man of a Thousand Faces deeply into an ocean of agony. Visibly shaken, he opened his mouth, his lungs involuntarily sucking in a great quantity of air. Teeth gritting, he tried valiantly to shake off the man's blow. But before he could successfully do so, Luke Cordray hit a second time, then a third and a fourth wallop, in that same vulnerable spot.

By now the Agent had doubled over in excruciating pain, his heart pounding like an enormous bass drum. Weird lights swirled before his eyes. Tears pooled around his eyelids. He knew he could take only a little more of

*** AUTHOR'S NOTE: Given Luke Cordray's knowledge of X's past, I believe it highly likely that some underworld elements have learned of the Agent's scar, possibly from police informants, and more likely, from police themselves, men who disgrace the very oath they swear.**

such punishment before he cashed in.

While the investigator bent double, Luke Cordray, dirty fighter that he was, kicked the Secret Agent in the jaw. The massive blow jarred the Agent's entire head, as if a church bell had rung inside his very skull. A millisecond later, the man-hunter toppled to the floor, barely conscious.

He lay there, battered and groaning. X was fortunate the blow hadn't connected with his trachea, thus severing it. But one thought kept him from fading out entirely. He needed desperately to end this fight with a victory. Only in that way could he save his own hide, and resume this campaign against his foe.

Luke Cordray had retrieved his gun from the place it had fallen, moments earlier. The .45 pistol in his hand, he bent down and rammed its barrel into the Secret Agent's temple.

X had one opportunity to survive, and that chance was now.

He had collapsed to the floor, such that his torso fell across his left forearm and, in the same manner, his left hand. X forced his left thumb to the base of his ring finger, the same digit that had sported that silvery band.

In haste, X had forgotten to doff the thing when he'd donned the guise of Luke Cordray. This case had already thrown him off-kilter, because of the sights he'd seen in Teutschland and and, worse, his possible exposure, on this case, as Elisha Pond.

Meanwhile, at Agent X's side, Luke Cordray gloated, "Looks like the end for you, Mr. X! If I hadn't been so mad earlier, I would have figured out that Calvert was signaling me. You remember? When he sucked his teeth, twice? Well, he does it once, if everything is jake. But two times, if something is rotten in Denmark. Like right now...."

X flipped the face of the ring around, such the face of it, a flat, plain surface, pointed outward.

Cordray grabbed the Agent's hair, in reality a toupee, thinking he would yank the investigator's head upward. The ex-athlete pulled with such force that he jerked the straw-colored mop from Agent X's skull. In the process he lifted the Agent's torso partially from the floor, so forcefully had he, Calvert's hood, hoisted the injured man. With the false hair removed from X's head, however, X felt his body drop abruptly downward.

Luke Cordray paused to look at the straw-colored thatch before he grabbed the Agent's real hair, lifted his body, and fulfilled his wish: to murder the Man of a Thousand Faces.

The gangster's aide didn't know that his foe had been regaining his strength all the while.

X touched a hidden stud near the ring's face, a feature thicker than was usual on such jewelry. As though by legerdemain, the ring's surface popped open to reveal a razor sharp knife, its tip doped with a fast-acting narcotic.

Like a striking snake, the left arm of the public defender shot around to Luke Cordray's right calf. As quickly, he stabbed the spring blade deeply into the man's flesh.

He promptly squealed like a stuck pig, dropped the Agent's upper body back on the floor.

The man swayed a couple of times, his dead shark's eyes paradoxically alive for once. But only long enough for him to drop, like a sack of floor, onto the tiled floor.

Still breathing heavily after his ordeal, the Secret Agent lifted himself from the floor, peered downward at the unconscious man.

When he'd regained his feet, he heard *it.*

Someone must have gagged. No—it was a cough. A cough?

No, that wasn't it, at all, the Agent decided. A sudden insight flashed across the brain of the brilliant investigator. It was a gun! X struggled to the side of the doorway, peeped quickly around its side.

It was the white-suited invaders, some four in all. They were standing around a form that was prone on the floor of the room. And they'd be on him, too, likely within a couple of minutes!

CHAPTER XII
AGAIN, THE WRATH OF GOD

BODY trembling and breathing labored, X lurched over to the discarded toupee. The public defender smoothed his hair back, such that it lay close to his scalp. Then as best he could, he repositioned the tousled mop over his mussed brown locks. His present look might thus convince his new foes he really was Cordray, post-struggle. In his condition, the real McCoy certainly couldn't offer any objections to that scheme.

He moved to Luke Cordray's former chambers and hugged the wall. From this new place he could briefly eavesdrop on his enemies. Also he could escape the promises if necessary.

A good thing it was that he'd retreated, as two of them, Tiny and Flame Hair, appeared before the door only seconds after his own departure.

From the room beyond, X heard these words, choking as though from a victim of strangulation. "That Calvert really dead?" It was Flame Hair, a man whose voice was unknown to X.

"Looks dead as a fossil to me," rumbled Tiny. He parted his lips in a slight laugh, his attempt at graveyard humor. "I think we did a good job."

"Then we can get back to the Resurrectionist?" Flame Hair asked. The twitching began again, much more severely this time. And the man's eyes grew ever wilder. He was clearly in a bad way.

The sight unnerved Tiny, in spite of himself. Still he regained his self-control and informed, "Yeah, I think we can. Better scoop up the stiff pronto, though, and scram. The police'll be here, any time now. And they're not part of our job."

Without warning a new thought exploded over the landscape of Flame Hair's mind. In between twitches, he quizzed, "What about Calvert's punk, Cordray? Remember what the Resurrectionist said? We gotta have a witness to what we've done."

Tiny exclaimed, "Damn! I almost forgot what the chief told us. Yeah, look around and see if you can find Cordray."

"What about that Agent X?" the man with the flame hair wondered. "He's the very one the Resurrectionist warned us about. We can't leave him at large. And I've—I've got to get—get that—that stuff, that 'sug—'"

Flame Hair unfastened the front of his bulky suit. Then he removed a handkerchief from an inner pocket. With the linen in one hand, he slipped the hood from his head and blotted his brow. Then he repositioned his hood on his head and returned his handkerchief to that pocket. These motions, simple as they were, required nearly all of the man's strength and control.

"Help—help me, Tiny," Flame Hair gasped. "Ya gotta, before I check out…."

Unnerved by the fellow's struggle, Tiny stammered, "I'll—I'll get on the horn with the Resurrectionist, right now. He'll know what to do."

Flame Hair had willed his shaking to cease for a time, his body tense with the mighty struggle. Then with a fury scarcely to be believed, the palsy revisited him. His form quavered like the trunk of a pecan tree shaken by a hard wind.

Outside that same room, X's friends kept careful watch on their silent opponents Chef Jules and Charles Atlas. These two crouched in the space between door and hallway, despite the fact that Charles Atlas had taken that hit to the shoulder.

Beckwith and Bates had seen the man suffer that gunshot wound. So they both suspected that his injury was a serious one. They had also heard Calvert's strange vocalization, which sounded, for all the world, like a kind of death cry.

It prompted Hiram Beckwith to probe, "What are we doin' sittin' heah, while dey just bumped dat guy down the hall?" an appalled Hiram Beckwith quizzed.

Fixing the man with his dark eyes, Bates responded, "Can't go out there right now. Too dicey. Birds in white know something is up, anyhow, because of that magnesium flare. Means that their friend isn't going to rejoin the party, anytime soon." He grew pensive for a bit; then he continued, rubbing his square jaw and thinking aloud, "Suspect something isn't making sense about this affair, anyhow. Going to send X a message. See if he's okeh. And tell him that something odd is going on with these white suits."

He reached inside his coat again to retrieve the compact UHF unit. A quick series of dots and dashes on the thing didn't produce any reply. The eerie silence threatened to crush Bates under its weight. To his mind something tragic must have befallen his mysterious chief.

Bates tapped out a second message. Again, he received no answer. To himself he thought maybe he and Beckwith should force their way into those inner offices, and lift the siege.

He shook his head. X had ordered him not to enter that area, unless it were absolutely necessary.

Hardly ever did he disobey an order of his enigmatic chief. The thought of obedience in this circumstance, though, chafed him to his core. But he left the unit on and, in a rare show of ill temper, rammed the device into his pocket.

Unbeknownst to him, the action twisted the transceiver's bandwidth dial clockwise, albeit ever so slightly.

As he and Beckwith plotted their next move, they both heard a metallic *something*. It emanated, seemingly, from nowhere, as though an etheric ghost.

"…Yeah, he's out of the picture, all right."

Then a pause ensued, followed by these words: *"Was there a witness?"*

"We haven't seen Cordray. Don't know where he is, right now."

Another pause met their ears. In that instant they realized they were eavesdropping on a conversation between one of the hoodlums and his leader.

With a speed belying his bulk, he jerked the transceiver from his pocket, increased the volume with a slight twist of the control.

The other speaker spoke tersely, *"You* will

find Cordray. If you don't, you'll be the next one to face the Wrath of God. It is the Death from Life—the Death which only I control!"

"*We can lay hands on Cordray with no trouble*," the voice—it was Tiny's deep tone—seemed to come from inside a well. He continued, "*Trust me, Sir. It's—it's just a matter of figuring out which is which....*"

Tiny's etheric respondent questioned, "*What do you mean?*"

Here Tiny came back with more confidence: "*He's here, too, Sir. Secret Agent X himself!... Calvert said he was posing as Luke Cordray.*"

"*You will know X from Cordray, fool, if you're observant.*"

The lightning of insight suddenly crackled in Tiny's eyes. He *did* realize, now, which one would be the real Cordray, and he softly told the Resurrectionist so. A buzzing, whether of agreement or no, wasn't apparent as it flashed through the transceiver.

At an unknown location many miles from the brownstone, a hooded man sat, obscured in shadow before a sophisticated radio sending set. He went on, softly, expanding on his scheme. Frustrated, Bates increased the volume once more on his gadget. He heard this statement: "*....You see how that will bring home the seriousness of my threat? And the reason I want the Man of a Thousand Faces to see what I can do, when he is in my power?*"

Tiny must have smiled underneath his hood, for his words of agreement carried a note of elation.

That tone evaporated, however, with this command from the Resurrectionist: "*Now get back to the reason why you weren't away from the building before now.*"

"*We were behind schedule, Sir*," Tiny stated, fearing reprisal and scrimping on details. "*See, we—uh—we had a scrape with two guys. But we—*"

A scrape?" the Resurrectionist interrupted. "*Elaborate, please.*"

"*A shoot-out. I think they were some of X's men, here to stop us and help their boss. They slowed things down for a little while.*"

Conveniently he omitted the detail of losing a couple of his own crew, one through death and the other through disobedience to orders.

His words prompted this clipped response from the other man: "*Slowed things down, eh? I see. Go on.*"

"*We got past those clowns. Then we found Calvert, only a little while ago. When he told me X was here, I—um, I cut Calvert's story short,*" Tiny related. In truth, he still hoped to divert attention from his men's less-than-perfect performance. After a pause, he resumed, "*Then I went ahead and bumped Calvert, as you'd ordered. With him out of the picture, I figured we had to get our people out of this place, before the law arrived.*"

Tiny's conversation partner, the Resurrectionist, husked a number of obscenities through the sending device. Then he gritted his next words: "*Get out of there immediately!*" he ordered. He resumed, less harshness and more resoluteness in his words, "*And bring your team back so that we can work out details of the next murder.*"

The criminal in white robes fell silent. Privately he thought to himself that it didn't matter that X was on to him or his plan. X represented nothing more than an obstacle to be surmounted. And the Resurrectionist had planned his revenge against the Secret Agent for years.

"Sir, you still there?" Tiny queried. *"I've got something else to tell you. It's about Petey. He's in a bad way and—"*

The criminal chieftain sidestepped the subject of Petey: *"Agent X is about to learn what it means to cross swords with me. He will rediscover something he believed to be lost forever: the power over death itself. And he will know, too, what it means to face exposure of his greatest secret. Now—depart that building immediately, and make sure Calvert's body is in tow. One of my street lookouts reports that the police are en-route to Calvert's brownstone, and that they will arrive there, any minute."*

The giant pressed, once again, the intelligence regarding his confederate, Petey: *"But you still haven't let me tell you about that red-headed squirt. He's in terrible shape. He needs his supply of the 'sugar,' as quickly as possible. Otherwise, he's a goner."*

The Resurrectionist laughed softly through the radio. *"Yes, it's his 'sugar,' again. Our friend Petey is far too careless and thus didn't do as he was ordered. You told him to take more, didn't you?"*

"I—eh, I sure, I did," came Tiny's shaky reply—not out of fear, but from the fact that he noticed a slight tremor in his own hand....

"He just wouldn't listen to me. That's all I can figure. He's one of those kinds who knows it all, Sir."

This cold-blooded response proceeded from the masked Resurrectionist: *"And because of his unthinking mistake, this time he won't be coming back from the dead. Too bad. I suppose I could summon the Wrath of God upon him. It would destroy any evidence linking him to us."*

Visibly shaken, Tiny pleaded, *"You don't need to tell me that! I've seen the Wrath in action...."*

"And you know, then, what it can do. Now, quickly—what was that question?"

Tiny stammered, *Wha—what do you—I mean, what are we supposed to do about the real Cordray?"*

Obliterate him with the Wrath. He's expendable, now, like Petey; and we can't have him connected to us. His destruction will let Secret Agent X know that we mean business...."

The Resurrectionist broke the etheric connection.

For his part the Man of a Thousand Faces had already heard some of this conversation, that which originated from Tiny's end, to be more precise. Also he'd contacted Hiram Beckwith, Bates being unable to take the message because he'd accidentally tuned his radio that other frequency. In a whisper the Secret Agent informed them of his plans. And he gave them clipped orders.

Promptly the two operatives ensured that the coast was clear. With the hallway still free of the invaders, Harvey Bates and Hiram Beckwith, a pair of tigers stalking prey, eased to the building's front doorway. The portal, the one they'd entered, still opened onto the white truck which had transported the men in the bulky suits.

X's friends couldn't risk departure from such an entryway, since more of the hoodlums might guard the white vehicle parked outside. But the door facing the street wasn't the only way out of the Calvert's brownstone.

Bates knew something of this structure, had glanced over a floor-plan of the place, in fact, before he and Beckwith had arrived. So Bates and his fat comrade raced back to the far side of the first room they'd entered and captured. From here Bates deliberately threw back a door onto a different hallway. They long-legged it down this one to a side entrance. Most likely it was one Calvert had used to elude his enemies in days past.

Still outside the criminals' line of sight, Agent X seized the reins of action.

He decamped, abruptly, from that other room where he had battled Cordray. This man X had slung over his shoulders in a fireman's carry. Now he and his unconscious enemy were in the midst of the white-suited hoodlums. And the men's eyes, already wild, fairly popped from their heads at this new vision.

"What are you doing here, Cordray?" Tiny gritted, not yet knowing the difference between the erstwhile opponents.

"I'm getting' outta here with Mr. X," the detective informed them, in Cordray's best style. "Gonna give 'im to the police, to make it easier on myself. None o' you's gonna be the cause o' *me* gettin' the chair."

In between a bout of severe twitches, Flame Hair, that is, Petey, threw back his head slightly. Then he stammered, "Think you're sm—smart, don't—don't you, Cordray? Think you're gonna—gonna get off that easy?"

Foolishly, Petey lunged at the Agent, thinking he would teach the public defender a lesson of sorts. In one fluid motion, X dropped the unconscious man to the floor and dodged the man's attack. The criminal's action worsened his twitching, and suddenly, he made the tile floor's acquaintance. A massive fit convulsed his body.

A prison of horror locked them behind its bars at sight of this.

"We're done—done with you, Cordray," a deeply unsettled Tiny told the Man of a Thousand Faces. The giant crook inched a little too close to Agent X. Tiny remained mistaken about the identity of this man until he, the big crook, recalled X's move of the previous seconds. He had seen X's wrist as he removed the unconscious Cordray from his broad shoulders and placed the man on the ground.

And he'd noticed nothing more extraordinary than a wristwatch adorning the Secret Agent's arm.

"Take X alive!" he pointed at the Agent. Screaming at the other thugs, Jules and Charles Atlas, he hollered, "And I'll finish Cordray!"

Atlas couldn't do much because of his shoulder wound, so X dispatched him with ease. But the fat hood took a plunge of his own towards the Agent. The Man of a Thousand Faces dodged to the side of the attacking man. As soon as the fellow scrambled back to his feet, he launched his form in a second assault. It too was unsuccessful, since the Agent snatched him from mid-air, hurled him away.

While this battle raged, Tiny pulled a bizarre pistol from one of his pockets. The weapon resembed a child's toy, in a Buck Rogers kind of way. Its maker had mounted a pair of canisters on it, one affixed to either side of the double-barreled and double-triggered weapon.

The skirl of police sirens accompanied what Tiny did next. He aimed the gun at the unconscious form of Luke Cordray and squeezed one of the triggers. Instantly a fine mist filled the air around the ex-athlete's body. With the second trigger he unleashed a silvery something, perhaps a dust, onto the man's form. Without warning a corona of bright, blue-white flame winked, no, exploded into existence, a veritable hell-blaze which raged over the frame of Pat Calvert's unconscious aid. In seconds the flames consumed the frame of Luke Cordray! Within seconds, he was a muscular, burning piece of flesh, as if he'd suffered the wrath of the Almighty Himself!

CHAPTER XIII
BAD TO WORSE

TINY, still hooded, rounded up the prostrate form of Pat Calvert, dragging the man outside the burning brownstone and onto the street, into plain view. Next he bolted toward the white delivery truck, and jumped through the now-yawning side door. Without warning, the thing rumbled into life. Obviously another man, one yet unseen, had stayed behind to stand sentry over the machine. Now it blasted off like a rocket, into the midst of the swiftly arriving bluecoats. The patrol and radio cars could not hope to stop the white truck, equipped as it was with a battering ram arrangement on the front. The reinforced chariot simply crashed through the police machines and made good its escape.

But that wasn't enough for the men in the truck, as it happened.

More mist gushed from the driver's and passenger's windows of the rolling juggernaut. Then that metallic something or other, an eerie silver glitter, spewed from the same points of origin. Blue-white flames were the horrible result, forcing the officers backwards. Some who were able dashed to their cars and rushed the machines out of the way, onto nearby sidewalks.

This second attack ensured the escape of the surviving white suits.

Amidst the crackling flames of the brownstone, X struggled with his opponent, Chef Jules. It didn't matter to the criminal that the room was filling with hellish fire, the bluish-white tongues of flame licking the overturned furniture or the walls themselves. And it was equally as irrelevant to the white suit that the stench of burning flesh pervaded the air. He wanted his man, no matter the cost.

Thus he threw a series of punches at the Secret Agent, blows that would have felled the ordinary fighter. But the detective had now recovered from the assault of Luke Cordray. As the fat hood moved in close to the Agent, X pivoted, and then hurled the heel of his left hand into the right side of the fellow's face. The blow practically caved in the cheek of the attacker, sending him, bawling, to the floor.

By now Charles Atlas had struggled to his feet for a final crack at the Man of a Thousand Faces. The Agent's head briefly averted, Atlas staggered towards the Agent, threw his frame at the detective. That hoodlum would not be deterred from bringing the man-hunter back, dead, to his master.

He jerked off his hood, an animal's fury gleaming in his eyes.

"By damn, I'm gonna get you, Mr. X, if it's the last thing I ever do!" he screamed at the detective. "You're the one who pinched my brother, Ned Smetana, when he was workin' for the Fool!* So damn *you*, and damn the Resurrectionist, if you think Timmie Smetana is gonna bring you in, alive!"

With his remaining strength, the man bit, scratched, and punched the Agent's upper

*** AUTHOR'S NOTE: Ned Smetana, a two-bit rat, served the cause of the Fool, who drove his victims mad with the chemical *wardat ashytan*, an exotic Arabic poison from the Crusades. Then the Fool gave them the choice of murder or extortion to escape his clutches. The Agent collared the Fool, as well as Smetana and many of his evil comrades.**

thighs and lower torso, with X returning numerous blows of his own.

Unbelievably, Charles Atlas scrambled to the Agent's upper body. At the same time the Agent hurled sledge hammer-like fists into his enemy's ribcage. Suddenly the muscular thug found a reserve of strength and speed. He freed himself from the detective's grasp; and like a striking cobra, he shot his hands outward, to grasp the X's throat!

Hands of iron closed inexorably around the detective's windpipe. He throttled the Secret Agent with a fury. As far as the grinning Timmie Smetana was concerned, this looked like the end for the Secret Agent. And it would have been thus, had he been anyone else.

The public defender knife-edged his hands. He airmailed both gifts right into the bundles of thoracic nerves, those at the base of the man's neck. Instantly a glassy-eyed Smetana loosed his grip, toppled to one side. When the stunned crook fell, his body landed at the very edge of a great mass of flames. Strangely they didn't burn his silver-white, bulky suit. That exhausted, wounded fellow attempted to rise, but he fell backwards, this time, into the very flames. They leapt eagerly onto his silver-white form even onto his battered and bruised face, while the man lay there, unable to move.

Agent X, coughing and gasping for breath, rolled to his feet. By now he had already inspired as much of the smoke-poisoned air as he could stand without suffering permanent damage. Also his eyes brimmed with tears because of the fumes which permeated the room.

He knew he couldn't do anything for Luke Cordray. That felon must be dead, now, nothing more than food for the monstrous blue flame which had hungrily consumed his body. When X looked over to Timmie Smetana, the story was the same. The armies of flame had first attacked his face, but now they assaulted the places where he'd torn the fabric of his silver-white suit. Clearly his life was almost done. Nonetheless, the Secret Agent might yet recover the other worthy, Petey, who'd attacked him earlier.

Staggering to the unfortunate man, Agent X hoisted him into the same carry he'd employed with Luke Cordray. Then the Agent, like Bates and Beckwith previously, weaved down that hallway, with one hand clutching the UHF transceiver.

By now coughing furiously, he halted occasionally, his ability to continue starting to flag. But his indomitable will impelled him, stumblingly, to his goal: the door through which his friends had passed. At the same time with his free hand he husked through the device's "mike": *"Be ready to receive me and an injured criminal, a red-haired man called 'Petey.' And Ba—Bates,"* a paroxysm of coughs stopped him, momentarily.

Here, Sir! Harvey Bates shot back.

"Tell one of your men to learn everything he can on this criminal I've recovered. He seems—he's—"

Came a *whoosh* of the bluish-white flames! Fingers of the conflagration clutched at every inch of the brownstone's first floor, reached for the Agent and his prisoner.

X stopped for another moment, grabbed a handkerchief from his coat. He briefly placed the man Petey on the ground and, as best he could, pressed the piece of linen around his, the Agent's, own mouth and nostrils. Once more he struggled to lift Petey over his shoulders, in order that he might bring them to safety.

His lungs were straining now. His breath was coming in short gasps. Normally steel gray, his disguised eyes, hidden behind the ebony contact lenses, resembled darkened pools, because of the tears filling them.

Then, gasping and hacking, he crashed to the tiles, his tired form partially striking an inside panel of the exit door!

The sound galvanized the antsy Harvey Bates into action. Instantly, he popped the heavy wooden portal and yanked X through the passageway. As forcefully, Hiram Beckwith grabbed the unfortunate Petey and pulled him, unresistingly, to safety.

Bates shepherded the Agent towards their vehicle's back seat, but the Agent insisted on sitting in the front, adjacent to the passenger door, in order to direct the two men. That criminal the Secret Agent directed to be placed on the rear seat. X promptly jerked the hood from Flame Head and threw the garment to the floorboards. The while, the man's breathing grew more stertorous.

In the automobile's relative safety X could now observe the criminal with more scrutiny.

Agent X's keen brain rummaged through his copious memory. He sensed something frightening had unfolded, something beyond the mere fact of hooded, weirdly-garbed men who committed criminal acts with a fiery murder weapon.

While the detective made sense of things, Harvey Bates cranked the cab, the battered chariot inching away from the burning building. In the next few moments they witnessed scenes straight from Dante's Inferno. They gasped at the torched police prowl cars and blackened husks that had been men, all in a veritable trail from Calvert's headquarters. They shook their heads at the screaming survivors, blistered as though from massive sunburns because of this terrible ordeal. The hideous tableau lacked only demons to complete the picture—and only their departure from the scene of the fire accounted for that detail.

Perhaps three score in front of them, police sirens played a horrible symphony. And several feet behind them, ten enormous fire engines accompanied the shrill performance.

Amidst more of the coughing and gagging, the Agent, head briefly pointed downward, whispered from the auto's front seat: "Bates—keep moving forward, so—so that we can get out of here. We—we've got to get this man to a hospital as fast as possible."

Harvey Bates, dark eyes screwed into pinpoints, did as ordered. Sweating from the heat and the intense pressure of the moment, he sent the hack slowly forward, in hopes that they could pass unmolested. But he and the other two men saw that hope dashed in the next instant.

They spotted Agent X's arch-nemesis, the forceful Inspector John Burks. He was leaning down through the opened window of a police radio car. Obviously he hadn't noticed them yet because of his conversation with the auto's occupant. But now with the *vroom* of the approaching machine, he launched his head upwards and spotted the oncoming vehicle. Outwards went his left hand, palm turned outward. It was as if he thought the very fact of his opened palm would, by force of will, halt X's machine. If tenacity and forcefulness could have worked such miracles, then Burks would have thereby proved his divinity.

The Man of a Thousand Faces thought

quickly. Burks' appearance there would be a bad break for the Agent and his two men under the best of conditions. But with the Secret Agent's weakened state, not to mention the criminal who had been convulsing in the back seat, the detective and his crew could ill afford a police search.

"We're going to have a tough time getting out now because of the traffic and the burning cars," the Man of a Thousand Faces softly observed, his energy rapidly replenishing in the clean air he now breathed. He whipped his head from one side of the street to the other, following which he ordered, "Stop the car as Burks directs. When he asks who I am, tell him I'm Secret Agent X. Then show him that badge in your wallet, Bates. Tell him you're a Federal man, taking me in Beckwith's cab to be questioned at the nearest F.B.I. office." *

"But, Sir!" a grim Harvey Bates protested. "Inviting trouble when you tell Burks something like that!"

"Not necessarily. See that ambulance over there?" he indicated the red vehicle, whose siren blared and whose red light whirled like a dervish. "They're hauling out some of the people from the building. I've noticed that at least three of them were covered with sheets."

Hiram Beckwith proclaimed, "Dat's right! Odds are that Luke Cordray was one o' the stiffs they removed from that blaze!"

"Or he *will be*, soon enough, like the man I just fought in there," the Agent predicted of Smetana. "Now, Beckwith, cover me with your pistol, as though I'm your prisoner. We've got to make this real, for Inspector Burks' sake."

With deepest reluctance on his fat face, Hiram Beckwith pointed his weapon at the Secret Agent.

They'd gotten even with the Inspector now. Bates took the initiative by rolling down the window and adopting, for him, a more cheery demeanor than usual.

Inspector Burks wasted no time with them. He wanted to know, immediately, who they were and what they were doing at this scene.

Grinning, Bates threw up a huge hand, announced, "We're Feds. Just picked up this bird for questioning, Officer—" he pointed his body forward and squinted dark eyes at the badge on Burks' sweaty shirt.

"It's John Burks, fellow," the inspector informed him, coldly. He gritted, "And I'm an *Inspector for the New York Police Department*, for your information. Now, you've already said you're Federal men. And that you have someone in custody. Mind telling me who this character is?"

Harvey Bates offered a slight smile, inclined his head at the master detective. "Sure. He's Secret Agent X."

John Burks leaned his bulky form forward and peered inside the cab. Then he threw back his head and grinned like a donkey eating briars. "Well, I'll be damned! I've been wondering where you've been hiding, you crumb."

"Glad to see you, too, Inspector," X replied with a cheeriness that, under the circumstances, was hilarious. "Did you miss me in my absence?"

"That's really funny, Mr. X. I suspect you'll laugh like a fiend when the State of New York finally executes you. And they'll do it this

*** AUTHOR'S NOTE: Both the Secret Agent and his lieutenant carry Federal badges, exact duplicates of those carried by the G-men. Technically speaking the badge of Bates is a counterfeit. However, in point of fact, the Agent himself *is* a Federal operative, though one working at the deepest level of secrecy, and answering only to his Washington superior, K9.**

time, too. You're the one responsible for this mess, aren't you? You're the Resurrectionist?"

Before the shocked X could reply, Hiram Beckwith joined the conversation: "You don't know that fa shuah, Burks. All's we know is this: He's Agent X."

Burks favored X's heavyset associate with a sneering laugh. "I wouldn't be too sure, Agent, eh—" he scouted the territory of the man's ample chest, seeking a badge or some other indicator of his name. "What's your name, Mister?"

The fat cabbie did the identifying work for him. He rasped, "It's Beckwith. And I'm *not* a Fed. I'm a hack driver, and I *work* for a livin'. Right now I'm losin' money because this Fed, here," he pointed a thick sausage of a thumb at Bates, "commandeered my cab. So I have to mark time, takin' him and Mr. Sunshine, here, to see a man about a horse...."

"I see. Fine attitude for a civilian to take," Burks sermonized. "A shame too, since I may finally have the evidence to nail Mr. X, here, for good and all."

"Oh, really," the Agent himself finally remarked, unconcerned. "And what evidence is that?"

Burks favored him with a most contemptuous smile. "Oh, just this little thing. I just found it, a couple of minutes ago, on Pat Calvert's corpse."

He extracted a small rectangle of pasteboard from his shirt pocket.

Into the hand of Harvey Bates the Inspector thrust the thing, the obverse, or front of it, facing Harvey Bates.

"Can't read this," a puzzled Harvey Bates declared, with a shrug of his enormous shoulders. He transferred the object to his chief. "Here, Mr. X. Might take a stab at it."

It might have been Inspector Burks' smug manner that tipped the Secret Agent something was up. But more likely than not, some sixth sense must have warned the Man of a Thousand Faces to be wary. He took the object from Bates' huge hand, pulled it close to his eyes.

It was no wonder that Harvey Bates couldn't read the inscription, αναστάσις, on this card.

"Someone has written one term in Greek," the Secret Agent told them, his brilliant linguistic ability coming to the fore. Softly, he glossed, "The word in question, here, is *anastasis*. It means 'resurrection.'"

This was bad enough, for some reason known only to X himself.

But the rest of the card's head was, for the Agent, almost as damning. It showed information he hadn't been able to see on the one from Lothian's wallet. Calvert's slip of paper displayed this legend: " 'Experience the life from death.' " And below it, he read this modest declaration: " 'I am the Resurrectionist.' "

X practically willed his hand to immobility as he flipped the card to the reverse side. On it the printer had inscribed a flower, this time a clear, though stylized image of a lilac. The Agent allowed his eyes to move below this drawing to the phrase, *LILAC-06*.

Courageously, he maintained a poker face. Indeed, had he been the focus of a movie camera, he might have won an Oscar for the lack of emotion on his disguised features. But in truth, his heart beat out a jackhammer's tattoo. And his hands finally commenced to shake ever so slightly. Burks couldn't help but notice the involuntary tremor.

Black eyes snapping with excitement, the

police inspector asked the detective, "See something familiar, Mr. X?"

X remained silent.

A smirking Burks answered the question: "I'll tell you what you see. It's like those newer calling cards you started carrying, awhile back, Mr. X. Remember leaving them at the scenes of your many crimes? I suspect you remember the little tricks they do. The writing always disappears after a time, doesn't it? I'd guess you're using a form of invisible ink that oxidizes on contact with the atmosphere. I'm betting the inscription on this one can do the same disappearing act."

He paused dramatically before drawling, "Let's wait a bit, to see if it does."

He continued with that smug smile, slathered like poisoned honey on his hard-bitten face.

And as though on cue, all of the writing on both sides of the card disappeared, all, that is, except for the LILAC-06 designation. It was just as Inspector Burks had predicted. And just as the Agent himself had feared would happen—for too many years to count. The past, it seemed, was giving up secrets that even the Man of a Thousand Faces might not withstand....

CHAPTER XIV
LORD OF LIFE AND DEATH

HAD the Resurrectionist seen the electric horror then crackling through Agent X, then that white-robed miscreant would have have gloated. Everything, to his thinking, proceeded according to his plan. It was, after all, the blueprint he'd been drawing and refining for years.

Of course, a bitter irony marked the site of his despicable strategy. He was plotting his malevolent affairs in a church, of all places. However, its parishioners had long since abandoned the once dignified edifice of granite. In the period following, commercial properties had almost overwhelmed the district, which formerly had been a robust residential area. Eventually, the commercial properties also fell prey to the vicissitudes of changing times.

The businesses which replaced them didn't exactly show the highest degree of public-spiritedness, either. Two-bit pawn shops, shady gambling dens, and ramshackle liquor stores stood all up and down the streets. Loan sharks, dope dealers, and mob types swaggered through at will. Only a handful of houses, mostly rickety affairs, made a last stand there. And their owners were mostly poor folk who frankly couldn't afford to leave the neighborhood. Thus this quarter of the city came to be a locale of death barely warmed over, of too many people forgotten and as many lives destroyed.

This rotten district, this hell of poverty and despair, served the Resurrectionist perfectly, however, as a base to build his equally wretched kingdom.

A king looking over his white-suited subjects, he insolently sat upon a throne of sorts within the very sanctuary of the former holy place. He had placed his seat of power at the most sacred portion of that large Romanesque structure, its high altar.

There the self-styled lord of life and death intended to live up to his own reputation, if his raiment were any indication.

He might have stolen his clothing from a bishop, so profoundly did he resemble one of these holy men. In that vein, he had currently mantled himself in a long, flowing robe of some unknown material. The hood of his vestment he had bleached to a state of purest white, titanium, though the rest of his garment was that silvery-white color. Nor had he neglected his feet, also garbed in sandals of the same glorious silver-white hue.

His face was a singular affair, a flexible, rubber-like mask of heightened reality, perfection, even. The device called to mind the handsome, beatific features and piercing blue eyes of a saint from a medieval painting in one of the European cathedrals. Indeed the wearer himself might have passed for the courageous St. George, immediately after he had slain the fabled dragon. Or he could have been mistaken for any of the so-called "warrior" or "military" saints, fabled for their martial prowess and their devotion to the Church's mission.

But this was all mere sham, if not blasphemy.

For the Resurrectionist, with his desire for unchecked power and limitless wealth, posed the greatest threat the city of New York had seen in years. Worse, he presented one of the most dangerous menaces to America itself. He could cause terror and destruction on a grand scale, with his Wrath of God, that is, the burning death. And coupled with his power to raise the dead and his plan to build an invincible criminal army, he just might succeed in achieving his goals. Especially if he removed the despised Secret Agent X from the mix.

A large group of his toughs had joined him in the church's former sanctuary, the men parked in the old pews at the foot of the former altar.

There they gazed upon the white-robed Resurrectionist with expectancy and excitement, the crime chieftain's men believing that he could and would help them to gain riches beyond measure. But some did indeed hold to that more grandiose scheme: eventual mastery of this nation, initiated through a campaign of murder and mayhem. And their hope in him was far from an idle one, especially given the reported burning deaths of Luke Cordray and those innocent bank customers and employees, not to mention the torching of those same commercial institutions.

The bloodlust and greed of the criminals only increased at the memory of such events. With the announcement that the Resurrectionist would shortly make, their heightened passion would soon hurl them into the realm of the bestial. Rumor had it that their arrogant chief would add a new ally to their ranks. Furthermore, that same new personage would reveal a traitor, within their very midst....

The white robed figure began, "My follower Tiny has radioed me from the truck to report good news. He and his men have killed Pat Calvert, and thus made him the latest recruit to my cause! Soon they will arrive here, in order that we might all celebrate their success."

From the throats of almost every hoodlum, a loud wave of approval swept through the former sanctuary. Of course, a few skeptics did inhabit that place, as would do so in almost any gathering. And those same naysayers made themselves known by a series of loud jeers from the middle of the room. But the white-robed Resurrectionist knew how to silence that bunch and how to bring this small group of malcontents into his fold.

His blue eyes blinked with greater rapidity. Then he unfolded his long-limbed frame from his throne, in order that he might look down upon the assemblage; increase his literal and figurative stature among them like that of a Titan. Before he addressed them he pulled a long rod-like affair, silver-white like his raiment, from behind his throne. A medieval knight might have borne the object during the Crusades. So sharp and shiny was the steel head of the object. And so perfectly balanced and beautifully carved was its long, wooden shaft.

"I see," he observed, "that most of you approve of Tiny's success! Excellent! You will also support the addition of a new friend to our cause."

Most of them did, in fact. But for the second time, almost on cue, the loudest member of the naysayers had to voice his opposition, much to the delight of a few other, like-minded souls. Nevertheless, the loudmouth's words prompted calls for him to clam up. He was, they countered, squelching their chance at a profit. And as far as some of the remaining fellows were concerned, he was also courting his destruction.

With his right hand thrown upward, the Resurrectionist ordered silence for the entire assembly. Then he stated coldly, "Before I can introduce our ally, though, I realize that I must deal with the protests of a few unbelievers in your number. They must, regrettably, be punished for their infidelity."

Mr. Mouthpiece, the most vocal skeptic, was now glaring through his little shoe-button eyes at the white-robed crime lord. Apparently seeking trouble, the hook-nosed unbeliever, a homely sort with a protruding lower lip, shrilled to the Resurrectionist: "Yeah, you're a real tough guy!"

Angrily moving closer to the front of the sanctuary, Mr. Mouthpiece pulled a burning cigarette from his mouth and blew a long streamer of gray smoke into the air. Then he used the same coffin nail to punctuate his next words, his tone redolent of Boston: "It's all the bunk, fellas! Use yer brains—if ya have any! He's running a cawn game, claimin' he can raise the dead. Well, he can't do it, any more than jackass can drive a car! Plus, he's been payin' us—all of us—on the cheap. Hell, I've a mind to turn snitch. Might even make some moolah in the process. If not, I could move on to a *real* payin' jawb with another outfit. Let's see how he likes that...."

He tossed the cigarette onto the floor, crushed the thing under his heel.

A low chuckle of derision echoed from beneath the beatific mask of the Resurrectionist. His blue eyes acquired dagger sharpness, penned the men to the pews. His optics grew compelling, like the orbs of a Napoleon, or any of the present European demagogues who dream of territorial expansion and grand conquest.

He motioned for a man who sat near the head of the toughs, a figure of scrawny form, also dressed in one of the silver-white suits, to arise and come near the altar. At a whispered word from his chief, this fellow departed the sanctuary by a side door.

In the meanwhile, some fresh murmurs issued from the lips of the men. Arch Fingeroth, Hobart's snitch, couldn't help but notice their barely concealed impatience, their complaints that the Resurrectionist was stalling for time. Fingeroth heard more than one of them agree with that loudmouth: Maybe they *did* need to question their leader's fitness to run the show.

In less than a minute the scarecrow of a man re-entered the sanctuary, one of those target pistols clutched in his right hand.

Fingeroth knew that something was up, for the scarecrow to be toting that pistol that looked so much, to him, like a target model of some sort. Along with that weapon, he was packing another handgun, one of those curious affairs with the small canisters affixed to the barrel.

When the scarecrow returned to his master, the Resurrectionist took a pistol into either hand. Then he descended the stone steps and delivered his latest command in peremptory tones.

"Come up nearer the front, all of you," he said, swiveling his head from one side of the group to the other. Finally, he fixed his fanatic's eyes on the complainer, the disbeliever from the middle of the room. "You, especially, Sir! Come stand at my side."

He cut his blue eyes around the room. Oddly, they lingered for several seconds upon one specific pew, and three of the occupants thereon. Those blue orbs of his fell first on a pair of pinkish eyes, those of Jonesy, the twitching albino. This worthy molded his thin lips briefly into a vampire's grin on seeing this attention from his chief. Next the Resurrectionist locked eyes with hazel ones, whereupon their owner, the man named Klinker, nodded at the Resurrectionist. Then the white-robed miscreant trained his peepers on a listener with bitter blue optics. They were the eyes of Arch Fingeroth, who watched the Resurrectionist with the same level of intensity.

He had not participated in the Resurrectionist's raid against Pat Calvert or a subsequent mass meeting of the Resurrectionist and his satellites. Fingeroth had pled the need to lay low for a while. His parole officer, so he'd claimed to his criminal chief, had been getting too close to Fingeroth's involvement with the Resurrectionist. That villain didn't know that Fingeroth was having nothing to do with his court-appointed officer. Moreover, the crime lord was unaware that Fingeroth had been slipping information to Hobart and his detectives who had, just now, successfully reached A.J. Martin via that UHF device, only to lose him again.

Cutting his eyes from one side of the sanctuary to the other, Fingeroth worried that the Resurrectionist might select him. In fact, the white-garbed villain cleared his throat as a preliminary to doing the very thing Hobart's man most feared. Yet strangely the Resurrectionist passed over him. Still, Arch didn't fail to notice that barest of nods the crime lord made towards him, Fingeroth. That act left him deeply unnerved and that much more hyper-vigilant. As a consequence he barely acknowledged the words of the stony-faced, swarthy Klinker to him. Nor did he pay but the most perfunctory heed to Jonesy's idiotic—and over-friendly—attempt at conversation.

Meanwhile, the Resurrectionist sent his blue eyes back to the disbeliever who had previously challenged him.

"You, there!" the white-mantled villain dramatically pointed at the Mr. Mouthpiece. "I have already ordered you to arise!"

Muttering all the while, Mr. Mouthpiece drew his upper lip into a sneer and rose. But he moved not an inch from his pew. Defiantly, he remained immobile until a couple of men shoved him into the aisle, where he decided, again, to imitate a stone.

Somebody pushed Mouthpiece a little further, but with not enough force to propel him more than a foot or two. After the Mouthpiece had gotten even with Fingeroth, Jim's man experienced the strange sensation that he knew the loudmouth. In addition, black-bearded Arch Fingeroth sensed the eyes of Mr. Mouthpiece boring into his own.

Meanwhile, chuckling eerily, the Resurrectionist then did something completely unexpected. He chose someone who'd voiced no opposition. This next subject seemed a timid soul, when a viewer considered his popping light brown eyes set amidst a pair of fleshy red cheeks and a Roman pug of a nose. He had been punishing a stick of chewing gum between his large, square teeth. But now that spearminty piece of chicle performed a Judge Crater, forever vanishing from the sight of men.

"Mu—me?" the now-quaking man gulped, biting his lower lip like there was no tomorrow.

The Resurrectionist bobbed his head. "Yes, you."

"I—I didn't say anything against you, Resurrectionist. I believe you can do exactly what you say you can! Honest!"

"Yes, I perceive that you are telling the truth," the villain agreed, his words dripping with contempt. "It is why you are so valuable to me. Now, stand beside me. Come and see my power of life from death! See and believe!"

Harder shoves compelling them, the fleshy gum chewer and the Mouthpiece eased towards their leader.

As they inched forward, their eyes locked on the fellow in white. While this drama unfolded, Arch Fingeroth rubbed his hand across more than two weeks' worth of his blue-black beard.

Surely this bird won't do what I think he's going to do, Fingeroth mused. *He can't do something like that. He* can't….

He thrust a hand into his pants pocket, ostensibly to retrieve a package of cigarettes. Actually he was transmitting one of his frequent radio messages to Sloan or one of his brother operatives at the Hobart Detective Agency.

An aggressive voice suddenly invaded his thoughts.

"Guess he's ready to make somebody pay the piper, now, eh? Just let *me* at that guy—I'd show the Resurrectionist how to keep 'im in line. Wouldn't put up with his kind! I *know* how to get a job done—and how to get somebody to shut his yap…."

Fingeroth turned his head slightly to the left, that is, towards his swarthy acquaintance Klinker. His combination of dark skin and impassive features lent Klinker the appearance of a cigar store Indian. His looks accounted, in part, for his nickname Chief Big Noise. But the Ring had named him thus for an even better reason: It was his loud mouth, which trumped his physiognomy. Fingeroth had already witnessed some of this behavior. The man did love to boast about his own accomplishments. Moreover he was forever dwelling on his own high hopes for criminal success, that is, for running an illegal operation of his own.

But right now Klinker, Chief Big Noise, revealed rare vulnerability. Indeed, his voice betrayed an anxiety that was palpable: "I'm not a loser, you unnerstand. Even pulled my share o' big jobs with a bunch o' different mugs. But things is tight, these days—have been for a lotta days, in fact."

He paused dramatically, revealing more of himself than he'd probably intended to disclose. "It's like I've told you before, back at Lothian's joint: I've been waitin' a long stretch for this kinda thing. If it's good, then mebbe the Resurrectionist can deliver on the other promises, too: security for me and mine. That's the reason I stay with this thing. I'm needin' that money, *somethin' terrible....*"

Jonesy, the albino, put a twitching hand on Fingeroth's shoulder. "I'm needin' the moolah, too, fella. Gots me a 'sugar' habit ta support—" he fixed the black-bearded man with those eerie, pinkish eyes, "and that dough the Resurrectionist supplies is the only way I can support it."

He is probably supplying that sugar, too, Fingeroth thought to himself. Inwardly Fingeroth was shaking his head at this human tragedy. However, he didn't offer such an editorial to the albino or to Klinker.

The bearded fellow merely gave a slight nod of acknowledgement. He whispered, "Guess it's like they say: Money makes the world go around."

"Yeah. You bet it does!" Klinker warmed to Fingeroth. "Bet you're glad you found your way into *his* world, too. It's the best chance you're ever gonna get, you know. Especially the kinda work you've done lately as a hired gorilla."

"Well, I suppose bein' hired muscle isn't much," the man with the blue-black beard admitted, "but it pays the bills."

The swarthy Klinker peered closely at him. "Kinda hard to pay bills, ain't it? I mean, movin' from job to job, and all, like you've said you've done."

Preoccupied with his own thoughts once more, the man with the blue-black beard simply grunted.

Chief Big Noise shot his eyes towards the altar. At that point he briefly caught the attention of the Resurrectionist, who gave the man another barely perceptible bob of the head.

The swarthy man elbowed Fingeroth's left ribcage. Then he posed this question: "Didn't you say your boss was Goren, before you skipped out on him?"

"Hey," the albino Jonesy joined in, "that's right. I thought you said Goren, too!"

Fingeroth mumbled something, but the dark-featured Chief Big Noise couldn't understand the answer. In response, the man with the blue-black jaw shrubbery restated, now testily, "No. How many times do I have to tell you two it wasn't Goren? It was Lowry."

"That a fact?" he peered sharply at Fingeroth. "I thought you told me it was Goren. My mistake. Just my goof."

Albino Jonesy glared at Jim, the colorless man's thin, vampirish lips curled into the cruelest of smiles. He became more twitchy and more bloodthirsty, as he stated, "*I* don't think it's a goof-up. Ast me, I think *he's* the one who made the mistake. And I'll wager *I* can squeeze the truth outta him," he rubbed his hands with relish.

Fingeroth turned his head right. There was no need to start something, he advised the belligerent Jonesy. They were friends—weren't they, he asked? It was a case of no harm, no foul. Plain and simple.

However, it *was* Arch Fingeroth's mistake, and the now-sweating snitch knew it. From then on he would be counting the seconds, wondering when the Resurrectionist would let the other shoe drop on his unprotected head. He decided, thus, on a last-ditch plan that might buy him some time to make an escape and get word to an operator at the Hobart Detective Agency.

In that vein he slipped a hand back into that pants pocket, whereupon it came out again holding his pocket watch, one smaller than the usual model. After he'd done something with the mechanism, he slipped the timepiece back inside his pants. He wasn't done yet, however, as his fingers manipulated the watch into a small container.

The Resurrectionist swaggered into the midst of his followers. He beckoned for the former gum chewer—someone hollered "Attaboy, Barney!"—to stand in front of him. Separated from his spearmint chicle now, he fingered the collar of his shirt and awaited the worst.

The Resurrectionist addressed Barney, "How loyal are you to my cause, Mr. Wyrick?"

Gulping, Barney Wyrick whispered, "Loyal like—like a hound dog, Resurrectionist. I'd do anything for you!"

"I'm pleased to hear that, Mr. Wyrick. Are you prepared to die for me?" the villain interrogated.

"Gawd! Don't make me do that, Sir! Anything but that!"

Sibilant laughter issued from beneath the Resurrectionist's beatific mask. "I think that *you*, Mr. Wyrick, should prove your loyalty to me. *You* should serve as the object lesson for everyone else."

He raised the target pistol, aimed the thing directly at the man's fleshy neck. Without another word, he squeezed the weapon's trigger. The projectile struck Wyrick's neck, and he uttered a gasp. Eyes enormous, he swayed once or twice and collapsed, dead, to the floor!

Despite himself, Fingeroth began to shake uncontrollably. A storm of unnatural fury broke in his blue eyes when he heard the Resurrectionist's cold utterance: "Carry him away. And see that his wife is duly compensated."

That finger of the Resurrectionist now beckoned Mr. Mouthpiece to come closer. This time the toughs pushed him irresistibly towards his white-cloaked master.

"My killing of Barney Wyrick was meant to weaken your resolve," the Resurrectionist addressed Mr. Mouthpiece. "He will return to this world, another partaker of the life from death. But you...*you* have doubted my power of life from death!" he exclaimed to Mouthpiece. "Thus I must make an example of you. I must subject you to the Wrath of God! You must be taken to the World of Inferno, to pay!

"But before I have sent you there, you will do as I direct. Since not everyone here knows your identity, you must share it with us," the Resurrectionist ordered. At the same time he allowed one eye, strangely, to shutter, then unshutter. Mouthpiece clearly saw this act, of course. However, people directly behind him, observers like Fingeroth, Jonesy, and Klinker did not.

But they *could* detect the strange calm with which Mouthpiece uttered, "The name's O'Marrah. Sean O'Marrah. I came down heah, from Boston, thinking ya was the comin' thing. Ya've at least proved ya can kill a man. Beyond that, I'm still wonderin' if I ya can do the other things ya've told me ya can do...."

"Such as raise the dead, Mr. O'Marrah? Or take over this country, after I've destroyed Secret Agent X and his organization?"

While the two men, the Resurrectionist and O'Marrah, tested each other's mettle,

Arch Fingeroth was frozen in place, fascinated by their exchange. Suddenly he remembered why this newcomer O'Marrah had seemed familiar to him—and why he, Fingeroth, couldn't afford to allow the two criminals to go much further in their exchange.

The Resurrectionist continued his interrogation of the New Englander: "Tell me something, O'Marrah: What would you say if I told you I could make you rich beyond your wildest dreams?"

"I might give it a listen," O'Marrah sneered—it seemed his default expression—but he had a question of his own for the white-clad being: "Theah's gotta be a catch to ya plan, though, right? I mean, ya're not gonna dole out free cash. So whadda I gotta do? Die like that sucker on the floor, theah?" he pointed down to the floor.

Condescending laughter rang from behind the Resurrectionist's mask. "Why, I thought you understood that was the case, O'Marrah. That was, after all, part of the deal we've already discussed.

"Now—if you want to bow out of the deal, that is perfectly all right. But you will then experience… the death from life, the Wrath of God! It is your choice, as it has always been."

O'Marrah peered around the assembly of men to either side of him. Finally he turned around to face those to his rear. During that instant his eyes alit on the form of Arch Fingeroth. The criminal from Boston gazed long and hard at Fingeroth before he, O'Marrah finally spoke again.

"That was my choice, like ya tol' me. But ya also said theah was anotha way," he reminded. "I could cough up somethin' on one of the guys heah. And ya'd still pay me off."

Nodding, the Resurrectionist stated, "I stand corrected, O'Marrah. Tell the people of our agreement."

"I'm squealin'. My life for his. And the rest of the agreement—all that money ya promised me—stays right in place."

When the Resurrectionist assented, Sean O'Marrah turned his back on the Resurrectionist and walked towards Arch Fingeroth.

Molding his sneer into a grin, O'Marrah stuck out a hand. "Hiya, Arch! Remember me?"

Of course, Arch Fingeroth remembered the man. Hobart's contact said that they'd worked together in that counterfeiting operation back in Boston, in '34.

"See that ya're workin' for a bettah class of operators, these days," O'Marrah commented, a smug smile crawling over his normally sour visage.

Fingeroth admitted, shakily, "Yeah, guess so. Makin' ends meet is pretty hard."

" 'Specially with ya medical bills," came the other man's response. "That cancer can be a tough nut ta crack, can't it?"

"Cancer? I, uh, I've beaten cancer."

O'Marrah laughed harshly. "Really? Ya battled it back in the old days in Boston. But I happen ta know it came back. That's why the law let ya outta prison. It was a mercy release."

The black-bearded listener felt his guts trembling, as though with palsy. He hadn't known of this detail—hadn't known that—

"—Arch Fingeroth is dead," O'Marrah completed for him. "So just who in the hell are you?"

"Why, who, indeed, Mr. O'Marrah?" the Resurrectionist interrupted. His voice acquired a note of triumph: "He is none other than the friend and associate of a nosy newspaperman, A.J. Martin. And allow me to add—he is an acquaintance of our foe, the illustrious Secret Agent X. In other words, gentlemen, meet Jim Hobart!"

CHAPTER XV
THE SINISTER CINEMA AND ITS CRITICS

"JIM HOBART, eh?" the criminal from Boston stated, more than asked. "Dammit, that makes sense now! Ya recognized me, all right! Hell, ya helped arrest me and send me ta jail, ya bum!"

Of a sudden he set his body to lunge against the black-bearded man, who immediately assumed a defensive stance. But the Resurrectionist's men grabbed the two and prevented the altercation.

Blue eyes snapping with anger, Black Beard insisted, "I'm not Hobart! I'm Arch Fingeroth!"

The Resurrectionist came into the midst of his followers, such that they formed a protective cordon around him. "Yes, you *are* Jim Hobart, all right. I have photos that prove it."

From a slit in his white cloak, the Resurrectionist produced one of those folders of he'd received, earlier, via the facsimile machine. He held them up for the entire body of his thugs to see.

As the pictures shifted from person to person, the series of events set the mind of Jim Hobart to racing. *This is nothing to fear,* the false mob gorilla thought to himself. *It's all a bluff. Just a big bluff and a trick, to get me to expose myself. I've got to keep my head. Got to! Got to!*

It was really a game he was playing with himself, a form of mind over matter. Unbidden, a massive wave of foreboding swept over Hobart, who'd embodied Arch Fingeroth as best he could.

But he willed himself to stay calm. And he groped, silently, for a way to explain to himself what had taken place. He hadn't known what had happened to Arch Fingeroth after he'd left prison. Certainly, he hadn't known the criminal had died from cancer. He had thought only about doing something, anything, to help his boss, Mr. A.J. Martin, since he was out of pocket. To Hobart that had meant operating alone, not subjecting his men in the Hobart Agency to such peril as this job would entail. It had involved his assuming a disguise as a notorious mob tough, then starting the investigation into the Resurrectionist's activities. Unfortunately Jim now realized, too late, that he should have waited for A.J. Martin to return from his lengthy sojourn before embarking, solo, on such a dangerous mission as this. He realized, more pointedly, that it was a matter of time before he *had* no time left, before the Resurrectionist claimed him as another casualty in this war.

Jim snapped back to reality as the pictures and the attendant insults towards him continued to make the rounds among the hoodlums. At the head of the group, the Resurrectionist explained the two factors which had tipped him off to Hobart's real identity: the way that Hobart stood in the pictures, for one; and the shape of the young private detective's body, for the other.

"Most people, unless they are experts, do not naturally bother to disguise such traits as these, in the real world. They think that such characteristics simply do not matter. But the expert master of disguise knows that little details do, inevitably, tell the truth. Mr. Jim Hobart, here, has failed to understand this truism of the art of disguise. And because of his failure, I now have him *right where I want him*. You, too," he addressed his hoods, "will realize what I mean when you study these pictures with the appropriate care and insight."

At this cue the men, as though famished, began to devour every morsel of detail in the photos of Jim. And each one of the shots depicted the young private dick with his natural crest of stiff hair, possibly light colored. They couldn't determine that his locks were actually red, of course, since the pictures portrayed him in black and white. Nonetheless, the people looking at the glossies could determine one specific fact, after the Resurrectionist had brought it to their attention. Namely, they all captured a unique mannerism of Jim.

He screwed his face into a tight mask of puzzlement, whenever confronted with information he did not understand.

"As I speak," the white-mantled crime czar pointed to Jim, "he is now doing that very thing!"

Involuntarily, Jim was indeed doing exactly what the Resurrectionist had spotted and what his men currently noticed him doing in the photographs!

But his situation became only worse in the next couple of minutes.

The man in white alluded to the second man in the photos with Jim, a fellow possessed of dignified carriage, handsome features, and iron gray hair. He asked whether a single one of them could identify that other subject. When none of them could successfully do so, the Resurrectionist said, "And that, my Resurgos, is why it has been so difficult to capture our enemy, Secret Agent X."

All of them drew in a collective gasp at that revelation. "But this guy is Elisha Pond!"

"He is, or *masquerades*, as Elisha Pond," the Resurrectionist insisted, "a personage of some wealth, power, and prestige in our fair city."

"You had us attacking that damn First National Bank, in hopes of smoking X out, huh, Sir?" shouted Chief Big Noise.

That question inspired a bob of the Resurrectionist's head. "At the time I launched my first thrusts against him, I did not know for certain that Pond and X were one and the same. I did though suspect it for reasons of my own. However this set of pictures provides me only further proof that they are. So, too, does an additional piece of evidence. You see, in my possession I have a rare piece of film footage which shows, conclusively, that connection between Elisha Pond and Agent X. In addition it establishes that X poses frequently as a certain AP reporter named A.J. Martin."

Secret Agent X, masquerading as his boss A.J. Martin! And facing mortal danger! The twin prospects sent shockwaves through the mind of Hobart. Yet everything of the past several years made *perfect* sense now. To prove this to himself, he mentally ticked off the more prominent characteristics of the two.

There was certainly the courage of Mr. Martin. But there were also his public-spiritedness, his boldness; his resourcefulness and most of all his loyalty and warmth. Agent X owned the same qualities too because Jim had witnessed them, once many years back.* He

*** AUTHOR'S NOTE: Jim deduced that a certain character Chelsia Bunn was actually the master man-hunter, as related in DIVIDENDS OF DOOM.**

recalled that he had never accepted the law's dark portrait of the man. And he still rejected it. By hook or crook, Hobart must somehow get word of the Resurrectionist's ruinous intent to the Man of a Thousand Faces....

He begged the Resurrectionist to allow him a cigarette, in order to calm his frazzled nerves. Though the man in white approved his request—a harmless one, in this circumstance—he ordered some of his men to train their guns, some of the Bolo Mausers, on the Agent's associate. That way, they could forestall any funny business he might attempt.

Jim allowed his right hand to drift towards that pants pocket. Here he had secreted the pocket transceiver, A.J. Martin's gift. At the same time the crime czar's men eyed him warily as his hand innocently fished around the waters of the cloth-bounded pool. As usual his fingers rattled the loose change in his pocket. And when they emerged again, they held a single object: a small cellophane package containing his cigarettes.

He feigned not having any matches or a cigarette lighter, a fact which was, of course, totally untrue. Nonetheless, for the moment they fell for his story. After a neighboring hood produced a lighter, Jim fired his coffin nail and placed the end of the paper tube in his mouth.

"You want the upper hand, do you, Resurrectionist?" Jim began. After drawing some of the acrid smoke deep into his lungs, he gave them a cool smile. "I could feed you some *real* information about Secret Agent X, if you were willing to cooperate with *me*, that is."

In this chronicle the young redheaded detective helped the disguised Secret Agent rescue Betty Dale from the machinations of the evil Achmet Karahmud and his ally Felice Vincart, the notorious Leopard Lady.

The Resurrectionist drew closer to him, such that only a tissue might have separated the two of them. "What information have you, Hobart? And what guarantee do I have that you are even telling me the truth?"

"That's a laugh! Think about this from my perspective for a minute. What would give me the idea that I can trust *you*?"

He took slow, cool drag from the cigarette—then blew smoke in the Resurrectionist's face. Next he stated, "Besides, what makes you think I have any love lost for that guy? He's cramping my style. I was this close," he placed right index finger and thumb less than a quarter of an inch apart, "this close, mind you, to nabbing that clown. And he escaped me, too, robbed me, a private dick, of the chance to bring him in. So the way I figure things, it doesn't matter who brings him in—as long as I can collect *my* due—some of the reward that John Burks and Charlie Foster have offered for his arrest.

"You want to finish X off? Fine. Just point me in the right direction, and let me do my job."

"And how do you propose to do that? More importantly, what is this information that you have on him?"

With his left hand, Jim put the cigarette back between his lips and sucked more of the tobacco smoke into his lungs. With his right hand he was fiddling with that something-or-other in his pocket. He knew beyond doubt that his moment of truth had arrived. So he made this proposition: "My proposal is this: I give you the Agent's real name and help you find him. You let me and any other prisoners here go free. No questions asked."

"I see. And suppose I do not agree to your proposal?" was the Resurrectionist's query.

Blue eyes calculating, Jim Hobart laughed coldly. "Oh, then I suppose," he suggested, hand wandering to his pants pocket, "I'll have to explode this bomb. It's already armed, by the way. And believe me, for its size, it will do *far more damage* than you have ever seen...."

From behind his beatific mask, the Resurrectionist cut loose with a laugh of his own, one beyond cruel. "A bomb, Mr. Hobart? You're bluffing."

Into his pocket Jim rammed his right hand, that member returning to view with a small oblong box of black Bakelite. He shook the thing once or twice in their faces, merely to frighten them. But one fact scared them more than meeting Count Dracula in a graveyard at midnight. And the man nearest him, Jonesy, realized just what made the small box so fearsome.

It was *ticking to beat the band.*

"Oh, hell, oh, hell, oh, hell!" the albino screeched. At the same time his muscular body began to twitch with more fury—much more fury. "It *is* a bomb—just like this gorilla said it was!"

Pop-eyed hoodlums began to back away from a grinning Jim as he held the box aloft. "That's right, it's a bomb, fellow," he addressed Jonesy, blowing more cigarette smoke upward.

Jim Hobart hated to say these next words, as though he were taking advantage of the dope fiend's problem. However, he had to play rough since that was the only way this bunch would or could understand the game. He delivered these next words slowly, deliberately as a physician giving a diagnosis of terminal cancer: "I'm itching to test this bomb's destructive power. And you'll be the first one to get it in the neck, Jonesy. 'Course, you won't escape it either, Resurrectionist.

"There's not a man among you who would want me to drop this little number, now, would you? Think about that for a minute. Your lives, your plans—everything. *Kapow!* You can't let that happen, can you?"

Unexpectedly he snatched the muscular wrist of the albino, who, for all his supposed toughness, squealed like a little boy being carted to the woodshed. Then Jim eased himself and the frightened, twitching hood away from the terrified group. Hobart planned to reach a side door of the sanctuary and possible safety.

A wary Jim and his prisoner had almost gained that door when the situation went straight to hell.

Out of the blue a stream of pained grunts poured from Jonesy's thin, vampirish lips. And a veritable cyclone of the shakes blew throughout his entire pale frame. Clearly something dire held Jonesy in its grip, as the next seconds revealed. His body began to shake uncontrollably. He rocketed a hand towards his pale throat. His lips opened and emitted a gurgling scream. Brownish fluid bubbled forth from his mouth.

Horrified, Jim Hobart stopped dead in his tracks. Then it happened.

Jonesy's colorless body became a rod of organic steel, stiffening in Jim's grasp. The albino's flesh turned parchment brown. He fell into one final spell of violent convulsions. With a last bloodcurdling scream, he died. His corpse became a desiccated sack of skin, a mummy of sorts, stretched over a bone frame. And it clattered like wind chimes as those hideous remains, a travesty of a human form, fell across the shocked Jim Hobart and onto the sanctuary's ancient floor!

Seconds passed in silence. Everyone was frozen, as though in amber.

Eventually the Resurrectionist marched arrogantly towards the Secret Agent's associate. The white-robed fiend seemed not to fear Hobart's declaration of previous moments.

It was no wonder he didn't.

Jim had involuntarily dropped the Bakelite box, yet it had not detonated its charge.

The Resurrectionist snatched the thing from the floor and shook it. When nothing happened, he put the object close to his blue eyes. They fell upon a tiny door with a clasp arrangement. He unfastened the thing and opened the box. Into it he plunged a finger. And out it came—with Jim Hobart's pocket watch.

"A fine piece of craftsmanship, this *watch*," the white-cloaked miscreant commented, turning the gold timepiece over and over in his hand. "But it's really quite harmless, no? It simply has a stopwatch feature underneath the crystal. And it was this which you armed, to counterfeit the ticking of a bomb's timer. That *is* what you did, wasn't it, Hobart?"

Jim merely glared at the robed criminal. When Jim's silence persisted, the Resurrectionist ordered Klinker to come forward. Briefly he praised Klinker for keeping a faithful eye on Jim Hobart, at which point the man in white ordered the unthinkable.

"Now, do your job—give him the life from death!"

Abruptly, the tough took careful aim, and he shot Jim in the neck. He stiffened and fell over, dead.

At the Resurrectionist's command, Klinker and two others strode to his body, to remove him from the sanctuary and inside a special room far beneath it. After they lifted his form, they briefly lost their grip on him, such that Jim flopped to one side. The resulting shift of position caused a number of articles, pocket change, a knife, some keys, his wallet, and one other item, to tumble from his pocket onto the sanctuary's floor.

The Resurrectionist ran to the side of the men, to see what exactly Jim Hobart had lost. And there it was: that UHF device, his one lifeline to the Hobart Detective Agency.

Scooping the gadget from the floor, the Resurrectionist gave it close attention. Obviously he admired the thing's workmanship. And though he couldn't decipher its intricacies, he understood its significance, its connection with Secret Agent X. Better than that, to the Resurrectionist's view, the fall had not destroyed the compact radio. Nor had its tumble altered the frequency along which he was sending his messages.

That UHF radio in hand, the Resurrectionist depressed the "on" switch, thereby activating the microphone. Instantly a male voice came on the line. It was Sloan, Jim Hobart's man imported from Boston.

"*That you, Fingeroth*?" he eagerly spoke into his mike.

A cruel laugh permeated the ether. "This is *not* Arch Fingeroth, or Jim Hobart, for that matter. This is the Resurrectionist. I have just ordered Jim Hobart shot—dead. It is the life from death! Tell your Mr. Martin—or whatever Secret Agent X calls himself these days—that I am coming soon to exact my vengeance. And when I have found him, I will burn him with the Wrath of God!"

The Resurrectionist held onto the radio gadget belonging to Jim. Meanwhile his men moved X's associate to that special room beneath the sanctuary. Eventually the remainder of the Secret Agent's friends would fall into the crime lord's waiting hands.

As far as the dead Jonesy was concerned, on the other hand, the Resurrectionist ordered the departing Klinker, "Put him out with the rest of the trash."

"God, he was a *still* a man, Resurrectionist. And he was my pal.... You can't just throw him—"

"He knew what this thing involved when he joined my cause. You do as I say, too; or suffer the Wrath of God. The rest of you," the Resurrectionist gritted, "join me in the refectory. We need to see that film, immediately. And one of you—bring Lothian and those two hypocrites Terran and Helmer into the refectory too. They should find our little cinematic presentation most instructive."

The Resurrectionist in the lead, the remaining men marched down the hall and into the church's former refectory....

As men filed down the passageway, Tiny entered the sanctuary. The Resurrectionist's men had emptied the place, only moments before. However, the big man could still hear the sounds of laughter and raucous conversation originating from a hallway to the side of the sanctuary. As a consequence he trotted down an aisle and passed through the door to the right of the old pulpit, that is, to the left side of the sanctuary. He immediately encountered people who asked him about the particulars of the raid.

Tiny drew a sketch of the events he and his men had initiated. But curiously he didn't mention anything about the disappearance and possible death of Timmie Smetana. The loss of Petey Tetwilder didn't escape his lips, either; nor did the death of Luke Cordray, whose death the Resurrectionist had ordered. These omissions might have seemed callous, all in the day's work for one of the Resurrectionist's assistants. However, because of his actions, Tiny was feeling qualms, some of which he had tried, for years, to suppress.

Nevertheless, when he finally squeezed into the vast refectory itself, he endured their hero's welcome of him, a reception which lasted for several minutes. The Resurrectionist himself briefly joined in on the accolades, making the perfunctory remark that it was a "shame that Petey had to die once more." Eventually the white-hooded villain drew all of this to a halt, however, by his next command: "Please take a seat, so that I might make some preliminary remarks about this film."

As they obeyed his orders, the Resurrectionist called Tiny aside and made some comment to him. The big criminal nodded his understanding, whereupon he stepped away from the Resurrectionist and kept to himself, near the back of the refectory.

His companions were finding seats in that great open space as another of criminal band straggled into the room. This worthy, the man dispatched by the Resurrectionist in previous moments, escorted Helmer, Lothian, and Terran into that less-than-august body.

Tiny watched that quartet take seats, with Stu Lothian offering greetings as raucous as those thrown his way. In contrast, the big man watched the two "respectable" businessmen, Terran and Helmer, offer tight smiles and forced nods but in general maintain a stony silence. Tiny figured that they were behaving in this manner from a sense of abject fear. For them, keeping mostly quiet was their only way to stay safe—and thus alive. Chuckling, Tiny couldn't offer much of an objection to their position. Terran and Helmer were, after all, in the very midst of the Resurrection Ring and its terrifying leader. *Hell,* Tiny conjured up a ghost of a smile, *we all are....*

Something most disconcerting forced Tiny to turn his attention back to himself. An unaccountable twitching afflicted his right cheek. Because he had already shucked his silver-white hood, he put his cheek through a brief though brisk massage. That motion quieted the fleshy area for a time. But he had no more than dropped his right hand when that appendage also displayed the same curious palsy. At first he thought nothing of the tremor, chalking it up to the stressful events at Pat Calvert's brownstone.

Maybe if he flexed the hand, he reasoned, that would stop its involuntary movement. So he did so, and indeed the exercise helped somewhat. The curious tremble didn't depart for long, however. When he brought the hand before his eyes, he noticed it was shaking like a cold, wet dog. Surprised, he shook his head with vigor. In seconds his eyes, pools of blackness, grew large when he realized the possible cause of the odd quiver.

Still Tiny tried to ignore the episode. He decided that socializing with his fellows would be good for him. So he walked casually between the rows of chairs seating his confederates. He chatted with them for a bit while the Resurrectionist walked proudly to the head of the assembly. Eventually Tiny returned to his original seat near the refectory's entrance. As he did so, the tremors besieged him afresh.

Not that the Resurrectionist cared a fig about his henchman's plight, of course.

In short order, the fiend in white took up housekeeping behind an ornately carved podium of mahogany. He ran his hands lustfully over its polished surface, stroked its four corners, each guarded by cherubim. Power was glorious, especially its capacity to give the holder control over the lives of lesser men, he whispered to himself.

Before everyone had fallen silent, he peered over his shoulder at an enormous movie screen, the silvery particles of its surface glittering like tiny diamonds. He cast his gaze to the refectory's rear. In back of the men, someone had parked a pricey Bell & Howell movie projector, a model renowned for its excellent video and audio quality.

Like a famous European paper hanger and arch manipulator, he raised his hands in a melodramatic gesture, shook them vigorously. The signal produced the immediate effect of silence in his men, and he began his harangue.

"What is the goal of ages?" he thundered to them, leaning over the podium. "For the common man it is the capacity to cheat death, to live forever. But the goal of the uncommon man, gentlemen, the 'overman,' is entirely different; for the Creator has appointed him to rule his fellows. This man and *he alone* can see the future and seize it because God has ordained it thus!

"I have in my hands the means to cheat death—and to gain power invincible. For with the life from death we can break death's bonds. And with the burning death, the Wrath of God, we can vanquish all our opponents. With these two abilities in hand, we can and will gain absolute power—even as the Almighty Himself wills it!" He paused dramatically. When he resumed, he addressed them in a mere whisper: "Still, one—and only one—obstacle will seek to block our way. And he is the Man of a Thousand Faces, Secret Agent X.

"Beside the refectory's door, you will notice the movie projector," he directed their attention to the place in question. "The film you will momentarily screen is a rare piece of cinematic art. Though a mere fifteen minutes, it is, purportedly, the only known film of Secret Agent X's real face! The notorious spy and master of disguise, Proteus, had shot this damning piece of celluloid, some two years ago." *

One of the men spoke up. He was a sleepy-eyed, lanky gent with loose, ill-fitting work clothes, denim shirt and pants, and straggly brownish hair. A newspaper cartoonist would have enjoyed a field day with this character, depicting him as a suffering member of the *demos.*

Sucking his teeth, he stated, "A friend of mine knows a blabbermouth from that newspaper, the *Herald.* And he heard that the Agent got hold of that movie and torched it. So what the hell are you doin' wit' a copy of it?" **

"Let us say, Vanderwaal," the Resurrectionist hissed, slick as a Fuller Brush man, "that I have my connections, men more than willing to sell him out if it means his utter destruction. All *you* need to know is this: Agent X neglected to destroy the copy you will now see. And now, let us watch—and learn."

He pointed his right index finger at Tiny, who arose and switched off the lights. Now he shifted over to the motion picture projector. En-route he struggled with more of the spasms; however, not a soul noticed. They all were frankly too enthralled with the Resurrectionist himself and the richness of his words. They did not question his reason for a mask and the poverty of his ideas.

With his left hand, Tiny attempted to hook the sprocket holes of the celluloid, the actual film, to the teeth of the drive sprockets. When he'd made the proper attachments, he could then start the projector, which in turn would pull the film into the mechanism.

His shaking hands accomplished the task, but with the greatest of difficulty. Truth to tell, he almost tore the fragile celluloid in the process. The projector's "on-off" toggle was thankfully a heartier device. But Tiny's left hand wouldn't stop its trembling long enough to activate the mechanism. He did it, therefore, with the other hand. He remained grateful the others still did not notice his struggle. To ensure they wouldn't see future episodes, he slid both hands back into their pockets and plopped his form beside the Bell & Howell.

The film *click—click—click—clicked* to a start. Tiny, in the meantime, skipped out the back, his twitching becoming unbearable. On his way out, he told another man to take over the film's projection.

Racing feet propelled Tiny to his vehicle, parked to the side of the building. Faster than you could say "jack rabbit," he'd cranked it and left the scene....

Back inside the refectory, after the leader, or the opening frames, had completed their march beneath the projector's light and lens, a grainy series of images flickered onto the screen. They depicted the Agent, a beaten captive, being interrogated by the faceless spy, Proteus. Early in the exchange the Red spy mentioned a dossier he had compiled on the

*** AUTHOR'S NOTE: A would-be ruler of Red Russia, Proteus captured and filmed a drugged Agent X in Washington, D.C. during THE FREEZING FIENDS.**

**** AUTHOR'S NOTE: In fact, the Secret Agent thought he had burned the original of this film. He may have burned the negative, not knowing that this print, a copy, had been left behind.**

Agent, but Proteus did not divulge its exact contents. To make matters worse, the sound quality of the film had degraded, at times severely. As a consequence the audience could barely decipher scattered words like " 'traitor,' " " 'treachery,' " and the occasional sentence, " 'Russia can be a most rewarding mistress.' " Clearly the Red spy intended to blackmail the Agent by framing him for treason, then exposing him to the government and the press. As a part of his grand plan, the villain pried two aliases, Elisha Pond and A.J. Martin, from the Secret Agent. In part this confirmed the depictions from those photographs they'd all seen, only moments before. It added corroboration to the hypothesis of the Martin-Agent X connection, too. But the celluloid roll unspooled what seemed more damning information. It seemed Proteus had wormed the Secret Agent's real name from the lips of the captive.

A strong wind of excitement blew through the assembly. That is, it did so until the man in white commented with utter calm, "I must point out that this is *not*, I repeat *not*, Agent X's true name—nor is this the Secret Agent's true face. That falsity of both emerged later, with details I won't rehearse here.* Suffice it to say, that Proteus failed to learn the truth about the Man of a Thousand Faces. And he didn't bother at all to discover his other great secret. *I*, on the other hand, will discover both because I have information Proteus would have killed to possess."

"And what would that information be, anyway, Resurrectionist?" Vanderwaal asked.

"I know, Vanderwaal, that Agent X himself is a living dead man, *like Stu Lothian, Henry Terran, and Wayne Helmer....*"

Vanderwaal's light brown eyes crackled with electricity. "Really? How did ya dope that out?"

"That is none of your affair," the Resurrectionist told him. "That is the business *only* of the one in charge. Let us say that I have my sources. One of them has already given me the location of the Secret Agent's headquarters. And the remaining person will lead us to the doctor we need to—"

"—Wait just a minute!" trucking racketeer Stu Lothian threw up hands of objection. "Sources? And one of them is another sawbones? How was that included in our deal? And will we have to pay for this mess?"

Men twisted their heads around in the direction of the trucker. And the Resurrectionist momentarily ordered the film stopped.

Lothian conceded, "I mean, I know you're keeping me and these other two clowns in 'protective custody,' as you call it," he looked directly at Helmer and Terran. "But we're no better than prisoners, as far as I'm concerned. Hell, we can't come or go, without your permission."

The Resurrectionist corrected him, "You are *not* my prisoners, Mr. Lothian. You are my guests. Pat Calvert will be one too, when he arrives. However, right now it is much too risky to allow your departure from this locale. I thought you understood that fact when you and I planted the lilacs. Less poetically, I thought you understood the time it takes to schedule proper, eh, 'corrective' cosmetic surgery."

Grinning like children in a toy shop, Terran and Helmer voiced loud, unctuous assent to the white-robed villain's words. But surreptitiously they offered each other the

*** AUTHOR'S NOTE: Actually, X had used a trick to deflect Proteus from learning his, the Agent's, real identity.**

slightest of nods. They thought it expedient for this crude trucker to do the talking for them—and perhaps get himself deeply in Dutch with their "host." Their thought was this: Who knew what might happen? Maybe the Resurrectionist would finish off Lothian and cut them in for a bigger piece of the loot.

Lothian, meanwhile, went on, "Okeh. So we cooperate with you. Then you'll put us on the first boat for Europe, or wherever else we choose."

"That is correct, Mr. Lothian," the Resurrectionist affirmed, his mask beatific but his blue eyes blinking and glittering with a fanatic's light. "And there you will be able to recommence your lives, free and clear of police or judicial molestation, especially the Federal kind. Think of it: new faces, new identities, and much fattened bank accounts. It will be paradise for you!"

"That still doesn't satisfy me about these sources you were jawin' about, a couple of minutes ago," the trucking racketeer objected. "Are they part of the deal, too? Or do we have to shell out more money for their services?"

The Resurrectionist stepped closer to Stu Lothian, at the same time pointing the lance directly at the trucker. In the next breath the crime chieftain grabbed the erstwhile dead man by the lapels of his suit and declared, "I have given you the life from death, *Lothian*. I can also take away your life, give you the *death from life* with a mere wave of the hand."

Lothian's blue eyes became, if possible, more contemptuous than usual: "Yeah, I guess you *would* do that. Make you feel like a real man, too, wouldn't it?"

A bomb of immense proportions exploded within the arch-fiend's brain. "Take him from my presence! When he's joined Hobart, persuade him of the error of his ways. And then see if he is appropriately humbled by the lesson you've shown him!"

Two more of the hoods manhandled the cursing Stu Lothian from the former refectory and down the hall.

Voice still trembling in fury, the white-robed crime lord resumed his address: "As I started to say before that interruption, two allies can help us to learn the truth about X. The first of them can lead us, I believe, to the Agent's sanctum sanctorum, if you will. And there, we can learn X's real name."

It was Vanderwaal's turn again. "Okeh. How are you going to find these two guys, Resurrectionist? Produce 'em from a hat like that magician guy, the Great Diamonte—or whatever ya wanna call 'im?"

"I see that you remain skeptical of me, Vanderwaal."

"Damn' right I am. I mean, for cryin' out loud—you're dealin' wit' Secret Agent X, for God's sake, a man who's unstoppable as a freight train when he's on a case! Besides that, he's practically a magician, disguisin' himself and gettin' in and outta traps. And don't forget trackin' folks, either. He could find a fly by the way it sneezed! They say that that big, rich doctor guy 'cross town is his only match. Or mebbe that laughin' spook with the black hat and the huge gats. Frankly, I wouldn't wanna meet any of 'em, 'cause I like livin' too much. And good as *you* are, what makes you think that *you* can produce results with this 'ally' of yours?"

The Resurrectionist was growing impatient under his mask. He blinked his blue eyes with a fury: "You know what I can do to those who oppose me, Vanderwaal! Do you want the same thing to—" he lifted that lance of his, pointed it menacingly at Vanderwaal.

Instantly the lanky man fell to his knees before his white-mantled lord.

When Vanderwaal spewed a fountain of apologies, the Resurrectionist delivered a terrible clout to the top of the man's head. Next the cruel boss turned his back on Vanderwaal and resumed his evil spiel. This other man, their ally, had once suffered imprisonment in the very headquarters of the Agent himself.

"Who is your stoolie, exactly?" inquired another man, an ordinary-seeming fellow who was balding, paunchy, jowly. He probably doted on steak, mashed potatoes, and thick gravy with his Rotarian's looks.

The Resurrectionist answered the fellow: "Perhaps some of you have heard me mention the name 'Ham Esler' some time ago. I had heard rumors about him. However, it was but recently that I have been able to make contact with him in prison and, eh, 'free' him from his cruel bondage."

Paunchy, the Rotarian, snickered, "The life from death?"

"Certainly not, Mr. Xavier," the Resurrectionist replied. "He did not have the money to afford a constant supply of it. A clever lawyer was much cheaper. I hired him one, and the attorney secured Mr. Esler's release. Needless to say, after he gained his freedom, he was most agreeable to assisting us.

"What makes him so special? He some kind whiz kid?"

"Oh, he is a cabbie. But he has a profound knowledge of the city."

"So does a map," replied the waggish Mr. Xavier.

The Resurrectionist was growing impatient. "Ham Esler has been a valuable source of information for us. Indeed he has already told me much about certain methods of our enemy. But an additional fact renders Esler infinitely more valuable.

"Two years back he was inside the very headquarters of the Man of a Thousand Faces.* Esler will locate it once again. And once inside it, there's another person Esler will help us find: another dead man, a doctor named Charles Darwin Osben. Years ago he worked under the guidance of a nameless Army intelligence officer, later a Federal investigator. After conducting brilliant, tireless research, this same doctor helped to create the man of mystery known as Secret Agent X!"

CHAPTER XVI
HOME OF THE BRAVE

CRIMINALS weren't the only ones plotting for the future. Across town, in that cab Harvey Bates piloted, the Secret Agent, too, strategized his own moves yet to come. These involved, most immediately, extricating his men and himself from the hands of Inspector Burks. But ultimately that strategy would rely on the Agent's own super-keen resourcefulness and his equally supernormal talent for misdirection.

*** AUTHOR'S NOTE: In DEATH'S FROZEN FORMULA, Agent X captured and questioned Esler, a crooked cabbie who served as a driver and field lieutenant for a dope ring. X conducted his interrogation of the hack man from within the Agent's headquarters, the Montgomery Mansion. Because of legal red tape and haggling heirs, this formerly grand house had been empty for many years. Via diligent investigations, the Secret Agent learned of the place. X, ever resourceful, modified the entire structure into a headquarters for his crime-fighting efforts. Presently the mansion harbors X's extensive crime laboratory, along with a number of remarkable technological devices. This advanced equipment equips him to prosecute his relentless war on crime and criminals. The Secret Agent used this edifice most recently in the chronicle MASTER OF MADNESS.**

He offered a taste of that dish, in this very moment, to Inspector Burks. And not even his two associates knew it was coming.

A deep groan, as of a soul tormented in hell, wailed from the back seat.

Abruptly the Agent reared upwards, astonishment at the sudden noise and Tetwilder's terrible plight written large on his disguised features. His widened ebon eyes merely underscored this pronouncement: "It's Petey, here! We've got to get him to a doctor, or he won't survive the day!"

Inspector Burks didn't exactly stand there, like a bump on a log. Coming to attention he quizzed, "Petey? As in the dope peddler, Petey Tetwilder?" he questioned. Suddenly in his right hand, a .38 police positive appeared, seemingly plucked from the netherworld itself. "That who you've got under that coat?"

The determined Inspector Burks whipped closer to the window, his gun at the ready. Now that he could clearly see the man's tortured face, Burks affirmed, with contempt, "Yeah—that's Tetwilder, all right. You didn't say *he* was in this rattletrap with you."

A stern look crept into his dark optics as Harvey Bates came back, "Wasting time, haggling with you about who's in the car and who isn't. Right now, trying to—"

"—If you ask me," Burks interrupted, by way of ruthless commentary, "you'd be saving New York a passel of money, to let him bite the dust."

Harvey Bates gritted slowly through clenched teeth, "Didn't ask you, Burks. Might not want to do it, but you *better* follow Agent X's instructions, and get this man to a doctor. *Then and only then* can we worry about X, here. I remind you that if Tetwilder dies, his blood will be on your hands. And you'll be found guilty of interfering with a Federal officer, in the line of duty."

Unnerved by such a prospect, Burks put up a hand to placate the supposed G-man, Harvey Bates. He, Burks, didn't want to stand in the way of a Federal investigation, much as he wanted to get X himself.

"See to it that you get appropriate credit, Burks," Harvey Bates assured him, rare impatience ratcheting his normally calm temperament higher and higher. "Now, tell your men to back off and let us through this line."

Inspector Burks bolted into action, motioning his officers and their vehicles to the side. This done, he trotted back to that original radio car. All of the police and the fire trucks on this street must move aside. This cab, license number 83NY42 was transporting two men, one critically injured, to the hospital. It was to be given a police escort to the nearest hospital, Dewitt Clinton Memorial, some five miles to the north of them.

Already Harvey Bates had thrown the cab back into "drive," thus propelling the machine slowly forward. After they and their police escort had left this street, the flow of traffic thinned to more of a trickle. Now they could move with speed.

For a period they drove with impunity through the traffic signals. The police auto's siren accounted for this, of course. But the atmosphere inside the cab remained tense, until Beckwith cleared it somewhat.

He simply couldn't believe that they'd gotten past Inspector Burks with such a minimum of trouble. After what he'd heard of the man's reputation, he, Beckwith, figured that Burks would have skinned them all alive.

"The Inspector *would* have done that, Beckwith," an unusually grim Agent X spoke up, "except that I used a bit of ventriloquism to divert his attention from us and make him think that was Tetwilder, doing that groaning. It was manipulative, I'll admit. But maybe it will buy us some more time, in order to get this poor man to a doctor. Even then, if my analysis of his condition is correct, he's going to die again—and horribly. The only question is 'when,' not 'if.'"

At that statement Beckwith pivoted his head around. There lay Tetwilder, whose body was drawn up in what resembled a *grand mal* seizure, the most serious kind of attack. Bloody froth collected in tiny pools at the corners of his mouth; his skin acquired a brownish cast. And his body seemed to be drying, like old leather, right before their eyes!

Horror widening his eyes, Hiram Beckwith stammered, "What's—what's goin' on with 'im, Boss? He's—he's dryin' the hell up, like a damn' raisin! And whadda ya mean, 'he's gonna die—again—and horribly'?'"

Agent X's voice remained strained, taut like a string pulled to the breaking point: "Petey Tetwilder is a notorious drug lord, probably one of the worst here on the East Coast, and certainly the worst here in New York. A mob button man knocked him off, three months ago, when I was still in Teutschland. That's part of what your men will find out, Bates, when they check this man's criminal record."

Bates joined in from the driver's seat: "May be the case, Sir. But don't see how this could be. Man's dead. So how can he be here in the cab, dying again?"

The Agent mused, "Yes, how *can* that be? And what was that reference that you heard, during Tiny's conversation with the Resurrectionist?"

"Dat's right!" fat Hiram Beckwith shot back. "Damn' Tiny character told the Resurrectionist that Tetwilder, here, needed his 'sugah.' If dat don't sound like a coke fiend to me, den I'll eat your hat!"

Curiously X didn't address this memory of "sugah" with his next statement. Instead he said to the two of them, "Bates, I want you to get to the hospital with him, and don't spare the horses. I'm going to leave you two as soon as we're a couple of blocks from it. When you get there, you'll know what to do about admitting Tetwilder here. Then as soon as you can, contact your operatives about this man: his drug operation, his enemies, his suspected murderer, that kind of thing. Beckwith, get this cab back to the garage where we store some of the other cabs. Then change the license plates on it, and send the car to the body shop. They can take it from there."

"But what about you, Sir?" Harvey Bates quizzed. "Be pretty tough getting away, with the police who'll be swarming around that hospital."

X merely stated, "You know where we are right now, don't you, Bates?"

Bates looked puzzled. But the Secret Agent, for his part, said nothing more. He thought it best that surprise would be the best reply for what was to come.

In the meanwhile, the police radio car was slowing from its faster pace of sixty miles an hour. Rapidly the towering concrete and steel shrine to healing, the hospital, came into view, immediately to their north.

Agent X could see, just below the medical center, an intersection, a traffic light, and a pedestrian crosswalk. When they received the "walk" signal, four men, two doctors in white lab coats and a pair of orderlies in green scrubs, strolled into the walkway and towards a delicatessen on the opposite side of the broad street.

On reflex the police chariot stopped. And in that instant that the Secret Agent acted.

"Luck, Bates, Beckwith," Agent X stated with a slight smile curling his lips. He pulled his gas gun from its place of concealment. Holding his breath, he squeezed the pistol's trigger, a snake of grayish vapor uncoiling full into the face of his lieutenant!

Surprised, a pie-eyed Harvey Bates felt his mouth, a trapdoor, pop open, entirely unbidden. Quickly, Agent X guided the slow-moving vehicle to the curb, in order that it wouldn't injure the passengers or any people from the street. As speedily he switched off the ignition. Then levering his muscular form past Beckwith and popping the passenger's door, the Secret Agent bolted through the opened portal and onto the roadway!

The stream of people, flabbergasted at the sight, parted to allow the running man to pass. Little did any of them suspect his real identity, much less the reason he fled the scene.

By now Agent X was recovered from much of the punishment he'd suffered at the hands of Luke Cordray. With the replenishment of his native vitality, he could run like an Olympic sprinter, yet dodge oncoming foot traffic like a tight end on the gridiron.

Legs pumping like biologic pistons, he moved deeper and deeper into this neighborhood of disrepute, a district as tough as the one he and his men had recently departed. Throughout his race he showed no sign of tiring, seeming to grow stronger, if that were possible.

The area grew more and more inhospitable, grim, even. Crumbling brownstones and decrepit rooming houses lined the streets on either side of him. Cheap dives, not classy nightclubs, guarded many a street corner. Human derelicts shambled up and down the streets, the light of hope having faded from their eyes. Some of the unfortunates were teens and young men. X would have expected them, too, to carry a heavy burden of hopelessness on their shoulders, given their straitened circumstances. But more than one of them looked wild-eyed, murderous, as if he'd kill grandma for a nickel. It was beyond depressing, to the Agent's point of view.

Then at a distance the man-hunter spotted a certain fellow in old, tattered clothing, a man who looked strangely cheerful in this district of despair.

An animate scarecrow, he whistled a tune and, surprisingly, acted as if he enjoyed the sunshine, the day's extreme heat notwithstanding. This fact would have shocked ninety-nine of a hundred people who witnessed such a sight. But it brought a smile of familiarity—and compassion—to the lips of the detective.

X stopped in front of the man, who in turn halted his own progress and faced the Man of a Thousand Faces.

"Mr. Robbins!" he greeted, a smile creasing his scarred, thin face. "I haven't seen you in a long time!"

"That's right, Thaddeus," Agent X called the man by name. "It has been too long since we've seen each other. Much too long, in fact. But I've been away for some time. Now I'm back here, hoping you can give me some help with a case. That is, if you're not too busy—"

"I was just walking to the market. But I'm happy to help you any way I can, Mr. Robbins," Thaddeus Penny replied, the smile still adorning his withered lips. And Agent X knew the cheery man was happy to offer his assistance. After all, that was the way of this blind fellow, a peddler of chewing gum, shoelaces, and other sundries.*

"Thaddeus," X began, "what do you know about the dope trade in this area? Anything to report?"

"There's the usual, Mr. Robbins. At least, that's what I've heard from the parents around here. They tell me those dealers are preying on the youngsters at will. No—it's worse than that. There've been several deaths lately, especially among the kids. You know, it's not enough that the neighborhood is dying—from that dope and from good old-fashioned neglect. What slays me is the fact that those dealers are trying to push this area into the grave. And neither the city nor most of the public care. Of course, I guess they've never really cared about us poor people anyway."

Agent X shook his head in sadness over the plight of these people. To him, they had as much worth as the wealthiest denizens of the city—but none of their power at City Hall.

Thaddeus Penny delivered some additional commentary about a couple of neighbors poorer than himself, older women whom he wished he could help, but he simply didn't have the money to do so.

X let the man finish, commiserating with him during the pathetic account. Then he continued, struck by one of Thaddeus' remarks, "Perhaps I can give your friends some help. But repeat something for me. You mentioned something about some dead youngsters. They were teenagers, I suppose, and not young children?"

"Yes, Sir, Mr. Robbins. Nearly every one of them. Died from that dope, too, from what their folks have told me."

"I see. Tell me: Have you heard anyone refer to the dope as 'sugar'?"

Thaddeus Penny threw back his head, as though to catch the rays of the sun on his scarred face. Normally such a move wouldn't have surprised the Secret Agent, since he knew of the blind man's great love of the sunshine and the outdoors. But in the present case the man was searching through that photographic memory of his, trying to recall any word, or person, that might assist the detective in his quest.

Mental lightning flashed across the mind of the blind man, as his words revealed: "Let me see, Mr. Robbins. 'Sugar,' eh? That's—yes, that was the word, all right! My neighbor Mrs. Sayre was complaining about it last week. She said her son was wasting some hard-earned money on that horrible stuff. But the son's not the real problem. She thinks someone's pressuring him into buying the stuff. And she believes it's her husband, back of it all. He's the one causing all the grief, and I *think she's right. He's* the one not giving an example to his boy. I've heard the way he talks to his son, and it's shameful—just as bad as the way he talks to his wife."

X nodded gravely. "A shame, this. But go back to the father and his use of the 'sugar.' You realize, don't you, that you're making a rather strong accusation?"

*** AUTHOR'S NOTE: Penny, who knows Agent X by the alias of Robbins, lost his sight in a tenement fire some years ago. Became of his affliction, Thaddeus Penny has developed his other senses, and his wits, to unheard-of heights. He can find his destination without the aid of a cane, for instance. Moreover, he can read books by Braille and can identify people by their voices or minute sounds they emit. Most recently Penny assisted the Secret Agent in fighting the Fool, as chronicled in MASTER OF MADNESS.**

Thaddeus shrugged his thin shoulders. "I'm sorry, Mr. Robbins; but based on some things which have happened recently, I stand by it. For instance, I can hear Mr. Sayre, or Gus, coming and going at all hours of the night. You know, I hear things the average person doesn't hear—or chooses to ignore."

"And you think that all of this has something to do with that 'sugar'?"

"Yes, Sir, I'm convinced it does. More than once I've heard his wife warning him in that soft, sweet voice of hers, cautioning him about 'something he's been taking.'"

"Those were her words?"

"They were. She warned him about getting Jake involved by taking it, too. He screamed that it was none of her business, since he was paying the bills. When she expressed worry about it, he slapped her, or threw something at her, I suppose, as she begged him not to hit her again. That's not all, though. I think he must have seen her last week, talking to me out in front of the tenement. He was talking to some man with a smooth voice that I didn't recognize. When the two of them drew near to us, the other fellow went on his way.

"They might have been fearful of discovery, Thaddeus."

"That's what I'm thinking, Mr. Robbins. Gus Sayre probably realized his wife was airing the family's dirty laundry to me. Well, lo and behold, that very night, after we'd spoken, the Sayres had another one of their fights. I heard him mention something about 'keeping her mouth shut around that blind man downstairs.' She merely told him that she needed to talk to some kind soul—that *her husband* would certainly not give her the time of day. And all she was trying to do was to prevent him from taking food out of their mouths and putting himself and their son Jake in danger."

"Follow up on this money angle, if you don't mind. He's spending lots of money. So he has to get it from somewhere, no?"

"She said something about that to me, outside that day. As fast as he can get cash, he spends it."

"Cash payments? How large? And from whom?"

"Sizeable ones, by all accounts. They're from some 'new employer' of her husband. Or that's what Mrs. Sayre said to me. She said that he was shut-mouthed about it, whenever she tried to get him to discuss it with her. Meanwhile this new boss of his had hooked the son with the same bait—and according to her, Gus Sayre didn't object. The fact is, he encouraged it. And the wife said it surely would be the death of them both. She was crying, Mr. Robbins, when she told me about her problems. She wanted all of it to stop: the fighting, the secrecy, the danger to her family. I wanted badly to help her, somehow; but what could I do?"

"You're doing her a great service now, Thaddeus, telling me about his and the young man's activities. Now consider this for a moment: Gus Sayre probably didn't stomach the kind of advice his wife was giving, did he?" the Secret Agent hypothesized. "In other words, he probably gave her more grief, wouldn't you say?"

Nodding vigorously, Thaddeus exclaimed, "That's *exactly* what he did, Mr. Robbins! He bellowed like a bull at her—something which comes easily enough for him—and he stalked around the apartment with that slow gait of his. I feel certain he slapped her some more, too, based on the loud noises I've heard."

"Surely you weren't lurking outside their door, Thaddeus?"

"Oh, no, Sir. Most recently I was below them. See, their apartment is directly above mine."

The Man of a Thousand Faces told the blind man of his, X's, great admiration for being such a concerned neighbor and citizen. Next, the man-hunter restated part of Thaddeus' narrative: "So Gus Sayre and presumably his son Jake are doing some sort of mysterious, at best dubious, work for an equally mysterious boss. In turn, they receive cash payments, large ones, for their 'services.' Someone has a large fund, too, from which to draw equally large pay allotments, apparently," he hypothesized. "Furthermore, no one wants the money traced, since otherwise, the mastermind would compensate his men with checks.

"Then consider her statement to you, namely that they spend their money on dangerous and illicit products, such as this 'sugar,'— and God knows what else. This is classic dope addiction, Thaddeus. The more of the drug a person uses, the more he becomes its slave. And the more enslaved to it he becomes, the more he must buy. That means having ready cash to make purchases—which inevitably go back into buying more of the drugs.

"Think about this, too: both of the Sayre men are prowling around at night, albeit they may be engaging in more of the same during the daytime. Whatever the case, neither of them will tell what kind of work he does, even to someone closest like a wife or mother. This suggests to me they're doing something illegal. Tell me: What kinds of visitors call at their apartment?"

"I *do* know that several different people have come and gone from their place, some of them in groups of two or three at a time. I'm guessing they're some of his fellow 'employees' for that mystery boss of his."

"Let me hazard another guess," the Agent suggested. "They always made such visits when Mrs. Sayre wasn't present, eh?"

Thaddeus cast his head upward, assumed a contemplative pose. "They did, at that. I've never heard her voice when these strange men were in the apartment."

"They would need to get her out of the way. She'd be a witness to their activities, of course; and that fact alone would render her a liability," the Agent stated, gravely.

"Mr. Robbins, you don't think he'd—he'd kill his own wife, do you?"

"In his frame of mind, and with the spur of dope to prod him? I don't think he'd hesitate to do so, Thaddeus, if she were bold enough to confront him. Or if she were in the wrong place at the wrong time...."

Knowing this could be a lead to the Resurrectionist, the Agent asked, "Can you take me to their apartment, immediately?"

"Sure, I can. She should be home right now because today is one of her days to take in wash."

Concerned for her safety, Agent X and the blind Thaddeus Penny marched back to the rundown apartment building and up to the ramshackle building's third floor.

Agent X marveled at the ease and the grace with which Thaddeus Penny moved. When the pair reached the proper door, the Secret Agent's nose detected a ghastly odor. Then his eyes espied a large round garbage bin, filled to overflowing. The cylindrical container crowded into a space immediately to the portal's left. The rubbish holder would necessitate a sighted person to move the thing aside before gaining entry. Or, maybe if the individual were agile enough, then that person could slip through the narrower opening. Only in one of these ways could the man or woman open the steel panel, which hinged outward.

The Secret Agent sped up, in order that he might beat Thaddeus to the door and make an opening for them. Instead, Thaddeus himself slipped past the Agent, slid the bin aside, and with a flourish, invited the Agent through the now-opened door!

The Man of a Thousand Faces gave a low whistle of surprise. He smiled broadly, "You never cease to amaze me, Thaddeus! I'll never understand how you do what you do. I'm just glad that you can do it."

They quickly mounted the stairs. Thaddeus replied, "And I'm glad, Mr. Robbins, that there are still people like you, who care about everyone—not just the rich folks in the city."

Agent X and Penny reached the third floor's door. On the hallway itself, Thaddeus Penny took the lead for the second time. X followed the blind fellow some ten doors down and to the right, where Thaddeus abruptly stopped before a closed door.

"This is the Sayres' apartment, Mr. Robbins. Shouldn't be any trouble, getting Mrs.—"

He stopped with the force of an automobile smashing into a brick wall.

From the apartment's interior a radio broadcast brassy swing music, perceptible even in the hallway. Clearly, in breaking off his narrative, the Agent's blind associate wasn't urging the detective to appreciate the blaring horns of the dance band.

"Listen!" the blind fellow whispered. "Hear that noise coming from behind the door? It's Mrs. Sayre, and she's arguing with someone. Sounds like her husband. And they're using the loud radio to disguise—"

The Agent *shushed* his blind friend into silence while the two of them listened a bit longer to the couple's war of words.

Apparently the battling Sayres were slinging more than words back and forth, however, as the next minute or so disclosed. The two men outside couldn't help but hear the loud *crash* of some object, as it struck its target. Then another projectile, glass or crystal, flew across the room and shattered upon impact. Evidently the second missile must have hit Mrs. Sayre, for she let out a feline scream of pain. Immediately on its heels she begged the man not to hit her for a second time. He could, she conceded, come and go wherever he wanted to; and she promised she wouldn't ever protest again.

The detective gently pushed Thaddeus Penny backwards.

In an eyeblink, the public defender rammed his muscular shoulder directly into the solid wooden door with such force that his blow actually splintered its surface! He aimed another devastating thrust of his shoulder at the wooden panel. As dramatically, the door blasted open, thundered against the wall behind it!

From the doorway the orbs of Agent X hastily took in the apartment's homely front room. Cheap, battered furniture, a shaky coffee table, a tattered sofa and three moth-eaten chairs, guarded one end of the place. On the opposite side of the room, a poor kitchen occupied a corner, an ancient coal stove ruling, poorly, as its monarch. In front of it a metallic kitchen table, a light-weight alloy, struggled to stand on three legs, with its much shorter fourth one shored up by a brick.

Agent X parted his lips, such that his teeth glistened like the fangs of an attack dog. Moreover his disguised eyes acquired a look of sheer fury, so frighteningly did they blaze. And they did so with good reason, on account of the terrible sight they located across the room.

No more than ten feet away from him, on the opposite side of the rickety kitchen table, the master man-hunter saw Mrs. Sayre. She would have been a pretty woman years ago—or perhaps in a different life. But rough circumstances had aged her. They had dug deep furrows in her once delicate features. They had also streaked her once lovely ash blonde hair with strands of gray. And worst of all, those same tough times had robbed all hope from her ice blue eyes.

Now, still on the floor she was kneeling and weeping amidst a flood of incoherent sounds that poured from her split, blood-flecked lips. Looming over her, Mr. Sayre, a big man slightly over six feet and many pounds over 200, was cursing up a blue streak.

He was Tiny, the Resurrectionist's chief field lieutenant, still garbed in that bulky garment of silver-white!

Eventually his vigorous behavior caused his shaggy black hair to fall into his wild coffee-colored eyes. The curses weren't enough for him, however, as he started next to taunt his victim. Stand up and say something, he screamed to his wife Annemarie, so he could knock hell out of her again.

Then the man happened to look up, spot Agent X speeding across the room.

Recognizing X, actually his disguise, the man gritted in a deep basso, "What are you doing here, Cordray? Think you're coming to collect your—"

Unexpectedly, Agent X took flight, a human missile sailing towards the big form of Mr. Gus "Tiny" Sayre. X crashed against the man, and the two opponents, arms flailing, toppled to the apartment's tiled floor.

This man was no fighter with style, X quickly discovered. He was a two-bit brawler, good with a smaller, weaker foe. But unfortunately for himself, Tiny thought he could behave the same way with Agent X. The tough grabbed at the Secret Agent's torso, intending to wrestle him into submission. Such a tack was a terrible move, for the enormous man was certainly no match for the Man of a Thousand Faces. Using the knife edges of both hands, X slashed at both sides of Sayre's neck. The Agent followed this move by hurling a quartet of punishing jiu-jitsu thrusts into the man's own midriff and head section. Tiny's dark eyes rolled back into his head. And he crumpled unceremoniously to the floor.

A wide-eyed Mrs. Sayre, still on the floor, watched the entire episode incredulously. No one had ever stood up to her husband. This stranger had stood up to her husband and bested him conclusively. She wanted to regain her feet and thank this mysterious Cordray, for that was the name she'd heard him called, for defending her.

Suddenly from one of the apartment's two bedrooms, the ears of the two people detected a series of five long sounds, then two shorts, and three long ones to close out the sequence.

The features of Annemarie Sayre registered complete puzzlement regarding the noise. That wasn't the case with her rescuer, however.

They'd heard, he told her, a Morse code call on a shortwave radio unit!

X shot his gaze over his right shoulder in hopes that the transmission might pierce the air again. It did, in fact, originating from a bedroom.

"May I?" he clipped to the woman.

She responded, "By all means."

He raced back into the bedroom. Immediately he spotted the two closets which guarded either side of a double bed. He knew that the opened one couldn't have played host to the radio, since this space was a nothing more than area for hanging clothes.

The other one, however, seemed a likely candidate for housing the shortwave unit. But the door was locked! And the shortwave had stopped broadcasting its message.

"You knew about the radio behind this door?" he asked.

"Not—not really," she stammered, her body a-tremble. She figured she'd better answer this man, however, tough as he had been. "Gus's been acting so nasty and so secretive that I was becoming more and more afraid to ask him anything."

"So I take it you don't have a key to this closet then?"

Her blue eyes started to brim with tears. "No, Sir. He's just started locking it, only in the past four or five months. I stay away from this part of our apartment when he's back here. Except for bedtime, of course. Oh, and I don't come in here when he's gone, either, to be frank. He—he takes out his anger on the boy and me, and—"

"Mrs. Sayre," the Agent altered his voice to its natural, vibrant tone, "you have nothing to fear from me. Let me show you something."

Who is this strange man? she wondered to herself. *He's not this Cordray that Gus thought he was. And he's not some other connection of Gus'.*

"Are you some—some kind of cop?" she probed.

X didn't answer her with words. Rather, he extracted his wallet wherein he showed her one of his cards with the brand of X.

"You—you're that—" she stammered, as the black X disappeared before her eyes.

Her comment elicited the most clipped of nods, along with a statement that he needed to get her and her son, immediately, to safety. Only in that way would they enjoy real protection from their dope-addicted husband and father.

From nowhere, the shortwave resumed its etheric pulse of earlier moments. Not only did it broadcast Morse code again, but the pattern spelled out an alphabetic-numerical sequence: *Calling LILAC-02! This is the Resurrectionist!*

CHAPTER XVII
SECRETS OF THE SAYRES

MRS. Sayre didn't know the whereabouts of this key to the closet. Neither could Agent X afford to waste time with picking the lock attached to the door. He whirled his right foot in a sweeping jiu-jitsu thrust at the door.

The wooden panel exploded from its hinges, blasted into the closet itself.

A roomful of sophisticated radio equipment greeted the Secret Agent's gaze: an expensive UHF outfit; a telegraphic sending set, just as pricey; and a radio direction finder, as high in quality as anything in the military.

With his right hand, X snatched the microphone from the table where it had sat.

"This is Tiny," the Agent mimicked the deep voice of Gus Sayre.

"You left while we were screening the film, Tiny," the voice of the Resurrectionist came with great gravity. *"Someone reported that you were shaking quite vigorously."*

Agent X displayed his supreme resourcefulness: "Wasn't feeling well. Thought I needed to get home," he lied, "and get some of my supply of 'sugar.'"

The Resurrectionist paused before answering him. Then the crime king responded, *"I will need you to meet our friend Mr. Esler at the Blue Streak Cab Company. Once there, you and he will proceed to location R-Zero-One."*

Not a real member of the Resurrection Ring, the Secret Agent couldn't have known, of course, the location in question. Thus he simply fished for information, in hopes that the Resurrectionist would take the bait: "Why R-Zero-One, and not some other place, like maybe my apartment?"

That question prompted a contemptuous response from the Resurrectionist: *"You must be joking, Tiny. Your apartment in particular would make us too vulnerable to interference. We must proceed to the fortified building in the Meatpacking District, down the block from Lothian's trucking office. There I will give you and your men orders for the next killing I have planned. Also you will receive directions about a certain act which must follow that killing. Therefore, Tiny, you,"* he directed, *"will be here—whether you have adequate 'sugar,' or not. Is that clear?"*

"Yeah, it's clear as crystal," the grinning Man of a Thousand Faces imitated in Tiny's deep basso. He'd gotten the information he needed, specifically, the locale for the meeting. "I'm guessing that I'll have to grin and bear it, if something goes wrong?"

Contemptuous laughter was the Resurrectionist's answer. *"If something does go wrong, it will be on your head. Remember: Be at the Blue Streak at seven o'clock pm promptly and proceed from there to the Meatpacking District. That is all."*

The Resurrectionist broke the connection, and the Agent replaced the microphone in its accustomed position.

The dope peddler Ham Esler? The investigator thought somberly. *He's supposed to be in prison. But he's out? And the Resurrectionist wants him for his knowledge of the Montgomery Mansion's location...?*

In the next instant while a surprised Mrs. Sayre stood there wide-eyed, the suddenly quiet man-hunter ventured back out into the living room of the apartment. There he found Tiny Sayre, still unconscious as a result of the Secret Agent's jiu-jitsu anesthetic. That news encouraged him, as did the fact that Thaddeus Penny had tiptoed inside the apartment. He was quietly waiting in the kitchen, ready to provide his friend with assistance.

X made a request of the street peddler: He was to escort Mrs. Sayre to the home of another neighbor, someone he trusted completely. From that person's apartment they could phone the police, the detective suggested, in the next ten minutes.

He escorted the two into the hallway to ensure they left safely. A glance at his wristwatch showed the Man of a Thousand Faces it was 3:30 pm. Though he still had several hours before Tiny's meeting, he knew he'd better get going.

Grimly he stepped back into the Sayre's apartment. But first he removed his pocket medical kit and in turn slipped a syringe from it. This article he charged with a powerful narcotic, all with the intention of shooting some of the chemical into the veins of the unconscious man. A thought crossed his mind before he executed this plan, however. Since that "sugar" was such a powerful and apparently dangerous concoction, the injection of his own drug might be putting the man's life in additional jeopardy.

Thus he decided to truss the man with a long, stout strand of cord he'd removed from a pocket of his suit. That way, unless Sayre were a modern Houdini, he couldn't effect an escape from these bonds.

As if Tiny were a child, X quickly hoisted him over his, the detective's, left shoulder. Smiling slightly, the investigator strode through the door of the remaining bedroom. Once he had placed the unconscious hood on the bed, he gained the door, and thrust the key into the lock from the outside. Next he locked it with one of those Oustini gimmicks which professional magicians and escape artists are known to carry.

In a trice he had moved into that bedroom next door. He passed into the combination closet-radio room. After he had closed its door, he thrust his right hand into one of the pockets of the seersucker suit. When his hand returned from its sojourn, it clutched that portable makeup kit which had served him so well.

From the receptacle he brought forth a fresh tube of his volatile plastic, in addition to a black toupee, a tube of skin dye, and a pair of coffee-brown contact lenses. He set up his kit on the table, began speedily applying the volatile material. The remaining articles he applied with equal speed, yet fidelity to his model. In short order he turned careful, yet critical eyes on the mirror from his kit. His face was now an exact twin to that of the unconscious Tiny. But the Secret Agent could not, under the present circumstances, duplicate Tiny's sheer bulk. The man, after all, outweighed him by a good forty or fifty pounds. To appear as him, minus the extra weight, was to invite immediate exposure by the Resurrectionist and his forces.

The Sayres kept a chest of drawers in this bedroom, so the Agent turned his attention to this piece of furniture. He rattled through several of its chambers before he found some of Tiny's undershirts. Quickly he doffed his seersucker garments, only to cover his muscular frame, first, in a quartet of the unconscious man's undershirts. This completed, he proceeded to don Tiny's silver-white clothing. X stopped when his sensitive fingers felt the composition of the material.

His disguised eyes sparkled with understanding, all of a sudden. He had a good idea of the clothing's makeup and its origin, and he was glad it was Tiny, not any random criminal, that he'd chosen to impersonate. Thus he completed his borrowing of the man's garments, in order to lend the final authenticity to his masquerade.

Agent X returned to that opened chest. As he was closing one of the drawers again, he happened to see a crumpled piece of paper, the edge of which was poking upwards from the drawer below.

He pulled the new drawer outwards, as well, in hopes that this paper might be some other clue. As it happened his act didn't quite free the object, since the document, apparently a pamphlet, was trapped by more clothing, as well as caught in the lower frame of the drawer itself.

Even though the paper was still trapped, X could see a picture of a gun's butt on the bottom edge of the cover. That image immediately piqued his curiosity, filled him, in fact, with more than a little excitement. On a certain level that simple brochure reminded the Secret Agent of the discovery of the Rosetta Stone. So excited was he on seeing more of the paper's actual cover that he accidentally tore the thing as he finally liberated it from its cloth and wooden captors.

Carefully he rejoined the torn ends of the little booklet on the chest of drawers.

It was a manual for the proper use of a certain kind of pistol, a Webley Mark II Senior. The thing was not a true firearm either, to be technical. The piece was actually an air gun, or a weapon which expelled its projectiles via compressed air or, occasionally, a gas. The present manual depicted all of the Webley's specifications, in addition to the various types of ammunition one could use.

Agent X permitted himself a brief nod. The use of this air gun would explain the reason none of the onlookers ever heard a pistol's report when the Resurrectionist's men murdered people. The bystanders all heard a sudden expulsion of air, a cough of sorts. In a sense air guns belched their projectiles from the barrel. Firearms, in contrast, exploded their rounds from their barrels, gunpowder being the active agent.*

Like a great musician, the Secret Agent felt his imagination inspired anew. The eyes of the man-hunter glittered brilliantly as he began mentally to assemble the information from the brochure and couple it with two other clues: the oily smudge and the tannish matter on the floor beside Lothian's corpse.

In the next breath, he quickly removed the compact UHF sending device from one of his pockets. After apprising Miss Arden of his current status and his intention to impersonate Tiny, he got off the horn with her.

He knew that he must still complete a thorough circuit of this room, must still locate evidence to build his case against this criminal concern.

Therefore he aimed gun-sight eyes on all points of that closet, starting with that fancy radio equipment. Into his capacious memory he placed the names of each piece of hardware, starting with the radio itself, and moving on, first to an expensive phonograph, and next, to a wire recording device. He also spotted a rack for holding several score record albums. And he noticed something else, a boxy sort of arrangement, with several glass dials decorating its face. Two long wires snaked from it, only to end in a pair of small speakers, their shells fashioned from the ubiquitous Bakelite. Tiny had attached this boxy machine to his wire recorder, too, with both of them linked by an additional pair of long wires to the UHF radio.

To one side of the desk, the disguised X noticed something else. It was a smaller bookcase of four shelves, like one a secretary might

*** AUTHOR'S NOTE: With a firearm, especially a small one, a small spring plunges its sharpened firing pin through the gun's breech bolt, part of its rear closing mechanism. That action, of a consequence, hammers the bolt against the primer, located at the flat end of the individual cartridge, or bullet. Once the gun has passed through these steps, the firearm's user cocks, or pulls back, the trigger, against a piece called the sear. The squeezing of the trigger causes the sear to relinquish its hold on the firing pin. That mechanism flies towards the primer, hitting it with great force. The resultant action of metal striking metal releases heat energy, in the form of fire. This then incites combustion in the gunpowder, which gives off gases. These gases literally blow the projectile from the barrel.**

use in an office. The detective allowed his eyes to trace each of its shelves. These contained a number of books on radio and electronics, proof positive that Tiny's interest in radio and electronics was far more than casual. The texts also bound him, ever more tightly to the Resurrectionist himself. However in what exact capacity was, as yet, unclear.

On the second shelf from the bottom, he focused his gaze upon a particular book, a great, green-backed monstrosity. He immediately lifted it from the shelf, fingered it open. The book housed an immense photo album of family pictures, all of which depicted the Sayre family in happier, or at least less tumultuous, times. Beside it he noticed another album, this one done up in plain black leather. It too occupied a great deal of real estate on the bookshelf. X wondered, naturally, if it were a heavy tome. But it was relatively light, he discovered, when he slid it outward.

He opened the cover of the book, to learn that someone had stamped the flyleaf with the year 1939. Moreover, on flipping through its pages, he found that only the first third or so contained any photos. Nearly all of them depicted besuited, dignified characters, each one of them the very image of respectability. He suddenly grew interested at these images because some of them depicted Henry Terran and Wayne Helmer. By means of tape, someone had also affixed the images of some other wealthy and shady men in the album, Pat Calvert and Stu Lothian being the most prominent among them.

X's eyes glittered with excitement. He closed this volume, but didn't stop his search. Running his left hand along other shelves, he chose additional thick books. X was playing the odds that these, too, contained photo albums, hopefully dated as the one from this year had been.

Sure enough he found more of them, two more thick volumes stretching back to 1937. They all contained the pictures of supposedly upstanding members of the community. In reality, all of these men had been facing Federal charges for tax evasion. And all of them had been murdered before they could stand trial. A perfectly slick racket, the Agent told himself with a slight nod. This Resurrectionist had been brazenly providing his clients a way out of their legal troubles with what seemed to be virtual impunity. The authorities could not prosecute a dead man, or so the Resurrectionist must have told his dupes.

So why had he only then revealed his intent to hunt down and to destroy Elisha Pond, that is, Secret Agent X?

The Man of a Thousand Faces pondered that puzzle for a bit. A sudden inspiration caused his mind to rehearse his cases of the past two years. During that time he'd barely utilized the Elisha Pond identity, and he had ignored it for a good reason.* Many of his recent investigations had taken him to cities and towns far afield from New York. Thus he had chosen to store this Pond role in mothballs, it being a masquerade better suited to the wealthy set in and around the great me-

*** AUTHOR'S NOTE: The Agent has worn Pond's face in only one recorded case of recent months, that is, HALO OF HORROR. However, he has told me of another instance he had to wear those features, a mere four months ago. During that exploit he adopted the wealthy philanthropist's features to nab a most cruel criminal gang. They operated a racket specializing in fake medical procedures and equally bogus philanthropy. Here it was especially appropriate that X impersonate Pond, since the wealthy man, the real Pond of the World War, received extensive training in medicine.**

tropolis. He'd practically done the same with his masquerade as the reporter A.J. Martin, having revived it only a few months back.*

Why, then, was someone hunting Pond? Why else, unless someone had made the connection among Pond, Martin, and X? Why, unless someone like a great cat had been lying in wait, ready to pounce on its prey?

But who might want him so desperately? This question would continue to bedevil him until he learned its answer. His deductions were no intellectual exercises, either, but life and death themselves, for him and for his friends.

He returned to the small bookcase.

Quickly he began to slide one book after another from the shelves, so that he might read the titles of them. Some strange sixth sense screamed to him to choose a relatively slender yellow volume, cloth-bound, from a place beside some of Tiny's references on electronics.

He would have ignored the thing earlier, but not at present.

Out he yanked the work, into his waiting left hand.

It bore nothing on the cover. But when he opened the tome, he uncovered an extremely rich vein of information.

It was a classic hollowed book, the stuff of too many detective novels to name.

Within its scooped out confines, Tiny had inserted one of those business cards from the Resurrectionist, with the slip being designated LILAC-02. Based on the Resurrectionist's transmission from previous moments, this code signified Tiny himself. X took this piece of pasteboard by its top edge and absently slipped it into his wallet.

Abruptly he removed the thing again because he'd seen something else on the card.

That other thing was a cartoony shape of some kind, rather like a fish in its general form. He peered closely at the article, possibly one of Tiny's creations, as it seemed to swim to the left, below the word LILAC and the digits "0-2." To the right of the entire affair, the cartoon and the lilac, Tiny, apparently, had scribbled, "Mine, once." He had also scrawled the words, "Like *they* were."

Back he slipped the card, into his wallet's pouch. He knew that that pasteboard would likely produce Tiny's fingerprints, and though these interested him, something else did too. This was the *ink* with which the Resurrectionist had printed the message. He suspected the writing fluid to be similar in composition to his own disappearing ink.

Below the business card from the hollow book, X encountered a photo of an expensively dressed woman with fine features, quite pretty actually, and a very young boy. To the picture someone had clipped a scrap of paper, obviously torn from a brochure of some sort. In a bold, likely angry hand, someone had penned the simple word, "Why?" along with three underlines. The handwriting, rough as it was, suggested that a man had scribbled the word.

Secret Agent X flipped the fragment of paper to its opposite side, in order to determine if anything of significance might be recorded there, as well.

Apparently Tiny had been the one to destroy most of the text the brochure had once recorded. Still, enough of it remained,

*** AUTHOR'S NOTE: X is remembering, of course, CURSE OF THE CRIMSON HORDE, CORPSE CONTRABAND, and another recent exploit YOKE OF THE CRIMSON COTERIE. In each of these adventures he had to revive his newspaperman's cover.**

such that the Man of a Thousand Faces could discern this sequence of letters to the right of the tear:

D
NCE
ON

Those letters might have seemed incomprehensibe at present. But the brilliant investigator knew that their apparent meaninglessness would prove most significant later. So he thrust this fragment into his wallet, along with that card.

Abruptly the sunlight of truth dawned in his disguised eyes. He had an idea what this sequence of letters signified, in light of the scribbling on that business card. But he couldn't test his hypothesis until later when he had the luxury of time.

In the meantime, X decided to make a final round of the Sayre's apartment. He wanted to discover if there were any supplies of drugs in Tiny's home. He wanted also to test them later in his Montgomery Mansion. But from experience, he knew the drugs wouldn't be in plain sight. Only in fiction did the addict leave his dope out in the open. In point of fact, the dope fiend always concealed his stash, oftentimes in some clever way: in something like that hollow book, for instance. Or he might stockpile drugs in a secret panel of a wall, or underneath a bathtub. Some dope users, too, had been known to conceal their illegal substances in a container with a false bottom, such as a suitcase, a chest, or if a small quantity, something like a jewelry box.

Something else was true of people like Tiny and his brother dopesters. They typically satisfied their addiction in some safe place away from prying eyes. For Tiny Sayre, this practice most likely pointed to his radio room. He kept the chamber locked to prevent his wife or others from discovering it. And there he could inject himself or swallow the vile chemicals to his heart's content.

Agent X reached out his right hand and tapped first the wire recorder. His efforts yielded nothing, as did a similar attempt he made with the boxy machine attached to it.

That wasn't true, however, with the phonograph.

The detective picked up the machine. On its bottom he spied a large clasp whose real purpose was to cover *something*. He gave it a twist, and his action unfastened a hidden panel at the machine's base. X knew he was on the trail of one of Tiny's secrets.

The Man of a Thousand Faces pulled out a drawer. In that compact den a most dangerous chemical viper was lurking, ready to strike.

It was a syringe loaded with a dark, almost chocolate-colored fluid. The same hypo perched atop a rectangular wooden container perhaps the size of a standard cigar box. X squirted some of the hypo's fluid out onto the table, sniffed the stuff. His hand strangely trembling a bit, he snapped open its lid. The receptacle contained nothing less than the supply of Tiny's infamous "sugar."

It was a variant of one of the chemicals which had helped him to create the mysterious identity, Secret Agent X. This fact he knew, all too well....

CHAPTER XVIII
DEATH BY "SUGAR"

IN ferreting out Tiny's cache of "sugar," Secret Agent X had discovered much to engender a sense of horror. He wasn't the only one who would experience such a feeling, as subsequent events would prove for his associates Bates and Beckwith.

Across town, in the emergency room of the Dewitt Clinton Hospital, the attending doctor had mobilized a virtual squadron of hospital personnel to save the life of the dope lord, Petey Tetwilder. Near these proceedings, the detective's men looked on, as the medical professionals grew more and more desperate in their efforts.

In the midst of these measures, Beckwith still couldn't believe what the Secret Agent had done, to abscond from the cab.

For crying out loud, Beckwith had told the giant Bates. At least Agent X could have warned them that he wasn't sticking around the place. By way of reply, the shaggy-haired Bates allowed his lips to curl into a slight smile. Then he calmly removed a square-bowled pipe from his pocket, filled it with tobacco, and lit the smoking implement.

This done, he drew a deep lungful of the cherry-flavored smoke between his lips. Finally he spoke: "Didn't expect him to do that, did you?"

"Well, no, I guess I didn't!" was Beckwith's sheepish reply.

Bates calmly asked the man to tone down the noise, and Beckwith complied.

"Expect the unexpected with Secret Agent X," Harvey Bates advised his fat associate. He took his pipe from his mouth and pointed with the mouthpiece. "That officer over there?"

Bates' motion directed Beckwith's eyes towards the bluecoat on the other side of the emergency room.

"Bought every bit of my story about X's escape, even down to our surprise at its coming. Plus, that John Law thinks the Secret Agent is a desperado on the loose. Doesn't know he's on the prowl for more clues about the Resurrectionist. Whatever the case, we won't disabuse that officer or his friends of their ignorance, will we?" Bates concluded, still smiling.

"So that's why he gassed us in the car? Damn, that Diamond Jim!" Beckwith interjected, using his pet name for the resourceful X. "He's somethin' else again, ain't he!"

"He's not called the 'Man of a Thousand Surprises' for nothing, Beckwith," Bates reminded.

"Amen to that, brother!" came Beckwith's vigorous affirmation.

Beside the operating table, the words of the doctor and the nurses grew vehement. Their reaction was completely understandable, in light of the events they witnessed.

One nurse, an older, graying woman, squealed. Another woman, a young, fresh-faced female perhaps two years out of nursing school, actually fainted. The doctor, for his part, drew in a sharp intake of air, whereupon he choked out a string of profanities. The astonished man wasn't so much trying to express blasphemy, as he was groping for words to describe this uncanny phenomenon.

Bates and Beckwith raced over to the table to see what had shocked the medicos.

In that portion of the hospital, horror ruled the day. Before their very eyes, Petey Tetwilder was slowly drying up!

Frantically his vocal cords vibrated, at the same time his lips contorting, horribly, to form the words he desperately needed to speak.

" 'Su'—'su'—'sugar'—damned 'sugar'... is the cause—cause of this whole damned thing..." he whispered to the assemblage, his eyes fairly popping in their sockets.

"Resurrectionist is your boss, Tetwilder," a somber Harvey Bates reminded. "What's he in this for? What does he hope to gain?"

The man was dying; that much was clear. He started to choke, and brownish fluid seeped from his mouth. A massive wave of convulsions swept over his struggling form again.

"He's trying to swallow his tongue!" screamed the older nurse.

The emergency room physician grabbed a slender piece of wood, a tongue depressor, from the top left pocket of his lab coat. He forced the wooden implement between the man's teeth. This action stopped him from swallowing his tongue, but it could not, of course, halt the onrush of the Grim Reaper.

Gradually the man's fit subsided, and he slowly swiveled his head back towards the shaggy-haired Bates. The big man realized that if he didn't extract the man's information now, then the grave would steal all of Petey Tetwilder's secrets.

The man started to whisper an indistinct something. Bates leaned down, such that he could either hear the man's dying words, or perhaps read his lips.

Tetwilder husked, "Thought I could beat it. Thought I—thought I could.... But there's no beatin' it. And no beatin' him, either."

"Who is 'he,' Tetwilder?" Bates questioned, intensity lending unnatural glitter to his dark eyes. "Who is 'he'? Come clean, Tetwilder, while you still can."

"Yeah, Tetwilder," Hiram Beckwith agreed, compassionately taking the man's withering left hand. Dropping his street vernacular, Beckwith spoke with correct grammar. And he became strangely philosophical in this most serious of moments: "I'm a friend. And you can unburden your soul to me, as you would to your own brother. Please do it, before it's too late."

A terrible grimace on his face, Petey Tetwilder summoned up his final reserves of strength, "Saw the truth about him at his hideout—awhile—awhile back, when he was—when he was givin' me some new orders. That mook had some kinda long rod with him, and he was playin' with the thing. Struck me why he'd be fiddlin' with somethin' so—so...." he trailed off, unable to continue.

Several seconds passed and he started again, willing himself to answer Beckwith questions. "There was somethin' else, too—some papers he hadn't meant for me to see. But—but I did anyway," the dying man reported in a whisper, proud of himself for his powers of observation. "Guess he'd knocked 'em off his desk, before I came in. When his assistant showed me into the Resurrectionist's private room, I musta walked in on him, pickin' 'em up from the floor and puttin' 'em back where he'd found 'em."

Now it was Bates' turn at bat: "This assistant of his. Name for the guy?"

"Can't remember it, right now. Seen that guy only once or twice. I—I hurt so—so damn' bad..." he whined, his body drawing up even more, his skin resembling old parchment. "All's I c'n remember," he recalled softly, "is that that clown was grinnin' an awful lot, like Bela Lugosi in *Dracula*. Just grinnin' and grinnin'. And gabbin' about the sweet stuff, that 'sugar.' Hell—it's all they talked about with some of us men. Or at least, the ones who used dope."

"Sugar" again! An admission of dope use this was, to Harvey Bates' mind. He sadly shook his head over the lives, that of Petey among them, this garbage called "sugar" had ruined. There was no point in condemning this dying man with a harangue about the evils of the stuff. It was already too late for that kind of thing. But it wasn't too late for something else.

Harvey Bates was conducting a criminal investigation under orders of Secret Agent X. To that end the giant had already assigned some of his own operatives, men and women of the Bates Detective Agency, upon his arrival at the hospital's emergency room. Likely these gumshoes would relate some of the same information to Bates, after he and Beckwith departed the emergency room. But equally as probable, they would report some additional intelligence.

In the meantime, Tetwilder continued to babble, unspooling a veritable roll of nonsensical statements. Neither Bates nor Beckwith stopped him. After a few minutes of this, Bates realized he would need to steer the conversation back to those papers Tetwilder had seen.

Features frozen in a grimace, Petey Tetwilder's head lolled like a doll on his scrawny neck. More seconds passed, after which he remembered, "Looked like they was some type o' legal papers—leastwise, I *think* they was legal—sittin' there. Couldn't—couldn't see nothin' but the top edge of one of them and the lower part of another."

"Any writing on them?" Bates queried, his dark eyes sharp like stiletto's tips.

Tetwilder gasped, "I don't read so good. Never saw much need of it. Anyhow, I thought I saw a seal on one of 'em. You know—like the seal they—they use for the State of New York," he paused between shallow breaths.

"Certain about that?" Bates clipped his question. "It really was an official document of the State?"

Seized afresh was the dope addict's body. That terrible convulsion shook his entire form. He hadn't long, Bates knew. Yet miraculously the fit passed. And somehow the redheaded man gasped out more words, more of the brownish fluid seeping from between his lips: "Hell, I ain't no—no damn' mouthpiece. But like I said, I fig—figgered it was the real thing from the State of New York. I'll say this: It wasn't like anything I'd seen since—since hookin' up with the Resurrectionist."

Harvey Bates was thinking through the man's words when Hiram Beckwith, much more intelligent than he portrayed himself, blurted, "He could've seen articles of incorporation or even a certificate of incorporation, Bates."

Beckwith leaned over the man, "Did any filigree run along the paper's edge?"

"What the hell is 'filigree'?"

"Tracery, squiggles. It's for decoration, especially on official documents."

"Mebbe so. I—yeah, yeah," he gasped, eyes brightening a little. "There *was* some squiggles, now that you mention it. Gold, I think. Anyhow, what the hell's that got ta do with anythin'?"

"The squiggles, the filigree, would mark it as a certificate issued by Albany, Tetwilder," Hiram Beckwith clarified, with his mention of the capital. "It would mean he saw a certificate of incorporation, Bates. It means, in other words, that the State had already allowed the Resurrectionist's scheme to become legal."

It was now Harvey Bates' turn: "All right,

Tetwilder, that's settled. Go back to the lower edge of the other paper. What did you see there?"

"Think it was a—a signature," the man gasped. "Actually a couple o' them. But I've told you, damn it—I don't read too good. So I couldn't make out the names."

This was a blow, since Bates and Beckwith had hoped the man might cough up a name in back of this mess.

Meanwhile, Tetwilder continued, "Ya wanna know somethin' else, though? This stuff let me onta the fact that the Resurrectionist was plannin' to do somethin' big. Then that set me to thinkin' about what he'd done—to me and to the others," he said amidst more of the shallow breaths. "Made me wanna get even, see, 'cause—'cause I was tired o'—his big damn' promises. And I was ready to do anythin' to stop all o' this pain and the seizures—day in, day out. You get me?"

Bobbing his head in agreement, Hiram Beckwith started the next line of questioning: "Which others do you mean, Tetwilder? Who else is involved with the Resurrectionist?"

Nodding ever so slightly, Tetwilder curled his desiccated lips into sad excuse for a smile. He informed, "More of the Boss' recruits. Fellas like—like me and Tiny and them other guys that offed Pat Calvert. Resurrectionist is gonna grab more of them workin' stiffs to do his dirty work. And them clowns like Pat Calvert? Boss has got some *real special* plans for 'em—and for the ones comin' later. But he's savin' the best for your friend, Mr. X."

"That so?" Bates posed.

"Yeah. Gonna ruin X, okeh? Learn his real name and his other secret—somethin' he's been hidin' for years. Then the Boss'll destroy him and his headquarters, with you two as part of the bargain. Resurrectionist has been planning this for years. Hell, I wish—" his hands worked in that wringing way of the dying, and he gritted through rapidly desiccating lips: "I wish I could be there to see the great Agent X get his."

A deeply troubled Beckwith looked quietly at his associate Bates. The giant was flat-cheeked with grimness. Sure, he and Beckwith heard this kind of thing before. Now however, a dying man was saying it. And he wasn't just any fellow on his death bed, but an opponent with connections to an old, though as yet unknown, enemy. It was unsettling, this man's account. And it just might come true, if they didn't get on the stick and locate their mysterious foe.

Gasping, Tetwilder went on, matter-of-factly: "Once all of you are—are outta the way, the Resurrectionist will remake the rest of us into his—his private little army—with every one of us bein' unstoppable. We'll—we'll take over New York, he promised. Maybe the whole damn' country. I ain't gonna see it. But I'm satisfied with one thing."

Harvey Bates wanted to know what that one thing might be.

"I know 'im," Petey Tetwilder gasped in pain, "I know who the Resurrectionist *really* is. Fact, I heard that assistant of his slip up and call the boss by his right name, when they let me in his office. I—"

Tetwilder's words rekindled the light of hope for Bates. He commanded the dying criminal with words of razor sharpness, "Answer me, Tetwilder! What is the Resurrectionist's 'right name'? Who is he?"

Pain-maddened, the man willed himself to focus on the question. Then he muttered through clenched teeth, the light in his eyes dying out: "He's—he's...."

He slid deeper and deeper into the abyss of pain. Suddenly he locked a death grip on the hand of Bates and choked out his final words, "Oh, God, the pain! The pain! Damn him! I hope that gadget barbeques him like a side of beef! Damn that Devil to hell! Damn that D—"

Bloodshot eyes bulging from his sockets, he expired.

And right in front of Bates, Beckwith, and the people from the hospital, Petey Tetwilder's body shriveled like an aged flower pressed between the pages of a book. The process left little more than something resembling a leather bag, his mummified flesh, which stretched most hideously over a collection of rather loose sticks, his bones.

Not normally a squeamish man, Hiram Beckwith practically fainted at the hideous tableau spread before his eyes.

"Damn it ta hell, big man," the horrified Beckwith whispered to Harvey Bates. "I've seen death and I've seen *death*. But this has gotta be the grand prize winner of all time."

Motioning Beckwith to one side where they would have privacy, Bates spoke with unusual frankness: "Gotten ourselves into a terrible fix. Agent X will want to know about Tetwilder's death as quickly as possible. Get outside to the car and use the radio in the console to call my detective agency. Tell them everything you've seen in here, as well as what we've heard. X will check in with them at the first opportunity—if they don't reach him first, of course. Must get to the bottom of this business before any more lives are lost. And emphasize that our club is at least two touchdowns behind right now, as it is."

"Gotcha, Bates," Beckwith nodded.

Sprinting legs carried the fat hackie outside the emergency room to the street beyond.

The physicians, meanwhile, collected a few final tissue samples and a vial of blood from Tetwilder's body. Bates marched over between two of them. The older of the fellows, the one to Bates' left, was tall, skinnier than a rail, wispy of hair, and coarse of features. A younger, baby-faced man with a fuzzy, strawberry blond goatee stood to Bates' right.

X's assistant promptly engaged the younger physician in conversation: "Need some of those tissue and blood samples, if you could spare some."

The doctor—his name badge showed Theodore Pontius—wasn't budging. Giving specimens to an outsider violated hospital policy in the worst way, he told Bates, eyeing X's assistant with unusual interest. "And anyhow, who do you think *you* are," he pompously questioned in a surprising baritone, "to think you have the right to ask for one?"

"Here, here," the older doctor—his badge read Cole Sipes—placed a firm hand on his younger colleague's shoulder. "You needn't be so rude to this man. He merely asked you a question."

Smiling, Bates pulled his wallet back out, flashed the Federal badge he'd used earlier with Inspector Burks. He let the physician get a good look at the silvery article.

"You see who *I* am?" he countered, his voice growing a bit stern. "Just one of your Uncle Sammy's favorite nephews."

The younger doctor immediately blurted, "My God, a Federal man! You're—then you're involved with this thing? I mean, the G-men are—"

"Right."

"That, um, that's different. Something big must be in the wind, I take it."

"Could say that."

"What will you do with the sample?"

Dr. Sipes politely asked, "I'm sure you'll be testing it at a lab, won't you, Mr.—?"

"Bates," was all the name Harvey would supply. "And Dr. Sipes is correct. I'll run it by the boys in the lab, here in New York. Be surprised what they can discover. Might even make your hair stand on end, especially if the guy was taking a new kind of dope, as we suspect."

Of course this statement hadn't strayed far from the truth, since Bates *did* intend to "run it by the boys in the lab." He simply didn't tell *which* lab or which "boys" would perform the appropriate chemical tests on the samples. And while he didn't know that Tetwilder was using conventional drugs, every piece of evidence pointed to his having been dosed with *something*. The magic word *dope* just might work the wonders that Agent X needed at the moment.

"Mind letting me have your samples, now?" he concluded, his massive hand extended towards the doctor.

The older sawbones happily obliged: "I've seen what dope is doing to the kids in this city—how those damned cravings have destroyed their lives. So I'm going to give you these two samples. But you've got to promise me that you won't tell anyone about this. I'm doing this strictly on the sly. You understand?"

Bates did, of course. At Sipes' direction, the giant followed Oliver Pontius to a nearby table, on which sat all manner of chemicals, medical tools, and other apparatus needful in an emergency room.

Cooperative and deferential now, Dr. Pontius related, "I'm going to stopper each one of these two vials, so that you don't spill the contents. Be sure to test them quickly, else they will degrade; and then you'll have to throw them away."

Agent X's associate nodding, Pontius reached for the cellophane holding the first rubber stopper. A quick rip tore open the package along its back seam. Next, though, he secreted something like a tiny pill in the vial. He did much the same the thing with the second stopper and vial, concealing both acts from Bates' dark eyes.

"Appreciate your letting me have them, Dr. Pontius," Bates smiled, slipping the two vials into the pocket of his coat.

With a shake of the physician's hand, he concluded, "Be going now, to join my friend outside. Might need to get in touch with both of you in the future."

Stepping closer, homely Dr. Sipes offered him an outstretched hand. "I'll be here if you need me. And I must say that it's a pleasure to help the G-men."

"Probably need your help, if the threat of this Resurrectionist continues, for any length of time."

For his part, a firm-eyed Doctor Pontius cut in, "You can count on it—I mean, you can count on me."

Harvey Bates gave him a single sharp look—it lasted but a second—whereupon he threw up his massive left hand in a quick wave and strode around the corner.

Muttering something about the Resurrectionist, the good Dr. Pontius, in the meantime, promptly marched past a large maintenance closet, the name "Grover Kelley" inscribed on a metal door plate. Just inside that panel, a scrawny, mustachioed, balding fellow, apparently Kelley himself, stood beside a work bench. There he was fiddling with the motor of a vacuum cleaner, starting it and stopping it every so often to determine it's the nature of its malfunction. Though busy with this project, he peered upwards, briefly, to wave and to offer a word of greeting to the man who'd rushed by him. Pontius, however, ignored the man's salutation.

That maintenance man, for his part, shrugged his shoulders and returned to his own task. But an odd glint animated his normally listless blue eyes, however briefly.

In the meantime, Dr. Pontius had reached a nearby phone booth. As with other large metropolitan hospitals, Dewitt Clinton had installed some for patrons' use. Quickly Pontius stabbed a finger into the rotary, dialed a number.

When he had reached the other party, the Doctor identified himself as Resurgos 15. The other speaker promptly passed him off to the Resurrectionist himself, who questioned: "What is your report, Resurgos 15?"

"That big guy brought Petey Tetwilder into the hospital, Resurrectionist."

"Are you referring to Agent X's associate Harvey Bates?"

"Yes, Sir. He introduced himself as 'Bates,' only a little while ago."

"Is he still there?"

"No, he's just left the emergency room—albeit with a surprise, courtesy of yours truly. He's going to curse himself that he didn't watch me any closer, when I gave that sample to him. Thought you needed to know."

"I admire your initiative, Resurgos 15. I will have a high position of power for you when I have destroyed Agent X. Now, I am accompanying some of our men, who were stationed near this hospital. We should be there shortly. And *I* will know exactly what to do with Mr. Hiram Beckwith and Mr. Harvey Bates when we arrive."

"Something else to tell you, too, Sir. I think I know who we're seeking now."

He whispered a name into the phone's mouthpiece, after which the Resurrectionist commanded, "Go back to your work, act as if nothing unusual has happened, and allow Resurgos 20 to take care of everything else. We will settle with the other one, shortly."

Pontius left the booth. The goateed doctor then traced his original path, past that closet. As he moved closer to it, he saw Dr. Sipes once more. That older doctor was standing around, and to the mind of Pontius, looking suspicious.

This caused the strawberry-blond man to ponder Sipes' behavior, and to smile mysteriously. He nodded and smiled at Grover Kelley, this time, too, as he, Pontius, passed that maintainence chamber. And for the second time Kelley trained his listless blue orbs on the doctor. He cracked a smile of his own, encouraged that Pontius had finally shown a sign of good cheer. *Maybe there is hope for that boy, after all*, a whistling Kelley thought to himself as he started fiddling with the vacuum cleaner for the umpteenth time.

From around the corner Harvey Bates cast suspicious eyes as Doctor Pontius strolled back to his post in the emergency room.

Bates would gain nothing in confronting the man, would waste time, in fact, when he needed to follow their latest leads. Still Agent X's associate knew that something suspicious was happening with Pontius. He carefully reached the door from the emergency room onto the street. Peering up and down the thoroughfare he saw nothing amiss. And Hiram Beckwith still awaited him beside the cab. He gave Bates the high sign to indicate that he'd shared the latest intelligence with the Bates Agency's operator.

Without preliminaries another hack pulled up, in this case a white Ford. Three people garbed in silver-white, bulky suits and hoods occupied the front seat: the black-haired driver; a droopy-featured man; and a fellow with a face like a wooden Indian. With his hood, robes, and saint's visage, the Resurrectionist himself claimed sole ownership of the rear seat.

When the vehicle came to a halt, the droopy-faced man stepped out of the cab and fired a single shot at the throat of Hiram Beckwith. Eyes filled with shock, he collapsed to the pavement, dead. The cold-blooded nature of the attack chilled Bates to the bone. Nonetheless, he somehow willed himself into action, running in what seemed like slow motion, towards the white hack.

As unexpectedly the Resurrectionist, too, disembarked the cab, holding two of those weird pistols. He aimed the one in his right hand directly at Bates' feet and squeezed the trigger. A thin snake of liquid hissed from the barrel. A small quantity of the liquid spattered Bates on the uppers of his shoes and the lower hems of his pants legs. Like a flash he stepped backward, prior to the Resurrectionist's next move.

It was a good thing he did.

The hooded miscreant fired his remaining gun, whereupon a cloud of that silvery dust, passed over the liquid; and all hell broke loose.

Blue-white flame *whooshed* all around the feet and ankles of Harvey Bates!

With the body of Hiram Beckwith in tow, the Resurrectionist and his hoodlum scrambled back into the cab and fled the scene.

"It was a good thing you used the two guns and not the one, Sir," the black-haired driver commented over his shoulder.

"Yes, the single gun with the adaptations isn't the safest weapon to employ—is it, Tiny?"

"No, Sir," the driver returned, his head pointed back towards the street. "I can attest to that."

The Resurrectionist questioned, "You are concerned for me, Tiny?"

"Absolutely, Sir."

"I thought so. I reward that kind of devotion with extra 'sugar' and other privileges, you know."

Coffee eyes impassive, Tiny gave a nod, while they continued their mad dash to freedom.

Back on the street fronting the hospital, Harvey Bates was fighting for survival. He had already dropped his frame to the pavement and set his body into a roll. His clothing still a-smolder, he doffed those burning shoes which threatened his very life.

Several men stood there agape with horror, unable to act in the midst of such horrifying events. A female Good Samaritan, a brave nurse, sprinted up to the scene, whipping off her navy-blue nurse's cape as she ran. After she came alongside the giant, the courageous middle-aged woman proceeded to beat out the flames, the risk to herself completely ignored.

In moments she and Bates had smothered the bluish-white flames, only because they had acted with alacrity. She stayed in command of the situation by whistling for one of the bystanders to re-enter the building, summon a couple of orderlies, and send them back with a trundling table. Soon the three of them had transported the shaggy-haired giant back into the hospital's emergency room.

The dark eyes of Harvey Bates were terrible to behold in those moments. He'd sent Hiram Beckwith out there to radio the Agent, and now he, Bates, believed himself responsible for the cabbie's death. He mentally cursed himself for what he perceived as his miserable failure.

The doctors promptly began to assess Bates' condition. Soon a round-faced, rosy-cheeked doctor, Antony Lockwood, came on the scene. A burn specialist, Lockwood ordered Bates assigned to a room, much against the giant's wishes. Still he grudgingly went along with the plan, in so far as they met two of his stipulations. First they must provide him a room with a phone. And second they must assign him police protection in the form of Assistant Inspector Timothy Scallot. That way, no one could come or go to the room, without first clearing it with this police officer.

Dr. Lockwood extended agreement to Bates' conditions, and a pair of orderlies then loaded him aboard a wheelchair. In seconds they had moved him into a private room.

In only a few more minutes, Timothy Scallot had joined him at the hospital; and they began to discuss the latest developments in the case.

Scallot had some new intelligence to report, in regards to those guns that the Resurrectionist's men were using. By all accounts they were target pistols of some sort, as some of the eyewitnesses had speculated. The question now was to determine what kind of weapon was being used, and why had it been chosen.

Bates remained grim over Beckwith's murder, throughout the discussion. Scallot, tough police officer that he was, softened over the loss of Beckwith. The assistant inspector assured Harvey Bates that they would nab the culprits. To keep himself focused on the case and off the man's killing, meanwhile, a tight-lipped Bates reached out and snagged the phone from the nearby nightstand. He needed to know if Miss Arden, his operative, had discovered anything new since the now-dead Beckwith had transmitted his message to the Agency.

Her voice was tense: "We've heard some news from an informant, Sir, something to the effect that the Resurrectionist planned to use Tetwilder's dope ring. We've even rounded up a couple of men who process that 'sugar,' formerly for Tetwilder. Now, they say they're working for that big shot the Resurrectionist. Unfortunately, they didn't know any other information of value—nothing like the location of his headquarters or anything about his identity."

"Makes sense," Bates spoke. "that that so-called 'mastermind' would commandeer someone else's operation. It's a classic case of 'Why reinvent the wheel?' Miss Arden. Tetwilder's would be the set-up to re-use, because he already processes and distributes poison."

Somehow much of Bates' analysis skated past Miss Arden. She reverted, instead, to the subject of Hiram Beckwith: "He—he paid my way through the remainder of business college, Mr. Bates. He was like—like a father to me. It's just like what happened to Mr. Hobart...."

Agent X's associate leaned forward in the bed. "What do you mean, Miss Arden?"

She began to sob. "Sir, we received word from—from Sloan, over at the Hobart Detective Agency. Mr. Hobart had infiltrated that Resurrection Ring, but they've—they've captured him. And that horrible Resurrectionist—oh, God, Mr. Bates, he shot Mr. Hobart dead."

Ever kind, the square-jawed giant consoled her. Once she'd regained her composure, Miss Arden told him that Agent X had transmitted a message over his compact radio. Had she informed the Agent, regarding Tetwilder's death and that of Hobart?

She had done so, she replied. Miss Arden had also told him about Beckwith's suspicion, that the Resurrectionist had already incorporated his Ring. All of this news had unnerved the Secret Agent, rendered him speechless, according to Miss Arden. Such news rendered Bates, too, momentarily dumbstruck.

"Where is the Boss, right now?

"He's at the apartment of a Resurrection man, Tiny Sayre. X said he'd subdued the man and was searching for more clues when we reached him."

"Has he found anything yet?" Bates husked.

"He didn't—didn't elaborate, Sir," her voice broke. "He just said that he needed to conduct this investigation solo from now, not to place any of us in such danger."

"Got to help him, Miss Arden," Bates uttered, steel in his tone. "Get myself checked out of this hospital, and I'll—"

"I'm sorry, Mr. Bates. But he emphasized he was going this one alone. Too much risk to—to you and the rest of us," she concluded, her voice stumbling again.

"Alone..." a solemn Harvey Bates repeated. He felt his square jaw go slack. And he muttered quite involuntarily to himself, "Boss is going to be completely alone...."

CHAPTER XIX
THE DEVILS AND BETTY DALE

X had left the Sayres' residence immediately after his unsettling communication with the Bates Detective Agency. Thus he had no idea about Bates' own return call to Miss Arden. In the same vein the giant had no inkling about the Agent's discovery of Tiny's cache of "sugar." This piece of information had so disturbed the public defender that he simply couldn't bring himself to mention it, even to his closest friends.

That communication he would probably share later on. Right now, he was racing the clock, trying desperately to complete his own research, not to mention keep that appointment with Ham Esler and the Resurrection Ring. Only one locale would afford him the proper safety to do this job.

It was his headquarters at the Montgomery Mansion.

The Agent knew he risked his life, driving out there. But it couldn't be helped in light of the situation's gravity. So he drove like the wind, flat-cheeked with seriousness, wondering what future calamities might befall his surviving operatives before this case was said and done.

No, he couldn't surrender to such despair. He must carry this investigation through to a successful end. This thought, above all, compelled him to press forward.

X pulled into the long street on which the stately manse rose. Still, he didn't park his vehicle in front of his headquarters. He never did this, in fact, as a precaution against those who intended him harm. So he halted his chariot some two blocks prior to reaching the site. From thence he nonchalantly exited his vehicle and assumed the demeanor of a neighbor, out for a walk. His casual though purposeful movement carried him past the Mansion's stately stone walls, its elegant roofs and gables. X came to a halt in front of the structure's wrought iron front gate. Casual observers would have regarded the gate as forlorn in light of that thin coat of rust around its handle.

A careful look to either side of his head assured the Agent that no one watched him. Now he did something most curious. He carefully examined the gate's lock. The outer mechanism appeared intact. A promising sign, this. Clasping the handle with strong, supple fingers, he assayed to lift the piece of metal. Yet Agent X wasn't trying to enter by this path, oddly enough. Rather, he needed to ascertain whether the lock had remained fused shut in his absence, rather than drilled out.

The lock still unharmed, a whistling Man of a Thousand Faces strolled around to one of the side walls. Thick and wide was a square, granite pillar which was the focus of his gaze. That stony support was wider than a football player's shoulders, as were all the posts which stood sentry around the yard's walls.

Again pivoting his head in both directions, the Secret Agent determined that no one was observing his actions. He ran his sensitive fingers around the top of the pillar in search of a certain *something*. Countersunk into the surface of the stone lay the object of the preying fingers' hunt: a circular button cast from polystyrene.

The Agent's right index finger stabbed the surface of that disk, at which point the stony pillar pivoted outward on a sophisticated hinge mechanism. This act revealed the grounds of the mansion proper. X cat-toed through the opened portal, reached to the inside wall, and touched a mate to the polystyrene button on the top of the pillar. As smoothly as a train on a track, the stone support glided back into its original position.

Up the cracked red brick walk and through a tired and neglected garden, the Agent trotted to the building's front door. This portal of the edifice, too, showed no signs of tampering. Unlike that outer gate, though, this entryway was operable. So without misgivings the Secret Agent unlocked another complex mechanism, using a special key he extracted from his pocket. Effortlessly, he glided through a spacious foyer, past a sumptuous dining room, and onto a long, wide hallway.

Along either side of this corridor, his extensive crime library, his archives, an armory, and a forensics laboratory awaited his beck and call. Right now he required the services of his laboratory and his library, more than he needed any other resources.

Into the laboratory he ventured, features resolute. Quickly he plucked that sample of tannish material from the envelope in his pocket. He also produced that business card retrieved from the body of Lothian and the piece of a pamphlet from Tiny's apartment. These would be easy to test, he thought. He saved that specimen of "sugar" for last, though. It would be the most difficult, not to mention the most disturbing, clue of all to analyze.

A nearby shelf held a glass bottle of a reagent. The detective removed a tiny, soft-bristled brush from a rectangular container in a drawer beneath the shelves. X inserted the implement in the bottle of reagent. His action thus moistened the brush for the task at hand.

Those bristles he swept, albeit delicately, over the surface of the card. His chemical brought out no alphabetic characters, no numbers, no images, nothing at all. He realized he would need another reagent, were he to render any of its information visible again. So he cast his eyes back to that same shelf which housed the original reagent. Next to this bottle he had placed another chemical preparation. He removed another of the small brushes from the container and repeated the previous procedure. Unfortunately this reagent produced the same result, as did *ten more tests with reagents*, all of a different class.

His features adopted a brief scowl. Scientists and inventors had devised over four hundred different agents for invisible writing. Still the average person would use only a handful of them, at best, usually settling on one or two. X had thought that he would hit it lucky, would discover, readily, the specific form of ink the Resurrectionist had used to hide his messages from prying eyes. The devastating truth abruptly hit the detective like freight train striking him, ninety to nothing. His enemy had adopted the same chemical for secret writing, or disappearing ink, that Secret Agent himself used before his recorded career, discarded, then lately resumed, for reasons unknown....

Shaken to his core, the man of mystery paused briefly before he turned to the next tests. These he would conduct on that oleaginous matter, tan in color, he'd salvaged from the murder scene of Stu Lothian. Out of the envelope came that gob, along with the crumbs located nearby.

An ungainly-looking piece of apparatus would perform the first part of this test for him. The gray steel object alternated a series of short, fat cylinders with long, slender ones. This entire affair concluded in a shell of sorts, which, if anything, resembled a pair of metallic punch bowls turned in opposite directions and placed atop each other.

The machine was an electron microscope, one of the most sophisticated and valuable pieces of equipment in his war on crime.*

Agent X carefully placed the pointed tan object in the microscope's specimen holder. Then he sealed the thing inside his machine. After another second he had activated it by a side switch.

He looked carefully at the image which appeared on its photographic plate, near the base. And he was glad he had built this powerful instrument. It showed him a few droplets of some sort, seeping, apparently, from the pointed article itself.

Of course, that mystery item might have acquired the moisture from the street. But he magnified the image a bit more, so as to gain

*** AUTHOR'S NOTE: This type of microscope is a fairly new weapon in the scientific arsenal, one which uses a beam of electrons, not light, to magnify the size of an object. Developed only eight years ago by German physicist Ernst Ruska and electrical engineer Max Knoll, this machine enables a researcher to see objects imperceptible to light microscopes, which can magnify something no smaller than 1/50,000th of an inch. In contrast, the electron microscope can enlarge an image much smaller than this. The device works in this manner: A high voltage beam of electrons is shot from an electron gun at the top of the microscope's housing. At the next stage the beam passes through alternating electromagnetic lenses, substitutes for the glass lens of a light microscope, and a pair of condenser apparatus. Eventually the beam of electrons strikes the specimen holder and magnetic objective lenses, picking up an image of the object to be studied. Ultimately the beam carries the image to a fluorescent screen-and-camera arrangement, enabling the scientist to see and analyze the object in question. The Agent tells me that the electron microscope will be a common device, not only in medicine, biology, microbiology, and virology; but also in crime analysis of future decades.**

a clearer picture of the specimen. Enough of it remained so that he could tell this about the clue: Someone had fitted symmetrical halves of the thing together while manufacturing it. Even in spite of this current damage, the Secret Agent could determine this much. And under the microscope's all-seeing eye, X could readily see something else: the remains of its hollow center. This had been the source of the object's seepage, and thus another factor requiring his analysis.

Carefully he removed the specimen from the microscope's holder and deposited that sample inside his spectrometer. As the thing beamed its light over it, he gathered a notebook for recording its findings and making calculations. Shortly the spectrometer had completed its work. X made some quick notations on his paper.

Now came the last one of his scientific inquiries: a chemical analysis of the "sugar."

With a shaking right hand, he poured a tiny quantity of the liquid into a basin specially fitted for the spectrometer. For the final time the machine subjected a sample to its analysis. When it completed its task, the tense detective pulled the basin from the machine. Here too he made the requisite notes on his paper. He was rapidly becoming antsy over his findings; but no matter the outcome, he couldn't stop at this stage of his investigation. The Man of a Thousand Faces knew he must press on. He must check his own discoveries against prior ones recorded in his extensive library.

Hence down the hall to the bookshelves the grave public defender marched, his long fingers pulling out numerous volumes. His choices might have seemed random to someone less versed in modern medicine. Certainly, they were a disparate lot, this gathering of scientific minds, under the covers of those books. Some of their writers were specialists in microbiology, the study of microscopic forms of life. Works by bacteriologists joined this number, too, as did additional texts by virologists.

X seated his muscular frame at a large desk. On thumbing the pages of his books, he decided he wasn't completely satisfied with the collection he'd chosen for the initial search. He knew that certain treatises were missing from this group, but he couldn't remember where he'd last put them. Suddenly he remembered the reason for their absence on the shelves. Agent X had separated them intentionally from the rest of the collection. Every one of them fell into the area of classified research, studies available only to government or military officials with a special clearance.

Arising, the Man of a Thousand Faces strode towards a corner of his crime library. In that area a single door guarded the entrance to a side room. He unlocked the portal in question. Switching on its light, he passed into the chamber, home to a large collection of government pamphlets. Among other things, these documents combined his digests or summaries of the strange weapons he'd captured through the years, along with government scientists' analyses of their destructive powers. They also contained material equally as top secret.

They preserved the scientific records of the project which had created Secret Agent X.

That was, in fact, what all of this affair was about. All of the killing, all of the destruction: It all revolved around Project Anastasis, the government program which had enabled

Secret Agent X to fake his own death and return from the grave.

Disguised eyes dark and forbidding as hell's pits, he slipped a pair of stiff, black cardboard boxes, both rectangular shaped, from the bookshelf immediately inside the door. His mouth remained a hard line as he put a box in either hand, turned off the light, and regained his chair at the desk.

Doctor Charles Darwin Osben's name adorned the cover of each folder he drew forth from the record boxes. Those cardboard sleeves shared the same byline with a number of the microbiology texts which the Agent had lifted from his bookcase.

Kind old Dr. Osben, the Secret Agent thought ruefully to himself. *He never knew how this thing would involve such violence, such murder and mayhem....*

X roved to the index of the first microbiology text to locate the topic he needed. When he'd traced it to the proper page, he wandered also to some of the folders, extracted some of these documents, too.

Osben had been a visionary in his views about the importance of microbiology, the investigator remembered. The physician had believed, even before X met him, that this branch of science would prove one of the most valuable to mankind in coming years. The medico had dedicated himself to it for this very reason, with the classic doctor's philosophy of, first, doing no harm, and second, of alleviating suffering and improving human life.

But Osben had felt such guilt over what he considered his failure, Project Anastasis. That was the reason he'd committed suicide, so Agent X had heard. He and his colleague Emel, later a murder victim, had developed a flawed scientific product when they'd studied the organisms they had chosen for the experiment.

X hadn't died from the experiment, though. In the absence of Doctor Osben, X had developed a treatment of his own, and it had done the trick. He was, after all, a scientist of no mean ability. Without warning his eyes suddenly acquired a compelling light.

His fingers flipped rapidly to the chapter in question. That section of the book and a corresponding set of folders both treated the microscopic organism known as the tardigrade, the "slow walker," or, colloquially, the water bear. They were fascinating creatures, these tiny beasts. And only a portion of their interest lay in the fact that the eight-legged, microscopic animals—for they *were* animals—resembled a member of the family *Ursidae*, or a bear.

Tardigrades, he read Osben's text, fall under the phylum Tardigrada. Tiny creatures, they usually measure only 1/100th-2/100th of an inch in length. Also they possess bodies of four segments, minus their heads; and they lack joints in their legs. Each one of their feet usually ends in either four or eight claws per appendage. And they periodically engage in molting, or the shedding of their skin.

In terms of food, some water bears consume plants and are thus phytophagous. Another category of them subsists off bacteria, meaning they are bacteriophagous. There is a final group of them which are predatory, that is, they feed off other microorganisms.

X's eyes roved through the paragraphs, only scanning some of the material about the animals' morphology, shape, and their reproductive habits.

He came finally to the discussion of their

habitats, underlining such material as this: The tardigrades usually inhabit water or watery mosses, though, biologists have discovered them in the Tibetan Himalayas, as well in solid ice and in sediments from the ocean. Osben concluded with words to the effect that tardigrades, water bears, were truly hardy little creatures. This was one of the rare comments that Osben made in his book.

Osben's textbook was a classic case of a medical treatise that was dry as dust—long on facts and analysis, but short on vision.

He himself did not lack that quality, however, as he'd explored it in some of those classified papers mined from the folder.

The Man of a Thousand Faces turned to the appropriate page in one of them. According to Osben's summary, scientists had observed a most unique ability possessed by tardigrades. Namely, the animals could survive extremes of cold and heat which would kill nearly all other animals. More specifically, some of them had survived temperatures verging on the so-called absolute zero, or -459 °F. Others, in contrast, had been subjected to temperatures of 304 °F. And in either instance, the animals had emerged little the worse for wear. Osben had to qualify this fact, of course, with the disclaimer that the animals not be placed in a high temperature environment for more than a few minutes, or a low temperature one, for more than a few days.

X continued his race against the clock, in order that he might make his scheduled meeting with the Resurrectionist later this night. Pencil and paper on hand, he scribbled copious notes as he pored over Osben's classified findings. They were the news which had actually driven the man of mystery to this doctor in the first place. The Secret Agent would need every bit of the physician's knowledge and more than a smidgen of luck if he, the man-hunter, were correct in his speculation: Charles Darwin Osben, like X himself, had faked his death and most likely assumed a new identity....

As the brilliant detective went about his research, his beloved Betty Dale conducted an inquiry of her own at the Caledonian Memorial Gardens. The staff was holding a late afternoon and early evening visitation for a deceased young woman. She had suffered an automobile accident with no connections to the Resurrection Ring. Acting most unconventionally, Betty regarded this event as her best opportunity to question the McGrieves about their connection with Roddy Shingle. Her arrival there might actually catch them off-guard, since they wouldn't expect her visit.

While she drove, Betty recalled what had finally happened at the Jazzy Kat, the night she had visited that club. There the beautiful Latin singer had briefly left the table where she and Betty had been talking. When she had returned, she told Betty more about Shingle and his connection to Butch Spangler. As it happened, the two men had indeed discussed a partnership before Shingle's murder. But his killing had ended that. And even before his death, Roddy Shingle had expressed great ambivalence about combining operations with another person. He was, she maintained, a businessman who needed to get his products to his customers. And he needed to do it without the interference of another person, namely Butch Spangler.

The Ramos woman described everything, Betty thought, in such commonplace terms. To hear Ramos tell it, Roddy Shingle might have built the most honest, commercial-minded reputation in New York. Betty couldn't help but say that he sounded like the envy of every pro-business person in the city.

X's companion had reminded D. Ramos that Roddy hadn't amassed the most honest record, though, and that he'd operated the most successful drug ring in the city. Further, the city and county authorities had indicted him more than once on charges of running a dope ring—transporting and selling the vile stuff. He had beaten back his legal opponents only by way of his clever mouthpieces, lawyers, and their legal maneuvering. Allegations of jury tampering and intimidation of witnesses also had dogged the man. Eventually the Feds had gotten involved in his activities, had intended to prosecute him for the most serious crimes. So he was, Betty related, not exactly a saint.

Dark eyes flashing with the heat of indignation, Miss D. Ramos didn't care about all of this, she told Betty. He hadn't been convicted on any of the charges. To her, Shingle was and would always be "*mi Rodrigo*"; and she loved him deeply.

Shaking her head in frustration, Betty had realized this would be a fruitless approach to the issue of Shingle's criminal enterprises. So she went about her interrogation in a different way. She asked for more information about Shingle and his ambivalence over the deal with Spangler. Why had Shingle wanted to join forces with the other fellow, only to back out several times?

"Someone—someone was 'putting the squeeze' on his *grupo*," she had admitted, using a Spanish word for an outfit or operation. Daubing at her tearful eyes with her handkerchief, she narrated, "I told him he should geeve een to them. They would keel him, otherwise. I think my worrrds finally perrrsuade him. But eet was too late. Too late," she whispered and cried.

After her brief, tearful outburst, she had resumed, "I think this is all Victor McGrieve's fault. He is responsible for this murrrder and all of the other crrrimes too. He and his son."

"Jay-Jay?" Betty had quizzed.

"No, Malcolm."

"But he's dead, isn't he?"

"No, he is alive. And *he* is the Resurrectionist."

The heart of Agent X's beloved had begun racing like a dog chasing a fox. She could hardly conceal her excitement by her sweet smile. Somehow, though, she thanked the Spanish beauty for clarifying the relationship between her, Miss Ramos', and Roddy Shingle. Betty Dale had then taken her leave from the Jazzy Kat, not cognizant of the fact that some of the Resurrectionist's men were trailing her, night and day.

She was more preoccupied with the Latin singer's use of the phrase, "putting the squeeze," on Shingle's drug operation. How was it that Ramos seemed to know an American gangster's idiom like this, yet she didn't know simple English words like *precious*, for instance? Perhaps it originated from her constant contact with mob lords like Shingle. But perhaps there was something more here.

Her car had now reached Caledonian Gardens. In a matter of seconds she had passed through the front entrance. Betty introduced herself to Viola Vye, Caledonian's female employee, as a writer for the *Herald.* X's companion expressed her desire to speak with Victor McGrieve. But Viola informed her that McGrieve the elder had gone out for an early dinner. He wouldn't return for another half an hour or so. But Betty could wait in Viola's office if she'd like. Viola cheerfully informed she would get them some coffee and return shortly.

Betty thanked her for the hospitality and on reflection, decided that waiting here for McGrieve was the best plan. In truth it would afford her the chance to question Viola too. Secretaries were often the ones with the most information about an organization, if Betty's prior experiences meant anything.

The Vye woman came back, two cups of java in tow.

Once she'd put them on her desk, Betty started her interrogation. How long had Miss Vye worked at Caledonian Gardens?

Since 1937, was the woman's response. And what types of work had she done before her time here? Viola related that she had performed secretarial functions for a number of businesses. Right now she was responsible for the usual things like typing and so forth, as well as arranging burials, selling caskets, that type of work.

Betty nodded as she wrote in a small notebook she had pulled from her purse. She swiveled her head around the room as Viola Vye went on. As Betty took in the sights here, the woman described in great detail the day-to-day activities of running a funeral home. It was all Betty could do, trying to stifle a yawn at such mundane affairs. Finally, though, the woman alluded to insurance. They sold it, or rather Miss Vye did, here at Caledonian Memorial Gardens.

The sapphire eyes of Betty brightened with interest. "Really? I didn't know that Caledonian sold insurance. I thought that Mr. McGrieve was—"

"—Barred from its sale?" Viola smiled. "He was, in fact, after the court ruled against him and sentenced him to jail. But after he'd completed his time there, he could return to the industry on a probationary basis. He's in that period now, near the end of it, as a matter of fact. Until he completes the last of that sentence, however, someone else would have to run the insurance end of his business."

"And I suppose you're the one doing that?" was Betty's next question.

Viola Vye offered a most lovely smile. "That, I am. I handle burial insurance and life insurance policies at a number of different levels of coverage. I couldn't interest you in one, could I?"

X's friend smiled politely. "I don't think so, right now. I would, however, like to know about their features: rates for premiums, levels of benefits, and anything else. Have you some informational brochures on hand?"

The woman opened her desk and pulled out one of the documents in question. She handed the crisp, white paper object, blue-bordered, across the desk to Betty Dale, who immediately noticed a heading: "Life from Death!" It was superimposed over a small, stylized drawing of a bluish lilac. Several lines of typeface followed the declaration, whereupon the booklet invited the reader to look inside.

Betty did so. And her lovely mouth failed to hide a perfect "O" of horror.

"I don't think this has anything at all to do with Caledonian, now, does it?" Betty suddenly fixed sharp blue eyes on the young woman and showed her the brochure.

Squirming in her chair, Betty's hostess stammered, her voice tightening to piano wire tautness: "Oh, I—I see I've given you the wrong advertisement. It, um, it contains a—a number of typographical errors, regarding the policies here. There are also errors in—in the rates for the premiums. Give me that pamphlet, and you can have one of these."

She extracted another brochure from the desk. This one was plain white, with the name Caledonian Life Assurance Company emblazoned across the top.

"I believe," Betty said, arising from the chair, "I'll hold onto the one I already have. Besides, why should a little brochure make you so uncomfortable, Miss Vye?"

"I—that's no concern of yours. Please return it to me now," the woman quavered, her hand reaching under the desk.

The Secret Agent's friend and companion came back, "I don't think I will. This policy will most certainly interest a friend of mine. He will find it *most* attractive—especially when he finds out the connection with the McGrieves—"

"You think that Malcolm is behind this. That's what you're implying," Viola said, resentfully. "You think *he's* the one who's really the Resurrect—"

Voice firm, Betty continued, moving away from her chair after the woman's interruption: "As I started to say: My friend will also be interested to know that *lilac* really means—"

"—It means, Miss Dale," a male voice from behind promised, "you'll surely die, along with Secret Agent X. Now please, surrender that brochure."

Betty remained adamant, holding onto the paper booklet rather than letting it drop onto Viola Vye's desk. Meanwhile, Viola Vye seemed to have become a block of ice; for she remained frozen. Something told X's companion to wheel around, to face this person. That individual was, to her, a complete stranger. However, Betty did recognize menace when she saw it, not to mention false courtesy, as expressed in his oily tone of voice. With his right hand, that newcomer clutched one of the target pistols. Pointing it at Betty's neck, the unfamiliar man stated, too politely, "I requested that you give me the brochure, Miss Dale. Now, I'm *telling* you to hand it over. I promise you, I *will not miss*, as close as I am...."

The public defender's friend threw a glaring look, first at this fellow and then at Viola. Betty thought about ducking beneath the stranger's gun hand or maybe throwing her purse at the man. The native intuition of X's companion caused her to peer a final time over her shoulder. But she knew any action towards her captor wouldn't have mattered anyway.

Without warning, the stranger squeezed the trigger. The bullet hit her, directly in the neck. And sweet Betty Dale died.

"I didn't say I wouldn't shoot her," the man rationalized. "I promised only that I wouldn't miss, being so close."

A strange expression suffused the pretty features of Viola Vye. She knew exactly who the man was. But Betty Dale wouldn't have known, of course, that this was the mysterious Mr. Ramond, who'd begun to grin and bray now, like a bearded jackass.

Secret Agent *was* indeed alone now, as Harvey Bates had predicted. Alone, but bound and determined to make his rendezvous with the minions of hell.

CHAPTER XX
DESCENT INTO HELL

ONLY moments after the pick-up time of 7:00 pm, Agent X had screeched to a halt outside the ramshackle structure, the Blue Streak Cab Company.

Garbed in a dirty, short-sleeved shirt of pea green and dark green pants, the hook-nosed Ham Esler was standing there at the ready when the disguised detective pulled up. As soon as he'd taken a seat in the auto, Esler complained that X was pushing his luck, cutting everything so close to their appointment and meeting with the Resurrectionist.

They zoomed off to their destination. Esler took a cigarette from a battered pack in his shirt pocket, shoved the paper tube between his waiting lips.

"I'm gettin' good money, sellin' this information, you know," he bragged as he fired the cigarette with a match, and crammed the coffin nail underneath his long, doleful upper lip.

The Secret Agent responded, "Sure you are, Ham. You're not the only one, either. But I had some things to do before I came out here."

Esler cut his cynical shoe button eyes to his left. "Yeah—betcha did. But if someone tells *me* he's gonna pick me up at seven o'clock, or any other time, then I expect him there *on time*. That's me—Punctual Ham Esler," he designated, drawing some of the pungent tobacco's fumes into his lungs. "Time *is* money. And money makes the world go around, as they say. I aim to get my share of it. Fact is, I know how to get at that clown, Secret Agent X."

They were coming after him, all right, this Resurrection Ring. Doling out numberless quantities of money to do their job, too, it seemed. Agent X maintained his role as Tiny to learn exactly what Esler meant by his declaration.

Crossing his legs there on the car seat, the crooked cabbie drawled in response, "Well, Tiny, it's like this: Two years ago I was runnin' the field operation for a dope outfit. They were a bunch o' losers, those guys—Wicker, Stien, and Nixon were their names. Anyhow Agent X figured out who I was, and he captured me. Drugged me too, and passed me off to the law. And the funny thing was, my thoughts were jumbled like lottery slips in a barrel.

"Way I figure it, the Agent took part o' my memory with that drug o' his. But that's okeh. Resurrectionist is better than my last bosses were, any day. A while back he got a smart mouthpiece for me, that Hamlet Marley, while I was in stir. Then after he got me paroled, some guy with a beard shot me up with some kinda dope. 'Course, he couldn't restore all of my memories; but his junk finally brought some of 'em back. One of them, especially."

"Really? Which one?" X continued to look straight ahead.

"The location of Mr. X's headquarters. Slick, huh?" the man concluded, his little shoe button eyes taking on a cocky glitter.

Secret Agent X felt his stomach fall, like a stone plummeting from a cliff. If this man remembered the whereabouts of the Montgomery Mansion, then it would be a matter of time before he'd be ponying up that same intelligence to the Resurrectionist. X had to ensure that Ham Esler never got the chance to deliver his message.

First, however, the Secret Agent must determine the location of their rendezvous without letting on his ignorance of its whereabouts.

"You still taking dope these days, Esler?" he interrogated the man.

"If it's snow you mean, then, yeah. But if you're talkin' about that 'sugar'? *Hell, no!* I ain't fool enough to take that junk. Heard too much bad stuff about it on the street."

A geyser of laughter could have erupted from the Agent's disguised lips. Esler thought cocaine was safe and "sugar" was harmful? The detective kept his editorial to himself but delivered this revelation, in Tiny's name: "Well, I'm taking 'sugar.' And I need some right now. Why don't I drive back to my place, and—"

"Hell, you don't have time!" a frustrated Esler blurted. "We'd have to go all the way back to your apartment, over in Hell's Kitchen. Then we'd be racin' like a horse, all the way back to the Meatpacking District, and that old warehouse near Stu Lothian's joint. Ain't no way in hell we can do that. Besides, I gots me a supply of it, anyway."

That took care of the low-down on their rendezvous, X thought to himself. Now he followed another trail, an interested light projecting from his eyes: "Say, what's this about your supply of 'sugar'? I thought you didn't use the stuff."

"That doesn't mean I wouldn't *sell* that dope," Esler snickered. "You see, I'm just a businessman, capitalizin' on an opportunity to serve the community."

He brayed like a donkey this time, as if this were the witticism to end them all.

X probed, "How did you get your stash?"

"One of your boss's men, that big blond Swede, uses hell out of it. And he stole a lot of it, too, when his boss wasn't lookin'. It's good, concentrated stuff, bound to keep the customers comin' back. Well, he sold me what *he* had, for some quick cash. He figured the two of us might peddle the rest of it and rake in a little of the green stuff on the side. Nothin' like a man pullin' himself up by the bootstraps, eh?"

"I'll say," the Secret Agent barely masked his fury, wanting to choke the man till a fly wouldn't light. "Sounds to me like you'd have a nifty racket going—selling information and selling dope, through your own operation."

Throwing his head back, Ham Esler removed the coffin nail from between his thin lips; and he blew a long plume of smoke from his mouth. He aimed a cynical laugh at his supposed ally. "Bet you'd like to get in on the ground floor o' my racket, wouldn't you, Tiny?"

They stopped beneath a red traffic signal. X turned his head briefly in Tiny's direction and said, "Depends on what's in it for me, Esler. I'm getting good money from the Resurrectionist already. Plus, I'm getting all the 'sugar' I want. You'd have to guarantee more of both than he can. And I doubt that's something you can do."

"I could make the deal sweeter than candy for you, big man. I could pay you more than he's payin'. And besides that, you wouldn't have to depend on the boss anymore for your 'sugar,'" Ham Esler claimed, giving the disguised Agent the hard sell. "Resurrectionist is usin' your muscle, anyway, from what I hear. I'd figure a guy like you would get tired o' that kind o' noise."

The rat's words held great interest for the Secret Agent. As the traffic signal changed to green, he remarked, "So you think he's got me for my muscle, do you?"

"Everybody knows it, Tiny," Esler related,

as though the big driver had been too dumb to catch on. "I thought you'd have known it, too. Jeez, you're *not* thinkin' straight, are you?"

At first the words caught Agent X by surprise. But suddenly he realized their significance and boomed, "Sure—sure. Guess you're right about that. Look—we're pussy-footing around too much, and I want to know more about this deal you have in mind. Are you going to stage a palace coup against the Resurrectionist? Maybe start your own outfit?"

Ham Esler countered, "Nothin' like that. I just thought you'd like to have somethin' to put aside for yourself, as a kind of insurance. 'Course, if you're not *inter*-ested," he ended, he cut his shoe button eyes around to the Agent, "then I can't do anything about it."

The Man of a Thousand Faces decided to play the crooked cabbie like a fiddle. "Fine by me. I don't give a damn anyhow."

Silence ruled the interior of the machine for the next few moments. Agent X knew this approach would entice the man if Esler thought he were dealing with a fellow hood. After all, the rat himself had broached the subject of a deal. And Agent X, knowing the man's greedy personality so well, realized the cabbie wouldn't let the topic rest.

Finally Esler stubbed out his cigarette in the ashtray, whereupon he lit a fresh one. "Look, the Resurrectionist hasn't paid me yet. I think he's a chiseler, if you want to know the truth. He offers one price for information, and then he backs away from it. So I'd consider sellin' you the information about the Secret Agent's hideout, okeh? And I'd throw in the Resurrectionist's plans for the place, once he learns its location. I'd even give you my own two-bits' worth, if it means anything."

His face impassive but his brain crackling with electricity, Secret Agent X reached behind his back into his left rear pant pocket. From it he extracted his wallet and, squeezing it open, permitted the hack driver to see the sheaf of bills crammed inside. As far as Esler could tell, it looked as though the Agent might be carrying the Denver mint on his person.

He reached for the object and exclaimed, "Damn, man! What the hell are you doin', drivin' around with that all those C-notes?"

Grinning, the Agent pulled the wallet away from his passenger and said, "You must not have been listening to me, Esler. I have money—lots of money. But you're not getting any of it, until you cough up the low-down."

"So now you're interested, eh? Then I'm gonna want, oh, five of those centuries for my trouble."

It was then the Agent's turn to laugh at him. "*I'm* not the patsy in this car, Esler. Tell me now—or I squeal to my boss what you've already related to me. I'm sure the Resurrectionist won't let you live long, when he finds out you're a dirty double-crossing *rat*, too."

Unnerved at this prospect, Esler puffed harder at his coffin nail. The tip of it acquired a cherry redness, and his words gained the scarlet of desperation: "I'm gonna—gonna tell him about the Montgomery Mansion, where the Agent hangs his hat. The Resurrectionist said that whenever he gets that information, he's—he's gonna imprison the Agent inside his own headquarters and burn both of 'em with that Wrath of God gadget. But not before cribbin' anything of value in the place."

"Such as?"

"I saw a few books around the joint, big books with dates scribbled on the spines. I'm guessing they're records of his cases. His real name is probably recorded somewhere inside that house, too."

Disguised eyes stern, Agent X reached his right hand towards the gas gun holstered underneath his left arm.

Esler saw the Agent's move and stammered this response, "What's—what's wrong, Tiny? I say something that—"

They stopped at another traffic signal.

"Oh, you've said *just enough*," Agent X now pointed the weapon at his passenger. He changed his voice from Tiny's coarse basso to his own deep, though pleasing tone: "It was all I could do, not to nail you, a few minutes ago. If I didn't have a bit of civilization in me, I would—"

Esler swore, "My—my God! You're X! And you did it to me again!"

"You didn't think I would allow you to get away with your scheme, did you?"

When Esler attempted to answer, X cut in, "Evidently you did, since you were talking as if that delightful bearded man—someone I already know, incidentally—had injected you with a phonograph needle."

"You—you know who he—"

"You're wearing me out, Esler," the Agent gritted his teeth in frustration. "Of course, I do. But that's the way it is with your kind of rat, isn't it, Esler? Always ready to shoot off his mouth and brag about his knowledge or his intentions?"

"Look—we can work this out, X! You can just turn me over to that big fellow in the tall building across town—that guy that makes 'em disappear after he catches 'em. Yeah! I wouldn't give ya any more trouble, 'cause he'd fix things up for me. He—"

"He's not going to help you were you're going, Esler," X said. Squeezing the gun's trigger, he stated, "Your days as an information broker are finished."

A grayish tendril of vapor spiraled from the gun's barrel, wrapped around the man's head. Staring, Ham Esler coughed once and fell over, unconscious, in his seat.

The traffic light changed to green. Not sparing the horses, a relieved Agent gunned his engine, shot the car down the block and towards a small theatre. Unused as this playhouse was in summer, it perfectly suited his purpose.

Quickly he tooled the machine into the building's empty rear loading zone. After he'd stopped his car, he jerked his pocket makeup kit from a pocket. When he'd pulled the requisite materials from its depths, he went to work, first with the volatile plastic.

Only seconds of work with the stuff lent a covering to Esler's face. That done, X dyed his features with special pigment from a jar. In no time the chemical preparation had altered Esler's skin to the color of old parchment. Then with his fingers the Secret Agent squeezed and prodded the plastic so that it became highly wrinkled, a fine-bladed sculpting tool completing the job.

X examined his handiwork. To his great satisfaction, Esler now looked exactly like a victim who was dying from the "sugar." And insensate as he was, he would easily pass muster with the Resurrectionist and his gang of murderers.

This wasn't all the Agent did, however. He made a quick search of Esler's pockets with the goal being to find some of the "sugar" in the man's possession. Sure enough, the man's inside coat pocket yielded several vials of the stuff. These containers he immediately transferred to his own clothing. They would play a critical role in his plan, once he'd infiltrated the Resurrection Ring.

The Agent now twisted the key in the coupe's ignition. Instantly the engine roared back to life. He threw it into gear, and his machine imitated a bullet from a gun, so quickly did it blast from that loading area. The Man of a Thousand Faces arrived there in the Meatpacking District at the former warehouse, an enormous, though squat structure of brown brick, only no light emanating from the windows.

As he alit from his car and drew closer, he understood why. The Resurrectionist's hoods had blacked out the glass panels, such that no light could escape from them.

Simultaneous to his arrival with Esler, another vehicle, one of the white delivery vans pulled up, as well. Several men disembarked from the thing, four of them carrying a tan burlap bundle, roughly the length of a long roll of carpet. When X saw this bunch, he simply fell in line behind them. They would, he knew, lead him to the correct entrance, and thus his appointment with the Resurrectionist.

Sure enough, the little band marched towards one of the side doors, the metal portal giving the appearance of long disuse.

"Boy, are *you* in for it," one of the men, a fellow with a thin face, thinning brown hair, and bushy brown eyebrows, warned out of the side of his rather broad mouth. He went on, "It's seven thirty right now. And you should have already been inside with the Resurrectionist."

Agent X pointed his head downward to check out his wristwatch. Before he could steal a look at the thing, a blond young criminal gained his side. He was a tall, muscular youngster of perhaps eighteen years. The light of the late evening didn't prevent Agent X from seeing a pair of icy blue eyes, colder than a well-digger in Idaho. Excepting his eyes, however, this young man bore little resemblance to the usual criminal type. In fact this member of the Resurrection Ring might have been a student at some ordinary, middle-class high school in any part of the city—or, for that matter, in any city in the country. If his appearance didn't square with this gang, then his next words proved equally incongruous—shocking, in fact, given their substance.

Eyes bugging with fear, he whispered, "Mr. Wexman's right—Dad. Boss will give you the business for being late again. Needing your 'sugar,' weren't you? Or were you—"

To stop the questions, the Secret Agent forced a series of twitches from his muscular form. These motions convinced the young man of X's supposed craving for his "sugar." But while he and the criminals unlocked the church's side door, X's mind was racing over the words he'd just heard.

Dad? the Agent thought to himself. *This was the boy Jake, whom Thaddeus Penny had mentioned. The youth was the son of Gus and Annemarie Sayre!* His presence in the midst of this body drove home, again, the need for the Secret Agent to spell *finis* to this hideous Resurrection Ring, before it destroyed another life, a young one in particular.

With no particular discipline the group strode inside the former warehouse with the detective in their very midst. After they had moved into its vast, nearly empty confines, they formed an impromptu line, which then marched towards a glassed-in area in the back. It must once have been the warehouse's conference room, for it still contained two pieces of its former accoutrements. One was a sizeable safe of the old-fashioned type, ornate and heavy. And the other was a long, rectangular table, which sat atop a rather thick platform of marble. The Resurrectionist's own chair, as befitting an emperor, guarded the center spot, and other chairs bookended it. Already the Resurrectionist had assembled much of his gang at this table. And in that moment he was haranguing them about the inevitability of their success.

X and his criminal traveling companions entered the sanctuary. Unceremoniously they threw the long burlap roll on the floor, and the Secret Agent did the same with the unconscious Ham Esler. At that point they all approached their criminal master, who stood, once more, at the head of this body. He couldn't fail to notice that the disguised Agent was with them, rather than with himself, the Resurrectionist.

Swiveling his beatific features around the room, he addressed the men from the delivery truck: "Some of you have acted expertly, bringing in this prisoner," he made sure to omit Tiny's name. "The one you have seized will bring that much more strength to our cause. With this capture, Agent X will know the seriousness of our intent—and the hopelessness of resisting me. To show my appreciation for your efforts, I will distribute extra supplies of the 'sugar.' You may find them behind this conference area."

Two criminals, a balding, dish-faced man named Merriwale and one called Poulos, a rat-visaged fellow with a receding chin, he ordered to stay behind. The Resurrectionist dismissed the rest of his satellites from his orbit.

Agent X had a premonition that the man wasn't finished with him, though; and the next events proved he, the Man of a Thousand Faces, was correct in his hunch.

"Tiny—you need to stay behind with me. I had ordered you to be here much earlier than you arrived."

In Tiny's coarse basso, Agent X offered the requisite excuse again: "It was my need for the 'sugar' that made me late. Sorry about that."

Fury tightened the Resurrectionist's own deep tone, made it like a bass viol's note: "You are 'sorry about that'?" Apparently you have forgotten who is in control. I directed you to be here to discuss my plans to kill Butch Spangler. I also commanded you to bring in Ham Esler. Yet you have thrown off my schedule, arriving late. And to top it off, you have brought Esler in, apparently unconscious. He is, I suppose, drunk, and thus no good to me?"

The Agent lied without a qualm, "I found him madder than a wet het and drinking straight bourbon, when I reached his cab company. He said you were a chiseler, Sir.

"A 'chiseler,' eh?"

"That's right, a chiseler. Said you didn't pay your debts," X said, watching for some angry reaction on the part of his listener. For the moment the villainous character didn't reply. So Agent X thought to antagonize the Resurrectionist with this: "I decided I needed to smack him one, you know, to correct him of his error. Esler got more and more worked up, though, and before I knew it, he was shaking like a man with palsy."

"Convulsing, eh? It is probably the 'sugar.' Is he dead?"

Agent X laid it on thick now: "I think he's two-thirds dead, yes."

"You, in the meantime, did not even try to get his information about Secret Agent X. You have succeeded in doing nothing, other than trying my patience," the Resurrectionist spoke tartly from behind those immobile lips. "And this is only the latest time you have committed such an infraction of my rules. As a consequence, you must now pay the penalty for your disobedience."

The man of mystery maintained Tiny's deep pitched voice. A patina of humility colored his tone this time. X had decided to push the sympathy angle to the hilt: "I—it won't happen again, Resurrectionist. I'll be here on the dot next time. You can count on me to—to—"

"You are pleading with me, Tiny Sayre?" the crime master quizzed. "That is *most* unlike you, this attitude of humbleness. Normally you are barely obedient, as if you think that *you* are running this operation. Something has happened to change your mind, perhaps?"

X allowed his form to fall into a spell of twitching, as befitted the addict. "I just—just need the 'sugar.' I've *got—to—have—that—sugar...*" he emphasized, booming through clenched teeth.

"Yes, you do need the 'sugar.' However, I want to know *why* you are always so late in reporting to me. Something else is going on. Are you hoping to betray me and perhaps trying to start a racket of your own? You know I will not tolerate such rebelliousness."

The Man of a Thousand Faces had no way of knowing why the real Tiny Sayre had been tardy in keeping his appointments with his chief. When the Agent mumbled a snide response to the Resurrectionist, the white-robed felon asked for a repetition of the words.

Deciding to play a bet, the Agent, who had briefly looked away, coldly turned to the angry Resurrectionist, "You must be deaf. I'm not going to repeat what I already said. Now, give me my allotment of 'sugar.'"

The Resurrectionist's features remained placid, the very embodiment of saintliness. But behind that mask, he was seething. "Exactly what I expected, Tiny. You will not address me in that fashion, either. You will be made to pay for this defiance when I send you to Hell...."

At his signal, Merriwale and Poulos drew their pistols, two of the ubiquitous Bolo Mausers. Promptly they aimed the business ends of their firearms at the Secret Agent. One on either side of him, they grabbed him by the arms and forced him outside the conference room. From there they hustled him through an old warehouse door and onto a hallway poorly lit with a jaundice-colored light. Throughout this involuntary trip, the Secret Agent remained silent, but hyper-vigilant, taking in all of his surroundings. He wanted them to think he was a dope fiend who, desperate for his fix, had decided against resistance. The truth was this: He was still manipulating the Resurrectionist and all of his crew, all in the hope of gaining intelligence about the crime lord's operation.

After almost three minutes of walking in that hallway, the criminals and the Agent reached a gray metal doorway which opened onto a staircase. This means of access in turn pointed downward to a basement. X, still feigning his need for the "sugar," didn't resist as they half pushed, half prodded him down the concrete steps to a second doorway. This portal, also of metal, popped open, seemingly of its own accord. Actually a new criminal—he heard Rat-Face call the square-jawed, hulking man Swede—revealed that the Resurrectionist had already called him via the UHF device.

Swede pulled the Secret Agent through the opening, following which he beckoned the two Resurrection men inside.

X marveled at this lucky turn of events. Here was the Swede, Ham Esler's double-dealing confederate, in the flesh! He was the very man X hoped to encounter and thus to turn the situation to his, the public defender's, advantage.

After studying the man closely, X decided he would be easy to manipulate. He based his conclusion on a couple of facts. For one, he knew about the tough's penchant for the "sugar." And for another, like the usual bully he guarded a coward's heart behind that tough wall he'd built for himself.

His lynx-like eyes the Agent then turned away from Swede and onto the upper walls of this long passage, also lit with that sickly yellow light. Up and down the hall's length, the villain in white had attached speakers immediately below the ceiling, in order to broadcast his words throughout the corridors. Those electronic devices represented another means by which the miscreant could contact his satellites, as well as torment those in his power. To Secret Agent X it gave additional evidence of the money which funded the operation.

A sarcastic remark from the Swede to Poulos and Merriwale brought the Agent back to the present circumstance. Rat-Face, Poulos, had asked Swede if he were busy. When the blond felon said he'd be free in twenty years or so, Poulos turned away, muttering under his breath. Swede changed his tune with the news that, sure, he'd join them and escort Tiny to Hell.

The smirking Swede thus fell in with the trio, the disguised detective at its center. Their shoving of the Agent impelled him towards one final door to the left, at the corridor's end. Here only a single bulb threw out its anemic rays in its struggle to stay alive.

That fact wasn't lost on the Agent, who prayed that the bulb would expire and perhaps turn events his way.

They stopped the twitching Agent, in the meantime, at the final door, beside which stood a tall supply locker. From that compartment Swede intended to pull a ring of keys and thereby unlock that panel.

Something caused that bulb to flicker on and off two or three times before it winked out, however. Swede cursed at this unexpected development. He fumbled at the locker's handle, thinking he might successfully unlatch the thing in darkness, as well as push the detective inside that room.

Simultaneously, Agent X delivered another convincing performance of tics. This time he, though, he took matters much further. In the darkness of the corridor, he reached hands inside his coat, hugged his sides, and commenced to twitch again. In the next breath he fell, seemingly convulsing, against the hulking Swede. The hand of the Agent dragged the man down with him to the corridor's hard floor.

Unleashing a new stream of profanities, Swede did his best to disentangle himself from the Agent's thrashing and apparent convulsing, both of which grew ever more pronounced.

Came the time Secret Agent X began to calm a bit, his twitching fading somewhat.

With a spent look on his disguised face, he tried to grab Swede's coat, so as to gain leverage in rising. Cruel as he was, Swede's mouth exploded fresh blasts of obscenities. Eventually Swede shoved the Agent away from himself, regained his feet more quickly, and aimed his brutish form through the opened door. He gave X the evil eye before he, Swede, slammed the metal divider between the room and the hall. After this episode one of the Resurrectionist's men locked and bolted the door from the outside. Not twitching but standing once again, the Secret Agent, smiling slightly, peered carefully around the room to gain the lay of the land.

They'd thrown him into a cramped room barren of ordinary furnishings, much less ordinary décor. The word *hideous* would most aptly have described what the Secret Agent witnessed in this room, for here the Resurrectionist had created a modern-day version of the medieval torture chamber. Indeed the place would have instilled pride in Torquemada or others of his ilk, what with its vast collection of diabolical devices.

Friend to tyrants and Inquisitors, the chamber's rack was one of these awful machines. It guarded one area of the small chamber, its long, wooden platform's restraints spread out in a terrible welcome. X mused grimly that the victim, too, would gladly welcome the Grim Reaper, once that same victim had been locked to the rack's restraints, and then stretched to death by its winch and roller arrangement. Nor was the rack the only diabolical device the Resurrectionist had positioned here. The man of mystery trained his eyes next on a large, iron cauldron, used to boil victims alive and thus to wring confessions from them, or, that failing, to execute them. Above it the Resurrectionist had suspended a stool for repeatedly dunking suspected witches or heretics. Here in this hell, the practice would persist until the victims either confessed their supposed transgressions against the white-mantled crime czar, or his executioner drowned the wretches. X now swiveled his head to another part of the area where he spotted an iron maiden. The villains kept its door thrown back for purposes of intimidating future victims, and with good reason. A rusty, brown substance discolored nearly all of its spikes, the tools for impaling its victims. And those stains' true nature left little room for doubt in the mind of the Secret Agent.

From a chain fastened to the ceiling, they had suspended the less-well-known coffin torture. The tormentor would force an alleged minor criminal inside this metal framework and leave the person for several hours, in the cold or heat. If the person had committed a crime like blasphemy or authorities suspected him of it, he would often be left inside the coffin for hours, to be eaten by animals, again in some extreme weather. Of course here that was not at all a possibility, since the device itself was indoors. However the Resurrectionist could move the cauldron beneath the coffin torture, thus roasting the person alive.

There were other machines for causing pain and suffering to victims, as well: thumb screws for crushing those digits; pliers for jerking the nails from fingers and toes; a simple, though effective whipping post for savage beatings. Taken together, the room was a veritable monument to human depravity and cruelty—and another argument for X to defeat the Resurrectionist, sooner than later.

The Secret Agent walked slowly from the

door towards the room's interior. There he spotted a device not as commonly used. In an eyeblink someone threw back the door, and X's three captors of previous moments entered.

Quickly they flanked him. And as speedily they pinioned his arms to his side and hustled the Secret Agent towards the object which had caught his attention only seconds ago.

It was a set of stocks for the feet, with an open-backed chair for seating the victim. Well-known for their mercy, the old-time Puritans had used a variation of this apparatus for punishing violaters of the Sabbath. And they had also employed it when they caught a person swearing or committing another relatively minor offense.

Those Resurrection men edged the Agent closer and closer to the seat. As Tiny himself would do, he struggled and cursed while they slammed him downward. Then a couple of the hoods locked the restraints over his feet while another one bound his hands behind his back. They had no more finished their deed when over the entrance, a speaker emitted a loud crackle and, next, the voice of the Resurrectionist himself.

"Welcome to Hell, Tiny! You are quite comfortable? Hmm? Know that you face my wrath for your early departures from meetings and your absences from others. Know, too, that you face this penalty for your late arrivals at our appointments. I have warned you, repeatedly, that you would pay a steep price for all of this defiant behavior."

These new details raced through the mind of the Secret Agent. Why was Tiny Sayre sneaking out of the Resurrectionist's presence? And why, indeed, was he such a threat to the Resurrectionist?

"However, I am not an unfair man," X's captor continued. While a grim smile played over the Agent's features, the voice of the Resurrectionist continued, *"I will allow you to redeem yourself, if you can withstand this punishment. It will be more interesting, and certainly more challenging for you to endure, than were the stocks of our Puritan forebears."*

His captors of the Resurrection Ring grabbed a smaller cauldron which was parked to one side. In addition one of them located a can of kerosene which had been propped against the cauldron; and a wire screen, which could be fitted over the cauldron, to block the heat and flames from escaping the pot.

Even from his uncomfortable angle Agent X could see that a pile of charcoal, much blackened, crowded to the very edges of the great iron pot. Swede bathed the charcoal with a generous flow of kerosene. This act completed, he lit the pile with his cigarette lighter; and a brilliant orange flame blazed upward. Finally he pushed the lip of the cauldron directly underneath the feet of the Man of a Thousand Faces.

"I know," the Resurrectionist resumed, "that you must be disappointed that I'm using this method on you, Tiny, instead of the Wrath of God."

"Just broken up as I can be," the Secret Agent gritted as the heat began to increase. This had to look convincing, he told himself, even if he didn't yet feel discomfort or pain.

"I suspected as much. However I think the punishment should always fit the crime. And since your crime is less severe than others, I think this particular means will serve as the appropri-

ate corrective, don't you?"

"Guess this'll teach me a lesson," X smirked at his foes.

Chuckling, the Resurrectionist came back, *"Oh, you will learn—and quickly, rest assured. Let me tell you what will happen. First—"*

"—I didn't fall off a turnip truck yesterday, you know," the Agent interrupted. "Swede or one of these other guys will give me a taste of the fire, to let me know how hot it is. After that, one of them will start pumping me for information: where I've been, who I was with, that kind of thing. If I give the right answer, one of my friends here will cover the fire with the screen. It will remain in place as long as I give you the responses you want. If I don't, then I can kiss my tootsies good-bye because you'll start burning the devil out of them. That accurate enough for you?"

"Oh, excellent! Excellent! You are much better informed than I ever had dared to hope! You know, too, that this constitutes a trial by fire. If you survive it, I might force you through a trial by ordeal, in which you must fight your way out of this room. But I state the obvious, eh, Tiny? Good luck."

His hidden lips issued a crazed laugh from behind that beatific mask. And he switched off his microphone.

With no more preliminaries, Swede and the dish-faced Merriwale yanked the screen back from the cauldron….

CHAPTER XXI
ADDICT X

MINUTES passed. In those first few sweeps of the clock, the Secret Agent could block the pain coursing through his feet. He did, after all, know the ancient Hindu trick of walking over hot coals, yet not burning in the process. But supernormal man-hunter that he was, even the Secret Agent could not stave off, forever, the horrible burns and eventual destruction of his flesh.

In the meanwhile, within the cauldron at his feet, that reddish-orange blaze burned with a hell-born fury. And as those tongues of fire licked hungrily upward, the Resurrection men, standing in front of him, pulled back their lips in cruel laughter, much as their chief had done, moments ago.

Swede taunted him with his predicament: "Hey, Tiny, yer not so tough now, eh, big boy?"

"Yeah, Tiny!" Rat-Face called. "Think this is hot enough to warm ya? Or do we need to add some more coals so that ya know the boss means business?"

Merriwale urged, "I say more coals! I can go outside and get more if—"

"Who said to do that, Merriwale?" Swede glared. "You'll go outside if *I* tell you to go outside. I'm runnin' this thing in here."

Great beads of sweat popped out upon the Agent's brow. His mouth grew taut, his cheeks flat with pain. He gritted, "Good to know you're running this resort, Swede. It's just—just like a nice steam bath, boys. It's really relaxing after a tough day on the job."

This statement elicited more laughter from those members of the Resurrection Ring. They were, in fact, guffawing, albeit more from their handiwork and the sight of another human's pain, rather than from X's attempt at humor.

Still, very ordinary human needs governed the lives of the Resurrectionist's ruffians; and one particular requirement ruled them now.

"This heat is makin' me damn' thirsty," Rat-Face declared, wiping the perspiration from his ugly brow with the back of one claw-like hand. "How's about I go and get us a couple o' beers, Swede?"

Merriwale wanted to affirm this request too. But the man's fear of Swede overruled his thirst.

Surprisingly, Poulos's suggestion met with the big blond's approval. Swede affirmed, fervently, "I'm all for some beer! But ya think it'll be safe to leave this clown here?" he posed, looking over at the now-squirming and grimacing Agent X. "I mean, that fire's gettin' hotter by the minute; and he doesn't show any sign of talkin'. He's just twitchin' like he needs his 'sugar,' and—"

Growing more unsettled by X's behavior, dish-faced Merriwale stumbled, "Better—better let him out of that chair, then, Swede. Maybe he'll come around. Then if that doesn't do the trick, I can always get him some 'sugar' from the doc. I'll bet that'll cure what ails him—"

Suddenly X's body stiffened. His eyes grew enormous like pie plates. A terrible series of shakes convulsed his entire frame. He uttered a terrible groan. And his form went limp in the chair. To their eyes he had died.

Poulos, Rat-Face, whispered, "Damn! I think—I think he's gone, Swede. Boss is gonna be more upset than ever if he can't learn the truth about Tiny! What the hell are we gonna do now?"

"Damned if I know, Poulos," Swede addressed his compatriot. "I say we unlock him from this contraption and throw his body over the cauldron. That way, we can always tell the Resurrectionist that Tiny struggled with us and then fell into the fire. Hell, busy as he is, the Boss will believe it anyhow. He won't bother to check out our story."

"I, uh, I don't know if that's the way to go, you two," Merriwale objected with a slow shake of his head and a slow rub of his blue-stubbled jaw. "After all, how's he s'pposed to have escaped the stocks?"

"That's duck soup, you knucklehead. Everybody in the Ring knows Tiny's a strong guy!" Swede declared. "So we say that Tiny snapped his bindings and unlocked the stocks."

Merriwale was skeptical. "Maybe so, but I don't think that excuse will wash. Think about it—how could he have the strength and the time to do all of that, plus take us on?"

"Fine," Swede sneered at him, his body swelling as if he wanted to strike Merriwale. "What do ya suggest, Mr. Smarty Pants?"

"Maybe we should just haul him outta here, and dump him somewhere, like a garbage bin, or, better yet, an incinerator. Then we'll tell the Boss that Tiny has left the Resurrection Ring."

" 'Tiny has left the Resurrection Ring.' Yer a regular genius!" Swede seemed to compliment his partner in crime. But then he changed his tune to one of utter contempt: "Are ya dumb enough ta think someone like the Resurrectionist will buy *that* story? I'm not at all a fan of Tiny, but he *is* the field lieutenant for this outfit. And since he's no longer in the land of the livin', I go back to my original idea of tossing him over the cauldron after a struggle with us."

"That's the best idea I've heard all day, Swede," Poulos, Rat-Face, approved with an arrogant grin. He looked at the Agent. "Let me make sure he's got no pulse; and then we can do what we need to do, to cover ourselves. After that, we'll get those beers; and the Resurrectionist can assign us to do the next job."

Shaking his head, Merriwale inserted, "And I'll get myself outta here. I don't want to be around when you two have to account for what happened."

He left the torture chamber with not another word.

Poulos said, "Say, you said somethin' about the next job. I thought we was gonna bump Spangler."

Swede agreed, "That was gonna be Tiny and some o' his crew. *We* were s'pposed ta get that undertaker."

"Ya mean McGrieve?"

"Yeah. Scuttlebutt is that this has somethin' ta do with the Boss's old grudge against his father. I tell you—I'd just write off the old man and be done with him. Case closed. Then I'd get rid of the dead weight like Tiny over there and get some new blood in this gang. Get tougher with everybody, besides. Especially the knuckleheads like Merriwale. That's what *I'd* do," he bragged, pointing both thumbs at his ample chest. "Boss could learn a thing or two from me."

Like a wolf, he bared his teeth, though a grin this was not.

Nodding, Poulos sidled over to the Agent. In the next breath the felon released the lock on the torture device. That done, he reached behind the Secret Agent's back, to feel his pulse. Though still bound at his wrists, the Man of a Thousand Faces struck with the fury of a hurricane. Reaching through the open back of the chair, he snatched Rat-Face's right wrist with his, the detective's, left hand. Closer he pulled Poulos's appendage, and harder he tightened his grip. His eyes terrible, the investigator informed over his shoulder, "Thought I was dead, didn't you fellows?"

"Tiny! I—we didn't—I mean, we wasn't gonna do anything ta harm ya!" was the fervent declaration from the mouth of Poulos, that is, Rat-Face. "I was checkin' ta see if ya was okeh. I was concerned about your welfare, is all."

"Like *hell* you were," the Agent countered in Tiny's gruff basso. "I may need my 'sugar,'" he fibbed, "but I'm not too out of commission to know what's going on around me. And I heard exactly what you intended to do. Now—since I've learned of your scheme to protect yourselves, I think the Resurrectionist needs to hear it, too. He *also* needs to hear some of *my* information, about Ham Esler and the illustrious Mr. X."

X began to squeeze Poulos's wrist with more and more pressure, until the blood felt as if it would pop from the vessels. Soon Poulos's wrist and lower forearm both took on the color of ripened tomatoes, ready to burst. Likewise Rat-Face's bones felt as though the Agent would snap them like green twigs. Every time the rat-featured hood tried to break the grip, the Secret Agent tightened his steel-like fingers and exerted additional pressure—and thus torment.

In the meanwhile Swede stood there like a bump on a log, growing more frightened that the supposed Tiny would not only harm Poulos, but himself, the blond crook. Indeed he believed, with good reason, that Tiny could actually break his bonds and settle the Swede's hash.

The Secret Agent warned, "Swede, if you're as smart as I think you are—and that's not saying much—you'll get on the horn and call the Resurrectionist. And while you're at it, both of you'd better make damned sure you're not guilty of anything else. *You know who* might be learning the truth about you, anytime now."

Swede had a good idea what the Secret Agent meant by his final statement; and as a consequence, he experienced an awful sense of dread. So much of this emotion did he suffer, in fact, that he wanted to be on hand when his chief returned. That way, the Swede could defend himself—or so he figured. Hence, he exited the room at high speed. Back in Hell, tense seconds passed, seconds in which Rat-Face begged and cried to be released from the Secret Agent's terrible grasp. X agreed to comply—if Poulos first released him. When the rat-featured miscreant initially demurred, the Agent offered an objection of his own. After all, he said, he had no guarantee that Poulos wouldn't stab him in the back, literally, rather than untie his bonds.

"We're in a Mexican stand-off, it seems, right, Poulos?" the Agent uttered a taut laugh, despite the increasing pain from his feet. "How about you release me, and I'll throw all of the blame to your loud-mouthed friend Swede? How does that idea strike you?"

At this offer Rat-Face eagerly agreed, quickly loosening the detective's bindings and releasing his ankles from the stocks. He painfully regained his feet and donned his shoes again, just as the door to Hell reopened.

Through it strutted, first, the Resurrectionist, in all his white-garbed glory. Like a loyal hound Swede trailed behind his master. The pie-faced Merriwale brought up the rear. He had been the one, in fact, who'd summoned the Resurrectionist here. It went without saying he'd been happy to do so, especially if his act would get Swede in Dutch with their master.

Perpetually immobile features belied the surprise in the Resurrectionist's voice: "You have survived your trial by fire, eh, Tiny?"

"I'm standing here, so I guess you could say that," X gave a sullen response.

"And I perceive that you are craving your allotment of 'sugar' more than ever. Am I right?"

The Man of a Thousand Faces continued to stand there, calmly. He dodged the question, "I think you'd better know how your flunky, Swede, here," X pointed at the blond, "was thinking he could run the Ring better than you could."

"That's right, Sir," Poulos said. "Swede said you should 'write off' your father. He went on to say that he would 'get rid of the dead weight like Tiny.'"

The Resurrectionist cast his hooded and masked head in Swede's direction. "Is this true?"

"Hell, no, Sir! I ain't said nothin' like that!"

"Well, what about your plan not to release Tiny, and get information from him?" Merriwale blurted.

Swede stammered, "That—that wasn't my plan... I just—just thought he was dead—"

"So that's why you wanted to throw him over the cauldron?" was the quizzical response of Merriwale.

The pie-faced hood countered, "*You* wanted to throw him in an incinerator."

Agent X stood by, calmly, awaiting his chance to lower the boom on Swede and create more dissent in the ranks.

"Gentlemen!" the Resurrectionist used the term loosely. "Silence! Now, Tiny—you wanted to say—"

The Agent lit a keg of dynamite. "So you didn't say anything about getting rid of me, eh? And you didn't say that you'd 'get tougher with everybody,' either, because you didn't think the Resurrectionist was tough enough to run his own gang? Hmm?"

"Ya liars! I never said anything like that!" he defended himself.

"This is most incriminating testimony, Swede," the Resurrectionist intoned with sternness. "You skirt the razor's edge of my wrath."

Swede wheeled around, aiming to flee the room. On the Resurrectionist's command, the other men, Poulos and Merriwale, forcibly restrained Swede, the ruffian sneering and cursing during these proceedings.

Eyes now glittering with excitement, Agent X reminded, "I warned you, didn't I Swede? But you *had* to play the boss." He turned to the Resurrectionist with a suggestion, "Sir, I think you'd better take a hard look at Swede's past dealings."

These words issued from the Resurrectionist's lips: "Why should I do that, Tiny?"

"He's making private deals on the side."

"With whom?"

"Ham Esler."

"You have nothing but *his* word?"

"True, Esler told me that. But there's more. The two of them cooked up a scheme to skim your profits. They intended to sell 'sugar' as independent vendors. Swede even filched a sizeable amount of it to start their operation. Odds are, he was going to steal as much as he could, as long as he could."

The eyes of the Resurrectionist took on that fanatic's light, becoming bloodshot. His hands shook. It was all he could do to restrain himself. His mental state worsened as Agent X spun more of his yarn.

"Esler also said that Swede was packing some special equipment."

"What kind of equipment, Tiny?" the Resurrectionist asked.

"He's been carrying a small lockpick kit on him, somewhere."

"My laboratory...." the Resurrectionist murmured. "He's been sneaking into it...."

Swede shook his head with a vigor enough vigor to make himself dizzy. "Ya lyin' crumb! I'm gonna nail ya for this, Tiny! I'll chew ya up one end, and down the other!"

His disguised eyes a-glitter, X chuckled. "You'd better come hungry then, Swede. I'll be waiting."

"I hope ya are, ya damned lop-eared clown! I hope ya are!"

The Resurrectionist stopped this exchange with a gesture. "What else did Esler tell you, Tiny?"

"He said he thought Swede possessed a listening device of some sort. But don't take my word for it—find out for yourself if I'm correct. And you should do it pronto. By the way, about Ham Esler: He told me where the Agent's secret headquarters is. But since Esler is practically a goner, it looks like *I'm* the only one who can help you locate it."

Curses hissed from beneath the mask, signs that the Resurrectionist had bought at least a portion of the story.

He raised his white-robed arm dramatically and directed, "Search him—*now!*"

Swede complained most vociferously, "It's a damned frame! That's all in hell it is, I tell you! It's a two-bit frame! He ain't nothin' but a liar! Hell, he's prob'bly makin' money off you, hisself, Sir! He and that Ham Esler and these other two mooks here!"

Like a vicious junkyard dog, he was straining to attack the Agent, baring his teeth and even throwing his share of wild punches in the Agent's direction.

X merely grinned throughout the episode.

Rat-Face, for his part, held his gun at the ready as Merriwale started a classic pat-down which would have done Timothy Scallot proud. At first Poulos, Rat-Face, located one of the Bolo Mausers, as would be expected, in the underarm holster. Poulos also discovered one of the target pistols, slipped into the Swede's waistband. But the next findings created the real shock in the minds of the onlookers.

Poulos reached the man's outside left coat pocket. His hand felt something oblong, soft. Into the white pocket Felps plunged his right hand. It dove back to the surface to reveal Agent X's leather kit of lockpicking tools, just as the Secret Agent had promised. Poulos took the pouch and passed it off to a sneering Merriwale. He gave the thing a once-over and, finished, rammed it into Swede's square-jawed, scarred visage.

"So, ya ain't a thief, then, huh?" he pushed the man backwards. "It's all a 'two-bit damned frame,' right?"

The man stood there in stony silence, his fists opening and closing like a pair of bony clamps. While this persisted, Poulos plucked another surprise from Swede's magic pocket. That new article was a part of the cache of "sugar" which the Agent had promised the Resurrection men would find. It and the lock-picking kit the resourceful man-hunter had inserted, secretly and ingeniously, during the time of his supposed "seizure" and his fall to the floor of that darkened hallway. None of the Resurrectionist's men could see these acts, of course. But everyone in the room could see—and hear—what the Resurrectionist coldly ordered done to Swede.

"Place him in the stocks, and leave him there to burn. If I am feeling generous, I might return, in an hour or so."

The Swede blubbered, "Ya—ya can't do that, Resurrectionist! These guys—they're framin' me, I tell ya! I was loyal to ya—never questionin' what ya told me ta do! I was even ready ta go after Spangler and that undertaker, McGrieve!"

"How did you know I would go after my father?"

The words exploded from his harsh mouth: "I—I heard it from someone! Can't say who told me, but—but somebody said you needed a new bunch to go after McGrieve. I wanted ta be part o' that group, is all!"

"You will go *when* and *where I tell you to go*," the Resurrectionist turned his back on the now pleading man. Motioning for the Agent to follow, the white-mantled crime lord departed his room known as Hell.

And X, horrified, knew exactly what would be the fate of this criminal; for the Agent had condemned the man to a terrible death....

In silence the Resurrectionist and the sleuth marched back down the hall. As they reached that door near the supply locker, the crime chief turned to his supposed lieutenant.

"You have proved your worth to me, Tiny. And you will be rewarded, accordingly, once we've reached the conference room. We will also discuss a topic of much interest to you, namely, your son Jake. I have great plans for the Sayres, as you will soon see."

The Resurrectionist saying nothing else, he and the Agent followed the corridor's path for a few more minutes until they'd reached their destination. When they gained it, the Resurrectionist offered a curt nod to a piggish man named Felps. After he whispered something to the thug, the criminal left the room in silence.

Silent again, the Resurrectionist strode right for the safe. X noticed the shaking right hand with which the Resurrectionist spun the combination lock. With the same appendage he lifted a small ebon box from the ponderous metal vault.

"This is the latest version of 'sugar,' Tiny," he announced, a smile in his tone. "You have the honor of testing it, *now*, as befits a loyal member of my Resurrection Ring."

Into the Agent's hands the Resurrectionist pushed the box. His heart working like a twelve-cylinder engine, the Secret Agent unlatched the container's lid and cast his gaze inside. There in a crushed velvet well, he spotted a short, brown leather strap. Its neighbor in that box was a vial of the chocolate-colored "sugar." And alongside the chemical squatted another recessed area, this one holding a fresh hypodermic syringe.

Here was the very chemical, or its variant, which had enabled X to rise from the grave. He knew this to be true, based on the analysis he'd conducted in the Montgomery Mansion. But that "sugar" had also come horribly close to killing him, those years ago. Now the supreme irony was the fact that the Resurrectionist urged it upon the Man of a Thousand Faces, as a reward for excellent service.

X couldn't avoid the stuff now, couldn't sidestep the injection that he must administer to himself, if he hoped to defeat this devil.

Hand shaking too realistically this time, he pulled both of the objects from the box and charged the hypo with the "sugar."

When he moved the now-loaded syringe towards his neck, the Resurrectionist stopped him with this direction: "No, you don't have to inject it there. You can shoot this into your forearm. Here, I will strap this piece of leather into place for you."

After he'd done this deed, the Agent knew this was the moment of truth.

The courageous public defender started the needle on its slow march towards the territory of his forearm. X gritted his teeth. Deeply he rammed the hollow needle into his arm and pushed the plunger to the end. The chocolate-colored fluid crawled down the inside of the hypo's glass tube, through the needle, and into his vein. Instantly he experienced a rushing of blood through his circulatory system. A much-heightened alertness invaded his senses, as did greater feelings of well-being and euphoria. In addition he felt invigorated with more energy than seemed humanly possible.

His symptoms strongly resembled those of the so-called "high" produced by cocaine.

But these were the conventional effects of a stimulant.

The "sugar" also produced a most weird sensation like synesthesia, such that the Secret Agent tasted colors and smelled light. Between this effect and the others, it was no wonder that the user quickly fell into an abyss of addiction.

"It is heaven, isn't it, the anastastralose?" the excited Resurrectionist posed to the Secret Agent. "It is the miracle which keeps you—and everyone else—alive."

X couldn't answer him for a brief time. He was trying to master his body and mind, for one. And for another, he was frankly shocked that someone would call the "sugar" by its medical name. Finally with a weak nod, he replied, breathing shallowly, "Su—surprised you gave it to me in this form."

"Well, its solid form *is* crystalline, as you are aware—and some of the men take it that way. But the liquid form enters the bloodstream much more quickly. Hence I—I mean, you prefer to use the liquid form. I'm surprised, Tiny, that you're so concerned, all of a sudden. You always take your 'sugar' in liquid form."

Interesting, this little slip-up of the Resurrectionist. Unsettling, however, was another, this one on the part of the Secret Agent. X wouldn't know about taking the "sugar" in liquid form, though Gus Sayre most certainly would have done so. So he, the Agent, decided not to press his interest in the drug's chemical structure, else he would fall into some *very* hot water with the gang's chief.

He did decide, however, to broach another subject: "What—what about Jake, Resurrectionist?"

"Yes—what about him, indeed? I want him to join you in the next killing, that of Butch Spangler. As you have already done, Jake must prove his mettle, as well as his loyalty to me. But first I want you and the boy to find Dr. Charles Darwin Osben, the man who raised Secret Agent X from the dead."

In the meantime, Felps had returned to the room along with Jake Sayre. The youth sidled over to his supposed father, the Secret Agent; though Jake remained quiet and more than a little scared. It was hard to tell if he feared Tiny Sayre or the Resurrectionist more.

The Resurrectionist addressed them, "All of you recall our contact Dr. Theodore Pontius, at Dewitt Clinton Memorial Hospital." Each of them including the Agent bobbed his head. Of course, the detective had never met the man. He had to continue his pose as Tiny Sayre.

From beneath his robes, the Resurrectionist produced a photo, another of the ones reproduced and transmitted by the facsimile machine. "Look carefully at the man depicted on this paper. His name is Cole Sipes. Pontius has reason to believe that Sipes is actually Dr. Charles Darwin Osben."

When he had his turn at the picture, X had to raise the following question: "And just why is that?"

"For one, Sipes has an extensive background in microbiology, as well as medicine. He is also a man of the right age, that is, the age that Osben himself now would be. And, most convincingly, Sipes has connections, or rather, former connections with Washington, as a government research scientist in biology."

Agent X's eyes grew sharp again, as his supposed cronies murmured their approval regarding Pontius' extensive research.

His finger wavering a bit, the Resurrectionist followed by calling another detail to the men's attention: "You will note the street number which is written below Sipes' image. This listing is the man's home address. I have decided that we will pursue him next. Sipes, rather Osben, has made everything most convenient for us, too, as he owns no automobile. Pontius gives him a ride to the hospital most days. We will simply use Pontius' car, and Osben will suspect nothing is amiss. After we have captured the good doctor, we can net the fish known as Spangler. Afterward, Tiny, you can privately share your information with me, regarding the location of Agent X's headquarters. It seems," he cast his head towards the unconscious cabbie, "I have thrown good money after bad in hiring Ham Esler. I will eliminate him at my first opportunity."

For the time being, Jake Sayre inadvertently bought Esler more time. Shyly, he reminded, his voice surprisingly high-pitched for a big youth, "Hate to be a punk, Sir, but I thought Spangler was scheduled to be the next hit."

The Resurrectionist made the pronouncement that his word was law, and that everything was settled. First they would pursue Dr. Sipes, followed later by Spangler. Esler would receive his, the crime lord's, personal attention....

X's unease only swelled the more. Now he must find Sipes, too, and spirit him to safety, away from the Resurrectionist's grasping hands. And Esler? What could he do, except perhaps counterfeit a means to take him out of this place?

That wasn't all X must do. He and Osben must counteract that drug coursing through his, the Agent's, veins. In his short time prior to joining with the Resurrectionist, Agent X had not enjoyed an adequate opportunity to amass the proper resurrection chemicals, much less to distill them for his own use. He was counting on access to a laboratory for processing the substances. Otherwise, as sure as God made green apples, X, too, would eventually become the latest victim of this "sugar," more properly this anastastralose, if he dawdled too long.

Felps intruded on the Secret Agent's thoughts with a remark about persuasion: Osben wouldn't exactly come of his own accord, would he? The man wouldn't exactly, Felps grinned, bend over backwards to help the Resurrectionist—especially if this doctor had once been an ally of Secret Agent X.

You already carry adequate persuasion, Felps, the Resurrectionist reassured, speaking to him of the Mausers and the Wrath of God. In addition, Felps had, the Resurrectionist reminded, the best field commander in Tiny, someone both fearless and resourceful. He would not fail Felps or anyone else, would he?

Like the real Tiny Agent X grinned. His supposed son Jake merely watched the proceedings and offered a polite though not terribly enthusiastic smile.

Ever observant, X noticed the youth's response and developed a means to solve the problem of both Esler and Jake Sayre himself.

The Resurrectionist dismissed the men in that next breath, with all of the men, save X and Jake Sayre, leaving the place until their rendezvous, early the next morning. Still in that former church, Agent X whispered a word into the ears of the white-robed czar of crime, in hopes the fellow would take this bait.

"You wanted Jake to 'prove his mettle,' by accompanying me on this mission. Suppose I give you a better way."

"Go on," the criminal whispered, intrigued.

"What if *he* offs Ham Esler? Hmm? Wouldn't that prove Jake is worth your trust?"

The Resurrectionist liked the idea. It would, he nodded, be a good way to repay Esler. And a good way, moreover, to test the boy's fitness to be part of this organization.

"Are you ready to kill for me, Jake?" the Resurrectionist turned in young Sayre's direction.

"Su—sure," he stammered. "I'll do whatever you say, Sir. Just need to get my Webley—"

"Kill him—do not shoot him with one of our special guns. Then dispose of the body in an incinerator," he emitted an evil chuckle.

Smiling again, X assured, "I'll do just what you've ordered."

Turning to the blond youth, the daring man-hunter laid a hand on the boy's shoulder and said with strange warmth, "Let's make man of you, Jake. We've got someone to kill…."

CHAPTER XXII
PROOF IN THE PUDDING

WITH that deal concluded, the disguised Agent, smiling inside, led the way out of the place, grabbing the unconscious Esler and heaving him over one of his broad shoulders.

The youngster gained his alleged father's side, trailed him to the street beyond.

When the two of them reached the car, X unlatched the door to the back seat, thrust the unconscious form Esler inside. X followed by boarding the machine, indicating, that Jake should, as well.

Once they were settled in, the auto whizzed away from the curb.

They hadn't motored too far down the block before Jake Sayre, formerly silent, protested that this wasn't their machine. But that was the least of his concerns, as he admitted, icy blue eyes warming somewhat. "Something funny's going on, Dad. You're acting friendly to me, out of the blue. You're concerned about my place in this gang, too, when you normally wouldn't give me the time of day. What gives?"

At first X wouldn't say a word to the boy. Rather, the Man of a Thousand Faces removed a pistol from his underarm holster, forced the boy to take the thing.

Voice becoming deathly cold, the Agent told Jake, "This is the way you're going to kill Ham Esler. Are you man enough to do it?"

Jake averted his head. "I—I guess so. Haven't killed anybody yet. I think I can—can do it, though," he finished, his right hand shaking a bit.

He thought he could, all right, but only because his seeming father suggested he commit murder to win his spurs in this gang. In all truth, the young man was wrestling mightily with his conscience, as was clearly evident to the Secret Agent. That being the case, the man of mystery thought the boy needed a chance to heed its call….

There in the inky darkness, they drove perhaps four more miles until they came alongside the former packing house. It was a perfect place for a killing.

He stopped his automobile there by the building's front. Getting out, he made immediately for the back passenger seat. When he'd unlatched it again, he pulled Ham Esler's insensate form out onto the street and laid him on the concrete.

"You going to help me kill this clown, or not?" he leaned back inside, where Jake Sayre remained.

The youngster got out too after several seconds of quiet and indecision. He clutched the gun with a trembling hand, an appendage that shook not from the "sugar," the anastastralose, but from the act which his alleged father had urged him to commit.

Jake Sayre went and stood next to Ham Esler. The younger man aimed the gun, caressed the trigger without squeezing it. But he stopped, unable to go forth with his seeming father's, X's, plan for him.

"I can't do—do this," he choked out, the gas gun dropping from his nerveless fingers. "I'm just doing this to please you, and I don't think you're my father. And even if you were, I don't think I can take another person's life. I wouldn't be in this gang, except that Mom wanted me to keep an eye on you—and besides, I thought maybe I could please you, somehow."

His crying, shaking form almost took a tumble to the pavement, but for the Secret Agent's strong right arm, snaking around him and bearing his weight.

"That's what I thought, Jake," his voice suddenly changed to something closer to his natural tones. "You did just fine. You acted like a *real* man, not the one who solves every problem at the point of a gun."

The younger man trained sharp blue eyes on him. "Who are you, anyway? And where's my Dad?"

"First things first, Jake," the Agent said to him, helping Jake to regain his footing. "I realized you didn't have a heart for killing, after I saw your behavior around the Resurrectionist. So it was simply a matter of getting you away from his clutches, yet making it seem as though you would go through with a murder. As for who I am—"

Understanding shone in the young man's eyes. "You—you're that man he's trying to destroy! You're Secret Agent X!"

Becoming dizzy from the "sugar," Agent X still forced a smile when he told the boy, "I'll admit that. But I'm really a Federal operative of sorts. And don't worry about your father. He's safe. But we've got to get you to safety, as soon as I drop off this garbage with someone from the city."

X promptly started the car again, and they departed that near-tragic scene. In nothing flat the two of them gained the Federal Courthouse. Agent X wrote a pair of notes, the first of which he affixed to the unconscious Esler. That other note, he directed the boy to take inside to Special Agent Weston. It would explain everything and, later, point the boy and his mother to one A.J. Martin, newsman with the Associated Press. Jake Sayre promised to do as the Secret Agent had instructed him, and that, for the moment, was that.

Now business would pick up. Secret Agent X motored quickly out to his Montgomery Mansion headquarters again, entered the site, and pointed his frame immediately towards his laboratory. He was twitching with more and more severity now, and he needed to distill those chemicals.

Quickly his eyes roved over the shelves holding his chemical compounds. But the metal platforms were barren of the anastastralose's key components, save the most critical. Gratefully, he pulled a jar of organic material, leaves of some strange plant, from its resting place. This done, he scooped a liberal quantity of it into a vial which he had already prepared for this purpose.

Refocused, he moved back into his radio room, in order to find out any news from Harvey Bates. The operator Miss Arden shared with him the news of Tetwilder's death, in addition to Bates' injuries and hospitalization.

"What is Bates' condition, Miss Arden?" came the Agent's query.

"It could have been much worse, Sir. But thankfully the Resurrectionist hit Bates only in his feet and lower legs. As it is, the doctors have covered his injuries in a paste made from a sulfonamide; and they foresee a speedy recovery for him.

This new intelligence inspired the Agent. Something was, happily, going according to his plans, he informed Miss Arden.

X now posed, "Did you get any statement

from Bates—anything about Tetwilder's final words or anything else pertinent to the investigation?"

"Very little, Sir. He was upset. He did *say that Tetwilder had seen some kind of documents, possibly legal papers, in the Resurrectionist's possession.*

"Legal papers?"

"That's right. Mr. Beckwith," her voice caught at mention of his name, *"Mr. Beckwith thought that Tetwilder had seen articles of incorporation."*

"Interesting. So possibly the Resurrectionist has established his concern as a business enterprise. It will be a front, of course, for the real operation, which is criminal."

"Those papers weren't all that Mr. Beckwith—I mean, Mr. Bates mentioned, Sir. He said he tried to get a sample of Tetwilder's blood and tissues. But someone had sabotaged it, as we discovered here at our lab. Mr. Bates suspects some doctor named Theodore Pontius, one of the Resurrectionist's spies, did the dirty work. Or it might as easily be another doctor named Cole Sipes who contaminated the specimen from Tetwilder."

Miss Arden stopped speaking for a time, at which the UHF device broadcast her soft sobs to the Agent's ears. This thing was becoming more than his operatives, or he, could bear. X hung his head briefly and rubbed his tired eyes.

After a long silence Agent X returned to the young woman at the other end of the radio. "I know what Beckwith meant to you, Miss Arden; and what he meant to all of us. We'll get the Resurrectionist and bring him to justice. Count on that...."

"It's just—it's just—I don't know whether I'm cut out for this kind of thing, Sir. We've never lost someone before."

The public defender offered additional words of consolation to her. He concluded with this: "Take some time off, if you need to do that. You don't have to make your decision when you're clearly bereaved. Will you do that?"

Miss Arden sniffed. She gave halting assent to his suggestion, and the Agent surprisingly moved the conversation in a new direction, one of action. He told her this new course would take her mind off the present tragedy and give her something constructive to do, some way both to bring in their enemy and to honor the memory of Hiram Beckwith.

In that vein the shrewd investigator asked Miss Arden to check the record of Dr. Cole Sipes, to determine when he'd joined Dewitt Clinton's Hospital's staff. She was also to do the same with any new people, including Pontius, who might have joined the staff in within the last couple of years.

He signed off and allowed her to do the requisite search of hospital records.

X, for his part, turned back to his medical tomes, in hopes of finding more information about Osben's chemicals.

The radio announced Miss Arden's return after a brief span. She related that she had made a call to a friend Eunice, who worked in the hospital's personnel office. According to Eunice, Dr. Pontius had joined the hospital's staff only a few months back. His employment had come on the heels of a dismissal at another hospital in New Jersey. They had let him go, Miss Arden related, because of accusations of stealing from the hospital's pharmacy. After linking Pontius new employment at Dewitt Clinton to the start of the Resurrectionist's crime spree, X came to the rapid conclusion that Pontius might have been the spy in the Resurrectionist's service. Miss Arden was to continue her research into the man's prior history, to determine, more conclusively, his real story.

That left another subject, Dr. Cole Sipes. He had come to work at the hospital in only the past year and a half. He had also done advanced work in microbiology for the United States government.

Exactly what had he done? the Agent posed. The woman stated that it was simple contract work for a hospital. The Secret Agent nodded. In other words, he came back, the man had done nothing of a classified nature. To this statement Miss Arden offered agreement, as far as Eunice's records showed. X bobbed his head for a second time. If the man had actually been Charles Darwin Osben, then he wouldn't have coughed up top-secret information so freely, his friendship with Pontius notwithstanding.

Who, if anyone else, might have gone onto the hospital's payroll, say, in the last year or so, especially in the last six to eight months? To this query Miss Arden said one name. It was a fellow named Grover Kelley. And unknown to Agent X, this fellow was the maintenance man who'd been working so diligently on the vacuum cleaner....

CHAPTER XXIII
THE MASTERS OF LIFE AND DEATH

X had assumed a new role, one familiar to Grover Kelley. But the public defender's hands, shaking as they were, had struggled to put the finishing touches on this masquerade. Thus the investigator's disguise, while far from inept, did not meet his usual standards of perfection. His cheeks were too gaunt in places, for one. And his toupee, though appropriately grayed at the temples, wasn't as crisply combed, as befitted the features he presently wore. Maybe he could pull this off, he chuckled grimly too himself, since he already looked as if he'd been rode hard and put up wet, as befitted the subject of his disguise.

There was a compelling reason for his condition, of course. He was fighting his own body in these moments, his form twitching with ever increasing violence, his organs struggling to perform their usual functions. He did his best to will his mighty frame into submission, but he understood exactly what was happening: he was succumbing to that modified version of the anastastralose, the chemical which had revived him from the grave.

Worse yet, certain activities placed him, and in the present case others, in dangerous circumstances.

Driving an automobile was one of them.

Normally he was a motorist with supernormal reflexes and judgment. Normally he was a man of unequaled experience and daring, a virtual "trick" jockey under the wheel. But under the influence of the "sugar," he was only another impaired driver. And his car, being a mere machine, did only what its driver forced it to do.

Thus he almost ran down an elderly woman who was crossing a street in the Tenderloin, the district to which he frantically drove in search of Kelley. The man-hunter nearly committed an additional—and tragic—mistake when a milkman opened the driver's door onto the street in the instant Agent X passed the man's truck. With a savage turn of his wheel did the Man of a Thousand Faces swerve around the yawning panel, which jutted directly into his path.

Shaking as much from nerves as from the "sugar," he managed to fight his coupe back under his control and push it the final two blocks to Kelley's address. He was gasping, was the Secret Agent. His very breath seemed to be leaking from his body, as he fought to master his frame, compel it out of the car, and past a weather-beaten pickup truck. Then it was a fresh battle to stumble up the broken concrete path to a little mother-in-law's cottage.

It wasn't much to impress an onlooker, this runty home with its chipped paint, its missing shingles, its screen door barely attached to its rusting hinges. But to the Man of a Thousand Faces, it was a vision of heaven on earth.

He was breathing stertorously as he reached the screen door. A scrap of paper in his left hand, X applied the knuckles of his right hand to the exposed panel behind it—and promptly fell, hard, against the door. Swirling lights flashed in front of his eyes. He knew these might be his final moments prior to taking that first step into the Great Guess. And then, abruptly, he knew nothing more at all....

A thin and mustachioed old man with chapped hands and a hang-dog expression met his gaze as soon as he, the Secret Agent, returned to consciousness. How long he'd been out of it, he didn't have an idea. The old-timer had been bathing his head with a damp cloth, and beside the bed, on a small night table, he'd left a glass of something.

"Captain Read!" he whispered. "My God, you gave me a fright! It was a good thing you had that formula for the counteractant in your left hand, and that vial of herbs in a pocket. I was able to analyze it, and synthesize its active ingredients from some chemicals I keep on hand. Guess I'm *still* a doctor—despite what my present job might indicate, or what I might tell myself."

The Agent endeavored to sit up from his position on that tired, broken-down old furnishing which hid out under the name "bed." He remained dizzy, however, spent. So his body slumped back into the pillow.

Kelley grabbed another pillow from the other side of the bed. With it he better cradled the head of the disguised Agent. "Now, be careful with the sudden movements. You mustn't tax yourself too much, after what you've just gone through."

"How long was I 'out'?" the disguised public defender euphemized.

"You've been, shall we say, 'dead,' for almost three days, until I revived you just then. There's something you need to know. I heard a radio news broadcast about some missing detective, a gentleman called Jim Hobart."

X listened carefully as Kelley took a chair, sat, and reminisced: "Back in Boston I once sewed up a gunshot wound for a young police officer, also Jim Hobart. I figured that he had a connection to you—even put you wise to him, back in '32. But that was before the police force removed him for graft. It involved some racketeer named Madder, I believe."

"Madder *framed* him for the crime. I produced evidence to clear Jim of those charges," the Agent corrected, offended that someone would speak ill of the young red-head.

"Yes, I expected you would discover the truth," Kelley stated with something like pride. "And that means he *does*, or did, have something to do with you."

Unnerved by Kelley's second statement, the Agent willed his head to rise from the pillow. "Is he dead?"

"Quite the contrary. The police evidently happened to intercept a portion of a UHF transmission by someone who, they believed, either didn't know how to switch off the device he was using; or couldn't turn off the device because it was broken."

"The Resurrectionist! He must have gotten hold of Jim's transceiver, and then switched it to a police band."

"They believed the same thing, since the transmission seemed intended only for their ears. Anyway, they heard this Resurrectionist gloat that he held Jim hostage in the 'life from death.' They'd also overheard the Resurrectionist something else: that if a certain Mr. X wanted to see Jim or someone named Beckwith again, he'd better bring Tiny Sayre back into the fold. Does this mean anything to you?"

Of course, it meant something to Agent X! It meant that both of his men still lived, and that, somehow, he could devise a plan to release them from the madman's clutches!

Grover Kelley went on, "There was something else in the news report, a brief mention of an attack on the home of the home of Dr. Cole Sipes. The Resurrectionist dispatched a band of his marauders there, and they shot the doctor's housekeeper Mrs. Meeker in the shoulder."

"How is she?"

"Mrs. Meeker will recover fully."

"What about Dr. Sipes himself?"

"They—the Resurrectionist's bunch—thought he was Charles Darwin Osben, from what the housekeeper reported. At least, that was what the raiders screamed at her, when they broke into the place. They carried Sipes off, but when they realized that he wasn't Osben, they killed him on his own front lawn."

Silently, the man of mystery cursed himself. Another innocent, in this case Dr. Sipes, killed because of this business.

Agent X pinned the man under his gaze, but the detective said nothing, in light of Sipes' murder. After a protracted silence, he declared, "To say you're Charles Darwin Osben seems unnecessary, now."

The maintenance fellow Kelley nodded, in a matter-of-fact sort of fashion. "I *was* Charles Darwin Osben before I had some plastic surgery. But I'm not the only one who has a different identity, these days, Captain Read. Or do you prefer Agent X?" he molded his hang-dog expression into a slight smile, trained now-kindly eyes on the Secret Agent.

Returning the man's friendly smile, the Agent replied, "X will do for now. Read is part of my past. And if it means anything, I haven't had *any* plastic surgery," he concluded with a chuckle.

"Still that boyish sense of humor, eh, Captain, I mean, X? Fine, then—X, it is, from now on. You know, I suspected everything would boil down to this, eventually—your rediscovery of me and our meeting, that is. In a roundabout way, that's why I decided to go to work at Dewitt Clinton Hospital, six months ago, albeit in the maintenance department. Pursuing medicine, frankly, didn't interest me as it once did—maybe because of your suffering during Project Anastasis or maybe because of my general disenchantment with the medical profession. No matter the case, even if I *had* gone back as a physician, my return would have made me a target of those characters."

"This Resurrection Ring *is* seeking you, all right," the Agent related. "They want your knowledge of the so-called "resurrection process," as some of the newspapers are calling it."

Osben's tone was grave. "And at some point they would have found me and wrung that information from me, or tried to wring it from me. So, on that end, I'm glad you located me first. At least I was able to provide you with some life-saving assistance. But to return to your enemy, I had already acknowledged to myself that I couldn't let this affair with the Resurrectionist proceed any further. With his knowledge of the resurrection sugars and that so-called 'Wrath of God' he possesses, this fellow represents, in my view, a dire threat to the stability and security of our society. In that vein it was the reason that I began to shadow someone I considered very suspicious."

"Sipes?"

He put up both hands, shook them vigorously. "Not at all, not at all. I mean Dr. Theodore Pontius. I had gotten a tip that something fishy was going on in the hospital where he works."

This news greatly interested the Agent, who struggled to sit up. "Who was the source of your information?"

"It was the strangest thing. I received it from a member of so-called 'respectable' society. This may sound cynical, but it was a member of the McGrieve family who put me wise to this thing."

"As in the McGrieves of Caledonian Gardens? You know them?"

"Yes, on both counts. They, or rather Victor, had buried my present wife, the woman I had married after my first wife died. I won't rehearse all of the details of that second marriage, except to say she, Kathryn, was a good woman. Moreover, she was well aware of my past, as well as my name change to Grover Kelley.

"I buried Kathryn after a protracted illness, leukemia, actually. This immediately preceded the time I joined the hospital's staff. I had driven out to Caledonian Gardens to check on the finer details of her life insurance policy, as well as mine. You see, both of the policies, actually the claims, seemed to me, to be most generous. That's in light of the amount we'd paid as premiums, as these were relatively low. Anyway, young Jay-Jay confided in me his misgivings about his father's dubious 'connections.' He also mentioned to me, and no one else, that he'd received some mysterious telephone calls. Every one of them, so he related, sounded like the voice of his dead brother Malcolm."

"So how did this relate to Pontius, at the hospital?"

"Pontius was a friend of Malcolm McGrieve. This fact was bad enough—if you know the history of the McGrieves."

X did, asking the man to go on. Osben stated, frankly, "Well, Pontius was also well known to me, as a fraudster. He was notorious for stealing drugs from hospital pharmacies, and later selling them, at huge markups, to poor patients. On the side he was also engaged in planting evidence of his own crimes, on members of the pharmacy staff."

"Frame-ups, eh?"

"Yes. So needless to say, I could in no way countenance such behavior. Jay-Jay even confirmed some of Pontius' actions, incidentally. He related that Malcolm had, more than a few times, been the beneficiary of Pontius' 'assistance,' that is, illegal drugs to support his dope addiction. It was tragic, what happened with Malcolm, dying in that prison riot."

He shook his head with sadness. "That wasn't all, though. Jay-Jay mentioned to me that he actually scheduled an appointment to see Pontius, since the man had once been his brother's doctor. And though Jay-Jay and his brother quarreled, the younger brother had some inexplicable love for the older one, more than Jay-Jay would have admitted, as a matter of fact. Jay-Jay told me that he had asked Pontius: Was there more than a snowball's chance in hell that Malcolm was still alive? And was Pontius at all responsible for his return?

"Pontius never would give him a straightforward answer, however. He merely said that stranger things had happened, and grinned like a Cheshire cat. You can imagine what sort of reaction this provoked in Jay-Jay."

"His father mentioned to me that he was a suspicious sort. I suspect he's high-strung, as well."

"That, X, is putting it mildly. Still, his words set me wondering about everything: a dead man possibly returned to life; the murders of several criminal or semi-criminal types, all buried by Caledonian Gardens and supposedly living too; and finally, Theodore Pontius' enigmatic behavior towards Jay-Jay.

"I thought I would get to the bottom of all this, if for nothing else than to satisfy my curiosity—and, I suppose, give my conscience some relief. So I finagled an interview to work there at Clinton Memorial as a maintenance man—I was always a tinkerer—and lo, and behold, I got the job. It was easy, then, to keep an eye on Theodore Pontius. But at first I could find nothing shady in his dealings. He simply covered his tracks to well to be caught.

"One afternoon, perhaps a month ago, I was bringing a repaired typewriter back to his office. As I reached his door, I overheard him, apparently talking on the phone with someone. He told the other person that he was stealing chemicals from the hospital pharmacy and bringing them to his house. The staffers at the hospital were, he boasted, too dumb to catch him; so he was safe. Well, I believe the other party was this Resurrectionist you're seeking. And I also believe that the Resurrectionist had hired him as an assistant of sorts. That is, the Resurrectionist needed someone to duplicate the formula which revived you from the dead. Unfortunately for Pontius, he couldn't seem to surmount the last hurdles for making the 'sugar' work properly."

The Secret Agent's understood where this narrative was going. "And that explains why the Resurrectionist wanted *you* in on all of this—to find the cure. Note this fact, though, Osben: He sought that remedy not for his minions but *for himself* since he, too, manifests the twitching, the drug's more obvious effect. But you, the developer of the 'sugar' were dead. Or supposedly so."

That wasn't all to the detective's hypothesis. Osben had faked his own death after 1932. Osben confirmed the detective's idea. The doctor noted that he hadn't been able to live with himself, in light of having condemned the Agent to a horrible death. X countered, though, that he'd lived. He had developed his own counteracting drug for the anastastralose. To this word, Osben smiled. The man hadn't heard anyone use that term in years. He had thought it was part of the past he'd left behind. That was something involving his revival of the Agent and, later, his, Osben's departure from the medical profession in perceived disgrace.

Surely, Agent X said, Osben must have known of the goodness he'd accomplished, helping the man-hunter to fake his death and prosecute his war on crime? X had, after all, brought down too many criminals to number, saved too many lives in the process. To this question the aged medico said he'd suspected, but wasn't certain, that Read had become Agent X. Still, the whole process of raising X from the dead had left Osben distressed, that maybe they were violating natural laws that human beings were simply not meant to do.

"With your synthesis of the so-called 'sugar' from the tardigrade, you mean?" the Secret Agent fixed his eyes firmly on the former physician.

Osben bobbed his head. "That's *exactly* what I mean. In the tardigrade, the sugar in question, trehalose, is produced as a part of the process of cryptobiosis."

X glossed, "The organism's ametabolic state achieved as a response to hostile conditions like a frozen or dry environment, or one lacking in adequate oxygen."

"Yes. Scientists had discovered, many years ago," Osben recounted, "that through the production of trehalose, the tardigrade is able to achieve the ametabolic state."

"What the general public knows as 'suspended animation,'" X elaborated. "The organism can achieve ametabolism through various means, cryogenic suspension, or the application of extreme cold being two of them. Either means will stop the organism's deterioration or possibly even its death."

Dr. Osben affirmed the Agent's summary. "With the present state of biological science, this is frankly impossible, at least in human beings, since ice crystals form between the individual cells. Thus were we to thaw a body which had been subjected to such extreme cold, something near absolute zero, we would find that ice crystals would still form. And the organism itself would begin almost immediate deterioration and eventual death. That would be the case unless we introduced one critical factor."

Here the Secret Agent rejoined, "The trehalose from the tardigrade, altered for human use. You had reasoned that its formation of this sugar acted as a so-called cryoprotectant, and prevented the formation of the ice crystals. Its effectiveness was predicated on a couple of criteria: first, that it not be toxic to the cells; and second, that it readily penetrate their walls."

"That's right. I worked with the tardigrades in the laboratory for some years, even prior to your finding out about my research through your own reading. But my resurrection sugars, the stastralose and its counteractant the anastastralose, as well as the process for distilling and delivering the two, were *highly* dangerous—completely untested on human beings. For some reason this didn't bother you, as I recall, as you were willing to go forward with them, no matter the consequences. I *still* can't determine how you were able to overcome the problems I faced with this, eh, 'sugar.'"

Agent X remained silent for several seconds, not willing to share his findings. Eventually he stated, "I'm not the person you originally injected with the 'sugar,' Doctor. I—after you gave me that 'death sentence,' I became a fatalist of sorts. That was especially true in the first month or so of my new career as an undercover Federal operative. But early on, as you had predicted, those cravings started—and, with them, that awful twitching and shaking. They became more pronounced, too; and they became chronic. I knew that I would have to do something, especially if I wanted to survive."

The public defender stopped the flood of his narrative, albeit briefly. How could he describe the real reason he needed to survive, no, to live? How could he describe the love of this good woman Betty Dale? How else, except to say to Osben, "I fell in love with someone."

This was summary enough for the old doctor, tempered as he was in the raging fires of human experience.

Resuming, X stated, shaking his head, "I went through hell during those four months you gave me as a prognosis. Eventually a rumor of a lost herb from ancient times sent me on a desperate trip to Japan, where I had originally learned jiu-jitsu. There I encountered a scientist who'd discovered the last specimens of that particular plant in the mountains. I also met up with a bunch of criminals eager to cash in on the stuff for reasons of their own.

"Well, the Japanese botanist and I developed a buffering agent for the anastastralose, since the old version of it was the actual problem. It caused a toxic reaction, resulting in the rapid deterioration of the tissues, followed by the failure of the organs, and the eventual death of the organism. The buffering agent stopped all of that. And it did something more, something I have never told anyone: it slowed my metabolism. In other words, I don't age like a normal person. Apparently I age at only half the rate, or thereabouts, of the average healthy man. It was an unexpected boon, I suppose. But I'm simply grateful to that Japanese scientist for pointing me to a cure.

One final time he stopped, but only long enough for all of this to soak in with Osben. Gray eyes glittering, X concluded, his words earnest: "Science brought me back from the dead, Doctor. But love gave me back my *life.*"

By way of answer, Osben offered a knowing bob of the head at the Secret Agent's words. This *was* the Captain James Read he'd helped, those many years past. This was the man of courage, daring, and fundamental goodness. Whatever could be done now, he, Osben, stood ready to assist the Agent by any means possible.

To that end the Secret Agent proposed a certain plan to Osben. But the man-hunter did not stint on telling the doctor the risks to both of them, especially if the he, the Secret Agent, should fail. Despite the inherent danger of the scheme, the doctor agreed to it without hesitation.

X trailed his request with a second appeal. He required a shot of a stimulant, in order that he might leave this temporary sickbed and return to his investigation. Osben cautioned strongly against such a plan, but the steely-eyed public defender remained determined. In short order the doctor left the room and returned. In one hand he clutched a hypo loaded with a restorative. In the second hand Osben held a small paper bag which he passed over to the Agent. The Man of a Thousand Faces compressed the bag enough to shove the thing into the pocket of his coat.

With this act of X completed, Osben promptly injected a dose of the liquid into the Agent's bloodstream. Quickly the stuff flooded his system with renewed vitality. And like a jack-in-the-box, the Secret Agent shot upward from that bed.

Revitalized, he grabbed his coat, thanked Osben, and directed him to repeat everything he, X, had said to Osben. Satisfied the doctor understood him, he was out the door and back into his coupe, zooming from the house.

Back across the city he whirred, the car breaking speed laws at every turn. Eventually he came to a halt at his Montgomery Mansion headquarters again. When he hopped from his machine, a sense of hope, his first hope in days, indeed, permeated his entire being. Jim and Beckwith, hostages, but still living. His own body, racing toward health, once more. And his investigation, taking flight, finally, based on some tidbits that Osben had shared. This was cause for him to take the offensive, namely, in the way that only the Man of a Thousand Faces could do.

He passed through the mansion's security devices and whipped inside the house. In a flash he had entered the Mansion's library and his own archive, to conduct some research. Mere moments passed while he collected the appropriate materials, all of them relating to Victor McGrieve's criminal prosecution, along with various records of case law, treating the subject of life insurance. All of this material he then carried over to a table, that he might peruse the information with more care.

Most of it was familiar with him, so deeply was he schooled in the law. However the fine details of McGrieve's case gained the greater part of his interest. He read these aspects carefully: the counts with which Victor had been charged, the jury's verdict, and, in the sentencing phase, the judge's ruling. It seemed too easy that Victor had earned the sentence he'd gotten, and then gotten out of the pokey so quickly. The man had been guilty as sin, certainly as guilty as his son Malcolm. That might mean that the judge had later taken pity on Victor, perhaps because of his age. Or it could signify that the fix was in, that is, that *someone* had engineered an earlier release for Victor, for reasons of his own.

Some detail of all this was still nagging at the Secret Agent. He ventured back into his library for another book, this one a directory of insurance companies currently operating in New York City. He rapidly flipped pages to its index, whereupon he found something most telling. Indeed this new information set his head to nodding. But only additional investigation could hope to clarify this detail or answer any of the remaining questions he had.

Thus he regained the wardrobe room of the headquarters, where he began to outfit himself with a new disguise. First Agent X applied a light brown toupee to his own dark brown locks. A fresh application of his volatile plastic, rubbed smooth, lent his features a somewhat waxy look, as of someone who stayed indoors far too much. Next he inserted special facial plates inside his mouth. These would puff his cheeks somewhat to make them fatter than usual. The Agent followed this with a deep cleft he pressed into his own rather smooth chin. A neatly trimmed mustache, blond, joined the entire affair thanks to the magic of spirit gum. Finally he donned an expensive linen suit, navy blue; a light blue shirt; a dark blue tie; and a pastel fedora—a dandy's touch. He now resembled a successful businessman with a $500 per day expense account. His appearance and attire would definitely serve him well, as would his fake business card. The little oblong of pasteboard would reveal him as a state insurance investigator. He would need such credentials where he was going. For he was convinced that some mysterious connection tied the Caledonian Memorial Gardens to the McGrieve family, their staff, and the Resurrection Ring....

Several minutes later he zoomed to a halt at the front of the funeral establishment. Once inside the doorway, he spotted Dean P. Morston and a sling-wearing Jay-Jay McGrieve, deep in conversation. As if attached to short strings, their heads popped up abruptly as he strolled in.

"Yes, Sir?" the smiling Morston cheerfully greeted him. "May I assist you in some way?"

Out of his pocket the Agent pulled his wallet, flashed a professional-looking card at them. In a high-pitched, though cheerful, squeak, he announced, "I am Buddy Doren, and I'm an investigator with the State Insurance Commission. Is Victor McGrieve in today?"

Dean Morston almost had a cat over the arrival of this Doren fellow. He embodied Dean's and Jay-Jay's worst fears: a state official who would come in and discover the fraud that McGrieve the elder was likely perpetrating. As a consequence, the pie-eyed Morston could do little other than stammer out these words: "I—I—I don't kn—know, Sir. I—Jay-Jay, is your father in?"

A storm of fright momentarily swept through the eyes of Jay-Jay McGrieve. Indeed, he practically swallowed his own teeth. His shock far from mastered, Victor McGrieve's son choked out a line that Viola Vye would know where his father might be. But then Jay-Jay remembered that Viola had not come into work that day. They hadn't seen her, in fact, since a funeral a day and a half previously. They'd assumed she was ill. The same was true, they remarked, with Mr. Ramond, who was also a no-show. Both Jay-Jay and Dean seemed completely unaware of the events that had transpired in her office, not least of which being the shooting of Betty Dale by Mr. Ramond. Or perhaps the Agent's movement towards Victor McGrieve's office had left them so rattled.

Whatever the case, a frantic Jay-Jay shot past the hall's entrance and perhaps three feet in front of the Secret Agent. As unexpectedly, he blocked the disguised crimefighter's path for a time.

Breathlessly, Jay-Jay conceded, "Maybe you—you *do* have something on him! I'm all for finding out the truth and seeing justice done. But you can't just—just barge in there, without him around! Or can you?"

"He can, Jay-Jay," Morston stated from across the room. "He's well within his authority, based on his state credentials."

X waited a moment to see what Jay-Jay would do. He'd already assumed a threatening position, as if he wanted to attack the detective. Why was Jay-Jay McGrieve acting protectively for his father's sake, or worse, suspiciously, on behalf of himself? What was really at play here? Such was the Agent's thought.

In the meantime, Dean Morston already rummaged around Viola Vye's desk. On it he found a note to the effect that Victor McGrieve had gone out with a client to examine the progress on engraving a headstone. If anyone called for him, the communication said, then the person could wait; and McGrieve would return within the hour.

"So, three members of your staff are missing today. How unusual is this?" Agent

X trained his eyes first on Dean and then on Jay-Jay.

Dean beat Jay-Jay to the punch. "Oh, we have to work short-handed sometimes. It makes our job that much more difficult. But we manage."

Jay-Jay commented, tartly, "Yes—despite the work of people like 'Old Creepy.'"

"Meaning?" was the sleuth's question.

"Oh, Mr. Ramond. He's spending our money frivolously and probably leading my father along the high road to crime."

Morston affirmed, "Yes, I'm sure that's true, as far as the spending goes. I've seen my share of company invoices. And I know that a great deal of money is leaving the company—and it's not being offset by the amount coming in, as far as I can tell. But I also know, Mr. Doren, that you didn't come to hear us air our personal grievances. Your visit is more professional in nature. And I'll be happy to answer any of your questions, after I've completed some paperwork in my office."

To the Secret Agent's polite smile and nod, Dean excused himself, whereupon Agent X was alone with Jay-Jay McGrieve.

Victor's son had by now returned to the land of calm. And wonder of wonders, he had apologized to the man of mystery. To show further evidence of his better humor, he invited the public defender to join him in his, Jay-Jay's, office rather than to talk in the edge of the building's foyer, where there would be no privacy. For some reason, Victor McGrieve's son had become willing to welcome this state investigator, a fact not lost on the Man of a Thousand Faces.

As soon as the two of them entered the office, Jay-Jay shut the door and offered X a chair directly across from the younger fellow's own spacious desk.

"I hope you can understand my frame of mind, Mr. Doren," Jay-Jay prefaced. "I'm torn, as I've said, between desire for justice and love for my father. Daily, this conflict puts me in a difficult position."

This knowing and compassionate response came from the sleuth's lips: "I have no doubt that it does. And far be it from me to exacerbate your own difficulties. I'm not here to cause family strife. I'm here," X clarified, "to assess the current level of your father's progress, towards regaining his insurance licensure. In other words, is he in compliance with the court's ruling, allowing a third party to handle day-to-day affairs of the business? Also, is he knowingly keeping free and clear of criminal associations and/or known criminals in his business dealings? There are other questions, as I'm sure you're aware, but—"

"—I'm *well* aware of such questions, Mr. Doren—and of such government inquiries, in general," Jay-Jay, frustrated, shook his head. "But to tell you the truth, I expected a Mr. Beckley, since his name is on all of Dad's correspondence."

"Beckley is busy with other cases," Agent X reported without missing a beat, "so I'll be handling right now."

Such words placated Jay-Jay towards the Man of a Thousand Faces. But in relation to Victor McGrieve's business dealings, Jay-Jay maintained a sense of moral outrage: "I've been warning him, almost daily, that someone from the government would come in here and give him and this place the once-over. He's had it coming, too, because of his little playmates."

He arose and strode over to the window, the one through which he'd leapt, several days back. While he looked through that new pane of glass behind its curtained barrier, the Agent pushed Jay-Jay, "His playmates? You mean—"

"*Hoodlums* are what I mean. Far too many of our cases involve their kind somehow, both in terms of burial and life insurance."

"No ordinary citizens?" X probed, already aware of the burial of Osben's wife.

Slightly smiling, Jay-Jay conceded, "Well, we *do* handle policies from upstanding people, true enough. So maybe I'm exaggerating. I do that, quite a bit. But we do sell our share of policies to the criminal element."

"Criminal element or no, your father isn't supposed to be handling the policies himself until his probationary period is ended. You *do* have someone who's doing that, and who is keeping the insurance business completely separate from the funeral home, I take it?" X questioned, hoping to inspire more openness from Jay-Jay.

"Viola Vye is handling that end—or is supposed to be taking care of that. But she's a figurehead for my dad, as far as I can tell."

X watched the man closely. "Are you certain of that? In other words, could she be acting on her own, or perhaps on behalf of someone other than your father?"

Forced to back down again from his dogmatic position, Jay-Jay came back, "I—I hadn't thought of that. But she couldn't be wrapped up with a gang of criminals, least of all this so-called Resurrection Ring."

"Really? When did she come to work here?"

"In 1937, in March of that year, if I recall correctly."

Agent X asked about her qualifications for the job: her educational background, her level of experience, her character references, and so forth. Jay-Jay related what Viola had told Betty, a day and a half earlier, about her prior secretarial work and the other details. X removed a small pocket notebook from his coat and recorded all of Jay-Jay's words. Without warning, an odd expression crossed the disguised features of the Secret Agent. Something about McGrieve's account was nagging at X, though for the moment he couldn't quite identify what that something might be.

The sleuth decided to steer Jay-Jay back to Victor's possible tie to the criminals. "Develop for me, if you don't mind, your father's possible link with the Resurrection Ring. What concrete evidence do you have, to bolster your claim?"

As if a heavy burden were removed from his shoulders, young Jay-Jay declared, "I have something that will count as proof, all right—proof that my father *and* my brother Malcolm are involved with these murders."

"I'd like to see your proof, then," came the Agent's utterance.

Wordlessly, McGrieve crossed the office, only to halt in front of a large bookcase immediately behind his desk. On a shelf above his chair and to the left, one particular book, a volume on classical ethics, occupied a sizeable piece of real estate. He slid the heavy tome from the shelf and deposited it on his desk.

When he opened the book, it disclosed a large hollow space inside. He scooped out that collection of papers, all the yellow legal pages and the two surviving envelopes, which he'd found in his father's office.

"My father was secretly holding these, albeit hiding them inside a picture frame in his office. But he should have realized that two can play at his game," he commented, handing the materials across the desk to the detective. Agent X then saw everything Jay-Jay had seen, starting with the envelopes. The investigator went over them carefully, his basilisk eyes missing nothing scribbled or stamped thereon.

He remained impassive until he allowed his fingers to wander into the territory of the letters.

"I noticed these two little drawings here," he pointed to the cartoonish fish, as well as the lilac. "What do you think is their significance?"

"One of them is obvious, to me, at least. Dad and Mother used to grow lilacs on our old property. So I'm thinking the drawing has sentimental value, even to a crook like my brother."

"You still maintain that this Resurrection is your brother Malcolm, come back from the grave, then?" he looked up at Jay-Jay.

Young McGrieve was convinced of it, though the Agent remained more noncommittal, asking if there were more proof than letters in Malcolm's name.

"These are clearly his handwriting, Mr. Doren," an impatient Jay-Jay insisted again, his voice climbing a bit in pitch.

X shrugged his broad shoulders. "Perhaps they *are* his. But they could be faked. Forgers spend their entire careers copying the signatures of other people, in order to commit fraud in the names of those people. The best forgers are good, that is, effective, to the degree they aren't caught. But even *they* suffer capture," he expressed, "because they ultimately make fatal mis-steps. You're aware of that, I assume?"

The younger man had to concede the truth of X's statement. X asked him to place the known specimens of Malcolm's handwriting on the desk, side-by-side with the letters of extortion and revenge.

In his left hand Agent X brought the top sheet of a letter up to his eyes, along with the received sample of Malcolm's hand, specifically his old letters to his mother, in the right hand. "There are clearly similarities in the two, especially in the way he forms the letters in the midst of words. They are delicate, almost like the hand of a woman. It's called Edwardian script, his mode of writing."

"He picked this up in college," Jay-Jay related. Somewhat wistfully, he went on, face slightly averted, "Prior to that, he wrote in an ordinary way. But he thought this was beautiful. Funny, isn't it?"

Agent X could see that Jay-Jay wanted closeness to his brother, despite everything negative that had transpired between them.

He thought it best, therefore, not to comment, only to acknowledge Jay-Jay's words, "Good to know this detail you've supplied me. But note this: In the known copies of Malcolm's script, your brother adds a flourish, at the beginning of each capital letter, whether in a proper name, or at the head of each sentence. In the revenge letter, the writer does this sometimes; at others he omits the flourish."

Fascinated at the Agent's powers of observation, Jay-Jay stated, "So you think this letter is not one of his. Do I understand you correctly?"

"Well, I would say only that the letter is, at best, suspicious. The fish symbol is also more regular on this letter, though not on Malcolm's known sample. Are fish significant in any way to your family?"

"Not really. That puzzled me too. I wondered if it might be some symbol he picked up in prison."

All the Secret Agent would offer to this puzzle was a dodge. He stated, "About your father's insurance business—my records show that it was called Caledonian Life Assurance Company. But in the aftermath of the court case, you dissolved that part of the business."

"I thought the people up in Albany knew about that."

"They do. Remember, however, that I'm new to this case. Now to continue: The court required your father to transfer control of his company, to a third party. It in turn would operate alongside Caledonian Memorial Gardens, but not be controlled by it."

"Correct, too. Miss Vye operates this firm, Life Assurance and Casualty of Long Island."

"Yes. Whose motto is, 'We cover Long Island,' as I recall."

"Indeed," Jay-Jay McGrieve affirmed. "And whose symbol is—"

"—a *silhouette of the island's shape*, isn't it?" X spoke. "In other words, it's that crude drawing, more like a sketch, which you thought was perhaps a fish?"

Jay-Jay's eyes lit up. "A fish? Would you let me see those letters again?"

X passed them off to him, and sure enough, the image in question did resemble a crude rendition of a finny creature—one roughly corresponding to the shape of Long Island itself.

"I don't think that's the only surprise, Mr. McGrieve," the Man of a Thousand Faces prepared him. "Why don't we go to Miss Vye's office and see if my hunch about the insurance company is also correct."

Encouraged and indeed electrified, Jay-Jay agreed to X's suggestion, leading him down the hallway. He produced a key, unlocked Viola's door. At first nothing suggested itself as an obvious explanation for X's hunch, despite Jay-Jay's search of the desktop, and a subsequent hunt through the bookcase. The detective then took control, since he was a more practiced hand at this sort of thing. He poked around in all the drawers of the desk for several seconds. Still he couldn't find that brochure that Viola Vye had accidentally passed to Betty Dale.

That is, he *was* unsuccessful until he stepped away from the desk and peered downward. His gray eyes toured its surface only briefly. In seconds he noticed that the edge of one corner, a heavy piece of ornamental wood, seemed too worn in comparison to its fellows. Agent X reached his hand towards that side of the desk and jiggled the wood. Instantly he noticed that a small hinge fastened the base of the thing to the desk. The investigator merely lifted the piece ever so slightly. Upon rising up, the thing must have activated another mechanism as X heard a slight *click*. At the bottom of the desk a hidden panel suddenly popped out.

Here a quantity of brochures nestled, with most of the paper circulars creased, as though shoved inside the chamber, in haste. X bent his limber frame over the secret cubby. His hand grabbed the pamphlets out of the drawer, and he looked at the one on top. At about the time he grasped it, a slip of paper fell out of the thing. On it a list recorded the name of every one of the criminals who'd been killed by the Resurrectionist. In addition the array of names listed the one remaining man, Butch Spangler, who had yet to be murdered. And alongside his name was today's date and a time, later tonight, during which the Resurrectionist's representative was to contact him and arrange the details of the hit.

This was a real find, to the thinking of the Secret Agent. As a consequence, he pocketed this slip with everything else he'd acquired here and elsewhere.

X could do nothing else for the time being, however, since Victor McGrieve strolled in through Caledonian's front entrance. Once he'd passed inside, he must have said something, as Dean Morston momentarily abandoned his paperwork. From Viola's office, X could hear as the young mortician informed McGrieve of the visitor's presence at the funeral home.

Victor McGrieve said that he didn't see anyone; hence Morston's intelligence puzzled him. Not for long did it mystify him, however, when Dean told him that the newcomer, a state insurance investigator, was down the hall in Viola's office with Jay-Jay.

At this point McGrieve stomped down the hall, eyes blazing.

"What are you doing in Miss Vye's office, Jay-Jay?" an angry Victor boomed. Turning his ugly face in the Agent's direction, he said, "And who are *you*?"

X looked towards the door and pleasantly replied, "Oh, I'm Buddy Doren, an insurance investigator with the State of New York. And I'm here to learn about your possible involvement with life insurance for criminals and people facing likely Federal prosecution."

Indignant, Victor McGrieve boomed, "I'm quite sure I *don't* know what you're talking about. Miss Vye handles all of that. I mean—she is *not* running a criminal enterprise. Her company is strictly legitimate and will continue to remain so."

Eyebrows arching and eyes a-twinkle, the Agent inclined his head, "That's strange. I thought it must have a connection with you, in light of your fondness for *lilacs*. That *is* the acronym for the company for which she's operator, isn't it, Mr. McGrieve—the *Long Island Life Assurance Corporation*?"

CHAPTER XXIV
SOJOURN IN THE HOUSE OF DEATH

OFFENDED, Victor McGrieve wouldn't have considered taking that "sugar," or so he rumbled to the three younger men. He maintained he was as far from being a dope addict or a drinker as New York was from Shanghai. It was his weak heart, he cried, that kept him from both of these vices. However, this revelation of the lilacs' true nature inspired the worst fit of shaking imaginable in the man. His twitching spell affected Victor as profoundly as it had done on the heels of Roddy Shingle's funeral. McGrieve moaned like a bow being slowly drawn across the strings of a bass violin. And large droplets of plain, old sweat, not mere perspiration, collected on his brow. The undertaker was in a bad way, to be sure.

His condition would worsen in the next instant, as events proved.

A loud *pop* assaulted the ears of everyone in the place. The loudspeaker system of the funeral home gave a deep hum. As unexpectedly, the building's lights surged, then died.

An unearthly voice declared from nowhere: "*I am the Resurrectionist!* "*You are defying me, Father—defying my will! Yet you know that I have cheated the warden of Attica prison of my presence. And I have cheated the grave, as well!*

Do you think you can continue to scoff at my plans? You will co-operate with me, or you will face the Wrath of God!"

Eyes glazing, a terrified McGrieve nearly collapsed to the floor. He would have, too, except that the Secret Agent whipped to his side and locked mighty arms around the man's form. As quickly he scooped the man's body up and draped him across Viola Vye's desk.

Dean Morston had heard the commotion by this time, and he joined the rest of them there. He blurted out an offer of help, despite the fear engraved on his handsome face.

Jay-Jay said that the old Army cot was still in his father's office. Therefore, Dean flew like a fighter plane from his office towards Victor's own. In the meantime, Agent X, Victor McGrieve draped over his shoulders, marched back towards the same destination. Once back inside the office they saw Dean, who had already removed the cot from the closet. In a trice he had unfolded the rickety thing for the ailing older man.

In those first few seconds Victor McGrieve was practically raving, so upset was he by the prospect of a criminal enterprise operating from his funeral home. X worried that the man would become apoplectic and thus suffer a stroke.

"That broadcast and the—the previous one that came—through the loudspeaker system, the other day," he gasped from his temporary sick bed. "It was my son—my son Malcolm, making those threats. I *know* it was. It was *his* voice, and no other. He *is* the Resurrectionist! And he's the one behind the business with those lilacs!"

The detective bent down beside the Army cot. In a kindly tone he asked, "Do you have any of your heart medication here at the funeral home?"

Shaking still, he couldn't respond to the question. Nonetheless the younger McGrieve knew the current location of his father's pill bottle: the top drawer of his, Victor's, desk. So X sent the fellow down the hall to get water, while he, the detective, retrieved the medicine. Once he'd seen to it that the man had his pills and water to swallow them, the Agent gave Jay-Jay McGrieve a friendly squeeze of the shoulder and pointed his form back down the hall. He had decided he needed to get out of the McGrieves' way for a bit. They needed their privacy. And at the same time he, X, could thus examine Victor McGrieve's office unhindered.

The public defender walked inside McGrieve's chamber. To the left of the door, he spied a large, glass water dispenser cradled in a frame of aluminum alloy. On a tray beside it, a supply of cups perched. On the opposite side of the door, from the visitor's perspective, Victor had placed a tall, sturdy hat and coat rack crafted from mahogany. McGrieve had slung three or four hats on its hooks, in addition to a rather large gray umbrella, which dangled from the bottom-most one.

Victor McGrieve's wall was a veritable art gallery for the death industry, with its many images of caskets and headstones, mausoleums and urns. Not all of the pictures depicted death, of course. Some of the wall's adornments consisted of nature scenes, like the usual "deer scampering through the forest" motif; or the "fish jumping from a lake" treatment. A copy of his diploma from the Indiana College of Mortuary Science also decorated a space, as well as pictures of his sons—both Jay-Jay and Malcolm—and four or five photographs of his deceased wife Millie.

A painting of a tree drew the onlooker's gaze to the center of the family photos. The Man of a Thousand Faces, curious about that watercolor, strode across the room.

That print did not depict just any woody plant, but a family tree of the McGrieve clan, with little blocks superimposed onto the various branches. According to the information thereon, the family traced its lineage back to late 17th century Scotland, when they had crossed the Atlantic and had immigrated to America. They had led distinguished lives, had this family, with some of them having served the country in almost every war; built up their communities; or distinguished themselves in education or business.

From Miss Vye's office Agent X suddenly heard a deep sigh from the elder McGrieve. Quickly the detective returned to the woman's office, only to be met by a heartened Jay-Jay McGrieve. Indeed he formed the index finger and thumb of his left hand into the high sign, meaning that the medicine was calming Victor McGrieve's heart. The Agent, too, breathed a sigh of relief at the man's remarkable comeback.

Earlier, while the crisis unfolded, unassuming Dean Morston had tried to stay out of the way. He had informed them, "I feel so helpless in this kind of situation." And his frightened animal look underscored that pronouncement.

Becalmed a trifle, he now tapped the manhunter on the shoulder and asked him for a private audience. Would Mr. Doren, that is, the Agent, care to accompany him to his office, where they had a bit of privacy? X agreed to the man's request, and they departed for Morston's space.

On the way down the hall, Morston expressed great unease over McGrieve's condition and yet greater discomfort over the possibility that Malcolm McGrieve might be the Resurrectionist.

They reached Dean Morston's office and the young man offered the Agent a chair across from his desk.

Ever kindly and optimistic as befitted his role as Doren, X expressed the hope that these events would end positively, that Victor McGrieve would recover and that the authorities would nab the Resurrectionist.

Dean Morston stated his fervent hope that this was so. He went on to say that he could never have foreseen something like the menace of the Resurrection Ring. Morston had, after all, grown up in a small town and lived such an ordinary life.

Where, exactly, had he grown up? was the Agent's question. McGrieve's associate related that he'd been born and reared in the small town of Pendleton, northeast of Indianapolis. When he was only a teenager, his father had died, leaving him to take care for an ailing mother, who already had the responsibility of running the family's funeral home. This business had emphasized, for him, the value and the importance of hard work. But it had done something else: It had shown him how much he enjoyed serving his community.

X observed, briefly, that such desire was commendable, to which Morston smiled.

Family was everything to him, he related. And he had wanted to make them proud of him by continuing his work in funeral homes. So to that end, he'd traveled from Pendleton to the big city of Indianapolis to study at the Indiana College of Mortuary Science. He had finished his education there in 1936 and gained his job with Caledonian, immediately thereafter. Humbly he related his belief, inherited from his deceased father, that he could do good for people even after their lives were ended. And his education and experience in mortuary science had provided him the means to do so.

Casting his eyes around the office, X noted first the man's bookshelves behind his desk. These contained the requisite texts from his profession: books on the history and practice of embalming, for instance; more volumes on the law, as applied to the mortuary business; and last, in enormous bound form, some trade journals which also treated the subject of this industry. Agent X also spotted the usual office bric-a-brac: some mementos, apparently from his school days; three or four plaques of appreciation from some charitable agencies, and one of those small globes, all of bronze-colored metal, which people stick on bookshelves. Propped on the side of the globe was a glass circlet of perhaps of no more than an inch in diameter, and to its right was a small paper box. From its end protruded a black strip of something or other.

Next, the Secret Agent turned his attention to the walls surrounding him. On them, he spotted Morston's many awards for community service, in addition to a picture of his alma mater, and that diploma from the Indiana College of Mortuary Science. He noticed, finally, a couple of photos of Morston, one with himself in front of an administrative building, perhaps at a hospital or a college; and another, with the man posed with the McGrieves, Jay-Jay and Victor, in front of the Caledonian Memorial Gardens.

Morston suddenly asked the Agent, "Mr. Doren, I need to tell you something. Under most circumstances I'm an optimist. And I'm public-spirited, too. That means I'd like strongly to help you. At the same time I really, *really* need this job to pay my bills. Frankly I'm worried about all of this—more than I can tell you, in fact. If Malcolm is behind these threats, or, worse, if his father is in league with him, then the State will shut us down; and I won't have a job. And the prospect of that scares me half to death."

"I'd reserve judgment regarding the culprit, Mr. Morston. Let the authorities proceed with the investigation. Then you'll have a better basis from which to pursue your own course of action."

"If Mr. McGrieve—or his son Malcolm—is involved with the Resurrection Ring, will the State go hard on him?"

"Well, that's assuming one of them is pulling the strings. It could be Malcolm. Everyone here seems to think he's back of these troubles. But it might be Victor, who might be exaggerating his heart trouble. There's also Miss Vye to consider. She is, after all, managing Life Assurance and Casualty of Long Island. It seems to be a front for that Long Island Life Assurance Corporation, which, I point out, may already incorporated under the laws of New York. And, suspiciously, she had those brochures for the Resurrection Ring in her desk."

He removed one of them from his inside coat pocket, where he had placed it on first encountering Victor McGrieve today. The paper booklet contained the Resurrectionist's watchwords, "life from death," "death from life," and an obligatory reference to the lilacs. There were also charts showing levels of premiums, amounts of benefits to be paid, terms of contracts—everything that a conventional advertisement for life insurance would contain. But there was an enormous difference.

"The lilacs are individual life insurance policies for criminals, according to the words of this pamphlet," an intrigued Agent X flipped through the little advertising circular. "The individual purchases one of these, and thus becomes the policy owner. If he buys it on his own life, he becomes both the owner and the insurer. The person, say the two are one and the same, then pays out regular premiums, or monetary amounts, as per the terms of the policy. This document then becomes the contract, at law.

"Next a contingent of hitmen murder their 'victim,' and the McGrieves handle all the burial arrangements, according to a prior agreement."

The young funeral associate quizzed, "What about beneficiaries? Someone must be cashing in on this thing, right, Mr. Doren?"

"As with legitimate insurance, the beneficiaries of the policy receive proceeds whenever the insured person dies. Here the benefits can total upwards of $1,000,000, depending on the level of coverage. Seems that this Resurrection Ring is a real moneymaker for someone, doesn't it?"

Dean Morston leaned across his desk, while his mouth formed an O of shock. "Who would the beneficiaries be? Obviously it couldn't be the dead men."

"That's *assuming* they've actually died in the first place, Morston. Most likely those beneficiaries *are* the dead men, now using aliases. But the police and other authorities don't yet know this, of course. Here's the reason why: The criminals have committed their dirty work on the Resurrectionist's clients—*in full view of witnesses*—and authorities have carted off the bodies to the medical examiner's office. Someone must have then signed fake death certificates for each one of them, if I'm correct.

"But that's only another rung in the Resurrectionist's ladder to the heights. To all eyes he is raising the criminals from the dead, and he's somehow harboring them in a safe place, out of police hands. This tells me that a large network of people is assisting him while he commits his various criminal acts. His many 'killings' of criminals are simply the most prominent and dramatic among them. And never mind that his clients *do* eventually die in most grotesque fashion, withering to death from that substance he calls 'sugar.'"

Dean Morston was petrified. "The stuff of fiction, eh, Mr. Doren? That is, something like a grand conspiracy?"

"All the earmarks of one, yes."

"I *really* don't like the sound of all this. It's ghastly, this whole plot. It makes me wish I had stayed in Indiana! Jove!"

Gravely, the Agent agreed, forming a steeple of his hands beneath his chin. "We all may wish we were doing something else before this is over. But I want to follow up on something Jay-Jay mentioned, back in his father's office. He said something about 'Old Creepy,' that is, Mr. Ramond. I still find it *most* convenient that neither he nor Miss Vye is here today. Strange, this turn of events—wouldn't you say?"

"I can't argue with that! Think there's anything to it?"

Agent X sidestepped the question with this response: "Well, right now, I'm just gathering information about the personnel and practices here at Caledonian. Tell me what you know about Mr. Ramond, if you don't mind.

I'd like to learn more about his background, his time of service here, his relationships with you and the McGrieves, anything else you consider relevant."

It was the young man's time to suffer a case of nerves, he said. Like Jay-Jay before him, Morston ventured from his desk to the window. Peering outside, he stated, "I can say of a certainty that Jay-Jay doesn't like him. 'He's leading my father back to crime,' I've heard him say, too many times to count. And I have to admit, the man is, um, 'strange' and, on reflection, a bit secretive."

"In what way is secretive?"

"He never discusses his past."

"That's not uncommon, you know. Many people jealously guard their privacy, especially when it comes to the past."

"Point taken, Mr. Doren. But he also works many late hours; and when I've walked in on him, in the lab, he says that he's 'conducting secret scientific research.'"

"In a funeral home?" X cocked his head an odd angle.

"So he's told me," was Dean Morston's response. "I didn't put two and two together until recently. Jay-Jay and I were embalming a Mrs. Leakey when Mr. Ramond and Mr. McGrieve—the owner, actually—asked us to leave the embalming room where we were. They came in and started to embalm Roddy Shingle, supposedly with a special secret process that Mr. Ramond claimed to possess. Now this Resurrection Ring and your investigation of it make me wonder if Mr. Ramond's not tangled up in the net too...."

"What about this specialized knowledge Mr. Ramond has acquired?"

"I know nothing about it, really. But could it be—"

"—Nothing less than the 'sugar,'" the Agent answered for him. "What else did Mr. Ramond do or say, when the subject of the process arose?"

"I have heard him use the phrase 'life from death,' to describe the process. It seemed to give him a thrill, as I recall, just the mention of it."

Agent X had a very good idea why it would cause such a reaction in the man. But the sleuth didn't share his thoughts. Instead X took the conversation in a new direction.

"You said that Mr. Ramond doesn't discuss his past. Yet to get a mortician's job in a funeral home, here in New York, he *must* have a past. In this case, he must meet certain educational requirements and possess so many years of experience, among other qualifications. What do you know along these lines?"

"He's a mortician, according to his diploma," Morston reported, as he stepped back towards his desk. "It's from the Mortuary Institute of Los Angeles. He came onboard here at Caledonian, a bit after I did. It was back in '37, as I recall. Prior experience? I'm not sure of that. You'd have to ask one of the McGrieves. I *will* say that he does the most professional embalming jobs of any of us—almost artistic, in fact. They all show a high degree of—how should I say—realism? Yes, that's it. They're almost *too* real, for my money."

The Man of a Thousand Faces threw Morston another pitch: "How old is he—Mr. Ramond, I mean? Do you know?"

"Can't say that I do. From his appearance, I'd guess he's, oh, fifty-five or maybe sixty."

"Interesting. If that's the case, he has either gained much experience in this field—or he was a much older fellow, when he started as a mortician."

Turning to face the Agent, Dean Morston shrugged his shoulders. At that point he walked back the handful of steps from the window to the desk. Then he offered this point, something he'd stated earlier, but developed, this time, with more substance:

"He certainly spends lots of money—Caledonian's money, I mean. Mr. Ramond says it's for the newest embalming chemicals. Who knows? I'll give the man this: He *does* know the latest science about the field of embalming... at least, to hear Mr. McGrieve tell it," Dean Morston related. Smiling, he finished his brief account, "Speaking of Mr. McGrieve, I suppose I should get back in the other office and check on my employer. If you'd like to stick around in here—or see Mr. Ramond's office—you're welcome to do so. I'm not sure it will do any good, though, to comb through his office. He probably won't have left anything incriminating behind that door."

"It won't hurt to find out if there's anything there, so I believe I will do that. Thanks," the detective said in the high-pitched voice he'd affected for this disguise.

"And thanks for listening," Morston stated. "I'll open Mr. Ramond's office for you on my way out."

McGrieve's young associate, on shaking X's hand, left his office to learn about the condition of Victor himself. For another brief instant, the Agent himself stuck around in the office, scanning the walls of Morston's space, and casting his gaze, at last, on the surface of Morston's desk. There he spotted some official-looking papers, documents from Caledonian. He removed several of these from the desk and found them to be nothing more significant than some claim forms for policies sold by the funeral home. Legitimate persons held every one of them too, as the Agent's informal search revealed. He replaced these policies on Morston's desk; and after a time, he wandered down the hall to Mr. Ramond's chambers. There the Secret Agent found that unlocked door.

X glanced around this place for a time to give himself the lay of the new territory.

He noticed numerous bookshelves here, as he had done in Dean Morston's domain. But in Mr. Ramond's space, only books and journals crowded the shelves, much as one would see in a library or a college professor's office. The man confirmed some of Morston's account, that of being knowledgeable about the latest embalming techniques.

He hadn't confined all of his learning to this discipline, however. On his shelves parked numerous books about culture: philosophy, world religions, music. And two final disciplines' works held honored spaces there, the worlds of art and sculpture. Their presence caused the Agent to nod strangely, as if he understood the books' real significance.

That inexplicable expression of knowing didn't fade from his face in the next heartbeat.

Agent X turned his attention to an enormous metal safe which Ramond kept, locked, beside his desk. Expert cracksman that he was, the Agent quickly breached the thing with a tool from his lockpick kit. The safe opened, he found more evidentiary food for thought in its confines. On its bottom and both middle shelves, he discovered several busts, parked thereon. They were all life-sized. Moreover, all of the plaster studies depicted the heads of women. And a couple of them struck him as eerily familiar, if not chilling.

Brows arching, he delicately lifted one from the shelf, examined it front and back, even to noting a tiny crumb of something which was clinging to the chin of one bust.

Someone had constructed these pieces for reasons far more sinister than artistic ones. And all of them sent him into a fury....

Making sure that no one had witnessed his doings, the Agent speedily replaced the bust on its shelf. Eventually he rested his steely eyes on Ramond's desk. He saw a wooden box with a small lilac engraved on the top. The entire affair rather resembled one of those intraoffice communications devices, complete with the screened oval which normally covered a loudspeaker.

The Secret Agent suspected the box's real nature was far less innocuous.

He tried first to lift the thing, but he could not do so. Someone had bolted it firmly to the desk, in order to prevent such action—or to stabilize the box. It was probably much of both, he decided. Then the Secret Agent made an attempt to open the thing, but he could find no latch on it.

He sent his eyes racing around the entire circuit of the desk, in the hope that he might find another of those concealed switches like the one in Viola Vye's office. While there were none of the ornamental edgings at the corners, he *did* locate something hidden. Someone had countersunk a tiny button into a recess underneath the desk's back lip, that is, at the place directly in front of the user. His left index finger offered the button only the slightest of touches. The box emitted a slight *click*. X lifted the box to disclose a control panel with numerous buttons and switches, all of them carefully labeled as to function.

One of these, a remote control device, he found particularly interesting because it squared with a mysterious electronic event he'd already witnessed. Another of the buttons, marked "closet," left no doubt about its function; but he quickly touched it anyway. The button activated the door to the closet, off to one side of Ramond's desk. The Secret Agent decided to touch another button, designated "closet panel." When he fingered this control, a large metal plate in the back slid upwards. The aperture beyond revealed an immense cubby with an array of radio and other electronic equipment. He thought back to the earlier power surge during which the Resurrectionist had broadcast those threatening messages.

Such an array of electrical apparatus, powerful and extensive as this stuff must be, could cause the electronic phenomena which the funeral home had experienced today and earlier.

X ventured inside the space before his eyes. He saw another expensive UHF outfit, more telegraphy gear, radio direction finders, and so forth, all of it like the stuff at Tiny Sayre's apartment. There was even a special effects machine like the one in Tiny's possession. This device in particular exploded fireworks of excitement over the horizon of the detective's mind.

Agent X left the hidden space and closed all of the hidden panels, via that control board. Now he trained his lynx-eyed gaze on a standard wire basket of gray, adjacent to Ramond's desk. Underneath the basket, the Agent spotted a torn piece of yellow paper, only the top third or so of the sheet surviving. Still, several facts informed him what the leaf had once contained. The columnar arrangement pointed to an invoice; and the page's title denoted a local business, Vox Populi. The Secret Agent already knew the nature of their wares. The outfit sold electronic and especially radio paraphernalia to enthusiasts in the field. It was another sign which pointed to Malcolm McGrieve. And someone had bought the surviving items—there may have been more—in quantities of one dozen for some things, and as many as four dozen for others. The individual had purchased vacuum tubes, for example, as well as capacitors, receiving antennas, and tuners. There was anything that the devotee would have wanted to build a powerful home radio set. But it was all conventional equipment, certainly nothing esoteric.

The Agent noted that the paper had been torn, however, across a word perhaps ending in "—fter" and another word whose last letters might have been combinations of "c-l-t," "c-i-t," or groupings of "e-i-t" or "e-l-t." However, the Agent wasn't certain which one was the correct choice. Immediately he thrust this paper into the pocket of his coat. His next move consisted of shifting some papers around on the desk. This hunt produced no prey, though; so he turned his attention to new grounds, the desk's interior. Agent X's search of the top drawer proved as fruitless as had the earlier places, at least at first. He roved through some purchasing orders, as well as more invoices, all of them dealing with some of the chemicals that Mr. Ramond had bought for Caledonian Gardens. This stuff more or less squared with Dean Morston's account, namely that the man was purchasing embalming compounds. None of them were unique, either.

But of a sudden the Agent's questing fingers brought to light something most singular: It was another sheet of paper, this one a white purchasing order, thus an original document, also made out to Vox Populi. Agent X removed the yellow copy from his coat pocket and set it side-by-side with the new white page. According to the tear marks, they were a match, showing exactly what the purchaser had bought, including the mysterious word ending in "—fter" and that additional word, or words, which actually stopped with the letters "—elt."

It confirmed his belief that someone here was buying this equipment, not as a hobbyist, but as a professional with something less than noble intentions in his mind.

Time it was, that Agent X should leave this office, check on Victor McGrieve's condition, and depart the funeral home. He would need to return to his headquarters and make sense of the clues he'd discovered here.

X thus started for the door, when his gray eyes caught sight of something glittering from one of the bookshelves. The Man of a Thousand Faces stopped, frozen in his tracks. He put forth a hand to the object. It was a small, unclasped gold bracelet, with two tiny diamonds inlaid in its surface. The Secret Agent's blood turned ice cold when he flipped the little circlet to its underside. There, these words were engraved, "Always, darling."

He had gifted Betty Dale with this golden circlet, some three years back. Its sudden appearance proved she'd been here, on these very premises. And the Resurrectionist had her!

CHAPTER XXV
THE NEXT DEAD MAN

WITH blazing speed, Agent X crammed the bracelet into his coat and marched, flinty-eyed, from the room. He barely ensured that Victor McGrieve was improving before he told Jay-Jay and Dean Morston that he would return later. Something, he stated, had come up; and it was imperative he leave immediately.

Hence, he quick-stepped outside to his coupe, started the machine, and zoomed away, in the direction of the Montgomery Mansion.

Back to his crime library he sprinted on arrival. There he placed the various clues—the bracelet, the brochures, the slip of paper from one of them, the purchasing order, and the invoice from Vox Populi—on the large table.

Prior to examining any of this material, however, he needed to phone Dewitt Clinton Hospital and hear the latest news on Bates' condition. He also required information from his associate or from Bates' operative Miss Arden.

A quick call connected him with the square-jawed giant. How was Bates doing, the man-hunter probed.

He was staging a robust recovery, which meant something, given Bates flair for understatement. The doctors said that the sulfanomides were wonder-workers, to which the Agent expressed the hope his friend would soon be back on the case.

Bates heartily concurred with his chief's wishes. He in turn wanted to know what the Man of a Thousand Faces had learned from his own investigation. With understatement equaling Bates' own, the man-hunter narrated his brush with death and the life-saving efforts of Dr. Osben.

"So you're okeh, then, Sir?" Bates posed at the conclusion, leaning forward in his bed and puffing his pipe with greater vigor.

"Fine, Bates. But my news is good only in a qualified sense: Hiram Beckwith is alive. But the Resurrectionist has imprisoned him and Jim Hobart, along with Betty Dale."

"God! Was afraid of something like this! Need to get the doctor to discharge me from the hospital, and then—"

"Listen to me, Bates," X commanded. "I understand your need to give assistance. Right now, though, you should recover a bit longer. I will need you, soon enough, from that hospital bed."

"Can't just sit around here and—"

"No, you won't be sitting around. You'll be working."

This statement engendered a measure of hope in the disheartened Bates. "Anything you say, Sir. I'm ready!"

"Good man. Now—I want to hear your account of Tetwilder's death, as well as anything else related to its aftermath."

In the clipped style for which he was so well known, Harvey Bates related all of the details. At present Bates' narrative offered nothing new. The rest of the intelligence squared with the usual death-bed pronouncements of criminals.

But the shrewd public defender thought there might be something more.

"I'm curious about Tetwilder's statement that he'd seen the Resurrectionist's real name."

"On those legal documents, yes, he said he'd spotted the man's signature," Bates told. "He damned 'that Devil to hell,' too, Sir."

"Think about it, Bates: That name Tetwilder saw wouldn't truly be the Resurrectionist's real name, of course. This would be an alias. I'm thinking, Bates, that this would also be the name of someone we already know."

Harvey Bates delivered one of his rare exclamations: "Say, you're probably right!"

"I'm *counting* on it. And I'm counting on all of this information to point backwards to the person who is *really* responsible for this whole devilish scheme. How would you like to make a phone call for me, and do some research?"

"Anything, Sir! Give the order, and I'm ready," the loyal Bates stated, eager to rejoin the fray.

"That's the spirit! Now listen: You have that friend Parker, who works as a clerk in Attica State Prison. Is he still employed there?"

"As far as I know. Need me to call Sam?"

"As quickly as possible. But tell me—do you recall a riot at Attica State Penitentiary, some years back?"

Bates was silent for a minute, poring over that capacious memory of his. He came back, "Certainly do! Bunch of those fellows died, as I recall. Guards there had a devil of a time, restoring order before all was said and done."

"Your memory is keen, as always. So here's what I need from your friend Sam: a list which records the name of every prisoner who died in that riot. I want to know causes of death, too, if possible. And tell him not to be surprised if there's a discrepancy in the figures."

"How so, Sir?"

X wouldn't answer the question, except to say, "Be prepared for anything he reports to you. And send my copy by the facsimile machine to the office of A.J. Martin. I'll pick it up there. Oh, and have Miss Arden conduct a final bit of research for me."

"What's that?"

"Ask her about any women who might be involved with the Resurrection Ring's so-called 'victims': Helmer, Lothian, Terran, Calvert, any and every one of them. I'd like photos of the parties who might be linked to them. If she can't find photos, you may send physical descriptions of them to my office too. Be sure that Miss Arden appends their criminal records to her findings, where appropriate."

"Done."

"Excellent, Bates. Get well."

"Will do, Sir," he promised, his very tone reflective of new vigor.

"X out."

The Man of a Thousand Faces moved back to that group of clues on his library table. He knew the secret of the lilacs, now. Also he had discovered the truth about the "sugar." That left the material scattered in front of him. And it left some more intangible clues, such as that year 1937, as well as the significance of Ham Esler's involvement with this entire thing. X wondered just what it might be, as he drew out a pencil and a long yellow legal pad. On its top sheet he divided the page into three columns, first listing the name of a person, then that man or woman's title or role, and finally the individual's possible significance to the case.

At the bottom of the page he drew a smaller object, a table of sorts, also partitioned into a trio of columns. The first of them he titled "clue," the second, "significance," and the third, "location."

As he was filling in the details of the page's top, his telephone rang. Agent X thought to himself that it must be Bates, as no one else would have been in possession of the number. The Secret Agent dropped his pencil and tonged the phone.

"Got Parker at the pen, Sir," the giant stated, his voice more confident than previously. "Found some interesting information, too. Seems that thirteen men bought it, during the course of the riot."

"Hmm. Let me guess—the number isn't correct, is it, Bates?"

"Just as you predicted! Parker told me that the prison officials swore by that number of thirteen dead, with the victims killed by massive head trauma, beatings, and so forth. They buried all of those men on the premises of Attica."

"That's a result of the fact that those men had no families; or they did, but the families wouldn't claim the bodies," X clarified. "I'm betting, however, that the records didn't jibe, somewhere along the line. In other words, if the other numbers are correct, then two more men must have died—or something else must have happened to them."

"Parker suspected as much. Said that he was surprised at the discrepancy, too, because Warden Hallan was the top cop there, at the time."

"I knew Warden Hallan. He was a good man. But Parker referred to him in the past tense. Has he died?"

"No, Sir. Said he had retired."

"Stay on this, Bates. Find out *exactly* what Hallan knows about that riot, especially as pertains to the two missing murder victims. It's highly likely they were claimed by so-called 'family members.' It's just as likely that someone, our friend the Resurrectionist, had those records falsified because *he* was one of those alleged murder victims.

"Claimed by a survivor, eh?" Bates anticipated X's line of reasoning.

"That's right. Oh, what did Miss Arden find out, regarding women and this crime ring?"

"Pretty disparate lot, Sir. There's Shingle's moll, Miss D. Ramos. You've already encountered her, of course. Also there's Spangler's woman, Monica Willens. There were some additional ones hanging around, before this Ring tried to pull you inside."

The news intrigued the Agent. "Really?"

"Wayne Helmer was squiring some woman named Charlotte Moon around to society functions. Just started to date her, according to the reports Miss Arden turned up."

"A little too convenient, that, Bates. What do you know about her?"

"Let's see—Nothing much for her, prior to 1937. Crazy, Sir; but she seems not to exist, prior to that date. Then Miss Arden finds her dating a Congressman, a Representative Dirk, who was in trouble with the law."

Bates' words flashed across the landscape of X's remarkable memory. The Agent responded, "I *remember* that! It was a big scandal. I think that a Congressional committee was already investigating him, and thinking about turning over its findings to the Justice Department."

"Man died unexpectedly, didn't he?"

Again the eyes of the Secret Agent shined with intensity as he told Bates, "Wait just a minute, and I can tell you more."

He re-entered his archives, running his eyes over his collection of newspaper and magazine clippings. All of them he had recorded by year and month. Once he'd produced the volume for 1937, he flipped pages until he reached the listings for June, more precisely for the 19th. In that month he found the article about Representative Dirk. He read to Bates: " 'Former Representative Logan Dirk of Pennsylvania, sixty-eight years of age, died today, as a result of a massive heart attack.

Prior to this date, witnesses had, for an entire month, observed an unaccountable *twitching which he seemed to have acquired*," Agent X emphasized.

He recited more from the article: "Readers of the Harrisburg *Courant* will recall that the Department of Justice had just filed racketeering charges against him, in his home state, especially since his dealings crossed into neighboring Ohio and West Virginia. The Federal indictment dealt with alleged fraud in his construction business, mostly in cement pouring and profit skimming, though labor contracts also figured into the government's decision to indict the former Congressman.'

"Later the same article lists the woman Charlotte Moon, who offered a gratuitous 'no comment,' when questioned," X summarized. "She disappeared from public view immediately upon his death. Nor has she been seen since his demise."

"Suspicious, Boss," Bates commented. "And as you said a minute ago, most convenient. But isn't it interesting, too, that Congressman Dirk didn't waste away to a bag of bones?"

"He died before he could. I'd heard the man had heart trouble already. So the 'sugar' may have precipitated his heart attack."

"Minus the heart attack and subsequent death, I'm thinking his case resembles Henry Terran's situation. His 'sweetie' Patrice Anders came on the scene, only three months previous to the man's death. And she disappeared quickly too, upon his demise. Police are still looking for her."

"I think we're onto something here," X posited. "I'll get going now and recover additional details from that list from my office. From there, it's on to Butch Spangler's apartment for more information."

"After that?"

"I'm playing it by ear for the present. Let's just say that some individual or group of individuals is acting as the intermediary between the Resurrectionist, Spangler, and the rest of the Ring's so-called 'murder victims.' This sort of arrangement maintains the aura of mystery and power hovering around the leader and protects him from discovery from them, much less the authorities."

"Still want to get a discharge from this hospital, Sir," Bates begged him. "Feeling better in the past couple of days. Ready for service and—"

"—I don't think you're able to—"X stopped him.

Now it was Bates' turn to cut in: "Please, Boss. You're going to require assistance and—"

The Secret Agent thought carefully for a time; then he offered, "Bates, how about a compromise? I'll leave my UHF device tuned to that different frequency, the experimental one for emergencies. That way, the Resurrectionist can't listen in on our conversations. If there's any danger to me, you and some of your men can come running. How's that?"

This plan satisfied the giant, who responded, warmly, "Fine by me. Good luck, Sir."

"Same to you, Bates. X out."

Secret Agent X returned to the tabular information he'd recorded on that sheet of paper. After poring over it for another few minutes, he drew a circle around the year "1937," following which he wrote "significance?" Daylight broke in his steel gray eyes when he realized the importance of that date. He reconsidered his capture and interrogation of Ham Esler that year. But that wasn't all the Secret Agent had faced during that period of time.

It was two years ago, when he'd faced Proteus. That meeting with the Shape-Shifter had almost cost the Secret Agent his life, its devastation magnified by the fact that the villain had filmed him *without any disguise.* Or so had the Shape-Shifter thought.

For the Man of a Thousand Faces had fooled Proteus, out-tricked the trickster. But there was still that film of his, in which Proteus had fingerprinted him and forced the information about the public defender's most important identities, Elisha Pond and A.J. Martin. X knew he must have divulged this intelligence in that cinematic record. And though the Agent thought he'd destroyed the single copy of that film, the Resurrectionist must have gotten his hands on another print of it. That particular motion picture must have been unknown to all but Proteus himself. To the Agent's mind, this must be the case. Again it emphasized the vastness of the Resurrectionist's resources, not to mention the depth of his ingenuity, his sheer ruthlessness, and his insatiable thirst for revenge.

X's mind was working like a finely-tuned machine now. He knew that everything rested upon that year 1937, possibly even the twelve months immediately prior to it. With that thought in mind, he scribbled these words on that page, underlining them with two bold underscores, thus: Ramond is the key to the mystery.

Mr. Ramond must be tied up in this affair, whether he had something to do with Jay-Jay McGrieve's bitterness towards his father or not. Indeed, the Resurrectionist might have been capitalizing on this very acrimony, from the very start. That didn't even take into account the so-called "secret process" for embalming which Ramond had developed, and which both Jay-Jay and Dean Morston had encountered, however indirectly. Also, there was the phrase "life from death" which Ramond had been heard to utter in the presence of Morston. And there were those busts Agent X had discovered. Yes, there *was* something here, all right, something that—

An eerie feeling came over the Secret Agent. There was, he realized, another angle to this mystery; and now was the time to check it.

Agent X roved back to his books. This time he chose a fat text, black-clad, from one of the shelves. The volume was entitled *Families of Old New York,* its subtitle reading, "Including Descendants, to 1910."

He sent his right hand quickly to the book's index. When he'd located the appropriate page numbers, he thumbed them leftward until he'd reached the objects of his quest. Next more scribbling filled the sheet of paper which mentioned Ramond.

Into his left hand the Secret Agent took that slip of paper. He knew this was the ideal opportunity to stymie his enemy's plans, indeed, to take the war directly into his camp. And X would do it by impersonating the illustrious Mr. Ramond himself.

To his wardrobe room he repaired. He slipped out of everything he'd been wearing, choosing, instead, a well-cut tan shirt and a conservative brown suit. Next he began prodding the volatile plastic material which covered his face. In subsequent moments, his face became somewhat drawn, though not extremely so. Moreover his nose took on a different shape, Ramond's slight bump included. He followed this detail by applying gray brows over his own previously disguised ones. And he concluded by adding a neatly trimmed gray beard, a Van Dyke, over his chin and lips.

Vibrant words rolled from his lips, resonated from the walls of X's sanctuary. He was satisfied with the result.

He had become Mr. Ramond, the fellow he suspected to be the Resurrectionist's chief mediator. Into his pockets he reloaded his special equipment, with the addition of some materials he hadn't been carrying earlier. His masquerade now complete, he bided some of his remaining time by scribbling more on one of those pages on the library's table.

After a while he motored to that office rented in A.J. Martin's name. From it he retrieved that list which Bates, or rather Miss Arden, had sent by the facsimile machine. A scan down its array of names confirmed that the prison recorded only thirteen people dead in that riot.

But Miss Arden, Bates' associate, had not sent the list by itself. The young woman had also wired some additional documents to the Agent, including a pair of black and white photos. Someone had made a snapshot of Patrice Anders in the first of them, and apparently the older woman—silver-maned, rather plain-featured, and double-chinned—hadn't considered photographic fame as an attainment to be pursued.

Much younger than the Anders woman, Charlotte Moon, the subject of the second picture, wouldn't have garnered many prizes, either. She owned the most pinched features, as if she'd caught wind of the most God-awful stench; and her tiny mouth suggested she sucked on persimmons for the sheer perverseness of it all. Wayne Helmer must have thought she was better than hotcakes and syrup, however. That picture, one seemingly spontaneous, showed him trying to twirl her at a charity dance, unadulterated glee writ large on his face.

X put these photos aside for a moment to peruse an additional record from Miss Arden. On seeing it, a transcription of a phone interview, he admired the young woman's sense of initiative and appreciated, further, the assistance of Bates' friend Parker. Somehow the man had reached the retired Vance Hallan, Attica's former warden. There the good news dribbled to a halt, however. Hallan's wife Myrna had been the only one who could take the call, since the retired man was on his deathbed after suffering a terrible stroke.

Myrna Hallan *could* confirm that a pair of bodies had been claimed by family members, but their names escaped her. All she could give was a description of the survivors and their deceased loved ones, based on her husband's account from three years ago. The manhunter nodded to himself. He suspected the first murder victim squared with Malcolm McGrieve, with the survivor being, most likely, Victor McGrieve himself who recovered the supposed body. This was no surprise to the Secret Agent.

The name of the other murder victim completely escaped her. All she could recall from the husband's description was the fact that the man had been "a good-looking fellow, a gentleman with fine features." At least, these were the words she'd stated to Bates' friend Parker. But there was no doubt about the two people who'd picked up the man's body. One of them was the ubiquitous Mr. Ramond—her husband had called him this—and, presumably, his wife, a woman who complained of aching feet.

Eerie lights flashed through X's gray

optics. He had a good idea who this woman was. And his hunch made it that much more imperative that he leave Martin's office post-haste.

Quickly he long-legged his way to the building's elevator and down to the street, where he had parked his auto.

Aboard the vehicle in mere seconds, he pushed the car's supercharged engine for all it was worth. It seemed that the chariot's might increased, the further and faster he pushed it.

In what seemed mere heartbeats, X zoomed to a stop in front of the Moderne, an apartment in the West Village, that is, immediately northwest of Washington Square. This new place must have made Spangler think he had hit the big time, since the structure was one of New York's ritziest new apartment buildings. A masterpiece of the French art deco style, the edifice showcased the art movement's bold outlines, its emphasis on rectilinear shapes.

As the Secret Agent prepared to disembark from it, another machine, a practically new yellow cab, rumbled up to the building, then halted at the curb.

A thuggish character—gum cracking and pock-marked of skin—sat behind the wheel, a dirty brown touring cap pulled low over his eyes. He made some remark, apparently humorous, to the passenger, who laughed at the man's witticism. In silhouette the erstwhile traveler could be seen to pass a quantity of money to the cabbie. This act completed, the fellow, a bulky man in gaudy dress—loud yellow suit and tie, along with matching yellow shoes—stepped onto the concrete walk in front of the apartment building. He gave a quick greeting to a doorman nearby, but wasted no more time entering the Moderne. On his end, Agent X understood the reason for the former passenger's haste.

The large man was Butch Spangler, who was obviously trying to reach his apartment in advance of his meeting with the Resurrectionist's representative.

Agent X let a few minutes elapse.

Satisified the time was right, the Secret Agent left his own vehicle for the apartment's foyer. To the right of the elevator, he readily located the number of Butch Spangler's place, 305, etched onto a fancy bronze plaque with scrollwork. The disguised man-hunter thumbed the elevator's "up" button, and in seconds the car emitted its rumble as it traveled downward. He jumped aboard it faster than seemed humanly possible, sent it back upwards.

The elevator car dinged to a stop at the Moderne's third floor. X whipped from the thing, out into the hallway. Spangler's apartment was only paces away, to his left. He reached it, and knocked on the door.

At first his effort garnered no reply. He tried two more times. Since he still enjoyed no success, X figured that the man were in another part of the apartment; or he might be on a telephone. X shot a quick glance at a watch, a pocket model, since Ramond never wore one on his wrist. It was the correct time, all right, 8:00 pm. He was about to give up when a bolt in the door emitted a sharp *snick*.

The metal panel slid back ever so slightly, and a man's voice, the coarse tones of Spangler himself, grated from behind the door: "Whatcha wantin', huh?"

The Man of a Thousand Faces had to act quickly, just as the real Mr. Ramond would do in the same circumstances.

He answered, "I bring you the 'life from death'—from the one who is resurrection...."

The words were an "Open Sesame" to the man on the other side of the door.

Instantly the metal panel flew back to disclose Spangler, in all his yellow-suited glory. "Hell, Ramond, I was wonderin' what took ya so damn' long. C'mon in, and grab a seat," he invited. "I was in the back, writin' somethin' down in a little book I keep for appointments. Got one of another one of 'em to keep in a little while, so ya better make it quick."

Another appointment? thought the Secret Agent. *With whom? And for what purpose?*

He decided not to dwell on such details, but to get down to business.

"You know why I'm here, don't you, Spangler?" he began in the mellifluous tones of Mr. Ramond.

"Hell, yes, I do, Ramond. It's about makin' that last payment to your boss, the Resurrectionist, isn't it?"

This was an interesting development, this reference to a final payment. X decided to play along. "Yes, your lilac is coming due—the final installment, that is. Are you ready to experience the 'life from death'?"

"Sure. I'm not wantin' to face a Federal trial any more than those other clowns were. I'm ready to get this show on the road, ya know? Yer boss gets my entire dope set-up—my manufacturing system, my connections, everything. That much, alone, is worth a fortune ta him. Then I get just what *I* want: He offs me, and he takes *all* the blame. After that, I get my new face, get outta Dodge, and start my new life, down in Mexico."

"I see. You have the path of your future life mapped out quite specifically, don't you?"

"Gotta make sure my sugar's taken care of, Ramond. And I'm talkin' about my gal, too, not that dope the Resurrectionist uses. Sure I want that stuff for my return—but no more after it. See, I gotta think about more important things, like providin' for my sweetie. Plus, I gotta have enough for myself—overhead is gettin' ta be too much, these days, what with hirin' gorillas, findin' a space for business, payin' off the law, runnin' my gamblin' and dope rackets. Just the everyday grind. Ya know what I mean?"

So this was it—Spangler's motivation for joining the Resurrection Ring in the first place. He probably cared about X's identity only in the most tangential way. In truth, Spangler was taking care of his own business affairs, however crooked they might be. Plus he was financing the expenses of his sweetheart, Monica Willens, simply to hold onto the alluring woman. It all made perfect sense!

Gray eyes crafty, X agreed, "I know *exactly* what you mean. What would you say, Spangler, if I told you that I had a proposition of my own for you?"

The tough guy slipped a package of cigarettes and a lighter from the left pocket of his robe. "Well, it depends on what kinda proposition ya mean, Ramond. I ain't got much time, since I gotta pick up Monica in," he dropped his head in the direction of his left wrist, "hell—I've only got about fifteen minutes till I cut out for Monica's apartment and we run back ta the Jazzy Kat. Gotta try out a new swing band tonight. Might steal 'em for myself, doncha see? Gotta keep the rubes happy. So ya'd better talk quick, or forget it."

This intelligence put the Agent into high gear. "I've got a quantity of the Resurrectionist's 'sugar' with me, as we speak. How would you feel about taking it right now—and doing your fadeout a little sooner than you'd planned?" he finished, his eyes glittering in a conspiratorial fashion.

"Yer awfully keen ta do this now, aincha, Ramond? What's in this for ya, huh?"

"Let's just say I'm going to sell my wares elsewhere. I know of a fellow who'll pay me more—much more—for my formula and for my services. And making a profit is all I care about, not his Resurrection Ring."

Butch Spangler's green eyes became hard. "This is too convenient, yer showin' up here, then askin' me to throw in with ya and renege on yer boss. Who's ta say ya won't turn on me?"

The right hand of the suspicious man suddenly dove inside the waistband of his pants, brought forth a .38 automatic pistol.

Under the gun, literally, X didn't have time to argue with him, much less battle Spangler and steal his identity in advance of Monica Willens' arrival. Meanwhile Spangler wasn't quite ready for this episode to end.

"See, I'm still not clear, why yer wantin' ta sell some 'sugar' ta me. Way I hear it, that stuff's death for the clowns who're takin' it. 'Course, that ain't stoppin' 'em from usin' coke or heroin, either," he chuckled cruelly. "S'ppose some people'll buy anything, eh? That's why I do what *I* do. I'm just a businessman, performin' a service ta the community—givin' 'em what they want. And ta tell ya the truth," he stated with a cynical grin, "that's what makes me *love* my business."

Spangler had trained the gun directly on the Agent's midsection, which the detective protected with his bulletproof vest. The man was smirking at the Secret Agent, daring him to do something like charge the gangster.

Smiling from behind his bearded, counterfeited features, X merely stood there, stock-still. "You're crazier than I thought, Spangler, if you think that I'm going to tangle with *you*. I know all about your reputation."

The gang chief—his ego was only slightly smaller than the state of Texas—returned the Secret Agent's smile with a broad grin. "Ya did right by that," he complimented. Keeping the .38 trained on the Agent still, Spangler walked over to an end table beside his sofa. From a drawer at its top he extracted a length of cord, his intent being to bind the Agent, pump him for additional information, and most likely murder him on the spot.

His smile had changed to a sneer of contempt. "Yeah, ya know my reputation, all right; and ya know what I do ta cheats too—especially when they come inta my home, like ya done. See, my mind's made up. I'm goin' through wit' this, and risks be damned. It's going to happen tonight, see, right after I leave the Jazzy Kat. When Monica and I are walkin' outta my club, right on the street, that's when some o' his guys are gonna drive up in one of those white machines. And that's when they'll plug me," he bragged. Laughing like a goon, he concluded, "Death never looked so good. And there ain't a damn' thing ya c'n do ta stop me."

The man ordered Agent X to put his hands behind his back. Suddenly X pivoted on his left heel, whipped around, threw up his left arm in a vicious bludgeoning motion. The devastating blow knocked the man to his knees on the floor of the apartment. In the meanwhile, his .38 went spinning off to the side, many feet beyond his reach. Cursing, the man warned Agent X of the certainty of his, Spangler's, revenge.

"Ya know what I've done to men in the past, Ramond!" he gritted, scrambling for his pistol.

Before he could rise, the Secret Agent blasted a punishing jiu-jitsu kick, right into the man's chin. He crashed, instantly, back to the floor.

X was desperate for time now, to make that appointment, as Spangler, with Monica Willens. Wasting no time, he divested himself of Ramond's Van Dyke beard, as well as the gray toupee he'd adopted for the present role. In the next instant he was rifling through his pocket makeup kit. From it he grabbed a dark brown toupee; the appropriate contact lenses, sea green, to mimic Spangler's eyes; and a small bottle of skin pigmentation. This would, of course, enable him to alter his own complexion to a more faithful approximation of Spangler's own.

He tied Spangler with the cord the gangster had meant to use on the Agent. Following this, Secret Agent X stripped Spangler of his yellow suit, and left the unconscious hoodlum on the floor. The Agent, suit in hand, made the man's bathroom his next goal. From its medicine chest he filched a small jar of Spangler's own pomade for his dark chocolate toupee.

All of these preparations made, the Secret Agent consulted a telephone directory for the address of Monica Willens. When he'd found the site, a mere two miles distant, he switched to his UHF device. Over that gadget he transmitted a call to the Bates Agency. He requested Miss Arden to send an operative to Spangler's address and retrieve his, the Agent's, auto. At the same time the Bates man should be prepared, X told Miss Arden, to hold Spangler for police questioning, in conjunction with the crime lord's possible involvement in the Resurrection Ring. X in turn would commandeer the gambling racketeer's machine and drive the thing to Monica Willens' apartment.

In moments the Bates detective executed X's order while the Man of a Thousand Faces winged his way to his rendezvous.

The detective reached the Cosmpolitan, Monica's apartment, in no time. In two shakes, the Secret Agent was piloting the automatic elevator to the fifth floor. As speedily he found himself outside her apartment door, announcing his arrival via a door-knocker at eye level.

Monica Willens wasted no time in answering the Secret Agent's summons at her door. She had donned a low-cut, sleazy dress of white satin and gold trim to greet this man she thought was her "sugar daddy." An aura of perfume, Lady of Jasmine, hovered around her lovely form. The scent imparted a feel of old Storyville, the former New Orleans red-light district, to the Secret Agent's encounter.

"Where have you been, 'Butchie'?" she balled her hands into fists, rammed them against her shapely hips. This didn't last long, however, as she practically knocked him down and kissed him most passionately. "You're late."

"Yeah, I am—ain't I?" the Secret Agent offered no excuse, other than a chicken-eating grin.

The woman grabbed the master of disguise by his lapels and yanked him into her apartment without another word. She wanted to know how everything had gone at his other appointment. And it was clear that she knew too much about the real Butch's meeting for this to be mere curiosity.

With a sly nod to his own facility for disguise, Agent X told her about the arrival of Mr. Ramond, painting the man as a money-grubber out to "pad his own damn' pockets."

"Cripes!" he went on. "Ramond even offered me some of his own supply of the 'sugar,' and he knows what it will do to somebody. But I stopped 'im."

"Meaning what?" Monica angrily came back.

"Ya've heard what that stuff does ta people—unless they get that antidote. Me, I ain't wantin' no part of that kind o' thing, anymore, after that first shot of it. See, I likes my life way too much," he concluded with a thick-lipped grin. "Mebbe I'll just go off on my own, and—"

This account shocked Monica Willens to her core. "I can't believe this! You're turnin' chicken! And to top it off, Ramond is pushin' plans of his own when he's supposed to be helping the Resurrectionist's cause! I can't believe either one of you is doin' this, Butchie!"

How instructive that she had become so heated, the Agent thought to himself. Perhaps *she herself* had something to gain by Butch Spangler's involvement in the Resurrection Ring. In his long war on crime, he'd certainly met more than his share of women who matched the menfolk for their ruthlessness and greed.

Something else might also be true of Monica Willens. She might actually be *serving* the Resurrection Ring, probably as one of its "ropers," or, "outside men," those who brought people into the criminal enterprise.

He could test his hypothesis immediately.

"Monica, what if I decide I ain't gonna follow through with all o' this mess? I mean, what if I decide I'm gonna stay solo, fight my own battles against Uncle Sam?"

"*You can't do that!* You've signed a contract, and you've got to go through with it, come hell or high water."

"That a fact, Monica? I was thinkin' 'bout us, uh, ya know, marryin' and all," he baited his trap. "We talked about it. Mebbe now's the time ta cut outta this racket the Resurrectionist is runnin'."

"Me—marry a clown like Butch Spangler?" she glared at him, the saucy beauty's light gray eyes crackling with hell-fire. "You must be kiddin' me! I'm just in this for—"

Throwing up his hands, open-palmed, the Secret Agent silenced her. An air of shrewdness permeated the Agent's next words. "Thought so. Well, since Butch Spangler just won't do as a spouse," he dropped his voice to its natural tone, "maybe you'll settle for someone else."

If a single look could kill, then Monica would have gladly tortured and murdered the investigator. She formed her lovely mouth into an ugly sneer. "And just *who* might that be?"

An arch expression on his disguised face, he replied, "I thought you knew already—Secret Agent X."

CHAPTER XXVI
PERIMETER OF THE RING

INFURIATED, Monica Willens hurled herself at the Agent, swinging punches like a boxer on fight night. Swiftly he backpedaled from her, but she came at him again, this time with even more rage than previously. X threw up his hands to guard his face from her clawing fingers. She continued to strike and slap in his direction, as if she herself were one of the addicts to the "sugar."

But the dope wasn't powering the engine of the woman's being. It was sheer, unadulterated hatred, which inspired Monica's vicious attack.

With blinding quickness he caught both her wrists and slammed them together. In the next second he'd removed a pair of handcuffs from a pocket and clasped the metal circlets around her wrists. The woman thus restrained, he carried her over to her sofa, a fancy, overstuffed antique affair with bone-white lace doilies on the armrests and back, and slammed her onto its downy bulk.

"He's gonna grab you! He's gonna inject you with the 'sugar' and turn you into a bag of bones!" she screamed at him. "Just wait and see if I'm not right!"

"Make me an addict, like the rest of them, and kill me afterward, eh?" the Agent deduced. "That's what he's already doing. Either the Resurrectionist—or Ramond—has introduced a powerful stimulant into the formula for the 'sugar.' That drug, coupled with the original chemical, makes the anastastralose that much more addictive—not to mention deadly."

"Do you think I care about that? Or that *the Resurrectionist* cares about that? *Do you*? He's been out for your blood for almost as long as I have—or as Ramond has, for that matter. I don't give a fig for what you and your kind represent."

The cold tone of her admission froze the Secret Agent in his tracks, all of a sudden. Why did she feel such a profound detestation towards him? The Secret Agent didn't even know her from Miss Astor's cat. She was ranting like a madwoman. Unless—

Down to her face his questing right hand drifted. In an eyeblink he scratched his hand across her left cheek, and the resulting motion didn't cut her flesh. Rather, it *peeled* a long swath of skin—three inches or so—from her very face!

Off the sofa Monica blasted. She began to fight him, throwing punches again at his face and shoulders. Even manacled as she was, the woman was a veritable wildcat in female form. Agent X dodged and parried every one of her blows. As unexpectedly, he slapped her cuffed hands downward with his left hand; with his right he snatched a handful of her hair.

The entire lot of her red-gold tresses came off, abruptly, into his hands! While she pitched her fit, the Agent could only stare in amazement at—Teresa Fox, the erstwhile assistant to Dr. Emel!

X drew his gas gun and with it hustled her back to the sofa.

Only because she was at gunpoint did she fear him enough to sit. Still she had to get in a couple of digs, both of them obscenities, before the Secret Agent spoke another word.

"Well, Miss Fox—you have a 'learned' vocabulary, don't you? Will wonders never cease!" X finally said, casually folding his arms. "I suspected something was up when I saw those busts in Ramond's office, over at Caledonian Gardens."

"You've got nothing on me, X," she gritted at him, her gorgeous face suddenly grotesque as a harpy's visage.

"I think not," X contradicted her with a sly grin. "Each of the busts depicted the faces of women who just happened to be tied up with the Resurrection Ring's so-called 'victims.' The women were all ropers, to bring the men into the Ring's orbit. Oh, and lest I forget, one of the busts was a representation of your own lovely features, those of the *real* Teresa Fox. And one other was the face of Monica Willens, the role you're playing—or were playing, gray contact lenses and all, to lure in Butch Spangler."

She sidestepped his statement of her disguise with a ridiculous declaration: "That bust of me you saw. It—it was just an artistic representation, a sculpture, and nothing more. I was a model for Ramond, and—"

"So you admit you've been working for Ramond—or Emel, hmm? For that's who he really is, isn't he?"

"My uncle is dead, X."

"So I've heard. Funny how people associated with the Ring turn up alive, though, isn't it, Teresa?"

Eyes bitter, she husked, "Okeh. So Uncle Morris is alive. He faked his murder years ago—as I faked mine. We had help, but what of it?"

"Morris, eh?"

" 'Morris Lorin Ramond' is his full name, if you want to be technical."

"Uh-huh. The ever-delightful Mr. Ramond. That's probably an alias too, isn't it?"

Teresa shot her head away from the Agent, tightly pursed her beautiful lips.

"Let's try a different approach, since you won't cough up his real name. You shot him with a dose of the 'sugar,' using a delivery method he himself designed. That specific method was a kid's target pistol, a Webley Senior airgun, used because of its virtual silence, but modified for 'special' service here. More precisely, your Webleys shoot *wax bullets*, tipped with hollow needles. In turn, your Ring has doctored these with the stastralose, a 'sugar.'"

"I'd like to see you prove this, especially in court," she sneered.

"Oh, my evidence against you would *certainly* hold up in court. And here is the reason: I made the discoveries of the bullets and the 'sugar' when I performed a spectrographic analysis in my own laboratory. The projectile revealed itself as a machined object, not something hand-crafted, with part of its seam intact. I was able to finish splitting it open and find a hollow within it. I also found some interesting liquid inside. Elsewhere, I discovered more fluid, whose chemical structure matched that of the 'sugar' your Ring is using. Of course, *none* of this information—the wax projectiles, the target pistols, or the composition of the 'sugar'—is revelation to you, now, is it?"

Her mouth suddenly became a locked gate, offering no ingress to the Secret Agent.

His only sign of emotion was a lifted eyebrow. "No comments this time, eh? Very well. Let's turn to your current disguise as Monica Willens. Will you admit to the fact that something like my own volatile plastic material, a crumb of it, was clinging to one of the busts in Ramond's safe?"

"I'm not saying anything to you, if that's what you're hoping for...."

"That's not surprising. You'll squeal like a stuck pig when the court is trying you for, oh, conspiracy to commit murder, racketeering, insurance fraud, no telling what else."

"You don't frighten me one little bit, Secret Agent X," she stated with amazing candor. "When the Resurrectionist is through with you, he'll—

"—Torture me and all of my organization, and kill us all," he sing-songed. "Frankly, I'm weary of those threats because I've heard them too many times to count, from too many two-bit rats to remember. You realize that, too, don't you?"

"He's got the ability to make it come true—unlike some of your previous enemies. You see, he's a step away from learning your real identity."

"Ham Esler is the way he thinks he's going to find it, I suppose?"

Teresa pivoted her head back towards the Agent. She favored him with a cruel laugh, one completely belying her loveliness. "Ham Esler is one of our allies. He'll do *anything* to help the Resurrectionist—and anything to get revenge on you."

"Oh, really? I hear he's too busy, at present. Word is that he's enjoying some sparkling conversation inside a police precinct house. I'm thinking Mr. Esler simply *won't* be able to pull himself away from such convivial hosts. You probably know their charms, too—don't you?"

The young woman fell silent. She slowly comprehended the challenge the Resurrection Ring had taken on in its battle against the Man of a Thousand Faces. Grudgingly she was forced to admit the unthinkable. X had begun to turn the tide against the Resurrection Ring, despite her master's best efforts to the contrary.

"You know I'm supposed to go back to the Jazzy Kat in a little while—"

These other details the Agent also filled in, concluding, "Your bunch thinks it's so sharp, but you trust people *too* easily, don't you—like you trusted me at first? Pretty naïve, if you ask me."

Sandpaper's grit spread over the public defender's next words, "Now—you'll slip that wig back over your head and play Monica Willens to the hilt. I'll even repair that makeup job for you to make the role authentic. We're going back to the Jazzy Kat, in Butch's car. And you'll gladly cooperate with any of my stage directions while you're acting in this little drama. That is, unless you want me to turn you over to the Resurrectionist."

"You wouldn't *dare* do that," she whimpered, her eyes darting back and forth in terror. "I mean—you know what that Wrath—"

"I see we both understand what that would mean, don't we? And I take it that you don't find the delightful scent of burning flesh a good complement to your beautiful hair and your white satin dress?"

Dismayed by the Secret Agent's suggestion, the woman became compliant, allowed him to repair her makeup. Some small embers of resentment still blazed within the lovely brunette, however, as the next moment revealed.

Teresa gave him a crafty look. "I suppose you're ready to leave?"

Her expression wasn't lost on the Secret Agent, no matter what the woman might have thought. He decided to play along with her, since he believed she intended him more ill.

Thus he said, with seeming naiveté, "Sure, let's get going. I think a bit of music will lighten the mood." He let this statement sink in with her, yet he followed it with one to chill her bones: "But remember what I told you a moment ago."

Her evil thoughts lent an unnatural beauty to Teresa Fox as she and the Secret Agent strode casually outside her apartment and to the elevator. Soon they had reached the ground floor and, outside, Butch Spangler's sedan. He had already uncuffed the woman, so now he merely allowed her to enter the auto under her own power.

This, the woman did, climbing in beside him as he cranked the machine and got it underway for their brief trip to the club.

"What do you intend to do, once you've reached the Jazzy Kat?" she purred, trying to entice him with her not inconsiderable allure.

Agent X informed, matter-of-factly, "What do you think? One: I aim to learn more about this Resurrection Ring. Two: I'm going to free my friends from their leader, in the process. And three: I fully intend to stop his threat to the public, once and for all."

"You honestly think you'll succeed, don't you, Mr. X?"

Confident, the Man of a Thousand Faces ignored her words and continued along his previous path: "The best way to accomplish all of these goals is to go straight to the next murder site—the Jazzy Kat," he told her.

Peering directly into her eyes, he scared her with the next remark, delivered in such a blunt manner: "When we arrive, maybe I'll shove you in between myself and the next bullet fired from one of the Resurrectionist's pistols. Or subject you to some torture of my own. A good pistol-whipping would mar those lovely features of yours. And as for that plastic surgeon your chief has hired? He'll be hard-pressed to correct what my pistol, here, would do to you. It's all metal, unlike some weapons. So you see, I have a couple of choices, right off the bat. And I'm sure I'll think of more...."

The prisoner was becoming antsy at the second of these prospects, this threat to her vanity. Her cheeks were taking on a deathly pale cast. Teresa's boss and the rest of his Ring had all claimed that the Secret Agent wasn't a ruthless man. His mercy and compassion were what made him weak and thus vulnerable. But here he was, talking like the most callous criminal she'd ever encountered—and she'd met or worked with more than her share of them. She couldn't know that he intended not a word of it, since his personal code precluded any intentional harm to anyone.

They continued their drive in silence until they reached the front entrance of the Jazzy Kat. From Butch's chariot, the Agent and his prisoner watched, tight-lipped, as patrons strolled in and out of the casino.

X wasn't pouting, of course. Instead he was scoping the site for the Resurrectionist's hit squad. As he played a waiting game, Emel Ramond's niece—she really *was* a member of his family—lit a cigarette and took a few slow drags on the thing. At the same time she tried to conceal the shaking in her hand, but she didn't do this too successfully. Her involuntary movements caused X to wonder if Teresa Fox, too, were an addict to the anastastralose, the infamous "sugar." Or it could be that she feared reprisals from the Secret Agent, or from the Resurrectionist himself.

Though Teresa hadn't finished her cigarette, she rolled down the window of the sedan and flicked the burning paper tube onto the sidewalk outside the Jazzy Kat. The cigarette's scarlet and gray tip gradually gave way to the palest of yellows. Eventually the end transformed into something on the Arkansas side of white. The object's metamorphosis wasn't lost on the young woman, who'd monitored the entire episode from the passenger seat. She lit a second cigarette, smoked it for a time, as well. And like that first one, number two bit the dust on the same sidewalk, but not without first turning that same color of yellowy white.

Finally, Teresa whispered to the Agent, "Look—I—I don't want to die—least of all because of that damned 'sugar,' or that Wrath of God he possesses. Maybe you'd like to know where the Resurrectionist really is—if it means I get to live without that beating you promised?"

"It's *not* a promise—*if* you don't lie to me."

"I won't lie."

"You really know the location of his headquarters?"

Teresa shrugged her slender shoulders just a bit. "I'm not certain of its exact whereabouts, but I've overheard my uncle Emel mention something about a 'Holy of Holies' somewhere near the Meatpacking District."

Agent X's eyes became sharp as pinpoints. "A 'Holy of Holies'? That sounds like a church. I know of an abandoned Presbyterian one, where that District meets the West Village. Since its windows are boarded up, no one on the street could see what's going on."

"Perhaps so," Teresa suggested. "Whatever the case, the Resurrectionist's crew will be going there. But that's after they finish with Butch. While they're whacking him, there'll be an additional team out there, making a hit on someone else. He made the mistake of not giving the Resurrectionist his just due."

"Someone else?"

"Victor McGrieve. That was the name I heard, yesterday."

"What time, exactly, will they pull the 'hit'?"

Tired of his questions, she replied with one of her own: "How should I know?"

X raised his gas pistol in a threatening gesture and allowed her to think he would as soon beat her like a yard-dog as not.

Chilled with fear, Teresa stammered, "I—I heard only—only the last part of the chief's words, and nothing more. Please—please believe me," she begged, hands over her lovely mouth. "But my best guess says they'll coordinate it with the attack, tonight, on Butch Spangler."

"This complicates matters," a frustrated X observed, knowing how much time it would take him and any possible allies to determine the exact victim, drive these distances, and thus prolong the danger for Betty, Jim, and Hiram. He decided to play the odds: "Do you know the location of Victor McGrieve's home?"

Head down, she muttered a street address, to which the Secret Agent said, "It's on the Upper West Side, isn't it?"

"Yes. But you'll need to follow the original plan, as Butch was supposed to do, if you hope to stop any of this."

"The original plan, as in, 'die,' by the 'sugar,'and then let the Resurrectionist's men take me there to that church, for a resurrection?"

Eyes crafty, Teresa pursed her mouth at him most enticingly. "You've done it before—back in '32. And you've got more incentive to do so this time, since we have nearly all of your friends in our possession.

"As we speak, the Resurrectionist has probably given all of them a few doses of the anastatralose since he captured them. They'll be craving it in the worst way, unless they can get a counteractant. And short of finding Osben, that's not going to happen.

"And don't think *you'll* get away, either, Mr. X. I've thrown a couple of cigarettes, actually flares, from this car, to identify your location to the Resurrectionist's killers. Also we still have an ace or two up our sleeves. So you see, you haven't a prayer against us...."

She laughed at his potential misfortune, and, all of a sudden, threw the door latch upward on the passenger side. Before she could make good her escape, Agent X clamped adamantine fingers on her left wrist. Reflexively, she shot her head in his direction, slapped his wrist in an attempt to break his hold.

"No, you don't!" the Man of a Thousand Faces exclaimed amidst her curses. "Your little games end—now!"

Up thrust the Agent's gas gun. A snake of grayish vapor hissed from the barrel. And Teresa Fox's perfect lips emitted a slight groan as she collapsed on the seat.

In seconds one of the Resurrectionist's infamous cars pulled onto the street from the opposite direction of the Secret Agent's machine. The position of the Resurrectionist's auto forced the driver to perform a U-turn, correct itself, and then seek a parking slot perhaps half a dozen spaces down from the Secret Agent and his passenger. Clearly the white machine sought a position for its crew to make the hit on Butch Spangler and depart the scene.

X thrust the key into the ignition's slot, and his borrowed machine roared into life. As promptly he cut the wheel hard to the left, the chariot's passenger door still opened. With a screech of his tires, he blasted Spangler's car back onto the street and around the corner to move the woman out of harm's way. Only two-score or so feet into the next block he whipped into the back parking lot of a Mom-and-Pop grocery which had long since shuttered its doors for the day.

Manner calm, the Secret Agent sent his right hand to the corresponding pants pocket for his UHF gadget. His device was still on, since he'd kept his promise to Harvey Bates to leave the thing activated.

X clipped to Bates, "Send some of your operatives from Station X-Twelve to my current position, post-haste. Ensure that they're wearing some of the new bulletproof vests, as I believe the Resurrection Ring will be armed with the Bolo Mausers once more.

"Also send another fellow to this other address," the Agent went on. "When the owner, a fellow named Grover Kelley, answers the door, direct your operative to show Kelley the proper credentials. Then have the owner give you a certain package and bring it to me."

"What about me, Sir?" Bates wondered.

The voice of the Agent, authoritative and resolute, was as close to his natural tone as Bates had ever heard: "You, too, Bates. Come if you're able."

The news left the giant elated like a faithful dog, ready to take up the hunt. He dispatched several men to the site, while the Secret Agent, inside the car, handcuffed Teresa Fox to the pedestal between the front and back seats.

Once he'd secured the woman, he rushed out of the automobile and back around the block. From behind a pick-up truck his gray eyes scanned the street. Less than five more minutes passed before some men from the Bates Agency—X spotted five of them in silhouette—swept around the corner in one of the Secret Agent's bulletproof sedans. After Butch's vehicle, an unfamiliar auto, departed, the Resurrectionist's men suspected a trick. So they decided to take charge of the situation and thus preempt the actions of any opponents.

Their car vomited forth four men, all dressed in the silver-white business suits. And because they stood underneath street lights, the Secret Agent could discern the types of weapons they carried. One of the supposed assassins carried a target pistol, one of the Webley kid's models. The remaining three men clutched handguns with short barrels and abbreviated pistol grips, the signs of Bolo Mausers.

X inched closer to the pick-up's hood as the quartet of white suits marched, arrogantly, towards the Jazzy Kat's entrance. The Secret Agent shot his hand back into his pocket, tapped out a message in Morse code to the Bates men. Harvey himself tapped back that they were ready. X told his men to form a cordon around the killers and to close their eyes briefly. At the same time he, the Agent, would attract the white suits' fire.

Keeping his eyes focused on his enemies, Agent X removed a small cylinder from the coat pocket of Butch Spangler's gaudy yellow suit. He gave a shout at the hoods. As they pivoted in his direction, he hurled the cylinder at the advancing men. Curses filled the air. Shots cracked in rapid succession. And the cylinder hit the ground, only to emit a blinding flash of white light, the sign of its magnesium charge.

Instantly a fresh cascade of obscenities washed over the street as the unseeing white suits fired everywhere around them. The gunshots couldn't help but inspire curiosity-seekers from the nightclub to venture to the front door, whereupon the same men and women, screaming like little children, raced back inside Spangler's casino just as quickly.

Meanwhile the gunmen's bullets continued to ricochet as the men from the Bates crew, eyes now opened, moved closer. Suddenly Harvey Bates caught sight of the Agent, standing near that pick-up truck.

Running towards the hoodlums, X pointed vigorously in the same direction. And Bates and his operatives charged the cursing white suits, driving them all to the pavement. The men, vision still partially blinded, balled fists and hurled them, clumsily, at their attackers from the Bates group. A lone fellow seemed near to regaining his eyesight as the Agent tackled him in the character's midsection. With a rush of escaping air, the white-suited tough clawed at the Agent for a second and collapsed.

In a few more seconds, Harvey Bates and his men had subdued their own foes, such that the entire group of white suits was vanquished.

In the next moment a young, dark-skinned operative with square jaw and handsome features passed that mysterious package from Grover Kelley, that is, Charles Darwin Osben, into the hands of Secret Agent X. He thanked the youth and said nothing more of it. Instead the detective held a private confab with the Bates crew and told them to disarm the Resurrection men. The Webley target pistol he momentarily retained for himself. In the meantime Harvey Bates' operatives would then transport the Resurrectionist's thugs, via the detective agency's own machine, to the nearest police precinct station. For his part X would notify Assistant Inspector Timothy Scallot of the group's imminent arrival.

With alacrity Harvey's men applied themselves to loading the toughs aboard the Bates Agency's car. Bates' detectives preparing now to drive away, the Secret Agent motioned for Harvey Bates to join him briefly. Preliminaries thrown to the winds, the master of disguise informed his associate of the Resurrectionist's next move. Bates promptly asked the Agent about their own course of action, to which the Man of a Thousand Faces, a sly look on his face, posed this: "How would you feel about killing *me*?"

CHAPTER XXVII INSIDE THE RESURRECTION RING

AT first the question perfectly horrified the square-jawed Harvey Bates. He couldn't imagine doing harm to his associate and friend—until Agent X clarified matters. In succinct, vivid terms the Agent explained his own brilliant scheme, one marked by both daring and simplicity.

Quickly the detective brought his pocket makeup kit into their midst. From its depths he fished a couple of tubes of his amazing volatile plastic, along with small bottles of dye for darkening a person's skin. Luckily X wouldn't need much of the stuff for the present disguise, he told Bates; as the giant owned a complexion close to the person he would need to impersonate.

And on grim reflection, X thought back to his conversation with Betty Dale and realized something else: Harvey Bates possessed a vague resemblance to Tiny that had nothing to do with Mother Nature. Agent X thus decided to make that similitude more pronounced. To that end he added more ingredients to the mix that would become Bates' disguise. The first of them was a pair of invisible lenses for altering a person's eyes. He slipped these bits of glass over the giants' optics and gave them tight scrutiny. They weren't quite a coffee brown in color. But they would suffice for the situation at hand, namely Bates' successful infiltration of the Resurrection Ring.

Now clutching the tube of volatile plastic, the man of mystery went to work on the giant's face, making the lines of Bates' face more classic and his lips more full. Gradually Harvey's own distinctive visage faded under the influence of the Agent's makeup wizardry. Without the original on the scene the Agent was performing his magic entirely from memory, but being the expert he was, X could conjure such a miracle effortlessly. After he'd inserted a couple of face plates in Bates' mouth, X finally ceased his labors.

He turned the kit's mirror towards Harvey Bates. X's associate trained his optics on the image which stared back at him.

"Tiny Sayre!" he exclaimed with uncharacteristic shock. "Face is just like his!"

Disguised lips curled into one of Spangler's grins, Agent X replied, "That's right—the Resurrectionist's chief contract killer, to the letter, if I do say so myself. And since you'll be impersonating him, you need to sound like him," X claimed. "Think you can pull off a credible imitation of his voice?"

"Refresh my memory, Sir," Bates requested, his trust in Agent X's memory readily apparent.

X repeated several phrases in the basso of Tiny, at the end of which Bates imitated them. After three or four tries he had achieved a creditable replica of Tiny Sayre's pitch and tone.

With clipped tones Agent X gave Bates one final directive. In the white truck he would drive to the address in the Meatpacking District and wait there for his chief's arrival. X in turn would remain in Butch Spangler's sedan, motoring to Victor McGrieve's home.

"For some reason, Victor is being targeted, as evidenced by his receipt of those letters. That's unlike Jay-Jay, who merely received a phone call or two. If I can drive to Victor's residence quickly enough, I intend to identify myself as X and remove him from harm's way. After that, I think I'll finally get to the bottom of this crime spree."

"Any way we'll know how to enter the Resurrectionist's headquarters, later on?"

The Secret Agent repeated the intelligence that Teresa Fox had shared with him. He concluded, "While Teresa didn't know the exact location, I believe that I can determine its entrance. But I'll require Victor McGrieve's services, equally as much. I think he can help me solve another of the mysteries involving the Resurrectionist himself."

With mutual wishes of good luck, the two friends zoomed away.

Bates reached the Meatpacking District in uneventful fashion. He parked the white delivery truck a block or so away from the aged building of Agent X's experience and the witness of Teresa Fox. And there Harvey Bates waited in the darkness....

Secret Agent X's trip across town, though a rapid one, was equally as mundane, that is, until he reached the spacious home of Victor McGrieve on the Upper West Side. Now from the upper end of the street, he spotted something he had hoped he might avoid: the presence of a white Chrysler sedan and a pair of the white suits. They lingered alongside the machine in wait for their confederates who had already stormed McGrieve's mansion.

In the darkness X pulled his borrowed chariot parallel with the street and parked the vehicle. As he was disembarking from it, he held his gas gun at the ready. On tiger's stealthy feet he padded across three different lawns towards the McGrieve residence. Lynx-eyed, he found cover behind a luxurious swath of hedge on the property of Victor McGrieve's next-door neighbor. The hedge stood perhaps three car lengths from the walkway of McGrieve's front door.

X watched carefully as two more men lugged a third fellow—it was Victor himself—through the opened and lighted front passage of the residence. The movers, if such they could be called, gritted a string of curses enroute to the white sedan.

The man of mystery heard snatches of their words:

"Sure knocked hell outta *him*, didn't ya?" the first one posed.

Muffled words followed this question, and the Secret Agent heard only a portion of the reply: "...unconscious cause that damn' gun of the Boss went on the fritz again!"

"Well, those Webleys can shoot the special bullets for only so long. Before you know it, that wax or whatever it is gums up the works. That's why I told you to clean out the barrel after every three or four of our hits."

So they hadn't used the "sugar" on McGrieve, if Agent X understood the hoodlums' conversation correctly. This news meant he could more easily revive the unconscious man, pump him for information, and bring him out of everything, alive.

X eased around the far side of the long, green hedge, such that he would come out parallel with the men hauling the undertaker to the sedan. The Man of a Thousand Faces crouched down a bit like a sprinter awaiting the starting gun. Without warning he launched his muscular body in the direction of the white suits, exploding into the rear figure with the force of a bomb blast.

The man went sprawling, with Victor McGrieve himself also crashing to the ground and dragging the third fellow down with him. Amidst this tangle both of the sedan's guards scrambled towards the other four. Before those newcomers could gain X and the rest, the Secret Agent had delivered a terrible jiu-jitsu thrust to the chin of a tough, who formerly carried McGrieve's head and shoulders. The blow threw the white suit's head backwards with whiplash force, sent him crashing back, unconscious, to the ground. In the meantime, his compatriot had by now regained his own footing. But X pivoted on his left heel, the right foot airmailed directly into the chest of the unfortunate. This worthy fell too before the surprise assault of the detective.

X went back on the alert even as used his left hand to palm something from one pocket while he trained his gaze on the scene to his front.

The remaining guards, Bolo Mausers ready, marched inexorably towards him. Only in this moment did they dare act. They would, they decided, flank and thereby capture the Secret Agent.

This plan the Secret Agent scotched with raised hands, the conventional gesture of surrender.

It was a good thing he did, since the man to Agent X's right, an angular man of hawkish features and harsh mouth, seemed especially bloodthirsty. To the Agent's left was another kill-crazed type, a horse-faced hoodlum. He had participated, of course, in the attack on Henry Terran, at the very beginning of the crime spree. Here at McGrieve's digs, Horse Face was taunting X, egging him on to try his hand at the two white suits.

"Come ahead an' try me, Spangler," he dared the detective. "Yer gonna wish ya really *was* dead, not just fakin' it, like the Resurrectionist fixed things."

His confederate probed, "Yeah, how come yer not laid out still, waitin' for the Resurrectionist ta raise ya?"

"That's because I got wise to everythin', boys," replied the Agent. "See, yer man Ramond showed up at my place and tried ta double-cross his boss. 'Fact of the matter is this: He was tryin' ta cut me in on a deal."

"Really?"

"Yeah, *really*. I squeezed th' truth outta Mr. Ramond. I finished 'im, right after that, too. He won't be squawkin' anymore, where he's goin," X stretched the truth. "And I decided then and there that yer big store wasn't much."

"Not much, eh?" was Horse Face's bitter question. He pivoted his head towards his thuggish companion. "He thinks the Resurrection's scheme is just a cheap con game, Hawk."

Horse Face's compatriot, the Hawk, normally a taciturn sort, opened his harsh mouth typically to fight his face, that is, to eat, or to cram a cigarette between his lips. Now his lips parted in a string of rasped obscenities, these ending in, "I'll make him think 'con game.'"

"Uh-huh—it's a con game yer boss is runnin', all right," the disguised Agent taunted the white suits as Spangler would have done. "'Specially if it allows a punk like Ramond to act like a roper for it. Yer damn' Resurrection Ring needed somebody more experienced, if ya get my drift."

Horse Face was becoming suspicious. "That a fact?"

"Uh-huh. I'm thinkin' if Ramond's on the double-cross trail, then he's prob'ly not travelin' it alone."

"And I'm thinking something else again," came the words of Hawk. He took over from Horse Face, "I'll burn ya down, right where ya stand, Spangler, unless ya drop that piece yer holdin'."

"Oh, I'll drop it, all right," Agent X promised the two men. "I'll drop it—right now!"

Down flew the gas gun in his right hand, the weapon taking a slight bounce onto the grassy lawn. With his left hand the Agent simultaneously hurled that object he'd palmed only seconds ago. The device, a small, globule of one inch diameter, crashed against the chest of Horse Face, shattered into an array of glittering shards. From these remains a grayish phoenix, a quantity of concentrated anesthetizing gas, slowly rose around Horse Face's head. A puzzled look passed through his muddy brown eyes. He coughed twice and keeled over. In the blink of an eye, the man of mystery jumped towards the lone survivor, bowling this man to the ground like his two predecessors. A couple of quick jiu-jitsu thrusts to the upper chest, and the Hawk changed his address to Slumberland.

At Victor McGrieve's side, Agent X determined the fellow's condition to be no more serious than a nasty abrasion and a Concord grape bruise, both of which he'd incurred to his right temple.

McGrieve was groaning a bit now, as if he were returning to consciousness. X brought the man around with a whiff of smelling salts from his medical kit. The sharp odor of the stuff caused McGrieve to gasp suddenly, blink his eyes, and raise his body a little. Agent X wrapped his strong right arm around the man and half-walked, half-pulled him to Butch Spangler's sedan.

Throughout the episode, the Secret Agent wrestled with endangering another life. But to achieve success, he must take this man along, into the very depths of the Resurrectionist's sanctuary.

Into the front passenger seat the Agent loaded McGrieve. After X had assured himself of the man's comfort and given him one of his heart pills, the detective took the wheel.

In short order the Agent started the sedan, whizzed the car towards the Meatpacking District.

X had been driving no more than five minutes when a deeply tormented Victor McGrieve suddenly mumbled, his deep voice seeming to originate from hell itself: "I'm sorry Malcolm! It's my fault for leading you and Jay-Jay on the wrong road! I'm sorry—so sorry—that everything came down to this! Please believe that I'll accept you," he finished, "and not just you. I—I—"

Spangler's machine wasn't one of the Secret Agent's super cars. Thus to drive the current machine at sixty and seventy miles per hour, on darkened city streets, was to push the chariot much harder than was natural—or probably safe. Moreover the circumstance compelled the Secret Agent to swerve, abruptly, around the parked cars and a number of delivery vehicles out at this hour. Indeed X's daredevil driving probably caused more tortured cries to pour from Spangler's back seat.

Eventually McGrieve bolted upright, parted his lips in a screech that would have awakened Lazarus. Agent X knew he needed to stop the sedan without delay, in order that he might check on the condition of his passenger. Therefore the sleuth whipped into a side street immediately prior to his arrival at the warehouse. Spangler's machine stopped, he checked the pulse in McGrieve's left wrist. It was remarkably strong, in light of his recent assault.

McGrieve, thinking he was still in the power of criminals, hung his head and mumbled to himself. He was begging this man Spangler not to harm him, assuring the racketeer that he, McGrieve, would comply with anything that the gangster directed him to do. After all, Spangler owed that much to Victor McGrieve, since the undertaker had already handled Spangler's final arrangements.

X realized his disguise was too good, especially as it related to the shaky condition of his "guest." Here, then, Agent X decided to reveal himself, immediately, as the Man of a Thousand Faces. Such an approach was more effective than continuing in his role as the criminal Butch Spangler. To that end the Agent removed a small card from his wallet, slipped it into Victor McGrieve's left hand.

The present oblong clearly wasn't something from Spangler, who wasn't known to carry such announcements with him. Nor was the calling card one of the Resurrectionist's own. He'd already seen one of those things.

A bold letter X branded this new pasteboard slip, though in seconds the character oxidized and disappeared before the eyes of the undertaker. Wide-eyed with shock, McGrieve rose up slightly from the passenger seat, at a loss what to do. He remained propped on one elbow till the investigator convinced him that he, X, was a Federal operative, and that he was trying to bring the Resurrectionist to justice. These last declarations and the Agent's kind assistance were ultimately proof enough for Victor McGrieve.

Rejuvenated now, McGrieve could relate the night's events to the Secret Agent. The older gentleman had gone to bed in hopes of reading himself to sleep. This was nothing unusual, he noted, since he followed the same routine every night. The phone beside his bed had interrupted his reading, but he'd decided to take the call. He knew he'd been—. No, he corrected himself. He had taken too many late-night calls in the past, so he figured this would be another. It might be someone who'd lost a family in a tragic accident.

X gave a nod to his statement, but he doubted the veracity of it. After all McGrieve had made a point to correct his misstatement. He had been on the verge of saying, X realized, that he *expected the call....*

This detail Agent X marked in his mind, intending to return to it momentarily.

Simultaneously, McGrieve was still relating the content of that phone call. The other person was threatening, hateful. It was, McGrieve believed, his own son Malcolm, who had come back as the Resurrectionist.

"You're sure that it was Malcolm's voice you heard?" X's words were abruptly sharp. "From what I've gathered, it is as distinctive as your own."

"I'd—I'd say it was, Mr. X. His pitch was certainly low enough, like mine. The tone was also close to Malcolm's, though perhaps a little off."

" 'Perhaps a little off,' eh? How so?"

"I'm not quite sure how to describe it. The voice seemed harsher than anything I'm accustomed to hearing from him, and I've heard him at his worst. This time, though, it was rather—I don't know how to say it—"

X had a sudden flash of inspiration at this last remark. Brilliant mimic that he was, the Secret Agent spoke a couple of sentences in Malcolm's voice, or more precisely, in the one Victor took to be that of his son. When the Agent had finished, Victor bobbed his head with enthusiasm.

"That sounds as if you're his twin! It's uncanny!"

"Thank you. Now, please continue, regarding the Resurrectionist's words to you."

"He told me that it was my time to die. And it didn't matter whether I was still in agreement with him or not."

He placed his account on hold briefly, and then restarted it: "He said they'd be out to my house to claim me, at any minute. They'd kill me and carry me away to his 'Holy of Holies.'"

"I've heard that term. Your assistant Teresa told me about it."

Uncomfortable, McGrieve rubbed his hands a couple of times. Following that deed, he averted his head and whispered a "yes."

He fell silent until, with X's urging, the fellow went on: "It might have been five minutes after that telephone call, when those men parked in front of my house. I left the window, but I was paralyzed with fear. Somehow, I made a run for the back of the house, since one of those white suits was marching towards the front. But I don't move particularly fast, so by the time I got to the back, another hoodlum was kicking the door down. He marched on in and took aim at me. But that odd little gun of his—"

"A Webley target pistol," X glossed.

"So *that's* what it was. Well, he aimed the thing at me and squeezed the trigger. But he couldn't make the gun shoot."

Once again it was the Secret Agent's turn. "When I reached your property, I heard them complain about using a gun that wouldn't shoot properly. Apparently its barrel was clogged with wax. I must tell you, McGrieve, that this kind of attack points to your involvement with the Resurrection Ring. You *were* tied up with them, weren't you?"

"I had been, yes—but he, the Resurrectionist, forced me into it," McGrieve admitted. "My heart and my fear of being involved with a criminal ring were driving me away from them, though. I just didn't know how to make my break."

"Interesting," Agent X commented. "This is the reason, a moment ago, you were about to say you were expecting that call from the Resurrectionist himself. Am I correct?"

Sad-faced, his lower lip turned downward, Victor McGrieve nodded his head. X decided to press him more strongly: "The Resurrectionist was blackmailing you, based on your previous criminal record, and the fact you believe him to be your son."

The older fellow said nothing this time, didn't even bob his head. But Secret Agent X's words painted additional details for this criminal portrait: "He was also counting on your not going to the police with your problems. In the meantime you were being compelled to work directly under the supervision of the Resurrectionist's chief intermediary, Morris Lorin Ramond. In fact the two of you were using that so-called 'special process' to prepare the supposed murder victims."

"Yes," the other one rumbled, his tone ashamed. He rubbed his eyes and shook his head. "I was using that procedure of Emel's. But I didn't know that the chemicals were so dangerous to the subjects. I swear that I didn't."

"They were extremely dangerous, deadly, in fact. Emel was addicting the Ring's 'marks' with a powerful stimulant, mixed with the other drug, the anastastralose," X deduced, his tone grim. "That additional concoction would make them dependent on the 'sugar,' such that they had to have regular injections of it, in order to survive.

"Emel knows this fact. He's known it all along, to be frank. It's the reason he's so keen on his 'special process.' Likely the Resurrectionist knows it too. From some of his behavior he leads me to believe he's addicted to the stuff like his followers are. But he would never admit it. He cares only about getting more criminal types to take the 'sugar.' That way, he'll always have a market for that devilish stuff, and rake in commensurate profits, besides.

"There's something else: That 'sugar,' as they call it, is important to me. I won't elaborate on the reasons—I hope you understand why—but suffice it to say that the formula is a variant of one I've encountered in the past. Under *no* circumstance can I allow it to go into the dope market. The risks to people, including myself, are far too great."

McGrieve was no dumb bunny. Moreover he was not an unkind, much less an evil man. Rather, he was one with more than his share of grief and heartache over his failed relationship with Malcolm. Truth be told, he was even regretful over his dismal relations with Jay-Jay. Hence the elder McGrieve answered the Agent, "All of your analysis makes sense, Mr. X. It fits well with the past history of my son Malcolm, who once ran a dope ring. I just wish, above all, that he hadn't gotten involved in all of this. God, how I wish that," he concluded, his lips quivering and his eyes dampening with sorrow.

The Secret Agent merely nodded his head but offered little additional comment, other than this affirmation: "I wish the same."

Both of them remained silent as Agent X restarted the sedan and eased it back onto the main street. Some blocks away he began to speak once more, almost as much to bring a sense of reality to these strange events, as to clue Victor McGrieve into his scheme.

X started with a bold assertion of his intent to penetrate the Resurrection Ring. Next, he asked McGrieve if he would consent to being anesthetized, albeit briefly. That way, he said, the two of them, teamed with X's associate Harvey Bates, could gain entry to the criminal operation. X related that the Ring would believe their plan to "kill" Victor McGrieve had succeeded. Last, Agent X would rescue his operatives and stop the Resurrectionist in his tracks.

Completely trusting the brilliant adventurer, McGrieve gave his assent to the Agent's plan. X thus removed that mysterious package of Osben from a place inside his coat. From the parcel he took out a small, specially treated bullet fashioned of wax. Its tip had been specially modified in the same manner X had deduced the Resurrection Ring's own bullets to be. And the projectile had been further altered, in line with Agent X's earlier request to Doctor Charles Darwin Osben.

Promptly X shot Victor McGrieve, point-blank in the neck, with the Webley.

Shortly, he and his comatose guest reached the proper street. He noticed instantly that it was poorly lit, with many of the street lights out or dim. X rounded the corner; but once out of the turn, he spotted not a single vehicle in his line of vision. For a moment he was worried that something might have happened to his giant associate. In other words, the Resurrection Ring might have found him, perhaps carried him into captivity as they'd done with Jim Hobart, Betty Dale, and Hiram Beckwith.

Agent X moved into a short side street as he done earlier. After stopping the racketeer's car, he parked it for a bit, Victor McGrieve locked up inside. The next breath found the man of mystery departing the chariot and venturing onto the side street. From thence it was back onto the main drag beyond. He trotted many feet down this thoroughfare though not quite to the front of the warehouse. All the while he was scanning the street for a sign of Bates. Out of his peripheral vision he spied an alley, and deep in shadow, a truck, facing the street.

It was the white delivery machine. But Agent X couldn't see Bates under the wheel.

Quietly the Agent padded over to the truck's cab. He pursed his lips. A soft, eerie whistle, bird-like in quality, permeated the surrounding air. The sound was the call of Secret Agent X, a token Bates would easily recognize.

Sure enough in a couple of seconds, Bates, a .38 automatic in his right hand, came around the back end of the truck and walked towards his chief.

The giant began, "Everything all right, Sir?"

"Yes. I stymied the attack on Victor McGrieve. He's in Spangler's car, around the corner. We'll retrieve him right now, and discuss what you've found while we run back to the car."

The plan was agreeable to Bates, so he and the Agent took off.

En-route to the sedan, X hypothesized, "You must have feared discovery by them, to be parked in that alley and not on the street."

"Heard some truck rumbling along on the next block, right after I arrived here. So I backed into that alley and peeked around the corner. Good thing I did, too."

"Were they some of the criminals?" the detective turned towards his friend.

"White truck pulled up down there," Bates nodded, pointing down the block. He winced suddenly because of the lingering damage the Resurrection Ring had caused to his feet.

"They're bothering you, Bates?" X queried, stopping.

"I can take it, Sir," his giant associate insisted.

Agent X was skeptical, so he decided to monitor his friend's condition with more care.

In a few more seconds they started running once more, whereupon the man-hunter requested, "Finish what you were telling me about that white truck."

His features still taut, Bates continued, "Machine drove away from this street, right afterward," he said, pointed fifty or sixty feet away from them. "But not before it unloaded four or five of their crowd."

"Did the driver or anyone else see you?"

"No, Sir. Seem to have eluded all of them, at least for the present."

"Could you tell where the foot passengers went?"

"Opposite end of the warehouse was their goal, best as I could tell."

X stated, "That makes sense. This particular entrance is likely near that conference room I've already seen."

"Been on the horn with some of my operatives, Sir," the square-jawed giant briefly changed the subject. "They have an idea who the Resurrectionist might be, and you're not going to believe it. Parker called Hallan's wife back, and she had found his diary, shoved deep into a chest of drawers. Anyhow she gave him a detailed account, stretching all the way back to that prison riot in 1936 and the two men whose names didn't show up in the list of casualties."

When Bates told X the two names, X bobbed his head. He had suspected these were the two men in question.

They were, by now, parallel with the property of Butch Spangler, that sedan hiding the unconscious Victor McGrieve.

X unlocked the car and removed the insensate mortician from the front passenger seat. He followed this deed by hoisting the man over his shoulder. Now the Secret Agent and Bates started back towards the alley and the concealed truck. During the return trip, the Man of a Thousand Faces analyzed Bates' account. His thoughts kept swirling around the real identities of the men killed in that prison riot. Something *still* didn't quite fit. The motive of the man in question *still* didn't square with the man Bates' friend Parker had fingered as the Resurrectionist. He wasn't someone X even knew. And yet....

They gained the delivery truck, and X promptly threw open the two gates at the rear. McGrieve he stored in the large area behind the double doors.

Names of enemies—scores of them, in fact—took wing, in the mind of the Secret Agent. Some of them were people X reasoned *could not* be the Resurrectionist. Such individuals were either imprisoned or dead. Abruptly the man of mystery had to smile at his momentary lapse. The Resurrectionist had apparently been both. And he'd still managed to cover his tracks in most devilish manner. This was a puzzle of epic proportions, indeed.

Still, such an insoluble problem couldn't remain thus forever. So the Agent laid it aside. At present he must tell Bates something far more important, namely information about their next move inside the warehouse. And that maneuver involved giving his associate the cue to play Tiny, in earnest.

Harvey Bates knew this was the trick up Agent X's sleeve. As a consequence, he became apprehensive. "Sure this plan will work, Sir?"

A smile curled X's disguised lips. "Nothing like the present to find out, eh, Bates?"

From his pocket he retrieved the Webley target pistol and shoved it into Bates' right hand. Next Agent X took his gas gun from his pocket, made a slight adjustment in one particular mechanism. This weapon, too, he handed over to Bates. X's words were serious: "I've reset a valve to release a much less concentrated stream of the gas's active ingredient. Now the anesthetic will keep me unconscious for only—"

Rumbling along the next block, another truck caught the attention of Harvey Bates. It would be only a matter of time before the thing halted in front of the warehouse.

"Now, Bates—before they can reach the warehouse and figure out the trick! Shoot me *now*!"

And Harvey Bates, dark eyes grim, squeezed the trigger of the gas gun....

CHAPTER XXVIII
CORRIDOR FOR KILLERS

BATES had loaded the unconscious Agent aboard the truck, cranked the machine, and flung it into the street.

His timing of the next moments was impeccable.

After his return to the main thoroughfare, the other truck rolled onto the street's opposite end. That second vehicle made a beeline for the warehouse. The square-jawed giant's truck rumbled towards them, Bates having donned a mask of impassivity that belied the violent churning in his stomach.

His truck halted immediately in front of the other vehicle while two more hoods climbed from the cab.

Dark brown eyes perpetually wearing a dying-calf look, the first hood, a young fellow, recognized Bates as one of his confederates in the gang.

"Hey, Tiny!" he greeted in a voice that was too old, too rusty for one as youthful as himself. "I see that yer bringin' that Spangler hisself as yer date tonight!"

This man, too, was already a victim of the chronic twitching, an indicator of his dependence on the "sugar." The same was true of the second ruffian, a little guy whose owl eyes missed nothing and whose small mouth convulsively jerked, every few seconds.

"Yeah, glad ya could finally make it to the dance with the rest of us," he spoke in a whispery sort of voice. "And don't Spangler look good enough ta take ta Chinatown, Volcker?" he guffawed to Calf Eyes.

Harvey Bates, not knowing how to respond, merely offered a slight smile to these men, his supposed allies in the Resurrection Ring. Evidently this wasn't the appropriate response for these two, as Volcker, Calf Eyes, remarked, "Tiny—whattsa matta wit' ya? Aintcha got a snappy comeback to t'row out at Siegen or me? Hmm?"

The eyes of Harvey Bates were hard as diamond. His mouth was grim. His voice, dark and deep like Tiny Sayre's own, boomed, "Guess I'm not feeling like it tonight. Got too much on my mind. So don't bother me, okeh?"

"Damn! Ya ain't gotta be such a grouch! Must not o' had yer 'sugar,' eh, boy?" the slight man, the Owl, opined.

"Yeah—no 'sugar' tonight And I'm mean as a snake when I don't get it, either," Bates declared, his hand suddenly gripping the front of the Owl's, Siegen's, coat, lifting the small tough a good foot from the ground.

Calf Eyes acted the peacemaker: "Look, ya two—ya better save that kinda thing for Mr. X, when we get him! C'mon now, and let's get to the entrance in the conference room. The Resurrectionist is waiting in the sanctuary."

Daggers of pure hatred stabbed from the optics of the owl-eyed criminal. But he backed down at the order of Calf Eyes, who seemed to be his immediate superior. With Calf Eyes, Volcker, leading, Siegen passed through the warehouse's door. Harvey Bates marched behind the other two white suits, the unconscious Agent X slung over one shoulder and an equally insensate Victor McGrieve thrown over Bates remaining one.

The weight of X and McGrieve were taking a toll on Harvey Bates, much as had the giant's brief run down the street, of moments past. He forced himself to admit he couldn't lug his chief and the mortician forever. Bates had to acknowledge, besides, that the Secret Agent must regain consciousness, and soon. Otherwise his ruse would not produce the desired results.

Siegen and Volcker made ridiculous small talk as they and the Bates' trio moved a door at the back of the warehouse. At this new portal they encountered another white suit of immense proportions—a man short, obese, balding, and thin-nosed. In a voice curiously child-like, he directed them to the conference area's rear. That long, rectangular table and several chairs occupied this piece of real estate. Had he been conscious, X would certainly have recognized the place.

Volcker found a seat at near the table's center, in front of the largest chair. He touched a button, recessed into the rectangular furniture's surface. Smoothly, as though resting on ball bearings, the table and its marble platform slid to one side. The space below disclosed a steep staircase that plunged deep into the ground.

With Bates lugging X and Victor McGrieve, Volcker and Siegen entered the passage to find themselves on a long tunnel which stretched interminably.

From the scores of pipes snaking their way along, Bates discerned that this was one of the many corridors through which steam heat traveled in winter.

Meanwhile Volcker halted them at well-worn portion, a panel whose top came only to eye level, even for a person of average height. There he tapped out a signal.

Sliding backwards, it revealed a much different passage from the one they'd recently traversed. For one, a crumbling, rust-colored brick, not concrete, lined the walls. In addition, the path owned a low ceiling which indeed forced the giant Bates to crouch for much of his journey. And last, the present passage was older, much older, in fact, if Harvey Bates' squinting examination of them was correct in the poor light.

They continued along this bricked passage for many minutes.

Calf Eyes, Volcker, drew them to a stop for one final time. Briefly they all stood there in front of that last wooden panel, after Volcker had given the special knock. By it, he spelled the words *lilac*, *prisoners*, and the names *Volcker*, *Tiny*, and *Siegen* in Morse code. In the meanwhile, in the pale light of the corridor, Harvey Bates caught sight of an inscription on the ancient wall. On it someone had etched these words: "Gunpowder, pistols, muskets, bayonets—for delivery to Major Benjamin Talmadge, by Samuel Culper. Date—August 15, 1777."

That second name struck Harvey Bates like a bombshell. In British-occupied New York Samuel Culper had served General George Washington as one of his spies, during the American Revolution! And like Secret Agent X himself, Samuel Culper was a complete fiction, the alias of one Abraham Woodhull.*

*** AUTHOR'S NOTE: Abraham Woodhull was a farmer and occasional smuggler during the Revolution. Eventually some agents of the Continental Congress caught Woodhull and some others and arrested them for their illicit activities around Long Island Sound. At this point Major Talmadge, an officer of the dragoons or mounted reconnaissance forces, realized the intelligence potential for a man with Woodhull's talents. Talmadge proposed that Washington employ Woodhull as an intelligence agent, upon the farmer's release from prison. Later the great General himself originated the word *Culper* as the name of the spy apparatus working on the Continental Army's behalf. He derived *Culper* from an abbreviation of Culpepper County, Virginia, his home, retooling the name as an alias for Woodhull, while he conducted espionage for the Army. Meanwhile, a number of New York's Patriots had already dug some of the aforementioned brick tunnels in order that they might secretly store supplies away from prying British eyes. Those tunnels gained added importance when the Culper Ring sprang into being, as many of its members sought refuge in those same passages.**

To the mind of Harvey Bates these passages had been mere fairy tales, the stuff of a child's storybook. For him to see one, to travel its path, was something else again. It was as if he touched history itself. He felt that he was breathing the very air and traveling one of the same routes by which Patriots had battled their fight to freedom. But now a white-mantled crime lord had commandeered that hallowed ground. No doubt this was the connector between that warehouse and the Resurrectionist's headquarters, that is, that abandoned Presbyterian church on the border of the Meatpacking District and the West Village.

As Harvey and the rest waited, another hoodlum eased the door back, peered beyond the portal and into the brick passage. He squinted at them through a pair of green-gold eyes. At the same time the tall, slender man licked his thin lips and rubbed his pointed chin as he asked them for more identification. Off to one side another worthy's tenor voice urged the stocky ruffian—his name was Junger—to let this bunch through the door. They'd already proved they were legitimate members of the Resurrection Ring.

Junger's response was a resentful, "I'm just playin' it safe for the boss."

Calf Eyes shoved the tall Junger out of the way, no mean feat as Junger was the bigger one of the two felons. Volcker followed by passing through the opening. The tired Bates, for his part, had already set Victor McGrieve and Secret Agent X onto the floor of the hallway.

When those other members of the Ring realized who lay outside, they wanted to rush beyond the door to bring in Spangler and McGrieve. They were under orders to haul both men, still supposedly unconscious, to cells away from the sanctuary itself. Exhausted as he was, Bates still vetoed this plan. He told them that he had a score to settle with Spangler before they shoved him in his cell.

Junger shrugged his shoulders. "Fine by me, ya big galoot. I'm just tellin' ya that—"

Harvey Bates stated that he knew *exactly* what Junger was telling him. But he decided to put the fear of God into the pointy-chinned offender, in order to let him know that he, Bates, meant business.

Eyes fearsome, he used his terrible strength and grabbed Junger by the lapels of his white suit. Junger tried throwing a punch or two, but Bates jerked him yet closer. He bared his square teeth: "Now, listen up! The chief doesn't have to know everything that happens around here, does he?"

The pointy-chinned hood, terrified now of the supposed Tiny, whispered, "N—no, he don't have ta! It'll be our little secret, Tiny. Honest to God!"

"We've reached an understanding, then," the hard-eyed Bates gritted at him. "So get this straight in your mind: Before I stash Spangler in a cell, I'm going to get even with that clown, come hell or high water. In fact, *he's* the reason I didn't get my dose of 'sugar' today. I had to go after *him*, instead. So if you know what's good for you, you'll stay out of my way. If not, you'll be thinking that *I'm* the Wrath of God, not that burning death gadget that the Resurrectionist has. Are we clear?"

Junger stammered, "Clear as mud, Tiny! Ya c'n do whatever ya wanna do!"

"I thought so," Bates replied. "I'll be one of the very people escorting him and the old man down the hall to the cells. But right now, just keep the two of them at the rear of the sanctuary, till I've seen the Resurrectionist."

Soon the giant had placed the Agent and Victor McGrieve on a pew, four rows from the sanctuary's rear. After he had deposited them there, he, Siegen, and Volcker strode to the head of the sanctuary, where the Resurrectionist presently held court, a good threescore of his toughs nearby. A pair of weasel-faced gunmen, one tall and the other short, flanked him. They must have thought they were chopping in high cotton, to be in his presence. And he milked their devotion and that of their fellows for all it was worth.

The two weasel-faced gunsels left through the back of the sanctuary, though to what place, Bates could only guess.

He turned his attention back to the Resurrectionist himself.

The crime lord had donned his white robes, as usual. But this time gold trim accentuated the gloriousness of his raiment and thus emphasized his elevated opinion of himself. He had even raised the throne yet again, such that it sat a good six feet above the erstwhile altar.

"Did you and the boy dispose of Ham Esler, Tiny?" he intoned to the Secret Agent's friend.

Unaware of the trick the Agent had executed to eliminate the former cabbie, Harvey Bates became momentarily unnerved. But he quickly recovered his composure.

"Yeah, we got rid of him, all right, Resurrection. I've captured Spangler and McGrieve, too, like you ordered. Stashed the two of them at the rear of the sanctuary."

The Resurrectionist gave him a suspicious look, but pressed forward: "You should know that you have redeemed yourself with their capture," he boomed, his voice echoing throughout the room. Eyes bloodshot as befitting the fanatic, he went on, "I was afraid I would have to use the Wrath of God on you—or perhaps on your son Jake. You would know then who is lord of life and death, eh?"

X's associate, ever resourceful, played along. "That boy knows what it's like to cross me. Way I figure it, all that counts is pleasing you. Jake pleases me, I please you, and everything is a-okeh. So that's what I'm trying to get the boy to understand."

This drawled response proceeded from behind the Resurrectionist's beatific features: "You are a wise man, Tiny. I'm glad to have your services—especially when they involve 'personalized' methods like yours. Your approach is *most* effective—especially with a small-timer like Spangler. He had become restless, skeptical of my power. But *you* have persuaded him. And you have done the same with my hated father, Victor McGrieve."

To Volcker and Siegen, the Resurrectionist then turned his head. To Harvey Bates, the Resurrectionist's voice, though deep, was oddly strained, perhaps because of the excitement of capture.

"Take him to the isolation cell until Emel has had time to examine him. After he has done that, I will raise him, a hopeless addict to the 'sugar.' Then," the Resurrectionist finished, "he will think about defying me!"

Both men, snickering, left with the unconscious Victor McGrieve suspended between them.

Triumphant, the Resurrectionist pointed his head back to the disguised giant. "Do you not feel elation, Tiny, over this latest development? It is only a matter of time before Agent X and his final henchman Bates fall before me! And when they do, New York and the nation itself will capitulate. It is inevitable."

Seemingly eager, Bates took in this statement, allowing his eyes stealthy trips to the room's various points of interest. He scrutinized the many criminals there too, albeit as surreptitiously. Certainly *he* couldn't hope to overcome such odds. But his boss the Secret Agent could outsmart them and thus win the day....

The Resurrectionist delivered a few more of his arrogant pronouncements. All of his statements revolved around more looting of banks and jewelry stores, additional burning of police and other government buildings, and of course further murdering of innocents. On the surface Harvey Bates continued to mask his horror with enthusiasm. Members of the Resurrection Ring, though, regarded their boss' speech as veritable inspiration, as if he were Moses, come down from Mount Sinai. Such was the villain's means of throwing raw meat to the animals, his followers, who were itching to devour Secret Agent X and, for that matter, all of society.

Dismissing Bates and his charge to the cell block, the Resurrectionist departed through the back of the sanctuary, via the old choir loft, for parts unknown.

At least his parting left Bates momentarily free of the Resurrectionist's presence.

Of course Harvey's immediate problems remained, that is, locating the cell block and removing X to the site, in accord with the Agent's intention. And conveying the investigator out of there reminded Bates of another equally pressing concern. Exhaustion mired him in its depths. Though treated, those burns on his feet and ankles also hurt, and severely now. Some of those wounds were even starting to tear open again. Hence X's associate had to put the disguised Agent onto the floor momentarily, while he determined his next move.

A piece of good fortune made a sudden appearance onstage. Bates looked around to see, coming from the head of the sanctuary, a notorious local hoodlum in the Resurrectionist's employ. The newcomer was a white-suit named Stoner, a blue-eyed fellow who always reminded Bates of a cartoon version of an angry mouse. His protruding ears accounted for a part of this uncanny resemblance. And the fellow's stiff, out-thrust tufts of hair, his pointed nose, and a set of bared teeth lent even more similarity to his ridiculous appearance.

A flabby, grinning hoodlum, an older fellow, accompanied Stoner. The grinning man lacked the wild gaze of the other ruffian, but the two of them could complicate matters unless Bates played his hand just right.

" 'lo, Stoner," a smiling Bates greeted the hood with the wild blue eyes. "The Resurrectionist wants me to lug this bird to the cells. I'm tired after picking up these two tonight; so I could use some help," he concluded.

Stoner sneered. "What makes you think I want to help you? Got my own rat killin' to do for the chief, and it don't involve hauling that goon over your shoulder."

"Ah, ya ain't gotta be so hard-nosed about it," his fellow countered, a pair of ill-fitting dentures clicking when he talked. He moved his hand over the head of the comatose Agent X, lifted him by the toupee. In so doing, he came within a hair's breadth of yanking the artificial hair from X's scalp.

While Bates sweated bullets over this development, the flabby offender quizzed, "Say, Tiny, this that Spangler ya bringin' in?"

"No, Cassel, it's Mizzus Roosevelt!" Stoner answered for him, in a voice brimming with sarcasm. "Who the hell do ya think it is?"

Cassel, the better-natured of the two, pulled the unconscious Agent X off Bates tired shoulders. He then hefted the Secret Agent's upper body into his own arms and pointed his head to the wild-eyed Stoner.

"You gonna grab his feet or not?" he asked the angry mouse.

Under protest Stoner complied with the request of his grinning confederate. They carried X towards a thick granite pillar, at the rear, not too many feet to the left of the entrance. Harvey Bates merely followed the other three until Cassel spoke again.

"Tiny, bend down and unlock the door on this pillar."

Bates, of course, had no earthly idea where to put his hand. "Kind of woozy when I bend down, you know. The 'sugar' and this overwork are doing me in."

"Sounds to me like those ain't all yer problems," Stoner commented, cynically. "Here, let me do it, 'cause of your 'delicate' condition."

He positioned his right foot over a small protrusion at the base of the pillar. Instantly, an entire segment—perhaps six feet of it—opened to reveal a yawning hole and a steep, spiral staircase, extending downwards.

Stoner and Cassel, X between them, slipped through the hole. Harvey Bates came on their heels as the little party traveled ever deeper into the ground, below the sanctuary. They came out, once more, on another part of a dimly-lit brick pathway, one in somewhat better condition than the previous corridor had been.

The quartet of men hadn't progressed more than forty or fifty feet before they encountered a trio. The first two gunmen, .45 automatics in hand, were the weasel-faced Resurrection men from the sanctuary. The cocky Junger was their companion, bragging about some exploit with which he'd once been involved. In one hand he held a pulp magazine of some kind, one of those detective books, by all indications. In the other hand, he waved a .38 automatic, the better to regale his listeners. Now with Bates, the supposed Tiny, on the scene, Junger had to show his tough-guy's mettle to the weasels.

"Well, what have we here?" he looked Bates and the others up one end and down the other. Left hand rising to his hip, he gestured with his pistol, "Goin' away party, huh? Why didn't ya invite me, too, Tiny? Or is this another secret yer keepin' from the rest of us?"

Growing angry, Harvey Bates stepped near to the man, thinking Junger might start an engine of trouble to rumbling, here in this narrow passage. The giant's shift in position put him adjacent to the man-hunter, Secret Agent X. And what neither Bates nor the rest knew was this: The Man of a Thousand Faces had returned to consciousness. He was simply biding his time until he could clean their clocks and rescue his captive associates.

X's right hand had dropped, such that it slightly bumped the left ankle of Harvey Bates. At first the giant thought the Agent had touched him by accident. The Secret Agent's contact with Bates was no fluke, however. In Morse code he tapped out a message to Bates to ignore the man Junger's taunts, and instead to prepare himself for action against this crew.

Emotionlessly, Bates thus threw off the punk's words, "We have work to do, Junger. This man has to be transported to a cell. If you want to come along, you can. It's no skin off my nose if you and your pals don't."

Chuckling wickedly, Junger returned, "Think I might just like that, Tiny. I want to watch these guys' faces when I tell 'em what you told me, outside the sanctuary. I think it's time *everyone* knows everything about you…."

CHAPTER XXIX
BETTY PLAYS SNITCH

HARVEY BATES broke into a cold sweat. He was neither a master of disguise nor an actor like his chief. Still the giant kept his composure.

"You're picking the wrong one to play this game with you," a stern Bates looked slowly at the man.

Cassel agreed. "That's right, Junger. He's an old hand at frame-up and blackmail games, aren't you, Tiny?"

When Harvey merely laughed at this new intelligence, Cassel, also smiling, addressed Junger again, "Say, why don't ya make yerself useful? Ya c'n give us a little culture while we walk—mebbe tell us about that latest story ya was readin' in that damn' pulp," he noticed a rolled magazine, which the man had now shoved into a side pocket. "What was that yarn called again—'Curiosity Made a Corpse'?"

"Yeah, wasn't that it?" Weasel One quizzed. "What the hell was that scribbler's name?"

"Tom Fleming," the resentful Junger muttered.

Weasel Two spoke up, "What's he know about the kinda life we lead, anyhow? Hell, he's just play-actin'."

"Ah, well, it's a good laugh—for kids and punks, eh, Junger?" was the laughing comment from Weasel One.

Junger doubled a fist, but Weasel Two ordered him to calm down and take the joke. So along with the weasel men, the loud-mouthed Junger, though none too thrilled, fell in behind Bates and his party. Now the little group resumed its journey. Every step propelled them closer and closer to the Resurrectionist's cell block. Bates, however, trailed behind, his strength still depleted.

During the trip the detective had allowed his own arms to dangle, thus furthering the illusion that he was out of commission. Unexpectedly his arms zoomed upward, to both biceps of Junger's arms. Deeply the Agent sank his thumbs into the punk's muscles. Here they found the proper nerves. And here, as well, Agent X's thumbs applied an especially painful jiu-jitsu hold calculated to birth maximum torture in a victim.

Screeching fiercely, Junger dropped the Secret Agent onto the floor of the passage. In advance of Stoner's attack, the sleuth gave a violent twist of his body. The move extricated him from the hand of his captor. X bent his free leg, kicked his enemy, Stoner, viciously, on the underside of the arm.

This blow quickly hurled Stoner backward, crashing him into the brick wall. As if by magic, the Agent regained his feet. He pivoted and then threw a rock-hard fist into the midsection of Weasel One, who had launched himself into the battle. This Resurrection man, too, collapsed in the face of the Secret Agent's punishing surprise attack. That left two of the men, Cassel and Weasel Two, to square off against the Agent and the exhausted Bates, who half trotted, half stumbled towards his chief. Unfortunately Bates collapsed before he could make another step.

Simultaneously Weasel Two aimed his .45 Colt at the detective. But the tough was much too slow, unlike Agent X. The public defender leapt at the man, throwing an uppercut off the gunman's glass jaw. He too went down for the count.

That left Cassel as X's sole opponent. He'd already seen how Secret Agent X had dispatched his fellows. And now he realized that this whirlwind of a man simply *couldn't* be Butch Spangler. Cassel simply gave up, his surrender emphasized by the pistol he simply tossed on the floor in front of the sleuth.

The criminal followed this move by throwing up his hands, as if to underscore his resignation. His next words were exclamatory: "My God! Yer that X fella himself, in the damned flesh! I'm not about to tangle with ya like these guys did. Fact is, I was kinda hopin' ya'd show up, so I could get outta this gang."

"So, you were, eh?" Agent X came back, skeptical.

The flabby hood nodded. "Hell, yeah, I was. If I turn on 'im—what are ya gonna do with me, anyhow?"

"If you really want out, then give me some information, right now," Agent X's eyes were stern, his tone still wary.

Evidently his very person frightened Cassel, as the flabby one stated, "Anything I know, I'll tell ya. Honest!"

"It's about the Resurrectionist's cells. Which ones hold my friends?"

"Ya mean that Hobart character?"

"Every one of them. Especially the one with Betty Dale. And don't lie to me about their location. You've seen what I already did to your friends, here."

"No, Sir, you'll get no lies from me—just the straight dope. They're—they're keepin' her in R-Nine with Miss Ramos. Maybe two hours ago, that weird doctor gave me a hypo with something different that the 'sugar.' He said it was like a knock-out drug. And he told me to give a shot of it ta the Dale woman."

"You injected her with it?" was X's inquiry.

"I, um—yeah, I'm sorry to say that I did. But there was no getting' around it. That doctor was standin' right there, watchin' me. And they took her out of the room, afterwards. Don't know if she's back yet or not, or if the Ramos woman is still there, either. Far as Hobart and Beckwith go, they're in R-Four. Been feedin' them fellas some of that 'sugar.' I was—was gonna, I mean, I didn't know—"

"What is, man? Speak up!" X commanded, as he shook him like a rag doll.

"Stop—stop for a minute!" Cassel begged, amidst the rattle of teeth. "The Resurrectionist assigned me ta give the 'sugar' ta your two friends. Wanted ta addict 'em, so he said. I did what he told me ta do—for a while. But I got ta thinkin' about that stuff, ya know, how dangerous it was. Some of the Resurrection Ring don't take that 'sugar,' well, not anymore. And some never started. I'm one of 'em who never got goin' with it. After I saw how Tetwilder and a couple o' them others was shakin', I thought that stuff wasn't for me.

" 'Course, that wasn't the only thing that made me stay away from it. That Dale kid and yer friend Hobart got me ta thinkin'. Got a couple o' daughters myself, one close ta her age, all right? A boy too, just a little younger than Hobart. Givin' 'em 'sugar' made me feel like I was givin' that stuff ta my own girl or boy. All that twitchin', them convulsions, those scary deaths. It was damned *awful*."

Cassel's voice cracked for a second; then

he whimpered, "I wouldn't hurt that Dale woman, Mr. X—or them other friends o' yours, either, now that I know the truth about that junk. Honest. I just took this job ta bring in some money and help my family. I don't give a damn what happens ta those crooked guys like Lothian and Calvert. Don't care much, either, about them rich clowns Helmer or Terran."

Despite his selective morality, the man was clearly struggling with what he'd done on behalf of his criminal master. Hence, X softened his tone a bit: "We can discuss what you've done later on. But right now I need your complete cooperation. Has anyone else dosed my friends since you stopped giving them the 'sugar'?"

Shrugging his flabby shoulders, Cassel confessed, "I don't know. Two of your little dancing partners," he indicated Stoner and Junger, "had orders ta give 'em 'sugar,' too. But that was after I'd stopped—after that doctor might have suspected I was fallin' down on the job, I mean. Anyhow, I don't know how much those fellas might've pumped inta their veins. As far as that second dose I gave the bearded guy? It was his last from me. Gave only one of 'em to the fat guy, too."

"At least two injections to Hobart, and at least one to Beckwith, then. Can you remember how strong the dosages might have been?"

"How should I know that? I'm not a chemist, dammit. That funny guy—Ramond—he's the one who developed this formula. He'd know how strong that stuff was."

"I see. What about that Wrath of God? He developed it, correct?"

"I'll bet he did," his respondent hypothesized with enthusiasm. "He's the *only* one who could have done it."

The eyes of the Man of a Thousand Faces acquired a stony look. All this incredible loss of life, and for what? To fatten the coffers of the Resurrectionist? To satiate his desire for revenge against Secret Agent X and his brave crew?

It was high time he whipped back to Harvey Bates' side. Fortunately the giant had not injured himself in the fall. So the Agent helped him to his feet, led him forward in the direction of the unconscious Resurrection men and their survivor, Cassel.

As soon as X and Bates reached the former scene of battle, the Agent directed his associate to remove a ring of keys dangling from Stoner's belt. The Agent then pocketed them for future use.

Ahead of the two allies, only a few feet away, the hall took a ninety degree turn to the right. Since the little traveling party hadn't yet reached any of the cells, the intrepid sleuth concluded these were along that next hall. Thus he extracted his gas gun from his pants and eased a few feet away from the recent carnage. Over his shoulder he told Bates to take Junger's firearm.

"I hope you understand the need for this pistol, Cassel. Tell Bates anything else you need to relate. I'll see what I can do for you after this thing is over...."

Unaccountably the Agent threw Stoner over his shoulder and resumed his quest. He moved with cat-like grace as he neared a better-lit area, far ahead.

More speed he put on his legs, Stoner's weight no obstacle to him. Something had killed most of the lighting, meanwhile; so he fired his cigarette lighter as a substitute. The passage thus better lit, he bent down. Something of interest had, it seemed, captured his gaze. At ankle level, he spotted a series of nozzles which projected outward, in groups of two, along either side of the brick corridor. That is, he could see one pair on a side, then corresponding ones on the other; a blank space of perhaps five feet, then another pair of the same nozzles. When he realized the purpose for the nozzles, chilly winds of horror blew over his mind.

X moved on with cat-like grace as neared an area still with lights. Once more he halted, and for the second time, he spied more of those protruding nozzles.

Onward he pressed towards a group of harsher lights that caused him to squint a little, despite the present distance. This area was the object of his search, he knew, so he quickened his pace. Some fifty feet away he made out a line of grim steel doors set along both sides of the brick hall.

X dropped Stoner unceremoniously on the floor, well in advance of the steel portals. From Spangler's garish coat X tugged his pocket makeup kit. Its depths produced a tube of his volatile plastic, along with two small appliances for pushing his ears outward, and a pair of blue contact lenses. In mere minutes he had assumed the guise of his prisoner. Next he stripped Stoner of his clothing, leaving the fellow clad, momentarily, in his underclothes. The audacious public defender practically jumped into Stoner's togs. Of course, X's disguise wouldn't be perfect, since the criminal lacked the Agent's wonderful musculature. This meant that the felon's white suit would fit Agent X much too tightly. However, only this means would enable him to rove the line of cells and not to create undue suspicion.

Hurriedly he slipped his former clothing onto Stoner and hastily disguised the man as Butch Spangler. This deed completed, X repeated the move of earlier moments, carrying Stoner on his shoulder.

He stopped in front of the steel-clad door of cell R-One. A single rectangular panel connected that metal door with the outside world.

Behind that portal, Henry Terran emitted blood-curdling screams. He was furious that he hadn't gotten his latest dose of the "sugar." And he complained that he hadn't gone under the knife for his plastic surgery. His words illumined the mind of the Secret Agent, who stopped briefly. Thus far, plastic surgery had enabled Charles Darwin Osben to escape detection too. As the detective had suspected, the Resurrectionist had made the same promise to *these* men.

Up and down the hall, the remaining prisoners expressed the same story, in much the same hostile fashion. They all wanted their insurance benefits on the spot, with their new faces and their new lives to start almost as quickly. But most haunting of all were their mournful pleas for the "sugar," like babies crying for milk.

One of them demanded all of these from behind the wall of either R-Six or R-Seven.

X recognized the voice as that of Stu Lothian; and the Man of a Thousand Faces halted, in order that he might hear the trucking magnate's rant.

Since he'd been revived, Lothian had demanded payment of his benefits, but the Resurrectionist had urged him to be patient. However, Lothian had raised the subject again and again. In doing so he had infuriated the Resurrectionist. So Lothian adopted a different tack, one he thought more effective.

The trucking king thought that he might buy his way out of this mess, as he'd often done in the world outside. That is, he would purchase the remainder of his contract if the Resurrectionist would only release him from this prison. No, that tack wouldn't work, he muttered. X heard him double or even triple his offer of a buy-out. Stu Lothian rehearsed his hypothetical bargain for a couple of minutes, but a desperate plea finally overwhelmed it. This was his need for "sugar." He couldn't take this anymore, he whined, the tics, the constant sensation of itching, the feeling that people were plotting against him. So the Resurrectionist would pay for this business, Lothian promised. He'd get out of there and—

Appalled, his head shaking, X passed on to R-Three, the cell with Pat Calvert.

From inside it the man was banging some heavy weight against the walls. Maybe he was even ramming them with his own body. Whatever the case, Calvert must have foolishly believed that he were still in control, that he could somehow fight his way out of here. He couldn't accept the fact that the Resurrectionist now held the whip hand. And dependent as he had likely become on the "sugar," he would probably start suffering the tics, and later, the convulsions.

Eventually X would have to level with these men, especially those who had long been taking the Resurrectionist's dope. He must tell them they were facing certain death, unless he could counteract the effects of the "sugar."

He wrestled with what to say to them when he came even with cell R-Four, the one belonging to Jim Hobart and Hiram Beckwith.

X crossed the hall and slipped the master key into its lock. He threw back the door, eager to free his friends.

Into the chamber he thrust his head. There was no one inside! But how could that be? Had the man Cassel lied, to save his own skin? Or had the Resurrectionist moved them, in order to ramp up the dosage of the "sugar"?

The Man of a Thousand Faces willed himself to a state of calm. He decided, now, to place Stoner in this room.

With the unconscious Resurrection man pulled inside, Agent X allowed his eyes to travel around that cramped, brick cell. Ancient, rickety cots on wooden frames supplied its only furnishings. At the edge of one of them, he spotted something, a blackish mass, on the floor. The thing was a small tuft of hair, mostly black, but *reddish* at the roots. These dyed locks must have been a portion of Jim Hobart's disguise as Arch Fingeroth. And most likely some member of the Resurrection Ring had ripped the organic filaments from Jim's own scalp.

Some additional sleuthing was necessary, X knew. He walked around the room a bit, only to hear a gritting sound, beneath his feet. Agent X lifted his right foot. Clinging to it, were tiny shards of glass. He roved to the end of the bed, where he spotted the glitter of another piece of the broken stuff, a larger one this time. The curved shape at one end of the fragment led him to make him think it might have been a remnant of a hypodermic syringe. That find set him to thinking, additionally, about Cassel's words.

Secret Agent X turned his attention to one of the cots. That larger, deeper impression in its surface suggested it was Beckwith's sleeping space. Agent X yanked the thin mattress upward. On it he discovered another clue. The thing was a scrap of paper, stuck to the pad by means of a piece of moistened, jellied orange candy. A receipt for this sweet treat covered the front of the paper. Beckwith's penciled chicken scratch littered the back. Secret Agent X realized that the man must have stolen the writing implement from one of his captors.* Then he'd used the fragment of paper, pulled from his wallet, to write a succinct report of their present condition.

Hiram Beckwith had been measuring Jim Hobart's tics with a pocket watch, also filched from one of their enemies. In the process he'd learned that the twitches were not as bad after the white suits had dosed him with the "sugar." He'd had Hobart do the same for him, Beckwith; and the result had been the same. Evidently fresh supplies of "sugar" would lessen the shakes the men suffered, or so Beckwith hypothesized in his note. But this could lead to a more sinister result, as the fat hack driver suspected. The men would grow dependant on the terrible stuff, just as the Ring intended. Only one maneuver had yet forestalled their foe's efforts, Beckwith mentioned. According to his narrative, an older criminal, their first jailer, had dropped a loaded hypo on the floor after administering Hobart's second dose. The fall had, of course, broken the glass. Another time the same fellow had simply squirted his allotment of the fluid onto the floor, sworn them to secrecy, and left the place.

*** AUTHOR'S NOTE: As related in MASTER OF MADNESS, Hiram Beckwith was a rum-runner during Prohibition. During that time he gained high proficiency with various kinds of firearms. What is less widely known is the fact that in the old days, Beckwith became most adept at all manner of confidence games, not to mention pickpocketing and other criminal acts.**

X's mouth couldn't help but dropping open like a trapdoor at these final revelations. Junger hadn't lied to him, then, about disposing of his associates' rations of "sugar." But where, exactly, were his two operatives? He had to learn that information, quickly, before the Resurrectionist killed them. As critically, he must locate Betty Dale and Miss D. Ramos, or they would suffer the same fate.

Willing himself to action and fighting his dread, he produced those master keys. His hand shook as he pushed the correct one into the lock of R-Nine. He prayed fervently that someone else hadn't subjected her to the "sugar."

The lock's bolt *snicked* backward into its compartment. He yanked the door outward. There, in the room beyond, he spotted a pair of unmade cots, with a small handbag on one but nothing on the other.

To the right he gave a turn of his head. There abruptly he discovered Betty, dear sweet Betty, her hair disheveled, her features drawn with worry and strain.

On seeing his disguised face, the features of Stoner, she clapped slender, *shaking* hands over her mouth. Her eyes shone in abject fear. So that no one else on the cellblock could hear him, he crossed his index fingers into the semblance of an X. Sapphire eyes now pooling, Betty opened her lovely mouth in a gasp. She jerked her shoulders upward. And she wilted in his arms, the hot tears streaming down her soft cheeks. Agent X grasped her close to himself, let her drink in his presence; and he, hers.

Mouth still quivering, Betty looked up at him. When he stuck his index finger to his lips, she whispered, "You! Finally, you! I've prayed you'd come for me! Hoped against hope that you'd finally make your way inside—"

He drew her closer to himself, his hands tenderly brushing her blonde locks out of her tearing, sapphire eyes. X whispered, "There, dear. It's all right. Everything is going to be all right now. I'll get you out of here, and then we'll locate Jim, Hiram, and Victor McGrieve—"

"We've got to find *our* way out of here first, darling," she advised. "Those white suits say it's impossible, because of the way they've modified these tunnels. They're Revolutionary War vintage, one of them told me."

Agent X curled his lips into a smile. His own eyes peered deeply into hers. "I discovered that only a little while ago. But what kinds of modifications did he mean?"

"The Resurrectionist can seal any passage he wants, by certain accordion doors that are located, strategically in the walls. When he closes off a particular hall, he alone will know the way out of a passage. He said something else about a 'special' surprise that he would reveal, when the time was right."

"You heard him say this, or one of his men?"

"Oh, he bragged about it to me. It was his way of showing his complete control of the situation and of me, I suppose."

"How, exactly, did his men capture you and bring you here?"

Before she could respond, the Secret Agent noticed a tiny piece of some unknown material, clinging to her left cheek. When she inquired as to the crumb's nature, X didn't reply. Instead he scraped it free. Next he scrutinized it with eagle eyes and asked her to return to her own story.

She rubbed her forehead, trying to collect her thoughts. Eventually she began, "It was all so sudden—the capture, the trip out here, everything. I had decided to visit Caledonian Memorial Gardens and learn what I could from Viola Vye. By mistake she passed me a so-called 'lilac,' or rather a brochure describing them. When I refused to return it, she somehow signaled that oily man to come into the office."

"The 'oily man,' eh? He's our friend Emel Ramond."

"Yes—he was *horrible*."

X added, "I've been told his name is Morris Lorin Ramond, or 'Emel' Ramond, after the initials 'Emm—Ell.' But I'm not too sure of that."

Betty resumed her narrative, her hands shaking a bit: "Well, he—he shot me with some strange pistol at the funeral home."

The detective exclaimed, "Oh, Betty! It was one of their Webleys...." He wrapped his left arm around her, pulled her close to himself. With his free hand he brought forth his pocket medical kit. In a split second he had loaded a hypodermic with fluid from container in Osben's parcel.

"This will hurt for a moment," he whispered, as he squirted the air bubbles from the glass tube. Before she knew what was going on, he had plunged the needle into her neck. Only seconds would pass as the counteractant to the "sugar" began coursing through her veins.

Dizzy for a time, she said nothing for many seconds. Following the silence she gave her blonde head a slow wag. Then her words came haltingly, "Oh—am—am I going to be o—okeh?"

"You'll need a few more shots of the drug, of course, over the next several days. But you should be all right. That's providing you received only a few doses of the chemical in the first place."

"I was starting to crave that 'sugar,' just as they promised would happen. I—I was afraid of becoming an addict, needing my 'fix' like some coke fiend. Now I know what it means for drugs to enslave a person, to steal her life, and her love...."

In her eyes shone utter despair. She'd been through hell, had this courageous woman. It was a wonder she could even articulate a portion of her feelings.

He held her tightly to himself once more and allowed her to regain her composure. Coming back to herself ever so slightly, Betty then resumed, "I regained consciousness in a lab which is located, I think, in a different part of this underground building. Anyway, that awful Resurrectionist didn't know I was conscious again. So I eavesdropped on a conversion he was having, via radio."

The Man of a Thousand Faces asked her, "To whom was he speaking?"

"I couldn't recognize the other voice."

"What were they discussing?"

"The other fellow was saying that he hadn't tried to be careless about something or other, but the Resurrectionist thought this wasn't explanation enough. He cursed that man and told him that his so-called 'carelessness' could have spelled the end to their operation."

"Really? How did the fellow respond?"

"He returned a few curses of his own. And he expressed some real trepidation about the chances of success for their life insurance scheme."

"That's what this *entire* thing is, Betty—a life insurance fraud, on a massive scale," the Agent affirmed. "The Resurrectionist, through the Long Island Life Assurance Corporation, is selling the policies, I'm guessing, at exorbitant rates which will fund his enterprises."

His beloved Betty nodded. "The policies start at $500,000 for their holders. I heard that figure quoted, when the Resurrectionist mentioned Spangler's name and those two business magnates, Terran and Helmer. No, I take that back. He mentioned Lothian and Calvert, too, but at different rates."

"They're *all* probably paying through the teeth—whatever the levels. Still, think of the dollars the Resurrectionist, their supposed benefactor, is hauling in, especially from people like Terran and Helmer. These people would be willing to pay out such outrageous premiums, without vetting their legitimacy. After all the policy holders are all known criminals or people facing Federal prosecution for their alleged crimes," X explained.

His eyes grew dark. "Consider this scenario: The Resurrectionist contacts his potential clients through one of his intermediaries, or marks, like Ramond. That middleman in turn gives the person, a virtual confidence artist's 'mark,' one of those little business cards with the lilac. Then this 'fish' bites at the prospect of the 'life from death,' the old faked death scam. It's just the prescription for what ails someone like the Resurrectionist's well-heeled criminal clients."

Those eyes of Betty Dale sparkled as an idea hit her. "Say, is it possible that this isn't the only part of the story? In other words, could that man in white be using the trucks of Stu Lothian to transport the killers around the city?"

"Yes, Betty!" X squeezed her hands. "And he could be using some of Calvert's union muscle for many of the hired thugs and killers.

Thaddeus Penny already told me the man or an assistant is visiting the tenements and enticing poor folks with his 'sugar. Next come promises of jobs. They take the one, the 'sugar,' and get hooked. And as for the jobs, they'll do anything he says, simply to keep buying the 'sugar.'"

"The Resurrectionist mentioned some sort of mysterious agreements in his conversation through the radio. What about those, dear?" she looked up at him.

"Possibly a client would simply sign contract that guarantees the 'murder' of the person, via the 'sugar,' or stastralose. He would pay the man in white for his services. Then as per the terms of the deal, the Resurrectionist would raise the person, or *claim to raise the person*, from the dead.

"You know how this relates to me, Betty?" he husked, turning his head from her. "Don't you—?"

Betty suddenly realized what X meant: This chemical was the one he'd used to fake his death, those many years ago.

"Oh—oh, my God!" she pulled him close to her, this time. "Now I understand why you were acting so strangely, a few days back. They've stolen the chemical from *you*, haven't they?"

"Partly from me, and partly from the doctor who helped me to simulate my own death, seven years ago. You see, now, why I use the alias 'Secret Agent X,' don't you? The phrase makes me the unknown personified."

She understood his reasoning for this: "Oh, darling, you can't afford to use your real name in the war you're waging. It's too much of a risk. But at least you're doing it for the right reason," she offered in a philosophical tone, her lips molded into a beautiful smile. "It's not like them. They're using aliases too, but strictly to hurt people. I heard them mention one of their fake names, in conjunction with that Spangler."

X's eyes acquired a strange light. "Of course! He'd have to employ a bogus name, after his so-called 'murder' and return from the grave. What name did they call him?"

"It was 'Samuel Wheelwright.' That was the name of the beneficiary on his life insurance policy, that 'lilac.' Terran had been renamed 'Nicholas Westmore,' if I heard that awful man in white correctly. And Stu Lothian was to become 'Fred Considine.' I'm sure there were others."

" 'Wheelwright,' 'Westmore,' and 'Considine,' eh? The Resurrectionist must have assigned those aliases and more to his clients, so that they could escape—or *think* they could escape—police detection. It's a common trick of people who engage in life insurance fraud," X glossed. "The fraudster and his conspirators will often name *themselves* as the beneficiaries, usually under aliases. You said that they'd signed another name on Spangler's policy?"

"Yes. It was 'Monica Willens.'"

"Another one of our illustrious friends. She's no more 'Monica Willens' than you are Jean Harlow or Thelma Todd. This Willens is, or masquerades as, Viola Vye."

The name exploded like a bombshell over the mind of Betty Dale.

More of them followed when Agent X informed, "She also presents herself as Teresa Fox, the niece of Mr. Ramond. But her repertoire is even more varied than that. Weeks ago she wore a mask crafted from materials much like my own volatile plastic. In fact, I think they stole it from me, when I first came back from the dead."

"How could that be?" she posed.

"Charles Darwin Osben, my doctor and Emel's former colleague, noticed, after my own resurrection, that certain papers were missing from his laboratory. Since Emel and Teresa Fox have turned up with a form of the volatile plastic, it's probable they borrowed a less-stable version of my own formula.

"They used it, or rather Emel used it, to disguise Teresa as one Patrice Anders, the 'friend' of soap and candle manufacturer Henry Terran. Needless to say, Anders disappeared, soon afterward. But she wasn't out of the game. Oh, no. After Terran's 'death' she became Monica Willens, to rope in Butch Spangler. Lest I forget, there's another member to this merry little band."

Betty was practically drowning in this flood of details. "Who do you mean?"

"She is, or was, Charlotte Moon, sometime back."

"Congressman Dirk's lover!" was Betty's shocked response.

"She even played the most unoriginal part, a woman named 'Mrs. Ramond.' That time she was the grieving cousin of a jailbird who was killed in a prison riot."

The sapphire eyes of Betty Dale became enormous. " 'Mrs. Ramond'? Not the wife of that man who captured—"

"That's right, dear. The ubiquitous Mr. Morris Lorin Ramond, once again. In other words, 'Emel,' or 'Em—Ell,' as his initials would sound when spoken. You know all about him, now, don't you?"

"I'll *say* I do!" she exclaimed, her eyes crackling with anger. "So he and this Fox woman get around, then?"

"Along with their compatriot, the beautiful, fiery singer—"

"—Miss D. Ramos!"

Agent X smiled drily. "That's right. She's actually Teresa Fox's charming kid sister, according to some information I learned from the Bates Agency and dug up on my own. Her name is 'Elyssa,' and she, like Teresa, also has a most lengthy criminal record. It includes jobs as diverse as Charlotte Moon, Miss D. Ramos, Patrice Anders, and probably some others I haven't yet identified."

"No wonder I had an odd feeling about the Ramos woman, then. I wondered about the fact that she spoke what I took to be correct Spanish pronounciation at times; and at others she slipped out of character. I wondered about something else, namely her good comprehension of American gangster parlance, but her lack of knowledge of simple English words. She didn't even know the word for 'handkerchief,' for instance."

This statement greatly interested the Agent, as did Betty's next remembrance. "There was something else unusual about her. Once her eyes seemed to tear up *after* she wiped them with her handkerchief. I hugged her then, to let her know that I sympathized with her loss. Her situation reminded me that I couldn't—couldn't imagine losing you," she choked back tears, "So, anyway, when I pulled her close to myself, I detected a sweet scent."

These memories set the Agent to thinking. "Those were fake tears, like the Ring's other tricks. They were caused by the application of menthol, likely in a paste form, and placed in the handkerchief by Emel Ramond. After that riot in Attica, Warden Hallan saw the supposed Mrs. Ramond wipe her own eyes. And *then* the tears flowed. His diary was specific about this detail, which was inspired by the death of her supposed cousin in that riot."

Betty inquired, "He probably had no connection at all with her, correct?"

"It's doubtful. But again, it fits with their known technique, especially with their talent for acting," he remarked. Now he let drop the proverbial other shoe: "And unless I'm totally wrong, the Resurrection Ring's final drama would have highlighted the talents of Elyssa, 'Miss D. Ramos.'"

She didn't follow his line of reasoning; so X drove home the point, his features grave: "She was to portray you, Betty."

"M—me?" she clapped her hands over her mouth.

The Agent explained, "That's also a technique of conspirators in life insurance fraud. They frequently hire only a handful of actors to play the roles of many different, grieving relatives or suvivors who hope to collect on the policies. That method worked with many of these men—at least with the ones who liked women and the night life. Some of them didn't, like Pat Calvert. Remember, there was no woman involved with him. He was too busy making his own money—and taking others' cash, besides. So they got to him through Ramond himself."

"Move forward to today. The Resurrection Ring captured you, in hopes of stealing your identity, then framing you for fraud, sometime down the road.

"How so?"

"Maybe you were to have been the lover of my identity as Martin—or of Captain James Read, the identity I used in becoming Secret Agent X."

"What if I loved only you, *Secret Agent X*? And what if I needed to die for you? Would you allow me to make that sacrifice, out of love?"

"Oh, Betty," he pulled her close to himself. Seconds of silence ticked by before he whispered, "Pray *that* never happens.... Just be thankful that I've gotten in here in time. Do you see what might have happened, otherwise?"

She did. And he made it worse, if such it could be, with his next words: "You were unconscious for a time, weren't you?"

"Yes, but I couldn't have been for very long."

"Emel could very well have used truth serum on you in that time. And it might be—and I stress the word *might*—that they pumped you for information about me—about my real face and name...."

The words galvanized her. "We've got to stop them, darling. But what—what can we do?"

Before he could answer, the Agent detected men's raucous voices from down the hall. One of them, the voice of the Resurrectionist, rang more loudly than all the others. As a result, the Secret Agent had only moments prior to his enemies' arrival on this cell block.

Agent X looked carefully at this loving woman who so deeply trusted him. Betty had given him an idea, as his question revealed: "What can we do, dear? Why, make a deal with the devil, of course...."

CHAPTER XXX
HOLY OF HOLIES

HE told Betty his intent before they exited the prison cell, so his general plans wouldn't surprise her. That didn't mean all of its individual details would be so obvious, of course. Nor did it mean that the

Agent himself could foresee all subsequent developments.

X and Betty marched out of the brick compartment, with the Secret Agent holding Betty at gunpoint. Down the hall the Resurrectionist himself strode towards them, along with his hoodlums and, of course, Harvey Bates.

On seeing Betty Dale, the Resurrectionist's men lost the little bit of humanity that lingered in their souls. Their leering expressions showed that they itched to force her down the road of addiction and depravity.

Sheer dread wrote its terrible signature across the lovely features of Betty when she saw them. Secret Agent X cut his eyes around to the shaking young woman, but only for a split second did they linger there. Instinctively the Secret Agent reached for a pocket where he might grab a magnesium grenade, detonate the device, and blind this diabolical crew. But he willed himself to calm as he'd done, moments earlier. For the present he had to allow the events to unfold on the Resurrectionist's terms. Otherwise, the sleuth would not keep a whole skin, much less bring off the rescue of his friends.

Chuckling eerily, the Resurrectionist strutted up to the counterfeit Stoner.

"We encountered a most interesting sight in the hall here," he noted to X. "Several men unconscious and more than a couple of them seriously injured. I'm tempted to say that Agent X was responsible. I'm also tempted to say that *you* might know the truth. But of course, you don't—do you?"

Agent X was prepared for such a query by his foe. "I don't know anything about any of that. But I *do* know that Junger got a little too big for his britches. He thought he would keep me from waltzin' down this hall and havin' a parley with the Jane here, Betty Dale. Way I figger it, she'll consider me *real* good company pretty soon."

"And why is that?" the Resurrectionist posed.

"When she realizes just how bad she needs that 'sugar,' then she'll do damn' near anythin' ta get it," he claimed, smirking. Winking at her and clicking his tongue in a lewd tough's manner, he inquired, "Wontcha, Toots?"

Feigning the shakes this time, Betty put on the dog to emphasize her condition: "Oh, yes—yes, Sir! I've got to have more of that stuff! Please—please give it to me! I'll die without it!"

The Resurrectionist's eyes were blinking with more and more rapidity. "Yes, you *will* die a most hideous death, Miss Dale, if we don't inject you with it. And, Stoner, I *do* hope that was the subject of your discussion in her cell. I trust you were not plotting some futile attempt at escape with this woman or anyone else here."

Agent X counterfeited a laugh. " 'Course not, Resurrectionist. I'm just thinkin' of my future with the cutie, is all."

All the while he was studying the man in white and his hop-eyed killers. He knew what they would do if he made any suspicious moves, so he had to continue his charade.

Suddenly the Resurrectionist addressed him once more: "Tell me, have you ever visited my Holy of Holies?"

"Doesn't sound like the kinda club I wanna visit, *anytime* soon," the Agent whined in Stoner's high voice. " 'Sides, I bet they ain't got no 'sugar' there."

To this response the Resurrectionist chuckled from behind that strange mask, "An appropriate reply, Stoner. For the 'sugar' is the 'life from death,' is it not? Still, I believe a visit to my Holy of Holies would be the sharpest of spurs to your loyalty and devotion to my cause. You *do* believe in my cause, don't you, Stoner?"

"More than I believe in Mamma and apple pie, Resurrectionist!" was the enthusiastic reply of the Secret Agent.

"I thought so. In a few moments I will try out a new version of the 'life from death' on three subjects: McGrieve, Hobart, and that disgusting cab driver Beckwith. This version of the 'life from death' will cause them to become dependent on it, after only a single injection. You and Miss Dale will follow all of us to my laboratory. Both of you will find the experience there most instructive, when you see what the new 'life from death' does to its newest 'devotees.' I dare say that you will then think twice before shifting your loyalty to anyone else…."

His masked lips immobile, the mouth behind them issued a repulsive laugh, like that of a de Sade.

Those guards of his offered laughs of their own, not to mention threatening waves of their guns. Clearly they, like their chief, suspected that the Agent was up to no good. Thus they were eager to prove their own devotion, never mind that it was a dope-fueled kind.

The Resurrectionist led the way back down the hall, past the cells. At the end of the passageway, he turned left. Immediately past that corner, he pushed one particular brick, such that the clay-fired object slid a good inch into the mortar. His move activated a door which slid back, into the very wall itself. He slipped through the door and into the bricked space beyond. This access he must have ordered built specially, as it was new, unlike the old Culper passage. Many paces hence, he stopped near a staircase and another pair of doors.

"If we go upstairs, we will return to the sanctuary. But at present that is not our goal. This first door," the crime lord pointed to the one before him, "leads to my office, where I store my records and communications apparatus. The other door leads to my Holy of Holies, the object of your curiosity."

Such was true for X, ever since Teresa Fox had mentioned the site to him. But he would allow his devilish host to divulge its secrets, in his own inimitable fashion.

They all stepped through another hidden door, activated by one of those brick switches. When X and the others entered this new place, they entered a new world.

It was a spacious area, this underground den. At its far side it might once have resembled a Christian's conception of Heaven, at least from a medieval artist's perspective. On one side's wall, the remains of an illustration depicted the souls of men and women, immediately after death, rising toward a light of blinding intensity. The next drawing might have shown them as they passed joyfully through the golden gates into Paradise. In number three the artist might have garbed all of those souls in gleaming white robes, while they clutched hymn books and apparently sang melodies of supernatural beauty. A final portrait might have visualized the new Heaven and the new Earth, at one in peace and harmony. God, represented as white light, might once have beamed over all.

The term *might* was the operative word here, since long scorches marked many square feet of the drawings, leaving them blackened and cracked. Something of great heat had created this mess, and the sleuth drew a terrible conclusion as regarded its real nature.

In that manner it resembled the condition of the images on the opposite wall. Flames had left long swatches of that divider charred, as well. And given the side which had suffered the damage, this was particularly appropriate. Indeed its pictures reminded X of that earlier room, the Resurrectionist's Hell. Here one image portrayed satanic legions who danced unholy jigs on a part of the wall. A different scene showed masses of grinning, crimson fiends who twisted their victims in knots. In scene three the hideous creatures tormented wretched sinners with long pitchforks or boiled others in enormous cauldrons. Looming over all, a giant rendering of the Evil One, Satan, shook one fist defiantly at heaven and out-thrust his remaining hand, open-palmed, as though to emphasize whose kingdom this *really* was.

As though to cap both sets of paintings, an ornate white throne, trimmed with gold and edged with seraphim, commanded an area equidistant from either wall. From this position the Resurrectionist could play the role of Almighty he had arrogated himself.

In another part of the room, a number of simple white operating tables, casters at their feet and restraints on the sides, lined a wall. At first the Agent couldn't quite determine their purpose. But he had a sudden inspiration: In the Resurrectionist's very den, the white-garbed miscreant used these tables as platforms for the temporary placement of his clients, before he had resurrected them from the dead. Most likely he also used the tables for some horrible experiments with the "sugars," the stastralose and the anastastralose. However, what specific purpose he had devised, X had not yet guessed.

Another wonder occupied the real estate beside the tables. This marvel was one more of the Resurrectionist's UHF radios, likely a sibling to the one in his office. This model had the added advantage of allowing the villain to continue his evil work, uninterrupted in his Holy of Holies.

Far away from the radio and the tables, the Resurrectionist had erected a glass wall around a large area. Through the glass Agent X could see a well-appointed biology laboratory which would rival his own in the Montgomery Mansion. He could see row upon row of chemicals, light and electron microscopes, a small centrifuge, spectrographs, anatomical pictures of the human form, and, if the bookshelves affixed to the walls were an indicator, a complete medical-biological-chemical library.

There was another wonder, atop a spacious desk: the third UHF in the villain's possession.

"Nice place you have here, Sir," the Secret Agent played the toady like Stoner. "Can't see what you have in mind yet, though. This is all beyond a guy like me."

"This 'Holy of Holies' is many things to me, Stoner, as I will explain. It is my room of reflection and meditation, where I pore over my books, gleaning their knowledge."

Agent X was hard-pressed to conceal his sense of irony: "Lots of reflectin' and meditatin', eh?"

"Indeed," the Resurrectionist hardened his voice with a bit of steel. "But this space is much more. It is, as you can readily see, a chamber of action and experiementation, where I prepare men to be raised from the dead. Here, too, I test new versions of the 'sugar' and, when necessary, new forms of the Wrath of God."

"That's something to see, I'm sure," Agent X said, with a slight decline of his disguised head.

"Oh, it is, most certainly. If you will turn your head upward, you will notice long slots in the ceiling, over in my Inferno."

X obeyed that command; and in the very spot indicated, he spied four long slits cut at right angles, such that they formed a rather large rectangle. He swiveled his head back to his host and awaited the next revelation.

"From those grooves I can drop walls of the most sophisticated materials imaginable—as I can do on some of the halls outside. Tell me—do you know about the properties of fireproof materials, such as asbestos?"

The Secret Agent did, of course; but he couldn't afford to portray Stoner as an educated, much less intelligent man. Thus the Man of a Thousand Faces allowed the Resurrectionist his moment of glory.

"Fire retardants, as they are called, are materials—chemicals or fabrics, rather than water—which reduce or delay other objects from bursting into flame. Such materials," the Agent's foe lectured, "may operate many different ways. They might, for instance, cool an object, perhaps chemically. Or they might form a cocoon of sorts around the burning article, and thereby stop the thing from combusting. Last they might even dilute the item in question with water or perhaps carbon dioxide, such that their action squelches the flames.

"Those walls are impregnated with a revolutionary fire retardant chemical. And the silver-white suits all of you wear? They too are fire retardant, thanks to a certain wonder compound which one day may replace asbestos. It should be obvious to you that Wayne Helmer developed this remarkable silvery substance, Helmerite, and that he has incorporated it in my glorious silver-white suits. You should also know that I have tested the Wrath of God on the suits, over there in that room. I'm pleased to say Helmer's advancements have made a most valuable contribution to my Resurrection Ring, certainly an improvement over earlier examples of the Helmerite...."

Agent X portrayed a cynical tone, but his humanity fairly shoved him towards this question: "I hate to ask, but were people—?"

"—wearing the suits when I tested the Wrath? Of course! I couldn't be expected to buy an expensive product without first testing it, Stoner. I must admit that the first two versions of the fabric didn't work quite as well as expected," the Resurrectionist shook his head with *faux* regret—and the man-hunter felt his stomach churn with new revulsion. He could have strangled this sorry excuse for humanity.

The Resurrectionist continued with a perverse sense of satisfaction: "Still, Helmer improved his textile, inspired by his desire to dodge prosecution; and I gained a new weapon for my war on Secret Agent X."

"The Wrath of God came along the same way, Sir?" X quizzed.

"Certainly. However, I will omit its details, as you could not understand the science behind it. Let's say that it came about, thanks to Henry Terran, another ally and would-be victim of Federal persecution. That is ever the way of the jealous and the resentful, towards visionaries like them—or myself. When I come to power, the day of such foolishness will end! It is just a matter of time...."

X cast his eyes around this room, his brain working on the puzzle of the Wrath.

In the meanwhile his enemy was still talking, "...and you will be one of the witnesses to my power, Stoner—you and the others in this room." He swaggered over to the radio atop that desk. There he seized the microphone and ordered his "clients," as he called them, to be brought here from their cells.

In no time more than a dozen Resurgos returned from the prison block, along with Terran, Helmer, Lothian, Calvert, and the man they took to be Butch Spangler. The false Spangler excepted, practically the entire bunch was twitching, with the first clients like Terran and Helmer exhibiting the worst symptoms of addiction to the "sugar."

The Resurrectionist ordered them lined up, such that they resembled a sideshow exhibit meant for the entertainment of these onlookers.

It was exploitative, downright hideous to the Agent, Bates, and Betty Dale, never mind the fact that most of them were criminal types and suspected offenders.

The situation grew much worse, indeed much more personal for Agent X and his allies in the next moment. Additional Resurgos emerged from the prison block, and this time a bruised Jim Hobart and Hiram Beckwith, both exhibiting mild tics, walked among them. Strangely Victor McGrieve wasn't part of this exclusive club, a fact not lost on the Agent.

Meanwhile, in his element now the Resurrectionist explained the action of the "sugars," which he called by their medical names, stastralose and anastastralose. He related everything that Agent X already knew, as well as some startling new details. First he was running short of his supply, his own men and the "clients" both needing it, in order to survive. Worse yet, they could all thank the Swede, the miscreant noted, for stealing a sizeable amount of it, then conspiring with Ham Esler to grab more. Still, all hope was not lost, he informed. He whispered words to a thug close at hand, Poulos. This fellow would, he directed, enter the lab and there retrieve certain numbered boxes for him.

Not well-acquainted with the lab, Poulos could do nothing but waste time in there, rummaging on shelves and looking underneath tables. Hence, this time the man in white ordered Tiny, actually Bates, and the disguised X, who volunteered, to find the proper boxes and bring them back.

When they entered that sector, Harvey Bates feigned knowledge of their new environs, all at the Secret Agent's undertoned command. X quickly shot his eyes over the space. And his intuition as speedily pointed him to a likely place for the boxes, one of the large metal supply lockers. Agent X unlatched the tall closet and threw back both of its double doors.

Sure enough, here were six of the boxes in question, all bearing the identifying number the Resurrectionist had already supplied for them. The Secret Agent requested that Bates and Poulos help him to lug the cardboard containers back outside.

During the removal process the Agent, ever observant, acquainted himself with the other inhabitants of that locker. Another of them, a cardboard shipping container from Henry Terran's outfit, suddenly captured his interest. He peered inside it. The thing held small rectangular metal boxes, a good dozen of them, filled with mineral oil, as denoted by their labels. The public defender slipped three fingers inside the topmost of the boxes. He created a miniature cyclone in the thing, so vigorously did he stir it. When he brought forth his hand once more, a granular substance clinged to it.

He pinned the glittering, gritty stuff under his sharp gaze, rubbed it around his fingers and palm for a bit, and slightly bobbed his head. More of the oil he spotted in a large glass bottle on a shelf, contiguous with a shorter stack of metal boxes. This container of oil and the gritty material were simon-pure proof of something he'd been seeking.

"Let's go, fellas," he turned his head back around to his criminal companions. "I thought I'd found more of the 'sugar,' but I was wrong."

All of them promptly left the laboratory and rejoined everyone else. The man in white personally supervised the removal of the "sugar," in addition to an ample quantity of hypodermic syringes from their places of storage. These hypos he then ordered to be fully charged with the "sugar," in this case the anastastralose, or resurrection "sugar."

X realized this was to be the crime chief's great demonstration, one more dramatic than all predecessors.

At the villain's next signal several of the hoodlums pushed and shoved the clients to eight of the tables there in the vast Holy of Holies. Under the Resurrectionist's order, X came over and stood nearby the head honcho, so that the Agent would have a front-row seat at this circus of evil.

Frost gathered in the disguised eyes of the Secret Agent. He watched as the Resurrectionist's so-called "clients" struggled to resist these minions of their supposed benefactor. He'd promised them plastic surgery and a new life in Europe or Mexico, not more treatment as lab rats. At least this was Henry Terran's complaint to the Resurrectionist. Wayne Helmer tried to stand his ground for a bit, refusing to move. But ultimately he adopted a look of defeat and a posture to match. He whined that he merely desired more of the "sugar" to quell his unending tics. No, he absolutely, positively needed it, he insisted; or that was all she wrote for him.

That wasn't the case with Lothian or Calvert, tough guys both. They tried to resist the move to the table, and in fact the two of them hurled a few ineffectual punches at the Resurrection men. They also made the obligatory threats, with Calvert rendering the more creative punishments he would mete out to this assemblage of crime. The villain in the white robes merely laughed cruelly in response. His mask remained immobile as always. But the Agent couldn't fail to notice the increased tremor of his hand, proof positive of the man's own addiction.

"You are about to witness a most unique exchange with some of these men," the Resurrectionist then turned to face the rest of them. "Aside from Agent X's associates, each one of these other 'guests' has chosen my generous offer of 'life from death,' so he may think, in order to avoid the G-men and the Federal prosecutors. But against his will, every one of them has become a devotee to my cause of destroying Secret Agent X and everything he stands for."

Straining at his bonds, Jim Hobart was fighting his own cravings but proudly raised his head, "You must be talking about those other pillars of the community like Spangler and Lothian! X isn't like them! He's a good, public-spirited man! I wouldn't betray him for all the gold in Fort Knox!"

From one of the tables Henry Terran strained at his restraints and shouted to Hobart and the Resurrectionist, "You both have it wrong! All I *really* want is the chance to begin my new life. Honest! I'm just ready to have Mr. Ramond do his plastic surgery on me so that I can leave the country—"

"But receive your periodic injection of the 'sugar,' first, eh, Terran? You are positively dying for the fluid which is the very 'life from death,' aren't you?"

"God, yes!" the candle and soap king swore, fighting his craving as vigorously as he struggled atop that table. He shrilled, "I've got to have it! I'll come unglued if you don't give it to me, right now!"

"Yes, you *will* 'come unglued,' as you've so vividly put it. And thus you will support my cause, for you will *pay any amount and do anything*," he emphasized, "to get that critical injection from me. That is the nature of the 'sugar' in its original form. It is a restorative from a death-like coma. But it exacts a most terrible toll on the mind and the body of the user. That is especially true when it has been regularly injected into someone, as I've done with these men.

"I now have, in my possession, a new version of the 'sugar,' a kind which, when introduced to the human organism, produces every one of the old benefits. That is, the man feels the euphoria, the heightened awareness, the increased motor activity, yet all magnified—*tenfold*. Unfortunately the individual suffers rather, eh, serious ill effects: near instantaneous addiction, for one; and much quicker physical deterioration, for the other. Indeed, according to my tests, he cannot expect to live more than twelve hours, at the most. A pity, this, because in losing one of these clients, I lose a paying customer. But I *do* gain a compelling weapon of terror against those who plot evil against me—X or otherwise.

"That makes the new 'sugar' most relevant for one such as you, *Stoner*," the Resurrectionist pivoted his head in the direction of the Secret Agent. "For I have not forgotten your unscheduled visit to the prison block, a few moments ago. Should you attempt to double-cross me, as Swede or Esler have done, I can make *you* one of the addicts to the new 'sugar,' as these others will soon be. It will not matter *one scintilla* to you that it will destroy your organs and reduce you to one of those mummies, so prominent of late in the press."

X's conscience was a veritable hurricane in that moment. Indeed he wanted to cloud up and rain on the Resurrectionist for what he intended to do to the Agent's men, and even to those criminals. For though they were offenders or individuals accused of crimes, they were still human beings. And as a consequence, they deserved to stand before the bar of justice.

Inside one of his pockets the Agent had secreted a small sphere of fragile glass. With that globule he could anesthetize everyone in his immediate vicinity. He thrust his right hand into the appropriate compartment. While he was pulling out his hand, the Resurrectionist was, in turn, reaching his own appendage for a hypodermic syringe. He was moving forward with his plans.

From the corner of his eye, however, the masked and hooded crime chief caught a glimpse of the Secret Agent's activities.

A cloak of suspicion covered his words: "What are you doing, Stoner?"

Agent X altered his voice to one entirely unlike that of the Resurrection man. His tone became rich and commanding: "You know I can't permit you to go through with your scheme, Resurrectionist. I aim to free my friends Hobart, Beckwith, and Miss Dale, for starters. Then I'll take your so-called 'clients' into custody so that the Department of Justice can prosecute them. In the meantime, you, my friend, will soon find yourself taking a trip to the death house!"

The blue eyes of the Resurrectionist became fanatical. He pointed his head at the Secret Agent and undertoned, "You're not Stoner. Who are you?"

The Secret Agent parted his lips in an eerie whistle which emanated from everywhere and nowhere at all. "Is that answer enough?"

Before the furious Resurrectionist could make another move, the daring Man of a Thousand Surprises had drawn his gas gun, jammed the weapon into the very face of his hypocritical opponent. From behind and with his free left hand, he locked a grip of organic steel around the throat of the Resurrectionist.

Simultaneously the miscreant's own assistants had yanked out their own weapons. "My, my, they're well-trained *dogs*," the Secret Agent smiled mockingly. He nodded acknowledgment at them, but a mysterious glance at someone else. Turning back to the crew of hoodlums he remarked, "Still I'm quite handy with this weapon. And I believe I could kill your boss before you could do a thing to stop me, or my friend—Harvey Bates."

Bates had already caught the Agent's signal and drawn a pistol of his own, that commandeered automatic from the hallway skirmish.

The Secret Agent jerked the Resurrectionist closer than before. Now the man was almost gagging as he tried to draw a breath. Only then did the Secret Agent resume, in a voice of diamond hardness: "Now, to our deal. You will release my men and Miss Dale, here, immediately. You will also bring Victor McGrieve in here, that he might accompany the rest of us, *and you*, from your so-called 'Holy of Holies.' I'm sure that deal will be most agreeable to you—if you want to live."

A chuckle of contempt issued from X's enemy. "Oh, I *will* live, Agent X—on *my* terms. And you, in turn, will face me again; for you have not, finally, bested me here."

He pointed to Poulos, Merriwale, and some other Resurgos and told them, "Untie the Secret Agent's associates, as well as the other men on the operating tables."

In the midst of all this exchange, the Agent told the Resurrectionist's "clients" to leave the room without delay. Betty Dale, however, pleaded with the Agent to let her stay behind. Knowing the risk of sending her out with those Resurrection men, the Agent decided to allow her to remain with him. Victor McGrieve, too, would stick by the Secret Agent, for a purpose as yet unknown to any of them, save the man of mystery himself.

This plan, of course, failed to pass muster with the villain in white. The Resurrectionist insisted, "McGrieve will not be part of our so-called 'deal,' Agent X."

"Oh, he *will* be part of the deal. I'll see to it."

He rammed his gas gun deeply into the man's temple, his finger becoming tighter and tighter on the trigger.

"Galvin," a nervous Resurrectionist addressed Weasel Two. "Bring Victor McGrieve from his cell."

Weasel Two left without another word. But the white-clad fiend was hell-bent to make the Secret Agent understand that old bitterness of years gone by.

"*He* was responsible for my incarceration. *He* made me take the blame for his crimes, and *he*, above all," X's prisoner underscored, "should necessarily pay the price. I will see to it that—"

"—You will see to nothing of the sort. The courts will determine his guilt, as they determined *yours*—several years ago," the Secret Agent reminded, his voice growing ever harder. "In your case it is only a matter of time before they do so, again."

Taunting words gritted from beneath the saintly mask: "You speak so confidently, Agent X. You act as if you and your little band will somehow remove me from my headquarters. In the first place you would become lost in these tunnels. Unfortunately for you, only I know them fully, thanks to the records of an ancestor of mine."

"And who might that be?"

"He was Angus McGrieve, the minister in the Presbyterian church above us. He was also a Patriot sympathizer and a member of the Culper group. In fact, he helped to dig some of these passages during the Revolutionary War. Before that conflict was said and done, he even left his pulpit, in the middle of a sermon, and marched off to join the Continental Army."

Agent X expressed utter contempt for his opponent, "You are a complete affront to all of those Patriots and to the brave men and women who supported them. You are nothing more than a criminal with a funny gun and a fancy suit. And I remind you again, I and my people *will* leave this place—*as will you.*"

Signaling Betty, Hobart, Bates, and Beckwith, Secret Agent X crawfished away from his position beside those operating tables, the Resurrectionist yet locked in the sleuth's iron grasp. As this scene played out, the Resurrectionist's men tracked every one of the group's steps with their weapons. They wanted desperately to free their master, but they took seriously the Agent's threat against him.

While they watched their boss's plight, the Agent pulled the Resurrectionist awkwardly in his, the detective's, wake. When the man in white saw the Agent's destination, that is, the laboratory, he involuntarily stiffened his form, as though fearful of entering that chamber.

"I caught that little move, Resurrectionist," X whispered to him, the detective's knowledge of psychology profound. "So there must not be a way out of that area. Too bad for you, eh?"

The megalomaniac executed a painful sideward turn of his neck: "I commend you on your nerve, Agent X. But I must warn you, again, that your attempt to leave is doomed to failure, even if you can make your way to an exit.

"Let us suppose that you make your way out of this room by a route other than the one you used for entrance," the villain conceded. "You will then face over four dozen of my Resurgos, scattered throughout my headquarters. Certainly you cannot hope to muscle your way past all of them."

X had shifted direction to the chamber's own version of the Inferno, whereupon the white-clad lawbreaker, formerly rigid of form, relaxed his posture. Agent X knew then that this was the way to proceed with his opponent, so the Man of a Thousand Faces kept inching forward. Still he held no illusions about the path he was following. The zone would likely be both death-trap and ark of deliverance for himself and his brave band.

As they reached an area between the two sets of paintings, a white suit, Weasel Two, returned to this den of danger with Victor McGrieve. Unmoving, the funeral home's director clearly had not yet thrown off the effects of Agent X's anesthetizing gas.

"He's dead as can be, Resurrectionist," Number Two related. "What are ya gonna do with 'im?"

"He cannot rise from the dead without the anastastralose—which only *I can give him*," the crime chief bragged. "Thus I hold the whip hand, Agent X."

Smiling, X addressed the former cop: "Hobart, reach into my pocket for my medical kit. It's time we draw this foolishness to a halt."

Jim Hobart sent his hand on its mission, but he couldn't stop its shaking, the result of Jim's injection with the "sugar." He retrieved and opened the case. Unfortunately a more vicious flood of tremors swept through his hand, and he dropped the medical kit on the floor.

And in that instant all hell broke loose.

The Resurrectionist exploded his left elbow twice into that scar beneath the Agent's heart. Reflexively, the Man of a Thousand Faces jerked his body upward in pain, a grimace branding his disguised face. And promptly he lost his grip on his foe.

With supernormal speed the Resurrectionist wheeled around to face the Secret Agent. The white-clad villain shot both hands at the detective's shoulder blades, pushed him violently backward. He stumbled several feet in the opposite direction before finally coming to a halt. Then the man of evil shouted, "This is your moment of judgment, Agent X! After all these years, you will finally pay for what you have done to me!"

Mobsters, briefly stunned, too, recovered their senses and hurled themselves in the direction of their master's enemies. At the same time they brandished their firearms, heedless of the danger of shooting each other, much less their leader.

In the meanwhile he raced for a portion of the wall depicting the white light which symbolized the Almighty. There the Resurrectionist had countersunk, ever so slightly, a rectangular panel, something roughly the size of a student's notebook. He pushed a concealed button at its base. The panel swung outward to reveal a control console littered with colored buttons and a mix of red and white toggle switches. Four cubicle pieces of Bakelite guarded each of the corners, a white, stylized lilac adorning the top of each one. Their style reminded the detective of the same engraving he had seen on that box in Emel's, Ramond's, office. He threw four of the white toggles in rapid succession, a fifth one, red, on their heels. And a concealed motor, somewhere, began to whir.

Startled at this sudden turn of events, Harvey Bates and Hiram Beckwith stood as bulwarks against the mob of hoodlums which barreled towards X and his associates. There was no way they could withstand an onslaught by this bunch, outnumbered as they were.

Still Harvey managed to lay hold of a magnesium flare from a pants pocket. Warning his friends to shut their eyes, he lobbed the thing at the first five or six of the Resurrection men attempting to overrun X and his crew.

The device detonated with a white light to rival the painted radiance on that wall. Members of the Resurrection Ring, blinded, dropped back, unable to proceed. His tactic didn't stop more men behind them, however, toughs who retained some their eyesight and used that sense to unload their pistols, albeit wildly, at Bates and the rest.

Panting hard from that blow to his midsection, Agent X heard those whirring motor and cast his tearing eyes upward. From those grooves the four hidden walls, their surfaces like accordions, slowly descended to surround him and his allies! And neither the Resurrectionist nor Betty Dale was anywhere to be seen!

CHAPTER XXXI
PROPOSAL FROM PERDITION

IMMEDIATELY prior to the Resurrectionist's escape, a half-blinded and grimacing Poulos had stumbled over to Weasel Two. Poulos had joined Weasel Two, and they half-dragged, half-carried Victor McGrieve towards the room of the Agent and his associates. Poulos had thought that perhaps he could pull an escape with the Secret Agent and his party, and thereby double cross the Resurrectionist himself. However, the walls, by this time, were a mere three feet from the floor. Poulos forced the Weasels to drop their burden. Then Poulos realized he could do nothing but perhaps get this man away from the vengeful Resurrectionist's crew.

He clutched this older man and drawing back with all his considerable strength, hurled McGrieve's insensate form along the floor. Just as the moveable barricade was slamming down into place, McGrieve came sliding through the narrow space that remained.

From behind the walls, the Secret Agent and his party heard the rapid fire of automatic weapons and a scream. Members of the Resurrection Ring had squeezed round after round into this criminal, this well-meaning criminal who still remembered human kindness....

Back inside that cordoned off chamber, a speaker in the ceiling emitted a *pop* and a *hum*.

"I have you now, X! You are trapped!" he gloated, his triumphant laughter echoing throughout that chamber. *"And I have someone most dear to you, in the person of Miss Dale!"*

Body shaking in fury, the Secret Agent clenched his fists until the palms turned bone white.

Suddenly on one of the panels depicting Hell, a panel yawned open. Through it a person on the opposite side slid the long barrel of some weapon. It was a long-barreled gun which fired Wrath of God!

A veritable fountain of blue-white flames gushed from the metallic discharging tube shoved through the opening. Fingers of fire clutched greedily at Jim Hobart, who stood closest to the grasping flames.

With the speed of a modern Hermes, X leaped, struck the body of his associate. The violent blow sent them both to the floor, bruised, but unharmed by the roaring blaze.

The gun's barrel shifted slightly to one side, this time taking aim at Harvey Bates, who by now parked next to the unconscious Victor McGrieve. The giant Bates pushed the older man as close to the wall as possible, following which he, X's friend, jammed his back firmly against the wall.

Watching these proceedings, a dazed, panting Jim rose slightly on one elbow. A crop of the bluish-white flames were springing up, no more than three feet in front of his long, raw-boned frame. Wiping his perspiring brow, he gasped to Agent X, "That's one—that's one ride I don't want to take again."

X undertoned his response too: "How are you holding up?"

"Twitching is pretty awful, about now," he informed, trying, in addition, to master his cravings by sheer force of will. "I know it must be that anastasa—anatrelo—oh, hell, that 'sugar' that's causing this. I need an injection of it, X, more than you can imagine. Yet I know that I'll wind up dying like that thug Jonesy, if I take it for any length of time."

"We'll get you fixed up after we're out of this place. I promise you that, Jim."

He sent his hand on a mission inside his coat pocket. The Agent shook his head because he had neither thermite nor concussive grenades to melt or to blast through the barrier. All he had were a few more magnesium flares and tear gas grenades, in addition to his anesthetizing globules.

"Looks as if I'll be stopping that thing manually, Jim," he stated with a grin to his associate.

"You—you can't do that! The fires will burn you to death!"

"What other choice do we have? If I *don't* do anything, we're sure to die. And there *must* be a way out of here, since our enemy took it, in order to escape us."

"What do you want me to do?"

"Be ready for my signal. I'm going to rush that door in a moment. After that, it's off to find Betty Dale."

"I think I might be able to help you there, X. Since I've been in this place, I wasn't always unconscious. And I'm sure they've carried me through some secret passages."

"He's going to use them to double-cross his men and trap all of us at the first opportunity," X declared.

"I'm certain of that," Hobart bobbed his head. "He aims to set fires in these passages and bring the walls down around all of us, including his own allies. Look—if we get out into the hall, I'll need to get my bearings for a moment. But we should come out onto that hallway that circles this room. One way leads back to that ladder to his office, but the opposite way will take you an alternate route. I think it will go to his office-radio room, and eventually to the old sanctuary."

"A radio room?"

"I was still pretty woozy when I arrived at this place. But I vaguely remember that they took me there when they first brought me back from the dead. They pumped me for information because they wanted to know the secret to my own UHF radio—the one I use for communicating with my detective agency. I didn't cough up much information, but you can't say they didn't try to get it from me," he rubbed that Concord grape contusion on his left cheek.

Grinning, the Secret Agent complimented, "Good for you, Jim. But listen: I'm depending on you to find that radio room again. Most likely, they'll have hidden Betty there, since its exact whereabouts are unknown, save to handful of our enemies."

Secret Agent X rolled away from Hobart, such that the man-hunter lay just outside the zone of fire. The detective's move placed him something near three feet from Hiram Beckwith. Another three or four feet separated this associate from Harvey Bates and Victor McGrieve.

"Beckwith, are you okeh?" X husked.

"Damn that Resurrectionist!" was the first statement he'd made to the Secret Agent in several days. "I thought that coke was somethin' else. But this stuff is *much* worse!"

"I suspect it is in the same family of drugs with cocaine," the Agent informed. "We're going to have to get you and Jim Hobart off this dope, as soon as we can get out of here. But I want you to pay attention. You will need to slip over there and get to Victor McGrieve. Protect him with your life."

The flames were roaring as he spoke these words, the heat increasing, to their minds, to the level of a blast furnace.

"I'm going to roll over to Bates. As soon as I do, I will tear the sleeves from my coat and use them to cover my hands. Bates will do the same. As soon as we've done this, we will grab that gun and then rush that door. If this coat is the miracle fabric the Resurrectionist claims it to be, then we should successfully withstand his fire."

Full lips parted in a huge grin, Beckwith promised, "Whatever you want me to do, Diamond Jim."

From the slot the bloodthirsty gunman abruptly fired his weapon again. A long shaft of the blue-white flames stabbed, this time, in the direction of the Secret Agent himself. Swift as thought he rolled over into a standing position. Just as rapidly he jumped for the position held by Harvey Bates.

This maneuver put him, like his giant associate, directly beneath the gunman's death port, and thus out of range of the Wrath. But he held this advantage only for a moment, as, on the opposite wall, someone threw back a second panel. And another weapon began firing the Wrath of God, as well!

X fished for his pocket knife, and finding it, cut a long slit in one of the coat's sleeves and followed with another in the remaining one. These coverings he immediately ripped from their seams and wrapped around his hands. Agent X then handed the knife to the giant, who knew to emulate his chief.

After they had protected their hands, the detective pointed his index finger first at Bates and then at the slit above their heads. His intent was plain to Bates: The giant would attack the gun on this side while X braved the fire of the other one from the opposite side of the room.

"Now, Bates!" X shouted at the man.

Upward the giant sprang. His huge hands, protected by the fire-retardant white fabric, grasped for the barrel of the gun.

Seeing this assault, the Wrath's wielder on the other side summoned fresh blue wrath upon this attacker of his criminal confederate. The hellish fires roared out of the barrel, some of them striking Bates in the back. But the material hardly earned a scorch mark!

X ducked and raced to that opposite slot. He wrapped both hands in a death grip around the gun owner's barrel, wrenched the hot object towards himself. The two combatants struggled mightily. The Wrath's holder tried at first to burn the Agent, the gun pointing at the regions of the Agent's body—head, arms, midsection—that he deemed vulnerable to his assault. He squeezed the trigger repeatedly. Just as often, the shooter failed to harm him, thanks to the flame retardant qualities of the Helmerite.

From the opposite side of the panel, the man gritted a curse. X bunched his mighty muscles. He jerked the weapon through the slot and out of the white suit's grip. And as unexpectedly he slammed the butt of the object directly into the hooded face of his attacker. He looked across the room. Harvey Bates stood there, smiling slightly, because he too had bested his own adversary and rendered the man unconscious. Likewise, he had recovered the gun formerly in the possession of their attacker.

The sleuth allowed himself a brief examination of his own unusual device. It looked rather like a conventional double-barreled shotgun, with a pair of horizontal tubes extending from the breech. The gun also sported a stock, triggers, and the other conventional parts of a shotgun. But the weapon and its twin differed from the usual weapon in the sense that the maker had mounted a pair of small metal tanks, apparently fireproof, to either side of the breech. These containers apparently held the components which produced the Wrath of God. And both chemical reservoirs had been utterly exhausted in the recent assault.

Across the chamber the Agent shot his eyes. Harvey Bates was coming his way. In addition, Jim Hobart and Hiram Beckwith had arisen; and the two of them, Victor McGrieve in tow, joined the Agent.

X intended to restore McGrieve to consciousness. But he still lacked his medical kit. This wasn't a cause for distress, however, for the Man of a Thousand Faces. He raised his right shoe—he'd retained his own foot covering for such an eventuality—and gave the heel a counter-clockwise turn. Inside a recess he had concealed a small hypodermic syringe. This device he popped from the heel. Charged with a restorative, the hypo would quickly return Victor McGrieve to consciousness.

The Secret Agent shoved the funeral home director's sleeve upward. He rammed the needle deep into the man's forearm. And in a second Victor McGrieve gave a gasp. He blinked his eyes several times to allow them to regain focus. Still at his side, the Agent determined that the man was recovering nicely from his time under the influence of the anesthetizing gas.

X and Bates helped the man to his feet; and once they'd righted him, the Man of a Thousand Faces gave commands. Bates and Beckwith would remove Victor McGrieve to the hallway. Next they would position themselves in between Hobart, who would lead the way out of this chamber, and the Secret Agent, who would bring up the rear and thus provide them protection.

Those keen eyes of the Agent shot over to the Resurrectionist's control panel. Luckily the man in white had affixed labels to the various toggles and buttons on its surface. With his right index finger the public defender flicked a particular toggle. Instantly his action caused a panel to open in the wall off to their right. Before they made good their escape, the detective ensured that he and Jim Hobart both carried the two portable versions of the Wrath weapon. Though emptied, these might intimidate an opponent long enough for the Agent's party to get past some of their enemies.

Now with Jim Hobart in the lead, the rest of the group departed the Holy of Holies. On the corridor, Hobart pointed them to their left, away from this room of doom.

Inexplicably, they encountered none of the

Resurrection Ring as they made their initial trek into the hall. The Man of a Thousand Faces realized a likely explanation for their good fortune. Since X and Bates had defeated both wielders of the burning death, those two hoods could not have warned their master of impending danger.

They moved in slow silence through the pale light of the hall. All that time, Hobart desperately applied his memory to the walls. He hoped to spot the correct panel which might have given their foes access to the radio room.

There came a time when Beckwith asked them to stop.

"Say, Jim," the fat hack whispered. "Do you remember any landmark along the passage? You know, somethin' like a light or—"

That was it, he exclaimed to Hiram Beckwith! Jim recalled a bulb which wasn't the same color as the rest of them. "It's up ahead," he told the rest. "It's green, unlike these others."

The Agent saw the simplicity of this. The green light was like the traffic signal which marked safe advance on a road.

They rounded a corner, and Jim saw the faint gleam of a greenish light, off in the distance. But as fast as he spotted its rays, he backpedaled to his previous position and promptly stumbled backwards, making a loud clamor in the process. When he arose, embarrassed, he informed the rest that he'd heard a fast *click-click-click-click* of footsteps from down the corridor. Someone must have heard him fall. Because of that accident, the other person was hastily closing the distance between himself and X's little party.

X bolted to the head of the group. He stole a look around the corner. It was the punk Junger, who'd regained consciousness. Now he moved relentlessly towards them, a belligerent look in his eyes. He probably desired to even the score with the man who'd defeated him, and at the very least, to re-establish himself in his master's good graces.

Junger was practically in striking distance of the corner. Suddenly the Man of a Thousand Faces stepped from around the bend and leveled his weapon at him. The eyes of the punk, already wild, couldn't help but pop now at seeing this diabolical device, which he couldn't have known was depleted. X milked Junger's reaction for all it was worth when he casually rammed the thing right under the white suit's chin.

"Well, well, if it ain't Mr. X!" he exclaimed, his words drowning in sarcasm. "Good ta see ya. But I didn't think it'd be anywhere, but a coffin...."

X slowly edged the gun upward, such that Junger's head also rose, like a balloon which gradually moved skyward. Coldly, he replied, "Uh-huh. Let me clarify something for you, Junger: The only imminent funeral will be yours—unless you lead me to the radio room and Betty Dale."

"Have it your way, Mr. X," the sneering Junger said, not with resignation but with a contemptuous glaze covering his words. "Boss figured ya'd break outta the trap he set for ya. Must admit, though, that the Boss is gonna be surprised when he finds out just how quick ya got out."

"Oh, just wait till I get going," a grim X pushed the gun harder by far, almost shoving a row of choppers out of Junger's head. "Now—take me and my friends to the radio room, or you're going to regret it, more than you'll *ever* regret crossing your boss."

Baring his teeth, Junger pivoted his head towards the wall above them. "All right, already!" He reached his hand upwards to that green bulb, its light lending all of their faces a monstrous effect, so eerie it was. Once Junger had placed his hand on the bulb itself, he pulled the thing downward! On a pivot, this mechanism, in turn, activated a door in the brick; and the panel slid quietly open.

Grinning like a bloodthirsty clown, Junger thrust out his hand in a flourish, chuckling, "Make yerself at home, *Mr. X.* Oh, and to show ya how hospitable the Boss is, he's providin' some special entertainment for ya and these other guys. Yer sure ta like it. It'll slay ya...."

Having caught up with the Secret Agent, Hobart, Bates, and Beckwith marched through the door, with McGrieve, pacing several feet behind the rest.

Immediately Junger locked the door behind them. To make matters worse, another of the hoods, Weasel One, appeared from a position to the left of the panel. He ordered X and his crew to divest themselves of any weapons, and to emphasize his command, he passed a cardboard box before them, holding them at gunpoint until they'd followed his command.

Hiram Beckwith, more than the others, was almost offended he would have to surrender a pistol he'd acquired from one of the thugs. Bates and Hobart, indeed, thought that the man might actually cry since he'd be without a firearm.

But this turn of events concerned the Secret Agent's least of all, in light of the tableau that they encountered here in that secret chamber, the Resurrectionist's sanctum.

Here a most sophisticated electronics room met their gaze, with expensive radio apparatus being only some of the machinery present. X spotted much of the stuff he'd seen in Tiny Sayre's apartment, albeit in much greater quantity. The man of mystery even saw another of the machines manufactured by Vox Populi, albeit this one was a more sophisticated model than the one in Tiny's possession. And X saw something else: a large television screen, on which a quantity of tiny black, white, and gray flecks—snow—was falling over the surface.

Their hoodlum guard told X to make a few adjustments to the television set. Agent X complied with the order, and in a couple of seconds the television's snow abated. But he nearly gasped when he saw the image on the television's screen: It was a shot of the altar upstairs, with Betty Dale, flanked by hoodlums! And in all his glory, the Resurrectionist hovered nearby, one of the Webley target pistols pointed at her slender neck!

He turned directly to face X—a camera must have been nearby—and he remarked, *"I warned you that you hadn't bested me yet, Agent X!"* the fiend gloated. *"And here is the proof: Betty Dale is soon to die. But I and I alone can raise her from the dead! Sadly, however, she will return to the world of the living a hopeless addict, a slave to the 'sugar.' And just as sadly, she will die from it, turning into a mummy."*

X's blood boiled. Storm clouds of fury gathered in his eyes. And he doubled his hands into fists, husking, "Not if I have anything to do with it. I'll—I'll stop you before you can do her harm...."

"You're not in any position to make those kinds of threats now, X. You will, instead, do as I have already demanded. That is, you will tell me what your real name is. Also you will unmask,

in front of me. Only by committing these two acts can you ensure your dear companion, Miss Dale, will live—at least for a time longer. . . ."

Thoughts raced through the mind of the Secret Agent. Betty Dale, to be rendered comatose and returned as an addict? Jim Hobart and Hiram Beckwith, already in the grip of the "sugar," and marked for death? Harvey Bates injured and promised the same fate? There had to be a way to beat this fiend in white at his own game. There had to be. And as if by inspiration, he recalled that plan he'd concocted in Betty Dale's cell.

"All right, Resurrectionist. Let me out of this room. You can have my real name, in exchange for the life of Betty Dale."

X's men were horrified. They couldn't believe he would cave in to this man of evil. Such words, however, played like a beautiful aria to the Resurrectionist, he stated, "*You have come around to my way of thinking, then, X?*"

"I suppose you could say that. So, do you let me out of here," he cut his eyes around to Jim Hobart, "or do I sit here and read the graphitti on your walls?"

"*Always the devil-may-care adventurer, aren't you, X? Very well, you may leave the radio room and accompany my man Junger directly to the sanctuary.*"

"What about my friends here with me?"

"*Oh, they may come too. They will find the disclosure of your true identity and your unmasking most instructive.*"

"That's fine," Agent X agreed to the plan. He turned his eyes on Victor McGrieve and mouthed the words, "now" and "Keep your head down."

At the Agent's signal Junger released the lock on the secret door, thereby allowing the prisoners to march down the hall and to a ladder. This device would in turn allow them ingress to the sanctuary, via another hallway.

In short order they reached the ladder, the Agent going up first, followed by Hobart, Bates, Beckwith, McGrieve, and the punk Junger.

As they traveled upwards, Jim Hobart was recalling something. He had met the Secret Agent, some three years ago. He was remembering, too, the connection that the Resurrectionist had made only days ago, regarding the Agent and A.J. Martin, the newspaperman. So the Agent and his boss were one and the same? Well, what of it? Hobart determined he would trust this honest, courageous, and resourceful man, no matter his real face, no matter the outcome, no matter the danger to his own life. . . .

They all reached the hallway and then, in short order, the sanctuary itself, loaded with the remaining mobsters and, of course, the so-called "clients" of the Resurrectionist. Without delay all of them parted, in order that the Agent and his party could move right in front of the man of evil himself.

The Resurrectionist began, triumphantly, "Welcome to you, Agent X. You are our honored guest—you and your friends," he looked over the bunch of them. "You have agreed to my proposal, and so I will now 'ask' that you uphold your own end of the bargain—the facts about your real name and face. Being the man of honor you are, I'm sure you will comply."

Victor McGrieve was listening closely to this pronouncement, taking in every word from the mouth of their captor, and realizing the truth. He was fuming over it, in fact. In that vein he bumped the tip of his shoe against the right ankle of the Secret Agent. But the Man of a Thousand Faces wouldn't be moved yet.

"As you wish—my real name and face, delivered into your grubby, little hands," the Secret Agent stated, his tone matter of fact, seemingly unconcerned in the very midst of this mortal danger.

"So pitifully defiant, even to the bitter end, eh?" posed his enemy. "I can accept that, as long as you give me your secret...."

Betty Dale, the only living being who'd seen his face, gasped in horror. She struggled in the grip of the hoods, begging, "Please—please don't make him do that! You'll destroy his effectiveness in fighting crime! And you'll destroy him, as well! You—you can't simply—"

"Oh, but I can and *will* do what you have just suggested, Miss Dale. That was indeed the whole point of my campaign against him. Or have you forgotten?

"Now, Agent X, I am growing *most impatient* with your attempt to stall for time. Who are you? What is your real name?"

"My real name," he frankly stated, "is Chip U. Herman."

" 'Chip U. Herman,' eh? I had expected something more dramatic from you, but an ordinary name *can* conceal the extraordinary spirit, it seems."

"Perhaps. But while we're at it, I'm asking you to cooperate, peaceably, and release Betty Dale into my custody. Then my men can take her safely from this place."

Pure viciousness gleamed in the fanatical blue eyes of the Resurrectionist. "I'm afraid you mistake me for a man of honor, X. You know that I won't do that."

"Not surprising, that revelation," X countered. "Well, it matters not, for Victor McGrieve, here, knows at least some of the truth about you."

"Hell, yes, I do!" he rumbled, his words cloaked in a mantle of fury. "And you're no more my son Malcolm than a jackass is!"

CHAPTER XXXII
REVELATIONS

IT was this word that the Resurrectionist had feared, this odor of exposure wafting from him to Victor McGrieve. And it would grow more pungent in the next few moments.

"Bad as he is—or was—my son wouldn't kill a woman. Now, I don't know who you are," McGrieve rumbled. "But I know exactly what you did. You used my son's voice to control me, to blackmail me, through the phone. And you wrote letters in his handwriting, thinking that you would achieve your ends. However, you did something much worse: You preyed on my guilt over what had happened between my son and me, years ago. *This* guilt provided you with the means torment me. This guilt—and nothing more."

The Resurrectionist spoke then, his next calm pronouncement, for once, the pacific complement to his beatific features. He turned his head somewhat jerkily to address the Secret Agent, not McGrieve himself. "I suspected you would pull some clever trick like this, before all was said and done. You grasp at straws to the last, knowing that you are defeated, knowing that I will take *all* of your lives and destroy your legacy, for all time!"

"If you live long enough," the Secret Agent drew himself up, inched closer to the white-garbed crime master.

"If *I* live long enough?"

"Correct. Your 'clients' won't let you live

when they know that you aim to double-cross them."

This disclosure lit a fuse of anger underneath the Resurrectionist. Amidst his clients' increasing murmurs and curses, the public defender pressed his advantage further: "You *never* intended to let them collect their insurance benefits from your fraudulent scheme. Nor did you intend to give them the cure for the 'sugar,' or at least what you perceived was a cure for its effects. Rather you wanted to find that doctor Charles Darwin Osben for your own reasons. You thought he possessed that cure, the formula for synthesizing the counteractant. You determined to gain that counteractant—preferably by stealing it—in order to benefit yourself."

X's opponent gave a cynical laugh. "How desperate you are, X! Why would I want the cure?"

"Because you're an addict too. And you knew that you'd die, unless you procured help. But there was an irony here, one you never realized."

"And that was?"

"That even *Osben's* cure was flawed. Let me apply your words: 'I and I alone' possess the only true counteractant for the 'sugar.'

His opponent's tone showed what the Resurrectionist only now would admit, "You—you have it?"

That's right—*I* do. My formula might work—and I stress the word *might*—provided that the user hasn't been injected with the 'sugar' for too lengthy a period of time. Without my counteractant none of you has a prayer, and every one of you faces certain, horrible death. I promise that.

"So you see, Resurrectionist, you do *not* own the whip hand. I do. And I urge these people here, these 'clients' and 'Resurgos' to join me," he said to the men, like a master orator. "Rise up against your so-called 'benefactor,' even as I do, this very moment!"

The murmurs from the clients and the Resurrection men themselves grew louder, more openly hostile towards this supposed lord of crime. He decided to squelch their objections immediately.

From within his robe he whipped out one of the deadly Bolo Mausers. "Kill the Secret Agent! Kill all of them—Betty Dale included—all who would stand between you and untold wealth and power!"

His harangue took on more violence and loudness. But he knew his action could backfire if his men, in turn, opened fire at this crowded altar. They might actually gun him down, not to mention kill each other. Hence the white-robed devil hesitated. But in that instant Junger unexpectedly acted.

The hood leaped at the Man of a Thousand Faces, the punk never having lost his desire to play tit for tat with the sleuth. Like a great cat, Agent X sent his body into a limber dodge, pivoted his form, and flipped the hoodlum over his shoulder with a violent jiu-jitsu move.

Another white suit, head down, propelled his body in X's direction. The man of mystery, back into a crouched form, grabbed the man's running figure and threw him hard to one side, right into the middle of a swelling mass of other white suits. Surprisingly they didn't join him in a counterattack against the Secret Agent. Instead, they trampled Junger and stormed the altar. There the Resurrectionist frantically attempted to shore up his position against the swelling tide of men about to drown him.

Harvey Bates and Hiram Beckwith cracked heads. In the process, the fat cabbie also liberated a couple of pistols, the Bolo Mausers. It was all Bates could do to keep the man from emptying one of the weapons on their opponents. Finally a reluctant Beckwith grudgingly began to use his pistol as Bates was doing, as a club to crack the heads of their foes.

X could see that his opponent's crime empire was teetering. He determined then to settle affairs later with this alleged mastermind of crime. Right now, though, the manhunter needed to evacuate from this scene of disaster before it was too late. Especially he needed to remove Betty Dale and Victor McGrieve from the danger. Otherwise, he knew that snakes like the Resurrectionist would try to bite their enemies, even when those reptiles were breathing their last....

Three more white suits clawed and kicked their way to the altar, immediately adjacent to the Secret Agent and his associate Hobart. The young ex-cop disabled one of them with a crushing uppercut. At the same time his chief buried his right foot in the stomach of one and, as quickly, his left hand in the jaw of the other.

He advised, "No more time to waste in here, Jim. Round up Bates and the rest, and then follow my lead."

Body relentless as a machine, the Agent pushed and shoved white suits and the Resurrectionist's "clients" until he reached his goal, the altar. There he could see a distraught Betty Dale, peering over the heads of the combatants and searching for the Man of a Thousand Faces. Her eyes grew wider and wider with terror while the Secret Agent battled his way to her side. Once there, he hurled another white suit out of the way; Betty, he placed, quickly but gently, into the cradle of his arms.

He raced the two of them behind a makeshift shield, a large pew, in the former choir loft.

X reasoned that immediate retreat onto the hallway offered them their sole chance of safety, especially in light of two factors. First the crowd of Resurrection men in here had lost any of the loyalty they might have once held to their chief, much less to their fellows. They became an unruly mob, striking and eventually stabbing each other with knives. From a vantage point in the former choir loft, the kneeling Secret Agent told Betty it was only a matter of time until someone fired a gun into the group. And as though following a stage direction, Betty and Agent X, joined by Bates and the others, saw and heard the prophesied gunfire, half a dozen rounds squeezed off in rapid succession. More of the loud booms marched behind this squadron, promising that other gun-wielders would soon follow suit with their own weapons.

Those gunshots and the four murders which resulted—two shots had missed their targets—were linked unbreakably to a second factor, one far more dangerous than loss of loyalty among criminals. This other issue was the amazing survival of the Resurrectionist himself! He had in fact fired his own Mauser to kill that foursome of his opponents, in this case, Lothian, Terran, and two members of the Resurrection Ring. In so doing he had hoped to save his own skin. Now momentarily freed from his enemies' grasp, he fled the sanctuary. And the Secret Agent intuited his foe's next thrust and its means of execution.

"This is it," he whispered to Betty, who

knelt on his left, and Jim Hobart, who, still twitching, knelt to his right. "We must leave here promptly, by the way we came in. We can follow that original path, or we might even get lucky and find another secret one out of here. Whatever the case, if we stick around much longer, he'll burn all of us to death."

He cut his head around to Hobart. "You're at bat, Jim. Ready for the pitch?"

"Anything you say, Mr. Martin," he slipped up. "I—I mean, X. Come on!"

X couldn't help but hear Hobart's *faux pas*, but the Secret Agent said nothing in response to it. Instead he rose up, at which point he and his associates bolted out of the old choir loft and onto that hallway. Mere seconds elapsed as their racing feet propelled them to that ladder. When X reached those vertical parallel bars, he wrapped his hands around the two sidepieces and moved himself downward two rungs. Suddenly he loosened his grip and his footholds, such that both his hands only partially clutched the ladder's sidepieces. His action started a hair-raising transit, perhaps two dozen or so feet to the corridor below.

"Hurry, Jim!" X shouted upward. "Put Betty on the ladder and tell her to follow my example. I'll catch her as she lands."

Teeth chattering like dice rattling in a cup, the shaking woman mounted the ladder with Jim Hobart's assistance. Then she did just as the Agent had directed. Her slender frame, a blonde arrow, shot downwards to its target. Cool air raced over her body. She opened her lovely mouth, as if to scream bloody murder. But she could issue only a choked squeak before arms of steel encircled her form and jerked her away from the steel sidepieces.

Jim Hobart assisted Harvey Bates onto the ladder as its next passenger, and the giant launched himself into space. His trip went off without a hitch, with the Secret Agent grabbing him, wordlessly, just above the lowest rung. Hiram Beckwith became a regular pansy went it came to such derring-do. Hobart almost had to force the "borrowed" pistol upon the man before he and Victor McGrieve could shame him into riding the ladder. Finally the fat hack driver half-glided, half-stepped, until he reached the bottom. Now it was Victor McGrieve's turn, and the old man came through like a champion, seeming exhilarated by the whole affair. Jim Hobart slid down last. But during his entire trip, he was twitching more and more. He knew that he needed that counteractant without delay. Still he put on a brave face when he thudded into the detective's waiting arms. Indeed Jim Hobart informed everyone that he was ready to go bear hunting with a switch. With all of them together again, Agent X started away from his friends.

"Where are you going, X?" a curious Hobart prompted him.

The detective turned to face them: "Back to the radio room, to retrieve my equipment."

"And after that?"

"To the Resurrectionist's office. That monster in white will follow through on his scheme to torch this entire site. Look along the walls, and see what I mean."

All of them obeyed his command. They spotted the parallel rows of spouts which someone had either punched through the walls from the other side, or maybe affixed to the walls from their end.

His tone serious, X pointed at the nozzles, "From some master control panel, the Resurrectionist will shoot water through those things. That will create a fine mist, one component of his so-called 'Wrath of God.' He'll follow that water treatment with another one—"

"—that silvery stuff!" a suddenly comprehending Jim Hobart cut in.

"That's correct. Some elements of thermite might also comprise part of the devilish mix. But its main ingredient is metallic potassium, reduced, in this case, to a particle form. When it combines with water, only a drop or two, the mixture will give off a violent blue-white flame of great intensity, in part the result of the hydrogen gas freed from the H2O. He might even throw in some fluorine, and cause the place to go up, like a bomb."

Betty Dale felt her blood freeze.

X, meanwhile, addressed Bates: "You remember our trip to the lab, and those boxes I found?"

"Yes."

"They were full of mineral oil. Manufacturers store potassium in this medium, and sometimes kerosene, to avoid mixing the element with water."

"All that damage from such a simple chemical reaction?" the giant Bates quizzed. "Begs the question: Where in heaven's name did he get all of that metallic potassium?"

"Why, from Henry Terran, the soap and candle manufacturer."

This revelation produced nothing but more puzzlement in the minds of his listeners.

X explained, "Manufacturers of soap and bleach both use great quantities of potassium nitrate to manufacture their products. The potassium renders the soap softer in texture, and thus more desirable for customers. The Resurrectionist understood its desirability too, hence his deal with Henry Terran to use his industrial potassium. Once the Resurrectionist had gained Terran's supply of the potassium-nitrogen-oxygen compound, he, or rather the so-called 'Emel,' could extract the nitrogen and oxygen from it and thus derive a fine grade of potassium. He could then pulverize the material and thus create a fine dust."

Additional words might have proceeded from the Secret Agent's mouth: the need for the Resurrectionist to overawe his followers, for instance, or the fiend's lies which covered his true identity. This was a double lie, a deception within a deception which Attica's warden had partially confirmed, and which Victor McGrieve had finally solidified.

No, the Man of a Thousand Faces could share none of this intelligence with his friends because of the next event which transpired.

Unexpectedly, a massive fit of tremors rocked the entire frame of Jim Hobart. Jim fell on the floor. His eyes became glassy, and he was unresponsive.

X clipped, "Bates—get to that radio room for our equipment. I'll try to remove Jim to the Holy of Holies, where we left my medical kit. If I can get to the counteractant, he might survive!"

So easily did the Agent scoop Jim up and drape him over his own arms, that the redheaded detective seemed no heavier than a child. Wordlessly, Agent X took off. Harvey Bates too sped away on his mission of recovery, with Hiram Beckwith left behind to stand sentry over Betty Dale and Victor McGrieve.

Down the hall the Man of a Thousand Faces ran. Around the corner from his friends, he heard a group of thugs moving towards his position. This bunch wasn't aware of the chaos in the sanctuary, much less the Resurrectionist's double cross of his own men. X heard them speak as if their chief yet controlled the situation above ground, and intended to reward them for their loyalty. X guessed that the corridors, like the laboratory, might be sound-proofed, thus explaining their present ignorance. Interestingly enough their words revealed that they *had* discovered the Agent's escape from hell, since they'd somehow opened that part of the lab. They were, as a consequence, out for his blood, if they could only catch him.

Quiet as a gnat walking on cotton, the Secret Agent deposited Jim Hobart on the path's floor. X allowed the toughs to edge closer.

Four of them popped around the corner—and the Man of a Thousand Faces popped the first one of them with a terrific kick to his midsection. Thugs Two and Three fared hardly better. They launched a brief, though largely ineffective, counter assault, thinking they could defeat the man-hunter. Number Two carved the air with a vicious slash of a switch-blade, the edge glittering like silver. His body a living weapon, Agent X blasted an elbow into the second hood's face; and the blow practically destroyed the man's cheek and upper jaw.

Number Three carried a set of brass knuckles, his emblem of the "real man." He found out how manly he was, much too quickly. Agent X spun his torso, launched his size twelve foot into a wide arc. The kick met the thug's face, which in turn made the immediate acquaintance of the hall's floor. That left one more thug standing.

Punk Number Four, a young, fat man, leveled his Mauser at the Secret Agent, thinking to pepper the man-hunter's body with his weapon. He didn't care that use of the gun might spell his own demise, thanks ricocheting bullets.

X dove for the feet of his enemy. He tonged the fellow's ankles with fingers of steel. The Agent pulled hard. Overbalanced, the punk toppled like a sack of corn meal, to the floor. A pair of blows to his head rendered the man unconscious. No longer harried, X returned to Jim Hobart. The sleuth snatched up his friend and resumed the final part of his trek.

They re-entered the site. Several dead members of the Resurrection Ring populated the lab, in addition to many who had suffered unconsciousness or injury in the Resurrectionist's escape to the sanctuary, several minutes previously. Probably others roved those corridors, as the previous four had been doing.

Needless to say the Secret Agent felt grateful about his foes' absence. But he knew he would sweat buckets until Harvey Bates had arrived safely. In the interim the Agent could accomplish his main goal, injection of the counteractant.

A quick search of the laboratory's floor showed him that his medical kit, although somewhat damaged, had escaped complete destruction. Even more fortunate, he was able to produce, unharmed, the vial for Jim's restoration. Faster than seemed humanly possible, the detective loaded a hypodermic with the miracle drug. When he was satisfied with the amount, he aimed the needle at Jim's neck. Just as X was set to slip the instrument beneath Jim's flesh and into a vein, another fit of the spasms carved Jim's bearded features into a veritable fright mask. Secret Agent X allowed this spell to pass.

As soon as it had subsided, the Man of a Thousand Faces plunged the needle deep into the proper vein. The syringe's entire load of chocolate-colored fluid Agent X injected into the young ex-cop's system. Jim Hobart lay there, still unresponsive.

Then his eyelids fluttered. After another second he turned his bitter blue eyes on the Secret Agent and gasped, "Thanks, X. I think that—that did it. I think those tics," he blinked his eyes again, "are slowing down a little."

"You'll need more of this drug over the next few days, Jim. But you should be fine, eventually."

Jim looked up at the sleuth, profound gratitude in his eyes. "You really are 'A.J. Martin,' aren't you? I mean, you're the newspaperman who got me that job as a detective, seven years ago. And you're X, too? This is too much for me to comprehend. I—I owe you—"

"—nothing at all, Jim. But we'll discuss this later. It's time we get out of here—"

Harvey Bates rushed into the room—just as Jim Hobart and Secret Agent X felt a slight rumbling beneath the floor.

Bates pointed a square index finger upstairs. "Can tell that something's going on," he related. "That Ring is growing more frantic, if the sounds outside the radio room were a sample. Think that their boss is up to more no good, Sir, just like you thought."

Instinctively the Secret Agent looked, not at Harvey Bates himself, but at the lower legs of the giant's pants. They were *damp*, as they would be if the fellow strolled past a yard sprinkler.

Agent X cocked his head to one side. A faint hiss sibilated from the air outside. On its heels a deep *whoosh* made its presence felt. That alternation of hiss and whoosh repeated for several seconds before it stopped.

The Secret Agent and Bates pulled Jim Hobart to his feet, and X guided both men towards the lab's exit door. When X had opened that panel, he and his associates could see a preternatural, blue-white light. The hissing and whooshing had started their song and dance number again. It was a performance none of them wanted to see. Yet they were frozen in time, all except the man of mystery himself.

Taking command, he said to Harvey Bates, "Follow me back to the Inferno room. Then get Jim and the others to the Resurrectionist's office, as quickly as you can."

"What about you?"

X responded cryptically, "I'll get there when I get there. Just wait. And by all means, *don't* re-enter that radio room till I've rejoined you."

Both the Agent and Bates led Jim Hobart back across the Holy of Holies to that room of doom.

He sent them on their less-than-merry way while he stayed behind. X remembered that the Resurrectionist had hovered near the side of the room which depicted the Heavenly court. Here he had disappeared. Yet X and his men had been trapped on the side portraying Hell. This meant that *both sides* harbored secret panels. But the controls for them had evidently been on the side of the angels, in more ways than one.

Over to that side he rushed, as a consequence. And he met with enormous good fortune, once he'd reached this new goal. The doorway to the control panel hadn't completely closed, being slightly ajar. X slipped a hand behind the thing and noticed the reason. The door had orphaned a small piece of white fabric from its mother—a white robe fashioned of Helmerite, the very garment of the monstrous Resurrectionist himself!

This was quite the find on its own terms, if for no other reason than its revelation of the the control panel. But the Resurrectionist hadn't labeled these, like those others. Still the Agent knew his opponent wouldn't have built his death traps without an override, both in his office, and in this deathtrap. After all, he, the crime chieftain himself, might someday need to escape his own devilish gadget. But what particular switch activated that shut-off mechanism? Which one—

Abruptly, on the hall the sounds of the hissing and whooshing resumed. X began to sweat when he thought about his friends, these loyal, faithful men who would give their lives for him. But they were now running to their deaths, unless the Man of a Thousand Faces acted with both speed and insight. In the next second he snatched that insight, seemingly, from nowhere.

The Resurrectionist was obsessed with that which is concealed, X knew, yet also, that which was baroque, or overly adorned. Therefore he posed this question, much as the white-mantled crimester would do: What better place to hide something, but in plain sight, just as he'd hidden himself all these years?

X turned his eyes on the four pieces of brown Bakelite with their lilac tops. He tried to lift the first one, which yielded an override control for the hallway's lighting. Agent X ignored this one for the time being. Cover number 2, however, gave up something much more valuable, namely a timer! Eyes crackling with excitement, he realized he was onto something, especially in light of the revelations from numbers three and four. He popped both of them open, the third to disclose a red button reading "Activate Wrath" and the fourth, a green circlet reading "Override Wrath."

He thumbed the green button with authority. And the sounds outside died, much as the Resurrectionist's victims had been doing for several weeks. The muscular hand of the Agent wiped the sweat from his brow. He had bought his friends some time, though exactly how much he couldn't determine. Nor could such minor vermin bother him, anyway. He had more important rats to kill.

The laboratory would have been the scene for his next action until he decided to throw additional spokes in the Resurrectionist's wheels. To that end the detective flicked the toggle which controlled the lighting.

Now he returned to his original goal, his foe's laboratory. From the miscreant's supply locker the Secret Agent ensured that mineral oil was in a can he'd found, beside the boxes. Along with the oil, he snatched a thin tube and a siphon, both of which went into the other pocket of his garment. Out of the laboratory he bolted, not by the way he and Hobart had entered. Instead, he took another passage, the same pathway that the Resurrectionist had taken when he had abducted Betty Dale!

Faster and faster X's feet pounded the floor of the darkened passage, the way of the manhunter lit only by the rays of his cigarette lighter. More and more collected the great globules of sweat on his brow. The hall took several curves as he ran forward. It followed this snaky track for a short span, whereupon it angled hard to the right, but as unexpectedly, it took a hard inclined path. This track made him think that he'd crossed over the other halls, much as a railroad overpass crosses a highway or a body of water.

Far up ahead and around another corner, the sounds of human voices created a buzzing in the air. It was as if someone had disturbed a horde of bees from their hive. He halted his progress and closed the cover of his lighter. Then he flattened his muscular form against the wall to let the chaos play out. He must have been no more than thirty or so feet from the Resurrectionist's office. More precisely he had stopped near the ladder that reached upward to the office from a recessed area, a niche of sorts, on the brick hallway.

Sharp curses sliced the air overhead. A series of shouts rendered the surroundings more jagged, if that were possible.

But then the Man of a Thousand Faces heard several fearful words from a woman's mouth. Her speech expressed deep distress over his safety, indeed, his very survival. In response he caught a man's tones—something about "fires are out now" and then this statement of encouragement: "Just hang in there a little longer, Miss Dale." These words, he recognized, originated from the person of the loyal, calm Jim Hobart. In response to continued Betty's whimpers, the fellow assured, "He'll be back in a bit. You can count on him."

"Yes—yes," she affirmed with the barest of nods, her sapphire eyes forming huge pools of tears. "I *have* to. He's going to be fine. I know he will."

So Betty Dale and his other friends had ventured closer to the Resurrectionist's office, X realized. He couldn't blame them disobeying his orders. They must have thought they were acting properly, to have moved from their old position to this new one. Likely Bates and Hobart, especially, had believed that this new vantage point afforded them a better chance to attack the fiendish Resurrectionist, particularly if something happened to the Secret Agent himself.

The lights suddenly came on again. To give them renewed courage, the sleuth popped into his friends' line of sight.

Meanwhile, another chain of shouts rattled the corridor. Indeed those angry screams permeated the space around X's band for several minutes before the blue-white flames began to blaze again, from behind. That strange fire crackled additionally, right in front of the Secret Agent, thus separating him from his allies. Their enemy had trapped them between walls of flame. Through the loudspeaker system, his twisted laughter echoed up and down pathway. Agent X feared that this time, the mastermind of crime would finally claim all of their lives.....

CHAPTER XXXIII DEATHMASK OF A PHONY SAINT

LIKE nightshade the strange bluish-white flames were beautiful—and deadly. Their radiance lit the hall, cast mysterious shadows off X and his nearby associates. The dark silhouettes seemed possessed of some bizarre almost-life, sometimes expanding, sometimes contracting.

In the midst of this crisis, Betty Dale attempted to show courage. But her heart pounded; and her body sweated under all of this heat and this terrible strain. She clapped a shaking, slender right hand over her mouth while Jim Hobart kept his strong right arm around her shoulders. Nevertheless, she was beginning to panic because the very breath of doom blew around them. Too, she started to suffer something like a claustrophobic sensation, the direct result of the fires in front and behind her.

X couldn't fail to see her rising dismay. He shouted at her, confidence in his exclamation: "Betty! I want you to stay close to Jim. *Do not move*! Everything will be all right!"

That next set of orders he delivered to the giant Harvey Bates, starting with a question: "Have you a stopwatch dial on your wristwatch?"

The man did. Agent X directed him to start timing the duration of each blast from the Wrath of God. His reasoning was obvious. Those streams must stop at some point, either because they would be turned off, or because they would have depleted their supply of potassium. In that interim, X would slip into the midst of the space and squirt a quantity of the mineral oil into the nozzles which fired the metallic potassium. His bold act would momentarily forestall the ability of the metal to combine with the water and thus create the Wrath. Then perhaps he and his men could mount that ladder and nab their foe.

Bates started his task, his dark eyes locked on the tiny stopwatch's face. He had begun his task in the midst of the flames' flow, during his initial attempt. But he got in on the ground floor of the fires' next pass, that is, the one in front of the Agent himself. As best the giant could determine, the flames burned for three minutes, then ceased for two—just as they did right now.

From that pocket the Agent drew out the long, snaky tube and fastened it to the offending nozzle. His hand steady as Gibraltar, he poured a generous quantity of mineral oil from the can and down the rubber hose. Some of the lubricant, of course, spilled onto the floor, since the diameter of the hose slightly exceeded that of the nozzle. Still, he had briefly stymied the Resurrectionist's efforts to shoot anymore potassium through that opening. At least now the Agent could climb the ladder. He could worry about the other nozzle, which burned with its devilish fire once more, after they'd nabbed the architect of crime.

At least, this *was* his intent, until someone addressed them from the loudspeakers below the ceiling. The voice sounded like that of the white-garbed fiend himself. That much was certain. But the monster's words came in a manner that betokened strain, breathlessness. He might have been in a fight, as far as the Agent and his friends knew. What *was* certain was the content of his message, an unvarnished threat.

"You think to—to defeat me, Agent X? I will finish—finish you, yet! For I am—I am still the 'life from death'!"

The mechanism which powered the Wrath of God commenced its devilish work again, regular as a metronome. A fine mist of water vapor shot from both sets of nozzles at the floor. That meant the other ones would squirt the metallic potassium dust particles onto the midst of the water. A taut couple of seconds passed. The hair stood up on the Agent's arms. He prayed his makeshift fix would work, practically willed the mineral oil to hold the potassium in place.

It did.

To the alcove he scrambled, that he might race up the ladder and root out this vicious crime lord who masqueraded as a human being.

Something stymied X's plan in the next

instant, though. And Hiram Beckwith caught wind of it first. It was another of the familiar and deadly sibilants which announced the Wrath of God's arrival. And unlike its predecessors this one didn't originate from the wall spouts. Beckwith felt a slight dampness in his bare scalp. At first he thought it was mere sweat caused by the intense flames of previous moments. The fat cabbie unfortunately was mistaken—badly so, as it happened.

His eyes raked the ceiling. The moisture dribbled downward, slowly at first; but eventually, a steady mist of it sprouted from tiny nozzles overhead! Victor McGrieve noticed it too, while the mist collected on his own balding head. Caledonian's owner knew what was slated to happen, but he maintained his courage.

"There's more of the water falling!" he boomed at Hiram Beckwith and Harvey Bates, who stood nearby with Jim and Betty. "Tell X! We've got to move the redhead and the woman out of here, immediately!"

Beckwith shouted up the ladder, "Got to get everyone in this alcove now, Diamond Jim! We've got no time to lose!"

Silvery dust particles began their downward journey, to the space between the brick walls. Because of the water the floor was growing slicker than a greased pig at a hillbilly fair. The moisture, now a small pool, separated Beckwith from his friends.

Then a bluish-white blanket of fire dropped over the edge of Beckwith's path!

Victor McGrieve and Harvey Bates hugged the bricks, gaped as the fires spread. X urging them, they linked hands, and McGrieve shot desperate fingers at Hiram Beckwith. Ever so gradually Jim Hobart and the mighty Agent X tugged the remaining two members of their party towards the alcove. Jim was giving out, however, because of his recent ordeal. He had to stop, catch his breath in the midst of their effort. As a result Agent X pushed him gently aside and supplanted the young ex-cop at the foot of the ladder. Then the Man of a Thousand Faces put his entire body into his life-or-death task. He set his weight. He bunched the muscles in his legs. With the strength of a modern Hercules, he edged McGrieve and Beckwith closer to the sheltering alcove.

Above them, from the loudspeakers, the Resurrectionist gloated, *"The fires are coming perilously close now, aren't they, my friends? They are eager to touch you, to wrap you in their deadly embrace! Rest assured, this is only the start of your misery!*

"Your flesh will soon begin to blister and peel from the intense heat. Your skin will turn black as tar. You will beg for release from the pain the fires inflict. You will share the torment of the victims who faced the stake, after the Salem witch trials. Exciting, no? Or is it, perhaps, terrifying? Let us explore your fate in greater detail," he chuckled. *"Your burns will increase from second- and third-degree injuries to fourth-degree ones. Did you know that they will even reach stages five and six?*

"By this time the fires will have burned through your flesh, to the very bone. Unconsciousness will already have claimed you, of course. And at this point you will face the inevitable and sad end, in other words, your death. I should tell you that it doesn't have to end this way, detective, at least for your friends. What would you give for them to survive? Would you give me your life, Agent X, in exchange for theirs? Would you?"

While he taunted them, armies of grayish-black smoke massed in the hall. Agent X and his allies watched them. He and his crew realized that it was a mere matter of time before the smoke overcame them, possibly even before the fires did. Still the tiny band continued their slow, though steady march towards the recessed area in the brick wall. Beckwith had already crossed its threshold. Then came Victor McGrieve into the niche, though the situation forced the man to extend his legs and thereby avoid another great puddle of water in his path.

In the meantime, blue-white flames inched closer to the fat man. And a simple, yet terrible, factor caused their advance. A thin bridge of liquid almost connected the pool to the mixture of potassium and water on the floor adjacent to it.

Beckwith reached the puddle that had blocked McGrieve. But the cab driver faced a distinct disadvantage. Not as tall as the older man, Beckwith possessed a shorter stride. One hand shaking on the brick, the hack man stretched his right leg over the puddle, such that the heel of his foot still touched the water's outer edge, the one opposite himself. Slowly upward he levered his obese frame. Just as he planted his weight on his left heel, his form nearly slid out from under him; and he almost fell to into the water. They grabbed him and jerked him into the alcove before he knew what hit him. And a sweating, trembling Hiram Beckwith rejoined his friends the safety of the alcove.

Nonetheless, Beckwith's near-tragedy was enough to agitate the waters, to link the source of the Wrath with the fresh puddle of water!

In those same moments, the bluish-white fires were spreading like mushrooms in a forest, the flames popping and hissing from nearly every square foot of the corridor. Moreover, the clouds of smoke gained choking denseness, immediately outside the alcove. Mere seconds would see them climb upwards into X's shelter.

Agent X and his friends had apparently gained nothing more than a momentary reprieve, since the Resurrectionist still maintained his advantage.

A new development put them in deeper danger. This was a deep rumbling and a series of loud cracks, as of wood splintering, which filled their ears.

Agent X responded, with a slow nod in Beckwith's direction, at the alcove's edge. "It's these fires. They've destroyed much of the church's wooden structure, though the stone and brick are hanging on for now. They won't do so for long, however. These flames and the building's age will eventually take their toll on the place. The Resurrectionist didn't consider any of this when he modified this building. He cared only about wowing his followers and 'clients,' not to mention providing himself a means of getting out of here alive."

Down below, the old church gave another shimmy that rocked the building to its very foundation. It was a clear sign the edifice wasn't long for this world. In addition, more of the eerie blue-white flames ran onto the stage that was the brick hall.

And the dense smoke, like a giant octopus, spread its tentacles, finally, into the niche.

Initially the stuff didn't bother them. But that respite, too, lasted only briefly. Victor McGrieve, older than everyone else, proceeded to cough a bit. Beckwith and Hobart also joined that chorus of respiratory distress. Before it was over, they all coughed; and their eyes smarted from the dust particles swirling around.

Somehow through it all, the man-hunter exuded a strange calm. He determined to move his friends from this niche in the wall and launch his final attack on the Resurrectionist.

From the ladder the detective pointed his head downwards, towards the entrance of the alcove. Those fires continued unabated in their fury. Outwaiting their enemy's supply of potassium was no longer possible, since the building might collapse around them. And even if the structure's eventual fall didn't finish them off, then smoke inhalation would assuredly do them in.

That meant going out into fresher air and possible safety, instead, via the trapdoor over their heads. Thankfully the Secret Agent noticed no lock of any sort in the hasp, so this hinged door offered them a viable, though dangerous, means to safety. And he was realist enough to know that they would have to possess the element of surprise. Only in that way could they execute a successful breach of this entrance, plus overcome their foe. X believed he could contrive just the trick to give them that edge they so desperately needed....

Suddenly the loudspeakers on the hall ceased broadcasting their rant and thus wrenched the man-hunter back to his surroundings. This didn't mean, though, that the Agent, Betty, or their friends heard nothing at all. In fact loud noises yet echoed off the walls of this protected recess. The man of mystery knew their foe hadn't switched off his highly sensitive microphone. As a result, Betty, X, and the rest commanded seats in the orchestral pit beneath the violent concert itself.

To their ears, it sounded as though the man in white, ferocious as a tiger, was battling some person or persons to the very death. X's crew heard the clatter of a chair or some other piece of furniture, as it apparently sailed through space and crashed against a glass object, perhaps the doors of a bookcase. Their ears made out, too, the violent collision of human bodies which struck with intent to do harm, indeed, to kill. They continued to hit and, most likely, kick each other, their bodies possibly rolling on the floor.

Several sharp, loud voices, maybe half a dozen of them, abruptly cut through the roaring blue flames on the corridor below. The words of the newcomers were harsh, commanding. And they ordered the members of the Resurrection Ring to surrender on the spot.

In the aftermath of those directives, probably because of them, the fighting in the office grew more pitched. More furniture took wing. More blows struck bodies. The screaming and cursing intensified. Shots pelted their targets. The conflict in that room had reached the stage of a young war.

And the voices from the hallway yet again ordered surrender or destruction.

This time a thrilled Jim Hobert almost flew from the alcove to the flaming hallway. He had to learn the source of the new voices. But the Secret Agent held him back with an outthrust hand, fearful the man would burn to death in the process.

It was ventriloquism, he whispered to Jim; and he, the Secret Agent was the source of the trick. The subterfuge inspired a brief smile from the young ex-cop. Only they would know the truth about X's desperate ploy.

They clearly needed something to believe, X realized. The gray-blck smoke had, by now, completely filled the alcove. These toxic fumes reddened their eyes, irritated their lungs. They all suffered constant coughing, barely able to breathe in the midst of the vaprous invasion.

A sleeve of the Helmerite material over his mouth, Bates hacked out, "Can't last—much—much longer here, Sir."

Bates was correct. X had hoped the police would arrive—John Burks himself would have been a most welcome sight—but no reinforcements had broken this siege.

Longingly the detective cast his eyes over to Betty Dale. Her eyes bloodshot, she exchanged a wan smile with him as she struggled to draw breath. Victor McGrieve showed the signs of labored breathing, his respiration being more pronounced because of his age. Surprisingly, though, he supported Betty with his own strength, the older fellow performing like a champion and never offering complaint.

"It looks as if we're on our own, Bates," the public defender declared. "But I need to do something before we go into the wizard's lair."

Betty Dale had stopped coughing for a moment when he called her close to himself. X whispered his plans into her ears: "You'll need to hang back, dear, when we break through. I will go first, along with Hobart and Bates. We'll try to disarm and disable anyone we find upstairs. Then, after we've finished our job, you can follow Beckwith and McGrieve."

Lips trembling with emotion, she cast her tearing sapphire eyes upward into his inflamed orbs, hugged him near to her own trembling form. "But you'll be shot—or worse, burned with that Wrath! I—I can't let you put yourself in such danger!"

"The alternative is much worse than that, dear," he smoothed back her dampened locks from her begrimed forehead. "You know what we'll face if we stay out here in the alcove. Bursting through this trap is the *only* way to reach that monster in white. I'm willing to take that chance. Otherwise, I'll lose the last opportunity I have to keep him from killing more innocent victims—you, especially. You matter to me, more than anyone else. And I've sworn to protect you—despite my *many* mistakes on this case. I should have taken more pains to ensure your safety. I should have—" he shook his head ruefully.

She countered, a slight smile adorning her lovely face: "But you *have* protected me! You removed me from that horrible prison of his. Maybe—maybe if we just wait a little longer here," she began to cough, more harshly, "then the police will arrive; or those people up—upstairs will—"

X marveled at the courage of this good woman.

He sent his body up the ladder, his two associates behind him. His gripped the trapdoor's hasp. X lowered the long metal fastener and in the next instant eased the trap upwards.

The sight meeting his eyes looked like a replay of the St. Valentine's Day massacre, so bloody it was. Several men lay dead on the floor. More of them clutched at wounds and emitted groans of agony. The Resurrectionist, his long robes now begrimed, peeped over the remains of a heavy table, where he'd taken refuge.

Across the room from him and barely in X's line of sight, another man, clearly shot, crouched beside a heavy desk and the remains of a large, ungainly swivel chair of leather.

Among the Agent's weapons was another tear gas globule. As he set himself to hurl the glass globule, a spasm of coughing overcame his lungs. Instantly the Resurrectionist's Mauser cut loose with a fresh volley. The Agent barely avoided being their target because he dropped his form beneath the ledge in the very instant he'd begun to cough.

Such retreat didn't prevent him from hurling that tear gas grenade, though. It sailed over the trapdoor's ledge into the midst of the radio room. More shots rang out from above his head, the Ring's surviving members firing blindly amidst the gas attack. From below him and on the corridor, there was more of the same, though *these* gun wielders didn't miss. Their bullets made meaty sounds when striking their victims.

X squirmed past his associates and down the ladder. From thence he wiped tears from his smoke-irritated eyes and peered around the edge of the alcove. Brave members of the New York police had fired those bullets at some of the Resurrectionist's surviving toughs! Those hoodlums had prepared to assault the police from the side X's allies had previously occupied. But the bluecoats had entered the corridor, somehow, behind the Resurrection men. And those same lawmen had promptly gained the advantage, picking off an entire flock of the white-clad jailbirds.

If the Resurrection Ring had seemed strange in their suits of gleaming white, so, too, might the police rescuers have seemed, at least to the untutored. They were dressed in glittering, bulky aluminized suits, their heads topped with square hoods of asbestos. Their bizarre gear bore an unearthly look, like the weird denizens of a cinematic nightmare. A team of firemen guided them along the path they had followed from the church's main floor into this underground complex, the Resurrectionist's very den.*

An entire squadron of the policemen and their brothers in red assumed the look of some futuristic army which eased warily through billowing clouds of smoke and over the bodies of their foes. All the while the brave rescuers shouted for survivors, Victor McGrieve and Betty Dale by name. However, truth be told, few of them thought they would find either of those parties on the scorched, brick-lined path.

Coughing again, X whipped back into the alcove. Back up the ladder he clambered, slowing only to weave around Harvey Bates and Jim Hobart on his way to the trap's hasp, overhead. Quickly the Agent thrust a cupped hand against the ear of Jim Hobart, whispered clipped instructions to him. Hobart gave a quick nod of understanding.

In turn Jim cupped his hands around his mouth and shouted these words: "Up here! Miss Dale and Mr. McGrieve are up here in the alcove with other survivors!"

That announcement caused the police and firemen to pick up their pace somewhat. Still within the alcove the Secret Agent whispered additional orders to Harvey Bates and Hiram Beckwith. Then for Bates, the Secret Agent speedily removed all of the makeup from the giant's features, much to the puzzlement of onlookers like Victor McGrieve and Betty Dale. Seeing the face of Harvey Bates now

*** AUTHOR'S NOTE: Developed only two years ago, these bulky garments have achieved great popularity and respect in the fire departments of larger cities like New York, Philadelphia, Chicago, and Boston. The outfits are more properly called "proximity suits," because they allow the firemen to get next to the flames themselves, as long as the temperatures do not exceed 500°F. Agent X tells me that the protective abilities of these suits will only improve in the future, especially when manufacturers add new innovations like Helmerite to the garments.**

disclosed, Jim Hobart gained a good idea of the Agent's intent.

When the man of mystery left the makeup, his masquerade as Stoner, solely on his own features, the act confirmed Jim's hypothesis. The Secret Agent did not want to compromise Harvey Bates' identity to the men of the law. X was willing to place only himself in danger of police capture and interrogation. Bates, no longer disguised as Tiny Sayre, could leave this former church without being bothered, except for routine police questioning.

That process of interrogation would likely begin in the next couple of minutes, since the advancing police had by now killed or gravely injured those hoods from the Resurrection Ring. X and the rest could see their shadows projected on the walls of the alcove, the bluecoats and the men in red less than a score of feet from the hallway shelter.

The gruff voice of Inspector John Burks sounded muffled as he shouted from the prison of his aluminized hood, "Miss Dale! Mr. McGrieve! You in there?"

X gave Betty the go-ahead to answer. Gasping for breath, she rasped, barely above a whisper, "Yes, Inspector Burks! There are six of us in here!"

"Come to the edge of the hallway, then! We have spare proximity suits for four of you! We'll get you and Mr. McGrieve to safety, along with two more who need to come out now. Then we'll come back for the remaining two."

Joined by Assistant Inspector Timothy Scallot, John Burks and a couple of firemen hauled the glittering aluminized suits to the niche in the hall. The rest of the fire breathers and lawmen stayed behind.

In the meantime, as Scallot, Burks, and the rescue party reached the niche, this side of the building gave a massive heave, a fountain of smoke and sparks spewing up, several feet in advance of the hallway's recess.

"There's no more time to waste in here, Miss Dale," Timothy Scallot shoved a proximity suit into the slender hands of Betty Dale. He offered her a friendly grin from behind the clear rectangular visor of his hood. "Just slip this jacket over your shoulders and button it tightly. Then we'll turn our backs while you slip the pants on. I'll help you fit the hood over your head last. All of these things will be a bit big for you, but just remember that it's not a fashion show you're attending."

At Betty's side, the Agent favored his companion with a slight nod and a look of deepest affection. She realized that protest over Scallot's comment was, thus, a waste of time in this circumstance. As all of the men turned their backs, Betty quickly donned the protective gear. Victor McGrieve did the same. So too did Jim Hobart and even Hiram Beckwith throw two of the proximity suits over themselves. Once that quartet wore the proper clothing, Scallot and the two firemen escorted them from the building.

That still left Inspector John Burks and some police officers there in the niche with the Agent and Harvey Bates. Burks kept a set of eagle eyes on Secret Agent X as soon as the lawman spotted the fake Stoner. This was a cue for Bates, who, though coughing furiously, gained Burks' attention. He needed, he said, to share some important information with the Inspector. Surprisingly the lawman was ready to hear it.

Eventually X's associate left the side of

Inspector Burks. And now the representative of John Law turned his hooded face towards the Secret Agent. His words were muffled but comprehensible to the Agent's ears: "The G-man Bates says your name is Myles, and that you're a city technician who knows these tunnels. He also says that this bunch of white suits captured and tortured you, to make you spill what you know. That right?"

X rubbed his irritated eyes and uttered a tired affirmative: "Yeah, Boss, I'm Myles. And I know these tunnels like the back of my hand."

"Just trying to see if you corroborate their account. A man with your description has supposedly been involved with activities of this Resurrection Ring. But that cabbie and the G-man tell me that you helped Miss Dale and Mr. McGrieve survive the fires. Also they said that all of you heard the sounds of gunfire coming through that trapdoor.

"Normally I'd be skeptical of such stories. But Bates has already shown me a Federal badge. If he vouches for you, his word is good enough for me. In fact, I'm thinking we'll need you and that Federal man Bates to take us upstairs where those thugs are holed up. Is this the best way up there?"

"Right now, it's—it's the only way," the Agent coughed.

"Then everything is beginning to fall in place, just like he said."

"Really?" the Man of a Thousand Faces questioned, his interest raised. "Like who said?"

"We got some mysterious call, a couple of hours ago, that this building was ablaze. The unknown caller said that if we went through a panel off the church's sanctuary, we'd find this hall. That trapdoor up there is the only place that could square with an office—that is, unless you know more than the caller did."

This was the Agent's rasping reply: "No, I agree. The—the Culpers stored gunpowder and bullets down here, spies too, during the Revolution. It could be that—that," he coughed, "the Resurrectionist's office originally served as a space for hiding people. The room isn't terribly far from the sanctuary, so that would be its most natural use."

His coughing grew harsh before he could finish. He resumed: "I'm thinking that a person would enter the church, supposedly to worship. But he wouldn't come out, unless it was safe to do so. If it wasn't, he could always leave by this corridor in front of the niche. Guess we won't know any of this for sure, until we mount that ladder—eh, Inspector."

Inspector Burks couldn't argue with this kind of logic.

By now the firemen and Scallot had returned with another pair of the proximity suits. The detective and Bates clothed their bodies in the glittering attire and steeled themselves for the trial to come.

At Burks' signal, the men on the brick corridor streamed into the niche, as, from the top of the ladder, the Agent eased up the trapdoor.

X lifted his body ever so slightly, such that he elevated only his eyes above the ledge. Through the remains of the tear gas and the smoke, his bloodshot optics struggled to see. Initially he believed the scene hadn't changed since his last reconnaissance. There were the same dead and dying strewn over the place, the same broken glass and furniture.

One factor distinguished this current picture from the previous one, however. Amidst all this carnage, the robed personage remained standing, miraculously, across the room. He was somehow propped between the remnants of the large swivel chair and that heavy desk X had seen. To the Agent's eyes, the white-cloaked devil looked as if he were plotting his next move. With a panther's stealth, the Secret Agent hoisted himself over the ledge. Meanwhile, the robed character stayed immobile.

X cat-toed towards his goal. Suddenly he launched himself at the large fellow. The two of them went crashing to the desk's surface, onto a small bundle of some kind. This wad of fabric and a hand-sized piece of something like rubber, a *mask*, shot to the floor. In that moment, the Secret Agent thought nothing of this. Rather, thinking that he had the Resurrectionist dead to rights, the Secret Agent flipped the strangely motionless fellow onto his back.

Breathing heavily after the exertion, the figure offered no resistance, even though the now-furious Agent jerked him upward by the cloak. X was fully prepared to beat this monster who had killed and maimed innocent victims, this fiend who had created such havoc in the city. In truth, X could have killed the man on the spot. But he stopped all of a sudden because neither the fellow's manner nor his face was right. In the first place, he was dying from gunshot wounds. And he simply couldn't be a suspect, if X's deductions were correct. Yet, here in the flesh was—

"Tiny Sayre!" the Agent husked. "I can't believe it!"

"Sur—surprised, aren't you, despite—despite his efforts to implicate me, all along," Sayre gasped.

"You could be lying, Sayre, to the bitter end," the man-hunter countered.

Giant Tiny Sayre coughed. "Hold onto that hood and the mask you knocked onto the floor, then, if you don't believe me. I have nothing left to hide, and only the truth to reveal."

That statement caused X to reach downwards to the floor, from which he removed the Resurrectionist's hood and that beatific mask he'd worn.

As a smile crept over his features, Sayre softly clarified, "I've lived as Tiny Sayre for several years now, but I want to make things right. I'm—I'm really Malcolm—Malcolm McGrieve, Victor's eldest son." His air sounded as if it were leaking out.

This response came from the Agent: "You are the other half of the pair who faked his death in Attica Penitentiary."

"Raised from—from the dead—like him, too," the man gasped. "He didn't have his 'holy lance' in those days. Just an injection from a hypo, disguised as a handgun."

X nodded, eyes glittering with understanding. "It makes perfect sense. That lance of his must contain a spring-loaded mechanism, concealed in the blunt end. With it, he would shock his 'client' back to life, by means of the anastastralose. But I'm curious about something. Since you don't look anything like your pictures, I take it that plastic surgery made you—?"

"—look like this? Of course. The Resurrectionist paid his ally Ramond to alter my features. But—but the Resurrectionist's plan went much further. He intended to frame Harvey Bates—as well as your friend Betty Dale and—and make it look as though both of them were wrapped up in crime."

The man's breathing was becoming more and more strained all the time, prompting X's solemn reply, "You've confirmed all of my own suspicions."

"Ye—yes, this was part of his plan—to destroy all of your organization, not just you," Tiny labored to tell the Agent. "After the Resurrectionist had done everything he could to bring your doom, I would have undergone another plastic surgery, in a place safe from interference. That final procedure would have enabled me to escape the authorities. Or so the Resurrectionist promised me."

Tiny Sayre, that is, Malcolm McGrieve, gave a terrible groan. "Look, those gunshots are about to kill me," he said, as the Agent looked down at a pair of them, one near the heart, and the other in the abdomen. Even the finest medico couldn't have saved him.

The dying man continued, his hand going not to his abdomen, but to his head, which seemed to cause him almost as much agony. "I want you to know what was going on behind the scenes: his intention to frame me for his crimes, his plan to double-cross me and everyone else in his group, the whole shooting match."

"I had already learned some of this. But confirm something for me: You were the one who phoned the police, weren't you?" the Agent asked. When the man admitted his act, the Agent pressed further, "And the letters sent to Victor McGrieve—they were supposed to have been yours. But you couldn't send all of them because you were hopped up on the 'sugar,' some of the time. So the Resurrectionist forged many of them, even to the postmarks and the stamps. Though he was an addict to the drug himself, he was tired of covering for your addiction. Yet that addiction wasn't your only problem though, was it?"

"No, it's—it's my head," the man admitted, his eyes shuttering tightly. "It's hurting right now too."

"Yes. You suffered these headaches from a terrible head trauma you incurred in prison. Between the headaches and your addiction to 'sugar,' you were ready to pull out of his gang, no?"

"Yes—yes," he labored to tell X. "My health was shot all to hell. That's why I called the police with my tip-off about him. I wanted out of the Resurrection Ring. Honest to God, I did. I—I had to leave it for my wife and kid's sake. I should never have hooked—hooked up with that pompous little pretty boy—in—in the first place," he gritted through his agony. He reached a pleading hand to the Agent's borrowed protective gear. "Tell my—my father and my brother that I'm sorry for everything—sorry about the way I turned out. And tell my Annemarie and Jake the same...."

He died.

Pivoting his head to face everyone, X saw Inspector John Burks immediately behind him. Burks had heard only the bits and pieces of the symphony—the parts about Tiny's head injury and his regrets about his family. So Burks accepted these statements as conventional death-bed pronouncements of a criminal feeling remorse. The Inspector's men hadn't even heard this much. They were searching the office, in hopes of unearthing more evidence. In the meantime, Harvey Bates had joined X beside the desk. On its surface X's associate spotted a piece of paper.

"Say—take a look at this," he suggested as he passed the square to the disguised Agent.

X read the handwriting on the paper: *"I am still the 'life from death'! And I will still be your end, Agent X!"*

Dark clouds passed through the eyes of the Secret Agent. The bottom was about to drop out of the sky. And X himself was the storm....

CHAPTER XXXIV
THE REAL DEVIL

IT was the first day after those fires destroyed the Resurrectionist's haven. As A.J. Martin, X had admitted both Jim Hobart and Hiram Beckwith to a special clinic which would help them to recover from their dependency on the "sugar." They were grateful for his help. And they fully intended to rejoin him, as soon as they could.

The representatives of the law also went about their work at the site of the fires. There they established a stout barricade around the church's burned husk. Only in that way could they prevent looters from stealing from it, or innocent victims from suffering injury or death there.

The police barrier did not prevent the newspapers and the radio people from covering the story, however, particularly in the two or three days after the tragedy. At every opportunity the press badgered the police and the firemen for information. All of this pestering wearied the men in red and the ones in blue. Hence the newshounds took their song and dance to police headquarters and to the city's main fire department. But persistent responses of "no comment" didn't deter the reporters one iota. They simply created stories out of thin air.

The most egregious of them was the tall tale that the Resurrectionist and his entire crew had perished in that burning building. For these journalistic moralists the place had become a hell on earth, and the criminals and would-be felons had suffered nothing less than poetic justice with their violent deaths. Those newsies changed their tune, albeit slightly, with the rescue of a few hoods including Cassel, the man who'd summoned the courage to help X and his crew. Now the state could prosecute and fry the remaining hoods. They had it coming, was more than one newspaper's frank opinion. The real tragedy, so those rags said, was the fact that the police hadn't recovered the body of the Ring's leader, the Resurrectionist. He must have burned to ashes in this fire. It was good riddance, as far as they were concerned. And no one arose to stop their persistence in this oft-repeated error.

Meanwhile, at the Caledonian Memorial Gardens the McGrieves tried to wrest normality from the tragedy, especially the death of Malcolm McGrieve. Sadly they realized there would be no return for him this time. There would be only the cold stillness of the grave and the mystery of the Great Guess which followed his interment.

That didn't mean the father and son couldn't start afresh, however. This, they were attempting to do, in that first full week after the Resurrectionist's presumed end.

Though Victor McGrieve arrived slightly in advance of Jay-Jay, both men entered the funeral home this morning with several purposes in mind. Sitting in Victor's office, they discussed the need to plan the next week's funerals, plus the necessity to review a stack of paperwork from the state. According to Victor McGrieve, they also needed to do one last thing: to show Ramond the door, and let the police handle him.

"You mean it?" was the shocked question from Jay-Jay's lips.

"That's right. He doesn't know it, yet; but today will be, for him, a most rude awakening," he said without further commentary. The older McGrieve went on, almost as an anticlimax: "In the next day or so we also have to handle some family business, as well as do something, finally, about that audio equipment which the Resurrectionist used for his own ends—never mind the fact that he bought it with *our money*."

"I say, 'Get rid of it and buy something cheaper,'" suggested Jay-Jay, with a note of finality. "Trust me—it will work just as well. And it will mean getting rid of something that the Resurrectionist used against us."

His father concurred, his right hand set gravely on his chin. He rumbled, "That's one of the chief ways that white-clothed monster tormented us, *you* and me both," he stated, much to Jay-Jay's surprise.

"You were worried about me?"

"I—yes, I was, sonny," Victor McGrieve addressed his offspring by the name he, Jay-Jay, had known as a youngster. Now in this new context he realized it was a term of endearment.

His father went on: "He capitalized on some old family problems, with Malcolm as his dupe. It's too late, unfortunately, for that wrong to be undone. Plus it's too late to undo some of that loss of business the Resurrectionist caused, thanks to his blackmail of me.

"Anyway, I want to rectify things—starting today. That's why I already called the people at Vox Populi, right before you arrived. Their radio engineer should be here," he consulted his wristwatch, "in another ten minutes or so."

Not much more time passed. Then from the hallway, a tall, blank-featured fellow in denim jacket and pants was knocking at the slightly opened door to Victor McGrieve's office.

Victor invited him inside, whereupon the stranger, a large leather bag in tow, inquired, "You the McGrieves?"

"Right as rain," Jay-Jay affirmed. "And you're—?"

"Zuiter. I'm the radio engineer with Vox Populi. You must be the son, Jay-Jay."

When the younger McGrieve gave a friendly nod and a handshake, Zuiter replied, "I'm here to remove the old loudspeaker system and replace it with a new one—that is, if you're still interested in doing business with Vox Populi."

The elder McGrieve came back, "Most certainly we are. But we have old, *painful* memories of the previous system. We hope you can understand. In any event, let me take you to the main chapel; and I can show you a part of the loudspeaker system. Then you can start dismantling it, and make recommendations for the new one."

Before they left Victor McGrieve's office, Zuiter asked if he could use the men's washroom. Luckily McGrieve had a personal one, whose doorway was there, in the office of Caledonian's owner. Zuiter ventured inside it; and seemingly in no time at all, he exited the place once more.

Now Zuiter and the two McGrieves started for their destination, a mysterious damp spot darkening the right sleeve of Zuiter's denim jacket.

En-route to the chapel, the trio encountered Dean P. Morston and Morris Lorin Ramond, who were then exiting the office of the older fellow.

Victor McGrieve introduced Zuiter to the other two men. Ramond seemed shocked that his boss Victor even wanted to remove the equipment. "Is it not working to your specifications?"

"Let us say it works *too* well," McGrieve

responded. "That is the reason Mr. Zuiter is here. He will correct it by installing a new, simpler loudspeaker system."

Zuiter elaborated, "And it won't drain as much power, either. But then, I'm sure you knew that already, didn't you, Mr. Ramond?"

"I beg your pardon?"

"I said that you knew that already. After all, Vox Populi has records of purchases you made, including the loudspeaker and a great deal of radio apparatus, in the name of Caledonian Memorial Gardens."

"Oh, I'm afraid that must be a mistake," corrected Ramond. "I've never bought anything from Vox Populi."

"Funny, that," Zuiter shrugged his shoulders. "I have some invoices here, all with your signature. Let's see," he bent down towards the bag at his feet. His hand wandered through the darkness of an inner pouch of his jacket. When that appendage returned to daylight, the hand bore some of the documents in question. "Yes, here are some of them. And they all carry your 'John Hancock.' Care to explain why?"

His voice absent that oily quality, Morris Lorin Ramond sputtered, "Why, it's—it's forgery. Plain and simple, it is."

Victor McGrieve asked to see the papers, so Zuiter transferred them to the hands of the funeral home director.

On examining the documents the owner of Caledonian stated, his eyes growing cold, "I'm not so sure about that, Emel. They look convincing to me. In fact, they indicate that you bought that equipment *entirely without my authorization*."

To one side of them, long-suffering Dean P. Morston gave every indication he would suffer a stroke. "Oh, God! I think I've had all I can stand! I can see it's time I pack my things and hit the highway!"

The younger McGrieve dissuaded Morston: "Don't leave us. We need you here, especially if Dad does what I *think* he intends to do."

Morston maintained his position of reluctance. With much persuasion, Jay-Jay called Morston aside, and the two of them left the hall. Jay-Jay McGrieve made certain, however, that they didn't stray too far from the scene of the action. That meant they stood only at the end of the passageway.

For their part, McGrieve the elder, Ramond, and Zuiter simply stood there for a moment before the radio engineer finally said, "I hate to be the bearer of bad news, but I'm on the clock. So if you'll just show me your loudspeakers in the chapel, I can get to work."

Angrily, Ramond inserted himself, "What about me, Victor? I think we need to settle some things now, not later."

Victor McGrieve would have fired the man on the spot until he caught, briefly, the steel-gray eyes of Zuiter. Something in the man's eerie optics compelled McGrieve to let this narrative spool unwind to its end.

As a consequence, Victor stated, "I can decide what to do with you, after Mr. Zuiter, here, has examined the loudspeakers."

Without another word he walked away from Emel, who stood there, still fuming.

Perhaps half an hour hence Zuiter came out of the chapel. He addressed Victor McGrieve: "Your speakers are pulling too much electricity. That's the reason you experienced the power surge and that momentary loss of power a few days ago. But it's odd, because the controls there in the chapel," he indicated a control board, near the double doors, "don't line up with such a powerful system. In other words, I'm thinking they're not the real culprit, if only a microphone and the loudspeakers are wired to that line. You wouldn't mind, Mr. Ramond, if I did some more looking around, perhaps in your office?"

Smirking behind that Van Dyke of his, Ramond urged, "Go right ahead. I have *nothing* to hide...."

A strange little smile adorned the features of the blank-faced Zuiter. Without acknowledging Emel's offer, Zuiter ventured down the hall into Ramond's office. As quickly, he circled the desk and planted himself in the chair normally reserved for Emel himself.

"What is the purpose of this box?" he pointed.

Emel Ramond smiled in that oily way of his. "It's an intraoffice communications device. Nothing more than that."

"That's certainly news to me that you're not using the one we put in here," McGrieve said. "I assume this gadget was another of your secret purchases, eh, Emel?"

Zuiter waited with expectancy while Ramond remained quiet. Shortly Zuiter passed supple fingers over the surface of that mahogany box. "There's a record for this device, all right; but it's no communications apparatus, according to *our* records. It's more of a concealment, a 'hidey hole,' if you will. You know about all about such things, don't you, Ramond?"

"I'm afraid I don't know what you mean."

"And I'm just as certain you *do*. This is *quite* the unique appliance with its *fake* speaker cover," Zuiter emphasized. "It's a singular piece of the cabinet maker's craft, to boot: a fine mahogany box, with four knobs, one at each corner; and a stylized lilac to decorate the surface. Lilacs figured in the recent flap over the Resurrectionist, as I recall. Any connection with your box, here?"

"Certainly not," Emel Ramond countered, his tone suggesting offense. "It's strictly coincidental."

"Ah, the ever-useful coincidence," Zuiter turned his eyes away from the box towards Ramond. When the man failed to comment one way or another, Zuiter cut his eyes back downwards, towards the four Bakelite cubicles at each corner of the box.

"I wonder—do any of these cubes turn or perhaps hinge?"

"No, of course not. They're stationary."

"And yet there is *still* the problem of the power surges, isn't there?" he pressed Ramond.

About this time, Jay-Jay McGrieve and Dean Morston eased outside Ramond's doorway. From this new vantage point they could see only what happened immediately inside the door, namely the movements of McGrieve and Ramond. Zuiter remained outside their line of sight. They could, however, hear his voice.

"So, they *do* work," he remarked about the Bakelite cubes. He had just found the hidden button underneath the lip of the desk and thus opened the wooden box. And in response to Zuiter's find, Emel Ramond also found something, a loaded .38 pistol, somehow hidden in his waistband!

"You're no 'radio engineer.' Who the devil are you?" Ramond sneered.

"I think you know *exactly* who I am, Emel—or is it 'Morris Lorin Ramond'?" the technician asked. "Oh, and I *do* hope you try to use that gun you're holding. I'm pretty fair with one myself," he concluded, his right hand lifting a deadly-looking pistol. Mysteriously his left hand remained hidden beneath the eye level of the men to his front.

"I'm sure you are, at that, Zuiter—or whoever you are," a high-strung voice to the side of the man-hunter affirmed. "I hope, however, you won't have occasion to use it."

The radio engineer, his gun unwavering, leaned ever so slightly, such that he was now facing Jay-Jay McGrieve, who'd addressed him, and Dean P. Morston.

Zuiter probed, "You think *I'm* the Resurrectionist, McGrieve? Do you *really* believe that?"

Desperate, eager to seize the advantage, Emel Ramond jumped in: "He is, Jay-Jay! He's the Resurrectionist, and he's somehow survived his shooting!" In response to this declaration of Ramond, his gun coughed up a single shot, poorly aimed, off to the left of the engineer.

Calmly the intended victim continued to stare at Emel. And the fellow, inexplicably, placed his own gun on the top of the desk. "If I *really* were the Resurrectionist, would I put this gun on the desk, Jay-Jay?"

He considered the engineer's deed for a while and, mastering his temper, he gritted, "I guess not. But that leaves only one possibility: You must be Secret Agent X."

"Guilty as charged. And I'm not the *only* one knows the truth about all of this death and destruction of the past few weeks, if not months. I'm also not the only one who knows the real story about those lilacs. I know that they are fraudulent life insurance policies, which our friend Ramond and his boss signed, and then doctored once more, after the fact."

Morris Lorin Ramond kept his own gun trained on the Secret Agent. His voice was cold as a corpse: "You're trying to protect yourself from me and from the Resurrectionist. But you won't be successful, this time. You're finished, X. We'll see to it."

The Man of a Thousand Faces ignored Ramond's threat and kept going with his explanation: "You and your master the Resurrectionist forged the signatures of your supposed 'clients,' in reality, those aliases; and you committed the same crime at other points, too, in order to funnel those enormous benefits from the policies to yourselves. At better than $500,000 per policy, that total would be quite a bit of money, wouldn't it?

"No wonder you were keen to involve the forger and blackmailer Roddy Shingle in your plans, and to allow him, at first, to hone Malcolm McGrieve's skills. When this approach failed because of McGrieve's addiction to 'sugar,' that obstacle didn't matter to the Resurrectionist. After all, he had already recruited Shingle to teach it to himself, that is, your chief, and you. And the two of you proved apt pupils. Thus equipped with your newfound forging skills, you could easily shift blame to others like poor Malcolm McGrieve, and thus keep the police—and me—off yourselves."

Ramond husked, "Keep it up, X! You are inching closer to the death I should have given you, back in 1932."

Calmly, as if delivering a college lecture, the Agent stated, "Unfortunately, you will find I'm at least as hard to kill as the Resurrectionist himself is. And I'm *much* harder to murder than some like Malcolm McGrieve. His first 'death,' his prison demise, made him the perfect fall-guy for the schemes of the Resurrectionist. Malcolm, or Tiny Sayre, seemed to have returned from the grave to bring revenge against his father, but also to exact revenge against me. It didn't matter that I had nothing to do with his original incarceration.

"The Resurrectionist held Malcolm in his grip by promising additional plastic surgery on him, besides assuring him of a chance at a new life, free, finally, of his criminal past. That begs the question: Just how did the Resurrectionist do it? That is, how exactly did he pose as Malcolm McGrieve for such a long time?"

Morris Lorin Ramond was being sarcastic when he said, "I'm dying to know that myself, Agent X. You seem to have deduced everything else."

X's steely eyes held a faraway look for quite some time. He was heightening the drama of this scene for all it was worth. When he remained silent, this soft interrogative came to his ears: "How *did* the Resurrectionist carry out such a successful pose? It's been bothering me for quite some time too."

X locked his eyes on his questioner and offered this reply: "I'm *sure* it has. It's a question I puzzled over for quite some time, too. But I finally answered it, definitively, when I happened upon some incontrovertible pieces of evidence from various sources," he continued to speak directly to the soft-spoken listener. "But I have *you* to thank for tipping your hand—*Dean P. Morston*. You are, after all, the Resurrectionist. Yet that name and your identity as Morston are nothing but fictions. In truth, you are someone else, someone I'd erroneously thought long dead."

His hands shaking ever so slightly and his eyes glittering wildly, Morston slipped into the Resurrectionist's laughter. "You have finally learned the truth about me, then?"

"Yes, I did, despite your best efforts and your years of planning," the sleuth grimly bobbed his head. "My evidence begins with those forged letters, a faked genealogy, and bogus credentials. Then there is the presence of that fancy recording equipment at Tiny Sayre's house. Oh, I mustn't leave out the wonders of plastic surgery, either, since they helped you to return to the outside world in a different guise. And finally, I learned how you'd a devised clever set of anagrams to disguise your *real* name."

The erstwhile Resurrectionist chuckled, "You've been busy, haven't you?"

X sidestepped the comment. "I'll begin with a little background. You capitalized on Victor McGrieve's past crimes by blackmailing him into thinking you were his son Malcolm, hungry for revenge. To that end you seemed to know the fine details of the family history.

"You claimed to have undertaken a 'holy war of vengeance,' like the McGrieves' ancestor from the Revolutionary War. But you didn't realize I knew the truth, namely, that the only McGrieve who served in that war, actually *deserted* the Continental cause. Thus, he brought shame on the family. But such attention to the facts never found a place at your table, did they, Morston?

"No, you dug your hole ever deeper, bragging to me about 'Angus McGrieve.' Remember him?"

"Why shouldn't I? He was a real man."

"True enough. But he was not from this branch of the McGrieves. He was from another branch, which settled in Pennsylvania, according to one of my reference books. Yet you concocted that story of Angus McGrieve, presumably to lend your narrative authenticity. You even went so far as to report to me, in my guise of Stoner, that Angus was the Presbyterian minister in that former church, later the Resurrectionist's headquarters. In actuality you stole that account from the history of Peter Muhlenberg, a Lutheran minister. In 1775 he is supposed to have left his pulpit during a sermon, in order to join the Continental Army. You weren't content with that error, though. You made another one with those forged letters sent in the name of Tiny Sayre, actually Malcolm McGrieve."

"You are terribly self-assured, detective."

"And you give me good reason to be thus. I know that your letters as Malcolm McGrieve were forged because of a couple of facts I discovered, sometime ago. You supposedly mailed a letter on May Fifteenth of this year."

"I've mailed many of them this year. What of it?"

"The letter contained a stamp that you arrogantly used, or rather forged, thinking no one would catch your mis-step. You had affixed a stamp, a depiction of baseball's centennial at Cooperstown, to one of your messages. But the U.S. Postmaster didn't release that particular stamp until June *Twelfth* of this year, almost one month after your May Fifteenth postmark. *Worse* than careless, this was. But it's just the beginning of your errors in forgery.

"There are the different ways you form the characters of your words: the closed letter 'e,' for instance in your own work, and the opened 'e' in his. The lack of a peak at the top of the letter 's,' in contrast to the peaks on that same letter in McGrieve's writing. Also I scrutinized a specimen of your handwriting, which was heavy and forceful, alongside a known sample of Malcolm McGrieve's hand, which was lighter, almost delicate. What made this all crystal clear for me, though, was something you yourself left behind."

"What was that?"

"I saw a collection of burial policies you were brazen enough to leave on your desk, when I stopped by here a few days ago."

"You! You were the insurance investigator Doren!" Dean P. Morston exclaimed.

"Yes. It was one of the many roles which gave me access to you. But the Doren guise was particularly helpful to me, for it enabled me to gain some critical intelligence about your criminal operation. You had, I learned, faked your credentials from the Indiana College of Mortuary Science, preparatory to coming onboard with Caledonian Gardens, three years ago. That begs another question: How did I learn this detail?

"A simple call to the college exposed that lie of yours. The Dean of the College was most angry, in fact, that someone would use his name and the name of his school to further an illegal enterprise. That, in itself, is a type of fraud. Some of your other frauds were much cleverer, though.

"The radio devices and sound equipment in Ramond's office fall under that heading. With those two kinds of machines working in tandem, you could seem to transmit messages, remotely, as the Resurrectionist; or your henchman Emel could do this for you, by hidden switches peppered throughout this facility. Viola Vye probably had a hand in some of these tricks too. Whatever the case this tactic could be especially realistic—and frightening—to those who feared your power over them. Then, too, you could use the radio devices and your sound equipment together to broadcast messages, even resorting to prerecorded communications on Bakelite disks.

You did that very thing in the funeral home to terrorize so-called 'mourners,' and the McGrieves. And you did it, also, in that old church, to your underlings, your 'clients,' and my associates. In every one of those cases you used that gadgetry to convince everyone that you were Malcolm McGrieve, back from the dead.

"How were you to do that, though, when you were not using your recordings, especially when you were simply talking to people and hiding behind your mask and robes? You must have reasoned that your guise wouldn't convince people you were Malcolm, unless they didn't already recognize his voice. And you realized that you needed something stronger, especially because your natural voice is not pitched as deep as that of the Malcolm. Indeed you tried hard to drop your voice's lowness, but at best you could manage sounds only two or two and one half tones above the correct pitch.

"As I put myself in your shoes, I recalled a device I'd seen at Malcolm's apartment. And I thought back to my search of Ramond's office and an invoice I'd located. That document from Vox Populi further heightened my sense that I was onto something. It recorded a sale to Emel for radial belts, for tuning the dials of your shortwave. In addition, it listed your purchase of a most unusual device for helping you to duplicate Malcolm's deep bass tone.

"Before he tried to bail out of your organization, Malcolm, a radio and sound equipment enthusiast, convinced you to buy a machine called a pitch shifter, a gadget from the motion picture and radio industries. This contrivance enabled you to deepen your own voice, and thus duplicate, quite faithfully and convincingly, the sound proceeding from Malcolm's lips. Your imitation of him proved so good, in fact, that you fooled even his father and brother with its authenticity.

"But at the last stage of the game, you became too clever, such that you outsmarted yourself."

Dean Morston was boiling by now, his eyes blinking as if he were in an Oklahoma dust storm. He had clenched his fists, too, ready to bash in the Agent's brains if he, Morston, thought this would halt the avalanche of revelation crashing down upon his scheme.

"I notice your frequent eyeblinks," the Secret Agent commented, his eyes and voice both unwavering. "Wearers of the new 'invisible' lenses suffer that very side effect because their eyes require more moisture than usual. Your lenses were—are—colored, to disguise your real eye color, which is most assuredly not blue. That wasn't your only cosmetic alteration, either.

"You put yourself under the care of a doctor, Morris Lorin Ramond, to undergo plastic surgery. Once that was complete, you looked nothing like your original self, a fellow of classic features. You were still a handsome man, but certainly not a fellow of movie-idol good looks."

"Jove, how I grow weary of your lecture, 'Professor' X! Are you quite done?" Morston grumbled.

"Not quite. I think the anagrams you used, the rearrangements of letters in words, were the final tip-off to your *real* identity. I noticed the names of certain figures in this drama: 'Ramond,' who I thought was the key to this mess; 'D. Ramos'; 'Dean P. Morston'; and the names of your female underlings 'Anders'; and 'Moon.' Notice that all of these names use only a small subset of letters: 'a,' 'd,' 'e,' 'm,' 'n,' and a few others. They set me to thinking about what names those same letters might also spell. They also made me consider something else. I thought about your all-consuming desire for revenge against me, yet I knew of no one I'd previously battled, under the alias 'Resurrectionist.' Then I received the diary list of the dead from the prison riot in Attica."

Laughing arrogantly, Morston, the Resurrection, noted, "Oh, I'd covered my tracks there. As far as Attica was concerned, I never died because I was never there in the first place."

"Unfortunately, Morston, you *did* 'die,' in a manner of speaking; and you hadn't covered your tracks, as well as you'd thought. Not at all, in fact. As I was about to say, when I received that list of casualties from Mrs. Hallan, it sparked me to consider the real identity of Dean P. Morston. So I rearranged the letters of your name, and I derived a new one—*Damon Preston.* And that is who you *really* are," the Man of a Thousand Faces declared with authority. "You are, without doubt, the man formerly known as *Thoth, Lord of the Dead.*" *

Damon Preston, the former Thoth and Resurrectionist moved closer to the desk, such that he stood on the left side of the seated detective. His eyes crackled with fury. "I should finish you and your friends the McGrieves right now, Agent X—in full view of everyone here. But I want you to die slowly, to satisfy my thirst for revenge and to serve as an object lesson to those who dare to defy me in the future.

"Get up from that chair," he commanded, his voice acquiring a gritty quality, his handsome features twisted into a devil's mask. "We're heading for the chapel now. You will find it rigged for death, too, even as my Holy of Holies was—before you destroyed it. We'll see how long you last, when I subject your unprotected body to the unchecked Wrath of God!"

It was X's opportunity. He blasted upward from the chair. With equally blinding speed, his left hand shot outward. As it did, his fingers clutched something strange: a long-barreled, gray water pistol!

Repeatedly he squirted the man's face, his shoulders, and his chest with the child's toy. The Resurrectionist sputtered and cursed, slapping the stream of moisture from his face as if it were a horde of attacking wasps. During the whole affair the other onlookers stood there, thinking that the man-hunter had lost his mind.

Ramond finally mastered his surprise, enough to sweep in and reinforce his criminal chief. With his own pistol the former doctor batted repeatedly at the detective's strange weapon, hoping to knock the thing from his hand. X fended him off, with a pair of well-placed kicks to the shins. These two blows sent the man crashing backward, in agony, to the floor.

*** AUTHOR'S NOTE: In the chronicle RINGMASTER OF DOOM, Damon Preston, Thoth, ran a kidnap and extortion racket of the most hideous kind. He discovered a means of causing artificial growth in human subjects by stimulating their pituitary glands. Having thus brought on artificial ostectis, a rare disorder, in his wealthy male victims, he began to extort money from them. He claimed he would cure them if they continued their payments to him. Along the way, Preston had deformed his victims by remolding their bodies and drugging their minds. His surgical and chemical treatments eventually gave them something like the semblance of Neanderthal men. However he could not return them to their previous state, since his process was, as he found, irrevocable. Agent X finally defeated Preston, wrung a confession from him, and, of course, sent him to Attica.**

In the aftermath of Ramond's attack, though, the sleuth tried to finish his job, that is, to dampen the face and body of the cowardly Resurrectionist. A grimacing Emel Ramond, too, earned his generous share of mist from the water pistol. In fact the Agent squirted the gun over the same general areas he'd already done with the Resurrectionist. The man of mystery couldn't hope to do this forever, since the gun's reservoir would soon become empty.

This detail was completely unknown to the man once known as Dean Morston. Terrified for his life, the man screeched more pleas for mercy, while he threw his body behind the McGrieves. They shared this house of fear with him; and Preston, the arch coward, knew the Agent would not intentionally harm these two innocents.

Humanitarian that he was, the Agent ordered them from the room, so that he could settle accounts, finally, with this fiend.

Preston vetoed this plan, however. Both of the innocent parties remained in the office with X, Preston, and the unconscious Ramond.

Meanwhile, Preston's cowardice became more apparent after X executed his next step.

In an eyeblink the man-hunter pocketed the water pistol. But he did not become idle. Instead he whipped over to the desk. When he pivoted to face the others again, he was clutching his other gun. Despite its appearance, this weapon was as far from being his usual anesthetizing pistol as Lake Michigan is from being the Atlantic.

He fired the device upward, so that Damon Preston could see the result: a long jet of glittering, silvery dust which spurted from the barrel. The stuff, tiny argentine snowflakes, drifted slowly, in a beautiful mass, to the floor. Though Ramond remained woozy, the mere sight of the glittering particles was enough to scare the devil out of Damon Preston, alias Dean P. Morston.

"Metallic potassium!" Preston hissed. "It's part of the Wrath of God! You can't—you can't use that on me—on Ramond! Have mercy! That's all I ask—mercy!"

Secret Agent X's eyes were like chilled steel. He asked scornfully, "Mercy? Where was *your* mercy when you burned innocents to death on the streets of this city? Where was it when you tortured other victims, even other criminals, in your so-called 'Hell'? And what about those men whose lives you ruined, or worse, killed, through addiction to 'sugar'? Rest assured, Preston, this gun is ready for more action. And the next two charges I will reserve for you and Ramond, unless you do *exactly* as I say," the Man of a Thousand Faces coldly finished.

"Anything, Mr. X! Anything! Just don't shoot me with the metallic potassium! If just a few particles of it hit me, damp as my body is, then—"

No words of comment, no flicker of emotion originated from the Agent. Instead X's free hand wandered back inside his jacket pocket while the other continued to hold the gun on Preston. Inside the Agent's hand, when it returned, was a vial of chocolate-colored fluid, though the liquid wasn't as dark as usual.

"I trust you know what this is?" the investigator held it up so that his opponent could see the contents of the vial.

Of course Preston knew what it was, he informed the Secret Agent. The liquid was the "sugar," which he so desperately craved.

"No, it's not just 'sugar,' Preston. It's the corrected version, the form mixed with the counteractant which I developed. If you aren't too far gone, it will help you to kick that dope. But you *must* surrender," X held out the olive branch to him, "so that I can start your treatment—"

As he made this announcement to the villain, the Agent observed the ever-increasing facial tics of Damon Preston. Alongside them X watched this once mighty crime lord as he slowly molded his hands into white-knuckled balls. Those appendages were shaking with more and more violence, by the second, despite Preston's strongest attempts to stop them. The rest of his body, too, provided its share of accompaniment to this chorus.

Suddenly while the Secret Agent guarded the desk, Damon Preston acquired the strength of the desperate man. He hurled his long-limbed frame in the direction of the sleuth. Grabbing at the Agent's hand, he shouted to the Man of a Thousand Faces, "I'll take that 'sugar' by force, if need be, Agent X!"

With his first blow Preston sent the gun flying into the air, where it eventually hit the floor and spun around a few times before coming to rest. Somehow throughout it all, the Secret Agent maintained his grip on the vial of "sugar," however, and kept it barely out of reach of his struggling foe.

While the two combatants struggled for their lives, Jay-Jay McGrieve and his father fled the room, the son wrapping an arm of protection around his sire.

Still at the scene of battle, Preston threw the Agent backwards, against the desk. The former mastermind repeatedly thrust forth his hands, with hopes of snatching the precious container from the hands of the detective. Every time he got close to the vial, the Secret Agent jerked the sealed glass tube in the opposite direction. A couple of times X resorted to throwing the object into his other hand, in order to keep the thing from Preston's grasp.

Ultimately Damon Preston scrambled up and away from the desk, dove for the floor. When he came up again, he gripped the Agent's weapon, the one firing the silvery mist. This gun he trained on Agent X, while the former criminal mastermind moved his frame backwards. His move placed him directly in front of the water cooler and that tray of mugs. By touch alone he maneuvered a cup underneath the spigot of the dispenser. And by the same sense he released a quantity of water into the mug, albeit more than a few ounces ran over the container's rim onto the tray.

"The shoe is on the other foot now, X!" he bragged to his foe. Grinning like a fiend, he hurled the clear liquid on his enemy, such that nearly all of it soaked the detective's face, neck, and shirt. "I have only to use your own trump card against you, to fire this gun; and you will finally succumb to the Wrath of God!"

His finger squeezing the trigger, the gun emitted a hiss. A tongue of glittering silvery dust licked out at the Agent. And nothing happened.

Preston screamed, "It should have burned you! Burned you to death!"

"Not if it is powdered aluminum, rather than potassium. It was a ruse to buy me time, Preston. And you fell for it!"

In a fury the erstwhile Resurrectionist threw the pistol at the detective, who promptly ducked it with supernormal reflexes. Preston wheeled to run from the room and make his escape.

Agent X launched his frame in a flying leap. He struck the man at the knees, brought him, hard, to the floor. Burning with fury, Damon Preston came up, to strike back at his hated enemy. And his body began to shake, much more violently than before.

The public defender immediately grabbed both of Preston's wrists in his own mighty hands. In the very instant he would have jerked the man to his feet and bound him, the body of Damon Preston stiffened. His features tightened into a grimace of excruciating pain.

The Secret Agent slipped his hands underneath the man's shaking head, the force of the convulsions becoming more and more violent with each passing second.

"You're responsible for all of this, Herman," the wild-eyed man gritted, addressing X by that name he'd used to bargain for his friends' lives. In between gasps for breath, Preston spat more venom: "I hate you for that and—and for everything you represent. You'll pay—for—for everything you've done—to me. I've seen to that, before—before you arrived here today. I sold—sold your name 'Chip U. Herman' to someone far—more dangerous than I."

"*Who* bought that name, Preston? *Who*?" was the Agent's earnest question.

"Hell is coming for you, X—he, who is—who is Hell itself!" he gasped with naked hatred.

His bloodshot eyes nearly popped from his head. The body of Damon Preston grew rigid as an I-beam, while his skin withered to the consistency of old, yellowed parchment. A froth of brownish fluid bubbled from his mouth onto his chin. A bloodcurdling scream escaped his lips. And this time Damon Preston, alias Thoth and the Resurrectionist, really died, his body a desiccated, crumbling wreck like the very empire he'd tried to build....

EPILOGUE
BOOK BURNING

ANOTHER ten minutes passed. Eventually, a blue police prowl car, its siren wailing like a tormented soul, rolled up in front of Caledonian Memorial Gardens. Inspector John Burks and Assistant Inspector Timothy Scallot hopped out of the vehicle almost in the instant Scallot stopped it. The two lawmen trotted to the front entrance of the funeral home where both of the McGrieves awaited them.

"Thank God you arrived quickly!" Jay-Jay McGrieve exclaimed. "We were told you were working another case and wouldn't arrive for another thirty minutes or so."

Inspector Burks spoke up: "A chance to capture the Resurrectionist, finally? We couldn't let this opportunity pass us by, eh, Scallot?"

"Absolutely, Sir," the younger man affirmed with an enthusiastic smile. He tactfully ignored the earlier belief held by his chief and the press, about the villain's demise. "We couldn't be happier over *this* news."

Victor McGrieve cut in with his deep basso. "Didn't the police dispatcher tell you the rest of the story, Inspector?"

Burks took a turn at bat. "What do you mean, McGrieve?"

"He's already dead, Sir—turned into one

of those mummies by the 'sugar.' And he wasn't even the person you or anyone else suspected him to be."

"That's right," Jay-Jay agreed. "He posed as Dean P. Morston, one of our employees. But in reality he was some old criminal named Thoth, actually a guy by the name of Damon Preston."

The hard-bitten Inspector, normally a cynical man, pushed his fedora back on his head. His features now formed a mask of utter incredulity as he muttered, "Well, I'll be damned! Where is the stiff, right now?"

The elder McGrieve pointed, "Down the hall, in my office. That radio engineer Zuiter overcame him."

This interjection exploded from Jay-Jay McGrieve's lips: "Man, I'll say he did! He saved our skins, and probably the lives of too many people to count."

They wanted to meet this lifesaver, did Inspector John Burks and Assistant Inspector Timothy Scallot. As they marched towards Victor McGrieve's office, Burks even commented, "I'll see to it that this Zuiter receives a commendation from Police Commissioner Foster! That's what I'll do."

The two men soon gained McGrieve's chambers. On the floor lay an unconscious Morris Lorin Ramond, who was still propped against the wall like a sack of potatoes.

"Bet this one will get the hot seat for what he did," Assistant Inspector Timothy Scallot commented, his pointing thumb aimed in Ramond's direction.

Earnestly, Inspector John Burks returned, "I'll see to that, Scallot. Damned if I won't. But where *is* that Zuiter fellow? I wanted to thank him for his help in bringing this mess to an end."

Off to one side of the two bluecoats, an opened window yawned onto the boiling hot, morning air which hovered outside the funeral home. That same window made a perfect complement to a dozen purple and white flowers and a small business card which Assistant Inspector Scallot located on the desk of Victor McGrieve. Eyes a-twinkle, Scallot read the wryly humorous inscription thereon: "I understand that Commissioner Foster's wedding anniversary is coming up, next week. Please tell him to accept this gift of fresh lilacs with my compliments. I don't think the McGrieves will mind my borrowing some of them for a good cause, either. Oh, and by the way, Burks," a now-grinning Scallot finished his recitation, plucking a single flower from the funeral arrangement, "you can take all the credit for everything—but catching me. Better luck, next time."

Scallot flipped the card to the reverse. On its surface a bold, black X slowly disappeared from view. And from outside that opened window, an eerie musical whistle gradually faded into oblivion....

Agent X waited a full two days before venturing out again, this time in his most common guise as A.J. Martin. He went around and picked up Annemarie Sayre and her son Jake, both of them dressed in their Sunday best. Her hair tastefully brushed onto her shoulders to frame her now-pretty features, Annemarie had donned a modest summer dress, a pale green affair with tiny sunflowers. Jake, on the other hand, had chosen a dark blue suit of simple, though tasteful cut. The Secret Agent had bought both garments for the family, donating the money to them with a check in the name of Elisha Pond.

For several minutes the trio drove in silence, and the Sayres acted thus for good reason. Both Annemarie and Jake knew where the Agent was taking them. But neither would have considered visiting a residence in this part of town, not even in the best of circumstances.

"Are you ready for this?" he asked them, reaching across Jake's knees to squeeze the pretty woman's hand.

Looking over at him, Annemarie Sayre responded with confidence, "I—yes, I think so."

"What about you, Jake? Think you can handle this, too?"

"Yes, Sir, Mr. Martin. I think I can do it."

"That's a good soldier," X replied, with a twinkle in his eye.

"You—you're," Jake Sayre almost called Martin X, "you're... an awfully good friend to Mom and me, Sir," he concluded.

They reached the front door of Victor McGrieve's mansion in the Upper West Side.

X parked his coupe, stepped out, and wheeled around to the side where his two guests had boarded his chariot. Annemarie Sayre opened the door before the Secret Agent could extend this courtesy to them. All three marched towards the front door, X leading the way. A nervous Annemarie momentarily faltered, but the Agent patted her shoulder as a sign of encouragement.

They gained the threshold. Victor McGrieve met them at the door, and strangely he had lost some of his hideousness when they stepped through the opened portal. As if in compensation, he seemed to have gained something else.

His heartfelt address to the woman said it all: "Welcome to my, eh, *our* home, daughter...."

She offered him a timid smile.

Slightly more assertive, Jake Sayre spoke up: "Wha—what about your heart problems, Sir? Won't we be a burden to you?"

"Doctor says I'm fine, including my heart," Victor McGrieve rumbled as he pulled a small bottle of pills from his pants pocket. After the Sayres and X passed inside the residence, McGrieve tossed the bottle into a nearby wastebasket while he informed, "I thought for years that I suffered from a weak ticker. So he gave me those tablets. When I visited him yesterday, he told me the truth, namely that my problem was nerves. He says I'm somehow better after this affair with the Resurrectionist, too. And he gave me the truth about those tablets: He said they're just innocent sugar pills, thankfully *not* that stuff which caused all of *this* trouble...."

"...or my own jealousy and self-righteousness, which compounded the problem," noted a contrite Jay-Jay McGrieve, who walked into the foyer to meet the newcomers. His eyes earnest, he looked, first to his father, and then to Annemarie and Jake, saying, "Maybe it's time we time we solve some of our problems together—as a family...."

Many more hours passed, after which the Secret Agent dropped the mother and her son at their soon-to-be former apartment in that scabby part of town.

Later, still playing Martin, he had stopped off at that special clinic maintained by a friend, an eminent neurophysician and sometime adventurer who occasionally treated cases of dope addiction. The Man of a Thousand Faces had journeyed there in order to visit the convalescing Hiram Beckwith and Jim Hobart. These two men certainly fit the bill of people who benefitted from the clinic's treatment regimen. But unlike the criminal patients the doctor usually served, these individuals, as law-abiding citizens, would not require transportation to the physician's larger, secret facility in upstate New York. They would need only medical help and patience for the next few weeks.

As the disguised sleuth navigated the central white-walled passage, a Mutt-and-Jeff pair, one short and apish, the other wasp-waisted and rather handsome, passed him. X overheard the apish character yell "shyster" to his chum, at which point the taller, better-looking man screamed, "freak of nature," or words to that effect. Behind them a giant of a man, lab-coated and golden-eyed, followed on their heels. He politely and earnestly apologized to X for the raucous behavior of the duo, especially in a venue like a hospital....

In only a few more seconds, the man of mystery rounded the corner ahead; and the doorway to his men's room met his gaze. After he knocked, the voice of Jim Hobart invited him in.

The Secret Agent offered warm handshakes to his associates, both of whom sat in chairs and listened to a baseball game over a brown, tabletop radio. For Beckwith, the man-hunter pulled a bag of jellied orange slices from the inside pocket of his coat. The Agent and the ex-rum runner laughed briefly, exchanging a few other pleasantries.

This done, the Agent turned his attention to Jim Hobart, who asked him to come outside the room for a brief time.

Hanging his head in shame, the raw-boned Jim began, "I, um, I need to tell you something, Mr. Martin. I'm—I'm sorry I went out on my own and tried to nab that Resurrectionist. I should have known better and left that kind of thing to you."

"No—no, Jim. Believe me, it's all right," he reassured his friend. "You did fine, infiltrating that gang and getting that information to your operatives. To tell you the truth, I would have been hard-pressed to do any better against him, especially in light of his intentions towards all of us, and his designs for that 'sugar.'"

"You—you knew what he was going to do with it?"

"I suspected his intentions to addict you and those poor neighbors of Thaddeus Penny, sometime back, yes," the Agent admitted. "But I needed you—*all of you, Jim*—to bring him to justice. Without each one of you, I can't say that I would have succeeded."

"You really mean that, don't you, X?" he slipped.

"I do. And it's high-time you know, for certain, that you work for me, Secret Agent X, and not simply for one of my disguises. That's part of trusting a person. And I could see you were a good man, a trustworthy man, before we ever met in person."

"How could you know this about me, before we met?"

"Dr. Charles Darwin Osben told me about you. He recalled treating a gunshot wound you suffered in Boston, when you were a young rookie cop. He'd said I should keep an eye on you, that you might be able to help my organization, sometime down the road."

"I—I don't know what to say, except this: Do you—do you have any work for an ex-cop who's trying to lick a bad habit?" Jim Hobart stammered, his tone humble.

A ghost of a smile haunted the features of Secret Agent X. He replied, "You'll be right at home with me then, since I like to put on other people's faces and pry into their affairs...."

That evening, in the silent basement of the Montgomery Mansion, the Man of a Thousand Faces found himself alone once more, facing the incinerator within his headquarters. He watched through the furnace's screen as the brilliant, red-orange flames, thankfully not blue-white ones, burned with an all-consuming hunger. He turned around to face a table, the seat of a certain small, leather-bound notebook.

It was the same tome whose pages had originally recorded his real name, the one he'd given up, in 1932. On that day, he had ripped the leaf from the notebook, as a means to protect his anonymity. Now from his right pants pocket, he removed the offending page, the very sheet which held the record of his *real name.*

Gray eyes staring into space, he thought briefly of the cognomen Chip U. Herman. It was no more his real name than Dean P. Morston had been the real identity of Damon Preston. In fact, like Morston, "Chip U. Herman" had also been an anagram, in this case for the phrase "human cipher."

In the flickering light of the incinerator, Agent X peered down at the scrap ripped from the notebook. What seemed like a lifetime ago, he had recorded this notation: "Today, I write my true name for the final time. I," he had scribbled his real identity, "have 'died,' that others might live. In staging my death, I understand that my own life will never be my own again. But I understand, too, that only in this fashion can I serve the cause of justice. Crime no longer reigns supreme. *The good work begins,*" it had concluded.

His pale eyes lit with eerie fires of their own, he pushed up the incinerator's screen. In the next heartbeat he balled the scrap and tossed the thing through the opened portal. The flames curled the paper's edges. At the same time an orange and red halo surrounded it with an almost supernatural light. Soon the paper blackened, and transformed to ash. After some additional thought, the Secret Agent decided to do the same with the entire notebook. The man-hunter threw it, spinning, into the hellish flames. In the process a few sparks leapt from the incinerator onto the floor beneath him before he could successfully lower the grate.

The public defender continued to gaze upon the incinerator, even though the scrap of paper and the notebook were now little more than memories. But to the hopeless, the helpless, and the oppressed—to anyone whom the burden of crime had crushed—he must remain far more than a mere memory. Anonymous though he now was, he must ever be the untarnished, indestructible sword of justice herself. Thus would always be the nature of Secret Agent X.

But what about that shadowy personage who had gained possession of his supposed secret, bogus though it was? That mysterious individual would learn one startling fact about the enigmatic crimefighter: that rising from the dead wasn't the only trick mastered by the Man of a Thousand Faces—and a Thousand Surprises....

THE END

Afterword

AND there you have it—the origin, in part, of Secret Agent X. I say "in part" for a reason which I will expand upon, later in this essay. Right now, thanks for reading this episode from his beginning. And thanks to you, Tom, for writing that Introduction, and to Matt, for publishing this little tale.

Now you and I gather in this coffee shop of sorts, while I try to offer some observations and thoughts about this yarn's composition. It was many winters ago, said Master Po, to Kwai Chang Caine, when—Oops. Wrong series, but right thought....

I'd intended to write an origin story for the Secret Agent for more than fifteen years. Honestly, I had planned this thing immediately after I scribbled the original version of *Halo of Horror* (long before its rewrite for Altus Press, that is), in the late 1990s. But a plethora of ongoing health issues, not to mention a return to college teaching and the loss of the story's outline, sidetracked my plans. After a while I thought I might never pen *The Resurrection Ring*. But I noticed the popularity that the character still enjoyed (cf. the volumes of new fiction from Ron Fortier and his co-writers at Airship 27, in addition to Matt Moring's fine reprint editions from Altus Press). And I received some great encouragement from friends like my publisher Matt and old pals like my original publisher and editor, Tom and Ginger Johnson. I gained many of the same good wishes from Ric Croxton and Art Sippo, the ever-gracious co-hosts of the *Book Cave* podcast. The time was right, everyone said, for me to set *The Resurrection Ring* to paper.

All of their well wishes I deeply appreciated—and still do. But I the problem itself still remained. How, exactly, could I approach this most unique challenge to Secret Agent X? My thinking was this: The Man of a Thousand Faces needed an origin, some etiological (or causal) narrative of the way he came to be. I was thinking of something along the line of *The Shadow Unmasks* or, long after the fact, Will Murray's *Skull Island* (which, by the way, I still have shamefully not read, because of a lack of time). Yet I knew I needed to preserve the aura of mystery surrounding the Secret Agent. I had to treat him profoundly, as some being greater than myself, if I might paraphrase the legendary Walter B. Gibson. If I followed this excellent advice, I would leave the readers panting for more. So I went to work, earlier this year. But a tall order this would be, as I soon discovered.

In the first place, writing *The Resurrection Ring* meant cooking up a plausible story germ for this landmark (and monumental) novel—and this constituted the easy part. Honestly, it did. The first entry *The Torture Trust* had established his backstory, that he had been officially declared dead, according to the records of the Department of Justice. It sounds as if someone and maybe something had helped the Agent fake his own death, those many years ago. I thought I could find some person to do this. I could create some character in whom the Agent would place his deepest trust, yet who would not reveal his deepest secret. I really did. But later you'll see how this presented its own problems. As far as faking his death went, I could easily concoct a viable means for him to stage his demise, at least with 1930s-era science and science fiction in mind. This was much, much easier to do; so I won't rehearse its gory details for you. Needless to say, you have already read the result. And it really does originate with George Thomas Roberts himself, more or less.

Indeed, his own work supplied the inspiration for the "life from death," which G.T. actually used in one of his earliest pieces of fiction, a short story entitled *The Death Master*. There he called his restorative "vital essence," something as melodramatic as my own "life from death," I must admit. In addition Fleming-Roberts loved to play with the idea of insurance fraud, particularly life insurance fraud. You can find this notion in the aforementioned *Death Master*, along with *The Poison Puzzle*, a novel of the Masked Detective. The idea crops up again in *The Corpse That Murdered*, one of the final recorded exploits of the Man of a Thousand Faces. Likely he used it in other yarns I don't own or haven't read.

Everyone might be as surprised to learn that he used a variant of the Wrath of God in a short story, too, in this case *The Scourge of Flame*, for *Thrilling Mystery*. There he used it to frightening effect on its victims. He even emphasized the supernatural angle whenever the resident villain deployed the Wrath. When I learned about both gimmicks, I was amazed at their dramatic potential, as you might imagine. I was almost as surprised that he never used them in the published Secret Agent X series. To be sure, he could have employed them in rejected plots or stories. But we simply have no way of answering that question at present.

All of this begs another question related to use of these devices. That is, why link the "life from death" and the Wrath of God to Secret Agent X? And as significantly, why set the events in 1939, after *Yoke of the Crimson Coterie*, the final number in his five-year run? I could say I placed *The Resurrection Ring* in this period, simply because I wanted to do so. In other words, it was my prerogative as the writer. And I suppose that's a possible excuse. But more compelling to me, I positioned *Ring* in June 1939 because of the dramatic events in Yoke. Here we finally meet Rex Durmont and Maurice Biers, who seem quite ordinary at first. As the narrative unfolds we learn they are two of the so-called "public-spirited men" who have bankrolled the anti-crime crusade of X since the dawn of his career. So it made sense to set my story only months after that key revelation. (And if you grab me off-mike, I strongly suspect that G.T. Fleming-Roberts himself might have revealed his own new facts about X's past, had the series survived a few more years.)

Another aspect of the story initially made me think it would be tough sledding to write an origin—exceedingly so. It would require that I avoid any mention of the master manhunter's real name, which is, along with his real face, his most closely guarded secret. But early on this turned out much easier than I expected. I simply revisited *Plague of the Golden Death* and revived X's old identity of Captain James Read, from World War I. And I avoided reference to any other name by simply calling him "the Captain" in the Prologue. Thus this problem actually solved itself. Readers even received a bonus. All of you have now seen a fragment of a first-person narrative from Secret Agent X himself. This was contained in the Prologue, of course. But as Ham Esler discovered, the Agent kept extensive archives over many years. The recorded stories were the ones which made it to print, of course, from *The Torture Trust* to *Yoke of the Crimson Coterie.* Inside the Montgomery Mansion, many more of those first-person narratives await our discovery....

So I had solved the problems of faking his death and safeguarding his name from public view. Yet I knew I would face another one with *The Resurrection Ring.* For authenticity's sake I needed to depict the tougher, more cynical, and more realistic tone and diction of the later stories, from 1937 to the series' end in 1939. As a result I re-read that last couple of years' magazines. In the same vein I boned up on some of Fleming-Roberts' short fiction from *Thrilling Mystery, Double Action Gang Mysteries, Ten Story Gang,* and many others. These books all pointed me towards one conclusion. Our author's other work had cross-pollinated his writing for Secret Agent X—and vice versa (much to my delight). In this vein I must say that reading his stuff was and is, still, a pleasure, what with its sophistication, its humor, its believable characters and (more or less) believable situations. To my mind he is one of the real superstars on the stage of pulp hero writers. And it's a shame, a crying shame, that he doesn't receive his just due with Dent, Gibson, Page, maybe Ernst, and a handful of others. I hope that *The Resurrection Ring,* though simulated G.T. Fleming-Roberts, helps everyone else appreciate his work, as much as I do.

I worked carefully to create that tone of voice you hear in *The Resurrection Ring.* There's a good reason I put in such effort. This is a different representation of our world, after all, than that of the Agent's earliest exploits. Tonally, those adventures are more "mannered" or "proper," for lack of a better term, probably because Chadwick served the ship as first officer, with Rose Wyn as captain. In contrast, by the time of the later numbers, G.T. Fleming-Roberts portrayed his world with more harshness, meanness, certainly more crudeness and cynicism than those entries we see, back to 1934. I'm guessing Wyn allowed him a slightly different hand. And I suspect this came about because she detected the shift in literary tastes, in this case, towards Fleming-Roberts' way of writing. Hopefully I captured some of that in Ring, what with some of my own sarcasm, irony, and the like, not to mention a less-than-respectful attitude towards certain players in the narrative. Again, you-know-who, the original and best model, inspired me. Perhaps I enjoyed his inspiration a little too much, if truth be told.

The diction (language) of the time, or Fleming-Roberts' presentation of it, is equally as tough, without, of course, being obscene. It occurs all over the series, though the last ones feature the tougher language much more prominently. Likely no one overlooked my own attempts at replicating his verbiage, particularly with epithets like "hell" or "damn," in addition to a favorite of our friend G.T., "jackass." Frankly I like that one, myself. It's particularly descriptive of a certain kind of person whom we all know. If G.T.'s word choice inspired me, then so, too, did his sentence structure influence me. This feature I tried with special faithfulness to replicate, using some of his favorites, the single subject and compound verb, as well as the inverted sentence, in which the object or the main verb may appear ahead of the subject, for purposes of emphasis or sentence variety.

I shouldn't omit another aspect of my inspiration's writing, realism of character. This meant I must depict my people as individuals with real hopes and dreams and believable motivations for their actions. Once again I knew that Fleming-Roberts highlighted the lives of more human-sized men and women in his later fiction (even in Diamondstone and The Ghost/Green Ghost). In actuality, he followed a pulp-wide trend, in presenting such characters. Readers will recall that among the hero pulps, Doc Savage, The Shadow, The Avenger, The Black Bat, and many others heralded that change, from the late Thirties, onward. And Secret Agent X was swept along on the first part of that wave, albeit only briefly. I could easily envision Fleming-Roberts having written situations like these in *The Resurrection Ring,* and then forced X to react to them. Along the same line X, this good and kind man, has seen a mysterious and horrible something in Teutschland, and that nightmarish something has profoundly affected him, as he first enters Ring. Thinking along the lines of G.T. Fleming-Roberts again, I have to ask myself, "What could Agent X have witnessed...?"

As I've so often mentioned G.T., many of you might be wondering why I chose to use his vision of the character, not, say the original one of Paul Chadwick. For one, Fleming-Roberts penned the bulk of the series. In more concrete terms this amounts to 21 known novels of the original 41 (with a couple of others being unidentified). And for another, more powerful reason, he wrote most of the best novels, those which gave the characters their humanity, made us honestly care about them as people. I wanted to follow his example for my own version of Secret Agent X.

Like G.T.F.R., I was compelled to pursue mimesis, or the imitation of the real. Mimesis is a literary term employed even by Aristotle, and developed, masterfully, in Erich Auerbach's perceptive literary study of the same name. (Buy it. Read it. We will have a brief quiz on Monday afternoon.) Fleming-Roberts himself worked out a similarly classical view of plot and character. He believed that all great fiction was built on well-conceived plotting that sprang from real life, and that made logical sense. And despite the occasional lapse in fictional judgment, his stories usually followed the same sound advice, featuring interesting and recognizable men and women, warts and all, who battled crime and somehow won through. So I knew I wanted to portray the minor criminals after the same manner. Many of them, poor people, became involved with the Resurrectionist because he promised them jobs, not merely because they were career thugs. I point out this fact not to excuse them, but to help us to understand people's motivations for the choices they make and the acts they commit. This push towards crime, incidentally, occurs still, in poorer communities, where job and educational opportunities are just as scarce as hen's teeth. And our response to those people—or to the mentally ill who may commit crimes—says much about us, as a people and as a culture. But, as the inimitable Stan Lee is wont to say, " 'Nuff said." I'm left with some other characters from *The Resurrection Ring.*

What could I say about them, the McGrieves? I felt much the same about this house, as I did about many members of my tale. The McGrieves were a clan of deep character defects—I won't enumerate them, since you've read the story—yet, as far as was fictionally possible, they were and are real. Indeed, I based them, if you must know, on some unnamed members of my own extended family. However I changed the sexes of all the players and used only two siblings instead of a larger number. Still I kept the same old secrets, old resentments, old slights, etc., to present their story. The resident heavy the Resurrectionist exploited similar issues with the house of McGrieve. They didn't come to terms with their past or with their reactions to it, until the narrative's end. Like thinking, that is, musing over people's hidden or secret pasts, led me to a comparable portrayal of Secret Agent X and his allies. He, too, possesses a hidden past and a series of questionable decisions, dating to his origin. Does this sound like heresy? Say it ain't so, Joe: Could the Man of a Thousand Faces be another flawed human being?

He could be. And he is—like each and every human being.

Think about it: If you harbor a minor secret of some kind, especially when it pertains to yourself, it will nag you like a fly buzzing around your dinner table. However, it will probably not give you qualms of conscience, unless you have a mental problem like obsessive-compulsive tendencies. If, on the other hand, that proverbial skeleton in the closet is a dangerous or devastating one, then you will travel life's road in isolation from your fellow human beings. Indeed, you will have not a life, but an existence. If you share your secret with only one person, it is no longer a secret, by definition. You will have paradoxically divided the burden you carry, as well as made yourself vulnerable to the other party. You hope, of course, that this individual is a trustworthy, supportive sort. But he or she might not be. Then you are potentially worse off than before.

Now walk in the shoes of the master manhunter. As such you will understand that Agent X has suffered the same dilemma throughout his career. Everything he has done rests on his decision, long ago, to fake his own demise. As such, he inhabits a dangerous place, and not merely one of hazardousness, but also a land of profound loneliness. He doesn't reveal his true face or name, even to Osben, after all. Yet Osben goes along with the plan of X to fake his, the Agent's, death. By all accounts, Osben further prevents Emel from discovering most of X's secret—the nature of his volatile plastic excepted. But this relationship with Osben is mostly professional. Agent X places the real value on his personal relationships. We see this first and most prominently with Betty Dale; but we witness it, too, with Harvey Bates and good old Jim Hobart. Such is true, throughout the series, despite the fact that most of the aides/ supporting cast disappear after 1938. (Their absence comes, most likely, from the severe editing to which the later stories had been subjected. It originates, too, from the greater difficulty in using New York-based characters when X is elsewhere in the country, solving crimes.)

I should disclose a key point, here, in relation to Jim and his relationship with the Man of a Thousand Faces. Beginning with *Octopus of Crime,* Jim Hobart's first appearance, the young ex-cop did not know that he even worked for the detective. Jim thought he performed investigative work for some daredevil, crusading reporter, A.J. Martin, the man-hunter's best-known alter ego. This arrangement worked for a time until *Dividends of Doom,* when Jim and the Agent suffered capture by that issue's villain. At this point Jim deduced that he had aligned himself with X. But notice this crucial detail: Hobart didn't yet know that he worked for the Secret Agent. Jim figured out only that the man of mystery and he, Jim, were working on the same case. The same situation persisted until *Death's Frozen Formula,* the only recorded battle where Jim and Harvey work together. After this, Jim disappeared from the series. (My own *The Freezing Fiends* explains, in part, why this happens. But the present story shows that Jim is back, operating on the Agent's behalf. He will come back in future entries, since I think he makes a valuable contribution to the series.)

Meanwhile, ahead of *The Resurrection Ring* I had made a decision critical to the story's development. I had decided to let Jim "in" on the Secret Agent's trick. That is, I'd decided to reveal to him, finally, that he actually worked for the Secret Agent, not simply some crusading newshound. This, to me, made perfect sense. You might think of my reasoning in these terms. Imagine a magician (Norgil, Blackstone, Bruce Eliott, or Walter Gibson) hires a young woman to do the old "woman sawn in half" gag. He tells his prop people exactly how the trick works. They then build the apparatus to his specifications. But he shares nothing whatsoever with the woman, who is, incidentally, helping him do the trick, but also assisting all of them to earn their daily bread. This would be the height of irresponsibility on the magician's part, not to mention the most unethical sort of business practice. Unfortunately X has been doing this kind of thing since he brought Jim Hobart into his organization. And I don't think he had ever honestly thought about the blowback that would result from it, if Jim didn't know the truth. After all, Harvey Bates knew he worked for X. And accidentally, Betty Dale sees his real face, for goodness sake. So it was certainly time that Jim learn that X was his real employer.

I've alluded to the business about X's deepest secret: his real face, but also his real name, something the original run never revealed. The constant threat he faces regarding exposure is the character's central conflict, perhaps better expressed as the classic self v. self, and spinning off into self v. society. In other words, thinking like X, I must protect my real name with all I have, no matter the cost to my own psyche. But the said walls I build around myself will, of necessity, separate me from my fellow human beings. This explains why, in the captivity scene, I put into the Agent's and Betty's mouths the words I did. It accounts, too, for my depiction of X's mounting fears throughout the narrative. These passages I tried to render especially terrifying for the Secret Agent. Hints of this unease go back, incidentally, to the earliest stories by Paul Chadwick and G.T. Fleming-Roberts, but also to my own *Master of Madness* and *The Freezing Fiends.*

All of this character analysis squares with the most striking feature about X. That is, much about him is a mystery of sorts because he has completely abandoned his real name. And his current designation Secret Agent X embodies that mystery. As his original editors often reminded us, his cognomen hints at the unknown (and the unknowable), in his person and in his previous experiences. But his appellation implies something else the series rarely explored. The term Secret Agent X suggests separateness, or the quality of being separated, in the old-fashioned sense of being "set apart for a special purpose."

I won't spend too much time here, discussing the many reasons why someone might be "set apart." That is a topic, an excellent one, for another Afterword. Nonetheless, I will say that X, too, has more or less willingly followed this path, becoming an undercover Federal operative, who just happens to be a nameless, faceless master of disguise. This in turn means that his days are mostly a tissue of fictions, a series of roles that he plays on the stage of life. (This is, in addition, a figure, a metaphor, for the varied roles, true, false, or otherwise, all of us perform, as we script our own lives.) We shouldn't be surprised at this revelation of X. As a matter of fact we forgive him for his constant deceptions because he is Agent X, working, in his way, for the greater good (and maybe even the common good). Paradoxically, however, his very approach underscores a problem inherent in all super-heroic fiction. That issue is the myth of redemptive violence. And specifically to the man of mystery, we see another equally pressing concern, one particularly relevant to us in the early 21st century. This is the expansion of the national security state, as embodied in the investigative and arrest powers vested in Secret Agent X himself. But these are subjects for future books....

If we lay aside such questions and consider the mind of X, we must acknowledge that he bears a heavy burden, what with all these portrayals, especially the criminal ones, so unlike his real self. And most likely they have inspired more than one crisis of conscience in this fundamentally moral man. The later story *Claws of the Corpse Cult* gives us one example in which X struggles with a decision he's made. I wanted to do something similar, in regards to his moral dilemmas. That is, I set out to write *The Resurrection Ring,* to show the consequences of X's long-ago choice to become nameless and faceless. And that meant I needed an appropriate villain to attack X at this point, paradoxically his strongest and his weakest. The narrative would require a criminal mastermind capable of fulfilling that role in classic megalomaniacal fashion.

I thought about creating someone wholecloth, for this story; but rather early on, I ditched this idea. Then I turned to the old chestnut, the recurring villain. Here, however, I would face a new, though not unforeseen, problem. Unlike Doc Savage, The Shadow, or The Spider, X never faced a major foe more than once. Sure, he encountered Felice Vincart, the Leopard Lady, in a couple of exploits (*Legion of the Living Dead* and *Div-*

idends of Doom, if you want to be technical). And though she was an interesting femme fatale, in neither yarn was she the main enemy. So I began to comb through earlier issues for an appropriate criminal mastermind. He must be someone who hadn't bitten the dust at tale's end—or hadn't seemed to do so. After a bit of searching I found him: someone conscienceless, absent of empathy, resentful/bitter, and certainly megalomaniacal. He was the perfect choice.

His first encounter with Agent X underscores my selection of him. The man-hunter had gotten on the trail of his enemy, through the fellow's underlings, men already the victims of hideous and irrevocable human experimentation. Eventually this crime king promises the same fate to the Agent, once the man of mystery is in his foe's clutches. This pledge and his own eyewitness experience convince X of his adversary's intent. In good weird menace form, both of them provoke a visceral reaction in the master sleuth. He is beyond horrified.

When I re-read that previous adventure, I couldn't escape the conclusion that X would have killed the man with his bare hands, if pushed much further. In comparison to other pulp heavies, the fellow was easily as horrible as Shiwan Khan and Benedict Stark, crime geniuses from The Shadow, for instance; Munro or the Living Pharaoh, enemies of The Spider; or John Sunlight and Jonas Sown, arch-foes of Doc Savage. And unlike, say, Sunlight, the genius gone wrong, the Secret Agent's opponent wasn't exactly a man out to do good. Rather he aimed to do the worst kind of harm. He hoped to create a virtual empire, if not a cult of crime, built around himself. What kept the Secret Agent from killing his enemy, the first go-around, was the exigency of that previous case. In short, he needed a confession from the guy! But X wrung the thing from him under duress—through something like "enhanced interrogation techniques," I might add. I had a real moral problem with this aspect of their battle, since I'm not at all a fan of such practices (or their devotees), much less the philosophy back of them. But I was trying to be faithful to the original characters and the original vision, once again. I hope that my efforts achieved success and that you found them entertaining.

I've covered a great deal of ground with this Afterword. And I've dropped some hints, earlier, regarding some future tales featuring Secret Agent X. That's right—to paraphrase the tags appended to the Bond films, "The Man of a Thousand Faces will return."

To that end, I have another surprise entry on the order of Ring, one that truly needs telling. Right now, I'm conducting some research for *Murderer's Moon,* which stars Agent X and doesn't star him, at the same time. This sounds like a contradiction of sorts, I confess; and it is. The tale will unfold early in the sleuth's career, probably in 1930 or '31—immediately before he becomes the man known as Secret Agent X! It will take place in my home state of Louisiana, specifically in New Orleans. The Mafia will appear in the thing, too, surprisingly enough. And I have a trio of good reasons to feature them as the main villains. First, it's always good to drop in on members of "the Family." Second and much more compelling, I've wanted to pit the Agent against them for years. Third, and luckily for me, it fits perfectly with the story's historical context. To be specific, New Orleans played host to some of their first activities in America, all the way back to the 1870s and 1880s. In those days they operated under the name the Black Hand, as a bunch of extortionists and murderers. I will possibly use the same designation or similar one for the New Orleans Mafia of the day. Nevertheless, my story will focus on other crimes they committed, besides the usual run of them. But that's not all. *Murderer's Moon* will feature the threat of an apparently supernatural creature which will battle the Secret Agent. This being, surprisingly, has a south Louisiana background. Yet it has deeper roots in Continental Europe and even in classical Greek legend. And once again, Fleming-Roberts used the beastie, or the threat of it thereof, in one of his earlier fictions. Oh, and let me provide a helpful hint to those who think they've deduced the villain(ess): Marie Leveau it's not. She's much too overpriced to make a guest appearance in my little tale.

Lest I forget, here's another yarn mentioned in *The Resurrection Ring*. This saga is, of course, *Hell's Haven,* the promised adventure from 1939. Further, it co-stars the legendary Captain Hazzard. This one, like *Ring,* I had planned to scribble, years ago, but didn't. It will be a globe-trotting entry, rather in the vein of *Curse of the Crimson Horde.* Harvey Bates will suffer badly in this one, I might add, as will one or more of Hazzard's men. But this adventure will provide another way to show the great compassion the Agent feels towards his fellow human beings. Hell's Haven will also feature the reason why the Secret Agent is so unsettled at the start of *The Resurrection Ring.*

The Blitz from Beyond the Earth will involve a person who should have appeared in *The Resurrection Ring,* but didn't, because the existing story was far too involved. As another teaser, this particular individual the writers sometimes mentioned, but never featured, in the original series. He will be itching for trouble with X, by the time we meet him in 1940. And this old enemy may hire the services of a super-powered henchperson to achieve his ends. More precisely, the superhuman fellow (or woman) will seem to do some pretty amazing things, like fly or hurl heavy objects. No, he's not that guy or that gal you might think. Nor is this outing going to be any kind of crossover. I want to let my hero X do the fighting, not fight lawsuits with unnamed comic book companies. I desire to demonstrate, too, who the master crimefighters of the 1930s and early '40s really were....

G.T.F.R.'s work inspired me to do some research for another Louisiana-based adventure, *Come, Taste the Terror.* This one I'll set in 1940-41, close to my own hometown of Ruston. On the map our city lies roughly seventy miles east of Barksdale Air Force Base, in Bossier City. BAFB is, of course, the inheritor to the long-ago Barksdale Field, the country's oldest bomber base. Here, a shadowy crime czar is ostensibly causing a string of mysterious, terrible murders, to take revenge on someone and perhaps to fatten his own coffers. That is, local authorities, the military police, and F.B.I. agents think these to be his motives. But the Man of a Thousand Faces isn't so sure.

Are you looking, for a Cold War entry as a change of pace? Then *Time of the Terrible People* may be the Secret Agent X novel for you. Set in 1949, this chronicle will be my take on the Reds' race for the Bomb. But unlike Dent's *The Red Spider, TTP* will involve a journey to a frightening world where resurgent Nazis have deployed the device against the US. Worse yet, our only hope for victory will lie with the scientists of that other Man of Steel—Josef Stalin!

Here's another Cold War piece, one which transpires in the same time-frame. Its title, evocative of G.T.'s Ghost mysteries, will hopefully whet your appetite: *The Case of the Red Report.* I leave it to you, the readers, to wring the truth from this heading. On my end, I can say only that someone, for reasons unknown, thinks it's better to be Red—than dead....

I have many, many more ideas for adventures featuring the Secret Agent. And they would enable the Man of a Thousand Faces to continue for quite a while to come—if you, the readers, want to see more, that is. Soon you can also drop by my Facebook page, *Secret Agent X: The Man of a Thousand Faces,* which I'm currently building. Here you will be able to give me your observations or suggestions about the Secret Agent and pulp matters devious or deceptive, weird or plain crazy. You can stay abreast of my upcoming plans for X, as well. Till later, thanks so very much for reading *The Resurrection Ring.* And X-pect thousands of disguises and thousands of surprises from Brant House and

Stephen Payne
December 2013